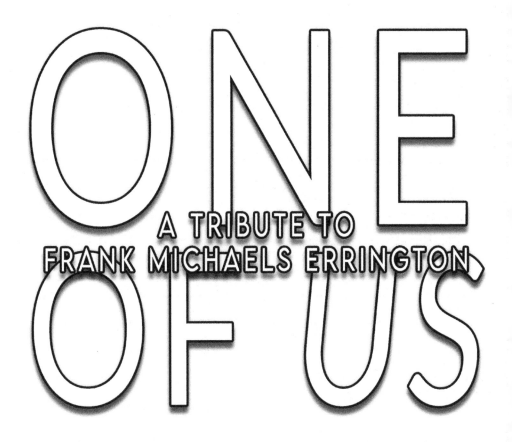

ONE

A TRIBUTE TO
FRANK MICHAELS ERRINGTON

OF US

EDITED BY KENNETH W. CAIN

BLOODSHOT
BOOKS

ONE OF US: A TRIBUTE TO FRANK MICHAELS ERRINGTON
ISBN-13: 978-1-947522-36-7

Edited by Kenneth W. Cain
Cover & interior design by Todd Keisling | Dullington Design Co.
Editorial Assistance by Somer Canon and Jacque Day
Photos by Frank Michaels Errington, Tony Tremblay, Kenneth W. Cain, Patrick Freivald, and doungjai gam bepko.

For Frank.

CONTENTS

FOREWORD

by Todd Keisling

Let's talk about Frank Michaels Errington.

I met Frank in person at the Northeastern Horror Writers Conference (NECON) in 2016. Prior to this, he was a name on social media, one of the many friend requests I'd received over the years. He reviewed books, loved horror, and lived somewhere in Pennsylvania.

That's all I knew about the guy, and if I'm being honest, I didn't recognize him when we passed in the hotel hallway. I've always had trouble with faces and names, but Frank's face was one that kept showing up in the crowd that weekend in Rhode Island. His name I slowly learned, thanks to our conference name badges, and over the span of days I began to equate that kind smiling face to "Frank."

We didn't really talk to one another all that much that weekend, but one conversation stands out in my memory. I was a ball of nerves, a nobody writer with a recent anxiety diagnosis attending my first writer's conference, and completely out of my comfort zone. Talking to complete strangers whom I didn't know very well wasn't part of my skill set. I had a few friends there, yes, but I'd lost them somewhere in the hotel. I found myself pacing the lobby, trying to get a cellular signal so my texts to them could go through, and I heard a voice say, "How are you doing, Todd?"

Frank sat in one of the cushy armchairs. He'd been watching me. I smiled, thought about shrugging off the question with one of those go-to platitudes meant to deflect the real question. *I'm fine, how are you?* And that's what I normally would've said to a perceived stranger, but when I looked at the kind man smiling at me across the lobby, I saw a friend. I really can't explain it better than that. Some people exude a kindness in their demeanor and voice, an outward glowing warmth. Frank was one of them.

"Not great," I told him. "Can't find my friends. Trying not to freak out."

He chuckled. "What do you mean? You're among friends here. You're one of us."

I don't recall what else we talked about in those few minutes before my friends passed through the lobby, but that statement, "You're one of us," has stayed with me ever since. I think it always will.

Our paths crossed over the years, from other book events to book reviews, but I really didn't get to know him until we began meeting regularly for the formation of the Horror Writers Association's Pennsylvania Chapter. Those meetings happened (and continue to happen) in Kenneth W. Cain's basement, usually one Saturday a month. My first time there, I had no idea Frank was going to be in attendance. I walked downstairs and there's Frank reclining on Ken's sofa, smiling and tapping on his phone. Whatever trepidation I had about that first meeting instantly evaporated.

We communicated more frequently after those meetings began. Back in 2018, I was going through a rough patch, and Frank reached out to me to ask if I was okay. I wasn't, of course—he had this uncanny ability of knowing when I wasn't doing well—and for the next hour, we talked on the phone about my troubles, my state of mind, and he reassured me that it would all work out, that I would be all right.

It did, and I was, but now that I'm thinking back on it, I realize how kind he was to reach out like that when he was struggling with his own issues. Frank had been living with kidney failure for almost the entire time I knew him. He'd been hospitalized multiple times due to various health complications, and for the last few years of his life, he'd been in search of an organ donor. Every time I saw Frank, he was a little paler, a little smaller, but he never stopped smiling. His personality never changed. He remained dedicated to the genre up until the end, writing and posting book reviews on his blog until a heart attack sent him back to the hospital for a final time. Even then, while waiting for surgery, he maintained his sense of humor. Who else but Frank would refer to angioplasty as a "balloon party?"

Losing Frank was devastating to everyone—his family, his friends, and to a greater extent, the horror genre which he loved and championed so much. One need only browse his Facebook timeline to see the impact he had on writers such as myself. In fact, the book you're holding in your hands is a testament to who Frank was and how much he meant to us. We've come together to create this tome and honor Frank's legacy.

Frank Michaels Errington was a loving husband and a devoted father. A dedicated book reviewer and horror fan. A kind and caring friend.

He was one of us.

Todd Keisling
Womelsdorf, Pennsylvania
8/22/20

IN EXCHANGE FOR
AN HONEST REVIEW

by John McNee

Well now. Here we are. The seventh and (please God, let's hope) final book in the notorious Ambassador for Evil series.

If you have deliberately tunneled your way down to this dank, sordid and lonely corner of the internet to find my neglected little blog, you must already be familiar with the Ambassador for Evil books and their author, the late Kel Astaroth. If not—if you somehow found your way here by accident—I can't begin to imagine what appalling sequence of inadvertent catastrophes must have befallen you to bring you to this point, but I'm happy (if you can call it that) to bring you up to speed.

I suppose the best place to start is with the man himself, Kel Astaroth—pen name of one Davit Stepanyan. The American-born son of an Armenian diplomat, Stepanyan was a qualified nuclear engineer, Satanist, practicing chaos magician and, to listen to him tell it, the greatest horror author of his generation. It pains me to have to tell you, but on this last point he was badly mistaken.

I love horror fiction. At least, I used to. For most of my adult life, nothing gave me greater pleasure than diving headfirst into a new book that promised monsters, murder, and mayhem. Sometimes they'd be incredible, sometimes dreadful. Most often they were derivative, middle-of-the-road diversions that passed the time in a gently entertaining way, even if they weren't particularly well written. But every time I cracked the spine on a new book, my excitement burned bright as before. Whether the work itself would turn out to be one I loved, loathed or felt completely indifferent toward, I never regretted making the decision to embark on that journey of discovery. I never regretted taking a chance on a book. Until I encountered Kel Astaroth.

I say "encountered," but "unearthed" might be the more appropriate term.

As I said, I love horror. And the last twenty years or so have been a fascinating time for the genre. Decades of stagnation, apathy and mismarketing led to a complete collapse of the mainstream horror publishing industry in the late 1990s, but the development of the internet, e-books, and print-to-order facilities prompted an explosion in the independent scene. Very quickly, self-publishing and an abundance of small presses made it possible for works by new, unheralded horror authors to access a global marketplace, completely bypassing the stranglehold of the Big 5.

For the horror fiction aficionado, it was a marvelous, energizing time. Overnight, our very small world of slick, highly marketable stories opened up into a vast universe of bizarre, unpolished, idiosyncratic wonders. And there were countless diamonds to be found among the rough.

In the excitement of this new age I, like many others, was compelled to share my discoveries—to spread the word about these dark delights that few readers (perhaps none other than myself) had chanced upon. And so, in the autumn of 2007, this humble blog was born.

I never expected it to become anything very big—and it never did—but over the next five years it did acquire its own small, dedicated, highly engaged readership, allowing me the chance to converse with all kinds of passionate horror fans from around the world, some of whom I came to think of as friends. It caught the attention of a few notable authors and publishers as well, enough that they were willing to provide me with the odd advanced reading copy in exchange for an honest review. I would have liked it if the blog had remained at that obscure level, not really bothering anyone, not making any kind of fuss. But then I discovered *The Darkness Sings Through Me*, the first book in the Ambassador for Evil series, and everything changed.

This was in 2012, by which point Ambassador for Evil was already a trilogy. *The Darkness Sings Through Me* was the first, but I checked out the other two— *Night of the Blood Snake* and *My Shadow Lies Screaming*—before purchasing a copy. It seemed he put one out every two years. All self-published. All available on Amazon, in paperback and e-book, all reasonably priced. All listed on Goodreads. And not one with a single review, anywhere.

I don't know the opinions of other reviewers on the subject, but I consider it a great responsibility, perhaps even an honor, to be the first person to review a book. Your opinion, voiced strongly enough, may come to define the very perception of the work itself. Perhaps that's why so many people balk at the thought of being first, preferring to wait until a book has a good five to ten ratings so their voice can be lost among the crowd or strike out through contrariness. To be the first, to be definitive, is too great a pressure.

This was not my philosophy. In any case, I was much too intrigued by the synopsis for *The Darkness Sings Through Me* to be put off by its apparent wallflower status, so I bought myself a copy and, before the evening was out, I had read it.

The Darkness Sings Through Me established a mythology in which the True King of Hell (aka Satan, Lucifer, the Devil) had been dethroned by a cabal of his underlings, working in concert with the forces of Heaven. He had been imprisoned in a separate underworld—a Hell beneath Hell—while his betrayers made an easy life for themselves, feeding on the steady supply of human sinners through their gates. Any potential conquest of Earth or the celestial realm beyond (surely a top priority for any self-respecting king of Hell) was jettisoned in favor of maintaining a status quo that allowed humanity to chart its own course towards extinction, taking its own sweet time. This had been the way of things for generations.

Only one man had the power and the will to upset the balance, casting all the designs of Heaven and Hell into disarray. His name? Special Agent Ezekiel "Zeke" Firestone.

Here's what you need to know about Zeke Firestone. Raised in a Texan orphanage by militant nuns, he was adopted as a teen into the Firestone family, an extended clan of multi-millionaire Satanists, becoming the protégé and sexual plaything of the aging patriarch and dark wizard Nathaniel Firestone. That's quite an origin story, but Zeke's young life, in the book, is painted in only broad strokes, providing vague justification for the incredible catalog of skills, achievements, and titles he had already amassed by the time we first meet him.

At the point he makes his grand entrance into the narrative of *The Darkness Sings Through Me*, strolling out of the shadows and snapping open a cigarette lighter as he prepares to inspect a gruesome crime scene, Zeke is: an alumni of both Harvard and Cambridge, fluent in over twenty languages, an Olympic gold medalist, the holder of three PhDs, a former marine, a former police office, a serving FBI agent, a gourmet chef, an unrivaled martial artist, the seducer of thousands of women, an active serial killer, a grand wizard of the dark arts, and twenty-four years old.

He is also—and this is revealed quite without preamble or explanation—an acclaimed rock musician and very successful recording artist. Subsequent books in the series would see him go on to further achievements in the spheres of film acting, reality TV, computer game design and, in the penultimate entry, literature, becoming—with the release of his first book—the most commercially successful horror author of all time (but I'm getting ahead of myself).

Talk about your renaissance man, right? Yes, Zeke is one of those perpetual tropes that plague indie fiction (and poor fiction, generally), the consummate overachieving badass, an insufferable Mary-Sue avatar for the author himself, engineered to deliver maximum wish fulfillment on every page. And honestly, the fact many of the author's wishes are apparently psycho-sexual in nature is one of the least troubling aspects of the book.

Zeke is a special agent in the bureau's occult crimes department, investigating a series of ritualistic murders. He is also a committed servant of the True King of Hell, spearheading a campaign to break the dark lord out of his extra-dimensional prison. To do this, he must capture one of Satan's betrayers—a bishop in the anti-church of the underworld—and believes whoever is carrying out the murders holds the key to achieving this aim.

All of which sounds like a lot of silly, demon-slaying mystical espionage fun. The synopsis promises an ambitious, whirlwind adventure full of action, escapism, and a liberal amount of gore. The book itself delivers on the gore and not much else.

In case you couldn't guess, I'll spell it out. The book is terrible. An absolute Grade-A travesty against the written word. Any pretense towards a plot is jettisoned within the first two pages. What follows is a mind-numbing string of opportunities for our antihero to show off in scenes that appear completely divorced from each other, following no linear path, with no actions having any impact on anything that follows, the same descriptions, plot points, and dialogue being repeated again and again and again, until at around three hundred pages the whole thing ends in a pathetic attempt at a cliffhanger.

It is a miserable, excruciating experience, compelling only in how bafflingly, astonishingly bad it is.

To break it down for you a little by way of example (without repeating my entire original review, which you can still find in the archives of this blog), the opening chapter finds our protagonist investigating the latest in a string of murders with his female partner, who has become suspicious of his interest in the case. She pledges to investigate him and uncover his motives (which you might expect to be a long-running thread in the plot) but almost immediately, Zeke gets the drop on her, seduces and kills her.

Chapter two finds him a bar (that's right) moodily drinking away his sorrows at a corner table and trying to ignore the attentions of a pair of drunk and horny college girls. When they persist, he spills a little (quite a lot, actually) of his backstory, impressing them so much they immediately engage him in an extended, exceedingly graphic and cringe-inducing sex scene, at the end of which he murders them and the bartender.

Returning home, he finds a beautiful woman has broken into his apartment. She's one of Nathaniel's latest recruits, sent to keep an eye on Zeke and aid him in his quest, proving herself most adept when a team of ax-wielding angels breaks in and (for no clear reason), they attempt to assassinate him. However, Zeke doesn't like working with partners, so, after the angels have been dealt with, he kills her (once he's seduced her, of course).

So it goes. On and on and on. Chapter after chapter. The plot never materializes. Nor do any significant characters. The prose is appalling—cumbersome and confusing, overloaded with poorly employed adjectives, by turns swinging for poetic and profound but lurching into coldly clinical, scientific detail whenever a sexual orifice is being explored or vital organ hacked out (one usually, very quickly, follows the other).

In my original review (which many have called scathing, but I would say didn't go nearly far enough) I struggled to find the words to adequately describe how truly dreadful *The Darkness Sings Through Me* is in every possible way. While ascending to the very peak of technical incompetence, the author plumbed the depths of his own worst impulses to create something sickeningly misogynistic, racist, homophobic, mean-spirited, puerile, pornographic, and nakedly narcissistic. It achieves the impossible by being both unbearably boring and incredibly offensive. *The Darkness Sings Through Me* is not just another bad horror novel. It is *the* bad horror novel.

Or it would be, if the next two weren't even worse.

That's right. After nearly burning the eyes out of my head by forcing them to endure *The Darkness Sings Through Me* in its entirety, I rattled off my rage-fueled review and then immediately got to work on *Night of the Blood Snake* and *My Shadow Lies Screaming.* Reviews for both, perhaps even more apoplectic than the first, followed shortly thereafter.

There's a certain assumption people have about critics—that we live for bad reviews. That nothing in this world brings us greater joy than savaging a piece of art, based purely on our own objective appraisal. I don't know if that's a fair comment to make these days. At least in the world of the online book reviewer, it's getting ever-harder to find someone willing to give anything less than three stars.

"If I don't like it, I just won't review it," they'll say. "Why should I give a bad review for something someone has worked so hard on? It's only my opinion. It's not worth hurting their feelings or their sales."

Well purely in my own personal opinion, this is cowardly bullshit.

It is not the job of reviewers to flatter the egos of writers. Our duty is to readers and to ourselves. If we can't be honest about the books we read, what's the point of reviewing in the first place? Quite apart from anything else, if you only ever give good reviews, how is anyone supposed to trust your opinion? No one likes everything. No one can be positive all the time. If you want anyone to value anything you have to say, you must be honest. You must be forthright. You must be unapologetic. You must say what you truly feel.

And anyway, people love to read a bad review. Nothing is more enjoyable to write or to read than a savage takedown, and that's important. It's human nature. In the week I posted my review of *The Darkness Sings Through Me,* it got more hits than the whole blog had over the entire preceding year. The review of *Night of the Blood Snake* doubled the number. *My Shadow Lies Screaming* tripled it.

Yes, I drew a tremendous amount of attention and praise for effectively ripping apart work someone had invested a lot of time and energy in, but did I feel bad for the author? Not at all. Because (and this is another overlooked truth of human nature) a bad review can often be a more effective sales tool than a good one. Every other comment I received on the blog was from someone declaring their intention to check the book out for themselves to see if it really was as bad as I'd claimed.

Over the next few weeks, I watched as social media chatter around the Ambassador for Evil series grew and grew. I checked in every so often on Amazon to find the books climbing in the sales ranks, beginning to amass a plethora of reviews, where previously there had been none (all gleefully echoing my own contention that they were some of the worst literary train wrecks ever written).

I can only imagine how Kel Astaroth must have felt when he finally decided to check up on his latest sales figures and discovered the eruption. How elated he must have been in the seconds between seeing the spike in sales and clicking through to Amazon to read the influx of reviews.

Well, no, I guess I don't have to imagine. I know how he felt, since he told me himself.

"Fatuous imbecile," he said. "Like a marble god descending from the pristine, crystal peace of Elysium into a quagmire of putrid mud and excrement is how it feels for me to be emailing you. And yet I would dirty my hands if only to pierce the balloon of smug, self-satisfied stench you might call an ego. It is obvious someone who would cavil with work of such obvious merit does so purely for the attention of their simpleminded peers. For the blinkered fools so devoted to your pathetic caterwauling, seeking to emulate your words with barely legible screeds of their own, I hold no contempt. They are not worthy, clearly having no minds and no talent for anything but licking the boots of a self-appointed gatekeeper. I will waste nothing on them. They and you will only impede my progress so long. Soon enough, my words will reach the eyes of those who recognize their true brilliance. My audience awaits. My reward awaits. My triumph awaits. And be warned, no milksop morosoph like you will stand in my way. I would wish upon you suffering and pain but am quite sure you already enjoy both in abundance."

In short, he did not care for my reviews, did not believe them to be sincere and thought anyone who agreed with me was just seeking my approval (as well they should, being the preeminent "gatekeeper" I am).

Incidentally. "Cavil" means "to find fault unnecessarily," and a "morosoph" is "a fool who puts on a pretense of knowledge or wisdom." I made sure to look up the meanings of both before copying the full email and pasting it on my blog.

Looking back, I see now this may have been a mistake. But the shock of an author lambasting me for daring to critically review his books, coupled with his ridiculous language and insane confidence in his own work, left me feeling compelled to share it. In doing so, I received the immediate support and validation I was seeking from others—and so much more.

To be clear: My original reviews of the Ambassador for Evil trilogy, when I posted them, were far more popular than anything else I'd produced to that date, but they did not go viral. The reprimanding email from Kel Astaroth, however, did.

If there's one thing the readers and reviewers on social media love more than a bad review it's an author or publisher behaving badly. Astaroth's email was hardly in the top tier of bad behavior, but it was so high-handed and lacking in self-awareness—this screed of bile from a nobody who believed himself God's gift to horror fiction—that it caught people's attention and prompted a fierce and exuberant dog-pile across multiple platforms. All across the literary blogosphere—and far beyond the horror genre ghetto—all sorts of people were asking the same two questions: "Who the hell is Kel Astaroth?" and (more pointedly) "Who the hell does he think he is?"

I enjoyed the circus from the comfort of my desk chair, reveling in the sudden influx of visitors to my blog and their interest in my reviews. My stature within the online community was growing, which was no bad thing. I never responded directly to Kel Astaroth, but nor did I hold toward him any lasting ill will. I assumed he would eventually calm down as his sales—prompted by the controversy—continued to climb and more reviews rolled in. Some of them were even complimentary. This was no surprise to me. One man's opinion is only one man's opinion. I never claimed to speak for the world. Astaroth had assured me his audience would find him. It seemed this was gradually becoming true.

I certainly imagined however much I'd upset him, it was surely water under the bridge by the time his fourth novel, *Saturn Wields a Golden Blade*, was announced. Continuing the adventures of Zeke Firestone (now working as a freelancer in the world of international espionage, pitting one government against another while simultaneously plotting an infernal jailbreak), this book was to be released by an actual publisher, which, it was announced, would also be printing new editions of the original trilogy with bonus content.

Well done Kel, I thought. Genuinely.

Which could have been the end of it, had I not begun to receive comments and messages from people wanting to know when I would be reviewing the new release. A trickle at first, then a flood. *Best not kick that hornet's nest*, I thought, right up until the moment Astaroth's publisher got in touch to ask if I would be interested in a review copy.

So I took a look. And by God, if it wasn't the worst one yet.

I had thought, now that he was working with a publisher, his work might have shown more polish, but it was clear from the opening pages that not one sentence had been altered by the hands of an editor or proofreader—no doubt at the insistence of the man himself. Everything in *Saturn Wields a Golden Blade* was 100-percent Kel Astaroth, i.e. pure sewage.

I said as much in my review, posted days before the book's official release.

The author's response—once again emailed to me directly—was illuminating.

"How would you like to be carved up like the fat pig you are?"

I have to admit to being a little taken aback. Even while I hoped, in the intervening period, he had realized a critical review was no bad thing, I had still half-expected to receive some complaint. Just not in those terms.

I confess it unnerved me a little. I did not reply. And this time, I did not share it. I didn't show it to anyone.

His next message came a few days later. "I asked you a question."

Soon after that: "Answer me."

Followed by: "Perhaps you'd prefer the skin flayed from your body and your exposed, raw flesh doused in salt? Maybe you would prefer to be slowly roasted on a spike? Or to have your throat flooded with live rodents so they can chew their way out of your insides? Any number of torments can be arranged. Do let me know."

And finally: "You interfere with my ambitions at your peril."

It can be difficult to gauge, in situations like these, how much of a legitimate threat a person poses to your well-being. Discourse on the internet is largely fueled by empty threats. How seriously should such vivid descriptions of violence be taken, particularly when they're coming from a horror author desperately seeking recognition for his evocative language and gruesome imagination?

I've never used my real name on my blog (still don't) or shared any personal details that could offer a clue to my identity. I've always been an incredibly private person and terribly careful about the things I share. So I didn't for a moment believe—even if the sentiment behind his threats was genuine—there was any likelihood I was in serious danger. Still, they were unsettling messages to receive and I eventually decided to share them with a friend in the community.

"Dude," he wrote back. "Have you even looked into who this guy actually is?"

It turned out I had not. Of course I had searched for the name "Kel Astaroth" and browsed through a few entries (mostly reviews and forum discussions sparked off by my original reviews). I had read the slight biographical information on his author pages. But for whatever reason, I had failed to journey down the rabbit hole far enough to reveal his true name, Davit Stepanyan. Five minutes was all it took, my friend, plus another five to dig up his life story.

Stepanyan, it emerged, was a highly intelligent nuclear engineer who had made himself all but unemployable through his devotion to the cause of Satanism. Specifically, a narrow sect of Satanism which believed the Devil had been locked up in Hell and it was their job to summon him to the Earth through acts of violence, blasphemy, and ritual magic. These were not beliefs or goals which chimed with the majority of modern Satanists, typically more motivated by their beliefs in progressive politics and religious freedom than in cloven-hoofed deities.

Following dramatic clashes with one Satanic sect after another, Stepanyan was eventually cast out from the congregation and tried to establish a church of his own. The small following he amassed soon drew attention—not least from local media organizations—for accusations of burglary, vandalism, and arson against both the Christian and Satanic churches, as well as sexual abuse within its own ranks. Stepanyan himself was never charged or convicted, but his involvement in all crimes—particularly the recruitment and molestation of a number of young women—was heavily implied.

The collapse of his own church (or cult, to give it a more accurate description) was followed four years later by the publication of the first Ambassador for Evil book from Kel Astaroth. From hunting around the discussions on various message boards in the intervening years, it wasn't difficult to ascertain his plan.

Stepanyan apparently believed in and practiced a very specific form of ritual magic based around the concept of visualization. Hardly unique to the occult, this is the idea that you can change your reality by thinking about it hard enough. Effectively "think positive and good things will happen," but with extra steps. Stepanyan supplemented his visualization strategy with rituals involving meditation, chanting, blood sacrifice, and sex magic (the details of which are far too disgusting to go into here). And, crucially, he was crystal clear about exactly the kind of reality he hoped to manifest. He wrote it all down. He published it.

Stepanyan's ultimate aim was not to become a beloved, bestselling author. That was merely a means to an end. His goal was to become Special Agent Zeke Firestone and raise the Devil. Revisiting the Ambassador for Evil series with this in mind, it is impossible to read it as anything other than a blueprint for an occult ritual. According to Stepanyan's understanding of visualization, any transformation of reality—no matter how absurd—could be achieved if the psychic signal was strong enough. A million or so people all reading his book, projecting its concepts, world, and lead character onto the cinema screen in their heads, he thought, ought to be enough.

To achieve this, of course, his books had to be critically successful bestsellers. And I—at least in his view—was getting in the way.

After learning all this, I made the informed decision that I would not be reviewing any more Kel Astaroth books. I didn't make it public. I continued to run my blog as I had always done, reviewing whatever works happened to catch my eye and doing my best to ignore the chatter as it began to build towards the release of the fifth book in the series, *Tread a Pestilent Path*. Beyond being a terrible writer, Stepanyan was quite possibly a violent criminal, at the very least deranged. I saw no sense in antagonizing him further.

But then he came to antagonize me.

"Dear imbecile," he wrote. "Don't fool yourself into thinking I've forgotten about you. For your transgressions, you have earned your place on my list. Damnation is assured. However, I am willing to offer you a single chance at redemption."

He said he wanted me to review his new book and this time he expected me to be "honest." He warned me not to test him again.

I knew what "honest" meant. And I admit to finding his demand insulting in the extreme.

But I reviewed the book. Honestly.

In truth, I may have savaged it just a little more than it deserved. But the condescending prick had riled me. I felt elated, almost heroic, when I posted my appraisal, ripping his latest travesty to shreds—and I enjoyed doing it. I knew his response would be swift and furious. But I wasn't quite prepared for how chilling his two-word email proved to be.

"NORRISTOWN, PENNSYLVANIA."

He knew where I lived. At the very least, he knew my hometown. My mind was overrun with thoughts of what he might do with this information. It wasn't long before I found out.

He started small, at first. I began to receive phone calls in the middle of the night. Dozens of voices whispering on the same line, saying nothing I could discern. Packages came in the mail containing strange charms fashioned from animal bones. On two occasions I returned home to find my front door open, things in my home moved around, but nothing missing. I would wake up some nights certain I could hear someone prowling around outside my window or creeping down my hall.

I never caught anyone in the act. There was nothing I could prove conclusively. But I was in no doubt what was happening. Throughout the ordeal I was passive, inert, unable to take action. I didn't call the police. I didn't reply to Stepanyan. I carried on as if nothing was happening, like everything was just fine, even as terror had me chasing shadows through the night.

Two days before the release of *Garden of Wilted Souls*, the sixth book in the series, I stepped out of my house to find a note nailed to my door. DON'T DO IT, it read. It had been scrawled in blood.

Surely not his own. I was certain he knew better than that. Blood he'd acquired by one means or another. Not enough to persuade me to finally tell someone what was happening. But enough to convince me not to review the book. That was the day, in fact, when I ceased reviewing horror books altogether. Somehow, all the joy had been taken out of it. All the passion I'd had was gone, to be replaced by a gnawing fear and anxiety. If that had been the purpose of his sadistic campaign, Stepanyan had certainly succeeded. I never reviewed *Garden of Wilted Souls*. I stepped away. I let the blog die.

So why am I back now?

Two months ago, in a hospice in the city of Meridian, Idaho, Davit Stepanyan passed away, the result of an inoperable brain tumor he'd endured for over a decade. Details are scarce, but what I'm led to understand is he limited knowledge of his illness to his immediate family. Apparently, the tumor did not directly affect him mentally. That is to say, it did not damage his brain or alter the way it worked. But I'm sure it motivated him in some way to write his series and bring it to a conclusion with his seventh novel, *The Vermilion Cantos*.

His publishers, at his request, agreed to withhold the release until after his death. This was not his only request. They also printed a single proof copy and brought it to his deathbed where, in one of his final acts on this Earth, he placed a curse upon it to ensure that whomever dared to give it a negative appraisal would meet with a terrible fate.

That book was then sent to me. Gifted "in exchange for an honest review."

In one of his final acts of petty vengeance, Stepanyan had set me a trap with three possible outcomes. I could write a negative review, a positive review, or no review at all, in effect leaving myself damned, a liar, or a coward.

Before I made up my mind, I decided to read the book, finding within its pages the blueprint for my own potential demise and Stepanyan's return. As I mentioned, by this stage in the Ambassador for Evil series, Zeke Firestone is an acclaimed novelist, beloved the world over for penning an epic horror saga based on his own exploits (subsequently adapted into a movie franchise in which he played the lead). He is also dead, having been felled by a poison dagger in the final chapter of *Garden of Wilted Souls*.

In the prologue to *The Vermilion Cantos*, Zeke returns to Earth to enact the final part of his plan, exploding from the pudgy body of a middle-aged book blogger after he posts a bad review of our hero's posthumous work, triggering the curse Firestone had the remarkable foresight to place upon it.

I must presume this is the same fate Stepanyan believes awaits me, should I dare to berate his fiction. A terrifying fate indeed.

Here then is my review:

> *The Vermilion Cantos* is the worst book I have ever read.
>
> As a stand-alone novel it is incomprehensible and exhausting. As the final chapter in a long-running saga it fails utterly, encapsulating only the worst traits of the previous six embarrassingly puerile entries, with little to no plot and prose so bad it carries its own hallucinatory stench—a pungent aroma of rotten fish and vinegar, seeping from its pages. Truly, it is so dreadful my own brain convinced me I could smell it. It quite literally stinks. This book deserves no stars, no attention, no readers, nothing. It does not even deserve this many words from me. It is an utterly irredeemable, steaming pile of shit.

So there you have it.

This will be my final post for the blog. There will be no more reviews. No updates to let you know how I'm getting on. It occurs to me that the moment I click "post" I could drop dead, my soul claimed by the minions of Hell, Stepanyan reborn from my flesh, and you would never know. I haven't told you my name. And the death of an unknown book blogger from Norristown, Pennsylvania, is unlikely to make headlines (unless it's especially gruesome).

So you will never know if Stepanyan's curse worked. If his magic, his religion, and all that he planned was real. I appreciate that makes this rather anticlimactic for you.

Except…you do know, don't you? We both know. Because however much we may love to read stories about it, all of us know the truth. There is no Hell. No demons. No magic. No witchcraft. Curses do nothing. The worst we have to fear in this world are the designs of evil men.

I would hesitate to call Davit Stepanyan evil (I think he would take it as a compliment) but he was certainly an unpleasant character. A hateful bigot with delusions of his own importance, obsessed with fantasies of wanton carnage and abuse. A bully, an abusive megalomaniac and an awful writer. I know he was capable of terrible things and believed him capable of far worse in pursuit of his repugnant, chauvinist agenda.

But he's dead now. Dead and gone. He can't scare me anymore.

And his fiction, for what it's worth, never did.

REMEMBERING FRANK

by P.D. Cacek

For years I knew Frank only as a Necon Camper—always smiling, always joking and always more than ready to jump in and lend a hand. It would be a bit later (hey, I'm slow, okay) that I realized Frank was also THE Frank Michaels Errington, reviewer, and that I'd been reading his reviews and buying the books he recommended.

Like I said, I'm slow.

Around that time I also discovered we not only lived in the same state, Pennsylvania, but pretty close to each other: he in Norristown, me in Phoenixville...ten miles as the crow flies. It was funny, but for a long time we never saw each other except at Necon and then, while preparing to read the following story at Fort Mifflin I looked up and there was Frank...sitting in the front row, smiling at me.

I think I had a "Where Am I?" moment, but don't think anyone, except Frank, noticed. The reading went well and he seemed to like the story. We chatted only briefly after and then he disappeared.

Fast in, fast out.

The next time I saw Frank was during the run of "Play On!" at Forge Theater in Phoenixville. I played the part of the harried, ill-tempered, hot-headed sound-light-scenic tech (typecasting) and was stunned when, during intermission while I was in my on-stage "tech booth," Frank walked up and said hi. He told me he loved the play and loved how I was playing character. I didn't tell him about the typecasting. After the play we said goodbye in the lobby and that was the last time I saw him.

I didn't know he'd been a pretty well-known actor in community theater until his memorial. It was a bit like old home week with Necon Campers, other writers I knew and actors I'd worked with...all of us with memories and stories about Frank.

I knew Frank as a Camper, but he was so much more.

And still is.

THE ENIGMA SIGNAL

by Douglas Wynne

But haven't you ever longed for the feeling that you're a part of something larger than yourself?"

Ricky wouldn't let it go. According to the latest Quinnipiac poll, more than half of the religious folks on Earth had questioned their faith at least once in the months since the satellite photos of Antarctica had hit the news, but Ricky "the Stick Man" wasn't one of them. I sighed, thinking of the five days at sea that lay ahead of us, of all the hours I still had to spend with this cat.

I relented. "Sure. And that's what I get out of music. What I get from jamming with a good band."

Ricky winced, like I'd just compared a Big Mac to filet mignon. But for me it was true and always had been. I'd never been a religious man, but I did get something spiritual from music, and that was enough for me. I didn't need the answers to Life, the Universe and Everything, just a sense of connection, a moment of elevation at the peak of a good solo. Getting a paycheck for *that* was all it took to satisfy *my* sense of wonder.

Ricky was a good drummer and a decent dude. I didn't understand why he needed more than that, why everything has to *mean* something for some people. Six days into the cruise I was trying to be tolerant, but even a big boat is still a boat. Not much personal space, and our trio was bunking in adjacent cabins. I wondered not for the first time why Ricky didn't nag Paul with his existential questions. Because Paul was a Jew? I never should have copped to being an atheist.

"That's not the same," Ricky went on, immune to my irritation. "Joining a band or the army isn't what I mean about being part of something greater. I mean like…when you look out from the deck of this ship at the majesty of nature, that pure white wilderness… Or when you look up at the stars and the aurora… Doesn't it make you feel small?"

"That it does."

"And do you ever get the feeling that that beauty isn't random? That there must be a creative force behind it?"

Kneeling over my guitar case on a bold-patterned carpet that reminded me of casino gigs in Vegas, I shook my head. I'd once had a music theory teacher who taught a whole lesson on the golden ratio and the Fibonacci sequence in Bach's counterpoint, the foundation of Western Harmony. The perfect proportions of a human face or a nautilus shell as reflected in art and nature. Bach's patron was the Church, and you don't even have to listen to the music to know their love for order and harmony. It's right there in the architecture. But one look at the cratered face of the moon will tell you that nature favors chaos and violence with brief intervals of peace and harmony that feel long to the flickering minds that inhabit them. We're just good enough at pattern recognition to fool ourselves into *believing* there's order in the chaos.

I said none of this to Ricky, just folded my guitar strap and laid it over the fret board of my 335 hollow-body, lowered the velvet-lined lid, and snapped the latches. Case closed.

But the drummer prattled on. "I hear spirituality in your playing, Marcus, I do. It's like you can't help it, it just comes out. I think under your hip modern skepticism, you're a deeply spiritual brother."

I winced.

"You say things with your axe that are spiritual, whether you know it or not. Like it's in your blood."

"What's that supposed to mean?"

"Well…you weren't *born* atheist, were you?"

"How do *you* know? You think all black people are Christian or Muslim?"

"I didn't say that, man." He raised a placating hand. Like I was threatening him.

I picked up my guitar case and looked him in the eye. "Sammy Davis Jr. was old enough to be my grandfather, and he was a Jew *and* a Satanist."

That twisted his brow for a second, but he recovered. "Sammy was a Satanist for like fifteen minutes in the seventies for the pussy."

A beat passed between us and we laughed and were just musicians again. At least Ricky could still joke about the devil. I swirled the ice in my glass, tossed back the dregs of my scotch, and winked at him. "If you'll excuse me, I'm gonna take in some of that majesty up on deck."

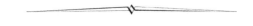

I lit a smoke at the port rail, downwind of the artists in their orange parkas with their sketchpads and easels. Mostly sketchpads, because paint tended to freeze at those latitudes. The subject of their studies was still distant—a monolithic structure jutting from a calved glacier. Everyone who looked at it saw something different, and what that was kept changing. Photography and video didn't work on it—some kind of electromagnetic interference, they said. When the military had figured that out, they'd enlisted this group of artists to capture it.

The cruise was funded by the U.S. government, with a pair of Canadian Coast Guard icebreakers enlisted to escort the cruise ship *Ortelius* through the Northwest Passage.

Most of the artists had been recruited from Hollywood art departments. A few of them worked in publishing, painting sci-fi and fantasy book covers. Apparently their usual work paid well, because the only way the government could entice them to freeze their tits off was to provide an open bar and entertainment, just like on a commercial cruise. That was how I fell into the gig, having worked the same route for Crystal Cruises out of Anchorage on two previous voyages. So far, this crowd was more interesting than the birdwatchers I'd played for on those runs. The tips were better, too. Probably because the drinks were on the house.

Looking over their shoulders on my cigarette breaks, I'd seen sketches of all kinds of improbable structures. Domed cathedrals with vented arches, stairs climbing to nowhere, faceted minarets, renderings in which construction and biology were fused in what looked like chains of architectural nucleotides. Crazy stuff.

As for me, when I looked at the horizon, I saw a black tree the size of a skyscraper, dripping coagulating ropes of oil like Spanish moss. An ecological disaster, always the same whenever I gazed north. I wondered if the seabirds migrating from the towering cliffs of Prince Leopold Island saw it that way, too. They foraged widely in this thawing region but gave the naked glacier a wide berth.

Down at the opposite end of the globe, the Antarctic city that had emerged from the melting ice on Google Earth last year was different. That structure had gradually revealed its contours to the satellite eye with no interference and no mutations. Before the UN resolution to block the satellite feed and ban journalists from the site, its public documentation had caused a tectonic shift in humanity's view of history. Granted, you'll always have your flat-earthers and dinosaur deniers. Psychological contortionists who will do anything to maintain a literal reading of Genesis. But now *thinking* people had to grapple with proof that mankind was not the first intelligent species to build a civilization on the planet.

You might have caught that clip of Neil deGrasse Tyson calling it the "second Copernican shift." Mankind—not just the Earth we inhabit—was no longer the center of the universe. Someone had come before us and they'd left their mark on an architecture undeniably designed to suit a different anatomy, sweeping all our creation stories off the table with a single image as iconic as the Blue Marble.

But at least you could study the properties of a lost city that didn't defy documentation, didn't defy the laws of space, time, and perception. At least reality was more or less *behaving* down there around the South Pole.

When the ice receded from this northern outpost, all bets were off.

Finishing my cigarette, I sensed an agitated uptick in the activity of the artists. The one closest to me at the end of the line was a portly white dude with long, snowy hair and a goatee that blended into the fur-lined hood of his parka. His eyes, just visible through polarized prescription lenses, darted back and forth between the approaching enigma and the sketchbook in his lap, a charcoal pencil racing furiously over the page. Before I could get a look at what he'd rendered, he flipped the page—so fast it snagged on the spiral—and started over on a clean sheet, leaning toward the railing with rapt attention.

He scribbled on the new page for less than a minute before flipping and starting over again. Wary of breaking his concentration, I edged closer for a look. In my peripheral vision, I detected similar urgency from his fellow artists down the line. If electronic drawing tablets had been reliable in these temperatures and conditions, the flurry of activity might have been less obvious, but given their tools, it was a riot of paper shuffling and scratching. Rough sketches tossed aside in rapid-fire iterations.

I flicked the butt overboard and walked behind the line of artists, glancing from the titanic structure on the horizon to their unfurling depictions of it. Out there, my black tree was morphing, the branches curling upward into a concave bowl, the hanging strands forming a net stretched between the boughs. And for the first time, I saw the same basic shape emerging on the sketchpads. Some of the artists stole glances at their neighbors' work, catching on that they were finally acting in concert, reaching a consensus.

A young woman wearing a Doctor Who scarf and fingerless gloves held up her drawing and said what I'd been thinking already: "It's a radio telescope."

The man beside her dashed out a triangular bracket pointing skyward at the center of his dish, blinked, and focused on her with the hazy demeanor of someone roused from a dream. "Or a parabolic antenna."

"What's the difference?" I asked, prompting both heads to turn. The man scanned my clothing quickly, trying to place my role on the ship—maybe to assess whether or not he was talking to a G-man. He shrugged. "Nothing, really. Just a matter of whether it's sending or receiving."

I nodded and strolled back to the stairs with no inkling at the time that I would be the one to tune in the first transmission later that night.

We were in the midst of the brooding noir groove of "Equinox" by Coltrane and I'd just stepped on my auto-wah pedal to add a brass tone to my solo when there was a loud burst of static from my amp. I thought maybe the pedal was on the fritz, but it cleared by the time Paul finished his descending piano lick and picked up the bass line again to support my solo. The audience didn't seem jarred by the noise like I was. They were deep into their drinks and conversations by that hour, well past midnight and nearing the end of our second set. They'd been more attentive earlier in the evening, coming off the exhilaration of a breakthrough day. But the booze had mellowed them in the trough of that adrenaline wave, and now only the dude with the white goatee—seated alone and doodling on a cocktail napkin with a felt pen—was still tapping his foot to our jam.

I remember watching him and thinking that my solo was starting out like a doodle on a napkin. Maybe that's what all improv is—a few lines out of context tentatively alighting on a suggestive shape, then maybe becoming something, taking on detail, themes, and emotion if it doesn't all just fall apart. I thought I knew where this solo was going. It was a familiar tune for our trio and I had a few licks I liked to touch on and weave together in this section. The auto-wah guitar is similar to a trumpet with a plunger mute; both sounds mimic human vocal tones. I used it a lot with the jazz trio, but that night, it sounded different. I was leaning in toward the speaker grille of my Fender Twin, eyes closed, fingers finding the winding path around the chord structures, like ivy climbing bricks, when I heard an overtone harmonizing with my guitar. I shot a look at Paul to see if he was playing it. Maybe he'd split the keyboard into two sounds: piano in the bass and some kind of synth tone in the treble register, but his right hand was just poised over the keys, giving me space.

The sound was both more vocal and less human than anything I could mimic, even with a stomp box, but I'll be damned if it wasn't coming from my amp.

In between phrases, I reached over and turned it up. The phantom melody continued on its own, like an echo or some kind of radio interference, like you sometimes pick up through a poorly shielded cable.

The past few nights of the cruise, I'd been surprised my amp worked at all so close to the enigma. We knew it interfered with digital equipment, cameras and phones, and our contract promised we'd get paid even if we couldn't play through the crackle, hiss, and hum. We were prepared for that, even though it would put an end to the tip jar real quick. This was the first malfunction we'd encountered, and at least it happened near the end of our set. We could wrap up early and I'd have time to troubleshoot my rig in the morning.

But as interference goes, it was just…too musical. Too harmonized with the song to be accidental and too alien to be a stray song roaming the arctic airwaves.

I reached around behind my amp, finger lingering on the power switch.

Ricky gave me a raised eyebrow. *Wrap it up?* But I couldn't bring myself to switch it off. I took the guitar pick from where I'd tucked it between my lips and struck up a new riff, digging in and playing off of the weird melody, mimicking and poking at it, as if it were coming from another musician on the stage, one I could coax into a lively exchange.

At first, the strange sound wave seemed to respond to my melodic flirtations. But the more I played around it, the less like a conversation it felt, and soon I was watching my fingers move of their own accord, compelled to find new shapes to support the exotic melody, building a scaffolding of chords I'd never played before, climbing the fret board on the trail of an alien acrobat scaling rarefied sonic heights.

I was lost in the music, eyes closed, when Ricky stumbled on a beat trying to keep up with me and I looked up to see the room clearing out. I don't know if it was the atonal sounds coming from my amp or the lateness of the hour, but the crowd was milling out of the lounge through a wedge of light from an open door. Only the old dude with the goatee remained, seated at his table beside the stage, leaning into the music and scribbling with even more intensity than he'd shown on deck that afternoon in his effort to capture the enigma.

The melody spiraled upward. My fingers couldn't keep up and the trio crashed in a jumble of notes just as my amp popped and fizzled out, leaving me slicked with sweat, my left hand cramped into a claw.

Paul leaned back from his keyboard and tossed his hair away from his eyes. "Dude. What the hell was that?"

I squinted at the glowing red power indicator on my amp and struck my muted strings. Nothing. I shrugged. "Dead power tube?"

Paul shook his head. "No, man. What you were playing. What the fuck was *that?*"

Ricky, sticks crossed on his knee, watched with interest, waiting for my answer.

Truth was, I didn't know. I'd played like a man in a trance. A man possessed. Turning to my microphone, I meant to apologize to the stragglers for cutting our set short. But we were alone in the room. Even the old dude with the goatee had left. I found myself staring at the ice cubes melting in his abandoned whiskey glass, at a loss for words.

I kept a spare set of tubes in my cabin. Swapping out the 6L6s in the morning brought the amp back to life. I'd slept fitfully, with a repeating phrase from the musical interference looping in my mind. I knew it was just a rhythmic pattern of static, but in that midrange of frequencies between one and six kilohertz, anything can start to sound like a voice. More of that pattern recognition. Except the words that had tumbled through my restless mind all night weren't in any language I knew. They sure weren't in English or French, those most likely to be heard on a transmission in this region.

"Tekeli-li. Tekeli-li." I said aloud to the empty cabin, pushing the last power tube into its socket with a bandana wrapped around the glass cylinder.

I'd skipped breakfast and made my own coffee. My stomach was growling when I switched the amp on and plugged my guitar in to the familiar crackle and hum that told me the signal was restored before I played a single note. There was no interference that I could hear at this volume level, which was just a fraction of how loud I played in the club. The bedside clock read 9:16. Early enough for my neighbors to still be asleep. I tuned up and fiddled with the cable, the same one I'd played through last night. Jiggling it in the jack didn't cause the rig to pick up any noise, either.

I let my fingers roam, searching for the exotic chord shapes I'd discovered the previous night and coming up empty. Both the interference and the inspiration had passed.

There was a knock at the door.

Housekeeping didn't do much to staff rooms, just replaced our towels and linens every few days, so I figured it had to be one of my bandmates. I opened the door in my boxers and Miles Davis t-shirt and found myself peering up at the big old dude I'd seen sketching in the club, his polarized lenses clearing as if he'd just been out in the Arctic sun and they were still adjusting to the dim corridors below decks. His goatee, white as ermine, concealed the contours of a smile, but his brow looked wrinkled more by uncertainty than age.

He offered his hand. "Joe Schumer. May I come in?"

"Marcus," I said. I gave his hand a quick shake and stepped aside, waving him into my messy lair. He entered, with a spiral notebook tucked under his arm, and cast around for a place to sit. I moved a pile of clothes and sheet music from the lone chair onto the unmade bed while he zeroed in on my amp and pointed an ink-stained finger at it. "You get it working again?"

"Yeah. Dead tube. I saw you in the club last night."

He nodded. "That was a hell of a jam." The words sounded less like a compliment than an allusion to some illicit act.

"Yeah," I said again. Then, thinking he might take me for an idiot if I didn't start speaking in more than single syllables, I said, "I don't know what came over me. My amp..."

"Picked up some interference, right?"

"Right. I tried to roll with it and riff on it. Jazz is about responding to the moment, you know? Whatever comes up. But it took me to some strange territory."

"We're *all* in strange territory on this ship, amigo."

"I saw you drawing while we played."

He nodded. It was his turn to weigh his words. "You know what synesthesia is?"

"Sure. Seeing sound, smelling colors, getting your sensory wires crossed."

"Something like that. I've always thought of it as more of a gift than a disability."

"You have it?"

He leaned back in the stuffed chair and drummed his fingers on his notebook cover. His Hawaiian shirt (octopus-themed) was neatly pressed, and I wondered who he worked for off the boat. He looked pretty L.A. to me, but for all I knew, he could be on the SPECTRA payroll. The once secret agency had become more visible following the Antarctic discovery and that business up in Boston in 2019, and word on the street was that they employed all kinds of specialists. I knew an audio engineer who claimed to have done some classified work for them for a big wedge of cheddar.

"My type is *chromesthesia*. That's a fancy word for seeing sounds as colors. Mostly they're clouds of color. *Your* voice is robin's egg blue to me. And when I first heard your lead guitar tone last night, it was amethyst purple—bright in the middle with a darker glow around the edges."

"That's interesting. Most cats talk about musical timbre as bright or dark, but it's not that specific."

Joe flipped his notebook open and picked through the pages. He continued his train of thought as if I hadn't spoken. "But after the interference joined the mix, and you started playing along with it, your color changed and took on distinct shapes. I keep a variety of ink pens handy and I did my best to capture what I could by the tea light on my table." He passed the notebook over to my perch on the corner of the bed, where I sat with my guitar in my lap.

The subject of the sketch was so intensely represented in the foreground— leaping off the page in bold strokes fringed with ink spatter from the pressure he'd put on the nib—that it took me a second to see my own silhouette in the background. He'd captured in minimal lines my posture while leaning over the neck when I'm really going for it. The focal point of the drawing—the *creature*, for lack of a better word—spilled out of my amp in a riot of iridescent fluid bubbling with lidless eyes and lipless teeth.

I searched the artist's face for a sign that this was some kind of punch line but found no humor there. Reconsidering his long white hair and Hawaiian shirt, I wondered how much acid he was enhancing his art with. "You saw this," I said.

He nodded. "I nursed one drink all night, if that's what you're wondering. Haven't touched drugs in decades."

"I guess you don't need them. You get enough enhancement from the synesthesia."

"Well. It's never been like this. Colors and shapes are normal, but this full-blown phantasmagoria. It was more like dreaming awake."

"So you tracked me down to see if…what? If I saw it, too?"

"Well, did you?"

"Nah. Not this. I saw shapes, like I usually do when I'm playing. Musical shapes in my mind. But they were different. Weird."

Joe looked from the guitar in my lap to the glowing power light on the amp, a bright red ember glowing in the dim room. I shifted uncomfortably. "You want me to play. So you can see it again?"

He swallowed, like a man afraid to ask for something he's not sure he wants, then closed the notebook. "It was flowing across the floor when your amp died. Had almost reached my table. I couldn't look away. Then it just…disintegrated, faded out, like your chords."

I didn't know what to say to that.

Now he met my gaze. "There was a theme you kept returning to. Mimicking that staticky voice. Do you remember it?"

I stepped on the auto-wah pedal and rolled the volume knob up on my guitar. It took a second of fiddling, but I found the notes. I played the phrase three times while he stared at the silver cloth speaker grille, his eyes widening until I stopped. "You see anything?"

"Bubbles. Play it again."

I did. And this time, when I stopped, the phrase continued cycling in the speaker. I checked the pedal board but the light on my delay box was dark. So where was the echo coming from? It morphed as it looped, twisting into something distinctly more vocal: *Tekeli-li…Tekeli-li…Tekeli-li…TEKELI-LI…TEKELI-LI…TEKELI-LI.*

Joe jumped backward, almost spilling the chair over. His notebook hit the floor, falling open to a random page: a sketch of the black dish on the horizon. Looking at the speaker, I could see it too, now—what he was retreating from: a black wave of rolling eyes reconfiguring itself with motions that looked divorced from the regular flow of time, like a stop motion video. I jumped, the guitar tumbling out of my lap like I'd found a scorpion crawling out of one of the f-holes. The inky pool spread around the amp. I knew shutting it off would probably make it disappear, but I couldn't reach the power switch on the back panel without stepping in the stuff, and the wall outlet where I might pull the plug was even farther away. There were mouths forming in the oil among the bubbling eyes. Teeth growing. Tongues lolling.

Joe was already in the corridor. I scrambled after him, shutting the door behind me as the living liquid overtook his sketchbook.

He clapped a big hand on my bony shoulder and we stared at the gap under the cabin door. I could still hear the chatter, as clear as it had been before I'd shut the door, only now it was reaching my ears in surround sound. I turned on my heel, following the sound to its source—an industrial gray intercom speaker mounted in a high corner at the end of the corridor. The grille dripped with more of the viscous, bubbling goo that had poured from my amp, drooling it onto the floor where it pooled and leapt with excited sentience. I grabbed Joe's hairy wrist and pulled him away from it, down a stretch of worn carpet toward the stairs.

He had a glazed look in his eyes, like a man in shock. I grabbed a fistful of his Hawaiian shirt, tugging him away from the discordant sound and its physical manifestation. "Joe! Look at me. What is it? Do you know?"

His thousand-yard stare passed right through me without focus, and I gave him a slap on the cheek. "Look at me, man. What the hell is that stuff?"

He blinked and I could see the rational part of his mind lumbering into gear, grinding against the paralysis of fear and astonishment. "The dish on the horizon," he said. "The enigma. It's transmitting a signal. And you picked it up."

"No shit."

"But it's a living signal. And when it made contact, when you tried to communicate back to it…"

"What? What happened?" I pulled him along, up the stairs.

"I think you woke it up, made it triangulate on us and manifest."

"I don't get it. Come on, man. Keep moving."

"When it first came through, it was subtle. Mostly made of sound." He spoke between labored breaths. Fleeing my cabin and running for the stairs was probably the most exercise he'd had all year. "Only I could see it. Because of my condition."

"Keep climbing, Joe."

A burst of semiautomatic gunfire ripped the air somewhere up on deck. We flinched and ducked in the stairwell.

"That must be why they chose me for the boat. Early detection. *Fuck.* I should've gone to one of the agents, not to you." He looked terrified. Not at the gunfire or whatever it was aimed at, but at what he'd done. He'd prompted me to provoke the thing.

At the first landing, I pushed him through a swinging door into an empty dining room. Tables lay overturned around a deserted breakfast buffet. Icy wind howled through a shattered window spanning the length of a wall. Faint shouts and screams reached us from the deck, almost drowned out by the alien chatter filling the room. Strings of inky iridescence dripped from the in-ceiling speakers. They pooled on the floor, merciless eyes in a rolling boil, percolating mouths chanting their ceaseless mantra with escalating urgency: *TEKELI-LI! TEKELI-LI! TEKELI-LI!*

I stepped through the broken glass and out onto the lower deck, buffeted by the stinging wind. The dining room overlooked the port side of the *Ortelius*. I could see the enigma, stark against the pale horizon, unfolding like a black flower against the icescape. A woman in an orange parka nearly knocked me over careening blindly up the deck in a panic, a scream trailing like a bright yellow ribbon from the fur lining of her hood. The gunfire was louder outside but no less difficult to pinpoint with the wind howling in my ears. Looking up, I saw runnels of red and black liquid washing over the side of the upper deck, staining the churning foam of the ship's wake some fifty feet below.

Joe and I had switched roles, him shoving me along behind the woman who'd just body checked me. She clambered up a flight of stairs, her boots slipping on the ice-glazed treads. As best I could tell, she was climbing *toward* the gunfire and chaos, toward the source of that wash of fluids that spoke of violence. And Joe wanted me to follow? It seemed insane until I looked aft and saw what she was fleeing. An exterior intercom speaker mounted in an eave of the upper deck drooled another monstrous form into being. Watching it lurch toward me, I froze, paralyzed by fear.

Joe shoved my shoulders with such force that I had no choice but to move or land on my face. My feet found the metal stairs and climbed. I wasn't dressed for the exposure and couldn't tell if my extremities were numbing from fear or cold. I grabbed the handrail to pull myself up and my skin bonded with the cold steel, leaving behind a layer when I ripped it free. I wiped my bloody hand on my shirt and focused on my feet. One shoe in front of the other, one stair at a time with Joe's firm hand on my back until we spilled out onto the upper deck.

One look and I knew it was over. The *Ortelius* would never complete the Northwest Passage, never reach the Atlantic or dock in Boston. I'd played my last set, cashed my last check, smoked my last cigarette. I thought of Cecilia, the girl I always imagined settling down with someday. The knowledge that that future had been canceled spread like hoarfrost in my chest. What was happening here would spread.

The speakers the crew used to pump music onto the pool deck in warmer climes were giving birth to the vast limbs of a massive creature, joined at a nexus in the bottom of the drained pool. I caught flashes of human faces and limbs in that roiling stew, white-eyed and terrified, twisted in a symphony of agony and awe as they were devoured or assimilated, and in a flash I comprehended the ecosystem laid out before me. Those who struggled were consumed for raw energy, while those who surrendered merged with the monster, their eyes and mouths bulging and stretching like ink smeared under an invisible thumb, taking on the curvature and coloring of those features I'd first seen depicted in Joe's sketch.

Men and women in white parkas and black Kevlar encircled the pool, firing rifles into the mess. Bullets plunked in the soup with no effect, except when they struck the heads of the victims swimming in the sludge. My stomach lurched when I realized those were their *targets*. Whether to prevent growth or end suffering, I couldn't say.

One agent had taken to firing at the big speakers, peppering the gray metal grilles with ragged holes. But the only result I could see was that the iridescent black tide poured faster from them. Whatever was manifesting here may have started with a sound only Joe could see, but we were beyond that now. The birth canals were open like sewage pipes, and there was no shutting them down.

Sensing that Joe was no longer at my side, I tore my eyes from the pool and scanned the deck for his print shirt. I spotted him at the railing, where passengers were jumping overboard into the icy water. Was our Canadian Coast Guard escort down there, or had they been overtaken, too? Were the jumpers choosing quick hypothermia over the gruesome transmutation unfolding in the pool? If they were, it was the right choice, and I embraced it as soon as I recognized it.

Joe sat on the railing like a man taking a load off on a park bench. He flicked me a resigned salute and tumbled backward, taking my stomach with him. Part of me still wanted to believe there was a Canadian Coast Guard life raft down there to catch him.

Walking to the railing through the tide of blood and oil, I thought I heard my name, and cast a final glance back at the pool. It was Ricky the Stick Man, I'd swear to it. Ricky shedding his flesh like snakeskin, melting and merging, his throat piping that ragged mantra, the incantation I'd invited into the world. And in that moment before the laser sighted rifles found him, I knew he'd achieved it. Apotheosis. A shade of ecstasy in his wild, rolling eyes. He'd become part of something larger than himself.

TRIANGLES AND MUSK

by Hunter Shea

L ookit right over there!"

"Where?"

"Follow my finger, hammerhead. There."

Ray Deevers, sweating under his Yankees ball cap, thrust his ramrod-straight finger at a moving, faint, glowing dot in the night sky. They'd hopped the fence with the 'No Trespassing' sign two hours earlier, setting up camp on the hillside of the Croton Falls Reservoir. Far from the ambient glow of streetlights, the depths of space were laid open for them, the stars appearing like swirls of luminescent lint on a black t-shirt.

"It's a plane," Scott, younger brother by a year and some loose change, casually declared.

"You're wrong. Look again."

Scott rummaged around through his backpack in search of a can of RC Cola he'd wrapped in tinfoil to keep it somewhat cold during their vigil. "Don't need to. There are red blinking lights at the back. It's a plane."

Ray nudged his brother's arm just enough to make some of the syrupy cola splash on his hand and leg. "I don't see any red blinking light."

Scott flicked droplets of soda on his brother. "Thanks, ass-munch. And put your glasses on. You'll see."

Squinting at the sky, Scott said, "I forgot 'em."

"You forgot to bring your glasses on the night we came out here to look for UFOs? How is that even possible?"

"Maybe it's because I was too busy trying to figure out how we'd sneak out of the house. I can't be expected to do everything."

Crickets chirped around them loud enough to drown out Scott's sarcastic reply of, "Big whoop, you picked the window we crawled out of when Mom and Dad fell asleep."

"What?"

"Nothin.' You want some?"

His gaze still targeting the tiny speck, Ray took the offered can and had himself a sip bordering on a gulp.

"Save some for me," Scott said.

His brother completed his drink with a belch that echoed over the still water.

"Nice one if I do say so myself," Ray said proudly.

"Just keep it coming out of that end."

Inside Scott's backpack was a bag of potato chips, two more cans of soda in their foil shrouds, some fruit roll-ups (cherry for Ray and green apple for Scott), two juice boxes, four Hostess mini fruit pies, and several long sticks of beef jerky, which gave Ray hellacious gas—Scott would never have packed the butt dynamite. He'd only found out when they got there that Ray had slipped them into his pack just before they'd crept out of the house while their father snored like a grumbling gorilla. With that kind of sound for cover, they could have stomped out the front door wearing mop buckets on their feet.

The UFO 'flap,' as the papers were calling it, had consumed the brothers' attention since it started in the early fall. Some days, when they would catch a report on the news or pore over an article about mysterious triangular objects hovering or zipping over the town, Scott was sure their UFO fever manifested in an actual fever. Some of the sighting reports sure made him sweat. There were whispers of abduction, a Chappaqua man saying he was floated out of his bed and taken aboard a ship where he was met by strange-looking beings and tall humanoids. Scott and Ray wondered what a tall humanoid could be. Basketball players? Could Larry Bird and Magic Johnson be extraterrestrials? They sure played like people not of this Earth.

"How about that?" Ray said, his right arm rigid at a fifty-degree angle.

Scott, who had the vision of a cat or an eagle or better yet, the Six Million Dollar Man, saw the slow-moving light and said, "Plane."

"Can all these jeez-damn planes just stay on the ground tonight? I mean, how are we supposed to find a UFO if the sky's full of stupid planes?"

Scott lay back on the grass. The air smelled sweet, the nearby water tinged with minerals and the promise of brown trout, bluegill, and largemouth bass. It was just past midnight and they were out here alone, and even if the UFOs didn't come, this was still a pretty special night.

"Don't worry. If they come, we'll know it. You see that picture in the *Brewster Gazette*? It looked like a pyramid, kinda, and they said it flew real low and slow and didn't make a sound. Then these red and blue lights came out of the bottom, and a little orange glowing ball like a tiny sun flew out of some porthole or something and zipped around the trees before joining back up with the mother ship. Then the whole thing just disappeared." The small hairs on the back of his neck tingled at the thought. "Anything like that happens, man, it won't matter if there are a hundred planes in the sky."

Ray swatted a bug off his arm. The insects were very happy for their company. "That would be awesome."

Neither boy considered the possibility that it would also be terrifying. They were out where no one could see or hear them. It was a definite disadvantage if they were to go toe to toe with a bunch of aliens. Or Larry Bird.

"Hand me the binoculars," Ray said.

"They'll limit what you can see."

"Just give 'em to me, bozak."

"Fine."

"Oh, and one of those beef jerkies."

Groaning, because there was no stopping the mad gasser now, Scott handed the field glasses and salty, cured meat stick over. As the younger brother, Scott knew he was smarter and more mature, but Ray was stronger. For kids their age, might was right.

"You think maybe we're too late? No one's seen 'em for, like, two weeks now?"

A gnat buzzed Scott's ear, and he flicked his lobe hard enough to make himself wince. "I had to bring something to Mrs. Macy in the teacher's lounge on Thursday. When I got there, I overheard Mr. Settecase talking to Mr. Grundling. He said he was pretty sure lots more people were seeing them but weren't telling anyone because they didn't want to get made fun of. They both agreed if one passed over their house, they'd keep it to themselves." Scott finished the RC and crushed the can. "Trust me, they're still out there. And they love water for whatever reason. We couldn't be at a better spot."

May had turned to June and school was almost over, summer beckoning them like a wanton siren. And here they were, free and unsupervised, waiting for the unknown to come calling at its favorite port of call. A majority of the local signings had been by lakes, reservoirs, and rivers. Did the spaceships run on water? Or were the aliens just plain thirsty?

"What time is it?" Ray asked, the binoculars practically glued to his eyes.

Scott pushed the small button on the side of his digital watch that activated the light. "A little after midnight."

"You think Mom and Dad noticed we're gone?"

A shiver ran through Scott. He sure hoped not. His mother no longer checked on them as she used to do when they were little kids. They appreciated the privacy, especially when they were paging through *Fangoria* magazine late at night or that porno newspaper they found in a dumpster behind C-Town that featured a very bosomy woman named Candy Samples. That was their secret treasure of treasures and was now under the loose floorboard beneath Ray's bed. If their mother ever saw that, she'd have a conniption. When their father got home, oh how his belt would sing.

"Nah. We're good as long as we get back before four."

Dad was an early riser because he owned a bread delivery route. The last thing they wanted to do was come sneaking in when he was walking out to his truck.

After thirty minutes of talking about the problems with the Yankees (Don Mattingly aside) and whether their math teacher, Miss Sanderson, was hot or not, Ray started to yawn. "I thought we'd have seen something by now."

Gazing up at the stars, Scott said, "Yeah, me, too. Maybe it's their night off."

"Or they're visiting Carmel or Somers."

"Could be."

They sat in silence for a while, the chirrup of dozens of frogs providing the soundtrack to the night.

Scott suddenly jumped to his feet. "Hey, I know something we can do. I read about it in *UFO Magazine*. Hand me the flashlight."

Ray rolled over and tossed him the flashlight they had pilfered from their father's workbench in the basement. It was the strongest one in the house. Scott knew they'd need it when they navigated their way through the woods and weeds.

"What are you gonna do?" Ray asked, intrigued.

Pointing the flashlight at the sky, Scott said, "I'm going to try to bring them to us."

With his thumb on the on/off button, he started flicking away, sending bursts of light into the heavens. He knew a little Morse code, and did his best to send the message, "Welcome space brothers." At least he hoped that's what he was flashing. He shuddered to think he might be saying something insulting that would make the aliens mad.

"Do it to the west, now. We have to cover as much as we can. There's no telling where they're hiding," Ray said enthusiastically. Then, came the inevitable, "Here, let me try."

He swiped the flashlight from Scott's hand, which was actually not such a bad thing. The button on the flashlight was hard plastic with these little ridges that were starting to rub his thumb raw.

Ray went to work, the flashlight a flickering star in his hands. The only message he sent was, "We're here! Come on over and say hi!"

Scott massaged his thumb and eyed the backpack. He considered drinking one of the juice boxes, but he'd just had the RC and they still had hours ahead of them.

And speaking of drinking, he had to take a whiz.

"Are you guys blind?" Ray said to the sky. "Just give us one triangle. Show us something that'll blow us away!"

"I need the flashlight," Scott said.

"Why? I just started."

"I hafta take a piss."

A cool breeze rippled the water's surface that blew Scott's bangs from his forehead and sent a shiver from his toes to his cowlick. Just what he needed—a chill to shake up his kidneys.

"We're in the middle of nowhere. You can pee anywhere. Just turn around and let 'er rip."

"I gotta find a...a spot to go."

Ray rolled his eyes and clicked his tongue. "You gotta get over that whole shy bladder thing. It's stupid."

"You're stupid," Scott shot back.

"Stupid is as stupid does. And stupid has to find the perfect place to pee when he's surrounded by trees and tall grass and darkness." Ray turned away from Scott and went to work on the flashlight.

A sharp pain started to build in Scott's back and lower abdomen. "Come on, Ray. Please."

Ray tucked the flashlight under his armpit and said, "Okay, but you owe me your *Iron Man* number two-hundred."

Scott recoiled as if he'd been slapped in the face. "No way! That's going to be worth a lot of money someday."

"It's worth your not peeing your pants right now," Ray said with the kind of chuckle only older brothers could master. Ray was both Scott's best friend and worst tormentor.

Scott felt a splash against the back of his teeth. He'd started to hop and was this close to pinching his wiener.

"Fine," he blurted. "But you have to promise to keep it in plastic."

"Duh. Here, go find your potty."

Scott snatched the flashlight from his brother's hand and whipped around, hoping there was at least a semi-clear path into the line of trees to their right. The flashlight's beam made a haphazard laser show on the local foliage. He was about to dart to an opening between two maple trees when he saw something that made him forget all about his overflowing bladder.

A pair of red eyes hovered in the pitch, slipping behind a tree when the light hit them.

"Holy crap, did you see that?" Scott exclaimed, his voice echoing to the other side of the reservoir and beyond.

"See what?" Ray replied. Scott wasn't a fan of bugs, so Ray probably assumed he saw a creepy-crawly and was freaking out.

"Something's over there." He jabbed a trembling finger at the spot where he'd seen the glowing orbs.

"Oh snap, is it a security guard?" Ray was on his feet, backpack in hand, head swiveling this way and that, searching for the best way out.

Scott could barely hear his own voice over the thumping of his heart. "I don't think so. Unless security guards are like ten feet tall and have red eyes."

"What? You're nuts."

Scott lifted the flashlight slowly until its beam landed on the exact spot where the eyes had been, presumably watching them the entire time. All he could see now was the bark of a tree.

"I don't see anything," Ray said, creeping up so close he made Scott jump when he spoke. "I bet it was a raccoon." He slapped Scott hard on the shoulder. "You're such a wuss."

"It wasn't a raccoon," Scott said, shaking his head. "No way."

"You still going to pee, or are you too afraid now?"

Scott couldn't answer. His eyes were glued to that tree. Was whatever he saw right behind it, waiting for them to drop their guard?

"Okay, keep your *Iron Man*," Ray said, taking the flashlight back. "We came here to see a flying saucer, not a raccoon."

As the light arced away from the tree, it landed on an enormous, hair-covered creature that stood on two legs. It had large hands, a broad chest, and a flat nose.

The worst part of it all was the eyes. They were as red as horror movie blood and glowed from within.

"Hoooly shit!" Ray screamed.

The creature, hearing his outburst, matched it with a howl of its own.

Scott's blood turned to icy slush. His feet grew roots, and his jaw dropped to somewhere around the equator.

Ray grabbed hold of his arm. "Run! Run!"

His brother's hard tug broke Scott's paralysis. The two boys set off in the opposite direction of the shrieking monster. They didn't know what lay ahead of them. All that mattered was that it was away from the...

"Freaking bigfoot," Ray said between pants. The backpack bounced up and down on his back, tapping the base of his skull on the upward swing. "There's no bigfoots in Westchester. No way!"

Scott didn't see the need to point out that Ray was quite wrong. There was a bigfoot, a very *big* bigfoot, and judging from the sound of loud, crashing brush, it was running after them.

There was no way they could outrun a thing with legs that big. Scott wasn't even sure they could put a safe distance between them and it if they were on their bikes.

Running blindly had its disadvantages. Their faces were whipped by low-hanging branches, and their shoulders bruised when they came in contact with tree trunks that seemed out to get them.

And then the inevitable happened.

"Agh!" Ray yelled.

His foot got wedged in a tangle of roots and he went down like a sack of softballs. Scott, who had been right on his heels, fell on top of him.

"I…can't…breathe," Ray wheezed, rolling out from under Scott. He lay curled on the leaf-littered ground, clutching his stomach, his mouth opening and closing in a desperate, fish-on-land O.

Lying next to him, Scott could feel the pounding of the bigfoot's fast-approaching feet. There was a tremendous crack, as if the creature had snapped a tree in half. It brought Scott to his feet.

He reached down for Ray. "We have to get out of here. Get up! Come on. It's almost here!"

Ray struggled to get up. The best he could do was strike a pose of prayer on his knees, spitting out long ropes of saliva.

The running behind them suddenly stopped. Ray gasped for air.

Scott felt the monster before he smelled its breath that stank of raw fish and moldy earth.

Don't turn around. Don't turn around. Whatever you do, don't turn around.

He turned around.

He screeched at an octave rarely heard in human beings.

Ray followed suit with the limited breath he had in his lungs.

The seething, reeking, muscular bigfoot glared at them, the cold malevolence in its incandescent eyes turning their bowels to liquid. In fact, Scott was able to pee in front of another person for the first time in his life. A river ran down his legs as he stared into the face of his eternal doom. There was no chance to get away now. Why had they come here? Was seeing a strange light in the sky worth this?

The bigfoot reached for him with its mammoth, hairless hand. By the light of the moon shining through the canopy, Scott saw its fingernails were as black as night. There was a one-hundred-percent chance each nail was full to bursting with all kinds of infections.

Scott also noticed its hair, which hung like one of those heavy metal glam band hairdos, was brown with streaks of gray. The sasquatch's mouth, thin lips slightly parted, was a cavern of jagged teeth.

Instead of grabbing Scott's throat, the bigfoot savagely ripped the backpack off of Ray, nearly dislocating his arm in the process.

"Ow!" Ray cradled his arm. From the corner of his mouth, he said, "Let's get out of here while it concentrates on your backpack."

The bigfoot tore the pack open, unfamiliar with zippers as one would expect from a legend of cryptozoology. Out spilled the silver sodas, juice boxes, beef jerky, fruit roll-ups, fruit pies, and chips. Keeping its blazing eyes on them, the beast bent down, its long arms easily swiping up one of the fruit roll-ups. It gave it a quick sniff and popped it in its mouth.

Seeing a bigfoot's face cringe would have been comical at any other time. It spit the faux-fruit gob over Scott's shoulder. A dollop of its rancid spit found Scott's cheek. He thought he was going to barf.

It appeared to like the fruit pies and pinched its nose at the fizzy bite of the RC cola (after biting the tops off).

It went for the chips next, but it gripped the bag too hard and popped it. Chips exploded everywhere, a few sticking to its fur. The bigfoot was startled, then angry. It sneered at the boys, exposing its deadly, yellowed eyeteeth.

And then Scott realized something.

How could they see the bigfoot so well? There was only a quarter moon out tonight and the tree cover here should have been enough to thwart any attempts at illuminating their demise.

He looked up and was blinded by a single white light hovering overhead. Its intensity increased and they were suddenly encircled with a luminescence brighter than the sunniest July day.

It wasn't just a light. Warmth was coming from it as well. Scott felt like a bag of french fries under a heat lamp at Burger King.

Even the bigfoot paused in its rummaging to cast its crimson eyes skyward. Ray, at the farthest perimeter from the cone of light, said with marvel in his voice, "Jeezus! It's one of the triangles! Look, Scott! Look!"

Scott tried and came away with burned retinas and teary eyes. When he blinked, an afterimage imposed itself against the backdrop of darkness and damned if he didn't see the outline of a triangle within that cone of brilliance. He turned away from the now-confused bigfoot to rub his eyes, confident the stinky brute was in just as bad of shape.

Then, as quick as the snapping of fingers, the light was gone. The end-of-spring air now felt like late fall.

With some of his vision regained, Scott turned around and saw the bigfoot's face was also stained by tears. That must have made the bigfoot angry—because whoever heard of a crying bigfoot—and the man-ape was taking it out on the nearest tree, smashing it with its fists while barking out a series of grunts that were like knuckle slaps to Scott's chest.

"Watch out," Ray shouted, pulling Scott away before one of those wildly swinging hairy arms took his head clean off and sent it flying to Poughkeepsie.

The bigfoot stopped, turning this way and that, trying to focus in on where the voice had come from.

"Be really quiet," Scott whispered in his brother's ear. The creature must have really gotten an eyeful of that light. Maybe red eyes were weaker than normal human eyes. No matter, this was their chance to get away. "Follow me and don't make a sound."

The brothers took one step. There were too many dead leaves on the ground. The soft crunch gave them away. The bigfoot yowled and dove straight for them.

Something moved to the right and left of the boys. A second before the bigfoot was going to barrel into them and turn them into tomato paste, two blurry figures intercepted the beast and slammed into its chest, sending it skidding backward.

The light came on again.

This time, Scott thought his eyes were going to fall right out of his head. Ray grabbed his arm so hard, it hurt.

"Am I hallucinating?" Ray asked.

Scott didn't know what to say. Maybe this was all a hallucination. Maybe, just maybe, some weird chemical had gotten into the soda vats at the RC Cola Company and the past ten minutes were nothing but some sort of psychedelic trip, like the kind they were shown in those "Just Say No" short films at school. If this is what LSD was like, Scott wanted no part of it.

Running from a bigfoot in a New York suburb was one thing. Watching it grapple with a pair of bulbous-headed, big-eyed, stick-skinny-armed gray aliens was the kind of sensory overload that could drive a person mad.

While the bigfoot was down, one of the aliens scrambled over its hairy body with the quick and disturbing movements of a silverfish and jabbed a needle into its neck. The bigfoot didn't appreciate that one bit. It backhanded the alien, sending it airborne for a good fifteen feet before a tree stopped its unscheduled flight.

The sasquatch leaped to its feet like a wrestler getting off the canvas, ready to turn the tide. It swiped at the second alien, but this one was smart enough to duck.

"We have to leave. Now," Scott hissed. The muscles in his legs jumped and jittered, ready to burn high-top sneaker rubber.

Ray wasn't of the same mind. "Are you kidding me? No way am I not watching this."

"Stop being a dumb ass. Let's…go!"

His brother wouldn't move. There wasn't a chance in hell Scott was leaving his idiot brother behind.

"Can we at least move to someplace safer where we can watch?"

The second alien produced a kind of laser gun from thin air and zapped the bigfoot in the knee with a yellow beam of light. The stench of burning, filthy hair was as nauseating as their Aunt Lori's tuna casserole.

Bigfoot punched the alien with the gun and sent it tumbling like a rock and out of sight. Luckily, the first alien had recovered and shot the other knee. It staggered the monster but didn't drop it.

Scott and Ray found a big rock a few feet away, close to the water's edge, and got behind it. If push came to shove, Scott was ready to jump in the water and swim to the other side. The bigfoot looked too big and heavy to be buoyant. As for the aliens, with their advanced technology, there really wasn't any way to avoid them. He just had to hope they were friendly.

"Holy shitballs, did you see that?" Ray said a little too loudly for Scott's taste.

The bigfoot grabbed one of the aliens by the back of the neck and smashed it face-first into the ground. Its head shattered, breaking not into shreds of goo and bits of skull, but hundreds of scraps of metal and glass.

"What…in…the…hell?" Scott said, gawping at the spectacle.

Not satisfied with decapitating the alien, the bigfoot stomped on its back. The whole thing fractured into a mess of metal junk with the sound of a car crash.

"It's a freaking robot!" Ray said.

Ray wasn't often right, but Scott was going to give him this one.

The other alien—or robot—or alien robot—ran around the bigfoot and grabbed it by the back of its head, pulling so hard, the beast fell over. The alien aimed its gun between the bigfoot's blood-red eyes, but before it could pull the trigger, the sasquatch lashed out and grabbed the alien's ankle. It flicked the alien away similar to how Scott would swat a gnat from his face.

This alien robot was made of tougher stuff. It struck the boulder they were cowering behind hard enough to break a man in two, sat on the ground for a moment, got up, and looked at them with its fathomless, almond-shaped eyes. The eyes blinked once with an audible click, and then it was back on the offensive.

Anxious for more, the bigfoot came rushing at the alien. They were on a crash course for disaster. When they hit, they made a sound Scott would spend lifetimes trying to describe. The closest he could come to it was a car plowing into a charging buffalo.

This time, the alien didn't fare so well because the bigfoot cocked its arm back at the last moment and delivered a kill punch to the robot's gut. Its head popped off and flew into the air like the puck dinging the bell at a carnival strongman game. The rest of the body disintegrated into mechanical confetti, showering the ground with flakes of gray, silver, and gold. It had the potential to be a wondrous sight, if not for the fact the boys were back to fleeing from a monster.

Ray stared at the cascade of alien parts with profound shock. "I really thought they'd win."

The bigfoot jerked its head their way.

Scott glanced at the water.

"Take off your sneakers," he said.

"Why?"

"'Cause we're gonna swim for it."

Thank God this wasn't winter where they would have been wearing heavy clothes and jackets and the water would be colder than the ass end of a well.

This time Ray was more than happy to retreat. Aliens from space were the only thing that could keep him in the presence of a killer cryptid, and now the space aliens were fit for the junkyard.

They flipped off their Reeboks and bolted for the water.

The bigfoot was hot on their tail, slobbering like a hungry bulldog.

Scott took a quick peek behind them.

They weren't going to make it.

The water was only ten feet away, but the long arm of the sasquatch was inches from getting ahold of their shirt collars.

"Faster!" he yelled.

No matter what he said, the law of physics was against them.

An instant later, the bigfoot had them. Its gross, bacteria-filled nails ripped down the back of Scott's neck and snared his shirt. He was lifted off the ground, his feet still running, now going nowhere. Ray was plucked into the air as well.

They looked at one another, eyes glassy with fear and resigned that this would be their last moment together. They would never flip baseball cards, sneak downstairs to watch horror movies on their new cable TV, argue over who was better, Ron Guidry or Doc Gooden, or a whole host of shared likes, dislikes, and heated discussions ever again.

"I'm sorry, we should have run when the aliens came," Ray blubbered.

The bigfoot twisted Ray around so they were eye to eye. Scott's brother lashed out and punched the monster in the face. Scott swore its eyes glowed even hotter. There was no point admonishing Ray for doing it. What did he have to lose?

While Ray endured the bigfoot's hot, horrid breath as it hollered directly in his face, Scott spotted a trio of bright, white lights moving above them. They weren't planes because planes didn't cruise the sky doing circles around one another.

They grew brighter and larger the closer they came.

He prayed they were dropping off some more of those alien robots, enough to keep the bigfoot distracted long enough for them to run like hell, find their bikes and motor home where they could change their underwear.

Then the lights up and disappeared.

Ray cried and called out for their mother as the bigfoot drew his face closer to its mouth. Scott tried to kick at the big ape, but it angled him just far enough away to miss.

Oh my God! It was going to eat Ray's freaking face off!

And then it's going to eat mine!

Scott felt no shame wailing for his mother right alongside Ray.

Snick! Fizzle! Blam!

Three sounds in quick succession preceded the harsh shaft of yellow light that blasted from the heavens.

That was followed by a feeling of weightlessness that made Scott's stomach do somersaults.

In fact, he, the bigfoot, and Ray were all tumbling in the now warm air, the ground rapidly fading from view. During one of his turns, Scott saw three objects above them, the one with the light beckoning.

He was terrified of heights. So much so, he couldn't even get on a ladder. Seeing the reservoir laid out a hundred feet or more below them made him hurl.

Unfortunately, in their state of limited gravity, his chunks formed a spinning cloud the three of them slipped in and out of as they tumbled upward. It was beyond gross and caused Ray to add to it.

As for the bigfoot, it had been struck mute, or maybe even, if they were lucky, dead.

Up ahead, an orange ringed portal awaited them, drawing them up like a milkshake through a straw. Scott tried to stop his spinning, to hold his hands out so he could maybe touch the edge of the portal.

Unfortunately, he lost consciousness before that ever happened.

When Scott woke up, he was greeted by the vacant eyes of one of the gray aliens. Its huge, black eyes looked like something that belonged on a bug that had lived through a nuclear detonation.

"Yaaaahhhh!" Scott squealed, jumping to his feet and running.

He charged into something soft yet sturdy. Hands grabbed him by the shoulders.

"Whoa, whoa, calm down, kid. You're going to hurt yourself."

He looked up into the pale face of a woman with kind eyes and short, dirty-blonde hair. She wore a brown leather jacket and tan slacks, like the kind his dad wore to work.

She wasn't exactly tall, but she was definitely a humanoid.

Trying to spin out of her grasp and see if that alien robot was near, he almost fell over when Ray came sauntering over. "Hey, you're awake."

"Ray!"

"And you must be Scott," the woman said.

Scott looked around. They were in a round room that resembled the bridge of the Enterprise in *Star Trek*, except all of the instrumentation was kind of clear looking, like it was there but not there. He wasn't even sure if the few chairs in the center of the room were real or some kind of hologram.

One thing that was real was the gray alien and several identical others. Their big heads were fixed on him and he didn't like it one bit.

"Where are we?" he said, breathless to the point of fainting.

Ray smiled. "Where do you think, dummy? We got saved by one of the UFOs!"

"What?"

"I have to thank you for finding our wild man," the woman said. "We've been looking for him for months. He may be big, but he knows how to hide."

"W-w-w-ild man?" Scott stuttered.

"She means bigfoot," Scott said.

"No, I mean wild man," she replied curtly, though Scott detected a note of humor in it.

"Did you kill it?"

She shook her head and smiled. "We wouldn't think of such a thing. No, he's back in his pen. Sugar makes him a little crazy. Good for me, because it brought him out in the open. Bad for you boys because it looks like he put quite the fright in you." She eyed Scott's still wet pants.

He looked at one of the aliens. "What about them? The grays? How can all this be happening?"

"Them? They just keep things running. Like mechanical mechanics. Hey, that's a good one." She laughed at her own joke. "There's nothing to be afraid of with them. Same as being frightened of your toaster."

"But, where do they come from? Are they going to invade Earth?"

The woman bent down to look Scott in the eye. She was so familiar. "Invade? Never. They just like to check on things from time to time. And in this case, accidentally lose a bit of cargo."

"But...but...but..."

"She said she's gonna take us on a spin around the moon before taking us home," Ray said with a grin from ear to ear.

"To the moon? But that would take days. We have to home before dad gets up."

"Oh, I'll get you home well before then. Take a seat and I'll open up a window."

Ray and Scott sat in clear seats next to each other. The woman ran her hands over brightly colored lights in the air and suddenly the entire night sky encircled the bridge. The lights of Westchester were well below them.

"You ready?" she said.

"Heck yeah," Ray replied.

Scott could only look at it all in wonder. He couldn't even remember his fear of heights. But as they zoomed into space, he did recall where he had seen this woman before.

A whole half a chapter had been devoted to Amelia Earhart in his history book.

"Are you?"

She gave him a wink. "I'm sure not your Aunt Tilly. I'll tell you how I ended up here on the way back. Let's just say I couldn't resist the chance to pilot the ultimate flying machine."

He had so many questions buzzing around his brain, it was like having a beehive in his skull.

All of that would have to wait for now.

The moon was right there, seemingly so close he could touch it.

He wondered if Amelia Earhart would take a request and cruise around the dark side.

PUT ON A HAPPY FACE

by Christopher Golden

The blood seeping out of the midget car was Benny's first clue that something had gone awry. The audience kept laughing—either they hadn't seen it yet or they thought it was part of the show—so Benny didn't slow down. He waddled on his big shoes, storming with exaggerated frustration toward Clancy the Cop, and slapped the other clown in the face with a rubber chicken.

It looked like it hurt.

The audience roared.

Back up.

The night before—a Friday—the circus had ended at quarter past nine on the dot. Appleby, the manager, was a stickler for punctuality. The last bow took place between ten and fifteen minutes past the hour every performance, and when the thunderous applause—which, honestly, wasn't always thunderous and was sometimes barely more than a ripple—had died down, the ticket sellers became ushers…ushering folks out of the tent as quickly as possible. The ushers didn't hurry people because anyone was in a rush to get their makeup off, but because once the little kids started moving, all the popcorn and cotton candy and soda and hot dogs started to churn in their bellies. Much better to hose the vomit off the ground outside than in the tent.

The clowns ran out of the tent the way NFL teams came onto the field, arms above their heads, whooping and hollering, before the last of the crowd had departed. Benny had always thought it looked stupid, but Zerbo—the boss clown and the troupe's whiteface—wanted to leave the straggling audience members with an image of the clowns as a kind of family.

Out behind the tent, the family fell apart. The tents and trailers that made up the circus camp were a tense United Nations of performers and laborers without any real unity. Like a high school full of jocks and geeks and emo kids, the clowns and workers and animal trainers and acrobats each formed their own caste, every group thinking themselves above the others. Friendships existed outside the boundaries of those castes, but when it came to conflict, they stuck together like unions. The acrobats were effete, the animal trainers grave and sensitive, and the workers gruff and strong.

But nobody fucked with the clowns.

"You mess with the clown, you get the horns," Zerbo was fond of misquoting, right before blasting you in the face with an air horn. His idea of a joke. Most people laughed, but Benny had never found the boss clown all that funny.

The Macintosh Traveling Circus Troupe had been playing sold-out audiences in a field in Brimfield, Massachusetts for a week. Normally, the grounds were used for the huge antique flea market the town held a couple of times a year, but the circus had been a welcome novelty, as far as Benny could tell. Not that Appleby talked to him about it. Clowns were beneath the manager's notice, except when it came time for him to talk to Zerbo about renewing contracts. Even then, nobody bothered to ask Benny what he thought.

In the hierarchy of clowns in the Macintosh Traveling Circus Troupe, Benny Martini was on the bottom rung. The runt of the litter. The red-headed stepchild. Shit, that last one was probably offensive in these sensitive modern times. No matter. The point was that Benny was an afterthought to everyone, even the audience.

He'd often thought about how much happier he would have been if, like Tiny and Oscar—two of the other character clowns in the troupe—he'd been too stupid to know it. But even Tiny and Oscar were above him. If the troupe had been a wolf pack, Benny would have been on his back, baring his throat for everyone who came along. And why?

It was all about the laughs.

Laughter and his status in the circus, nearly always the only two things he thought about, were foremost on his mind as he followed Zerbo, Oscar, Tiny, Clancy the Cop, and the rest of them into clown alley. Tiny bumped Oscar, then clapped him on the back—they'd successfully completed the Hotshots gag after having totally bungled it the night before. On a façade so rickety even old-time Hollywood stuntmen would've shied away from it, three-hundred-pound Tiny dressed in drag and pretended to be a mother trapped with her infant on the third story of a burning building. The fire effects were minimal—gas jets, a low flame, a lot of orange lighting, the whole thing designed by a guy who'd helped put together the Indiana Jones Stunt Spectacular at Disney World, before he'd been fired for drinking on the job—but it looked great, as long as Tiny didn't set his wig on fire.

Oscar, in character as a clown firefighter, pushed a barrel of water back and forth across the ring, exhorting Tiny to throw him the infant and then jump into the water. The culmination of the whole thing was that Tiny's aim would be off, forcing Oscar to step into the water barrel in order to catch the baby—only a doll, of course. At the moment he caught it, the trap door would give way beneath the ring, dropping Oscar and the baby and the water through and giving the audience the impression that the baby had been heavy enough to drive him into the ground. It was a pain in the ass to set up the gag, but when it went off, the surprise always led to real laughs, especially when Tiny theatrically threw up his hands, mopped his sweating face with his wig, took a deep breath, and blew out the fire around the windows like candles on a birthday cake. The lights would go dark. Cue the applause.

Thursday night, Tiny had stumbled, throwing off his timing. The doll—to the eyes of the crowd, an infant—had tumbled down to splat in the middle of the ring while Oscar stood watching like a fool, until the trapdoor gave way and shot him down into the space beneath. The audience had to know the baby wasn't real, but they'd screamed all the same.

Timing was everything, Benny always said.

How Tiny and Oscar could screw up the gag so badly and still be above him in the pecking order, he would never understand.

In clown alley that Friday night, he washed off his makeup without a word to any of the others. Most of the time he shot the breeze with them and tried to ignore the fact that, four years since he'd joined up, they still treated him like a mascot, but not tonight. The cold cream took off most of the makeup and then he splashed a little water on his face and dragged on a pair of stained blue jeans and a Red Sox sweatshirt—it had been strangely cool the past few nights, uncommon for July in western Massachusetts.

As he left the others behind and went out to wander the grounds and clear his head, he ran into the lovely blond contortionist, Lorna Seger. There were tears in her eyes and she gave him a helpless, hopeless glance that made him think maybe she wanted to talk about her breakup with the stunt rider, Domingo.

"Hey," he said, shaken from the reverie of his self-pity by her sadness. "You okay?"

Lorna smiled and wiped at her eyes. "Could be worse, I guess," she said. "I could be a clown."

Benny flinched. Lorna chuckled softly to let him know it had been a joke. He hoped Domingo ran her down on his motorcycle.

"You're such a bitch," he said.

Lorna rolled her eyes. "Why is it clowns never have a sense of humor?"

He walked on, fuming, wanting to scream, wanting to get the hell away from the circus but crippled by the knowledge that—like everyone else who performed under the tent—he had nowhere else to go.

Put on a happy face, his mother would have said. Remembering did make him smile, but it faded quickly.

The wind picked up as he walked the grounds, which were rutted and pitted with tire tracks from decades of vehicles moving through the fields in all weather, turning up muddy ridges, which had then dried and hardened. Loud voices came from the trailers where the workers had made their own small camp, and he could smell sausages cooking on a grill. When he passed a tent, he saw them, standing in a semicircle, drinking beer, a small radio picking up a static-laced broadcast of tonight's Red Sox-Yankees game. Summer in New England. These guys looked like their entire life was a tailgate party. They worked hard and were content with the cycle of labor and paycheck, beer and cookouts and Red Sox games. In a way, Benny envied them.

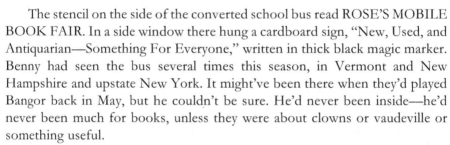

The stencil on the side of the converted school bus read ROSE'S MOBILE BOOK FAIR. In a side window there hung a cardboard sign, "New, Used, and Antiquarian—Something For Everyone," written in thick black magic marker. Benny had seen the bus several times this season, in Vermont and New Hampshire and upstate New York. It might've been there when they'd played Bangor back in May, but he couldn't be sure. He'd never been inside—he'd never been much for books, unless they were about clowns or vaudeville or something useful.

Tonight, he just wanted a distraction.

The accordion bus door was open and a sign indicated that the mobile book fair was as well, so he went up the couple of steps, ducking his head though he'd never be tall enough to bang it. Oddly enough, he didn't notice the woman right away. At first, all he could see were the books, and he wondered how she managed to keep them all from falling off the shelves while she drove the old beast of a school bus around the northeastern United States. The metal shelving units had been secured to the walls and lined both sides of the bus. Each shelf had an ingenious device, a bar that went across the spines of the books to hold them in place and could be locked into different notches to accommodate racks of books of different sizes.

"Looking for something to read?" the woman asked, and he blinked and stared at her.

She'd been there all along, of course, but it felt almost as if he'd dreamed her into being. Slender and fit, perhaps forty, she wore black pants and shoes and a tight pink tank with a bright red rose silhouette stretched across her breasts. Rose—for how could she have been anyone else?—had an olive complexion and a proud Roman nose, and she wore a kindly expression, her gaze alert and attentive. Though the interior of the mobile book fair was lit mainly with strings of old white Christmas lights, he could see that her eyes were icy blue. It both pleased and unnerved him to have someone study him with such intensity—such intimacy. People looked at him all the time when he had his clown makeup on, but he couldn't remember how long it had been since anyone had really *seen* him when he didn't have it on.

"I doubt you'd have anything for me," he said. "I'm not a big reader."

"Didn't you see the sign," she said, amused. "Something for everyone. What do you do here?"

He almost lied, but she would've taken one look at his little potbelly and stiff shoulders and known he wasn't an acrobat.

"I'm a clown."

Her eyes lit up. "I've got a small section back here. Not a whole shelf, but a handful of interesting antiquarian books I picked up from an old guy in Cheektowaga, when his carnival went belly-up."

Most of the books were things he'd seen before. Way back in high school, he'd researched Grimaldi and Tovolo and Ricketts, studied the Fratellinis, and watched the films of the great movie directors who had started their careers as circus clowns, like Fellini and Jodorowsky. Charlie Chaplin had become his god, and he mastered the rolling walk of the Little Tramp. There were many schools of comedy, but Benny had never been much interested in telling jokes or doing stand-up. In his heart, he had always been a clown. Though some of them were probably quite valuable, none of the books Rose's Mobile Book Fair had on her shelves were unfamiliar to him.

He'd just begun to turn away when he noticed the frayed spine of a book lying on its side atop the dozen or so she had shelved at the end of her boys' adventure section. The worn, faded lettering was almost unreadable in the shadows, but when he slipped his slender fingers in and slid the volume out, the cloth cover made him stiffen in surprise. The comedy and tragedy masks were there, along with the initials G.T.

Quickly he leafed to the title page and a warm feeling spread through him. *Charade: The Secret to Being a Clown*, by Giovanni Tovolo. He had never even heard of the book, had not run across it in any of his reading and research, even in the biography of Tovolo he'd read. The famous Italian character clown had retired after a horrifying accident had taken sixteen lives in a big top fire outside Chicago in 1917. All but forgotten, Tovolo had been a particular fascination of Benny's because the man had earned his reputation doing characters. Most of the famous clowns were whitefaces or augustes. Tovolo could do anything, at least according to what Benny had read…but now, to read it in Tovolo's own words.

Maybe Tovolo could help him figure out how he ended up spending four years at the wrong end of clown alley. He glanced up at Rose, unable to stifle his excitement and hoping she didn't take advantage of him.

"How much do you want for this one?" he asked.

She took it from his hand, opened it to see the price she'd penciled on the first page. "Twenty-two dollars."

Benny swallowed hard, knowing his smile was too thin. Did she not realize that, to certain collectors, this book would be worth a hundred times that? Or did she simply not care, having paid next to nothing for it herself.

He smiled. "I'll take it."

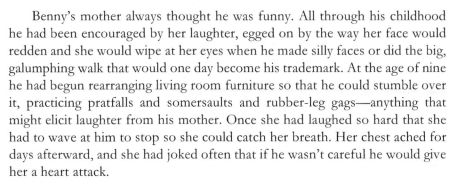

Benny's mother always thought he was funny. All through his childhood he had been encouraged by her laughter, egged on by the way her face would redden and she would wipe at her eyes when he made silly faces or did the big, galumphing walk that would one day become his trademark. At the age of nine he had begun rearranging living room furniture so that he could stumble over it, practicing pratfalls and somersaults and rubber-leg gags—anything that might elicit laughter from his mother. Once she had laughed so hard that she had to wave at him to stop so she could catch her breath. Her chest ached for days afterward, and she had joked often that if he wasn't careful he would give her a heart attack.

That's how funny Benny Martini was as a kid.

He loved to make her laugh. He watched the Three Stooges and the Marx Brothers and forced his friends into helping him reenact their gags. Mrs. Martini took young Benny to the circus every year, and when the clowns made the audience roar with their hilarious antics, he watched with fascination and a dawning envy. For weeks after a circus trip, he would mimic the clowns, practicing the faces they pulled, their walks, their timing.

In school, he put whoopee cushions on the seats of teachers and thumbtacks on the chairs of the girls he liked. In the eighth grade, he had taped a sign to Tim Rivard's back that read HONK IF YOU THINK I'M A MORON. Only other jocks had been brave enough to make honking noises when Rivard walked down the hall, but it took the football player until fourth period to really start to wonder what all the honking was about. He'd slammed Benny's head into a locker, but the sign alone hadn't been enough to prompt the violence. That had come when Benny had pointed out that Rivard going most of the day without noticing the sign pretty much proved his point.

When Benny told his mother what he'd done, she'd put a hand over her mouth to hide her laughter. And when he confessed that he'd been suspended for three days—even though he was the one with the black eye—she'd laughed so hard she had cried, tears streaming down her pretty face, ruining her makeup.

Benny had become the class clown by design. He knew every class had to have one, and he'd be damned if he let some other guy take on that role. His classmates—hell, the whole school—would remember him forever as *that guy*, the one with the jokes, the one with the faces, the one who couldn't be serious for two seconds.

There were dark moods, of course. Who didn't have them? Who hadn't spent a little time studying his own face in the mirror, trying to recognize something…anything of value? Who hadn't tested the edges of the sharpest knives on the hidden parts of their skin just to see how sharp they really were, or sat in the dark for a while and wondered if people were laughing with him or at him?

By the time senior year of high school rolled around, Benny didn't know how to be anything but funny, and he didn't want to learn. His mother had told him he ought to try to do birthday parties, paint himself up as a clown and make children laugh. Benny would rather have cut his own throat. He didn't want to do gags at birthday parties for a bunch of nose-picking brats; he wanted to perform in a circus.

The Macintosh Traveling Circus Troupe came to town in the spring of his senior year. The Macintosh was small enough that it still relied on posters hung at ice cream stands and grocery stores and barber shops to pull in an audience. In a little town like Corriveau, Vermont, that sort of thing still worked.

He'd gone to the circus every day, hung around before and after shows, talked to the workers, the animal trainers, the ticket takers, and eventually worked up the courage to talk to the clowns. By the third day, after hours, they invited him into clown alley to talk with them while they removed their makeup and hung up costumes and props. Benny could barely breathe. It had felt to him as though he had stepped into a film, or into history. He could smell the greasepaint, could practically feel the texture of the costumes, could hear the roar of the crowd, even though the tent had stood empty by then.

The second to last night, his hopes of an invitation fast fading, he confessed his hopes and dreams and begged for an apprenticeship. The clowns had indulged him, patted him on the back, told stories of their own glory days, but none of them had encouraged him. It was a hell of a life, they'd said, something they would never wish on anybody. It was brutal on family and worse on love. Circus life set them apart from the rest of the world, created a distance that could never be bridged. Once you were in, you were in. They were trying to scare him off, but Benny had persisted.

Two hours after their final performance, as they were packing to move on, Zerbo—the boss clown—had given him the word. They'd take him on for the rest of the season, no pay, just food and a place to lay his head. If he was good enough to take part in the act by the season's end, and could get some laughs of his own, the circus manager—Mr. Appleby—would hire him on. If not, he'd be sent home.

Benny had given it his all, pulled out every gag, every funny face, every silly walk he had ever learned. He had studied the troupe, could stand in for almost any of them if someone fell ill. At the end of the season, on the fairgrounds in

Briarwood, Connecticut, they were as good as their word—a spotlight of his own, a chance to prove himself.

The laughs had been thin and the applause half-hearted, but Zerbo had given him the thumbs up. Tiny had told him later that it had been a near thing, but he'd worked so hard they had wanted to give him a second chance.

Now, four years of second chances later, he still felt like an apprentice.

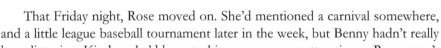

That Friday night, Rose moved on. She'd mentioned a carnival somewhere, and a little league baseball tournament later in the week, but Benny hadn't really been listening. Kind as she'd been to him, a woman as attractive as Rose wasn't interested in doing more than selling him a book, and she'd done that already.

He stayed up all through that cool night, reading Tovolo's words over and over until the battery of his flashlight began to give out, the light to dim. By then, the horizon had begun to glow with the promise of dawn, but Benny read the final chapter of the book over a few more times. At first, he'd thought the whole thing was some kind of joke, Tovolo trying to pull one over on the reader, or attempting some tongue-in-cheek social commentary about circus life that didn't quite translate in his imperfect English. The book had been broken down into thirds—part one a memoir of his life, part two a kind of compendium of what he considered the funniest gags, and part three a reminiscence about his lifelong interest in the darker aspects of the history of clowns, everything from suicides and murders to haunted circuses and black magic.

The final chapter concerned Tovolo's lifelong struggle with his own talent, and his belief that he had never been funny enough. Two small circuses had merged, forcing him to perform alongside his longtime rival, Vincenzo Mellace, and every time the audience laughed for Mellace, Tovolo had wanted to set himself on fire. The reference to self-immolation made Benny shiver every time he read it, and he wondered if it had been written before or after the tragic blaze that had led to the Italian's retirement.

Tovolo had befriended a Belgian fire-eater who had come over from the other circus and who shared his hatred of Vincenzo Mellace. The fire-eater's mother traveled with her son, and sometimes told fortunes on the show grounds after the audience had gone home and the circus folk had drunk too much wine.

She had been the one to instruct him as to the ingredients for the elixir, and to explain to him precisely how to summon the spirit of Polichinelle, the patron of clowns, the demon known to children as the jester puppet Punch.

As the circus folk began to rise that Saturday morning, the day arriving overcast and bleak, Benny read Tovolo's final chapter over and over. Each time, he held his breath as he read the last few lines.

Mellace's routine was a disaster, he had written. *He has performed Busy Bee thousands of times, and yet it seemed like his first. Laughter was sporadic at best, and mostly sympathetic at that. There were boos. For myself…I could do no wrong. They laughed at a simple chase on the Hippodrome Track. They howled when Rostoni and I performed the Shoot-Out. And when I went out to do the Cooking Class gag on my own, it felt like a dream of how smoothly I have always wished for a performance to unfold.*

God, how they laughed.

I cannot say for certain that Polichinelle was in my corner tonight, but he was certainly no friend to Mellace. If offering the demon a little of my blood and a handful of days at the end of my life is all that is required for me to become the greatest clown in the world, it is a small price to pay.

When Benny heard Oscar and Tiny calling for him, he closed the book, yet as he went about his morning, he could think of nothing but the elixir and the summoning spell that the fire-eater's mother had given to Tovolo. One line kept repeating itself in his head.

God, how they laughed.

The blood seeping out of the midget car was Benny's first clue that something had gone awry. The audience kept laughing—either they hadn't seen it yet or they thought it was part of the show—so Benny didn't slow down. He waddled on his big shoes, storming with exaggerated frustration toward Clancy the Cop, and slapped the other clown in the face with a rubber chicken.

It looked like it hurt.

The audience roared.

He'd asked the demon Polichinelle for his heart's desire—to be the funniest clown in the circus. As blood flew from Clancy the Cop's split lip, Benny began to have second thoughts. He staggered backward, tripped over his own big clown feet, and let himself roll with the fall. His whole life had been spent performing such antics, so if there was anything he knew how to do, it was fall. He rolled on his curving spine, then flipped back up onto his feet and executed a fluid bow.

Clancy, snorting like a bull, eyes bulging with his fury, barreled toward him running on an engine of vengeance. Benny saw him coming just in time, spun in a circle to avoid his outstretched hands, and whacked Clancy in the back of the head with the plucked, frozen chicken—it wasn't made of rubber anymore. The impact dropped Clancy to the ground, where he began to spasm and seize.

Benny lifted the chicken by its legs, examining it in full view of the audience. From their seats, they couldn't have seen the blood on the chicken, would presume his horror just a part of the act. He turned and looked at them, a wide-eyed clown mugging for the paying customers, and they ate it up. The stands were shaking with laughter.

Stunned, a dead, frozen chicken dangling from one clenched fist, Benny remembered the midget car. He turned, saw the blood dripping from the door seam, and started to run toward it. A scream filled the air and Benny spun to see Tiny standing in the window of the Hotshots building façade, his striped dress and blond wig both in flames that spread quickly to his arms and the baby doll bundled in his arms.

But from the way Tiny stared at the swaddled infant—and from the high, shrieking noise that could really be nothing else—Benny had the terrible idea that maybe it wasn't a doll in Tiny's arms. Not anymore. Not thanks to Polichinelle.

Burning alive, screaming baby in his arms, Tiny jumped from the façade, which was now engulfed in flames, and plummeted toward Oscar, who stood knee deep in the water barrel below. Too late, Oscar realized his situation. He tried to climb out of the barrel, but tripped on the rim and fell half-in, half-out of the water, where he lay when Tiny and his baby struck Earth in a comet-like blaze. The trap-door opened and all three of them crashed through, water barrel and all. Steam and smoke rose with a hiss and the stink of burning hair and flesh began to fill the big top.

The applause was deafening. The laughter rolled through the tent like a hurricane.

Bobo shot Zerbo through the head during the Shoot-Out. The guns were supposed to be made of rubber. When Zerbo's only bullet went astray and killed a young father, passing through his popcorn tub on the way and spraying butter and popcorn onto a dozen people, the laughter turned to breathless, teary-eyed hysteria that reminded Benny of his mother.

Numb with shock, Benny staggered over to the midget car—what the public called a clown car—and vomited across the hood. Crimson leaked from every crevice in the miniature vehicle, pooling on the floor and running across the ground. The stink of blood and offal wafted off the midget car, and he felt as if he stood in an abattoir.

The driver's door popped open. A colorfully-clad leg slipped out, and then Polichinelle climbed from the car. He wore a red and black jester costume, complete with ruffles at the shirt cuffs and bells atop his pronged hat and at the toes of his shoes. His alabaster skin did not appear to be makeup, nor did the bright red circles like burn scars on his cheeks.

Benny caught a glimpse of the carnage inside the midget car. The trapdoor meant to be beneath it no longer existed. Eight clowns had been broken and twisted and jammed together to make sure they could all fit in a space that would've been cramped for two, and somehow Polichinelle had fit into the driver's seat.

Bobo stood in shock above the corpse of Zerbo, shaking and weeping. As Polichinelle pirouetted toward him, Bobo could only stare, but as he looked into the demon's eyes, he screamed.

Polichinelle plucked a trick flower from Zerbo's corpse and held it as if offering it to Bobo for a sniff. When he squeezed the rubber bulb dangling from the flower, an acrid-smelling liquid jetted out of it, coating Bobo's head. His scream rose to a shriek as his face began to melt and his eyes sank into his skull. When he crumpled to his knees and then toppled sideways to land beside Zerbo, his scream died.

Benny had never heard laughter so uproarious. The audience cheered. Some stood and others doubled-over, clutching their bellies. Some slapped hands across their chests as their hearts burst and they slid into the aisles, gasping into cardiac arrest. Throats went hoarse, faces turned red, hands blistered from applause, but they couldn't stop. Their faces were stretched into grins that split the corners of their mouths and they wept tears of terror and pain and amusement, but they simply could not stop. It was, after all, the funniest thing they had ever seen.

God, how they laughed, Benny thought, and then, at last, he began to laugh as well.

Polichinelle performed a mad, capering little dance, part ballet and part mincing, mocking swagger, and then mimed a curtsy to the audience.

Through his laughter and his tears, Benny managed to choke out a single word. "Why?"

Polichinelle gave him an apologetic shrug, an angelic look on the demon's face. "You wanted to be the funniest clown in the circus."

Trying to catch his breath, Benny forced out the words. "All…all the others…are dead."

Polichinelle giggled. "Don't blame me, Benny. Blame your mother for all those years of lies."

Benny stared, eyes widening in horror. "My…my…" he gasped, but he couldn't get the word out.

"Sorry, pal," Polichinelle said. "But you're just not that funny."

The giant mallet seemed to appear from nowhere. Polichinelle gripped it in both hands as he swung, and Benny knew it wouldn't be made of hollow plastic or rubber. The crowd roared, laughing themselves to death.

God, how they laughed.

REMEMBERING FRANK

by Jason Parent

Frank reviewed many of my novels, and it was through this context that I first met him. We always got along great online, but it wasn't until my first NECON that I had the chance to meet Frank in person and see for myself what a warm, genuine, and devoted friend he was not only to me, but to the whole horror writing community. Like many writers, I can be socially awkward and extremely introverted and maybe even come across as antisocial. Going to the convention as a day camper, knowing of people but not really knowing anyone, I didn't feel like I was part of the community, that I belonged there or anywhere. But Frank, with his wry smile (I think he was usually smiling, even at times when it was must have been hard for him to do so), approached me, opened his arms, and gave me a huge welcoming hug. He knew me by my face and told me how much he liked one of my titles. Those who know me and my aversion to physical contact might have laughed at that sight, me looking awkward and probably blushing, him with his admirable and unabashed earnestness filling the room with warmth. When I felt like no one, he made me feel like someone.

I spent most of my time at the convention with or around Frank and a few others, and I considered him a dear friend from that point on. I headed back the next year, primarily to see the people who make our community great, Frank at the very top among them. Sometimes, I still get those doubts, that I don't belong, and then I remember Frank and that hug and all the conversations about books and life we had after, and I wish I could tell him how much it all meant to me and how much he, too, belonged.

He was one of us. He was my friend. And I miss him greatly.

THE LOST PROPHECY OF URSULA SONTHEIL

by Catherine Cavendish

How many families can boast about having a bona fide prophetess in their ancestry?

This, I can assure you, is no idle claim. Growing up I felt blessed by it, but now?

Mine is a strange story, but tonight I must tell it. For tonight is a special night. A momentous night.

As I have done every year at this time, I unfold the sheaf of papers my mother first gave me sixty years ago. I settle myself and begin to read…our story.

The legend captured me from the first time I heard it. The fifteenth-century witch, born in a cave, possessed a remarkable gift for prophecy. According to tradition, she predicted everything from an archbishop's untimely demise to submarines and space travel. All of this is well known, but in our family, we have a lesser tradition concerning Ursula Sontheil—the woman known to the world as Mother Shipton.

We are told she had no children, so there could be no direct descendants, but there is another reason why this story has been faithfully handed down from mother to daughter for generation after generation. More of that later. For now, dear daughter, on this Halloween of your sixteenth year, I must pass it on to you.

October 31 in the year of our Lord 1552 saw icy blasts of wind, hail and rain scything through the forest of Knaresborough. Tall trees bent and swayed so violently, they might topple and crush the old, misshapen woman who scurried as fast as her bent, arthritic legs would allow. She wrapped her cloak tighter around her, wishing the cloth were warmer. In a sudden gust of wind, her hood blew off. To her dismay, a small group of children, approaching in the opposite direction, pointed at her and laughed.

"Dirty old hag. Dirty old hag," they chanted. "Old Mother Shipton's a dirty old hag."

The woman tugged her hood back over her head and tried to ignore their cruel laughs. *I should be used to it by now.* After all, it happened every day. "Have a care, young Master Shepherd," she lisped through broken teeth. "Remember, I know who you are. I know your parents. And yours, Master Fairclough."

As their paths crossed hers the children fell silent, but their eyes never left her. She felt them burning into her. Her lips formed a twisted smile. In her mind, she could hear their parents cautioning them, *"Don't cross the witch, or 'twill be the worse for us all."*

What a shame they had chosen to ignore the admonition. Ah well, one more score for her to settle. But, for now, she had more pressing matters to attend to.

She peered up at the sky. Would this cursed weather ever change? The rain never cease?

Shivering and soaked to the skin, she reached her destination—a deep cave where her fifteen-year-old mother had birthed her sixty-four years earlier. These days, she only came here on the important feast days, and they didn't come greater than Samhain. The aches and pains of age meant she enjoyed the comforts of her cozy little home in town but, for magic, she returned to her origins. The cave provided the special, timeless atmosphere she needed to commune with the spirits of the dead.

She busied herself with building a fire, collecting kindling and branches from the piles of wood at the back of the cave, wincing as the rheumatism throbbed through her joints, making her jolt and stumble and long for her younger days when she could scurry and bustle. The job would have been done by now and she would have been warming and drying herself by a welcome blaze. She sighed for those faraway days while she reached into a niche in the rock and pulled out her tinderbox.

The dry kindling caught quickly and flames soon licked at the logs. At last. Ursula eased her aching limbs down onto the smooth, worn rock a few feet from the cheery blaze and warmed her hands. They throbbed as the feeling returned to her numbed fingers while the flames burned high enough to illuminate the rock walls with dancing shadows. She fancied she could see leaping fauns and dancing goblins entertaining her, while the steam rose from her sodden clothes. A smell of damp wool wrinkled her nose, and in a far corner of the cave, she swore she saw the shadows move. She reached behind her and picked up a warm blanket she always kept here. Wrapping it around herself, she reveled in its cocoon-like comfort, soothing away the torments of age as it always did.

But today was different. Today the atmosphere had changed in the cave. It seemed to weigh her down, as if another presence had joined her. She frowned as she strained her eyes, staring at the walls, searching the shadowy nooks and crannies.

Nothing. No one. Nevertheless…

Her cracked voice echoed around the cave walls. "I know you're there. Come out and show yourself."

A rustle.

This time an unmistakable movement in the shadows at the far end of the cave. A figure. Ursula caught her breath. The firelight sent flickering reflections of orange and red, striking through the gloom. A tall man stepped out of the shadows and moved toward her.

He towered over her diminutive, hunched frame. As he came into better focus, she saw he was strongly built, his face framed by long, black hair, his eyes dark. They gave him a magnetism. Had she been a young and pretty girl, he could have stolen her heart. Such a man didn't belong in a cave. He belonged in polite society where he could captivate all around him.

When he spoke, his voice matched his appearance. Rich, deep, enigmatic. "Forgive me," he said. "I did not mean to startle you. I have come a long way to meet with you this Samhain, Mistress Shipton."

Ursula eyed him carefully. Her fingertips prickled, a sure sign something was amiss, but was it to do with the man himself or the manner of his arrival? He couldn't be from around Knaresborough or he would never have presumed to enter her cave. The locals always gave it a wide berth, frightened she would put a hex on them.

"I am known by that name… and others," she replied. "I do not believe we have met before."

"I have known of you for many years. Your reputation as a seer and a wise woman has spread far and wide. It is said that the young king himself has praised your powers. Your many predictions during his father's reign came true on every occasion. Yet, despite your fame, you still choose to return here…" He spread his arms wide.

"It is the place of my birth and the place where I can be close to she who bore me. On this night of all nights, I must be here."

"So I see. I have need of your counsel. As you say, this is a special night, and the only time my need can be fulfilled."

The stranger sat on another flat rock, opposite his hostess. Illuminated by the flames, she now had her first proper view of his angular face. His gaze captured her, but only served to remind her of her own awkward features. His dark— seemingly black—irises held depths that drew her in.

"You wish to commune with the dead," she said, never breaking eye contact.

"You presume correctly, Mistress."

"It is Samhain and you come to visit me, it wasn't hard to guess the reason."

The stranger smiled, showing white, even teeth. He had still not introduced himself. Clearly, by the quality of his cloak, he possessed some fortune. Maybe he held an important position and didn't want anyone to find out he had consulted a wise woman. No matter. It was no business of hers.

Ursula made her decision. "I will prepare the altar."

The man stood and helped her to her feet. He watched in silence as she limped to a piece of protruding, rocky wall that formed a natural ledge. She felt his eyes follow her every move while she positioned the human skull her foster mother told her had been owned by her birth mother and countless previous generations of Sontheil women—the identity of its original owner now long forgotten. Ursula lit a tallow candle and placed an ancient bronze dagger in front of it, along with her yew wand and offering cauldron. Next she poured a small quantity of cold water from a clay jug into the cauldron.

She picked up a small earthenware flask, removed the stopper with a resounding *pop*, and sprinkled in a few grains of powdered human teeth she had obtained from a corpse buried in the churchyard. She recalled the shards of incessant pain that had coursed through her fingers and up her arm as she ground the teeth as finely as her mortar and pestle would allow. She flexed her stiff fingers. It had been necessary work, for the most effective magic.

She sighed and moved on to her next task, adding some of the mixture she reserved purely for use at Samhain—a combination of mugwort, valerian, chicken blood, a special kind of marjoram, and a miniscule sprinkling from a small jar she only used for Samhain summonings. Even she didn't know what the mysterious gray powder consisted of, only that, whenever she removed the cork, her nose rejected the appalling stench. Highly concentrated, it came from the mysterious east, far from England's shores. The tiniest amount was all that would be needed.

Ursula replaced the cork and wafted the smell away, took up a small wooden spoon and mixed the concoction together.

Satisfied it had all blended, she turned back from the altar and rejoined her guest. "Now we must wait until full darkness."

Outside the wind howled, fanning the flames of Ursula's fire, making her draw her shabby cloak ever closer around her. Hail showered the rock like hundreds of tiny pebbles as a wild evening spread outside the cave. Ursula spoke little, merely answering the man's questions. He revealed nothing of himself but seemed keen to learn about her birth mother.

"She entered a convent when I was two years old. I never knew her," Ursula said. "But from her I inherited my gift. Some might say my curse."

"Your *gift* of prophecy, of second sight. And your powers." The stranger stared into the fire. "Yes, your powers." The flames rose a little higher. "And you married?"

Ursula didn't want to talk of *him*. As his question brought the image of the man she hated more than any rushing into her mind, she once again felt the stinging slaps and ringing blows on her face, arms, chest, back, anywhere he could reach before she ducked out of his grasp or he fell down dead drunk—only to awaken and begin the torment anew.

Until the day he didn't.

"He died."

"Toby Shipton."

"You *knew* him?" How could someone like this know anyone like the low scum she had married?

The stranger smiled. "Merely a passing acquaintanceship. You do not mourn your loss, I see."

"A man who beats his wife is not one to be grieved for."

"And now you are alone."

Ursula did not reply. A serpentine ripple of apprehension wound its way up from the pit of her stomach. Suddenly she had to know more about the identity of this stranger.

"Am I to know your name, sire?"

"In good time, Mistress. In good time you shall know both my identity and be well rewarded for your work this night. I have a special gift for you."

That would have to satisfy her for now, but this unaccustomed apprehension she was feeling did not sit easily with her.

"I believe the time has come for us to begin," he said, gesturing to the blackness at the mouth of the cave.

"Indeed." Ursula struggled to stand, her knees creaking and reluctant to obey her. The stranger held out his hand and she took it. He gently helped her to her feet. She thanked him and limped back to her altar where she placed gnarled hands over the cauldron and her lips mouthed the ancient incantation to summon the dead. She must not repeat it out loud, fearing he would hear, learn and remember. Then he would gain power and could turn the spell back on her.

Ursula ended her invocation and picked up the small cauldron. The mixture had hardened into a thick paste and she scooped some out and flicked it on the fire where it spluttered and spat. A green flame shot into the air and she staggered backward, almost tumbling to the floor. The man watched calmly, as if he had been expecting this but Ursula had never seen the like. The strange flame writhed and twisted like a sensuous woman performing a seductive dance.

She pointed a shaking finger at him. "You are responsible for this."

A deep, rumbling laugh rang out through the cave. It seemed to have emanated from deep within him. "You are correct, Mistress Shipton. Let me show you more."

The flame grew in luminosity, casting an eerie light over the cave. In its heart, strange shapes formed: a black dog with flaming red eyes and scales on its back, culminating in a forked tail. The creature rose up from the fire and opened its mouth. Cruel, pointed teeth gnashed. A snake's tongue protruded. Ursula clapped her hand to her mouth to stifle the scream that threatened to escape.

The dog vanished. The flame writhed and twisted once more. Hideously deformed beasts that were neither human nor animal thrashed in its depths.

71

Creatures no more than two feet tall crawled on spindly, bent legs. Evil, twisted faces, black as charcoal, eyes that were only orange pinpricks. Their long, pointed ears stood upright on their circular heads, while their dragons' tails thrashed. They opened their mouths, and each issued an earsplitting shriek, revealing twin rows of ugly, malformed fangs. They lunged at her, taunting her with claws that narrowly missed flaying her skin.

Ursula recoiled and stared at them in horror, yet the man beside her laughed. The flame died down and the creatures stood either side of the fire.

"Come, my imps," the stranger said. "You have had your fun. Now leave us."

The creatures vanished.

A heavy silence filled the cave. "Who are you?" Ursula asked, not daring to speak above a whisper.

"Oh, I think you know who I am. The question is, who are you?"

"I am Ursula Sontheil, known as Mother Shipton, but this you know already."

"Your name is not important. Your gift is who you are, and I am here because of it."

"I don't understand."

"I am here to show you the future. The future the Master will create and you, or those who come after you, will prophesy. This is my gift to you."

The man waved his hand over the fire. The green flame shot up high, writhing and twisting as before. This time no creatures appeared. Blurred images grew firmer and more sharply defined.

A man with a small moustache stretched out his right arm, while crowds of oddly dressed men, women, and children cheered and copied his strange salute. They waved huge flags with an unfamiliar symbol emblazoned on them. Fires burned out of control. Buildings fell. In the air, impossible machines flew and dropped cylinder-shaped objects which exploded on impact with the ground.

The picture blurred and another scene took its place. The flying machines were different than before. Much bigger. Gleaming metal. Ursula watched in horror as one hit an impossibly tall building which stood next to its twin. Black smoke. Flames. People ran for their lives. Some jumped from such heights, they could never survive. Everywhere lay covered in thick, gray ash.

Again the scene dissolved, to be replaced by another. More flying machines, but these looked very different. Gone were the wing-like protrusions. They were smooth, triangular, with long, tapering noses. No visible sign of how they were powered, yet hundreds of them flew, filling the skies. On the ground, people wandered helplessly. They seemed confused; many held their heads and wept. Everywhere the dead and dying littered the streets. Buildings lay in ruins, their metal frames twisted and pointing upward like so many broken and mangled fingers.

The scene darkened and the sky grew thick, clogged, a drab brownish-gray. In such a fog, she could see no flying machines. Or maybe they had gone away.

On the ground, no one moved. Skeletons lay strewn on sidewalks, roadways and in the doorways of long-abandoned buildings. No sign of life. Not a bird or animal. Not one human.

"And this is how the world will end?" Ursula asked.

"Mankind will be wiped out and *his* kingdom shall rise up."

Surely he couldn't want her to… "You want *me* to prophesy this? You want *me* to tell everyone there is no hope for them?"

"It will not come in your lifetime. Not for many lifetimes. You have been chosen because you have the eyes to see. Your gift."

"You are placing a terrible burden on me."

"Not so terrible. You are strong, Ursula Sontheil. Your mother was strong, and her mother before her."

"I thought you had come this night to commune with one who had passed over. You said this is the only night you could do this, but this isn't communing with the dead."

"But it is the dead who know what is to come. Once released from the burden of their earthly bodies, their spirits are free to travel in time and space wherever they desire. Those who travel to the future bring their visions back with them. But they can only share them with the living on this one night a year when the portal between this world and the world of spirit opens. You know this to be true. You come here each year at this time and you receive visions of the future."

"Not like this." Ursula pointed at the fire where the green flame continued to display the cataclysmic scenes.

His voice was gentler now. Tender, as if indulging a child. "You always forget. It is meant to be but… Ursula, we meet every year at this time. Tomorrow you will have forgotten all about me."

"I doubt that."

He laughed "And every year, you say the same thing."

"Are you telling me I will have forgotten what I have seen in those flames?"

"No. You will remember that. You won't remember the flame, or how you witnessed those visions, but you *will* remember them. You will cause them to be written down, just as you have dictated your previous visions. Like them, you will keep these revelations safe. Unlike them, you will not reveal these yet. Maybe *you* will never reveal them, for to do so is to summon *him*.

"Your dark master?"

"The Lord of Darkness himself."

Ursula stared at him. Unable to read and write, Ursula always recited her prophecies to herself in verse form until she had memorized them. Then she would speak them to young Master Fenchurch who wrote them in his neat hand. The resulting scroll was rolled up and placed in a tall earthenware jar. Over the years, she had amassed quite a few.

"Who are you? A devil come to taunt me?"

Again, his laughter rumbled around the cave, echoing off the walls. "Not a devil, Ursula. Merely *his* servant. And your father. Your mother, Agatha, gave birth to you in this very cave."

"You are my *father?*"

"Of course. Another reason why this can only happen on this night. I have long been of the other world. From my appearance you can tell I was younger than you when I passed."

Ursula tried to take it all in. She knew nothing of her real father. This man was surely a complete stranger. Yet...

"You can see the truth of my words, can't you my child?"

Ursula slowly nodded. "Yes...father." The word sounded alien on her lips.

He smiled and stood. The green flame extinguished.

"And now I must go. It is almost midnight and I must return."

Ursula felt an inexplicable wrenching in her heart. "Don't go. Not yet. I have many questions."

"But I must leave now. I told you. You will not remember me in the morning. Only that which you must keep safe. We will meet again next year."

Once more, he waved his hand over the fire and the green flame shot skywards. He spread his arms and stepped forward.

Ursula stared in disbelief as the flame embraced her father and enfolded him. "*No!*" But he and the flame were gone, and the memory of him dissolved like salt in stew.

Once more, Mother Shipton gazed into her warming fire, as her eyes grew heavy.

She awoke, her head burdened with sleep. Outside, pale sunlight held little warmth. Ursula struggled to her feet, her legs numb from the position in which she had slumbered. She tried to remember—it felt crucial that she did—but, try as she might, she couldn't recall any detail of how she had spent the previous evening.

From somewhere, fresh prophecies had imprinted themselves on her brain. She shook herself and dry leaves fell from her cloak. The fire had almost died, and she kicked ashes and dirt on it to smother the meager flame.

She looked about her. All seemed normal. The altar was still laid out. She must have cast some spell last night. No matter. She would remember if she needed to.

Ursula made her unsteady way out of the cave. Normally, she shunned a walking stick but today a slim branch, lying near the entrance of her cave, would be a blessing to lean on with her joints so stiff and sore. As she tested it, she was relieved to find it to be precisely the right height for her.

She began her return journey back to her little house in the town.

A few yards from the cave she came upon the Petrifying Well—a place of magic. The water that dripped from the rock seemed clear, but if you placed any item in its flow—a glove perhaps, or an old shoe—that very water would turn the item to stone within days or weeks. No one could explain it, but it happened every time. The old woman smiled. There were some who whispered that it was all her doing, that she had bewitched the well so it would not produce fresh water for the inhabitants of the town. Those were the same people who crossed themselves whenever they came upon her.

Ursula resumed her walk, easier now that she had the stick. She must get home as quickly as possible so young Master Fenchurch could write down her latest visions before they became blurred in her mind. Why she must secret these particular ones away until the time was ripe for telling them, she couldn't imagine, but she must obey the voice in her head, however heavy its instructions weighed on her. She had never felt so anxious about a prophecy before. But then, never before had the vision been so momentous.

Ursula knew young Master Fenchurch was only too happy to do her bidding. She would reward him with bright, shiny pennies. At sixteen years old, a young man could enjoy himself well on a few coppers. He happened to be one of the few people who wasn't wary of her and she enjoyed his company, albeit only for the time required to write down her prophecies. Then she was glad for him to go and leave her alone with her thoughts and visions.

An hour later, he sat across from her in her comfortable parlor. A fire burned in the grate, warming the room. On the table in front of him lay a couple of sheets of paper and a quill pen. Ursula had also filled an inkwell ready for him to begin.

She closed her eyes and allowed her latest visions to swim back into her mind. As soon as she began to speak, Simon Fenchurch dipped his pen in the ink and began to write.

Chaos will reign when the devil shall rise
To claim his throne and seduce with lies
Hell's fires shall all the earth consume
When the dead from their graves, he will exhume

No man nor beast nor living thing
Shall raise their voice in praise to sing
For on the earth no peace sublime
Shall herald in the end of time

To parody the virgin birth
Shall come a tyrant, not of Earth

The horned one shall he usher in
Destroying all that lives therein

Then shall the devil's work be done
When here on earth there number none
That walk and crawl and swim and fly
As all that lives he'll cause to die

Then shall his kingdom truly reign
And man no more shall wake again
Of further times, no more be said
For none shall live among the dead.

Her head rang with the crowded images and the utter despair and desolation of the final act.

The boy left soon after and a wave of exhaustion sent Ursula off to her bed. She lay there, her mind still reeling. With a rush of fear, she gazed down at her prone body. A second later, her spirit soared up and out across time. She smelled sulfur, burning flesh, heard screams and moans. In the swirling images that came to her, women wept and clutched torn and battered babies to their breasts. Flames shot up into the sky from hundreds of explosions. A young girl with dark skin held out her arms, tears streaming down her face. Ursula reached out to her, only to shrink away in horror. Where her hands should have been, the girl had merely bloody, blistered stumps.

The awful scene dissolved, and she stood in a peaceful graveyard. Around her, tombstones—some carved with ornate angels—stood at crazy angles, as if they could fall at any moment. Under her feet, the ground lurched, quivered and sent shockwaves up through her feet.

A rumble began deep underground. Gravestones toppled, the earth raised up. She willed her spirit to rise high above the ground, terrified she might be trapped and swallowed up by some earthquake. She might never be able to return to her body, and be left here to wander aimlessly in this nightmare world she knew formed the future of mankind.

Still the ground bucked and rocked, sending showers of earth upward. Ursula's spirit cried out as coffins were flung out of their graves, some so rotten they burst and released their skeletal contents. Soon the graveyard became littered with the dead. White bones, tattered shrouds, skulls with gaping jaws.

Above it all, the sky turned red—a vivid vermilion reflecting a thousand conflagrations.

A horned figure towered over the ground, its eyes burning red flames, its body black, with huge scales, clawed feet and hands. Ursula willed her spirit to leave that place but she wouldn't be released yet.

The evil one spoke to her. "To you has been entrusted this vision of my world. Guard it well, lest I come for you. Destroy it and I will return sooner. Now, be gone from here."

Clouds swirled. The vision retreated, spinning backward from her. Ursula's eyes snapped open. She breathed relief at the familiar surroundings of her bed and room. Had she fallen asleep? But she knew that had been no dream. She had been burdened with that vision of man's ultimate destruction and the boy had written down her words that very morning.

No, this prophecy could not be shared. She must keep it safe. Guard it. The truth of the destiny of the world would be too much and, almost certainly, she would be arrested for blasphemy, tried, convicted, and even put to death as a witch or heretic. After all, she had predicted the rise of the Devil's kingdom on earth. The church wouldn't appreciate that, and priests were all too powerful.

Ursula stared for many minutes into the flames of her fire. Then, cursing her uncertain limbs, she took up the sheet of paper from the table and folded it carefully before sliding it into a narrow earthenware jar she then sealed with a stopper. She reached up above the fireplace and removed a loose brick. She laid the jar on its side, eased it inside, and replaced the brick, making sure it would be impossible for anyone to detect. That hidey-hole had come in useful on a number of occasions before. Now it would have a permanent purpose.

Nine years remained to Ursula and she guarded these prophecies well. Only on her deathbed did she share the secret with another—the woman believed to have been Ursula's half-sister.

Only in her final year, on her last Halloween, did her father permit her to remember him. He has never appeared to any of us since—as far as we know.

On a blazing hot July day, he came for her—as he will come for all of us. One day.

For the rest of his life, Simon Fenchurch protested that there existed a prophecy Ursula had never shared with anyone except him. He could never remember it sufficiently for it to make any sense and, as he grew older, his faculties waned and people smiled indulgently at the old man's fantasies.

So now, my dear daughter, you know it all. Except where to find the lost prophecy. You know, of course, that this house is many centuries old and has been in our family for hundreds of years. Tonight, at midnight, you will receive the gift handed down through the generations. Tonight, I shall show you the loose brick and you will hold in your hands the lost prophecy of Ursula Sontheil.

One day soon, the time will prove right for you to warn mankind by uttering the prophecy. And it will come to pass. Perhaps then the world will understand. Its fate is its own doing—and its undoing. That is its curse.

I fold the papers carefully and retrieve the ancient scroll from its hiding place.

So much has happened in this world since Ursula Sontheil's day. She would recognize precious little of what remains here, except for the vision her father showed her that fateful Samhain.

Now it has come to me, for I am to be the one who utters the prophecy that will summon the Lord of Darkness. The world is fast destroying itself.

Has destroyed itself.

It is time.

With the scroll in my hand, I reach for my phone.

WHEN THE DEAD LIE

by Brett J. Talley

I'm one of five or six people in the world who can talk to the dead. But that's not the hard part. The problem is they lie so damn much.

That surprise you? It shouldn't. The dead aren't all that different from the living. If anything, they're worse. Their material needs are satisfied. Permanently. Don't have to worry about food or shelter or how they'll afford their next ride. When you're dead, all that matters is your reputation. People worry about how they'll be remembered after they're gone. But when you're dead, that's *all* you worry about. Turns out that's quite the incentive to lie, and even more of one to cover up the lies you told when you were still alive.

I'll give you an example. This woman found me once. I'm not sure how they find me, how they *know* that I can see them, hear them. Sometimes I imagine there's an arrow over my head, a beacon bobbing up and down, like in a video game. But it's not that bad, really. It's not like you might imagine, what with several billion people having lived and died on this earth. I'm not constantly surrounded by ghosts or anything. Truth is, there aren't actually that many around.

I've spent some time debating why that is. I'd like to believe most people float up—or down—to their eternal reward, leaving a handful of folks behind with unfinished business. But sometimes I wonder if maybe it's worse than that, if maybe most people just dissolve away after death into the emptiness of eternity. Maybe only the strongest, stubbornest souls survive. Or maybe it's random, who knows?

Anyway, this woman finds me. You can tell right away when they're dead. No, they don't float or glow or anything. They aren't transparent or whatnot. No chains. No blood or broken bones or missing limbs. It's the eyes, really. There's no life there, no light. Otherwise, they look just like you or me.

She was a pretty one. Long blonde hair falling down over her shoulders and a rack you hate to see go to waste. I'm not saying a dead chick was turning me on, but a dead chick was turning me on. So when she explained to me that there was a flash drive in her bedroom with some photos of some family she wanted to see one more time before she passed on to the next world, I fell for it. The next couple of hours involved me breaking into a house, getting chased by a dog, and barely evading the police, but I got the flash drive. When I popped it into my computer, I wasn't too surprised to find a couple dozen videos of her riding a guy who clearly wasn't the husband I'd seen in the photos hanging on the walls of her home. This was one time I wasn't upset about getting lied to. The lady didn't even apologize. She just asked me to destroy the files for her. I told her I would. Eventually.

I don't do the work for free or out of the goodness of my heart. Spirits know things. Sometimes it's as simple as giving me access to a hidden bank account or a pile of money stashed away somewhere. Sometimes they have the encryption key to some Bitcoin or even, one time at least, know where some gold is buried. More often than not they direct me to where they hid the weed they never had a chance to smoke. What I'm saying is, I may have to put up with their shit, but this job is totally worth it.

Not that I'm rich. I'm very good at blowing dead people's money. That's why I've got this gig, the checkout guy at the local Real-Mart ("It's not good unless it's Real good!"). R- Mart's not doing great. Our store's been in the process of closing for six months now. Every day the shelves get a little bit barer. We haven't had fruit or vegetables for as long as I can remember. Still got some wine, if you like it out of a box.

Customers have pretty much dried up, too. I stand here under the cold fire of the fluorescents, their light cooking me from the inside out. It's quiet enough to hear the buzz of those lights, the occasional metallic *clink* of their slow death. Not too many customers when you have nothing to sell. And tonight, it was dead. No pun intended.

Which meant my lane was empty when she walked up.

I say walked up. That's how it happens in a sane world. But she was just there, like she'd burst into existence. And she had, in the way they do. She ran her hand along the torn conveyor belt, and I wondered if she felt it, or if she just did it by habit from when she still had fingers with which to feel.

"Slow day at work," she said, and I noticed her voice was clearer than most of her kind, more solid, as if it came from an actual throat instead of the void.

"Every day's slow," I said.

She stopped in front of the payment terminal and looked up at me, her blue eyes peering into my soul. "I've heard about you. From the others. I can't tell you how long it's taken me to find someone like you."

"Oh yeah? Happy customers?"

"For the most part," she said. "That teenager from the canyon had some choice words." *That* kid. So I'm not always successful, what can I say? "But I think you'll do. You up for the job?"

"I get off in twenty, if you can wait."

She grinned. "I've got nothing but time."

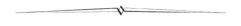

She was in the parking lot when I stepped out of the now-rickety, barely functioning sliding doors. As they closed behind me, the fluorescents of the store went dark. With so little cash to count, my manager was already locking up and hitting the road.

I saw her leaning against one of those yellow poles we'd installed ten years back after an old lady in a station wagon plowed through the plate glass window at the front. Old buzzard had opened the door cussing like a sailor, complaining that we hadn't "marked the parking spots" better, whatever that means.

"Do you feel it?" I asked.

"What?"

I pointed at the pole.

She grinned again. "It's hard to explain. Not like you do. But I know it's there, all the same. I feel things you can't imagine."

"Haha," I laughed awkwardly, reliving that time in high school when Jennifer Upchurch suggested we go swimming and I innocently replied that I didn't have a bathing suit. "Neither do I," she had said.

"So, you'll help me?"

"You haven't told me what you need, yet."

"I need something…removed. Something that keeps me from crossing over."

"Huh. That's a new one. Okay, what sort of something?"

"It's difficult to explain," she said. "It's something you really need to…see for yourself."

"I feel like I'm going to regret this. Is it illegal?"

"Not at all."

"Dangerous?"

"I doubt any more dangerous than your average job. Less so, likely."

"All right," I said. There'd never been any doubt I'd do it. Truth is, I've never turned one of them down. I might see ghosts on the regular, but the idea of being haunted by one for the rest of my life gives me the willies. "I'll do it. When do we start?"

"Tonight," she said. "But you're going to need a shovel. And probably a crowbar."

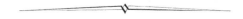

We were heading down Highway 25. I'd popped back into the R-Mart and grabbed the last shovel we had in stock. I keyed in the code to shut off the silent alarm but didn't bother to call anybody and let them know I'd shut it off. I doubted anyone really cared anymore.

I already owned a crowbar.

She was sitting in my passenger seat, looking as real and solid as any woman I'd ever had in that truck. Not that I'd ever had anyone as good looking as her climb up into the cab before. She was *hot*. Probably thirty, that perfect age where the girl is gone but the youth isn't and a real, honest-to-God woman emerges.

She was dressed simply. T-shirt and jeans. Not sure about the shoes.

"I have a question," I said.

She was staring straight ahead, watching as my headlights cut through the darkness. "Shoot."

"Your clothes. Why those in particular?"

"You'd prefer if I were naked?" she said, cutting her eyes in my direction. I felt myself blush.

"No, that's not what I meant."

She grinned. "It's a decision. Not sure if it's conscious or not. You just decide."

"You weren't wearing those when you…"

"When I died?"

"Yeah…"

"No. Not at all. I think I can say for certain that I've never worn this or anything like it."

It was difficult for me to even imagine having never worn denim. But I knew rich chicks who wouldn't be caught dead in jeans like that. No pun intended, of course.

"In a couple of miles," she said, "there's a road that intersects with this one. You'll need to turn down that road."

I frowned. We were already in the middle of nowhere, and it was about to get worse. "Right, huh? We going to The Bottoms?"

She nodded. "We are. Is that a problem?"

"No problem at all," I said. "Just wondering what in the world you'd want in a swamp."

"There are old things in the swamp. Lost things. But it's not the swamp that I want."

It was dark with no moon, and I almost missed the turn. I swung the truck hard to the right onto the bumpy, broken pavement. The dust and the bugs dimmed the beams of my headlights, and I could see nothing to either side of me. If there'd been a hard, sudden turn either way, I'd probably have ended up in a ditch. Or worse.

"You'll want to take a left in about a half mile. It's not much of a road, so be careful."

"Worse than this?" I said, as the car bounced through a pothole deep enough to lose a tire in.

"Just make the turn."

I did, and indeed, it was worse. Branches whacked the side of the truck, and not for the first time I was glad I drove a clunker. We continued bumping down the path—she was right, you couldn't call it a road—in silence for another five minutes.

"It's up here. On the right. No need to pull over. There won't be anyone else along."

I didn't doubt that, and I pulled the truck to a stop next to an old tree of unknown variety, its ancient limbs heavy with Spanish moss. The air was thick and cloying, the late hour having done nothing to lessen the weight of the humidity. Beyond the tree were two broken piles of stone. It looked like a gate might have once hung between them, long since rusted away to nothingness.

"Where are…"

"Grab your shovel," she said, suddenly beside me, "and follow."

She passed between the piles of stone, and I followed. The ground was solid, but I knew the swamps were somewhere just beyond. I hoped we'd stop before we reached them. I'm not afraid of ghosts, but snakes and alligators are another thing altogether. I wished I'd brought a flashlight. You forget just how dark it is outside of the city on a night where there is no moon. I'd have been unable to see anything at all, were it not for that unnatural glow of the swamp that has always given uneasy sleep to those unfortunate enough to spend a night within one. And there was her glow, too. She *shone* in that darkness. I'd never seen it before, not with any of the others.

We were in an uneven field, sparsely covered with trees. There'd been a path there once, but it was long gone. I stumbled along, nearly falling more than once in the shallow depressions that dotted this haven of solid ground in the midst of the swamp.

"What is this place?"

"You don't know?" she said, stopping next to a small slab of stone, driven into the ground. "You, of all people, don't recognize it?"

I looked around. And I realized that slab of stone wasn't the only one in the field. There were many, spread out here and there, some standing, some having fallen, all around those interesting depressions I had noticed before.

"Well shit."

She grinned. "Come now, surely such a place is of no consequence to one such as yourself. A seer of ghosts, afraid of a cemetery? How quaint."

"Just what exactly am I supposed to use this for?" I threw the shovel down, and it clanged across the stone-covered ground.

She grinned again, and this time I thought it tinged with the sinister. "You know. Follow me. We're close."

I stood there for a moment, as if I was going to turn and leave in a huff. I'm not sure who I thought I was fooling. She never turned around, never expressed any concern that I wouldn't follow her. I cursed under my breath and picked up the shovel.

She spoke as I followed. "My husband put me here. Dug the hole and did what he did so he could sleep at night."

"Are you saying he murdered you?"

"My husband? The man was a coward. He would never lift a finger against me, not in life at least. He was afraid of me, for the same reason he fell in love with me." She stopped under the oldest tree we'd seen yet. If a grave were there, no stone was left behind to mark it. "Dig here."

I dropped the crowbar to the side and drove the blade of the shovel into the ground. The soil was soft, sandy. Befitting what everyone I'd ever known called The Bottoms, the swampy area that surrounded the city. It was a blessing. Within minutes, the pile of dirt next to the tree had begun to grow.

"He told me once, early in our courting, that he found me exotic. Maybe even dangerous. Once we were married, exotic became frightening. Then I truly was dangerous. I suppose he thought marriage would tame me, or that the ring he gave me was a shackle. A chain to bind me to his will. But I always served another."

I don't know if you've ever dug a grave—Check that. You've never dug a grave, and I can tell you, it's not like it is in the movies. Hours passed as the mound of dirt grew. My hands were raw. My back ached. All the time she stood, staring down at me, waiting.

"When the sickness struck, I could have cured it. I could have saved my life. But my husband refused to allow it. He locked me away in my room until life left me. He brought me here and did what he did. And when the sickness came for him, there was no one who could save him. He cut his own throat when he cut mine."

My shovel struck something solid. Thirty minutes later, and I'd cleared the dirt from the solid sheet of wood that was the cover of the casket. It hit me only then that this grave must have been very old indeed. No one had used this cemetery in ages, and the coffin I was standing over was made in the old way. This was no Heritage 3000, if you know what I mean.

"And so it is," she said. "I doubt you can imagine what it's like, looking down into your own grave. When you open that casket, you'll see what's left of me. We'll both see."

I reached up out of the hole and grabbed my crowbar. "You ready for this?"

She didn't respond, but her dark eyes flared, and I knew it was time. I jammed the crowbar into the thick wood and pushed down until the cover cracked and the stale air within rushed out and enveloped me. The putrid stench of ancient death filled my nostrils. Then it filled my lungs, too, as I gasped at what I saw.

I've seen death before. Plenty of times. And worse death than this. Dead bodies bloated and decayed. This was just a skeleton. A skeleton with a wooden stake driven through the chest, an iron nail hammered between the teeth, and a curved iron bar pinning the throat to the earth.

"As I said, my husband thought me dangerous. Even in death. Superstitious fool. Can you believe it? Consumption stripped my lungs until every cough was bloody. Until the fool decided I was something more than human."

"This grave... When...?"

"As I told you, it took me a very long time to find one such as yourself. You'd be surprised just how rare you are. Months became years, years became decades, so on and so forth. I don't even know how long has passed. Time has a way of melting into itself. I think you can see now why I can't rest."

I looked back down at the implements of her soul's torture. She stood over me, at the edge of the grave.

"So, you want me to just..."

"Yes. Remove them please, and free my soul."

I admit the superstitious part of me wondered whether that was such a good idea. But then I thought of her husband, the madness that had taken him. I reached down and grasped the end of the wooden stake. With a jerk, it came loose.

I heard her inhale sharply above me, and I wondered why a ghost would inhale at all. "Yes," she said. "That's it. I can feel the change coming already."

I threw the stake over the side of the grave into the pile of dirt beside. I took the crowbar and jammed it under the curved bar that held down the skeleton's throat. It was awkward, avoiding the bones. I worked it back and forth until it gave way with a pop. I threw it next to the stake.

"Almost there," she said, and I could hear the wanting in her voice, the desire, almost sexual.

I reached down and grasped the end of the iron nail. There was no room for the crowbar, not without destroying the skull, and somehow I felt as though she would frown upon that. I pulled...and nothing happened. It didn't even budge. I pulled again, and nothing. I adjusted my grip, sliding my fingers between the teeth of the skull for better purchase. I pulled again, and I felt it move. Just ever so slightly. I pulled again, and it moved again. I tugged, and it slipped another quarter inch.

"It's about to come out," I called out, so she could prepare for whatever was coming.

"Do it!"

And so I did, pulling once more until the iron nail came free and the teeth of the skull clapped shut, falling forward with the force of gravity. I waited a beat, but nothing happened. I looked up at her, and she was smiling. I reached up and pulled myself free of the grave to stand next to her.

"Well?"

"Give it a moment," she said. "And witness the glory."

I didn't know what that meant at the time, but I was about to learn. I felt it coming before it came. There was a sharp shattering sound, like breaking glass. Then she started to laugh. There was a crack of electricity, and her spirit glowed like it was on fire. The light burst from her and flowed like a waterfall down into the grave, surrounding the skeleton. I watched as her spirit was consumed by that fire until there was something like an explosion, and I felt myself picked up and thrown backwards. I landed with a thud in the pile of dirt. Then, silence and darkness.

I heard a sound, and I looked in its direction. Toward the open grave. Up over its edge came a hand, delicate and feminine, followed by another. She lifted herself up with a grace and elegance I would not have expected. Then she stood before me, as youthful and beautiful as she had been as a spirit. But this time, completely and utterly naked.

I'm not saying a dead chick was turning me on, but a dead chick was turning me on.

She smiled knowingly, her elongated canines as plain as day. "I'm sorry if I misled you. I'm sure you understand." She took a step forward. "But if it's all the same to you, I can think of a few ways of making it up to you…"

The dead, man. They are absolutely full of shit. But sometimes, this job is totally worth it.

HIS OWN PERSONAL GOLGOTHA

by Geoff Brown

gol•go•tha (n). A place or occasion of great suffering.

D arkness and dirt.

After he'd woken in the small, muddy cavern, he'd scrabbled uselessly for what felt like hours, but it was all still darkness and dirt.

He didn't want to die today. He'd find out soon enough whether the choice was his to make.

His fingertips scraped against something unusual in the dirt as he struggled in the direction he hoped was up. Smooth and rounded, it fell from the earth as he pulled at it. In the darkness, he couldn't see what it was, but later, as he climbed back down to rest for a moment, he grabbed it from the floor. He scraped enough dirt from it to feel eye sockets and teeth. It was a skull, small enough to be that of a child.

He placed it back on the floor and continued his journey to the surface.

Clawed at the earth, he hoped he was still heading in the right direction. The longer it took, the harder it was to breathe, and the dirt around him seemed to draw closer. A knot tightened in his chest as his lungs cramped and his heart pumped faster. He had to get out, so he increased his effort, until he broke through to the world above. Still, darkness reigned.

He'd been without light for so long that he could see fairly well. Everywhere around him, nothing but gravestones.

Low hills surrounded the valley that held the graveyard, and the dead, ragged trees that crested the hills appeared as skeletal hands reaching for the stars.

He dragged himself out of the grave and tried to brush the clay from his rumpled trousers, but the cloth was covered in it. He was shirtless.

Near him was a headstone.

Words were engraved upon it.

Unum Qui Patitur

'One who suffers'

Suffers?

He cringed without knowing why.

He looked up at the night sky, unsure of just where he was and hoping the pattern of the stars would look familiar. No such luck.

A blood-red moon hung low in the sky, silhouetting the scraggly trees that lined the distant hills. He had a lot of walking to do and wished he knew which direction to take.

All around him, decrepit gravestones lurked in the dark like murderers, huddled and hunched, waiting for unsuspecting victims to stroll by. He could just make out the words engraved on the ones nearest where he stood.

Manet Vilior 'Worthless remains'

In Parva Mors

'The Little Death'

This second phrase was engraved on a smaller stone than the others. He looked around and saw that most of the nearby graves were child-sized, covered in images of tragedy and loss. As he moved closer, he saw on one the image of disembodied hands from Heaven reaching down to pluck flowers from the earth; and on another, small lambs, lost and alone. Cribs were carved on a third grave, one that was laid out in size as though for three children. The cribs on the edges held images of sleeping children while the third was empty. On the ground beneath some of the gravestones were toys: raggedy dolls and faded dollhouses; wind-up metal cars now rusted or with paint peeling; in front of one, an old-fashioned spinning top with a spiralled auger.

Ravens rested on some of the headstones, a glint of red shining in their eyes as they watched him trek through their home.

Gluttons. Harbingers of death. He could recall no more.

Why can't I remember?

He looked behind him to the earth he had clawed his way out from under and found another small grave. No image or text on this one. No toys at the base.

He shook his head and followed a sudden compulsion to move on, to move away from where he was standing. He walked slowly forward, along a roughly defined path that had to lead somewhere. He didn't know where he was going; he just knew he had some destination in mind.

As he moved through the graveyard, he gradually found his bearings. Some hills lay ahead. They looked like a scabrous spine exposed in a shallow grave, the bony processes regular and symmetrical. Beyond the third vertebra from the left lay a light. It was a glow rising beyond the hill, a sign of life and a possible destination. He knew what it was, somewhere deep in his mind. A name floated up from the depths of his memory: *Necropolis*—City of the Dead.

Home. I think it's home. A way to the truth. A place of knowledge.

He yearned to know.

Desiccated leaves littered the path he walked. Every footstep crushed more of them into dust; red, brown and gold. Slush-piles of dirty-white, half-melted snow lay here and there between the graves, a sign of impending winter. Sudden flashes of an image invaded his consciousness; a young girl, clad all in white, almost glowing, skipping though an orchard on an autumn day. The leaves scattered with every step she took; red and gold and brown, to match the leaves he walked through now. The vision vanished, yet something remained with him. *Regret? Desire?* He wasn't sure.

Shaking his head and sinking back to his own reality, he lengthened his stride, heading towards the spinal hills and the light in the distance.

So far, yet too close at the same time.

The leaves fell behind him and the snow became more prevalent. Goosebumps rose on his torso, and he found himself wishing for more clothing. He wanted to feel warm, for once in his miserable memory.

A tickle in the back of his throat caused him to cough. After a second, it formed into a hard lump, packed in his throat and blocking the air from his lungs. Gagging, unable to breathe, he dropped to his knees. Leaning forward onto his hands, he tried to hack whatever it was up and grew dizzy from lack of air. Finally, with one harsh, wracking cough, he felt it move inside his neck and brush the back of his soft palate. He strained to open his mouth as far as he could and reached inside with a muddy hand, managing to grasp something soft and fibrous. He dragged it out, inch by painful inch. White fabric; lacy cotton. At least fifteen or twenty inches of what seemed to be part of a dress. A few blowflies were caught in the material, buzzing weakly.

One last lump remained in his throat, and no matter how hard he tried, it wouldn't shift. His lungs were bursting, and his head spun. Darkness started to seep into the edges of his vision, and he fell forward onto his hands once again. No matter how much he tried, he couldn't breathe. Darkness engulfed him.

He awoke in agony, his throat burning but now clear and empty. He was in the mud where he had fallen. His nose was filled with slime, and he could barely draw breath, but he had more oxygen than he'd had just before he blacked out. He lifted his face and snorted his nostrils clear. Pain streaked through his neck, and his breathing was ragged and shallow. It hurt to breathe too deeply.

Gradually, his mind cleared, and his heartbeat slowed.

He looked around to gain his bearings and was taken aback by the changes.

How long have I been out? Where am I?

Red was everywhere. Red leaves now littered the ground and lay over the gravestones that surrounded him. The blood-red moon had sunk lower in the sky, yet seemed to have grown. It looked so close he imagined he could reach up and touch it.

A childish giggle rang out through the still air, echoing amongst the graves and the crypts, making it impossible to identify its source.

"Who's there?"

"Caitlin..." The wind carried a whispered name.

The smell of roses wafted through the air, underscored with the pungent aroma of musk. Potent yet seductive.

Another giggle rang out, more blatant than the last, from a different location. He whirled towards from where he thought it came, but again it was impossible to pinpoint.

The scent of rose and musk grew stronger, visceral yet sweet. He felt a stirring in his loins. He looked down at his erection in wonder. It was a physical reaction, but to what, he had no idea. The combination of the innocent laughter and the sexual undertones of the perfumed air aroused him. His penis tingled and grew even harder, to the point where it became painful. He reached down and unzipped himself, freeing his engorged member. It throbbed as the cold night air hit, straining to grow beyond its limits.

The smell grew stronger, now infused with vanilla and the scaly smell of old semen, and swirled through the air, almost visceral enough to touch. The temperature suddenly dropped even more. Cold seeped into every inch of exposed skin, causing his erection to shrivel and die.

"No. Please. Stop. You're hurting me..."

The voice was now distant and pleading, where before it had held a more mocking undertone. This part of his journey was nearing an end.

Where did that thought come from?

What journey?

Another peal of laughter, even more distant, tinkled like bells in the now-frigid air, followed by a fading voice.

"No more. Please, just let me go. I won't tell... I promise."

A sudden red desire ran through him in a wave, followed by a sense of regret.

Follow the voice!

He took a step towards the direction he guessed the voice had come from. Towards the hills. Towards the glow of Necropolis.

Towards the truth.

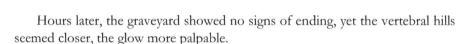

Hours later, the graveyard showed no signs of ending, yet the vertebral hills seemed closer, the glow more palpable.

His feet were beginning to ache. He'd need to rest soon. He'd hunted the girl more than halfway towards the hills, but the nearest he had come to finding her was bubbles of tinkling laughter floating through the air.

The landscape had changed as he neared the hills. Palm trees spaced here and there between the graves. Once, he had seen a bonnet spiralling in the wind, drifting aimlessly through the sky.

Soon, he could walk no further. He slept for a while, exhausted.

He dreamt he sat inside a cage of bones.

Outside, a young blonde girl sat amongst dogwood trees, eating sweet, red berries and watching him.

"Who are you?" he asked.

"I am the victim of your desire," she answered. "I am your lust, and I am death. I am named Caitlin."

"I don't understand," he said, although he thought maybe he did, somewhere deep inside his heart. His mind rebelled at a memory he couldn't quite grasp.

"You hurt me very much," she said. "You took from me that which I didn't want to give."

"What did I do?" he asked.

Caitlin parted her lips to answer, but no words came out. Instead, she closed her eyes as a fountain of deep red blood poured from her mouth and nose. Her jaw stretched wide, and then even wider, accompanied by the cracking of bones and the snapping sound of ligaments stretched beyond their limit.

He stared in horror as her chin bent down far enough to touch the lacy collar of her pristine white dress. A scream built up in his throat, but refused to be voiced.

The blood spilled down the front of her dress, soaking the fabric and turning it a vivid red. She opened her eyes. They were as red as the blood; no white of sclera, no black of pupil. Pure red.

He looked at her. She looked at him.

She leaned forward and passed something between the bones of the cage. He managed to break away from her gaze, and looked down to find that he held an old stuffed toy. An owl; tattered and torn.

"For wisdom," she said. "For redemption."

By the time he looked up, she was gone.

Everything was gone: the cage; the girl; the blood; everything.

He awoke, lying on his back and staring up at the stars. They still didn't look familiar, but he had a sense of *déjà vu* that almost crippled him with its strength.

Why am I here? What have I done?

I'm sorry.

This last thought hit from nowhere. He felt a twinge of regret, but wasn't sure he was ready to face what it was he regretted. Shame filled him.

He stretched and sat up. Looked down. By his side was the owl from his dream.

Reaching down, he picked it up. It was old. Two worn and chipped buttons represented eyes. Rough stitches held it together, now ragged with age. There were spots the colour of rust here and there on its body.

Blood? It looks like blood.

He knew he'd seen it somewhere before.

Where?

He remembered an orchard in autumn. Leaves covered the ground between the rows of apple trees, and shrivelled pieces of fruit lay forgotten from the harvest. He remembered the red, the blood.

He could recall nothing else, but he knew that, in time, it would come to him. Standing up, he stuffed the owl under his arm and walked towards the glowing hills.

He walked for what felt like a full day this time and drew closer to the hills. Sweat hung heavy on his brow, despite the coolness of the air. Still no sign of dawn. Nothing but endless night and an ongoing desire to reach the far side of the now-closer hills.

He had a sense that his desire was to be avoided, but he couldn't control it. Somehow, he knew it would be more trouble than anything, but he had always been weak in the face of his longings.

Another few hours and the graves had started to thin out. Finally, there was nothing between himself and the hills but a vast meadow, laced here and there with apple trees. He wondered if this related to his memory.

Have I been here before? Will I be back again?

Why did he think that? It made no sense. Nothing made any sense.

Who was he? Where was he, and where was he going?

The vertebral hills lay ahead, much closer now. The light behind them was brighter. It was a soft, pearl-like colour, with traces of red and black around the edges. Like no light he had ever seen before.

"Don't. Stop. Don't stop."

It sounded like Caitlin again. She seemed a fair distance away. Somewhere in the hills, up near the ridgeline. He pressed on, determined to find the source of the voice.

He reached the end of the meadow. The apple and cherry trees had given way to silver birch. Sparse patches of shrubs poked up above the grass here and there. The hill itself, the third from the left in the range, seemed made of rounded, strangely uniform white rocks.

It was only when he got close to where the grass ended that he saw what the hill was really composed of.

Skulls.

Thousands, tens of thousands, maybe even millions of skulls. The hill was a pile of bone two hundred metres high. He looked left and right, but the other hills in the range seemed normal. They were covered in grass, and the silver birch continued up the slopes. This hill, the one he needed to climb, was a barren pile of skulls.

Interlaced within the pile were other bones: long, thick femurs; delicately curved ribs; flat, axe-like shoulder blades; and stumpy spinal vertebrae. Millions of bones, piled high enough to contain every skeletal structure from every grave in the endless cemetery he had walked through to get here.

"Don't stop. Keep going. Climb and achieve knowledge. Face the truth that lies within."

Again, that voice called out to him. Again, the compulsion pulsed though him, an almost sexual feeling that stirred his loins and raised the hairs on his back and neck.

"Keep going and you shall find the meaning and the memory. Don't forget the owl."

Looking down at the stuffed toy in his hand, he realised he'd almost forgotten it was there, yet had managed to keep hold of it.

He looked up towards the crest of the hill. There seemed to be a large white box there, the size of a coffin. On it, a white figure reclined.

"Keep going."

He stepped onto the first of the bones, expecting them to shift beneath his feet, but they proved more solid than he expected. It was as though they were firmly fixed in the ground underneath; purely a decorative layer.

"That's it. Come to me. Don't stop."

"Who are you?" he cried out.

"I am temptation and punishment. I am your weakness and your desire. I am what lies within. I am innocence lost and the child of stolen dreams. I am diminished by lust."

A hidden memory surged forward at these words.

[flash] Stalking her, stealing her, taking her amongst the budding apple trees.

He remembered what he had done. He dropped to his knees, shame and regret warring inside.

What am I? How could I?

After a while, he came back to his senses. He had to make amends. He had to make things right. He had to find Caitlin.

"Where am I?"

"Where you need to be."

"That answers nothing," he said. "Where do you lead me?"

There came no reply, and the figure stood up from what he now saw to be another grave. It turned away and walked down the other side of the bone-hill. The last he saw, her fine golden hair was billowing as though wind-blown, yet there was no breeze.

"Caitlin," he called.

There was no response as the figure disappeared over the crest.

"*Caitlin!*" he called louder. Nothing. She was gone.

"I'm sorry," he whispered.

He increased his pace, and soon enough he reached the tomb she had been sitting on. A square of white stone, large enough to hold a coffin and protect it from the elements. There was no headstone; just one word engraved on the top slab.

Tu

'You'

Me?

Beneath the word was a carven symbol—a serpent, in the form of a circle that was swallowing its own tail. He had seen it before, but had no idea what it signified.

Rebirth? A cycle?

The tomb was sealed. He had no desire to open it. The very idea terrified him even more, if that was possible. He turned to follow the girl. He reached the crest of the hill and stopped, staring in wonder at what lay before him.

A massive city, marbled and lit throughout by what appeared to be torchlight, lay in the valley past the hills. It went for what seemed to be miles; houses made of stone interwoven with crenelated towers and castle-like fortresses built of massive basalt blocks. He could see movement in the distant streets. Crowds washed through them like water moving through a series of creeks; fluid and full of motion. Surrounding the city was a towering wall, interspersed with gates that stood at least thirty feet high. All seemed closed except one, which stood at the termination of a snaky road that led from the base of the bone-hill to the city itself. It was lined with torches and strange-looking trees.

Necropolis. *City of the Dead.*

He didn't know how he could be sure, but he was still certain this was the city's name.

A breeze lifted the hairs on his head, cooled the sweat on his brow. It carried with it the scent of vanilla and old sweat. Somehow, it seemed both arousing *and* abhorrent.

He started down to where the road began at the bottom of the hill. He was close now—he could almost feel the possibility of resolution. The toy owl dangled from his hand as he scrabbled down the bone-hill.

Soon, I will know who I am and accept what I have done. Soon, I will be whole again. Soon, I will live again. Soon, I will say I'm sorry, and she will know I have found the way.

He reached the base of the bone-hill and looked along the road. What he had taken for trees were actually poles, wrapped around with barbed wire that held up many children's toys. The poles were spaced about a hundred feet apart, all the way to the city.

A voice whispered in his ear.

"Look at me. I'm bleeding."

He whirled, trying to find who had spoken.

"I'm bleeding for you!"

He dropped the owl and clutched at his ears, spinning again, but there was no one around. The breeze picked up, strengthening the smell of vanilla and sweat, but this time it was laced with the tang of copper and old blood. Still, it managed to arouse him once again. His penis grew erect, and sweat sprang from his pores.

He stumbled along the road for a few metres before he remembered the owl. He went back to grab it. It looked different. He couldn't work out what it was for a second, and then noticed the eyes. Before they had been old buttons, but they were now tarnished pennies, sewn on with metallic thread.

Pennies for eyes, or to pay the Ferryman?

He walked towards Necropolis. *Not far now. I'll be there soon. I'll find out what lies beneath the bones and the blood and the dreams and the graves. What lies beneath the earth. I'll remember what happened, and I'll find a way to change it all.*

"Soon. You'll have it all very soon. This time, things will be different."

There was that voice again, but this time he ignored it. He cared for nothing but to reach the gates and find that which he sought. Knowledge.

He walked past the barbed toy-trees and the lit torches; he walked until he reached the city gates. They were closed, although he was sure they had been open when he had gazed down from the bone-hill. Old and worn, the wood they were made from looked ancient, yet they seemed solid. The gates were black and arched, and were graven with one phrase repeated in many different fonts.

Virginem Portam

'The Virgin's Gate'

He pushed against them once, and then again, but there was no give. He took a step back and kicked at them. Nothing.

"If you want to enter, you must take them by force! The city does not want you to enter. I don't want you to enter. I want you to not want to enter."

Caitlin's voice, saying those words, brought back everything. He recalled walking through an orchard. He remembered seeing her walking alone one row away from him, maybe on the way home from school. He remembered his lust, and he remembered what followed. He remembered... God, he *remembered.*

Anger and shame ripped through him. This was a lie. *He would never do that, would he?*

He charged the gates with all of his strength, uninvited yet undaunted. Angry and suddenly unrepentant.

At the last second, just as he reached them, he heard the voice once more.

"We all must bear the burden of the choices we make."

He tried to pull back.

No! I won't do this, he thought, but it was too late. The gates flew open. He fell through them, into darkness.

Darkness and dirt.

After he'd woken in the small, muddy cavern, he'd scrabbled uselessly for what felt like hours, but it was all still darkness and dirt.

His fingertips scraped against something in the dirt as he strived in the direction he hoped was up. Smooth and rounded, it fell from the earth as he pulled at it.

Caitlin? Why did that name spring to mind?

He placed it on the floor and continued his journey to the surface.

Soon enough, he broke through to the world above.

Still, the darkness reigned.

Behind him was a headstone. Words were engraved upon it.

Circulus Fatorum 'Fate Circles'

He leaned forward and laid the stuffed owl at its base.

He didn't want to die again, and hoped this time would be different.

redemption (n). The act or process of redeeming or of being redeemed

CHRYSALIS

by Stephanie M. Wytovich

A chrysalis in a bed woven from sticks,
I twitch, suffer against the mold I've been
cast in, the tapping behind my eyes,
a soliloquy, a midnight silhouette.

The hanged one calls to me,
a familiar voice,
           reversed in the wind

But I am a reflection, a mirage,
my body the liquified dream reanimating
in nakedness, this underworld dance
my spiritual disrobement.

He rocks me to death, a lullaby
turned dirge
           hidden amongst the trees

I sleep to echoes of his blood, this
pumping, a circulation of nightmare,
I am torn to shreds, my spirit a ripped
gossamer gown, a forgotten glove.

Please, feed me the wings of seraphs.
Someday, I too,
           want to fly.

REMEMBERING FRANK

by Greg Chapman

There were many instances of Frank's legendary love of the horror genre, but one memory I will carry of Frank is the time he went out of his way to let fellow author Todd Keisling know about a piece of potential book cover artwork I had created.

I posted it on my wall and Frank saw it and immediately knew it was perfect for Todd's book, *Devil's Creek*. Within minutes, Todd and I were working together. And that was Frank's gift—that he could bring authors, readers, and artists together, and that he wanted to help all authors succeed. He was the glue that held us all together.

I'm sad Frank is no longer with us, but I am happy to have known him, for him to have read and reviewed my work, and to have been a part of his life, even for a short time.

We all miss you Frank.

You can read this interview I did with Frank in 2017 on my website here - https://darkscrybe.com/2017/07/07/interview-with-reviewer-frank-michaels-errington/

HACKIN' AT THE PEACH

by Paul Tremblay

Ty Cobb.

The Georgia Peach.

One of the greatest baseball players to play the game.

And one of the meanest son of a bitches according to my granddaddy, William "Pepper" Schaefer. He played with Cobb from 1905 to 1911. During the off-season Granddaddy was a successful vaudeville performer and even invited Cobb on stage with him for a couple of acts. He never did consider the man a friend though.

Not at all.

Granddaddy took me to the corner of Michigan and Trumbull, grand old Tiger Stadium, to see my first ball game. Our seats were right behind the home dugout. I'll never forget that day. Sun shining and all my favorite players were within arm's reach. Almost like seeing a daydream become real.

But the Tigers—who weren't as good as my littleboy eyes said they were—lost to Ted Williams and the Red Sox 9-3.

And my granddaddy was madder than a fistful of hornets.

"That's no way to play ball. Everybody swings for the fences now. No bunts, no base stealin', no thinkin'. That Williams ain't so hot. Now when Cobb played, he'd go from first to third on a grounder in the infield and then steal home with spikes high," he said when we got home.

Teddy Ballgame was a secret hero of mine. And it had to be a secret in my Detroit Tigers family. But, for some reason, I shook up that fistful of hornets by telling him that I enjoyed the game.

Granddaddy grabbed two cokes from fridge, eyeballed me with gray eyes, and smiled. His mouth was a rusty trap of stained-brown teeth and not-so-silver fillings. Clumps of wispy white hair clung to his leathery scalp like fading clouds.

"Now lookie here, boy." He touched the side of his nose like he usually did before he spoke. And that bulbous nose of his showed the years of boozing and ballplaying—and in that order. "I hope you don't think that flashy Williams kid is anywhere near as good, or more importantly, as much of a character as Cobb."

I said, "No, sir."

"Because he ain't. Williams is a brash, braggart that Cobb would've beat into the ground like a tent pole." Still a large and muscular man, he clamped a thick left paw onto my shoulder, almost knocking me to the floor. "You've heard all my usual spikin', fightin', and cussin' stories, isn't that right?"

"Yes, Sir."

"Well then. I got a tale for ya that I ain't told anyone. Not Grandma, not your daddy, no one. It ain't a nice story. It's nothin' that you'll see in any book or newspaper." He pulled me close and I smelled the ballpark sausage and onion on his breath. "But it can be our tale, boy.

"So, do ya wanna hear it?"

His smile faded into a more serious and stern look. Must have been the same look he used to rattle pitchers in his day because it intimidated the heck outta me.

But I still wanted to hear his story.

"Okay, boy." He touched his nose again. "Storytellin' time. First, you should know all them tall tales, even the ones I've told ya a thousand times, about Ty Cobb are true. Even the ones that aren't true, it wouldn't surprise me a bit if they were.

"Now, I can guarantee that my story really happened. 'Cause I was there."

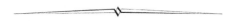

1906.

Spring training in Augusta, Georgia, which just happened to be the hometown of Ty Cobb. The year before had been the Peach's rookie year and despite the promise he showed, he was still fightin' for a spot on the club.

Even at that young age...nineteen, I think...no one on the team liked him much. You just couldn't kid around with the fella. Now, we usually gave rookies a hard time during their first year. Playin' jokes on 'em and the like. Harmless stuff. But with Cobb, each barb and prank was a challenge to his manhood and he lashed out at everybody.

It was like we were pokin' a stick at a pissed-off rattler.

A couple of veterans, Matty McIntyre and Ed Killian—a couple of louts—would hide his clothes and saw his favorite homemade bats in half. Cobb would come runnin' out the locker room, yellin' with his southern drawl, challenging the world to a fight.

That was another sore spot for Cobb. His southern-ness. Me and him were the only southerners on the team. And me being from Virginia, I really wasn't as southern in my ways as he was. Lookin' back, he was just a kid out on his own for the first time, and we didn't help the situation too much. Though I tell ya, we toughened up that son of a bitch.

Maybe we did too good of a job.

Two seasons later he was the best, toughest, and meanest player in baseball.

Well, that spring of 1906 was a bad one for Cobb. First, his mother had accidentally killed his father. A mess of an affair that I don't want to get into, at least not until you're older, boy.

Anyway, Cobb missed the start of training camp because of it. He was broken up something fierce, and embarrassed too. The papers made a big deal out of the whole sorry scene. So his frame of mind wasn't all there to start the spring.

He caught up with the team in the middle of our exhibition tour in Birmingham. Despite the home heartaches, damn if that son of a bitch didn't play his way onto the team, getting two or three hits a game and runnin' the bases like a jackrabbit.

We continued our tour up north, playing exhibition games just about every day. That two-week stretch was cold and rainy, just like March always is in the heartland. And Cobb got sick. By the time we reached Cincinnati, he had an awful case of tonsillitis.

Cobb had only confided in me, as McIntyre had just about the whole team feudin' with him. I told him to ask Armour for a couple of days off, but Cobb refused. He was too worried that he'd be givin' the skip an excuse to cut him.

So he played on. But the tonsillitis got worse.

It got to the point where Cobb only ate bread and milk because swallowing hurt too much.

We finally had some scheduled days off when we hit dreary Toledo. That first morning we had off, I stormed into Cobb's hotel room.

"Come on, Ty. Let's go," I said.

Cobb was curled up in his blankets with all the shades drawn. It was like I walked into a big old hole where animals crawled to die.

"Leave me alone. I'll sleep it off," he said. His voice rasped like he'd been gargling bleach and had chased it with rusty razors.

"No way, Peach. Let's go."

He didn't fight me. I pulled the blanket off his bed and I felt a wave of heat. He had such a fever, grabbing his arm was like squeezing a hot water bottle. Cobb struggled to his feet, and I turned on a lamp. Good God, I had woken a dead man. His fire-red hair dripped sweat and his normally sharp blue eyes were glazed and bloodshot.

"Damn, Peach. I've scraped better lookin' things off my shoe."

I led him downstairs to see the hotel doc.

The infirmary was right next to the greeting desk. I knocked, with Cobb leaning on my shoulder, the big son of a bitch. You might not be able to tell from the old pictures, but he was a big man. Just over six feet, which was tall back then, and about 180 pounds of wiry muscle.

I had to knock again. "Hello, anybody home? We got ourselves a sick man here!"

An older man opened the door. Late fifties or maybe even early sixties. Skin as white as the belly of a fish, bald head with only tufts of hair perched above his ears, and dark eyes so brown they were black. Beady too, like a hawk's eyes. And he was heavy, with jowls dancin' on the side of his face.

"Sorry, I was engrossed in my anatomy book when you knocked," said the smiling doc.

His accent struck me. He spoke too well for Toledo. It felt wrong, as if this guy was trying too hard to sound like he was soundin'.

"Come in, young man, come in."

I put Cobb down in a large chair next to an examination table. The infirmary was really nothing more than a small office. Not much more to the room other than some bookshelves and a cluttered oak desk.

Doc shook my hand and said, "Dr. Jonathan Wells."

"Pepper Schaefer. And this here unfortunate kid is Ty Cobb. His throat has been hurtin' him something fierce for the past couple weeks."

I noticed it then, but didn't think much of it at the time. Doc's eyes widened like an owl's when I had mentioned Cobb's throat.

"Really, the throat is such a troublesome area," he said. Doc grabbed some stuff of his desk.

Cobb tried to speak, but Doc shushed him.

I tried to stay in the background as much as I could. He turned a light on directly above Cobb and then put on that light-reflecting hat those docs wear. I don't remember what those are called, but anyway...

"Open wide," Doc said.

He pried and poked around Cobb's mouth while clucking and muttering to himself, until he called me over.

"Mr. Schaefer."

"Call me Pepper," I said. "I hate being called Mr. anything."

"Pepper then. Come take a look at this if you please."

Cobb closed his mouth and whispered, "What is it?"

"No, no, no, NO talking, Mr. Cobb. Please," Doc said and he again opened Cobb's mouth and held down the tongue with that Popsicle stick-thing.

I looked inside to see two, bright red swollen tonsils that almost filled the back of Cobb's head. Christ, I could even see them pulse with his heartbeat. "Damn, it's a wonder he can even breathe."

Cobb whimpered and wheezed with his mouth held open, but I couldn't understand him.

Doc nodded to me and said, "Yes, right you are, Pepper. I'm afraid these will have to come out right away, right away. Today. Right now, in fact." He ran back to his desk, knocking a stack of papers and books to the floor before rummaging around a clanky top drawer.

Cobb croaked like a bullfrog. "Okay. Let's get it over with."

What else were we supposed to do? We didn't know any better, and in 1906, whatever Doc said, you did. He started right then.

"Pepper, I need you to hold down young Mr. Cobb, as this will not be pleasant." Doc had an apron on and held a small scalpel in his hand.

"Doc, isn't there anything we can give him for pain?"

"There's no time and even if we did give him something, it doesn't take well in the throat. As I mentioned, the throat is a problem area."

With that, and with me holding down Cobb's shoulders, Doc cut into those swollen tonsils without any painkiller.

Now you gotta remember, we just didn't know back then, boy. Neither me or Cobb had been to a surgery before.

I felt Cobb's body tense as the scalpel sank into his throbbing tonsils. I tried not to look, but my damn eyes were drawn to the bloody mess. There Doc was, just hackin' away at the Peach, and he seemed as calm as a summer's day. An amazing amount of blood filled Cobb's throat and it was enough to make me sick, boy. So I leaned back and focused on Cobb's twitching face instead.

Boy he was tough, didn't groan or shed a tear. All I heard from him was tired, watery breaths. We worked out a system where Cobb would tap my arm if the blood had filled his throat and he couldn't breathe. Doc would let him up and Cobb then spit out a mouthful of blood and rested a bit. I also stopped Doc twice, when I thought Cobb looked like he was gonna pass out.

Doc worked on him for two hours before stopping.

"He'll need to come back tomorrow. Let the area heal overnight and then I can see if there is anymore that needs to be done," he said while wiping bloodstained hands on his apron.

I couldn't speak. On the examination table next to Cobb's head, lay chunks of pulpy flesh and the red scalpel.

Without a word, I helped the half-conscious Cobb back to his room. He collapsed on his bed. I pushed him onto his side so if he bled some more, he wouldn't choke on it.

Boy, that was one of the worst things I had ever seen, but we still had to go back.

Cobb brought his favorite bat with him that next morning. He was a very superstitious man and told me that it would bring him luck that day. I figured it couldn't hurt.

Doc was waiting in his doorway as we shuffled on down to his office. His eyes were wide again, looking too eager, and as I stumbled in with Cobb, I saw the freshly cleaned instruments sitting on the table.

"Good luck bat, eh Mr. Cobb? Don't worry, I'll take care of you. Now, let's see how our patient is doing?" He just about pried Cobb's arm off my shoulder and put him in the chair himself. After a quick inspection, Doc sighed and said, "There's still more, more to be done here."

Cobb slumped with disappointment but didn't fuss. Doc grabbed his scalpel again.

This second session, I kept my eyes on Doc. The look of pure joy on his face made me uneasy. It bothered me more than the bloody surgery. So I asked him a question. "You ain't from around here, are you Doc?"

"Whatever makes you say that, Pepper," he said without taking his gaze off Cobb's throat.

"Your accent," I said.

He looked at me and I thought I caught a flash of anger, but brushed it off. It could've been Doc was burned 'cause I was askin' him questions during surgery.

"I was born in England but moved here shortly thereafter, Mr. Schaefer."

I knew there was something to his speech and I also knew that he was pissed at me. It made sense not to rattle the cage of the guy doin' the cuttin', so I didn't ask him anything more.

The rest of the morning passed like the first did. Cobb gettin' up to spit blood every once and a while. And after another two hours, Doc said he was finished.

"I'm sure we're finished, but come back tomorrow, just to check up." He then gave us the bum's rush out the door.

Cobb remained in bed for the rest of the day.

Listening to myself now, I can't believe what we did. I can't believe we didn't go to the manager or another teammate and talk about what was happening. But, you just gotta remember boy, that despite some of the uneasy feelings I'd had, I didn't know there was anything wrong.

That next morning—the last we spent in Toledo as the team was supposed to be on a train headed for Columbus early that afternoon—we again went to see Doc Wells.

Cobb was awake when I went to his room and he seemed to be feelin' better. I looked at his throat best as I could in the dim light of his room and tried to say something comforting.

"I'm sure Doc will say you're done."

"Yeah, let's hope so, Pepper. But I'm still bringing the lucky bat."

Again, Doc was waitin' and ready for us. Cobb actually was able to move and sit at the chair under his own power.

I was sure Cobb was done. But after a quick look, Doc said, "Well, Mr. Cobb, there remains only a little bit of swollen tissue left. It shouldn't take long to remove the pesky remaining tonsil."

Unbelievable as it sounds, Doc was soon starting a third session of butchery. And on this morning, Doc seemed anxious. Sweat beaded on his head, his eyes were crawlin' around the room, and his lips were moving too, like he was mumbling stuff under his breath.

"You okay, Doc?" I asked.

He shot me a look with those horrible black eyes.

I had just about made up my mind to put a stop to this. Doctor or no doctor, I knew this wasn't right. I let go of Cobb's shoulders and noticed his eyes were closed.

The Peach had passed out.

"Doc! Cobb is out!" I yelled, and Cobb didn't even flinch.

Doc pulled his scalpel out of Cobb's mouth and said, "Pepper, go get me that glass of water over there on my desk. Quickly now." His voice cracked with panic, like the screeching of a cornered cat.

I ran toward the desk but—for some reason that I still don't remember or understand, boy—I stopped and turned back to look at Doc.

And there he stood, with Cobb's naked neck in his left hand and scalpel held high in the air with his right. He was gonna kill the Peach! I jumped and tackled Doc into the wall. He was raving like a mean drunk while I struggled to knock the knife out of his hand.

"It's still there! It's still there! Don't you see? It's spreading! It's spreading!"

Now, I probably sounded like a madman too. I was yellin' at Doc using language I can't use in front of you. I had never been so scared in all my life, boy. While pinning Doc's arms to his chest, I was kneeing him in the stomach. He was too old to take me, but I had a sense that he was a strong, strong man once.

The scalpel fell to the floor.

And Cobb gasped for air with blood spillin' out of his mouth. My grip on Doc loosened and he ran out of the office. I grabbed the lucky bat, went to Cobb, and helped him into the lobby where I spied a teammate lounging about.

"Take Cobb upstairs, get 'em some bed rest, but make sure he gets on that train this afternoon, or you have to answer to me," I said and shook the bat like I meant it.

I didn't answer any questions and ran out of the hotel after Doc with the lucky bat in tow. He was nowhere to be seen on those crowded Toledo main roads.

I went back into the hotel and had the manager call the police. I met two of the Blue Boys on the hotel steps and the three of us went to Doc Wells' apartment that was only two blocks away. I told them my story as we jogged to Doc's.

He lived on the second floor of a ritzy apartment building, or as ritzy as downtown Toledo could be back then. The three of us stood outside his door for a bit. We heard coughing and choking noises inside. The two cops banged on the door, but Doc didn't answer. Taking turns smashing into the door with our shoulders—the cops even gave me a couple of cracks seeing as I was bigger than both of them—I finally busted through the door.

Doc stood in the middle of his dark apartment while in front of a full-length mirror. Old and yellowed newspaper clippings, each with blazing headlines covered much of the surrounding walls and lined the mirror's frame.

The cops rushed ahead of me, but stopped when they saw Doc had a scalpel in his hand.

Ignoring the cops, Doc smiled such as smile of evil when he saw me. His mouth dripped blood. He was shirtless and red stained his pasty British chest. I thought I might lose it right there, boy. Truth be told, I was no hero and I wanted nothing more than to run screaming from that place.

And I still see those clippings and Doc's smile in my nightmares.

"It's spreading, Pepper! Be careful. It used to only be in those whores that I had cured. All those awful, dirty whores back home in England. But they spread their disease, Pepper. They spread it all the way across the pond. I didn't stop it, after all. And it was in Cobb."

"You should've let me finish. And now it's in me and I have to get it out."

Even though his voice gargled with blood, I heard the accent change. He sounded like a cockneyed Brit, just off the boat from London.

Doc opened his clenched fist and I saw a red lump of flesh that could only have been a tonsil. Boy, I'm not too proud to say that I didn't lose my stomach right there on the floor.

And I dropped the lucky bat.

The cops approached slowly, with billy clubs in hand.

Doc screamed, "Let me get it out!" He jammed the scalpel into the base of his throat and sliced down his chest. I won't go into it too much, boy, but there was a lot of blood. The cops jumped him.

I was told they managed to bandage him up without much struggle.

I didn't see that, 'cause I ran from the apartment and back to the hotel like the devil was chasin' me.

I ran back to the hotel and sat on the front stairs. It was all I could do, boy.

Eventually, other police found me and asked more questions. My teammates had already put Cobb on the train out to Columbus. I managed to convince the police that they didn't need to pester Cobb.

I arrived in Columbus the next day. Cobb, incredibly, played seven innings and got a hit as we beat the American Association team. While in the prime of his youth, he soon recovered from the horror that visited him in that Toledo hotel.

And boy, I never told him about what I found or saw.

I had my reasons. As I had said, Cobb was an extremely superstitious man. If I had told him the truth about Doc Wells, I bet it would've ruined him. No amount of knocking on wood and evil-eye protection would make a guy forget that. Believe me, I know. He also had a terrible time with his teammates that year and he probably would've thought I was joking him.

Two years later, though, when he was a bona fide baseball star, I did bring up the surgery, during a rain delay.

Sitting next to Cobb on the bench, I told him a part of the truth. I said that Doc was placed in a mental asylum shortly after the surgery.

The Peach looked at me with his wild blue eyes and hook nose curled above a sneer and said, "Well, he got the job done, didn't he?"

I didn't say anything more.

I was convinced, and still am to this day, boy, that the Peach was as crazy as that son of a bitch Doc.

I had nightmares about Doc Wells for a week after Granddaddy told me the story. Horrible nightmares where Doc reached into my throat and pulled out my tonsils with his bare hands.

Still, it was our story and that made it special.

I'm gonna tell my grandson that story today. Right after the ball game. Tiger Stadium is gone now, but the Georgia Peach and my granddaddy will live on through all the stories.

Including this one.

You know, in thinking about that story over the long years, I have my own opinions, but I won't tell my grandson who I think Doc Wells really was.

He'll have to sort that out himself.

Besides, that's all a part of what Granddaddy would say was "Storytellin'."

THE DEADLIEST REVIEW

by Jeff Strand

Frank Michaels Errington is going to review your new book in Cemetery Dance."

I almost spit my mouthful of Dom Pérignon onto my gold-plated laptop monitor. "Excuse me?"

My servant, Edward, took a step back. He knew to give me space when I became cross or apprehensive, lest I lash out at the nearest warm body. Frank Michaels Errington? A review? In Cemetery Dance?

No. It couldn't be. I had to have misheard.

"Speak that sentence to me again," I instructed.

"Frank Michaels Err—"

"Blast!" I shouted. "Blast and hellfire!" Frank M. Errington was one of the most powerful reviewers in the industry. He'd destroyed many careers, cackling with mad glee as he did so. Upon reading that his latest horror novel didn't meet Frank's lofty expectations, Jonathan Janz had kissed his family goodbye and then hung himself by the neck until dead. His family was right there and could have stopped him, but they knew it needed to be done. In fact, Mr. Janz had used too much rope, so that when he knocked over the chair his feet landed on the kitchen floor, leaving him unharmed; his children had to tug on him to complete the neck-breaking process.

Worse, immediately after a middling review of his latest tome was published, James A. Moore gazed outside his window and saw a pitchfork and torch-wielding mob. "You have disappointed Frank!" they shouted, kicking down his front door. Mr. Moore's high-pitched girlish shrieks echoed throughout the night. Bits of him turned up in the town's water supply for the next several years.

So, yes, I was uneasy with the thought that a work of mine had found itself into his vicious crosshairs.

I had reason to worry. My latest novel, *Whizzy McWiener Buys a Chainsaw*, was not my best. My private island had been overtaken by crustaceans, forcing me to write this book within the confines of my mansion, cursing every moment. My servants had done their best to make me feel pampered during this ordeal, especially Monique the Maid, whose reward system for my writing progress was unsurpassed. Yet writing by an Olympic-sized swimming pool with a water slide could not compare to writing in a hammock by the sparking blue waters of the ocean, and my writing suffered accordingly.

Perhaps Frank Michaels Errington would be kind.

I knew this to be a lie.

I'd met him but once, at one of those wretched conventions that forced me to interact with authors ("the poor") who'd achieved far less success. I was not there by choice; my agent felt it was best for me to attend at least one of these events per calendar year, to give back to the community. Hearing my inferiors say flattering things about me should have been pleasant, but I was overcome with a sense of intense pity for them.

Frank Michael Errington did not say flattering things about me.

He walked up to me, looked me directly in the eye, and said, "I find your work...unworthy."

My hand went to my open mouth. Had anybody overheard? They had not. Frank held my gaze, his cold, black eyes conveying a sense of menace beyond anything I'd ever encountered. I wanted to look away, but I dared not.

I'm unashamed to admit that I stuttered for several seconds without completing a word. Frank smiled at me—oh, that demonic smile, how it chilled me!—and then walked away.

That had been six years ago. I'd known this day might come, the day he put his thoughts about me into actual sentences that others might read, but I'd prayed for my reprieve to last until I was about to die from natural causes anyway.

"Leave me, Edward," I said. "I must brood."

And brood I did. For ten long months I brooded from morn 'til eve, until that accursed day when Cemetery Dance Online published Frank Michaels Errington's thoughts regarding my novel.

It was actually a pretty good review.

I let out the breath I'd been holding for these many months. "Edward!" I shouted. "Fetch me Monique the Maid and two cans of whipped cream, for today I celebrate!"

Lest you think I grew complacent after that, I assure you that the opposite is true. I knew I had to improve my craft, for fear that Frank might deem future works unworthy of the high standards set by *Whizzy McWiener Buys a Chainsaw*. Each word would be meticulously selected to be sure it was the proper choice.

That's why I'm only on Chapter Three of *Whizzy McWiener Buys a Chainsaw, Part II,* six years after I started writing it. And though Frank Michaels Errington has sadly passed on, I can feel his gaze still upon me, watching over my shoulder, ensuring that I produce only my finest work.

I shall not let him down.

I dare not.

I, CREATOR

by Tim Meyer

Troy Mantley had just finished typing "The End" on his newest manuscript and headed over to the fridge for a celebratory beer, when a hollow knock came at the front door.

Who the hell could that be, all the way out here?

His personal writing retreat had taken him to a log cabin in Upstate New York, and his closest neighbor was almost a mile away. He had no friends or family in the area, and there was no reason for anyone to come out here when everyone closest to him knew he was working on a new novel. Plus, they would have called or texted him. This had to be someone else. Someone he didn't know, or someone who was confusing him for someone else.

Maybe the cabin's owner?

The man he rented from lived in California, and he doubted he'd send a maid while he was still here, especially since Troy specifically instructed him not to.

As he made his way to the door, he wondered if it was the local police. His creative mind started conjuring up crazy scenarios, immediately drifting toward the more far-fetched. *What if the police are investigating a local murder, and I'm their number one suspect?*

He balked at the silly notion and gripped the doorknob.

Opening the door, he was surprised to find a guy, mid-twenties, standing on the porch, sporting a leather jacket and tight black jeans despite the blazing summer heat. He turned toward Troy and as soon as the writer saw the man's face, he knew something was gravely wrong.

"Can I...can I help you?" Troy asked. He recognized the face, even though he'd never seen the man before.

The man pushed his hair back, away from his eyes, and smirked. "I don't know. Can you?"

"I'm sorry?" Troy scanned the tree line. He was waiting for a whole crew of people to come popping out of the surrounding forest, the publishing team, maybe his agent. Hell, maybe his daughter and her husband, practical jokers they were, put them up to it. "You knocked on *my* door."

"Yeah, I did. You gonna invite me in or what?"

"I'm sorry. I don't think I know you."

The man burst out laughing. "That's a good one. Come on, Troy. Quit playing around. Let's get to the part where you invite me in, we sit down with beers, and I tell you all about what I'm doing here."

Troy shook his head and began to close the door. "No, I'm sorry. This isn't…"

What? What are you going to say? This isn't RIGHT? Of course, it isn't. This man cannot exist. Can't possibly.

Before he could close the door, his guest stepped on the threshold. Troy closed the door on his foot, but the man didn't blink. Didn't respond.

"Please move," Troy told him, "or I'm going to call the police."

"Go ahead. Call them. How're you gonna explain where I came from?"

"Where did you come from?"

"You know damn well where I came from." The man clicked his tongue. "New York City, 1975."

"Impossible."

"Come on, Troy. Don't give me that shit. Invite me in. Let's have a beer. I'm fucking parched."

Troy didn't exactly open the door, but he didn't resist when the figure he'd dreamt about, the man he'd envisioned so many times in the past, pushed him out of the way and let himself in. Once inside, he took in the cabin, sniffed the air, and nodded.

"Helluva a nice place you got here, Mantley. Hell of a nice place."

"You're not him."

"What?"

"I know what you're trying to do, and you're not him. You need help."

The street kid faced him. Troy could see the heavy bags around his eyes. The bruises on his face. Someone had recently pummeled him, maybe a week or two ago. Troy knew that for a fact because he'd just written the scene around the same time.

"Quit horsin' around, Mantley. We've got work to do. Get us beers."

"You may think you're Vinny Sangriani, but you're not."

That trademark smirk found life again, and Vinny planted himself down at the wooden table in the center of the room. "You're a funny guy, Mantley. I like you. They said I wouldn't, Tony and Mikey, but I do. Fuckin' hell, I like you a lot."

"I can call someone. Get you help."

Now he looked annoyed. "Listen, I know you're trying to process this thing, mentally or whatever, but you really need to sit the fuck down and chill out. I've got to tell you something important and we ain't got a lot of time."

"Prove it."

"Prove what?"

"Prove you're really him."

"How the fuck am I going to do that? Didn't exactly bring my driver's license with me, you know what I'm saying?"

You know what I'm saying? One of Vinny Sangriani's trademark quotes. *Christ, if this is an act... it's a goddamn good one. Hand this kid an Oscar right fucking now.*

"When was Vinny's birthday?"

"Holy shit, writer-man. You're gonna test my bat with that softball? June 1st, 1953. My mother's name was Maria, my father was Luigi, God rest their souls. I was raised by Don Romano Sagarelli. Anything else, wise guy?"

"Who shot Bucky Archibald?"

Vinny smirked again, waved his hand. "Everybody knows Ricky Dimples pumped that bastard full of lead after the Don put the hit out on him. No one missed the fuck either." He wiggled his fingers, asking for more.

Okay, those were easy. He could still be a fan. A crazy, out-of-his-fucking-mind fanatic. Those questions could be found in any of the five published books in the Grand Mafioso series. Give him something new, something that hasn't been published yet. Hell, give him something that hasn't even been written yet. Something you've been planning for the sixth book.

"Who kills Don Roman Sagarelli's son, Angelo?" he asked, folding his arms, feeling confident.

Vinny smiled. "Yeah, figured you were going to go that way." He held up his hands, which were stained crimson. They hadn't been moments ago, and now that they were, it caused the writer to almost wet himself. "I did. That was me. Did the fuck dirty, too. Popped his head like an oily pimple. No open casket for him. I spit on his mother." He spat dry air to illustrate his point.

"Jesus Christ." Troy stumbled into the cabin's wall. Without the timbers there, he would have gone to the ground, easily. "Holy fucking shit, this is real. I've finally lost my mind."

"You ain't lost your mind. Look, I'm here on some very important business."

He felt himself break out into a cold sweat. Looking toward the front door, he wondered if he could outrun Vinny, make it to the car before Vinny could react.

"You ain't going anywhere," Vinny said. "Sit the fuck down."

God, he's in my head.

"I am in your head, remember? Shit, you really need to calm down. What I have to say is life or death, you know what I'm saying?"

Slowly, Troy managed to sit down across from one of his own favorite creations. Vinny had always been fun to write. He'd changed so much over the course of five books. In the planned sixth and final book, Vinny was set to finally become the man he'd always meant to be—head of the crime family.

"Now look at me," Vinny said, staring at his creator. "You've got a bad heart. I don't know when it's gonna happen, but if you don't get your ass to a doctor right now, that heart is gonna seize up like an engine with no oil, and you're gonna be fuckin' dead. And you know what that means?"

Troy stared at him blankly.

"Means you die, I die. You fuckin' prick. I can't have that. So you're gonna pack up your shit, and you're gonna hit the nearest hospital and have them check out your heart. Then you're gonna get to writing that sixth book, my friend. Yeah, the one you've been putting off for years because you don't want the journey to end or some such bullshit—look, bottom line, finish the fuckin' story, man. Don't die, either. We definitely don't want that."

Troy took a moment, collected his thoughts. It wasn't easy because they were scattered in a hundred-thousand different places.

"I'm going to die?" he finally croaked.

"That's right, cupcake. So pack your shit. Let's get going."

"I'm not going anywhere."

"Was afraid you'd say that." He sighed deeply, then stood up. "Come here. Take a look outside." Troy made his way to the window, pinned back a curtain with his hand. "Come on, let's go."

Reluctantly, Troy dragged himself over to the window.

His heart skipped.

Near the tree line, shadows emerged from the forest. Dozens of them. Maybe a hundred.

"What the…"

"See, if you die," Troy said, "we all die. And how do you think that makes us feel, to hear you're not going to take care of yourself? To *save* yourself."

The shapes materialized. He spotted Dick Croggins, an old-timer from a literary fiction book he'd written several years ago. Old Dick was walking on his cane, the one with the bald eagle head atop it. He saw Miss Andersen, a fourth-grade teacher from a coming-of-age horror novel he'd written in his twenties. The Sagarelli crime family was present. They chewed their gum and watched intently. Misrande, a female warrior from a fantasy novel he'd published under a pen name, was also among them. She held her magical staff and crouched down, as if about ready to charge into battle. The four ghost hunters from his comedic-horror series—basically a rip-off of *Ghostbusters*—were also there, looking at him, unhappy to hear about his decision to take his medical matters lightly.

"I don't know what they're gonna do to you if you *don't* go to the hospital. But I have a feeling they'll be very convincing."

"Okay…" Troy said, eyeing his creations, hating the way they returned his gaze. "Okay… I'll go."

Two days later, Troy had four stents put in to open up his clogged arteries. The doctors thought it was pretty amazing how he came to discover this, out of the blue, with no symptoms. Troy told them it was *a feeling,* and he couldn't explain it.

You have an angel looking out for you, one doctor had told him.

Troy wanted to tell him he had hundreds.

"Now," Vinny told him from the seat next to his hospital bed, "about that sixth book. I have some requests."

REMEMBERING FRANK

by Tony Tremblay

Frank and I first crossed paths at Necon, a convention for horror writers that was held every July in Rhode Island (now it's held in Salem, Massachusetts). Though Frank and I were friends on Facebook, we had never met, but we knew enough about each other to feel more than comfortable in each other's presence. When our eyes met, we both were clutching cameras, and our smiles were bright enough to illuminate the foyer we were standing in. Laughing all the while, we immediately took pictures of each other. We spent quite a bit of time together that July, mostly talking about horror novels and the writers we admired.

Frank was a reviewer of horror novels, and prior to us meeting, he had done a review of my collection The Seeds of Nightmares. The review was glowing, and when I asked Frank if I could use a portion of it for a blurb on the hardcover, he was in shock. He hadn't realized how many people were reading his reviews—and how many people enjoyed his insights. After a short discussion, he agreed to be part of the hardcover release. When I was selling the book at that Necon, he was first in line to purchase one. I'll never forget the look of pure delight when he saw his blurb on the back cover.

When my novel The Moore House was in ARC form and ready for reviews, Frank jumped at the chance to read it. If I remember correctly, Frank was the first to review the novel. He praised the novel so highly, his review stoked the flames of other reviewers wanting to read The Moore House. Word of mouth about the novel spread, much of it starting with Frank's review. The Moore House made the final round in the First Novel category of the Bram Stoker Awards. It didn't win, but if it had, Frank was mentioned in the acceptance speech.

My fondest memory of Frank has nothing to do with writing or reviews.

One day, while pouring scotch into my favorite scotch glass, my hand slipped, and the glass fell to the floor and shattered. I had really liked that glass. I had it a long time, and it felt like I lost an old friend. As I am prone to, I went on Facebook and shared my loss and sorrow with my friends. After that, I switched to another glass, poured myself a scotch, and forgot about the incident.

Two days later, I received a package in the mail. It was from Frank. I had no idea what it could be as I didn't think Frank would be sending me a book. I opened it up, and was stunned at the contents. Inside were four scotch glasses. You couldn't have wiped the smile off my face with sandpaper. I went back on Facebook, thanked Frank, and all of us on the thread had a rather humorous discussion. What I hadn't realized was that Frank was once again at the start of something that would snowball.

Days later the scotch glasses started arriving. I believe seventeen other people also sent me a scotch glass to replace the one I had broken. There were so many I had to go back onto Facebook and plead with people not to send me any more. Frank found this delightful, and he had quite the laugh the next time we met up.

Like most people reading this anthology, I was concerned when I first learned Frank needed a transplant. We conversed a few times after this, but for the most part, I followed Frank's medical progress on Facebook along with all of you. When he passed, I was prepared, but still saddened. I consider myself fortunate that a small part of Frank graces the back cover of my first collection. Whenever I read that blurb, I see Frank smiling, and that makes me smile.

RIVER BUGS

by Anthony J. Rapino

D an Thompson threw another rock into the woodland river and cursed the marred summer day. Damn his mom for making him watch Timmy. Damn his dad, too busy at the computer to weigh in. And double-damn that dumb river Timmy always wanted to play around.

Barely a river, Dan thought. He mapped the jutting boulders in the water, estimating a mere six leaps would carry him across without so much as a wet shoe.

Trees surrounded the river on all sides, blotting out the rest of the world. Golden sunlight winked through the canopy, and the day buzzed like a lazy bee. Not so long ago, when Dan had still been Danny, the abundant summer magic would have embraced him like a mother's hug. Now, he could only see another wasted day with his bothersome brother.

Timmy plunked a stone into the water.

"Your turn, Danny." He pushed a rock into his big brother's hand. "Throw."

"Stop calling me Danny, twerp."

Dan should have been at his buddy Finn's house, not in the forest playing kiddy games. He threw his rock with all the force of adolescent frustration behind it. The stone sailed over the river and landed on the opposing riverbank. Not such a long distance at all.

"Danny."

"I told you to stop calling me—"

"Look." Timmy pointed beyond the rushing water. Two young girls stood on the bank.

"Where'd they come from?"

Though the distance wasn't far, he had trouble making out their features. He heard his mother's voice nagging him about needing glasses, saying that's why his grades had dropped (and not because he spent most of his class time fantasizing about Tina Drake).

The taller of the two girls waved, then called out sweet and tender. She looked like a pink and violet smudge. He squinted hard, trying to make out any singular feature, but the girls remained mist and mirage. Just barely there.

Timmy tugged on Dan's arm. "Hey, I want to go home."

"What?" He knelt beside his brother. Timmy's eyes were squinted against the sun. There were red spots on his face where mosquitoes had feasted. "*Now* you want to go?"

He nodded emphatically.

The river murmured along a rocky bed. Summer's sleepy buzz joined this midday song as if some faery realm called from beyond the trees. The girls waited in the water's shimmering light.

"Come on, Timmy. There's a girl your age too. We can go say hi, maybe throw rocks with them."

"I don't want to."

"What's wrong with you?"

"No, what's wrong with *you*?" Timmy stomped away and picked up a rock. He ran to the bank of the river and threw as hard as he could. Dan could tell he was trying to hit the girls. Luckily, he hadn't the strength, and the rock plopped into the water.

Timmy said, "You never want to hang out with me anymore."

His accusation thrust through Dan's veil of hormones and pierced a heart of truth. He had a point. They'd always been best friends until something inside Dan changed. He had snapped in half like a broken bone, but try as he might, he couldn't fuse the grating pieces back together.

Timmy pointed across the water again. "You don't know them."

Dan squinted at the two girls, waving him over. Calling to him with sweet voices. The river tinkled like bells. A woozy patina coated the world. The lone figures watched and waited. No, he didn't know them. But he sure wanted to. He'd seen the sex sites on Finn's computer, and while the precise mechanics of what he'd witnessed eluded him, he knew he liked it. Maybe the older girl would know more about sex. Maybe she could show him.

"I'm going across. Stay here."

Timmy grabbed him around the waste. "Don't!"

Dan shoved Timmy, who fell hard.

"Ow." He looked at his skinned palms. "You're stupid," Timmy muttered, the sound of a boy losing his hero. Another stab into the heart of truth.

"You're fine." Dan stalked to the edge of the water where the nearest boulder lay. "I'm sorry, okay. I just want to say hi."

"Don't leave me alone. Something's wrong with them."

Though thirteen and a man by his estimation, fear still lurked in the shadowy corners of Dan's mind. Some nights—though he'd never admit this—Dan put his old night-light on, dug from the bottom of a dresser drawer. Because sometimes, in the inky black, creatures watched and crept and crawled. Hungry things who liked the flavor of children best.

His brother's words—*Something's wrong with them*—tugged at the childish part of Dan's brain. The part that housed fear and doubt. Gooseflesh prickled his skin despite the heat of the day. He shrugged away the thoughts, not liking the feel of them. Like last year's winter coat, too tight and stinking of mothballs, he'd outgrown these absurd notions. Besides, across the river stood two young girls in the sun of a warm summer day. No shadows or creeping things to fear there.

Dan made up his mind. "I'll be right back."

Timmy groaned in opposition, but it was no use.

Dan jumped onto the first rock. His foot slipped, but he had agility and youth on his side. The girls clapped and cheered him on. Their voices carried over the rambling river, tickling the nape of his neck.

He turned to see Timmy watching from the riverbank, rubbing his skinned hands.

Dan hopped two large boulders in quick succession. Water rushed all around him, muting sounds on the banks. The sun dipped behind an errant cloud and the day dimmed.

Although Dan was halfway across, the girls were still smudges. They wavered in the broken light cast through the trees, their features fuzzy like frosted glass. Dan decided he'd let his mom take him for an eye exam after all.

He hopped to the fourth rock, which was small and covered with moss. His foot skimmed the slippery surface and zipped out from under him.

He catapulted into the air.

Water, sky, rocks, and the girls blended together like a wave of spiraling colors, then exploded in a bright flash as he plunged into the cold water. He shut his eyes tight. Water rushed around his ears. He extended his legs to stand, but his feet kicked free in the water. How could that be? The bottom of the riverbed was visible where he fell, only a few feet under water.

Dan opened his eyes as he kicked. The sun broke behind the clouds and shimmered through the surface of the tumultuous river. A strange twinge of panic entered his throat, which felt tight from holding his breath. His chest began to ache.

He continued kicking, but the surface came no closer. Maybe he'd become caught on some underwater obstacle. Dan checked but saw only the riverbed far below. *Too* far, lost in the murk as if he'd dove into a deep lake and not a shallow river. A slippery shadow slithered by in the cloudy depths, tickling his ankle. Dan kicked away and swam up. And up.

And up.

Dan's oxygen-deprived brain manufactured flashes of light and splotches of dark. He imagined giant water snakes and tentacled creatures hunting the woodland river, slipping around his frantic legs, embracing him with slimy bodies.

He reached, striving for open air, kicking for freedom. The panic shifted to biting fear. A mind-rending dread, tearing his thoughts to ribbons.

His lungs throbbed and eyes stung. The surface eluded him with every kick. Dan's throat convulsed, threatening to open and welcome the surging water if only to quench the fire in his lungs.

The river encased Dan, unwilling to release him. His attempts to resurface turned to terrified spasms as something clamped around his ankle. He didn't dare look down. Dan continued to kick and thrust and reach. The rippling surface taunted him, inches away, yet miles. The thing holding his ankle yanked, and he lost precious momentum.

He opened his mouth to scream *no*, but only the last remaining air escaped in bubbles. Head-shaking, water-tearing fury overtook him as he channeled this last frantic energy into an escape, kicking free of the gripping thing, soaring through the water.

And just as he sensed release, his body betrayed him.

Dan inhaled a lungful of cold water as he emerged close to the riverbank. He sputtered, taking another deep lungful of air on top of the water, then unceremoniously evacuated the contents of his stomach in a splash of runny vomit. Dan kicked and dragged himself onto the shore as he rasped more air into his starved lungs. Everything around looked glazed with scum. The world had turned to an expressionist's painting, blotches of color making up his surroundings in blues, greens, and browns.

In the distance, Timmy screamed interrogations. He called Dan's childhood name, wanting to know if he was okay. Was he alive? Why had he stayed under so long?

Dan sat up, dazed. He wiped water from his eyes and with foggy vision glimpsed the girls standing a few feet away.

Their faces were all mouth, hanging open and lined with hooked teeth. Drool cascaded over thick and quivering lips. A hungry sound like bugs being crushed under foot emanated from their convulsing throats.

Dan yelped and kicked away. He rubbed more water from his stinging eyes and when he looked again, the girls weren't there. They had probably run off when he botched the landing on the last rock. He must have imagined the grotesque creatures, his eyes not yet readjusted to terrestrial life. Perhaps the obscene vision had even been a hallucination caused by oxygen deprivation. Whatever the cause, Dan decided he wanted to go home. Back to the comfort of his bed. He suspected his hidden night-light would even come out to play when the sun abandoned the sky.

Dan stood and shook water from his hair. As he wrung out his shirt, he gazed around for the girls. He saw only the rocky shore, weeds, and trees.

"Gone." He wiped water from his face. "I'm such an idiot."

From the far side of the river, Timmy called, "Danny!"

The sound of his little brother's voice drew a line of fire up his back.

"Danny!" The call, a squeal of terror. A *warning*.

Dan swiveled, suddenly sure the drooling creatures were real and had sneaked up behind him. He could still feel the place where some unseen thing had gripped his ankle. But the shoreline harbored no slithering snakes or any other waterborne creatures. He checked again, but no one stood on the shore with him.

"Danny!"

Dan turned to address his brother's calls with a few choice words. He'd had enough of the annoying twerp and was done with obligatory brotherly outings. Dan was grown up, and if he wanted to hang out with his friends and go to parties and talk to girls, by God, that's what he'd do, and no one was going to stop—

The curses and attacks stuck in his throat. Dan felt as if he were still trapped under the cold water. The summer sun did nothing to warm his shivering body.

On the other side of the river, the two girls held Timmy by his arms. Only, they weren't girls at all.

They'd *never* been girls.

Timmy screamed and yanked, but couldn't break their grasp, because they didn't hold him with hands, but enormous clamping pincers that bit into his skin, sending rivulets of blood running down his thin arms. Little Timmy cried and screamed, pleading for his big brother to save him.

Dan could see them clearly now. Perhaps he didn't need glasses after all.

"Get them off! Please! I promise to never call you *Danny* again! I promise!" His words broke into wet screams.

Dan opened his mouth to speak and river water poured out, like some hidden well had been tapped. He gripped his throat, gagging, spewing, watching his little brother squirm and cry.

Slime dripped along the creatures' plated bodies. Tiny skittering legs grew from their torsos, twitching and stabbing. They heaved Timmy between them, gurgling obscene laughter. The creatures cackled as their pincers dug deep. They smiled with enormous, hungry mouths.

Mouths that tricked Dan's teenage brain.

Mouths that had lured him away from the intended prey.

Mouths that preferred the taste of young children best.

PANORAMA OF MADNESS

by Sara Tantlinger

Fleshy garden of delights,
crisp clarity burnt the ends off
swallowed our crystal rivers up
       the only light here is fire
       the only promise is one of Hell.

We're all Judas in the lost paradise,
spinning sins like ashy webs
caught in the stick of deranged erotica,

blink once, your lover is damned
shake slightly, the animals sniff you out
mutated muzzles savoring fear
       the only taste here is human flesh
       the only temptation is survival.

Everything pulsates, darkness and lust
coagulated into hemoglobin rituals
a painted panorama of madness,

blink twice, your hands are burnt vines
wrapping around the neck of light,
squeezing earthly delights to death
       the only peace here is oblivion
       the only promise is one of Hell.

KEROSENE

by Pete Kahle

Fifty years after some dude named Norman Morrison doused himself in kerosene and lit himself on fire to protest the involvement of the United States in the Vietnam War, Traci Pickering did the same exact thing in the Dunfield High School cafeteria during second lunch. Except for the Vietnam thing.

Needless to say, they cancelled Homecoming.

———————————✕———————————

I only knew about Morrison because we had just covered Vietnam two weeks earlier in U.S. History class and I remembered wondering at the time what could have possibly caused someone to do something that stupid. I still don't know.

Traci's official cause of death was listed as self-immolation, but her reasons for choosing that way to die were unknown. I was familiar with all the usual methods of suicide: gun, pills, hanging—we have at least one school assembly on that subject each year—but burning yourself alive? That's just insane. Forget about how much it would hurt. What about watching your skin bubble and char? Or feeling your eyes boil until they popped? Somehow, she sat there silently as she died, even as the cafeteria erupted with shrieks of horror around her. And the smell... I still remember it. Burning hair and a meaty odor that coated my sinuses, reminding me of hot dogs that had been on the grill too long.

Now, I would never even consider suicide, but it isn't hard to see some kids gravitate toward it. Enough shit exists in the world today that it's easy to empathize with anyone who feels like killing themselves—even Traci, who had been one of the most popular girls in school—but there are certainly much better ways to end it all.

School was shut down for two weeks while they gave us time to deal with our shock and grief or whatever emotions we were feeling. Most of us were just numb. It didn't seem real. Bereavement counselors were made available to anyone who needed them. My mom made me go because I knew Traci, and she thought it would help me come to terms with my demons. She actually said that—*demons*.

If she only knew.

The first day back was pretty surreal. Teachers and students travelled the halls somberly in small packs, huddling together as if for protection from any demons that might still be stalking DHS. An industrial aroma of lemon and bleach lingered in the air, especially near the cafeteria, as if the act of cleansing would somehow remove the stain of what Traci did and purify the school grounds. Maybe it was my overactive imagination, but I was sure I could still smell the burnt hair and hot dogs. Eventually, though, normalcy prevailed and the undercurrent of disquiet faded. By lunchtime, the hallways seemed to have returned to the ordinary tumultuous routine. Relieved that nothing had occurred, herds of students milled around and gossiped before the mad rush right as the bell for the next class sounded.

As seniors, we had first lunch, so we were the first students allowed to enter the cafeteria since Traci had taken a flaming kerosene shower. Surprisingly, it looked exactly the same. Kinda disappointing, to be perfectly honest, but I don't know what I expected. A scorched outline? Soot stains on the ceiling? I was quite impressed at how they had managed to erase any sign of the fire. I looked at my friend Charlie Livermore and could see he felt the same way, a bit let down by the routine appearance of the room.

As far as I could tell, the only evidence that anything had changed was a small section of floor tiles. They were in the school colors—blue and gold—like the rest of the floor, but these tiles appeared slightly newer, less dingy. Over time they would fade in with the rest of the floor, but now, with just the right angle of lighting, you could see the difference.

I headed for the deli line, maneuvering around Jonny Whitlock as he mopped up a spill right at the edge of the newly tiled section. Jonny was the newest custodian here. Most of us already knew him, because two years ago he had been a student here as well. He had squeaked out a diploma on the five-year plan at age nineteen, and now he was back working at his old school. I guess the job market sucks for pot-smoking slackers whose main set of skills revolves around video games and internet porn.

As I did my best to avoid the wet spot, I saw him kneel down and pick up a small white object. At that point, I didn't really care about whatever he had found, but it looked cylindrical and thin as he held it up, like a stray chicken wing bone. I forgot about it as soon as I lined up for my sandwich.

Five minutes later, I paid the cashier and headed over to our table where Charlie sat with Dave Spurlock and Jessie DeSantis. They grunted in greeting while Charlie winged a tater tot at my head and blurted out "What took you so long, fuck-o?"

"Your mom," I responded. That never failed to shut him up, so I always had it ready in a pinch. It was probably a low blow considering she had left him and his dad last year and now lived with some roided-up moron ten years younger than her, but he would get over it eventually. He always did.

I sat down and elbowed him in the side to show I was only fucking with him and then joined the table banter. Morbid as we were in my circle of friends, the conversation quickly turned to Traci, and soon after, we were arguing over what were the best methods of suicide. Dave thought the best way was the trusty shotgun-in-the-mouth routine, but the rest of us agreed it would leave a huge mess for someone to clean up. There was also the chance the blast would only blow off the front of your face, leaving everything else behind it remaining intact. *No, thank you.*

Jessie was a firm believer that pills were the way to go. "I'd go into my mom's medicine cabinet and swallow a handful of Ambiens," she proclaimed. "You'd never have to worry about waking up again." She smiled when she said it. I don't think I was the only one who thought it was kinda creepy, like she had been saving her idea for a while.

Charlie, as usual, was approaching this topic with a bit too much enthusiasm. He wanted to go skydiving without a parachute and hit the ground at terminal velocity.

"I'd wear a GoPro all the way down until impact so the video could get posted to YouTube," he said. I considered pointing out that the damage to the camera would destroy any recording but didn't feel like putting the effort into actually speaking.

When he finished, he looked in my direction, signaling it was my turn to reveal my plan. I just shrugged and took another bite out of my sandwich. I had some ideas, but I didn't want to share any of them.

The other three sat there for a few seconds until Charlie blurted out, "Dude, that's lame. Come on, Brian, you heard ours. What's yours?"

I looked around the table. All eyes were on me, eagerly awaiting my scenario, apparently certain I would blow them out of the water with a ridiculously cool idea.

But I had nothing. Nothing that matched the perfect statement of Traci's death. Nothing worthy.

I tilted back my Mountain Dew and finished it in two long swigs before crushing it into a flat disk and lobbing it into a trash can. The lunch monitor, Ms. Ludwig, glared in my direction and shook her withered little head at me. She didn't bother coming over to reprimand me, though. Sometimes it really helps when your father is the principal.

I turned back to my friends, ready to mollify them with visions of me diving headfirst into an industrial woodchipper, but the bell rang and the mass exodus to fifth period began. Gobbling down the rest of my sandwich, I emptied my tray into the trash barrel and headed reluctantly for the door. Next class was my least favorite, Chemistry with Mrs. Howles, so I lagged behind everyone as they swarmed into the hall.

I muttered a goodbye to Jonny as I passed him on my way out. Usually he flashes a thumbs up, but he didn't respond at all to me, not even with his trademark "Du-u-u-de." His eyes were even more glazed than usual, and he appeared thoroughly distracted as if he were listening to his music, but his ever-present headphones were hanging around his neck. I didn't think anything of it, though. He was probably stoned out of his skull.

Three days later, we heard the news. At the tail end of sixth period, Mr. Yancey was in the middle of expounding upon the joys of trigonometry when the loudspeaker crackled and I heard the voice of my father, known to everyone else as Principal Gentry, echo through the halls.

"Please excuse the interruption," he said.

As soon as he began speaking, I knew it was going to be bad. My dad might have a reputation for being an uptight prick, but he does have a soul that occasionally makes an appearance when he has to deliver bad news as part of the job. In the days following Traci's fiery demonstration, he pulled me into a stiff hug whenever he had to leave the house. It was beyond awkward.

After a drawn-out pause and a nervous cough, he continued, "It is with deep sorrow that I must relay this to you, especially considering the events of the past two weeks." A sharp burst of feedback shrieked through the speaker, causing a few students to wince visibly as he waited for it to subside. He continued, "This morning, I received a call with the sad news that Jonathan Whitlock, a former student who had recently joined our custodial staff, lost his life in an automobile accident late last night. Whether you knew Jonathan personally or not, he was well liked, and universally thought of as a genuine and friendly member of the DHS family. Mr. O'Dwyer and the rest of guidance department will be available to speak with anyone if needed."

Most of us, myself included, tuned out the rest of his comments as we digested the news in stunned silence.

The rest of the day passed quickly. Since it was too late to dismiss everyone to go home, the teachers allowed students to gather in the cafeteria or the library during the final two periods. Some chose to stay in class in small groups, but I headed to the cafeteria. As expected, Charlie was already sitting at our table where he was busy tapping away at his phone.

He glanced up and greeted me with, "Du-u-u-u-ude, have you seen them?"

"Seen what?"

"The pics." He held up his phone and showed me the image before continuing, "Somebody—no one knows who—posted pictures of Jonny's car just after the crash. It's fucking gruesome, man."

"Wait, what?" I struggled to process what he had said as I snatched his phone from his hand. "No way. Who's sick enough to do something like that?"

I looked and winced. The tangled mass of twisted, scorched metal looked more like someone had taken a blowtorch to a soda can than a car wreck.

"Check that out," Charlie said, pointing to the lower right corner of the screen.

I expanded the image and swiped left so it centered on the license plate—4204EVA. Definitely Jonny's car. Everyone knew that plate and the car that wore it. It was unmistakable, even if the rest of the vehicle was unrecognizable. There were other pictures, taken from every possible angle, even a close-up of the driver's side where Jonny's charred corpse was curled. His mouth stretched wide in an eternal scream, lips broiled away and blackened. His eyes had burst and leaked down his cheeks. Disgusted, I shoved the phone back at Charlie.

"Dude, I didn't post 'em!" he protested.

"Obviously," I sneered. I turned away from him and glared at the students at the tables around the cafeteria. Nearly all huddled in their own groups, ghoulishly studying the sickening slideshow. I felt guilty at having done the same thing only seconds earlier. I turned back to Charlie and apologized. "Sorry, man. Where did they come from?"

"That's the weird part, Brian. Someone posted them to Instagram and you'll never guess whose account posted it."

I shrugged, but as soon as he spoke, I knew whose name I'd hear.

"Traci Pickering's."

I didn't respond. I couldn't. For the next few minutes, all I was capable of doing was staring at the rectangle of new tiles where she had sat quietly as she was engulfed in fire.

That night I had the first dream.

I sat on a wooden plank bench in what appeared to be a council hall surrounded by a dozen or so men and women huddled together on benches of their own. The sounds of rain drummed on the roof above us. The walls were stained white, bare except for several flickering oil lamps suspended from hooks. The floor was built from the same rough planks as the benches. I looked around at the men and women who were in attendance and recognized none. They were dressed in simple homespun clothes, dyed in shades of brown, dark blue or forest green. All were silent, attention on me as if waiting for a signal; some had their heads bowed in contemplation or prayer. I turned my head and saw a massive wooden cross, rough-hewn and taller than a man, affixed to the wall behind me, and I realized this building also served as a church.

Eventually, I stood—or rather my body stood—and I realized I was not "me." I was simply a passenger, a spectator tagging along to witness some event, and I would just have to wait and see what would happen. All eyes looked at me expectantly. I approached a simple pulpit and turned to face them. My hands rested on the wooden surface, and I saw how gnarled and twisted they were, like the roots of an old tree. I was old, older than any of the other attendees by far.

"Brothers and Sisters," said a deep voice. The voice resonated, and I understood that I was the speaker. "We all know why we have assembled here at this hour when we should be with our families and beloved."

At the mention of families, one of the women, frail with sunken eyes and a pinched mouth, began to weep silently. After a pause, the person through whose eyes I watched continued to address the others. "We have seen how this cursed woman has corrupted our God-fearing community. How she has seduced our men and beguiled our sons and daughters with her demonic charms. Sarah Gormley—how I loathe that name as it passes my lips—Sarah Gormley has put a blight on our fields and made barren our stock. We have witnessed the misfortune that comes to those who oppose her."

At least half of the people on the benches turned and looked at the weeping woman.

"Weep now, Goody Pickering. You, of all people, have experienced her hate firsthand. When your Jeremiah was taken from you, we all knew who caused your mule to be possessed, killing him instantly with a kick to the head. It was Sarah Gormley."

A straw-haired man with a crooked nose stood and spoke. "Why is she not charged with witchcraft? We know her to be a witch, do we not? What stops us, Brother Marrow?"

"What we know and what can be proven are quite different," he responded. "Spectral phenomena have not been accepted as evidence against a witch for over a decade. After the events in Salem Village..."

"Salem Village?" spat a fat ruddy-faced man. "They should've finished what they began. Governor Phips be damned for pardoning them! He should've been hanged next to them. They invited this evil into our homes by suffering them to live."

A clamor arose in agreement as they all began to speak at once, but one voice cut through the noise. A young woman's voice shouted, "Brother Peale... Goodwife Furness... Brother Whitlock... All of you! Listen to me now."

As one, we all looked back at Goody Pickering who now stood defiant, tears staining her face as she stared at each of us.

"We know what must be done," she whispered quietly. "Only one thing will end this all."

Wisps of smoke curled from under her collar. Her face turned scarlet and began to blister. Within seconds, her eyebrows had singed away and her eyelashes curled into ash. A black mark slowly expanded on her left cheek until, suddenly, a charred hole appeared as the skin peeled back and her entire face burst into flame.

I wanted to run, but I was still just a passenger in this old man's body. No one else appeared to notice the girl's head was wreathed in an inferno as she walked towards me. Molten fat sizzled and dripped down her neck. Her lips bubbled and curled like bacon in a pan. She came closer and I could see the bones of her skull as her flesh flaked away in charred clumps.

"All witches must burn, Brother Marrow," she hissed. I saw scorch marks on her teeth. "You see that now, don't you? We must burn Sarah Gormley."

I woke in my bed, wheezing with the stench of smoke and charred meat in my nostrils. The names Brother Marrow and Sarah Gormley echoed in my ears.

Over the next week, I had some version of this dream every night. Each night, I was forced to watch through Brother Marrow's eyes as the same events unfolded. Each morning I woke with ashes in my mouth and tears drying on my cheeks.

Even so, the dreams never followed a set script. On the second night, the straw-haired youth with the crooked nose burned—his name was Stephen Downes, I learned. The next two dreams featured Cyrus Peale, the loud red-jowled man, and then Goodwife Pickering again.

I felt helpless, unable to stop these nightly visions, and I began to lose sleep. I withdrew from my friends and walked through the school halls like a zombie. After several days, it began to affect my appearance. I skipped taking showers, wore the same clothes, and I'm sure I smelled like a hamper filled with sweaty gym socks. I also started smoking pot more often. Before, it had only been an occasional bong hit every couple of weeks, but now I got stoned every night to try to fend off the nightmares.

So far, it hadn't worked.

My friends noticed, I'm sure, but, not surprisingly, my parents didn't see any changes…or maybe they just didn't care. They rarely paid attention to me normally, so why should these recent tragedies change that? Admittedly, my father was preoccupied with the school, but my mother? During the day, she was too busy with her obsession with CrossFit, constantly talking about how many burpees and box jumps she did or how much she hated doing lunges, never realizing it was just another manifestation of her obsessive-compulsive disorder. Later, after dinner every night, she would finish off a bottle of merlot while watching *The Good Wife* or *Mistresses* or some other stupid-ass show that only appealed to chronically depressed middle-aged white women who feel trapped in a cycle of tedium…in other words, women exactly like her.

Ironically, despite her apparent inattention to anything outside her own personal bubble, my mother was the one who clued me in to something I never had known before—something that tied my family history to the dreams.

When I'm stressed, one of my coping mechanisms is doodling on any available scrap of paper. I fill notepads with poorly drawn pictures of people around me, random intricate designs, and any word that pops into my head. Since the dreams, my doodles had become frantic and, unbeknownst to me, they had meaning.

It was on the second Monday after Jonny Whitlock was cooked alive that I learned about our connection. I was filling a monster-sized mug with coffee that, hopefully, would stop me from passing out in class again. A couple of days earlier, I began snoring halfway through U.S. History and Mr. Lowdermilk thought it would teach me a lesson if he dropped a textbook on the desk next to my head. I hadn't found it amusing, so now I was determined to drink as much caffeine as possible without triggering a cardiac arrest.

I heard my mother before I saw her, racing down the stairs so she could get to her latest CrossFit class on time. She hustled herself into the kitchen and opened the refrigerator to grab her "bug-out bag"—a bottle of flavored water, some salted chia seeds, and a Tupperware container with some baby carrots— essential nutrition for those who needed to burn calories at the drop of a hat.

"Have you been digging through the old family albums?" She turned around and looked at me with a smirk as she pulled her hair into a ponytail.

"Huh?" I grunted. I had no idea what she was babbling about.

"Marrow?" She pointed at the pad where I had unconsciously scribbled his name a dozen times. "That's my great-great-grandmother's last name. I think the Marrow name goes all the way back to the seventeenth century in this town."

Dumbfounded, I couldn't come up with any other reason, so I nodded.

"What brought this on?"

I shrugged and muttered something about a school ancestry project.

She pursed her lips and continued as she put in her earbuds. "Well, okay, but please be careful. Some of those books are well over a century old. Put them back when you're done, and next time ask first."

I nodded, and she rushed out the door after kissing me on the forehead.

That's a good boy, I thought. Seconds later, I climbed the stairs to where all the family albums and heirlooms were stored.

One of the best features of our house is the enormous walk-up attic. I had loved coming up here and digging through the piles of boxes and old furniture when I was younger, but it had been at least a year since I had climbed the stairs and looked around. Bare rafters ran the entire length and width of the structure, from the ridge twelve feet above me running down the center of the ceiling to where it slanted down on both sides to meet the dusty floor.

It took me several minutes to remember which boxes had the albums, but finally I found them behind a stack of milk crates filled with my dad's old vinyl records and a couple of garbage bags containing years of Halloween and Christmas decorations. Dragging the box out from the corner, I set the stack of photo albums to the side and immediately opened the book that had been secreted beneath them, what I had really been looking for—my mother's family bible—in the back of which was the Pritchard family tree.

My mother's maiden name was Pritchard. Unlike my father, she had lived here her whole life. The Pritchards had made their home in Dunfield for well over two centuries and some of the side branches of their family tree reportedly went back to the original establishment of the colony. Opening the heavy tome carefully, I turned it to the back section and examined the entries that listed the names of my ancestors. I traced the line of her maternal branch up to the top of the page, and just as my mother had said, her great-great-grandmother was named Olivia Marrow. She was buried on the outskirts of town at Peale's Hill Burying Ground, the old Puritan cemetery.

The next morning, I ditched school and drove to Peale's Hill. It was a grey day and the sky was leaking rain. As I sat in my car outside the grey granite gates, my phone rang on the seat next to me. I glanced at the screen and saw it was my father trying to track me down, so I ignored it. This wasn't the first time I had skipped classes. He would have to deal with me later.

After listening to the rhythm of the raindrops on my windshield for a few more minutes, I took a deep breath, stepped out of the car, and began trudging up the hill. It was unusually steep, especially for a graveyard, as if the land was swollen and bloated. I imagined the ground filled with the rotting corpses of centuries of Dunfield's dead, all biding their time until they could claw their way to the surface.

The graveyard was designated as a national historic site, since most of the graves were well over two centuries old, but it didn't appear as if anyone maintained it more than once a year. The grass was well past my ankles, wet leaves covered the cracked pathway, and more than a few of the gravestones had fallen over. The oldest of them were made from fieldstones, barely legible from erosion.

I had no idea where I was going as I walked deeper into the graveyard, but I noticed the dates on the gravestones were getting progressively older as I headed further up the hill on the path to the right. I felt compelled to turn in that direction, so I followed my urge without a second thought, reading the names as I climbed. Colburn, Howles, Furness, Swayne—some were familiar names I had seen around town on street signs while others were unknown to me. The path was slippery with mud and I nearly fell to my knees once as I lost traction. The air was redolent with the odor of decaying leaves underlain with another scent, reminiscent of ashes, bringing to mind the remains of a campfire after it had been doused with a bucket of water. I thought nothing of it until, nearing the summit, I stopped to catch my breath and saw a rough circle of blackened earth exactly where I was headed.

Moving closer, I noticed the grass had been completely burnt away and the remaining ground was covered in a thin layer of wet soot. The smell of the ashes did not block another familiar aroma underlying it all—gasoline. An unknown arsonist had set this area on fire, and judging by the fact that it was not disturbed, it had to have happened in the early hours of the morning.

At least half a dozen gravestones were within the black circle, but only one was situated dead center. The rest were in plots near the edge. I hesitated as I placed a foot on the circle's border and looked left at the nearest stone marker. Somehow, I was not surprised when I saw the name Olivia Marrow engraved in the surface. Beneath her name, the dates were illegible, obliterated by erosion. Slowly, I walked around the circle, examining the other ones. All bore the Marrow name. The center gravestone was larger than the rest, more ornate, yet older. The etched name was shallow, weathered from centuries of exposure, but once I touched the surface and traced the lettering, I was able to decipher the name of the interred and the measure of his life.

Enoch Marrow
12 May, 1619 – 20 November, 1716
A STEADFAST SOLDIER OF GOD

Once his name took form in my mind, I knew this was the man in my nightmares, and I was certain he was my ancestor. Though many generations separated us, I knew this to be fact. But what drew me to the grave of a man over three centuries dead? Something connected this man to Traci's and Jonny's deaths? I needed answers.

I lowered my head and gazed at the stained earth between my feet. My shoes were ruined. Black soot was embedded in every crack and crease of the leather. The laces were a lost cause. Normally I would have been furious at their condition, but this time it barely registered in my thoughts. Something else had caught my eye.

Protruding from the dirt between my feet was a small ivory object, roughly cylindrical with markings covering its surface. I reached down and pulled it from the grave's grasp. It was smooth, approximately two inches long, and it looked like it had been through a fire.

Of course it had, I realized. Looking at the ground around me, the entire area must have been burning just a few hours ago.

Turning it over in my hands, I struggled to recognize the marks that were cut into its sides. There were wavy lines, concentric rings and a scattering of what appeared like primitive miniature lettering covering one side, while on the opposite face only two larger symbols were aligned vertically. I looked closer and realized a number of things in succession. A dark, reddish-brown residue—maybe blood—was caked inside the two larger symbols. I scratched some of it away with my thumbnail and rubbed the pad of my thumb over it to clean it off. Immediately, I felt a sharp sting and I realized I had cut myself. On instinct, I stuck my thumb in my mouth and I flipped the object upside down. The blood from my cut and the substance from the markings mixed on my tongue. It was bitter, like coffee left at the bottom of the pot. My mouth tingled as I realized what it was and the symbols finally took shape in my mind.

It was a finger bone.

The symbols were letters. Familiar letters. SG for Sarah Gormley, the woman accused of witchcraft in my dreams.

Shadowy images overwhelmed me. I collapsed to the ground and everything faded as the rain collected on my face.

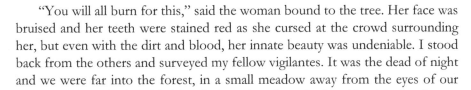

"You will all burn for this," said the woman bound to the tree. Her face was bruised and her teeth were stained red as she cursed at the crowd surrounding her, but even with the dirt and blood, her innate beauty was undeniable. I stood back from the others and surveyed my fellow vigilantes. It was the dead of night and we were far into the forest, in a small meadow away from the eyes of our community. We had decided to eliminate her threat by breaking into her house, abducting her and marching to this clearing in the center of the woods.

Here was where it all would end.

The fog swirled through the oaks at the edges of the clearing and pressed in around us like a shroud. Unlike my previous dreams, I knew all their names in this vision and I remembered their secrets.

"Burn!" Sarah Gormley repeated. "You're all foul murderers and you will burn in Hell's darkest pit for what you do."

"Shut your sinful mouth, whore!" screamed a bony grey-haired woman at the front of the throng of witnesses. "We know what you are!"

As soon as she spoke, I also knew who she was—the widow Prudence Howles. Her husband Thomas had hanged himself last spring after he had been caught buggering a goat—a male goat at that—but Goody Howles had accused Sarah Gormley of addling his mind with a curse. Her Thomas was a good God-fearing man.

Cyrus Peale, the red-faced toad of a man from my previous visions, stood on the other end of the mob, holding a glowing whale oil lantern above his shoulder.

He adjusted the shutter and aimed the beam at Sarah Gormley's eyes, momentarily blinding her. Laughing, he spat a greasy wad of phlegm, hitting her on the left cheek. He was a drunkard, but he hid it well. He justified his weakness to himself with the belief that it helped drown out the voices of her demonic familiars who constantly exhorted him to commit unnatural acts.

Behind him stood the town farrier, Jephtha Horne, bald, bearded, and glowering fixedly at Sarah Gormley. His grievance against her was of a more personal nature. Unbeknownst to all but me, despite no signs that she had ever been interested, he had attempted to convince her to marry him for well over a year. Most recently, she had burst out laughing at the absurdity of the idea.

As I stood there, a silent passenger in Enoch Marrow's mind, I could see the secrets of each of them as if they had committed those sins out in the open. Wrath…jealousy…greed…pride…perversion…infidelity. All became evident as I watched the crowd. Well over a dozen folk were there, more than had been at the meeting in the church. Unbidden, the rest of their names came to me: John Guilford, Elizabeth Furness, Edward Chadwick, John and Dorcas Brownlee. And on the other side of the circle, Giles Whitlock, Samuel Masters, and the twin spinsters, Remember and Rejoice Smith. In the lantern glow, their features were cast in flickering fire. Some gazed upon her with fear, others with self-righteousness, but all of them were seething with hatred for this woman—except for one. Amid all this bloodlust and religious fervor, I sensed that Enoch Marrow was overcome with sadness, that he knew this was wrong and yet necessary to bring it to its conclusion.

He cleared his throat and, holding a worn, leather-bound bible in his arthritic hands, spoke, "Exodus makes it clear—chapter 22, verse 18—'Thou shalt not suffer a witch to live.' What say you, Sarah Gormley, in response to the charges of witchcraft? Will you finally confess and repent, so you may enter the Kingdom of Heaven?"

"You are the ones who need to confess for your sins," she snarled.

"Sins?" shouted Cyrus Peale. "A foul creature such as yourself has no right to accuse others of wrongdoing." He spat again and turned to the others. "Let us end this sow. I can no longer abide her tongue." Peale looked over his shoulder at Marrow.

I felt a second of doubt pass through Marrow's mind, then he nodded.

Peale grinned and, without hesitation, hurled the lantern at Sarah's feet. The glass panes shattered and flaming oil splashed onto the gathered branches they had placed around the trunk. The branches caught fire, and the blaze rose past her knees and licked at the bark. Her torn, muddy shift ignited and the flames climbed quickly up her torso to her head. Soon the entire tree was wreathed in flames. Her hair was gone, burnt to ash in seconds, and her eyes melted down her cheeks. She shrieked until her voice whistled and broke. The leather lash around one arm broke from the heat, and she reached toward the crowd in a desperate plea for mercy as gobbets of charred meat fell from her bones and her jaw gaped in a final silent scream.

At her death, the crowd initially cheered and reveled, but soon their voices subsided and they all stood there taking in the sight. Forced to witness through Enoch Marrow's eyes, I could not turn away. I was unable to avert my gaze, nor did I have eyes to close. If I had been able to speak through him, not a word would have left his mouth. The light of the flames cast flickering shadows over all their faces and for a moment, I saw the features of people I knew. Goody Pickering's face shifted and I saw Traci. In Giles Whitlock's eyes, I recognized Jonny. Cyrus Peale's piggy nose lengthened and transformed briefly into the face of my Chemistry teacher, Mrs. Howles. Others I recognized but couldn't place.

We stood there for a while, watching as the flames died down. Sarah's corpse was twisted, contorted and black like the tree to which she was bound. Except for her hand, the one she had extended towards us in her final throes. Outstretched, it had been completely flensed with only small fragments of burnt skin, ligaments and tendons remaining. The finger bones were all that were left behind, ivory white and curled as if pointing in accusation at the individuals who had stood there while she was burned alive.

Muted, now that the spectacle had ended, the witnesses began to disperse until only Enoch Marrow remained. He sank to his knees on the wet forest floor and prayed for a long time.

I woke on the wet ashes with the bone still clenched in my hand and immediately walked to my car in a daze. The rain had stopped, and the sun was turning the day humid and unbearable. I was tired, clothes stained black and smelling like gasoline and smoke, and I wanted to shower before I figured out what I had to do next. As I opened the driver side door, I heard sirens off in the distance, down in the valley near the center of town. A dense plume of black smoke rose skyward. Starting the engine, I looked at the clock and saw that it was just past noon. I had been unconscious next to Enoch Marrow's grave for nearly four hours.

Driving down the hill into town, it dawned on me that the smoke was coming from the direction of the high school. I looked at my phone and found dozens of missed calls and texts from my parents and friends. After reading a few of them, it was obvious that my fears were true—a fire had broken out at school and my absence had them scared.

I decided to wait before responding and headed home. Even though I wanted to know what had happened, showing up in my condition—covered in ash and reeking of gas—would not have been a smart idea. Regardless of what had caused it, my appearance would immediately arouse suspicion. Plus, my parents already thought I was screwed up, and I didn't want them getting any more ammunition for their paranoia. Not now.

I had things to do.

Luck was with me. My mother wasn't home to interrogate me for not being at school, so I quickly changed into another black-on-black ensemble and tossed my filthy clothes in the washing machine with a load of laundry, adding a little extra detergent to take care of the stains. I headed for my car when my cell buzzed again. Jessie was texting me again. I finally responded.

Me: hey, 'sup?

J: OMFG! Brian, where r u? been txtng u all day!

Me: Home. I drove around, then fell asleep. slept all morning.

J: something happened at school again!

Me: just saw the smoke. what was it? more fire?

J: howles blew up in chem.

Mrs. Howles? I thought. *She was in my vision at the graveyard.*

Me: WTF

J: no joke

Me: stop fuckin w me, Jess. srsly?

I reached into my pocket and touched the finger bone. It was hot, almost too hot to grasp, as if it had recently been exposed to a flame. The carvings on it were especially hot to the touch.

J: srsly. no lie

Me: u saw it?

J: no. it was in daves class. 2ⁿᵈ period. she lit the gas line for some xperiment. it xploded in her face and her hair caught on fire and she ran down the hall screaming and fell down the stairs.

Me: OMG that's fucked up

J: dave sez they put her out but it was way too late. broke her neck in the fall

Me: you still there? I was headed over

J: no. they dismissed evryone. most of us are at the mall. meet us in the food ct

Me: K, I'm on my way. CU in 20

J: hurry

I stuck my phone on the passenger seat and pulled out of my driveway. The bone was still searing hot as I stroked it, but I didn't stop. I liked it. It felt like something I needed.

In my opinion, the local mall was a plastic corporate shithole, but at least the food court was a good place to meet. It was packed to capacity today, with probably more business than they had seen since the Christmas holidays. Each table was full and, in some cases, groups of students huddled or sat against the wall and gossiped about the latest death. Some looked frightened, but the majority of faces I saw seemed to be glowing with excitement. There's nothing like a few horrible deaths to get the heart pumping, I guess.

Dave called me over to a table in the corner, right next to the Wok & Roll. Charlie and Jessie were there, as well as a skinny girl with braces I didn't recognize at first. They pulled their coats and bags off a chair they had been nice enough to save for me, and Charlie offered me an egg roll as I sat down. I eagerly wolfed it down since I hadn't eaten anything since breakfast.

We all were quiet for a second, listening to the din of voices around us, when Jessie spoke up. "You remember Shawna? She has something to show us."

I looked closer at the girl and suddenly it clicked. Shawna Pickering—Traci's little sister. I only knew who she was because she was friends with Charlie's sister Gina, and I had seen her hanging out at his house over the past few years.

Mouth full of egg roll, I grunted in greeting. I was somewhat embarrassed because I hadn't even thought about how Traci's death had affected her and her family since it had happened. Looking around the table at my friends, I realized they were waiting for me.

"What? Am I supposed to say something?" I said.

Shawna answered, "Have you been having any dreams, Brian?" She reached to the middle of the table and placed an object. At first, I was confused. I reached into my pocket to confirm that Sarah Gormley's finger bone was still there. It was, as hot to the touch as it had been before, but on the table in front of me was its twin. No, not its twin, but very similar. The markings were nearly identical, but it was shorter, broader. A thumb, I realized.

I pulled out the one in my possession and placed it on the table next to Shawna's. Seconds later, the others followed suit. Three more finger bones, differing from the others in only slight ways, lay there in a semblance of a hand.

"Sarah Gormley?" I whispered.

Lips pressed together in a tight line, Shawna nodded. The others looked down at the bones.

"We've all been having dreams, Brian," said Jessie. "It wasn't until Shawna contacted each of us, though, that we realized we weren't alone."

"Traci was the first," interjected Shawna. "I don't know when she found this, but …afterwards, when I was going through her things, it was in her treasure box."

"I never told anyone this because I was kind of embarrassed," said Dave, "but Jonny was my cousin. Our grandmothers were sisters. We never mentioned it. Anyway, his keychain just appeared in my locker the day of the crash. You know, the big green one he always had hanging out of his pocket?"

"Who put it there?" I asked.

"That's just it," he answered. "I don't have a fucking clue. The finger bone was attached to it with a piece of leather. Jessie had hers mailed to her, and Charlie found his in his backpack as he left Chemistry last week."

"I think Mrs. Howles just snuck it in there so she could get rid of it," muttered Charlie.

Jessie spoke up, "Let's not bullshit each other. These aren't just any fingers. They're Sarah Gormley's."

"So?" I asked again. "What does that mean?"

"We need to make it right," whispered Shawna.

"Make things right? How?"

"Traci and Jonny died. Mrs. Howles died. They didn't listen and they were killed for it. We need to balance things and maybe she'll spare us."

I was silent, unable to voice my exact thoughts. Around us, hundreds of students, each in their own cliques and social groups, were probably discussing what had been happening these past couple of weeks, but as I sat back and gazed around the room, I felt removed from them. They were less real, unimportant. They were shadows, and the five of us at this stained table in a shitty mall, we were the important ones. Instinctively, we all reached to the center of the table and interlocked hands while touching all five bones simultaneously. A cooling energy seemed to flow into all of us.

We would survive.

Together, we made plans to make things right.

The next night, I pulled into the parking space outside the Dunfield Community Center, where a town meeting had been called to address the recent deaths. Serious consideration was being given to the idea of moving classes to another school while they investigated what could have caused the gas explosion. The place was at full capacity. Ironically, even more people were there than the fire code should have allowed. All our parents were there, along with anyone else who considered themselves important in this town.

The meeting was in full swing. I had made sure we would show up after everyone had gone inside. Charlie was waiting on the sidewalk, so he helped me carry everything once I removed it from the trunk. As we walked around the side of the building, I saw that Shawna and Jessie were already on the roof. Dave had brought his father's ladder, and he was in the process of handing up gallon jug after gallon jug as quietly as possible. While he did that, Charlie and I went around to all the exits and chained them shut with a dozen bicycle locks I had just bought at Walmart. Once that was done, Jessie, Shawna and Dave, who had joined them on the roof, began pouring the kerosene and gasoline through the vents into the community center below. Charlie and I did the same, pouring it beneath the doors so it pooled at the entrances. When we were done and everyone was on the ground again, all five of Sarah Gormley's finger bones were placed in a pile and drenched with the last gallon.

Within a minute, we heard some yelling as people started to smell the fuel, and then screaming when they realized that every exit had been chained shut. I think I saw my father's face at one of the reinforced windows in the main entrance. He yelled to me in panic, but I couldn't be certain what he said. All I could hear when I lit the flare and tossed it next to the pile of finger bones was the thunderous pounding of my heart.

TROUT FISHING AT GLEN LAKE

by Tony Tremblay

I think September is the best time for trout fishing. Trout are more likely to take the bait when the water is cold. Unfortunately, the beginning of September is when fishing season ends. It's also when school starts.

I'm a sophomore at Goffstown High this year. There are only twenty-five kids in my class, and I've been sharing homerooms with almost all of them since I was seven. It makes me smile when I think about how I used to grab at Vivian Auclair's hair to tease her—now I grab something else of hers. She's my girlfriend and I'm gonna live with her someday, though she keeps telling me to hold my horses.

Viv can't spend time with me today, so I grab my pole and tackle box. I plan on doing a little solo fishing at Devil's Rock. It's about half a mile down one of the trails into the woods. It's at the start of that trail where I see John.

John's family moved up here from Haverhill, Massachusetts, last spring. He hasn't made a lot of friends yet, but from what little time I spent with him in class and in gym, he seems to be an okay guy.

"Hey, John! What's up?"

Phone in hand, John is headed up the trail. He has his earbuds in and I guess he doesn't hear me. I wave my pole to catch his attention. He notices me and pops the earbuds out. I ask him again.

"Nothing, Billy." John wasn't much of a talker.

"Oh." Not that I'm much of one either.

We both look around. Like me, I'm sure he's pretending the scenery has something to catch his interest, but that lasts about ten seconds. I decide I have to say something at the risk of straining my neck.

"I'm going fishing. Want to come?"

John's eyes brighten. "Sure."

He pockets his phone and earbuds and walks beside me on the path. John and I don't say much while we make our way. I ask if he fishes. He says he never has. I tell him that next spring I'll let him borrow my extra pole. He says thanks. Neither of us minds the lack of conversation, though. It feels natural being out in the woods. When we come to the spot in the trail where we have to veer off, I point with the pole and we turn onto a narrower path, full of crabgrass. We walk along it until I see the lake and the huge boulder I call Devil's Rock. I hold out my arm to slow John.

"Okay," I say in a hushed voice, "we need to stay quiet."

John scrunches his face. "Why?"

"'Cause I don't want the fish to hear us."

He snorts. "Fish don't have ears."

"Maybe, maybe not. What I do know is that if we're too loud, they'll know we're coming."

After a moment, he shrugs and nods.

I've come here so many times I could probably get to it blindfolded, but I slow down to make sure John doesn't trip over a root or get whacked in the face by a branch. The area around the base of the boulder is bare, trodden down from all the people fishing here. When we get to the rock, I put my hand in front of John again. We both stop. I cock an ear to the lake.

"Do you hear something?" I ask.

John tilts his head and listens. "Yeah, I do. It sounds like people talking."

We walk lightly and go around to the side of the rock where the voices are coming from.

About a hundred feet down shore, there are three men in a small clearing. They're to the right of us, which means we must have passed them on the trail walking in. Two of the men are standing, and the third is on his knees, facing the water, his back to his companions. The men standing are dressed in black suits, white shirts, and black shoes. Their hair is cut short—I can see their ears from here. The man kneeling is also wearing a white shirt. It has large red stains on it. I lower the fishing pole and tackle box to the ground and push John back behind the rock. Our eyes are wide and we aren't sure what to do. We lean in closer and listen.

"Please, don't. I have a family."

"You should have paid Sullivan the money then."

"I will this time, I promise!"

John's mouth opens and my chin drops. I recognize one of the voices. It's Mr. Day, our gym teacher. We hunker close to the ground and inch our heads around the rock. We have a good view, and despite the kneeling man's wailing and head shaking, I confirm it is Mr. Day.

One of the men in black, taller than the other, replies to Mr. Day.

"You've promised us way too many times before, Bob."

The tall man nods to his partner. The shorter guy lifts his arm—he's holding a gun. He steps forward and places it against the back of Mr. Day's head. A second later, we hear a muffled pop. The top of Mr. Day's head flies off into the lake. His body wavers for a few moments, and then collapses forward, facedown into the water.

"Holy shit!" John cries.

My face goes blank for a second, and then I turn to look at John. Shaking, he turns to meet my gaze. The palm of his hand covers his mouth.

We stare at each other for a second, then peer back at the men.

They are looking our way.

"B-Billy, I'm—I'm sorry."

I twist around and grab John's head with both hands. "Shhh. Be quiet!"

John nods and we chance another look at the men.

They're not there.

By the time I yell "Run," I'm a step ahead of him.

My heart has never beaten so fast in my life. I want to pick up speed, but the path is too narrow and the overhanging brush slows me down. I can't focus more than a few feet ahead because the ground is uneven and there's a risk of turning my ankle. Twice I feel my foot slip, but both times, I manage to shift my weight and avoid twisting it. Any thought of dodging branches while I'm flying down the path is long gone. I don't even think to make sure the ones I push aside don't whack John on the head when they swing back. I keep my ears open, though, making sure he's behind me. As long as I can hear his footsteps and heavy breathing, I know he's there.

Our ten-minute walk from the main trail to the rock takes us less than half that to get back. Instead of taking a left, which would lead us to those men, I take a sharp right shouting, "This way!" The thud of John's sneakers hitting the dirt behind me is all the reply I need.

Though I'm running as fast as I can now that we're on the main trail, John catches up. We're side by side, shooting up the path like scared deer running from wild dogs.

"Where we going?" he asks between breaths.

"Around that bend, up there, is another path," I reply, pointing and gasping. "A side path to an old storage building." I wait a few breaths before going on. "That storage building is on Church Street. We can follow Church Street into town."

"You think they're following us?"

I turn to him, and he looks back at me. "Yeah," I say between chest hitches. "I think they're coming for us." John's eyes go wide and his face tightens. Next thing I know he's ahead of me.

The urge to slow down and check for those men is fierce, but the path leading to the storage building is coming up; a quick turn of my head when we round it should satisfy that impulse.

"That rock ahead," I shout. "Turn onto the path after that!" John makes it to the boulder, but as he slows for the turn, I hear a sound. John's back straightens. His head flies up and he seems to get a few inches taller. He collapses at the foot of the path.

I stop at the rock, turn to look back, and I see them: the two men. One is standing, but he's not moving. The other has one knee on the ground with his arms out straight, a gun pointed at us.

I lean over and pull John behind the rock. I let go of him—one of my hands is covered in blood. Turning him over, I see a dark spot on his back, near his left shoulder. The area around it is turning a deep red, and it's growing larger.

"John, can you run?"

"Not sure. I can try." I can barely hear him; his voice is so soft.

I wrap my arm around his good shoulder and lift him to his feet. "Lean on me—the building is only fifty feet away. Come on man, we gotta do this."

John nods, and together we head down the path. He doesn't last long before he falls limp against me. I don't have time to explain to him what I'm going to do. I lift him, throwing him over my shoulder. I brace him as best I can, then take off.

The small man shot John from about a hundred and fifty feet away. If they stop at the beginning of this path and fire again, we'll be sitting ducks. With John over my shoulder, he would take the bullet. I'm ashamed for thinking this, but I know it's my only hope if they catch up to us.

I run as fast as I can. John slips, but I push him back square on my shoulder. My legs ache like crazy, and I'm breathing so hard, I worry I won't catch any air. I see the end of the path, and beyond it the storage building on Church Street. A few feet in front of me, a small patch of dirt and twigs explodes off the ground. I run past, and it happens again. That's all I need to spur me on.

I burst out of the woods and take a sharp left to the building. There are two large swinging doors at the rear, but they're closed, an oversized lock hanging between them. I keep moving. When I reach the front corner of the building, I round it, and come to a dead stop. What the heck? The front of the building is different from what I remember, and I saw it only two days ago.

It used to look the same as the back of the building, the only difference being small windows on either side of the wooden doors. Now, enormous tinted glass windows line the front. Farther down in this sea of windows is a set of double glass doors sitting in the middle.

I need to make a decision. Do I waste more time here to see if someone's inside, or do I make a run for it down Church Street? I'm sure I won't get far carrying John. I look up. The new owners had put an awning up over the doors. There is an inscription on it. In big black block letters, it reads GOFFSTOWN PAWNSHOP. What are the odds of a pawnshop being open on a Sunday?

I rush to the doors to find out. I push, they open, and I charge through.

"Help," I shout, "Help!" The doors swing shut and I lean back against them. John moans and I lower him to the floor.

"What brings you into my establishment, young man?"

I can't tell where the voice is coming from. Except for racks full of stuff lining the walls, the pawnshop is empty. To my left, a counter runs almost the entire length of the wall. I follow it with my eyes, and that's when I see him, standing at the far end of the counter. He's a tall, thin man, and despite the distance, I can see his eyes. They are bright gray, gleaming like polished steel. From the way he is staring, I swear he can see inside me.

"Please, mister, you've got to help us. These two guys are after us, and they shot—"

Bolts of lightning strike the back of my head. I pitch headfirst toward the floor. My nose hits the cement, crushing the cartilage and adding to my agony. My forehead makes contact a split second later. For the first time in my life, I know what it means when people say they saw stars. The pawnshop is getting fuzzy, fading to black.

I'm about to pass out, but a blow to my ribs turns the lights back on. I crawl forward a few feet to escape more pain. Moaning, I stop and struggle to turn over. I squint through my haze toward the front doors.

The two men have followed us in. The taller one stands by the doors and stares at something outside. He calls out, "A cable company truck pulled up across the street. Looks like we have to hang tight for a while."

The other man nods. He hovers over me but his gaze is elsewhere—he's staring at the guy at the end of the counter and pointing a gun at him. Without taking his eyes off the guy, the short man says to me, "Get up, or I'll kick you again."

Every muscle in my body protests as I pick myself up off the floor. The room spins a little when I stand, so I focus on a spot on the wall to make it stop. My eyes land on the top shelf of a rack. There's a picture frame there, and what looks like a metal box behind it. The frame appears to hold a modern art painting. I stare at it for a few moments and the room stops spinning. My gaze wanders to the door and I see John, spread-eagle on the floor.

John!

I'm wide awake now and take a few steps toward him. The shorter man swivels and points his gun at me.

"Look," I tell him, "I just want to help my friend. Please?"

The man looks to his partner, who nods. The tall man then turns to the guy at the counter and asks, "Hey, how do you lock these doors?"

I bend down to John. He's moaning and there's a pool of blood underneath him. I look up to the tall man. "He's bleeding bad. He needs help."

He looks to the guy at the end of the counter and says, "After you tell me how to lock these doors, help the kid with his friend."

The guy at the counter doesn't say anything; he doesn't even move. He stares at the tall man so hard it makes me uncomfortable. I have to say something. "Come on, mister. Please?"

The tall man reaches into his suit coat and pulls out a gun. He aims it at John. "You've got five seconds to answer me."

The guy at the counter remains silent.

The tall man leans forward and raises the gun until it's aimed at John's head. "Please, mister!" I beg.

A reply finally comes and the guy points at the counter. "Okay. I have a switch—a button. When I press it, the doors will lock."

"Does that button also call the cops?"

"No."

I could swear the corners of his lips turn up slightly when he answers. The tall man must not have seen it because he hurries over to where the guy pointed. He scans the counter. "Is this the button?"

The guy nods.

"Then get over here and press it."

The guy moves to that end of the counter, but before he can get behind it, the tall man says, "Nope, you stay on this side."

If I had doubts that the corners of the guy's lips curled up a moment ago, there's no question they drop when he's told to remain on this side of the counter. He hesitates, and I can almost see the gears turning in his head. But it doesn't take him long to sort out what's going through his mind. His face returns to its steely expression, and the guy walks to the center of the counter.

"Remember," the tall man cautions. "No police."

"Oh," comes a reply, "I guarantee there will be no police."

The guy reaches over to the counter and presses the button.

I'm not sure what to expect. In spite of the guy's comment, I thought for sure that after he pressed the button, red lights would flash, a siren would wail, or steel bars would drop from the ceiling to cover the doors and windows. Instead, all I hear is a thunk. It's loud, though, and I catch its echo at the far end of the shop.

The tall man jiggles the door handle. "All right, help the kid if you want."

The guy walks over to me and John, taking charge right away. "We're going to lift him up and place him on the counter. What's your name, son?"

"Billy."

"Okay, Billy, grab his legs; I'll take the arms. On the count of three, we lift and put him there." He motions with his head to a space on the counter. "One—two—three!"

Because John isn't heavy, we manage to move him with little effort. We place him on the counter with his bad shoulder facing the wall. The guy goes to work on John as soon as we put him down.

"Are you the owner of this place?" I ask.

"Yes," he replies without slowing down.

"When did you move here?"

"The shop moves around a lot." What might have passed for a smile crosses his lips. After he removes my friend's shirt, he inspects the wound.

"Hey!" It's the short man. He is over by the racks on the far wall—picking up, looking over, and then replacing various items. "What kind of place is this?"

The guy replies without turning his head. "It's a pawnshop. Didn't you read the awning?"

"Doesn't look like any kind of pawnshop I've ever seen. This is some weird-looking shit."

The pawnshop owner bunches up John's shirt and hands it to me. "Billy, press this over the hole. Hold it tight. We need to keep the blood from flowing out. The wound looks worse than it is. It's nothing that can't be taken care of if we get him help soon." As I take the shirt, he turns to face the short man.

"I have a discerning clientele. They don't walk in off the street. Almost all of my business is done by other means."

"You mean like the Internet?"

"Yes … and word of mouth."

The tall man is quiet while everyone talks, staying by the doors and looking out the windows. His gun remains drawn, and he holds it close to his chest.

"Hey, what's this?" The short man holds up a rectangular black box. From what I can see, it's almost two feet long and about a foot square. At its end a round hole in the center takes up half the space.

The pawnshop owner's eyes brighten. It's the first time since we burst into his place that he's had a full-on smile. "That's a faience box!" He answers in a tone that has a hint of admiration in it. "It's two thousand years old—a relic of the Kush kingdom in Sudan. King Amanitore himself commissioned that box as a testament to his royal power. The faience boxes of the era were usually manufactured to assist those in the afterlife. The one you are holding, however, is different. Not only is it lacking the traditional depiction of a set of eyes that warded off evil spirits, it's devoid of color. As you can see, it's entirely black. It also differs in its purpose."

The short man's eyes widen. "No shit! It's two thousand years old, huh?" He calls to his partner at the door. "Hey Randy, this must be worth a fortune! Mr. Sullivan would love this, I bet."

Fury burns in the tall man's eyes, and I think I know why. We now know his name is Randy, and his boss's name is Mr. Sullivan. This isn't good. My hands shake while I apply pressure to John's wound. The short man is oblivious to his mistake, which also can't be good for us.

"What's its purpose?" the short man asks.

"The records made it quite clear that it was a loyalty device. It was common in those days for a king to be deposed, usually by family members. As a way to thwart assassination, the king instructed his holy men to infuse the box with the ability to make an assessment on those who would succeed him. When the king died, his soul would transfer into that box. His would-be successor would be required to place his arm inside. The king would pass judgment on him from the afterlife."

The short man's eyes squint. "What do you mean?"

The pawnshop owner sighs. "It means if the soul of the king decided his would-be successor would govern the kingdom with a steady hand and a pure heart, the king would imbue the man with special gifts."

"Special gifts? Like what?"

The pawnshop owner shakes his head. "We don't know for sure—the records on this particular faience box didn't say. Other boxes were said to impart the ability to foreshadow and to grant the power of invisibility."

"Foreshadow? What does that mean?"

Heck, even I know what that means. But if the pawnshop owner is put off by the short man's ignorance, he doesn't show it. He answers the question without looking irritated. "It means he could see the future."

The short man is delighted by the answer. "Wow! What a lucky bastard that guy would be! He'd know who was coming for him, turn invisible, and kill them."

He brings the box over to the counter, placing it on top, the hole facing him.

I have to admit I'm also caught up in the story, but there is one important piece of information the short man didn't ask for. I was about to ask it myself, but as I open my mouth, the pawnshop owner shoots me a glare so fierce I shut up right away.

The short man places his gun on the counter and then pulls the left sleeve on his suitcoat up as high as it will go, bunching it up around his elbow. He unbuttons his shirt sleeve and rolls that up to his elbow, too. As I watch the short man stick his arm out and wiggle his fingers, it dawns on me why the pawnshop owner glared at me. It looks as if I'm about to get my answer without even having to ask the question.

"Hey, Randy," the short man sticks his hand into the box and says between chuckles, "watch me turn invisible."

I can't help myself—I lean closer to see what happens.

But nothing does.

The short man stares at the box. He doesn't say anything, but I can tell from the way the corners of his mouth dip that he's disappointed. Looking toward Randy, he shrugs and laughs.

His left shoulder jerks. It jerks again and the box slides toward him a few inches. He struggles, like he's trying to pull his arm out, but he can't. After a few more tugs, he holds the box down with his free hand, and tries again.

"Hey, asshole," he says, "I can't get my hand out of this thing."

Randy shakes his head. He looks at the pawnshop owner. "Can you help him get his hand out of that box?" The way he says it doesn't sound like a question, though—more like when my mom is pissed and wants me to do something without yelling at me.

The pawnshop owner faces Randy, staring at him. "No," the pawnshop owner says, "I can't. King Amanitore is passing judgment."

The short man's eyes go wide. His voice rises. "What? What the hell are you talking about? Get me out of this—ahhhhhh!"

All three of us stare at the short man. His screams bounce off the walls and his body shakes so much it looks as if he's plugged into a power outlet. Blood pours from his eyes, spraying the counter and floor in weird patterns. He opens his mouth and chokes out dark clots that collect on his chest. I gasp as his legs lift from the floor. They arc out to the side, rising until his body is horizontal with the box. Blood pools on the floor beneath him.

"Make it stop!" Randy shouts. "Get it to stop!"

The pawnshop owner replies, "I can't."

Randy rushes to the counter and places the tip of his gun against John's forehead. "You better find a way. Do it now!"

With a slow shake of his head, the pawnshop owner repeats his answer. "I can't."

Click—bang! A second later, my face is covered in blood.

The top of John's skull and the upper portion of his face are gone. Some of his brain drips down into a cavity above his mouth, settling in a dark soup of red with bits of white fragments that poke through the surface.

The tension in my arms drains. I let go of the shirt I was pressing against John's shoulder.

This can't be real. None of this can be happening. I must be at home, tired and confused, watching a movie, maybe.

The view around me recedes. I'm elevated, looking down at all of us. John looks so small from up here. I turn away from my dead friend and see the owner staring at him. There is a man with a gun standing close to me, and I know I'm the next to die. At the far end of the counter is another man with his hand in a box. He's levitating, and vibrating like a cellphone on silent. He's spraying blood everywhere. I can't stop blinking. I focus on the pawnshop owner. Between snapshots of light and dark, I see the man's eyes. They burn with fury. I concentrate on them. Part of me welcomes the hate I see in them. I blink, and I see all of us again. Another blink, and I'm back on ground level, standing over John. His eyes are missing.

This is no movie.

There's a sound at the end of the counter and our heads turn to the short man. He isn't vibrating anymore. Like an old photograph, he's still, captured in a moment. We hear the sound again, a crackling, like someone twisting an ice cube tray fresh from the freezer. The noise intensifies. Thin black lines appear over his body. There is a bang, and the short man shatters like glass, crumbling to the floor in thousands of little pieces.

Without a hint of sarcasm, the pawnshop owner says, "It looks like King Amanitore is a pretty good judge of people."

Randy, eyes huge and mouth hanging open, pivots to him. Gun leveled at the pawnshop owner, he backs up to the glass doors. Reaching them, he yanks on the handle. The door is as frozen as his partner was.

"Unlock these fucking doors!"

The owner doesn't reply. He stands tall, his eyes cold.

Randy rushes to me. His free hand wraps halfway around my neck as he places the barrel of the gun against my temple. Without taking his eyes off of the pawnshop owner, he walks backward, taking me with him to the far end of the counter. We step over pieces of his partner. I can feel him under my sneakers. Randy jabs the barrel twice into the side of my head, forcing my neck to twist to the right.

"Unlock the door now or I swear, I'll kill this kid."

The owner sighs. His eyes dim and his head drops.

I'm ashamed for thinking this, but I want him to unlock the doors. I don't want to die right now. I know there's no way Randy is just going to walk out of here and let us live, but still, I'll be alive that much longer.

The pawnshop owner lifts his head. "I will, but let Billy go."

"Not until you unlock the door."

The owner walks to the counter where he pushed the button earlier. He lifts his hand and holds it over the button. His arm trembles as if he's not sure he can do this. I'm breathing so hard I think I'm going to pass out. Come on, push the button. The owner rests his hand on the button for a few seconds, longer than when he pushed it the first time.

Click.

Randy continues holding my neck. The pressure increases. "Go to the door and ease it open. If you run out, I'll shoot you first, then the kid."

The owner nods and approaches the door. Reaching it, he pulls it toward him a few inches, then lets go. The door glides shut.

As the pressure on my neck lessens, Randy's arm withdraws completely. I lean against the counter and massage my neck, taking deep breaths. That's when I see something on the counter.

The pawnshop owner walks toward us, taking small, deliberate steps. "I've unlocked the door and I assume you will now leave us."

Randy chuckles. "No, that's not going to happen."

The pawnshop owner seems unfazed by the response. "I didn't think so. Before you kill us, there's something you should know." He continues his slow pace toward Randy, who doesn't appear to be bothered by it. In fact, he takes a few steps forward of his own with his gun pointed toward the man's waist.

"Oh yeah? And what would that be?"

"I have an associate. His name is Rex. If you kill me, Rex will hunt you down. You won't believe how much you will suffer when Rex finds you. I will also add, we have implements here to ensure your agony will be eternal."

"This Rex guy will have to find me first."

"Rex has been around for a long time. He knows how to find people. He will find you."

Randy doesn't reply. His back is to me, so I can't see his face, but the man's words chill me to the bone. I hope they have the same effect on Randy. After seeing what happened to Randy's short partner, I have no doubt the pawnshop owner is telling the truth.

Randy laughs. It's a hardy laugh. I'm stunned. He doesn't believe the owner. I watch him as he raises his arm. The gun is now aimed at the pawnshop owner's chest.

"I'm not scared of you. I'm not scared of this Rex guy. He'll have to get through Mr. Sullivan to find me, and there's no way that'll happen. Say goodbye."

Randy's body stiffens. A second later, he's twisting, falling to the floor. His gun goes off, but I don't flinch. The bullet hits something on one of the shelves against the wall. It breaks and tumbles off the rack. I look down at Randy and notice the large hole in the back of his neck. It's black, and a steady stream of red flows from it. I catch sight of a gun in my hand. It's the short man's gun, the one he put on the counter. For the life of me, I can't remember having reached for it—or using it to kill him. I gaze up at the pawnshop owner. He's staring at me. His neutral expression throws me off guard.

"You did good, Billy."

I nod.

Behind him, the pawnshop's double doors swing open. Standing in the doorway is the biggest man I have ever seen. He's only visible from his chin down. He has to be almost seven feet tall and takes up the width of the doorway. He leans forward and takes two steps inside. My arm is shaking badly, but I manage to raise the gun.

"No, Billy. Don't shoot him," the pawnshop owner says in a calm voice. "That's Rex."

Rex remains standing by the doors. He is taking in the carnage and, I imagine, looking for threats. After a bit, his gaze settles on the pawnshop owner.

"You're a little late, Rex. We could have used you earlier."

The giant man nods.

An image of Randy suffering in eternal agony comes into my head. It doesn't bother me a bit.

The pawnshop owner shifts to me. "I want to warn you—you are not to mention what has occurred here. You must never mention me, Rex, or the pawnshop. Not to your parents, your friends, or the police."

"How will I explain what happened?"

"That'll be taken care of. I need you to tell Rex and me where you ran into these men."

I tell him everything that happened since I met John at the beginning of the trail. He asks me to elaborate on a few things, but other than that, he doesn't interrupt.

When I finish, he stares hard into my eyes. "Billy, never walk into this pawnshop again."

Any sense of bonding I had with the man vanishes. I find myself taking a step back from him. He closes the distance and touches my forehead. My eyes close.

I hear men talking and radio chatter. I open my eyes. There's a young woman in a white uniform peering down at me; I see the tops of trees and the sky behind her. She's all excited about our eye contact, and calls out to someone that I am conscious. Where the heck am I? I sit up, forcing her to pull back. Craning my head, I try to figure out what's going on.

There are police all around me, walking back and forth, searching the ground for something. I recognize the area. I'm at Glen Lake. Looking past them and to the left, I see a white sheet lying over something on the ground. That's where the two men shot Mr. Day. In the opposite direction is Devil's Rock. There are more police there. And there's another white sheet on the ground. Someone taps the back of my shoulder and I look over. It's a policeman.

"Hey, son. I need to ask you some questions. Are you up to it?"

Gazing around, I see that everyone has stopped in their tracks, looking at me. I nod.

"Good. First, I need to know if it was only you and your fishing buddy involved with this man and the teacher."

Fishing buddy?

John!

My stomach churns when I remember what happened to him.

Wait. This man?

I'm about to tell him that there were two men, then the warning from the pawnshop owner comes back to me.

"Yes," I reply.

The policeman sighs. "Okay. One more question. Did you or your fishing buddy have a gun with you?"

I'm not sure why he's asking me this, but I make the mistake of looking at my hand before I answer.

"No."

He stares at me. He knows I'm hiding something. "One last question before we take you to the hospital. Do you know who would have called to tell us you were out here?"

I shake my head. Meeting his gaze "No. I don't."

He won't look away from me. It's a contest I know he can't win. Finally, he understands this, too.

"All right," he says. "We'll talk again later."

It's been three weeks since John was killed. I've since learned they found the bodies of John and Randy on the ground by Devil's Rock, and the body of Mr. Day in the lake that afternoon. They also found two guns at the scene, one of which had my prints on it. That gun was used to shoot Randy in the neck. I told them I had no memory of the event from the time John and I made it to Devil's Rock until I woke up with the emergency people around me. The detective in charge of the case didn't believe me. He said there was another set of fingerprints on the gun, that there had to have been another person at the scene. I continued to tell the detective I couldn't remember. He made me go back to Devil's Rock with him. He said it was to spur my memory. We took the same route John and I had when we ran away from the two men. I took note that the building on Church Street was still there, but the pawnshop was gone.

Word spread quickly that I was a hero. I had killed the man who had murdered John and Mr. Day. I told my parents, the kids at school, and the newspapers the same story—that I didn't remember anything from the moment we arrived at Devil's Rock. It didn't matter though; everyone treats me differently now. Everyone wants to be my friend and my old pals want to hang around me more. Heck, even Vivian is willing to let me go further with her.

The thing is, I'm different, too, now.

When I'm outside walking around, sometimes I see a shadow. I catch it out of the corner of my eye, and when I turn, it takes on the appearance of a huge man. The shadow man stares at me until I look away. It's never there when I look again. I've also seen the pawnshop. It's now in the bottom of a three-decker in the center of town, next to the bridge. It has those same tinted windows so I can't see inside. Any temptation I have to go into the pawnshop and speak with the owner is dashed when I think of the shadow man.

Rex.

I do my best to avoid that area.

FORGOTTEN MEMORIES

by Kelli Owen

While it felt like a lifetime, I knew Frank Errington less than a decade, but it made those years so much better. He didn't just review my books, he was a friend. *Sure, he came to my signings, but he also delighted me by showing up for my birthday party. Beyond reviewing my books, Frank sent me lovely messages about the blogs he thought were more "story" than blog. He was a good man, he is dearly missed, and this was not only one of his favorite entries, it seems somehow* apropos. *This was an older essay, from before Frank and I ever met, and has long since been offline. But the random name choice made us both giggle, and it feels right to share it again with all of you, for Frank. I give you "Forgotten Memories."*

———————◆———————

As I was walking down the steps to the lake this past Saturday, I thought about the generational vacations I was witnessing over the Fourth of July weekend, and how to blog about them. My own children were off at summer camp, but the remaining family segregated themselves as if assigned. The older generation sat on the porch, enjoying the sounds and feel of nature and happily chatting on any wayward tangent that presented itself. The younger non-campers planted themselves in the living room, plugged into their various portable games—a huge difference from when my generation was their age and you couldn't keep us inside with even the best of bribes. My generation's habit is to "porch with intent," as we enjoy the older and try to include the younger, but occasionally walk away from both to hit the lake. At that moment, mine included fishing gear. But by the time I had settled in on the dock, the tiny details of my own location took over and I gave no further thought to the generational gaps up at the cabin.

I have many fond memories of the cabin, such as walking through the woods with my grandfather collecting samples for a school project. Other memories have emotionally changed with time and while I was frightened then, I smile at them now—like my father convincing me at twelve that the Old Ones lived in the woods surrounding our lake. (For the record, I'm still not entirely sure they don't.) The cabin is a place of peace, with no bad memories (or do we erase those from our happy places?), but too often it provides specific memories that will then be forgotten until triggered. Take, for instance, the woodpecker this weekend, who caused the long dried out pine to finally give in and topple to the lake with a thunderous crash—which I will forget all about witnessing by the time I finish writing this. Until I see a woodpecker again. My fishing time Saturday was also one of those moments, and I accept this, but for the time being it's fresh in my mind.

The lake that day was the quintessential canvas of nature, and a picturesque reminder of why I put up with the winters here. The crystalline water provided a clear view of the tiny black minnows surrounding me on all sides—which *should* have been a dinner bell for the larger fish—as they happily darted between my swinging feet and the safety of the dock's shadows. Above the surface, a herd of dragonflies serenaded me with their buzzing wings. A mother loon used our back slough for training purposes, as she taught her two children how to dive, much to their squawkish displeasure—I'm sure they would have preferred sitting in the living room playing Nintendo DS with the others of their generation. And just out of eyeshot, there was a constant barrage of unattainable fish splashing at the surface to catch bugs. It was perfect. The lake belonged to me—with no boats or other humans in view, the peace was mine alone—as I slaughtered night crawlers in the name of pan fish everywhere. And then I made a new friend.

The water is high this year. The dock is literally right on top of it, and if you didn't know there were stanchions underneath you'd swear it was floating there. The occasional boat caused slight waves that washed across the top to soak my lower half and rolled underneath in a rhythmic thump. Until the thump was accompanied by a clanking sounded. At which point, I turned to locate the rogue stick that had *obviously* become snagged on the low dock and found nothing. Turning back to my bobber, a large snapping turtle came from under the dock and passed right between my calves. Frank, as I decided to call him, was in no hurry. He wasn't hunting, diving, fishing, or even remotely acting as if he had a plan. He was out for a casual stroll and paid no attention to the woman above him.

Now I've had plenty of experiences with the snappers on our lake, two clearly come to mind. When my sister and I were fishing in the boat and gabbing like loud teenage girls do, a lull in the conversation offered a strange breathing sound that scared both of us. We turned to see twin snappers had paused beside us. Their heads above water, they sucked air with heavy determination and eyed our stringer with intent. Yes, we left their territory in a quick hurry, giggling the entire time in an effort to overcome the fact they'd startled us. The other was a day much like this weekend, where I was, alone on the dock, and actually caught a snapping turtle on my fishing line. Today I would simply cut the line and call it good, but at the time, my sixteen-year-old reaction was to scream bloody murder until my dad came down and severed the line by biting it. Unfortunately, the snapper decided it really liked our area and immediately swam under the stationary wooden dock at the shoreline (not to be confused with the aluminum one we put out each spring, like a pier, which I'm sitting on to fish). Having much younger brothers who swam near shore, I watched as my dad grabbed a rake and leapt into the water to battle the snapper hiding in the shadows underneath.

This weekend was different though. This snapper hadn't interrupted an easily shaken teen, nor was he a threat to swimming children. Instead, there was something majestic about Frank and his nonchalant attitude. I sat and talked to him while I continued to toss my line in the opposite direction. I offered to throw him the little ones if he would stay far enough away and not spook the fish I was attempting to lure with waterlogged worms. And as he ignored me, his tail lazily swishing back and forth, I realized I was watching a dinosaur. I found myself suddenly overcome with a sense of awe and appreciation. I was witness to a casual leftover from when the spring-fed lake was nothing more than a puddle—if it existed at all. An ancestral remnant of brutal global climate changes and shifting paradigms. Frank not only has memories he's forgotten, he himself is a memory of a forgotten time.

Normally, I spend this weekend thinking of why we celebrate Independence Day and quietly contemplating the men who have fought and died for our freedom over the years. Don't get me wrong, I'm patriotic the rest of the year as well, and come from a very proud military-speckled family, but I've celebrated the Fourth of July with a touch of sadness for as long as I can remember. As a parent, I have traditionally reminded my children how the fireworks, while beautiful in the night sky above the lake and *clearly* my favorite part of the festivities, are symbolic and such knowledge needs to be remembered in the midst of the oohs and ahhs. But this weekend I was humbled by a completely different celebration. Not of freedom, but of survival in general—specifically the survival that comes with change. And for whatever reason, it continues to resound in my mind.

In the end, Frank slowly drifted out of sight toward his destination—which I imagine was a favorite fishing hole—while I continued to sacrifice nightcrawlers and contemplate the miracle of the majestic snapper, cataloguing yet another cabin memory to be forgotten, until prodded. A handful of too-small-to-bother-cleaning bluegills and pumpkinseeds later, I walked away with an empty stringer. I hope the dinosaur had better luck.

Unlike the woodpecker (which I had forgotten until rereading this), I have thought about that turtle often. I've thought about the myriad memories we make that only last a moment, and those that become part of who we are, like Frank Errington. He was a wonderful human, with a kind heart, who looked out at the harsh world with the softest of eyes. Eyes full of wisdom and knowledge, and patience. A dinosaur's eyes. We need more like him. And the world is so much worse for losing him. But we will remember him. Always.

Author's Note: the name in the blog is a happy coincidence. Frank, the man, intentionally appeared as a bit character in Deceiver, *and then as a recurring character in the* Wilted Lily *series.*

REMEMBERING FRANK

by Tim Meyer

There are people who like horror fiction, and there are people who love horror fiction, and then there are people who love horror fiction; it's safe to say Frank Michaels Errington belonged to the latter. Few people match up to his brand of fandom. A reader, a reviewer, a promoter of the genre—Frank was everything to the horror community. Sadly, I only had the pleasure of meeting the man and his legendary smile exactly once.

BEERS N FEARS is an annual book tour myself and three of my best friends (Armand Rosamilia, Chuck Buda, and Frank Edler) embark on. We usually hit about four stops, one being Spellbound Brewing in Mount Holly, New Jersey. It's typically my favorite brewery on the tour, and in 2017, Frank Errington reached out to tell us he was planning to come. I'd known Frank only through the powers of social media, his blog, and of course, his reviews on Cemetery Dance. I thought it would be cool to talk to someone who loved the genre as much as I did, someone whose reviews and opinions I greatly respected. I could tell he was a guy who breathed horror fiction, and someone well read in tales of the macabre is always a hero in my book.

But then, a few days before the signing, Frank fell ill and was admitted to the hospital. He didn't know how long they'd keep him, but it put his attendance in serious jeopardy. Not long after, he told us he probably wouldn't make the signing and that he was bummed about it, but wished us a happy and successful night. Obviously, we wished him the best, a speedy recovery, and told him that there was always next year. But Frank's stay ended up being shorter than previously thought, and surprise, surprise—he actually made the trip across the Delaware River, to a little brewery in the back of an industrial complex in southern New Jersey.

My memory of that night is hazy at best (thanks to three Double IPAs and that delicious Oatmeal Cookie Stout) but I do remember one thing—Frank Michaels Errington was genuinely one of the nicest, supportive people I've ever been around. I distinctly remember hanging out at the bar, Frank next to me, chatting it up about our favorite books of the year, the ones we were looking forward to, the must-reads from previous years. Above all else, I remember him always smiling, an infectious gesture that brightened an already spirited atmosphere. Less than a day released from the hospital (if I remember correctly) and Frank was there to support and shoot the breeze with people he'd never met before. I can't imagine many folks—biggest fans, even—would do the same. But Frank was different. We all know that. He was more than just a fan of the genre. He was us. We were him. We share the same horror DNA.

In the following months I kept in contact with Frank. Whenever I had a new release coming out, he was the first one in my inbox asking if he could grab a review copy and offering a guest spot on his blog. He reviewed everything I wrote and did so with care and professionalism. Best of all—he was always honest, a trait every writer should look for in a reviewer. His analysis was always helpful in some way.

In 2018, Frank had to skip BEERS N FEARS. I can't remember if it was for a medical reason or a personal one; in the end, it doesn't really matter. His absence definitely left a hole in that signing, and I think I speak for the other authors when I say that hole traveled deep.

Once again, we're left with a hole. This time, in our hearts. Frank is missed by many. I'll always remember the man who showed up despite the odds.

I'll always remember my friend.

IN THE END

by Tim Waggoner

You walk into the hotel room, leather satchel slung over your shoulder, con badge hanging from a lanyard around your neck. You don't pull the door shut behind you as you enter, allow it to close on its own. The sound is loud—*ker-chunk*—and somehow final. It reminds you of the noise that prison doors make in movies when an unruly convict is shoved into a cell by a guard and locked away.

Ker-chunk.

What are you in for, buddy?

"For being an idiot," you mutter.

When you reach the foot of the bed, you lean to the right and allow the satchel to slide off your shoulder, over your arm, and onto the mattress. There are a couple notebooks in there, black gel pens, and several manila folders with printouts of notes for various projects. One of those folders contains a short story you had planned to read aloud at the con. But when you went to the room where your reading was scheduled, which was located in a different hotel several blocks from this one—it's a *big* convention—no one was in the room. You waited for twenty minutes. During that time a young woman stuck her head in the door, saw that aside from you the room was empty, and left. A security guard passed by soon after that. He glanced into the room, saw you sitting alone at a table with a microphone and a pair of speakers, decided you were no threat, and walked on. You waited a little longer before sliding the satchel's strap onto your shoulder and getting the hell out of there. You told yourself you shouldn't be surprised. This isn't a con celebrating the written word—especially not the strange sort of stories you write. This is a con focused on cosplay and paying hundreds of dollars to have a photo taken with a pseudo-celebrity. Even that low level of renown is more fame than you'll ever know. You wonder why you came here, why you agreed to participate in the programming. You got a free membership out of it, sure, but it hardly seems worth it.

Last night, when you were hanging out with some other writers at the hotel bar, one of them said, *If you weren't a big name when you got here, you won't be a big deal when you leave.* Depressing, but true. You're living proof.

You remove your con badge, toss it on top of the wooden dresser next to the TV, then take off your shoes. You're tempted to lie down, close your eyes, and vanish from existence, completing your journey to absolute and total irrelevancy. Instead, you walk to the window. It's a big one, stretching from wall to wall and floor to ceiling. The window, of course, doesn't open. *Too bad,* you think. There are two layers of curtains over the window, one light brown, one sheer and gauzy. You draw both and gaze out at the cityscape before you. You're on the forty-fourth floor and you can see for miles. It's early afternoon in late August, and the sun is bright. You're glad the room has air conditioning. Not for the first time when you've had a high view like this, you wonder what the people of the distant past would've thought if they could've seen the world from this height. Would they think they'd been ensorcelled by demons and were in danger of losing their immortal souls, or would they instead believe they'd been elevated to the status of gods? Maybe this view would've been incomprehensible to them (likely) or maybe it would've terrified them (possibly) to the point where they went mad. Maybe, maybe, maybe…

You lean forward until your forehead touches the cool glass and you look down forty-four floors to the street below. Good thing you don't suffer from vertigo; if you did, you'd probably be nauseated right now. You expect to see tiny toy cars rolling along a tiny street, and you do, same for the insects scuttling along on the sidewalks. Pedestrians, en masse. Probably heading off to the other hotels to discover no one has shown up to *their* fucking events, either. You smile unexpectantly, and you're pleased to learn that after being a writer for so many years, your skin has thickened into a nearly impenetrable rock-hard hide. It's the artist's primary survival mechanism, after all. Movement catches your attention then, and you shift your gaze to the top of the parking garage across the street from the hotel.

You see—you do a quick count—ten vehicles parked on the roof, a mix of cars and SUV's, four black, five white, one silver. But what drew your gaze to the building are the two figures standing among the vehicles. One wears a red hat and a blue jacket. The other is garbed completely in black, making the person look like a shadow that's somehow broken free from its caster and obtained independent life.

You're not especially interested in the people, but you watch them because they're there. Shadow remains stationary, but Red Hat paces back and forth. You can't tell if the two are facing each other, but you think it likely. Red Hat stands about ten feet from Shadow. There's no way to tell from this distance what the gender of these two beings are, or if either *has* a gender. You can't even tell if they're human, for God's sake. Human*oid*, sure, but human? Who knows?

Red Hat turns toward Shadow, gestures with both hands, turns away, turns back, gestures some more, turns away, and starts walking. The ten feet between them becomes fifteen, twenty, twenty-five, and then Shadow starts following Red Hat. Red Hat walks toward the edge of the roof, not running but walking rapidly.

You can't tell if he—something about the person's movements make you think male—glances back to see if Shadow is coming after him, but you think it likely. Neither has made a threatening move toward the other, but your gut tightens anyway, and there's a cold prickling on the back of your neck. If something bad *is* about to happen, you wonder what you'd do. There's no way you could stop it from happening, not so high up, not with a window that won't open. And if you could somehow open it and shout down to Red Hat, warn him to get the hell out of there, would he be able to make out your words—assuming he could hear you at all over the traffic on the street? And even if he *did* hear and understand you, where the fuck would he run? The stairs that lead down to the street are positioned in the center of the roof, housed in a small rectangular structure. Shadow lies between Red Hat and the stairs. No escape that way. Whatever's about to happen, all you can do is watch.

If something bad does occur, you'll be a witness, maybe the *only* witness. You look at the two, try to discern specific details so you can relate them to the police later. But you can't see any details beyond what you already know. Red Hat. Shadow. You imagine telling this to a police officer, imagine the look of disgust you'd earn for being no help to the investigation whatsoever.

Didn't you say you were a writer? I thought you guys were supposed to be good at observing.

You expect Shadow to walk up to Red Hat, and since there's nowhere else for the latter to go, you imagine Shadow shoving him over the edge, imagine watching Red Hat's already tiny form get just a bit tinier as it plummets to the pavement below. He'd only fall three stories. He might survive. Maybe. You wonder if there would be blood, and if so, how much? Would his shattered limbs jut from his body at awkward angles? Would his abdomen split open and his internal organs spill out? That seems unlikely, but you've never seen someone fall to their death, so who knows? You figure there's a better chance his skull will burst like an overripe melon, spilling red fruit onto the ground. Now *that's* a detail you'd definitely notice, not that it would help the cops.

Yeah, we saw his brains splattered on the sidewalk. Hell, I probably got some of the mess on my shoes.

You don't *want* Red Hat to get hurt, don't *want* to be a witness to murder, but if it's going to happen anyway and there's nothing you can do to stop it…

You could call 911 right now. The police wouldn't get here in time to save Red Hat, but they might get here before Shadow can escape. You don't reach for the phone in your pants pocket, though. You just keep watching.

Shadow stops before he/she/it reaches Red Hat. Once more, there's ten feet between them. Weird. It's like they're magnets of opposite polarities, able to only get so close and no closer. Is Shadow saying something? If so, does Red Hat respond? There's no way to know, of course, but you don't *want* to know. Knowing closes off possibilities, and to a writer, possibilities are everything. Schrodinger's cat is only interesting as long as its box remains closed. Once you take off the lid, and see what's inside, the story's fixed. It's known. And once known, it's over. All of it.

Red Hat and Shadow stand like this—ten feet apart—for several moments, and you start to think they know each other. Not friends, maybe, but acquaintances. Maybe they work at the parking garage. Or maybe they've come for the con. Shadow's all-black outfit might be some sort of cosplay. But whatever the nature of their relationship, there's a brittle sharpness to their movements, a barely restrained tension to the way they stand—moving from side to side, shuffling feet—that makes you think there's animosity between them. If they were going to fight, though, they'd have gone at it by now. A friend once told you that when two people face off, as long as they're talking, they're not fighting, and if they talk long enough, they aren't going to—

Shadow starts toward Red Hat, walking fast, purposeful.

This is it, you think. *Red Hat's going over.*

You press your forehead harder to the window, as if by doing so, you can somehow see better. You should look away, you know this, but you can't. Not because you're fixated by the horror of what's about to happen, but because you want so badly to see what happens next. Isn't that what all stories are about at their core, the ultimate question: What happens next?

But at the same time, you also want to close your eyes. You don't want to be a vulture, a cold-blooded scavenger that hopes for misfortune to befall others so you can swoop down and pick over the corpse, and use bloody bits of its meat and bone to build your stories from.

You remember an incident, over twenty years ago, when you were working on a short story about a closeted gay man who refuses to accept who he is and creates an illusory life as a heterosexual husband and father to help him deny his sexuality. A gay friend once told you of a terrible experience he had in college. His roommate was straight, and one night—when the roommate had too much to drink—he asked your friend to give him a blowjob. When it was over, the roommate ran into the bathroom and began vomiting loudly, sickened as much, if not more, by the sex act as by the alcohol he'd ingested. You decided to use this experience as part of your main character's backstory, but while you were in the middle of writing that scene, your friend called to tell you his mother had died. You talked for a while, gave him your sympathy, and when the conversation was over, you returned to your computer and finished the scene. So if Red Hat is thrown over the building's edge, you know you'll use it in your fiction. You won't be able to stop yourself. Does this mean that you want Red Hat to die? That you're wishing for it, wishing so hard you hope to make it happen?

You don't want to know the answers to these questions.

But before Shadow can reach Red Hat, the man starts moving again, circling around Shadow, still keeping that ten-foot distance between them, and heading for the stairs. You picture Shadow running after Red Hat, catching up to him, grabbing him by the shoulder, spinning him around, punching him in the jaw. You see Red Hat going down, Shadow bending to rain blow after blow on him. No, better yet, once Red Hat's down, Shadow stands over him, pulls a gun, points it at the man's face, and fires, reducing his features to bloody paste and blowing that hat right off him.

But Shadow doesn't increase his speed, and Red Hat reaches the stairs and disappears. A moment later, Shadow follows and is gone as well.

You watch for several more minutes, but neither returns.

You tell yourself that you aren't disappointed, that you're glad nothing happened to Red Hat. You almost believe it.

You hear a knock on the door then, a single sharp rap. You have no idea who it could be. Housekeeping has already taken care of your room today, and you came to the con alone.

Another knock. Louder this time, sharper, insistent.

You turn to face the door. You look at it, consider, then start walking toward it. When you reach it, you stop. You wait for a third knock, but none occurs. You look through the peephole, but you see nothing. It's dark, as if the hole's been painted over.

You're tempted to reach up and touch your head, see if you're wearing a red hat, but you don't. You stand there, anticipating, savoring… You tell yourself you shouldn't open the door, because once you do, you'll see what's out there and you'll *know*. But you could remain standing here like this, waiting, wondering, infinite possibilities swirling around in your mind, each more tantalizing, more terrifying, than the last.

But you reach for the metal handle anyway, turn it downward, hear the lock click, pull the door open, and it's over.

21 GRAMS

by T. Fox Dunham

Arthur fused the knee to the cartilage, securing it to the leg. He aimed the tip of the infusion gun, shooting gel into the bone cavity. The microscopic workers labored, connecting tissue, locking cells in hibernation, tending and weaving and nurturing like tiny nannies.

"There you be, son. Tick-tock. Good old legs for kicking a football, for running, to keep you tall and skyward—but don't look to the skies. God made the blue fields into His new hell."

Arthur dragged the pulsing shield over the operating table, scanning the vessel, illuminating the vacant flesh in violet rays. The light highlighted the grid of scars crossing down the six-year-old's rebuilt body. Tubes fed through the chest, snapped onto copper valves between his ribs. A pipe clamped directly over its heart, pumping blood through the construct's system. The lungs inflated, deflated. The muscles twitched. The arteries pulsed. The brain slept, frozen in stasis.

He leaned over and whispered, "Do you dream now, Tommy? Or does one need a soul to dream?"

Pain shot through Arthur's left leg—courtesy of an angry mob. He grabbed a nerve blocker from the med bag and shot himself in the lower back. He set the injection gun on the table with his saws, meters, and surgical tools.

The pumps stilled. Blackness fell in the delivery room. Arthur manually cranked open the portal, stepped through, and quickly sealed it, keeping the rats out. They scurried at his feet. The mines teemed with surface animals escaping the fury up above. He climbed the iron ladder built into the stone wall of the derelict mine shaft. He grabbed a kerosene lantern from a hook, ignited it with a match, then he read the rusty dials on the wall below the outer hatch. The gauges indicated safe radiation levels and no more than the usual electromagnetism ambient to Alaska. He spun the hatch, braced his legs, lifted the steel door and climbed out onto the cement bunker roof.

The northern lights cascaded across the canvas sky, burning night into day, casting lambent glow on the dirt fields, the hills, the gray peaks of Mount Hayes in the distance. Hoary powder layered the cement floor and mixed into the dust, remaining from the last storm. Spectral radiance flowed in a rainbow, and he paused to appreciate the rich hues, the greens and reds and violets, delighted, forgetting for a moment what forces were harbored.

In the valley below, the town of Walsh Stream—the windows, the streetlights, the few headlights—glittered. Few folk came into the town since the sky fell. Some had already died from the collapse of society. When the stormfront finally arrived they would all die together.

Arthur hurried to the shack and unlocked the padlock. He checked the generator, changed a faulty spark plug, then yanked the cord to start it. The engine groaned to life. He spied the sky one last time, then he climbed down the ladder, sealed the hatch, and returned to the lab. He slipped off his boots and tied his neck-length silvery hair into a ponytail. He piloted the scanner over the waiting vessel, checking for any cellular damage in the body he had built. It showed some cellular necrosis, but for the most part, the transition nanites had maintained preservation. He kissed the vessel's bald head and rubbed his fingers over the closed eyelids.

"Won't be long now 'til you come home to us, my son."

He checked the memory core dump, the matrix of energy where he'd copied his son's brain pathways when they still lived at the compound. Inside the photonic sphere, his son dreamed. He opened a side hatch into the habitat and climbed through the oval portal, joining Tildy in the family module of the bunker. She sat back on the loveseat, head nearly touching the curved wall in the tight quarters. She darned socks over a basket—socks to fit a boy's feet.

"Tommy is coming home, soon?" she said.

"He'll be getting into all sorts of trouble, running about the place, driving us out of home in no time. We'll almost wish he still slept."

She'd not combed her hair in weeks, and stray hair spun over her forehead and neck. Her waxy skin glowed sallow in the dull halogen light. Operators muttered on the short-wave. Their voices distorted then clarified, speaking of the devastation down south when the storms came through California and ripped open the atmosphere to space, to solar rays. The operators speculated on the cause: everything from natural phenomena to aliens, humankind's attempt to play god with technology and control the weather, thus incurring divine wrath.

"In a few hours, he'll open his eyes and be with us again," he said.

The emergency-band radio keened over the shortwave:

> Attention residents of eastern Alaska. FEMA has just issued a Red
> Storm Warning for your region. For those of you who can get underground
> or find heavily shielded—

Arthur opened a seal in the family-room floor, grabbed a basket with water and nutrient packets, and climbed into the tight lower shaft. Tildy lit a lantern and followed, then he sealed the entrance. They huddled together, unable to lift their heads.

"He won't have a soul," she said.

"A lot of nonsense," Arthur replied. "It'll be our boy."

"You atheists killed the world, opened the skies and created the zipper storms by trying to control the weather. Souls are real. They have mass. You ignore the evidence."

He lifted the patch over his right eye and rubbed the empty socket. He couldn't find a compatible second eye in the stock material he'd harvested across Alaska—so hard to find good parts.

"Duncan MacDougall proved nothing with his scale," he said to her as he had before. "Weighing bodies at death, such fantasy, even for the 1900s."

In her youth, she'd worked for the Bradbury Online Library System, before the storms fried the core mainframe.

"Twenty-one grams of weight the body lost at the moment of death," she said. "The soul has mass. It is a divine creation."

"He mutilated the bodies of TB patients, perverted death."

"He did nothing compared to your perversions, Doctor."

"Then our son sleeps forever," he said.

The ceiling vibrated. Dust spewed from cracks in the cement. He wanted to hold his wife, but instead she curled up on the floor.

The storm cracked the cement on the top of the bunker. They heard it snap while hiding in the pit. They waited, huddled like naked children in the elements. If the storm had hit them dead on, they would have instantly burned to ash.

Arthur fed electrodes through skull holes. The micro-wiring intuitively linked to the vessel's neurons. He fetched a jar from the workbench. A gray gland pulsed inside a clear solution, and he popped open the skull. He fit the pituitary gland into the woven brain, then he applied the nanite mixture. He initialized basic brain function, booting the brain stem. It surged microvolts through the brain stem, a progressive stating sequence through the motor functions and finally the frontal lobes.

He had used his influence at the Progressive Science Foundation to setup this private lab in Alaska when the mobs moved through the cities, burning down hospitals and research facilities. They finally broke down the compound gates, demanding blood sacrifice to appease the vengeful God who had burned the world. They had ripped his son from his arms and offered his blood to the heavens. Manna did not fall. The storms failed to calm.

His wife stepped into the lab. She cradled Tommy's plush turtle.

"God forgive us," she said.

The vessel opened his eyes—one silvery blue like hopeful skies; the other, cold green like the old forests before they burned. Both candles needed to be lit. He gazed at his parents with soul-hungry eyes.

Arthur disconnected the pipe to the boy's chest, freeing him to stand. He'd stimulated the muscles into shape, and the boy slid off the table to his feet. Arthur stared through his wife in a daze.

"Liar!" his wife yelled. "You promised me my son."

Arthur yanked out the keyboard on the memory dump tower. He initiated the neuron training program. Tommy's mind—memories, experiences, learned behaviors—flowed through wires, stimulating nerve patterns in the vacant higher areas of his patchwork brain. Arthur watched the boy's eyes, spitting awareness.

"Tommy?" he said. "You know me?"

Awareness evaporated. The sentience drained from his eyes. The child lunged, ripping the wires from his bald head, tearing the skin. He clawed at his father, shredding his shirt, slicing down his stomach. Arthur tumbled backwards. He fended off the little boy, trying not to bruise the perfect body he'd constructed, the vessel he'd made for his son to live again.

"Tommy, don't!" his wife yelled. "Remember us. Arthur don't hurt him. You're hurting him!" She rushed forward to break the two apart, but Tommy lashed out, knocking her into the wall.

"This soulless thing will shred you, my husband," she said. She dropped to the floor in the room corner. She folded up and passed into a fugue state.

Arthur kicked out the vessel's legs, giving him enough time to get to his feet. He grabbed the med bag off the table and popped a sedative into an injector gun. The boy ran for him, his eyes spinning maelstroms. Arthur shot the sedative into the vessel's shoulder. The flesh vessel dropped. Arthur picked up the weak body, collapsed like a stringless puppet, and laid him on the operating table.

"The neural imprint didn't take. According to this, it downloaded. Your God is robbing me of my achievement." Nausea overwhelmed him, and he vomited brown lumps of his yeast meal from the day before

His wife mocked him in silence.

He knelt down before her and brushed the auburn hair from her forehead. "Something in the equation is missing, an element I didn't calculate. You can't be right. If there are souls, then there must be a God. Twenty-one grams."

He left the vessel on the table, his wife collapsed on the floor, and he retired to the living space.

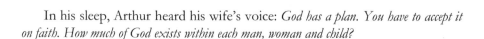

In his sleep, Arthur heard his wife's voice: *God has a plan. You have to accept it on faith. How much of God exists within each man, woman and child?*

"Twenty-one grams," Arthur whispered, stirring from sleep.

Soft voices broadcasting over the shortwave woke him from his stupor. He sat up on the cot. His wife had never come to bed. Arthur changed out of his old clothes, replacing the torn shirt, and into a pair of gray scrubs. His leg ached, so he got up and opened the hatch to the lab to grab a nerve blocker.

The failure had to be the neural matrix transfer. The EM field replicated the exact paradigms in the vessel's brain. He'd miscalculated; of course, he was working in the theoretical field of this science. Organs, bodies had been generated with this technology, but neurological regeneration was thought to be decades from application. He'd kept his progress to himself so no one would try to steal it. He alone possessed the key to immortality, the ultimate power over life and death. Once he'd bottled it to sell, he'd ascend to godhood.

He stepped into the lab and slipped in a burgundy pool. He caught himself on the equipment shelf. Tildy leaned against the wall with their son. For a moment, he remembered his wife sitting on the carpet and reading to Tommy. The vessel bit into a femur still covered in flesh at the far end, crunching the bone and sucking the marrow. Blood stained his bare chest. Flesh chunks and bone dropped from his mouth.

"That's right, baby Tommy," Tildy said. Without legs to lean on or arms to brace herself, her torso and head rested upright against the shelf. Blood oozed from her stumps, staining the surgical saw still spinning on the floor. He picked up the pain blocker. No charges remained.

"I never meant—" he yelled, squeezing the oozing limb. Blood poured down his clothing. "Why did you do this, Tildy?" Tommy calmly ate, a civilized child enjoying his dinner. His eyes calmed and studied the room, registering intelligent interest, looking with purpose."You mutilated yourself for superstition," he said.

He knelt by his wife. Her eyes drifted off. He grabbed the scanner from the med bag. Her vitals barely registered. She'd used technology to preserve her life, but the nanites quickly reached their limit.

"The soul has mass," she said, slurring her words. "It's in the body. He just needs to eat enough of it."

Arthur reached to take her hand, but Tommy had already devoured it.

"He's better," she said.

Her vitals failed. He lowered her eyelids, and she looked serene, at peace.

Tommy looked up to him with sensitive eyes.

"You're there," Arthur said.

Tommy studied Arthur's face. His eyes jumped, marking recognition moments.

"Tommy. In your mind, you know me as your father. Can you say my name?"

Arthur attached electrodes to the boy's skull and monitored normal brain activity. He sat in the blood pool and spent the day showing the boy flash cards, old photographs, even manually working his mouth, trying to trigger the neural download. Arthur's heart jumped whenever he recognized one of Tommy's mannerisms, like the way he'd scratch his ears when something confused him. After a few hours, the awareness vanished, and the vessel clawed for Arthur, all traces of Tommy's soul dissipated. Arthur sedated Tommy, laid him on the table, then he carried his wife's torso out of the bunker. He buried her in the parched dust, then he laid on the grave and gazed at the sky lights. He'd mourn his wife later, together with their restored son.

He didn't understand the science of it, not yet. He needed to experiment more, to monitor the progression. So, he returned to the bunker, packed his rifle, some rations, and the sedative gun. He used the crane to raise a Harley motorcycle out of the storage bay on the side of the hill, filled the tank with gas and began his search. Finally, after driving through the dead lands of Alaska, he found a scavenger rummaging through an abandoned house.

"It's my son," he said to the mad old man, who was half naked, drooling down his chin. "He's ravenous for souls, so hopefully you are still in possession of yours." He shot a sedative into the old man's shoulder. "All twenty-one grams of it."

He returned that night and descended into the bunker. Pain shot up his leg, but he ignored it, numb to it. He used the crane to lower the old man into the bunker, then Arthur severed each of his limbs and fed them to his ravenous son. Arthur carved up the old geezer like a roast. The boy chewed and munched, tearing away strips of flesh and slurping them down.

"A placebo effect, mayhaps," Arthur said.

The intelligence returned to Tommy's eyes, the presence of spirit, of understanding. He sliced up the geezer's heart and served it to Tommy a silver charger. His son took such pleasure in eating, Arthur took three portions and sipped their last bottle of red wine.

At times through the night, the boy mouthed words, whispered syllables. Then, the brain waves distorted on the monitors. He laid his son to chemical sleep and climbed out of the bunker to search for another lost soul. The satellite radio phone equipped on his motorcycle chimed a warning:

A severe atmospheric EM disturbance is building over the state of Alaska and the Pacific Northwest, Japan, and parts of China. All residents are urged to take shelter deep underground. The storm will hit at—

Arthur scoured the dust until his fuel thinned, and he drove home to the bunker.

He scanned the sky. Cloud banks suffocated the horizon. Azure lightning discharged on their surface, igniting the night. The wind carried the juggernaut directly for the bunker, and the shockwave pulverized hills and houses. It would make short work of the bunker. He climbed down the shaft, joined his son in the lab, and woke him with a stimulant injection. Tommy thrashed against his bonds.

His wife had used all the remaining nerve blocking agent, but Arthur no longer needed it. He'd dwelled in a life of quantified results, in fact, not faith. In the last moments of his own consciousness, he no longer had such comfort before oblivion; or perhaps, his soul would face judgment for his blasphemous life. Just let it end. He longed for sleep.

He injected himself with nanites to extend his fortitude, enough to finish feeding his son. Then, Arthur stripped and ran the surgical saw. It sliced though his flesh, sticking at the bone then cutting through. His vision blurred, and he focused on holding the limb to Tommy's mouth. The boy chomped down flesh, bone, soul-mass, and he calmed. With his good arm, Arthur activated the release code, and Tommy sat up. Arthur sat in the corner, and his son sat in his lap. Arthur sawed off his leg and handed it to the boy.

The bunker trembled. Concrete popped, then crumbled. The walls of the lab cracked. Arthur tasted metallic ozone on his tongue. Azure sparks arced between the walls and the floor, and his equipment ran wild like a slot machine announcing a winner. The light died, leaving father and son in the dark.

"Daddy?"

THE PAINTED PANEL

by Mark Allan Gunnells

H anna spent the car ride home in a crisis of anticipation. When her mother had arrived to pick her up from school, she told Hanna there was a surprise waiting for her at the house. This made the twenty-minute drive feel like an eternity to Hanna's ten-year-old mind. Impatience thrummed through her like an electrical current, causing her to bounce up and down in her seat and constantly ask for hints. Her mother remained tight-lipped, the smallest curl of a smile suggesting it was going to be something good.

Oh, Hanna hoped it was a new dollhouse. Right now, all her dollies lived in an old trunk with a broken lock that once belonged to her grandmother. Not exactly the swankiest of accommodations. She'd seen a beautiful two-story dollhouse that opened right down the middle in the window of the toy store downtown when her mother had taken her to get new shoes last week. Hanna had spent a couple of minutes staring through the glass with longing in her eyes. Perhaps her mother had gotten the hint.

When they finally arrived home, Hanna ran into the foyer, chanting, "Where's my surprise? Where's my surprise?"

"In your room, but take off your coat and shoes first."

Hanna thought she probably broke the record for the fastest removal of coat and shoes then darted down the hall to her bedroom, her mother trailing along behind her. She burst through the door and scanned the room, looking for the dollhouse. Disappointment stilled her when she realized it wasn't there. She didn't see any new toys at all. Her room seemed exactly as she'd left it this morning.

Except for a dingy plank of wood with faded flowers painted on it hanging on the wall opposite her bed.

"Do you like it?" her mother asked, stepping over to the plank and running her fingers lightly down its grainy surface.

Hanna frowned. "What is it?"

"It's a painted panel. I think it used to be a swinging door, looks like it once had hinges at the top and bottom. Anyway, the lady at the antique store said it dated back to the 1930s, and this is hand painted. She told me a lot of people hang these things on the wall like art, and I thought your room could use a little livening up. Isn't it lovely?"

Hanna tried not to show how let down she felt. Since her father had gone to be with Jesus earlier in the year, her mother had been so sad. Hanna was sad too, and she felt like her mother spent most of her time trying to make Hanna feel better. Even at her age, she could appreciate that and wanted to return the favor when she could.

"It's real pretty," Hanna said, forcing her lips wide into a grin that felt like a mask.

Her mother didn't seem to notice and smiled back, hers looking genuine. "I think so too. The price tag was a hundred dollars, but I haggled her down to only sixty. I think it cheers up the room."

Hanna nodded. "Thanks, Mom."

"Yeah, cheers everything right up," her mother said, though Hanna noticed the moisture in her eyes. "Okay, I'm going to see about supper. Why don't you change out of your school clothes and come help me?"

"Yes, ma'am."

Once her mother was out of the room, Hanna allowed her smile to wilt then stood staring at the panel. It was mounted on the wall just above the baseboard, definitely taller than Hanna but maybe not quite as tall as her mother. It had a sloped top, and delicate tulips, daisies, and lilies were painted all over the thing, the stems inter-tangling. The colors were faded, but that pale quality seemed to accentuate the delicacy. Hanna had to admit that the panel was in fact very pretty.

Still, she would rather have had the dollhouse.

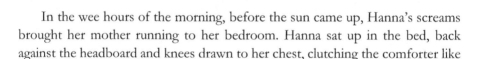

In the wee hours of the morning, before the sun came up, Hanna's screams brought her mother running to her bedroom. Hanna sat up in the bed, back against the headboard and knees drawn to her chest, clutching the comforter like a shield.

Her mother turned on the lamp by the bed and settled next to Hanna on the mattress. "Honey, what's wrong? Did you have a bad dream?"

"I woke up and there was a man standing in the doorway, watching me."

Her mother's head swiveled to look back to the door into the hall.

"Not that door," Hanna said, pointing. "*That one.*"

Her mother's gazed followed her finger to the painted panel. "Honey, that's not a door. It's just a panel hanging on the wall."

Hanna shook her head so that her hair flew around her face like whips. "It was open, and there was a man standing there. At first I thought it was Daddy."

Her mother put an arm around her and pulled her close. "You know that Daddy has gone to live in heaven."

"I know, I only thought it was Daddy at first, but when he spoke I realized it was someone else."

"He spoke to you?" her mother said, the skepticism and placation clear in her voice. "What did he say?"

"He called me Gertie. I think he thought I was someone else too. When I realized it wasn't Daddy, I started screaming and he stepped back and let the door close."

"Honey, I think you were simply dreaming."

"No, Mom, I wasn't. There was a man standing in the doorway."

Her mother let go of her, stood and walked over to the panel. She then lifted it off the screws that held it in place so Hanna could see there was nothing behind it but the wall. Her mother then rehung the panel and returned to the bed. "See, nothing there."

"There was. Can I come sleep with you in your bed?"

With a sigh, her mother sank down onto the mattress again. "We've talked about this. Right after your father…well, it was okay for you to sleep in my bed for a while *after*, but I think it's important you start sleeping in your own room again. You're a big girl."

Hanna looked again at the panel. She'd been so sure she'd seen a man standing there, and she'd heard him speak that strange old-fashioned name. Then again, she also knew the panel wasn't a door, and her mother had shown her there was nothing behind it. Perhaps she had been dreaming. She'd had a lot of nightmares in the weeks following her father going to live with Jesus.

"Okay, Mom. I'm sorry I woke you."

"Don't worry about it," her mother said, leaning down and kissing Hanna on the forehead. "Do you want me to read you a story?"

Hanna snuggled back down against the pillows. "Yes, please. Something with princesses and dragons."

Her mother took a moment at Hanna's bookshelf to pick out the first book in a series about a princess with a pet dragon, but before she even finished the first chapter, Hanna had fallen fast asleep again.

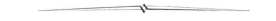

Two days later over breakfast, Hanna's mother asked her standard morning question. "How did you sleep, honey?"

Hanna shrugged. "The man was in the doorway again last night."

Her mother paused with a forkful of egg halfway to her mouth. "The man who came through the panel?"

"Uh-huh. He asked me my name this time, said I reminded him of his daughter Gertie. She got sick and went to live with Jesus like Daddy did."

Her mother let the fork clatter back to the plate, and Hanna instantly regretted mentioning her father. It always made her mother so upset.

"The man's name is Robert," Hanna said to change the subject. "He seems nice. Kind of sad, but nice."

Her mother wiped her mouth with a napkin very deliberately then cast a serious gaze Hanna's way. It reminded her of the way her mother looked at her the day she'd explained about her father going away. "Hanna, honey, this is some story you're making up, right? Like your friend Piper, the pink elephant?"

Hanna laughed. "No, Mom. Piper was *imaginary*."

A frown twisted her mother's lips. "You know there's not really a man in your room at night, don't you? The panel isn't a door. So you're either dreaming him up or you're playing some kind of game. Which is it?"

Hanna shrugged again, crunching into a crisp piece of toast covered in jam. With a full mouth, she said, "Robert says no one believes him about me either."

―――――――――――〜―――――――――――

The next week, Hanna was having a tea party with her dollies when her mother came into her room. Her mother smiled at her as she grabbed Hanna's clothes hamper, but halfway to the door she stopped suddenly and glanced back at the party.

"Hanna, where did that doll come from?"

"Which doll, Mom?"

"That one," she said, pointing.

She wasn't pointing at Barbie or Raggedy Ann or Talking Tina. She was pointing at the limp cloth doll with the dirty face and tattered bonnet.

"Oh, this is Stella," Hanna said, taking the doll into her arms. "Robert gave her to me."

Her mother dropped the hamper and walked to Hanna, towering over the girl with hands planted firmly on her hips. "Don't lie to me. Did you get that from someone at school? It almost looks like you scrounged it out of the garbage."

"No, Mom, I told you, she was a gift from Robert. He said she used to belong to his daughter, but now that Gertie is living with Jesus, she doesn't need Stella anymore. He gave me the doll last night when he came through the door."

Her mother bent and jerked the doll right out of her arms. "I don't know where you really got this piece of trash, and I have no idea why you are making up stories all of a sudden, but I won't stand being lied to."

"But I'm not lying, cross my heart and hope to die."

"Fine, be that way. No TV all weekend, young lady."

"Mom, that's not fair!" Hanna whined, but her mother had already stormed from the room, leaving the hamper full of dirty clothes behind.

―――――――――――〜―――――――――――

Several nights later Hanna woke up needing to go to the bathroom. She glanced at the panel on the wall, but it was closed. The clock said it wasn't yet midnight and Robert rarely visited this early. She got out of bed and padded down the hall to the bathroom. After she had done her business, she flushed and washed her hands. On the way back to her room, she heard a soft and wet whimper coming from behind her mother's closed door. Hanna hesitated only a moment before opening the door and stepping inside.

Her mother sat up in bed, the bedside lamp casting a frosty glow across her face as she stared down at her iPad. She was crying.

"Mom, are you okay?"

Her mother started then laughed shakily. "Hanna, honey, what are you doing out of bed?"

"I had to pee. Why are you still up?"

"I was just looking at some old photos and videos of your father."

"Can I see?"

Her mother scooted over and patted the mattress. Hanna ran across the room and leapt on the bed. She'd seen these pictures and videos before, but not in a long while, and it was great to see her father's face again.

"Hanna," her mother said, running her fingers through Hanna's hair, "has the man from the panel been to visit you lately?"

Hanna stiffened. She hadn't talked to her mother about Robert since the day her mother had gotten so angry, taken away Stella, and punished her with no TV for two whole days. She wondered if her mother were laying a trap for her, and if she said yes then she'd be punished again.

"It's okay," her mother said as if reading Hanna's mind. "You can tell me. I won't get mad."

"Yes, he comes to visit me every night."

"Is he…I mean, does he look anything like your father?"

Looking down at a photo of her father smiling at the camera on a sunny day, Hanna said, "Not really. He's older than Daddy, and shorter. His hair is darker and kind of a buzz cut."

"What do you two talk about?"

"He just asks me about my life, school and my friends and what I like to do, stuff like that. He says he misses his daughter something awful, and talking to me makes him feel better."

"Does talking to him make you feel better?" her mother asked.

Hanna nodded. "Yeah, I guess."

"I wish I had a friend like that."

Hanna brightened and took her mother's hand. "Next time I see Robert, I'll ask if he can come visit you too."

Her mother smiled, but tears streamed from her eyes again.

When Robert Fredrickson arrived home at five in the morning from his shift at the mill, he did what he always did. Made a beeline for the bedroom at the back of the house, the one that used to belong to his beloved Gertie. Only as he approached the room this time, a cold shock coursed through him like ice water in his veins.

The swinging door with the flowers he'd painted himself was gone, replaced by a plain regular white door.

Behind him, he heard footsteps and turned to find his wife Maggie, wringing her hands with worry.

"I'm sorry, Bobby, but I had to do it."

"You had no right. None!"

"We're both grieving for Gertie, but you're losing it. All this talk of there being a room that isn't Gertie's on the other side of the door, a girl that isn't Gertie, sometime in the future. It's a delusion, and it scares me. I thought if I got rid of the door maybe that would snap you out of this."

Turning away from his wife, Robert twisted the knob on the new door and pushed into the room. His dead daughter's room, now cleaned out of all furniture and toys and clothes. Just an empty space with blank brown walls. Not Hanna's room, full of bright yellow wallpaper and the vibrancy of life.

"Where's the other door?" he asked in a hoarse voice.

"I got rid of it," Maggie said behind him, her tone firm and resolute. "It's gone. I need you to stop living in a fantasy world and come back to me."

Slowly, Robert sank to his knees and began to sob. After a while, his wife left him alone with his tears.

———————✕———————

Hanna spent the next several weeks lying awake, staring at the painted panel, waiting for Robert to visit her again.

He never did.

She tried to open the door herself, to go looking for Robert, but she only succeeded in tearing the panel off its hooks. Her mother was furious and moved the panel out of her room and into the den. At night, after her mother was asleep, Hanna took to sneaking out to the den, sitting in front of the panel, praying it would open. After her mother found her sleeping curled up on the den floor a few times, she got rid of the panel altogether, donating it to Goodwill. Hanna cried for days.

She wrote letters to Robert, but of course had nowhere to send them and just kept them in the bottom drawer of her dresser. As she got older and made new friends at school, started to become interested in boys, discovered her love of ballet, her memories of Robert began to fade. It started to seem unlikely to her that his visits had been real, and she wondered if he was just a psychological manifestation of her yearning for a father.

By the time she turned thirteen, she referred to him as her childhood imaginary friend, though for the rest of her life she wondered if the door would ever open again and Robert would step out.

REMEMBERING FRANK

by Douglas Wynne

Like probably most of the writers represented in these pages, I first got to know Frank through his kind and thoughtful reviews. He'd been reviewing my books for a few years before I finally bumped into him at Necon, but by then he already felt like a friend. Small press publishing can feel like howling into the void. You know somebody is out there reading the books, but writing is often a lonely pursuit. Finding friends and allies along the way, people like Frank who invested countless hours for very little reward supporting a genre he loved and raising his voice to help readers and authors find each other…that's something rare and special. Something that can keep an author going when the goal posts for work in progress look like a mirage.

I think many of us who have chosen writing as a creative outlet are also, shall we say, less than adept at socializing. Putting bodies to JPEGs at a convention can be a little awkward. But meeting Frank in that hustle and bustle was easy. There was no bullshit in him, just the same honesty and genuine warmth that came through in his reviews. That authenticity made it easy to fall into conversations with him over the long weekend, whether it was at breakfast with a group or just the two of us drinking in a quiet corner of the quad late at night while the festivities wound down around us.

I wish there'd been more time to deepen that friendship, more conventions and books shared with him, but I'm grateful for the little time we had. Frank was especially kind to my SPECTRA Files books, so I've contributed a story that makes reference to that world here. I hope he would approve. I learned along the way that life had not been easy on my friend, not in his younger years and not in his later health struggles. And yet, those trials failed to make a cynic out of him. He remained a positive force, an encouraging voice, a man with perspective and heart. Like many of the finest people I've met in the horror book biz, he shined a light that was as bright as the stories he loved were dark. I'll miss him.

COLD

by doungjai gam

It's knee-deep in winter on the Connecticut shore and the few beach houses on this cul-de-sac aren't in use right now. There are no streetlamps along the road, and the light reflecting off the crescent moon makes a dull impression on the snow-mottled ground. I lean against the side of a small house that has seen better days and peek around the corner. The houses are dark, the driveways unoccupied.

There's no one here to see me, and that is exactly what I want.

I scurry through backyards and come to a halt when I see the beach house of my childhood. Using the key I swiped from my dad, I let myself in the back door and grimace at the musty smell when I step inside. I fish around in my backpack and find my flashlight, but its batteries are old, the light too dim. I leave it on the kitchen table, knowing my parents and their reluctance to change anything. I should be able to make my way around the house on memory alone.

Relics from the past offer me comfort as I walk through the house. The fleece blanket folded neatly over the threadbare couch reminds me of the chilly summer nights when, as a kid, my mom and I would sit on the deck, wrapped up together for warmth as we watched the tides go out. Near the staircase is a small hutch of figurines my mom collected over the years. I reach in and run my hand over a particular piece that has a slender and shapely form. When I reach the figure's neckline, I feel the glue that keeps her head attached to her body. Inside me, a familiar anger rises.

Step away. I've already failed once tonight to suppress my rage.

I need to get upstairs, because I don't have much time left. I take the stairs one by one, making sure to skip the tenth one with the creaky board my father never bothered to replace. In complete darkness now, I count the paces to my bedroom—*one two three* watch out for the table by the bathroom door, *eleven twelve thirteen* there's the doorknob. My hand lingers on it for a moment before I swing the door open and find that—much like the rest of the house—nothing has changed.

Interesting, how there's comfort in stagnancy.

I glance at every corner of the room, a mild panic ready to burst wide open. I spot the item I'm looking for: the conch shell I found on the beach when I was eleven. Holding it again for the first time in years, the memories rush over me:

the excitement of finding a near-intact shell larger than my hand and the way my mom held it with reverence as she gave it a thorough exam to make sure it wasn't inhabited. My fingers run over the surface, mostly smooth with the occasional hole or crack that no doubt holds secret stories of what it's like to live in the ocean.

And then, a new sensation—a hard, ragged line that feels like the same glue used to keep my mother's figurine together. One tear, followed by another, starts a deluge as more memories rush to the surface for air. The sadness in my mom's voice as she reminds me that I'm a good boy. The way she spent most of her summers in scarves and sunglasses. It wasn't to look fashionable; she had to be creative to cover up my father's handiwork. In my case he liked to aim for my legs, usually the upper thighs so my swim trunks could cover the bruises.

For a moment, my grip tightens on the shell as I glare out the window. At the end of the road, a car drives by slowly. Too slowly. My heart sinks as I see the headlights become brighter as the car turns onto this road.

My time is up, but they're not going to catch me. I race down the stairs and into the kitchen. I place the shell next to the flashlight. I pull a note from my pocket and leave it unfolded on the table. One last time I rummage through my backpack and find my father's gun, which I place on top of the note. I leave through the back door and run across the beach. I'm calf-deep in the water by the time the police have parked. It's so fucking cold, but I keep going. Behind me, voices yell for me to come out of the water. In my head, voices echo in cacophony: my mom crying as she was beat by someone she trusted, my father bellowing that I would never amount to anything, my own screams as a frightened child. The one I hear the loudest is also the one that is the quietest…my mother telling me she loved me more than anything in the world. They were the last words she spoke to me before her "accidental" fall down the stairs into the basement. I still wonder if I could have saved her if I hadn't gone out that night.

My body is numb but my face is hot with tears. Waves slosh at my chest and neck. In my mind, I keep seeing my father dead in his bed by my hand and his gun. I try to think instead of warm days, of the shell I forgot to bring with me so it could go home again. As the waves push harder, insistent that I join them, I mutter the words written on the note left behind:

"I did this for my mother. This was not self-defense."

MÉNAGE À TROIS

by J.F. Gonzalez

D oug Richards smirked as he scanned through messages on the Survivor Bulletin Board.

Most of them were lame. Chatter talk and bored confessions of what most people had done before the epidemic. Doug didn't give a rat fuck about them. *Before the epidemic I was a Senior CEO for Viacom International, Inc.* Fuck you. Other soppy ones consisted of snippets such as *I was a housewife and I had three wonderful children.* Yeah, right. Little fucks were probably out right now chewing through somebody's asshole to get to their innards. Others were too sick and stupid to even deserve life in the thereafter: *My wife died in childbirth six months ago and I can't bear to put her out of her misery. The baby, too; she's so beautiful* (at this point Doug can just imagine the guy sobbing). *Won't somebody please help me? I don't know what to do, but I can't part with them…I can't…kill them…I keep them chained up so they can't…do any damage…but I just can't stand hearing them…* What a dimwit. Fucker deserved to have his brains blown out. If Doug knew the guy was within a three-hundred-mile radius, he would drive over himself and blow away wifey and baby before turning the Luger on the pitiful buttwad.

People were such morons.

He didn't have to worry about putting up with mankind's stupidity up here. Nestled in the crags of the High Sierras, Doug Richards' split-level cabin was the only sign of civilization for fifty miles. The last human activity in the area was two months after the epidemic when one of the forest rangers was killed by his partner over a game of gin rummy and the ranger rose from the dead and ate his partner's brains out through his eye sockets. Doug had used the zombie for target practice; the zombie ranger had lasted a tad under a month, even after Doug had blown most of its extremities and torso into mush. Once he closed the game with the headshot, he knew he wouldn't be in for such delightful amusement for some time. Being over fifty miles away from civilization did have its drawbacks.

The messages on the bulletin board contained more of the same. Doug sighed. "Stupid fucks." He clicked out of the general chatter line and locked in on the private talk board. This was where the action was. The topics were heavy in this arena. Organizers of Skin Game events advertised their wares within these lines, along with promoters of underground dance clubs (*The Zombie Zoo invites you for an evening of music, drinks, and games*). Something had to be happening somewhere. Despite liking solitude just fine, he needed occasional human contact. He was tired of winging his flesh torpedo to the stereophonic sounds of porno actresses getting tit fucked.

Doug had this cabin built in '83, a year after he got lucky with some wise business investments. Ten years before he had won a large cash settlement from the city of San Francisco and the ACLU after arriving home from 'Nam. A clash of anti-war protestors had attacked Doug and two other veterans as they arrived home from the war. The injuries he suffered in the melee—a concussion, a hundred stitches along various sections of his noggin, and six broken ribs—were worse than any he'd endured during two tours of duty.

He ended up suing the city of San Francisco and the local chapter of the ACLU, which had organized the demonstration. The out-of-court settlement from both parties was enough to ensure Doug the next decade of peaceful, easy living. He put the money in Swiss accounts, wise investments that yielded nice returns, and lived off the interest. By the time the eighties dawned, his wheeling and dealing had amassed a fortune of thirty million dollars. He had owned three automotive repair companies, a large retail comic book store, two bars (one of them was a way-cool strip joint on Hollywood Boulevard and Fairfax), four video arcades, and a small cable TV channel. He also held stock in two finance companies, four clothing firms, and a racetrack. Life was good.

But he didn't really like the people he had to deal with. Frankly, he didn't like dealing with people at all, unless the deal was to result in some gain for his ownself. And when his purse was lined with enough green to ensure a lifetime of doing absolutely nothing, he checked out, sold his companies and his share in stocks, and hightailed it to the Sierras where he commenced the construction of his dream house.

He equipped it with the latest in modern technology. Why deal with people when you could have the world delivered right to your door? He almost never had to leave the house; the satellite dish he installed outside beamed in two hundred stations worldwide; he subscribed to thirty different magazines, belonged to two different CD clubs. He had been one of the first to cash in on the computer craze, and was hooked up to bulletin boards at day one. Books were bought via mail order dealers, as were videocassettes and DVDs (better variety with those, too). The only time he really had to leave the house was to take the fifty-mile trip into town for his provisions and to pick up the mail. Anything he didn't have he could get by phone or mail. And when it came to women, he met many through the computer bulletin board sex clubs. Arranging rendezvous in the city had been a monthly occurrence. It had been his only contact with mankind.

But with the coming of the epidemic, most of this was shut down. Half the cable stations and radio stations were now completely off the air. Some were resurrected by survivalist types who ran them as twenty-four-hour news-lines. The mail system ceased to exist, and while the phone lines were down for about three months, it was resurrected successfully in certain parts of the country by some enterprising survivors who had the intellectual candlepower to flip a couple of switches. Granted, he still couldn't hook up to the places he was able to before, but it beat being totally cut off.

Big cities had it worse. The widespread panic following the epidemic produced mass hysteria, which resulted in anarchy. After the initial damages, it was deduced that it would take years to get technology back to the degree it had once been before. Most of the big cities Doug had traveled to since the epidemic lacked the basic necessities of running water and electricity. It was almost like living in the Stone Age. He had forecasted something similar transpiring a decade ago, and made preparations. The only difference was that back then he was a hundred percent positive the end would come via nuclear annihilation. Who would have thought that seventy percent of the population would have been stupid and slow enough to allow themselves to be eaten by their dead brethren?

The generator that churned away five hundred feet from the rear of his home was powered by a stream that wound its way down the lush, green mountain. Doug had channeled the stream to various degrees, harnessing enough waterpower to run his hilltop abode. Running water was channeled through a separate system, which funneled into the main water supply system of the house. He enjoyed all the modern comforts of the way things had been before; electricity, running water (hot and cold), and the telephone. He cooked his food with an electric stove, and he heated the house in the winter with a woodfire stove. While most modern comforts had failed in urban areas, Doug prevailed. Life hadn't really become that primitive for him since the epidemic.

A bulletin came over the private chat line on the computer. Doug zoned in on it, his blood pumping with excitement:

INDUSTRIAL GLOOM

DANCING

GAMES

FOOD AND DRINKS

SENSUAL ENCOUNTERS FOR ALL

CLUB DEAD

DOORS OPEN AT EIGHT P.M.

An address flashed on the screen. Doug jotted it down. It was in Hollywood, near Sunset and Vine, and the festivities started tonight at ten. The digital clock in the computer read two thirty-seven. He had just enough time to shower, hop in the four-wheel drive, and head on down to L.A. Tonight wasn't going to be so bad after all.

Doug turned off the computer and was in the shower a moment later, soaping his body off, his mind dwelling in anticipation of the evening ahead. It had been close to a year since he'd been laid, and the need pulsed in his veins stronger than ever. When the plague hit he'd remained in his lofty fortress, venturing out only for food and supplies. In the first few months, the walking dead outnumbered the living, but as weeks flew by they fell to natural decay and headshots. Because of the scarce population in the area, it was rare that he came across the walking dead. Those that he did come across were blown to raspberry slush. He hadn't come across any dead folks in close to six months. He'd probably exterminated all those that were in the area.

Less than an hour later, Doug Richards was fully equipped and heading south to Los Angeles.

It looked like the world's biggest New Year's Eve party had just gone down on Hollywood Boulevard. The street was littered with debris: chunks of concrete, broken glass, and garbage. Dilapidated cars sat among the boulevard, some tipped over and gutted. Doug had been seeing pretty much the same ever since he hit the San Bernardino County line. Pretty much all of civilization had been reduced to rubble.

The few people he passed were all equipped the same way he was; double thick work boots, provisions belt with a canteen and Bowie knife, a pistol slung in a holster, and a larger automatic weapon slung over their shoulders. Some had rounds of ammunition slung over their shoulders, too. Those that Doug passed by recognized him to be among the living and sane; they nodded as he drove by. Doug nodded back. Those that survived the plague and its immediate aftermath usually welcomed those that were living. Their kind were now a dying breed.

Doug found Sunset easily and parked the jeep behind an abandoned van. Heavy electronic music boomed out of a narrow doorway set almost indiscreetly among the dilapidated buildings. The faint swell of laughter could be heard as Doug approached the entrance. He grinned. Tonight was going to be fine.

A low moan averted his attention and he whirled toward its source. A puke-green dude in a Rolling Stones jersey and tattered jeans hobbled toward him. A thin hypodermic needle stuck out of his inner elbow. His eyes were sunken and dead. He smelled like stale pig shit.

Doug grinned and withdrew a Luger nine-millimeter semi-automatic pistol. Green Man was a good twenty feet from him and as slow as a fly stuck in molasses. The dead guy groaned hungrily and flayed his arms out toward him.

Doug raised the Luger casually. "Sorry, Charlie," he said, and pulled the trigger. The shot was loud. Green Man's head exploded in gray and red crap and splattered the wall of the building. His body stood rigid for a moment, his arms flailing confusedly as if he'd just stepped off the bus in the wrong neighborhood, and then he went down. Doug chuckled as he stepped over the prone body and made his way to the doorway. Not a glimmer of candlepower in any of them zombie fucks.

Doug stepped through the threshold. A huge guy with a bushy black beard and bulging, tattooed biceps guarded the door. Doug caught a glimpse of a Remington pump shotgun behind the counter. The bouncer nodded as he recognized Doug as one of the living. Doug nodded back and stepped inside the club.

Someone with some smarts must have gotten the power running in this part of town. The strobe lights in the club were on, basking the black interior in a steel gray, gloomy look. Ministry howled over the club's sound system. Doug stood near the entrance for a moment as his vision adjusted to the gloomy interior. He grinned. He liked what he was seeing.

The building itself looked like the interior of an old warehouse. The ceiling was high, with huge industrial-like fans whirling. The floor was concrete, with tables and chairs grouped around in a semicircle along the right side. A good fifty feet of floor space in the middle of the room was devoted to the dance floor. Two dozen couples were dancing. A large bar flanked the right side of the room; bartenders were filling drink orders. Cocktail waitresses didn't seem to exist in this place. Doug stepped farther into the club and surveyed the folks mingling. Most of them appeared college-aged, dressed in hip, upbeat, tight clothing; the guys wore baggy slacks and shirts; the women short skirts or tight pants and tops that showed lots of cleavage. Despite the fact that civilization had gone into post-apocalyptic times, you wouldn't know by stepping in this place. In here, it still felt like a pick-up joint from times forgotten.

Doug moved to the bar and sidled up casually. A tall geeky-looking guy with a crew cut approached the bar and took his order. Doug ordered a shot of Black Jack and a Miller. The bartender set him up and Doug felt the first shot fire through his veins. He turned around on his stool, watching the crowd as he nursed his beer. Marilyn Manson moaned that we're all stars in the dope show.

Two swigs into his beer and he was being hit on left and right. Doug laughed and went with the flow. He ordered drinks for his new female companions, talking aimlessly, cracking jokes. There were as many as six women within a twenty-foot radius that conveyed heavy interest signals. It was obvious that they were hitting on him, yet catfights seemed to be far from the making. Most of them seemed to be hitting on other guys as well; the demand for folks who wanted to spend the evening with another able-bodied soul was higher than days bygone when AIDS, egos, head games, and emotions had to be wafted through to get down to the nitty-gritty. Doug knew that those he passed on tonight would wind up with someone else. No hard feelings.

Five beers later he was in deep conversation with a drop-dead gorgeous blonde. She stood no taller than five foot two and had wonderful breasts. The minute she blinked those big baby blues at him he was hooked. His head swam from adrenaline and the buzz from the alcohol and music.

Three beers later they were in Doug's jeep heading toward Tiffany's condo in West Hollywood. They were accompanied by her friend Andrea, who was tall, willowy, with big brown eyes and great breasts (*Face it*, Doug thought. *Every female is going to have great breasts since you haven't seen any in over a year since all this zombie shit started.*) As Doug drove, Tiffany related how her complex was one of the only buildings in L.A. that still had workable electricity and running water. Their apartment was on the top floor, via the elevators. The walking dead were too stupid to man the elevators, and both women carried nine-millimeters and extra clips with them. They were both getting to be pretty good shots. Doug grinned, hardly paying attention to their banter. All he could think about was what lay ahead.

Moments later it came. And Doug came with it, along with Tiffany and Andrea, all over each other, in the comfiness and elegance of the girls' penthouse apartment on the thirty-second floor.

"Why don't you come with me to my place?" It was one of the few complete sentences Doug had spoken to them since arriving at their apartment. All of last night and most of this morning had been spent frolicking in their king-size waterbed. It was now high noon, and Doug had popped the suggestion after another seemingly endless round of sex. Andrea looked at him quizzically from his right, her long lashes masking the confusion in her eyes. Only Tiffany, grinning ferally at him from his groin, responded. Doug grinned down at her. "Whattaya say?"

Tiffany slithered up over him. Andrea ran her finger lightly over his right earlobe. "And why should we go to your place, lover?" Tiffany grinned.

Doug nodded toward the expansive entertainment center opposite the bed. It was equipped with a twenty-four-inch color TV, a VCR, a DVD Player, and a high-tech stereo system. None of them worked, due to the faulty electrical system in the building. The elevators and lights were about the only thing that worked in the building. "I've got stuff like this back at my place, and my stuff works."

Andrea flicked her tongue in his ear. "Really! How so?"

Doug felt fingers of pleasure rock through him as Andrea ran her tongue through his ear. "Come with me and I'll show you."

"Where do you live," Andrea whispered. She kissed his earlobe.

"A few hours drive. High Sierras."

Tiffany sat up in bed. "Geez, that's a long way."

Doug rose, too. "At least just come with me for a couple of days. I've got all the conveniences of modern technology and everything works." He spilled out a rough list of how his place was set up, including the generator, the phone line, and the computer setup. Both girls perked up at the sound of it. Doug grinned and rubbed Tiffany's shoulders. "Just for a few days. You'll love it."

"I don't know," Tiffany said. She turned to Andrea, who was lying on her stomach, her rump jutting in the air, legs bent upward at the knees. "What do you think?"

Andrea pursed her lips in contemplation. "Sounds okay to me." She looked up at Doug. "You'll bring us back in a couple of days?"

"Honey, after seeing what I've got at my place, you're not gonna want to come back," Doug chuckled.

Tiffany and Andrea traded glances. Doug smiled and Tiffany giggled. "Well, then, let's go."

An hour later they were winging their way out of the empty, dead city of Los Angeles to the mountains.

He was right about their reaction when they got to the house. They were more than amazed; they were astounded.

The girls looked in awe at the massive living room, the huge dining room, and the downstairs rumpus room filled with toys, pinball machines, a large pool table, and other electronic gadgets. They marveled at the widescreen TV and the fact that it worked; they *ooohhed* over his massive collection of videotapes, DVDs, compact discs, and books. They were equally impressed with his massive kitchen and its supplies. Andrea squealed with delight when she opened the freezer and found a frozen pizza. To appease her, and their growing appetite, Doug put the pizza in the oven. Then he steered his guests out toward the back patio.

Once at the patio, they *ahhed* at the awesome sight his perch had over the mountain range. His house was situated on a crag that overlooked the main pass coming up the Sierras, and if you looked due west you could see the rolling hills of the San Joaquin Valley. It was an awesome sight to behold.

He took them down into the woods that consisted of his property and showed them the generator. He showed them the stream that ran by it and explained how it worked. He pointed out the massive satellite dish that sat next to his home; it brought in the phone line, and it used to bring in over five hundred channels from all over the world. The girls were doubly impressed.

They ate the pizza Doug had put in the oven with all the zeal and excitement of children spending an afternoon at Chuck E. Cheese. Neither of them had had a pizza in …well, gosh, in over a year, since the first zombie rose from its grave and bit through the first wandering human. In Los Angeles there had been plenty of frozen pizzas that had thawed out when the electricity died but with all the power gone, savoring their taste was something that could only be reminisced. Doug smiled and put another pizza in the oven and brought out two cases of Dos Equis. He reached underneath the cabinet in the kitchen and produced a bag of powdery substance that brought a squeal out of both girls. Pizza, beer, and coke—three great tastes that taste great together!

They munched and drank, babbling excitedly. Doug grinned. The girls were acting like they were in Donald Trump's mansion. And to them, this *was* a mansion. Those who had survived the zombie plague sure didn't have luxuries like running water.

When they had eaten their fill, Doug rolled up a crisp, ten-thousand-dollar bill. Tiffany nearly babbled with excitement. "Jesus Christ, Doug!" Her eyes sparkled, her smile dimpled her cheeks. "So that's how you were able to get such a bitchin' place?"

Doug handed her the rolled-up bill and winked at them. "There's more where this came from, baby. Not that this money stuff is worth anything these days."

Doug was right about Tiffany and Andrea wanting to stay longer than a few days.

The first two weeks at the mountain retreat was spent languidly fucking, eating, sleeping, snorting coke, fucking, sleeping some more, fucking again, eating, drinking, partaking in some more toot, fucking some more, and, well, fucking. The two of them provided a workout that Doug never thought he would go through again with a woman. After the first night he thought his dick was going to fall off from the sheer exertion of the strange contortions they were putting it through. He was having sex every day, if not with both of them at the same time, then with one or the other. Because they were bisexual, it spurned him on even further. There were moments when all the energy was drained from his body, but the sight of Tiffany eating Andrea's pussy with her tender little ass poking up in the air brought the divining rod between his legs to full attention. It was always enough for a quick romp from behind.

Doug drove them down to Los Angeles two weeks later to gather their things. They really didn't need that much, Tiffany said, just their keepsakes. Photos of their late boyfriends and parents, friends. Trinkets. Doug didn't mind, and they were back at the house by darkness, enjoying another night of sex and coke.

The days seemed to pass quickly for Doug. Mornings consisted of awakening to the smell of frying bacon or perking coffee, one of the girls in the kitchen while the other lay nestled next to Doug. He would awaken and sometimes, if the mood was right, make love to whoever was in bed with him. After breakfast he would do immediate chores while the girls lounged in the den, watching a movie on the big screen TV, or blasting the stereo. Andrea was the bookworm, and preferred quiet mornings in the library. Tiffany usually warmed up in the morning with a Cher video, and around noon they met at the back porch for a light lunch usually prepared by Andrea. Then it was whatever struck their fancy for the rest of the day and evening. Sometimes they went on romps through the woods, or accompanied Doug into the little town fifty miles down the winding, steep valley road to stock up on provisions. Movies and music were almost always on the agenda, and Tiffany told him that she could probably watch every single videocassette and DVD he had for a year and still not get through all of them. Doug had what amounted to a store full of videos and DVDs; his collection had grown since the plague.

But more often than not, their evenings ended up engaging in sex and partying, usually until the wee hours of the morning. The coke that Doug had was one of two dozen kilos he had accumulated over the past two years, gained from a dealer that also supplied him with a steady amount of marijuana, which Doug had started growing himself shortly after the zombie plague. The girls dipped into that stash too, usually in the early evening. Getting stoned always helped arouse the nerves and brought heightened climax to their lovemaking.

To Doug, it was heaven. How many guys would love to be able to fuck two gorgeous women with perfect breasts every night, anytime they wanted to?

And so the lifestyle continued into the summer months.

———————————————◦——————————————

Doug began to sense that something wasn't right toward the end of August.

The past couple of weeks had been filled with slightly tense moments. For the first time in almost two months, Tiffany started suggesting insane ideas that they pop down to Los Angeles and bring some of their friends out. Doug squashed that idea in a hurry. Andrea seemed to side with Tiffany, and they went around that topic for a good portion of a night. *We just want to see some of our friends again*, was the excuse. *Well then, we'll drive down for the day and visit*, was Doug's reply. No, they wanted to do more than that. They wanted to bring people up from L.A. to party. *Well, what's the matter with what we have already?*

"Don't get us wrong," Tiffany said. They were seated on the cream colored couch in the recreation room. The VCR was unrolling *Terminator 2*. "We love it up here, and we love *you*." She winked at him, smiling broadly, and Andrea seconded the motion with a kiss on his cheek. He was sandwiched between the two women as they explained their situation to him. "But …well, we kind of miss our friends, and we just thought it would be nice to have a big party up here."

"And then they would want to stay, and you would needle me into letting them." Doug knew what they were getting at and, by God, he wasn't going to let that happen. "The reason I built this house in the first place was to avoid all that live-fast-make-a-pretty-corpse bullshit lifestyle. So, no way, I am not throwing a big raging party for hundreds of people I don't even know."

"Don't you even want to talk to other people, get to know what's going on?" This, from Andrea. "Make new friends, meet new people?"

"I don't want to make friends and meet other people."

"Well, suppose *we* do?"

Now Tiffany joined in. "We love it up here, Doug, and we like being with you, but we just can't stay cooped up here. We need to ... interact with other people every once in awhile. Play the field."

Doug snorted. "Ha! So that's what you wanted all along."

Andrea sighed. "All the old moral codes are gone now, Doug. We're not legally bound to you in any way, nor are you to us. We don't mind that we're sharing you, and personally, I would like it if I had more than one male lover right now."

"Me, too," Tiffany said, quietly.

This threw Doug into a rage, but he contained it. His cheeks grew beet red, his eyes flared righteous anger. He rose suddenly from the couch, his hands curling into fists. "It figures. I give you everything you could possibly want, yet you still want to . . .want to—"

"Fuck other guys?" Tiffany's tone was ice. She leveled her sea blue eyes to meet his. Both girls were wearing shorts, bikini bras and nothing else. Couple their looks with their tone and anger, and they looked like Amazon bitches who weren't going to take shit. "Yeah, to be quite frank with you, Doug, I *would* like to fuck other guys. Just as I'm sure you'd like to fuck other women."

"That's not true," Doug retorted.

"Bullshit." Now Andrea rose and stormed toward the French windows that overlooked the back deck. Tiffany joined her, leaving Doug to pace the floor of the recreation room. What the hell was wrong with them? He had given them everything they could possibly want, or need, and now they wanted to sample other pleasures. He had been nothing but kind and generous to them, loving and caring. The last few months had brought Doug to a feeling of closeness with them. Andrea and Tiffany were the first women he'd ever felt this way towards; if the institution of marriage still existed, he would have done it with them in an instant. Because marriage was now a long disposed of issue, bigamy could only be much easier. You could love two women equally, and he loved both of them more than he had ever loved anyone. He told them that time and time again. Didn't they understand that?

For the first time in almost three months they spent the evening in near stony silence.

They took Doug that night.

Doug seemed to switch from brooding, to lustful at the moment Andrea stroked him beneath the covers. Doug had tumbled into bed by himself, leaving the girls to simmer downstairs. Now they joined him in bed, waking him up with their expressions of affection. Doug woke up to a raging hard-on, Andrea's hand stroking him expertly, Tiffany's lips and tongue trailing wet kisses down his bare stomach. Doug turned over and took them into his arms; the argument was all but forgotten now.

The girls played this out, leading him along a cascade of endless sex as positions were switched, orifices were probed and entered, nipples and lips were kissed. Doug surrendered completely to them, yielding to their every whim.

When it was over the girls watched Doug slip into a deep sleep and traded glances. Neither had made verbal plans, but the same thought was running through their minds. They were acting on pure instinct now, letting everything run its course.

Andrea scrambled off the bed and out of the room. She emerged a moment later with a baseball bat. Tiffany scuttled off the bed quickly as Andrea cocked the bat behind her head like Hank Aaron poising for a homerun and then *whack*! The fat end of the bat hit the top of Doug's skull. The impact sent reverberations of the blow up Andrea's arm. Doug made a choking sound and was out, his breathing seeming to rise quickly, then stopped altogether. There was dead silence for a moment as the girls stood frozen with bated breath, waiting for some signal of death to emit from Doug's now bashed head. Tiffany could barely make out the trickles of blood oozing from Doug's skull in the gloomy darkness, but she knew from his crumpled look and still chest that Andrea's first swing had more than done the job. Doug was deader than a doornail.

Tiffany looked up at Andrea with rising glee. Andrea raised her left hand in victory, the right still holding the bloodstained bat. She let out a war whoop, and a moment later both girls were laughing, hugging each other, laughing so hard that tears spilled down their cheeks.

"We did it!" Andrea squealed. She kissed Tiffany, *smack*, on the lips, and Tiffany returned it enthusiastically. Andrea beamed at her lover, their arms encircling each other's waists, their breasts touching. "We did it, babe. We did it, and this place is ours, the jeep is ours, everything is *ours*!"

"And we can go back to L.A. and bring Bruce and Janie and everybody from Club Dead back," Tiffany echoed.

"And we'll have one big fucking party, and we can bring anybody we want to." Andrea was so happy, she was practically glowing.

The implications of what their lives would be like now in this castle-like abode hit Tiffany like an explosion. It would be wonderful, like heaven. The warmth of their lovemaking still coursed through her veins, and she could still feel Doug's seed trickling between her legs, inside her. The feeling bubbled within her, made her take Andrea in her arms and kiss her passionately. Andrea cupped Tiffany's face in her hands and kissed her back, remained lock in her embrace as the kiss waxed and waned.

When they came up for air, they were panting. "I love you, Andrea," Tiffany breathed.

"I love you, too," Andrea said.

"Let's get Doug out of here now."

They did it. They rolled Doug's body off the bed and dragged him by his arms across the floor and out of the house. They dragged him out to the porch, down the stairs, and laid him to rest beside the big oak tree that towered next to the cabin. Tiffany laid a green tarpaulin cover over him and smiled. Both girls were still nude, their skin goosefleshing from the cool mountain breeze. Tiffany tweaked Andrea's puckered nipples and kissed her again. "We'll bury him tomorrow," she said. She was beginning to feel hot for Andrea all over again. "Right now, I want you to take me down."

Back into the house, through the kitchen, and that was as far as they got. They didn't even make it back to the bedroom, their passion and hunger for each other was so strong. They took each other in the kitchen, on the big table, and made love to each other until they sank into deep sleep.

Morning.

Tiffany emerged from the bathroom wearing one of Doug's chambray shirts and nothing else. Andrea was just beginning to stir in the early morning sun. They had fallen asleep in each other's arms on the living room floor, and now the sun beat golden light through the window on their makeshift bed. Andrea smiled up at Tiffany, her eyes lush with love. "Hi!"

"Sleep good?" Tiffany asked, smiling down at her.

"Mmmm. Never slept better." Andrea raised herself up on her elbows. "And you?"

"Like a baby." Tiffany moved into the kitchen and rummaged around for a glass of water. Andrea rose and retrieved a T-shirt that had been tossed on the sofa a few days before. She slipped it over her head just as Tiffany came back from the kitchen. Tiffany was sipping on a glass of water. "Well, I guess we should take care of Doug."

Andrea nodded. "Yep."

Tiffany set the glass down and together they moved outside and down the steps to where they had laid Doug down last night.

They both stopped at the same time. Tiffany's heart pounded in her chest. Her limbs felt suddenly light. She traded a fearful glance at Andrea, who looked like she'd just witnessed a ghastly crime. The same thought popped into their heads at the same time, sparking an instant rise of fear. "Oh, Jesus," Andrea said.

Doug was gone from where they had left him last night. Only the tarp remained, with a few dried bloodstains.

It felt like an eternity passed before Tiffany could muster her collectiveness together. "Jesus, Andrea, why weren't we fucking thinking?" She turned and began trotting up the steps to the back deck. Andrea followed her, more out of fear of being left alone. Tiffany strode across the deck and into the house, Andrea trailing right behind her. Tiffany's thoughts were running like wildfire. He was dead, he had risen from the dead because he *was* the undead, they had killed him but not in the way they should have. They needed to arm themselves and find him before *he* found them. She darted through the kitchen toward the back den where Doug kept his gun collection. One good headshot would be all it would take. "We've got to —"

"Got to what, babe?" The voice came from Tiffany's left, just as she was entering the threshold to the den. Tiffany started, the fear lodging in her throat and stifling her scream.

Doug stood in the darkened hallway, a Remington pump shotgun cradled in his arms. His flint gray eyes blazed with a maniacal fury. Blood caked the left side of his face and stained his left shoulder and chest in a gory mess. Tiffany thought she could see slivers of his skull from the ruined mass of his head. Doug grinned and shambled forward, bringing the barrel of the shotgun to a careful aim. His left arm appeared partially paralyzed, and he rested the barrel of the shotgun across it, holding it firmly with his left hand. He had them frozen in its sight. "Didn't even check to see if I was dead, did you?" He snickered. "Stupid air-headed bitches."

The girls stepped back. Tiffany's throat felt locked up, but she still managed a few words. "Doug, please —"

"Enough." Doug gestured with the shotgun. "No excuses. You tried to take what was mine and you almost killed me for it. Although I think that the worst part about all this is that you did it in such a cowardly manner that you felt you needed to blindside me and leave me for dead." He regarded them with his blazing eyes. "Shows how goddamn stupid you are. If you'd had any brains you would have blown my head off with one of the guns, and that would have been it." He leered at them. "Suppose I *had* died? Suppose I had died and come back? What would you have done?"

"I—" Tiffany tried to answer that they were in the process of doing that just now, but stopped. He was right. They'd been stupid, not to mention careless. Any excuse she came up with would only make her appear more dimwitted.

"Thought so," Doug muttered. "You have no answer for that. Isn't that right?"

The girls said nothing. They remained frozen, paralyzed with fear.

Doug tittered, grinning. The shotgun was still trained on them. "Believe me, but I know your kind well. Knew it even when I met you at Club Dead. Living for today, for the flesh, for desire. Nothing else mattered. Not peace of mind or spiritual peace. Not even for the beauty of life itself. Drifting from one party to the next blow of coke, to the next stud."

Tiffany could see that he was running on pure adrenaline that was fueling his energies to keep him alive from his head injury. A flap of skin permitted a brief glimpse of the shattered bone of his skull. "Doug, please," Tiffany said. Her hands were held up in a peace offering. Andrea stood beside her, a smile trying to worm its way on her face. "Doug, put the gun down," Tiffany said, her voice calm. Smooth. "Put the gun down, and we'll get help for you—"

The barrel of the shotgun raised to mid-chest level. "From where?" Doug's eyes narrowed as he focused in on his target. Sweat stood out in shiny droplets amid his blood-crusted forehead. "I'm gonna die, Tiffany. I'm gonna die, and then I'm gonna rise and walk the earth in limbo. Only problem with that is there ain't gonna be nobody around to satisfy my new craving."

Tiffany started babbling again, joined by Andrea. "*Shut up!*" Doug blurted. His finger was tightening on the trigger. "Just fucking *shut up!* If you were going to kill me, you should have blown my brains out, but you didn't and I'm gonna die. I'm gonna die and come back and I'm not gonna let you get away with it . . ." He was almost crying, his voice now coming in hitching rasps. He took a deep, collective breath. Focused them in with his gaze. Determined. "I'm not gonna let you get away with it."

With a swift move, he gripped the barrel of the shotgun and brought the heavy stock down on Tiffany's head. She collapsed to the floor, her eyes rolling up in the back of her head. He grimaced at Andrea as she stood in numbed shock.

The introduction of shotgun stock to Andrea's skull produced similar results. Doug stood over them for a moment panting, his panic-stricken mind racing.

Five minutes later he was limping down the steps to the woods and up the mountain, dragging each girl behind him by the ankles.

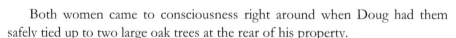

Both women came to consciousness right around when Doug had them safely tied up to two large oak trees at the rear of his property.

It had taken every last ounce of strength he had. After he dragged both girls up, he'd trudged back to his place and rummaged in his workshed for some rope, or preferably something more heavy duty. He found some heavy-duty steel cable and rope, and after pausing for a quick rest (and to let a bad bout of nausea pass) he headed back to where he'd left the girls.

He tied them up carefully, taking care that they were trussed up securely.

He also made sure they were a good thirty feet apart.

Then he waited for them to wake up.

They came awake slowly. Andrea was the first to focus in on what was going on. She saw Doug and immediately started to cry.

Tiffany came awake thirty minutes later.

Doug stood up and approached both women, shotgun in hand. His breath wheezed in his chest. Already, he could feel his limbs growing weaker, could feel his equilibrium give out. He knew he had a serious head injury, and that it was only a matter of the next twenty-four hours if he lived or died. And if he died, he knew he would be back.

The thought of eating them sickened him.

Funny he would think that now, he chuckled to himself as he brought the barrel of the shotgun up and took aim. He sure loved eating them out before.

Tiffany's left eye widened in horror as the barrel of the shotgun aimed at her midsection; her right eye was closed shut and swollen. "*Nooo! Doug!*"

Doug pulled the trigger and the shotgun exploded, propelling Tiffany back against her bounds. A large hole exploded between her breasts, blowing chunks of flesh, bone, and skin. She fell back and hit the trunk of the tree limply and slid down, her eyes wide and vacant. The blast snapped Andrea from her shock, and she struggled in her bonds, eyes wide with fear. Her full lips were open in terror as she looked from Tiffany's corpse and up to Doug.

Doug jacked the pump on the shotgun and took aim at Andrea, fixing her baby blues in his gaze. Her face screamed white fear. "No, Doug, oh *please,* God *no —*"

"Goodbye, Andrea," Doug said, and pulled the trigger. Her right breast exploded in a shower of viscera. The impact flung her backward over Tiffany. Doug pumped another shell in the chamber and stepped forward.

Andrea was still alive. Her left side twitched spastically. Her eyes locked on Doug as he approached her, and she moved her limbs in a half-assed attempt at escape. Blood ran out of her mouth and was pouring out of her chest, staining Tiffany and the forest floor. A mewling sound rose in her throat. Doug stood over her and took aim, a slow grin beginning to spread on his features. A perverse sense of elation swept through him as he stood over her. She twitched in pain beneath him, still trying to get away. A massive hole of ruined flesh gaped where her once luscious right breast used to be.

Doug smiled and aimed at the center of her chest. Where the heart was. "Goodbye, Andrea." He pulled the trigger.

He stood there in the thicket, listening to the echo of the shotgun blast reverberate through the forest.

Tiffany had ceased her struggle. Doug kicked her body with one booted foot. She was dead.

And so was Andrea.

He felt himself growing weaker, but he knew he had to wait. He had to wait to see if what he had hurriedly planned would work.

Andrea's fingers twitched. A moment later Tiffany's foot moved. Doug fought back a wave of nausea as he squinted at the two girls lying before him, trying hard to keep his breathing even.

Andrea was trying to sit up. Her dead eyes locked on him and she opened her mouth and hissed. Doug smiled. He knew that look on her face well. He had seen it on hundreds of them before. It was a look of undying hunger.

A moment later, Tiffany joined her. Both women strained against their bonds, their arms outstretched, jaws opening and closing, teeth gnashing into bottom lips in hunger. Doug laughed. He supposed it was like tying a starving man in front of a filet mignon, teasing him with it.

Doug took a dozen steps back, feeling himself growing wobbly. "Bye bye, girls." He sat down heavily on his rump, the shotgun almost flying out of his grasp. He could feel himself growing faint. The shotgun seemed suddenly heavy, but he still managed to bring the barrel to his mouth. He stretched his lips over both barrels, his teeth scraping against the cold steel. He stretched his arm out and his finger found the trigger just as he felt another wave of blackness wash over him.

The sound of the shotgun blast was loud and echoed throughout the valley.

The wailing and gnashing of the hungry went on for much longer.

AT MĀRATOTŌ POOL

by Lee Murray

Maratoto: garden spring
Māratotō: river/gushing lifeblood

I'd carried the bike for a kilometre through the sun-brittled hardwoods, forced to put it down each time I helped my mother manage the dusty inclines, or step over the dried out ponga trunks. She was nearing seventy, after all. I would leave her to catch her breath while I went back for my trusty Trek.

"For God's sake, just dump the damn bike, Viv," she shouted after me.

I refused to give it up. It was all I had left; the only thing connecting me to home. Instead, I slipped my arm through the frame and hoisted the bike up, ignoring Mum's whinging and the pedal digging into the middle of my back. When I reached her, she made that *tsk*ing sound, like some vintage schoolmarm. "You're so bloody stubborn. Just like your father," she grumbled.

He hadn't been stubborn enough though, had he? Not enough to go the distance—taking his own life mere months after my brother Michael had got himself riddled with holes in a senseless shootout. So now there was just Mum and me, trudging through clouds of dust, towards an imaginary sanctuary somewhere up Māratotō way.

"Come on. Let's just keep moving," I said. "How much further to this lake, anyway?"

"Not a lake. Māratotō is a waterfall. Or at least it was, when I last visited."

"When was that exactly?"

"I don't know. A few years back, in thirty-four or thirty-five."

More than two decades. I didn't bother to roll my eyes. "Everywhere else is dry," I said.

"There'll be something there," she insisted. "Māratotō is Māori for 'gushing lifeblood,' so there has to be water. Stands to reason, doesn't it?"

There was no *reason* about it. I imagined an arid and dusty hole, its steep banks crumbling with desiccated moss. "Tell me again what they said at the water tap."

I'd missed the story, leaving her to hold our place in the line while I'd tried trading our last two Paracetamol caps for food.

Her tired eyes brightened as she told the story again. It had been nothing more than a whisper really, rumours rippling down the line at the township's last remaining water tap. The tale of a place with water where they welcomed everyone, not just able-bodied folk who could pay with their labour. Well, people talked, didn't they? What else was there to pass the time while they waited for their daily ten…then five…and now three litres of water, the quantity strictly enforced by two men with guns.

Of course, the sanctuary was a myth. It had to be. Because if a nirvana like that really existed, why would anyone leave it to come back into town and tell the story? It was just another rumour to add to all the others. A dream to dwell on while people wished away the hours. When I'd said as much to Mum, she'd just shrugged.

"Well, I'm going," she'd said, proving that the stubborn gene existed on the Braid side of the family, too. She waved her hand about what was left of our garden. "What's left for us here, anyway?"

I'd glanced at my precious crop of runner beans, shaded beneath their wilted too-white leaves, everything blanketed in dust, and pressed my lips together. The beans had been doomed, but I hung on another week—until someone broke down the fence and got away with half the crop.

After that, going to Māratotō was all Mum talked about. "If you don't like the place, you can always come back."

I helped her over a rut in in the track and wondered if she'd have got this far on her own. An *easy* half-day bike ride from home. I stifled a snort. Life was full of paradoxes, wasn't it? Nevertheless, I hoped Māratotō still had its waterfall. A waterfall would be something.

We rounded a corner and my breath caught in my throat.

Tents of all colours. People. So there *was* a commune here. And I couldn't see any weapons either. But the people turned to look at us, and there was something slow and glacial about their movement. Their smiles were too wide, and their demeanour screamed of practised casualness.

The skin on the back of my neck prickled. "Mum," I said, hoping she would catch the warning in my tone.

"Shhh," she replied.

"Welcome to Māratotō, the garden spring," said a woman. She was my age and unremarkable—mid-thirties, brown hair pulled into a ponytail—but standing beside her was the most beautiful man I had ever seen. Not hard like the men in town. I could barely keep my eyes off him.

"So, is it true, then?" Mum's eyes glistened. "The falls are still here?"

"They're up the track a bit. In a grove of trees."

My knees trembled and I had to steady myself against a tree. There *was* a pool. They had water here!

The beautiful man smiled. "The falls might not be exactly as you remember them—they're hardly Niagara—but the pool is still there. Marelle and I will take you up there if you like."

They were going to let us see it! It had taken us three days to climb into the hills. We were weary, dusty, and as parched as stone, but we had to see the waterfall.

I left the bike behind and we walked a kilometre to a grove of four solid fruit trees, their trunks as wide and straight as young kauri. Beneath the trees was a pink-brown mud pool fed by a dribble of water which trickled down a narrow incline on one side.

Half a dozen people, mostly older women, lounged in the mud, their heads laid back on the flattened stones at the edge of the pool.

I felt myself colour as Mum took off her clothes, dropping them where she stood, and climbed right in. "Mum!"

Marelle touched my arm. "It's fine. There's a well further up the valley that we use for our drinking water, so we allow the older folk to indulge," she said. "It reminds them of the past."

My heart did cartwheels in my chest. There was a well! Not just this muddy wallow, although I could understand Mum's urge to get in. I'd only been small—maybe four or five years old—but I remembered swimming in fresh water. We'd gone to Lake Taupō, Mum, Dad, Michael, and me, before the crater lake had been pumped dry to slake the thirst of the country's six million gasping citizens. We'd walked an hour over the pebbly sand to the water's edge, where my brother and I had plunged into the icy water and come up shrieking and laughing. Our whole bodies, *immersed* in the water. I could still recall the sensation, so cool and calming on my skin, and with no crusty seawater sting. Just thinking about it raised goose bumps on my arms.

Mum lay back in the pool, mud rolling over her shoulders, and closed her eyes. I'd never seen her so serene.

Marelle said, "Why not let her soak while Phillip and I find a place to set you up back in the village?"

They are going to let us stay. Why? The goose bumps lingered.

Mum's eyes barely fluttered. "Go on, Viv," she said. "I'm not going anywhere."

Marelle, Phillip, and I trudged back along the track to the cluster of tents, Marelle veering off to chat with someone when we neared the commune, while Phillip showed me to a dusty grey tent. A couple of camp beds had been stacked to one side, clean bedding folded on top.

"Surely this belongs to someone?"

Phillip shrugged. "They left."

Not knowing what else to say, I busied myself setting up the beds, relieved when Marelle returned carrying a basket of fruit resembling pomegranates. She offered me one.

I hesitated.

"I don't blame you," Phillip said. "Can't stand them myself."

Perhaps to reassure me, Marelle bit into one, its red juice staining her teeth and lips crimson. "Blood fruit," she explained. She showed me the inside: the flesh blood-coloured with sharp white pips.

I couldn't help narrowing my eyes. None of this felt right. It was all too good to be true. *The well.* This tent. The beds. And now this offer of food. Even with New Zealand's population dwindling to less than a million, there was still barely enough to go around. No one gave away food. Not without getting something in return.

"They say you let anyone in here," I said warily. "Is that true? You'll welcome anyone who turns up?"

I caught Marelle's shifting glance. "Not just anyone. We're careful."

"Why us then? You don't know anything about my mother and me."

Marelle pulled that slow smile, the one she'd given us when we arrived. "Well, that's just it, isn't it? You were willing to bring an elderly woman to a sanctuary this far into the mountains with no idea of what you might find here. That kind of thing says something."

"Yeah. It says she's a bossy old woman and I'm an idiot."

Phillip grinned. "Well, yes. There is that. But it also showed us you were kind."

It didn't seem nearly enough.

In years gone by, a commune of sorts would pop up anywhere people located a water source—survivalist groups, religious nuts, even a few local authority regimes, all demanding you toe the line for a share of whatever resources they had on offer—but with so much demand, overcrowding and disillusionment meant many communities had imploded in violence. When munitions had still been available, people with guns had rampaged through the settlements. It hadn't been so much survival of the fittest as much as survival of the armed. Thousands had perished in that Great Cull. Nowadays, almost no one had bullets, but there were other ways to die, so people remained cautious.

Marelle's giggle cut across my thoughts. She handed me a blood fruit, then picked up the basket. "Well, if you *had* planned to kill us in our beds, you could hardly make a quick getaway with a seventy-something in tow, could you?" Smiling, she left in a swish of brown ponytail.

I had to admit she had a point.

When she was out of sight and we could no longer hear her chuckling, Phillip leaned over and nudged me with his shoulder. "If you must know, it was your bike."

"My bike?"

"Remember, that well we were telling you about? The one further up the valley? We drag the water buckets up by hand."

Understanding dawned: properly harnessed, the mechanical power of my bike would make it easier to bring the water to the surface. My unease dissipated.

Of course. For all Marelle's talk of kindness, the bike had been our ticket into the commune. The quid pro quo.

I took a bite of the blood fruit and let the sweet juice drip down my chin.

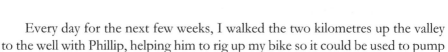

Every day for the next few weeks, I walked the two kilometres up the valley to the well with Phillip, helping him to rig up my bike so it could be used to pump well water to the surface, and then taking my turn in the saddle to contribute to the commune's daily supply. During those walks, and over the course of our days together, I learned a lot about the commune.

"It's not so much a commune as a retirement village," Phillip joked as he adjusted the bike seat to accommodate his height. "There are close to sixty residents, most of them living in tents in the village, but one or two live dotted about on the surrounding ledges and plateaus. Half of our residents are in their sixties or above."

"I haven't seen any children."

His expression grew sombre. "No, you won't have."

Had they set up a school somewhere? Was that why? Surely, I would've heard the kids playing?

Phillip climbed on the bike and pushed down hard with his legs to get the wheels spinning. "There are no kids at Māratotō."

None at all? Children were rare enough, but in a community this size, I would've expected a few.

"Dunno why exactly," Phillip said before I'd even asked the question. "For some reason, new arrivals tend to be older. The drought taking a toll, I guess." He puffed heavily, getting into the cadence. "Or maybe it's our Māratotō population that's skewed. It was bound to happen; while we don't advertise it, people hightail it here pretty fast when they find out we don't require our seniors to work."

I arched a brow. "Nice life for some," I quipped.

My mother was certainly revelling in it; getting up earlier and earlier every day to make the one-kilometre trek to the falls where she would while away the hours, lounging dreamily in the mud pool like some kind of hallowed hippo. It was a wonder she hadn't dissolved, she spent so much time submerged. Marelle said there was something protective in the mud. A tourism industry had been founded on it. Way back in the 1900s, apparently. Then, last night, when I'd gone to collect Mum for dinner, she'd refused to get out and come back with me.

"Let her stay," Marelle had said kindly. "It can be a long walk for our older members. There are a couple of tents up here for those who prefer to stay close."

"But she hasn't eaten anything since breakfast."

Smiling, Marelle had laid a hand on my arm. "You're a good daughter. It can't have been easy looking out for your mother all these years. A lot of people took the easy way and abandoned their parents, you know? You deserve some time out. Cassie and I will make sure she eats."

So, I'd left my mother there and walked back to the village with Phillip. Then, after we'd eaten, the two of us had spent the evening beside the fire. We didn't talk much; just sat there enjoying the crackle and tangy scent of burning mānukā. From time to time, Phillip added another log, which stirred up the embers, sending frenzied sparks into the dry air. Bathed in flickering firelight, his skin had turned a dark bronze. Today, under the sun, it gleamed gold. He'd been pedalling a while now and the sweat was beading on his shoulders and back, fascinating me.

"Is that why elders get indulged here?" I asked, handing him a cup of water. "Because there are no kids to dote on?"

Phillip sat up in the saddle, his feet braced on the pedals, and took the drink. "Possibly. I never really considered it that way. I always thought it was because Marelle's great aunt Eremia founded the community and the old lady was part Chinese, part Māori." He handed me the cup and went back to his pedalling.

I had some Māori in me too, so I got his drift: in both Chinese and Māori cultures, elders were revered and respected. They were cherished family members to be nurtured into their old age, not just shunted into retirement homes. Since the drought had started, those values were wearing thin. It was refreshing to find they still existed here. Marelle's great aunt must have been a force to reckon with.

"Did you get to meet her?" I asked.

"Eremia?" Still pedalling, Phillip wiped the sweat from his forehead with the back of his hand. "Eremia is still here. In a way. The spirit of her, at least. She's like a kind of overarching presence. But no, I didn't get to meet her in person. The old lady was long gone by the time I got here."

I didn't ask him to elaborate. Once upon a time I might have, but it had become impolite to ask about people's origins, and even more rude to inquire about their past. These days, everyone was entitled to a skeleton or two in the closet.

The bucket reached the top of the well and Phillip stopped pedalling. I tried to lift the bucket off the crossbar, but it slipped through my fingers, precious water slopping on the ground before I could recover.

I stared aghast as the silver droplets seeped into the earth.

"Here, let me help," Phillip said quickly, hopping off the saddle, his fingers brushing mine as he grabbed the bucket.

"Sorry I wasted some," I said.

"It was an accident. Don't worry about it."

I held the container steady, while he poured the water from the bucket, his reassurance not making me feel any better.

Phillip hooked the bucket back to the pulley. The rope creaked.

"Where does the water come from, anyway?"

"No way of knowing," he replied. "An underground stream. Maybe an aquifer."

"Aquifers are finite."

"All water is finite."

He must have seen my alarm because his face softened. "Let's hope it's not an aquifer."

We didn't speak again until we'd loaded the last filled cask onto a wheelbarrow contraption, each of us lifting a handle to push our cargo along the trail back to the village.

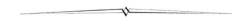

Three months after our arrival, Mum emerged from the pool, brushed the drying mud from her skin, and hitched a ride on one of the wheelbarrow-contraptions for the kilometre journey back along the track to our tent. I hadn't been expecting her, so her arrival sent me into a frenzied panic. Mum sat on a camp stool and clucked her tongue while I separated the camp beds, changed the bedding, and shooed Phillip off to another tent to make space for her.

Mum rolled her eyes cheekily. "Don't mind me."

I was too happy to let it bother me. I suppose my relationship with Phillip had been inevitable given the time we'd been spending together. Perhaps it was because for the first time in my adult life I'd gained some independence—*I'd taken control of my own life*—now that Cassie and Marelle and the rest of the commune were helping to take care of Mum. And despite looking a little thinner than usual, Mum appeared to be thriving, although she moved about less, and when she did, her gestures were slow and graceful as if she were practising tai chi. I watched her with fascination as she teased drying mud from her hair. Perhaps this languidness was my mother's natural state, and it being so long since I'd seen it (if I'd seen it at all), I no longer recognised it.

"It's good that you're happy with your young man," Mum said, stopping her grooming for a moment to lift my hair off my shoulders. "I'm happy for you. For both of us. Coming here was the right thing to do: the people and the pool..."

I crouched beside her. "What's it like in the pool?"

She curled a mesh of hair around her fingertips. "Viv, it's blissful. Almost sinful." She breathed deeply and beamed at me, a rapturous schoolgirl describing her first crush. "I can hardly describe it."

"Try me."

She took my hands in hers and closed her eyes. "Being immersed in the pool makes me feel youthful again. My skin feels soft, even smoother than yours is, and my bones don't ache anymore. The pool, the mud, it lifts me up. *Uplifts* me somehow, cradling me to it. It's as if your father's still with me and holding me close." She sighed softly, then went on. "I'll spoon him, my cheek warm against his back, and breathe in the scent of him. It's so wonderful, the two of us lying there together in the cool where everything feels solid and safe. It was always meant to be like this." She opened her eyes, tears welling at the corners. "It's how our lives would have been, if the drought had never come."

My heart lurched with sorrow for her. What she was describing was pure fantasy. For a moment, I considered preventing her from going back to the pool and forcing her to face reality. But I stopped myself. If she'd said these things while we'd been back in town, I might've done exactly that, but now that we were here, it seemed too cruel. After years of hardship, my mother was finally content. What harm did it do to allow her to daydream? After all, I had Phillip now.

"You're sure you're not bored spending all day up there?" I asked her.

"Bored? Of course not. There's so much to talk about! We're always chatting."

I smiled. The times I'd been to the pool to see her, she'd almost always been napping, her body in the mud and her head resting on a stone, eyes closed and her chest gently rising and falling. More often than not, she hadn't even registered my presence. Although, lately I hadn't been there as often as I would've liked. Perhaps I'd just picked the wrong moments.

I lifted my hand to her cheek. "Well, if you're happy, then that's all that matters."

Tilting her head to one side, she covered my hand with her own. "Viv, I really am. It's why I made the trip here to the village. I wanted to let you know that I plan to stay out at the pool permanently. I love it there."

My skin prickled. "You want to leave me?" My voice sounded petulant, needy.

"Viv." My mother pinched me gently under the chin. "You're thirty-six years old. A grown woman. You don't need me under your feet playing gooseberry."

Since she'd already made her decision, all that remained was to make the most of her visit. I prepared her a cabbage tree heart wrapped in an omelette and told her about the commune's poultry farm and its skinny yet overconfident rooster. I made her a tea of steeped mānukā bark and told her how some of us were rediscovering the Māori process for making glue from tarata bark, which we hoped might come in useful for mending the aging tents. When I asked if she'd like to finish her meal with a wedge of blood fruit, she shook her head.

"Too sickly," she said, and I smiled because Phillip and I didn't eat them either. I didn't care for the way they made me feel; some compound in the fruit making my head spin and my teeth go numb.

After dinner, Mum said little, content to sit by the fire and let me natter on about this and that. Indulging me, I guess, since she was moving away.

The next morning, after she'd left and I was changing the bedding, I found the note. It had been written on a sliver of stick and hidden in the hem of one of the blankets. I might not have discovered it at all, but the stitching on the hem had unravelled and the stick had worked its way out. Someone had written shakily in purple biro: *Beware Māratotō!*

"What's this?" I asked Phillip.

His head whipped up and he snatched the stick from me. "Is that your mother's writing?" he demanded. Last night's tent mate had been a snorer, so he was crotchety from lack of sleep.

I shook my head.

Phillip threw it in the fire pit. "Buggered if I know. That stick could've been there for ages. You nearly ready?"

Draping the bedding over a line to air in the sun, I hurried to collect the water casks for our daily trek to the well.

In autumn, I awoke one morning to learn one of the elderly women who shared the pool had died overnight, so I delayed my daily trip to the well in favour of a detour to the pool to check on Mum. As always, I found her with her head resting on a flat stone, eyes closed and her shoulders submerged, although this morning a thin line of pink-brown clay smeared her cheek.

"Mum?"

"Hmm?"

"They say one of the women passed on last night. I thought I would check you were okay."

"Okay," she repeated, her voice distant, as if she were waking from a dream.

I slid my hand into the lukewarm mud and squeezed her shoulder. "I wanted to make sure you weren't upset about losing your friend."

"It's fine. She's fine." Beneath my hand, her shoulder twitched. Perhaps she'd intended to raise her arm but found the effort of lifting it out of the mud too much and changed her mind. In any case, she didn't open her eyes.

"I suppose she's gone to a better place," I said. It was a platitude, but what else could I say? I hadn't known the dead woman.

"Something else springs forth," Mum murmured. "Decay and renewal. It's the cycle of things. She's still here with us." She opened her eyes and stared hard at me. "Just in a different way."

I jumped backwards, startled. Could she tell? Did I look so different? I left her, heading across country to meet Phillip at the well. My detour hadn't taken long, but already he'd filled and loaded a barrow of water casks.

"Everything okay?" he asked when he saw me.

"Yes."

"You don't sound so sure."

"I'm pregnant," I told him.

When Phillip announced he was leaving the commune, my heart skipped a beat and my knees buckled.

"Not for good. Just for a few days," he said, gathering me to him. "Marelle has asked me to go down the mountain to get some supplies. Someone goes every six months or so to trade."

"Why you?" I whined. "Can't someone else go?"

He nuzzled my neck, hands on the small of my back. "They could, but Marelle's asked me because she knows I'll be careful about what I say. If news spreads about the commune, we'll be deluged with people looking to join us."

"Let them come," I said flippantly. It was how we'd come to be there, after all.

Phillip stepped back. "You're too trusting. Not everyone appreciates the way we live here."

That's when I remembered the stick hidden in the bedding. The people living in the grey tent before us had decided to up and leave. What hadn't they appreciated exactly?

Still, I didn't want Phillip going into town. Things had been bad enough when Mum and I were still living there, and no doubt they'd have deteriorated since. "What's in town that we can't make here?" I said. "We've got everything we need."

"Well, medicine for one."

"What's wrong with the old Māori remedies?"

"There are other things." He read off a list written on in the margins of a page pulled from a textbook. "Firelighters, a new chain for the bike, a pair of tweezers…"

"Phillip—"

"I have to go, Viv," he insisted. "Whatever you do, don't lift any water casks, and don't go getting in the pool—we don't know what the mud might do to the baby."

The days were endless without him. I couldn't get any peace. Since ours was the first baby born to the commune in close to a decade, everyone fussed about me. They meant well, but it was stifling.

"Sit down, Viv," they said.

"No reaching."

"Here, let me leave this water here for you."

I sat cross-legged outside my tent and made twelve flax baskets, ground a mountain of pikopiko fronds, and mended a craggy hole in the fly sheet. When I couldn't bear it any longer, I walked up the track to the pool to sit with Mum, only to face a scolding from Marelle the moment I got there. But even she could see I was going stir crazy, so she let me hold the basket while she harvested blood fruit from one of the trees.

A week crawled by.

Phillip had been gone ten days when the fire broke out. I was napping and might have slept on, but the shouts and screams woke me. I emerged from my tent to find the village shrouded in smoke, the plastic smell of burning tents polluting the air. And everything was ready to light up like touchpaper. Already, half the tents were engulfed in flames.

A man staggered from the wreckage of his tent, burning fabric seared into his shoulders, and plunged into the bush, a trail of fiery carnage spreading in his wake. Charging through the commune after him was Cassie, her hair ablaze.

"Cassie!" The smoke choked me. I pointed to a cask of water, but either she couldn't see it, or she was too crazed with pain and fear because she ran right by. Only a few tents remained now, the fire melting them like candyfloss. I'd waited too long. It was closing in. I needed somewhere safe from the fire. Somewhere Phillip would find me.

There's only one place, and it's a kilometre away.

I couldn't just run. The fire would get me first.

Dashing back into my tent, I snatched up a blanket and carried it out to the water cask, where I leaned on the container, tipping it over and drenching the wool. Then, pulling the damp fabric about my head and shoulders, I ducked under the smoke and crouch-galloped clumsily up the track.

My lungs were heaving, and the blanket was dry by the time I reached the pool. I didn't hesitate; dropping the blanket, I stepped in beside Mum and the others, mud squelching through my toes. My shoulders had only just slipped beneath the surface when the fire arrived, hissing and cackling and burning the bush in patches of blurred orange.

I dowsed my hair in the muddy ooze, leaving only my nostrils and eyes on the surface. Still, the hot smoke stung my throat and eyes.

Suddenly, at the edge of the pool, the largest of the blood fruit trees groaned, the sound loud despite the mud caked in my ears. Was it really crying or was it just the sound of the wood drying and splitting in the heat? Cringing, I cradled my belly in my hands and did my best to close my mind to the tree's desolate shrieking. With no escape, the tree dragged its limbs back, away from heat and the creeping, licking tendrils.

Then Marelle was there, running up the scorching track, her bare feet slapping on the dirt and a bucket thumping at her hip.

I dragged my already heavy body up against the sucking mud and lifted my shoulders from the pool. "Marelle," I shouted. "Get in the pool. Quickly!"

But either she didn't hear me, or she chose to ignore me because, taking her plastic bucket, she scooped up a load of mud from the pool and slathered it over the trunk of the tortured tree.

What was she doing?

"Marelle!" I could only sputter.

"I'm here, I'm here," she crooned.

But the fire was here too, and her ministrations were not enough to prevent it from razing everything in its path. The crafty flames bounded from a nearby treetop, jumping across a gap to devour the blood fruit's papery leaves and bite into the white flesh of its trunk.

"No!" Marelle screamed.

She took off her cardigan and slapped at the trunk with the fabric, desperate to beat out the fire. All she did was fan it, the flames leaping and ducking out of reach. It caught her by her hair and in seconds she was burning. I expected her to run, like the man and Cassie had done. Instead, she sank to her knees against the blood tree, her body overrun by fire, and howled.

If her screaming was agony, her silence was worse.

I lifted my eyes, unable to watch any longer. Above Marelle's immolating corpse, blood fruit blistered on their stems, eventually shrivelling to black pits which rained into the pool. I thought I heard my mother moan, but with mud in my ears, I couldn't be sure. I sank further into the warming mud. *Please!* I begged the pool. *Help me! Save my baby.*

My skin tingled and a feeling of calm swept over me. It was if I was stretched out in a hammock, rocking gently, with the cool air lifting my hair and tickling at my neck.

Phillip wrapped his arms about me. "We're going to be a family," he said.

No, that couldn't be right. Phillip had left Māratotō. He'd gone to town to scrounge for supplies. We'd squabbled and he'd gone...

Perhaps I was dying. People have delusions when they're dying, right?

"It's Eremia who has perished," someone whispered in my ear.

"The pool will sustain us yet," another said. "Others will come. We'll survive."

"Yes, yes, Māratotō will go on."

Someone giggled. I was missing the joke. I tried to turn, but I couldn't move.

The trees reached into the pool, their roots smothering me, suckling from me. Soft mud enveloped my limbs, flooding me with warmth. Somehow, the pool could leech away the pain.

Did I want this?

"Why must you insist on being so stubborn, Viv?" my mother said. "Give in. It'll be easier."

No.

A feeble protest because I didn't really mean it. Phillip's bronzed limbs stroked my stomach and my thighs. In the end, I lay my head back on a stone and let myself drift.

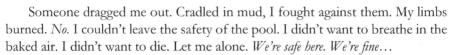

Someone dragged me out. Cradled in mud, I fought against them. My limbs burned. *No.* I couldn't leave the safety of the pool. I didn't want to breathe in the baked air. I didn't want to die. Let me alone. *We're safe here. We're fine...*

Water splashed over me. Water? My eyes flew open.

It was Phillip.

"Viv. Baby, we have to get this mud off of you."

"But it's nice in the pool," I croaked. "Soothing. Get in with me, Phillip. Try it."

Phillip just pursed his lips and threw more water on me. The cold was shocking. I shivered even as warm blood sluiced down my thighs and mixed with the water at my feet. The slurry seeped into the ground. Seeing it, something in me stirred. Letting fluid drain away like that? It was wasteful.

Phillip's slap stung my cheek. "Viv! Come on. Snap out of it!"

Barely able to lift my head, I gazed around us at the devastation.

The trail to the village was nude, the trees scorched to the ground leaving only an occasional black stump, wisps of white smoke rising from them to curl into a grey sky.

I turned, though it took all my strength to do it, my movement slow and sluggish. Why were my limbs so heavy? I felt like a Golem, with ponderous limbs fashioned from rock and mud. At last, I was facing the pool. I shuddered. To one side, near the largest blood fruit, Marelle's body was little more than a pile of dusty charred bones beside the tree's burned-out husk. Three sister blood fruit trees still remained, although their leaves were singed, and the fruit was shrivelled.

"You were lucky," Phillip said. "The wind shifted."

"The baby?"

He shook his head.

I'd lost her. Deep down, I'd already known it. I wasn't going to be a mother after all.

Mother!

I dragged myself to the edge of the pool, plunging my arms back into the mud, searching for her. "Mum!"

"No!" Phillip yanked me back and doused me again with water, washing away the mud.

I struggled against him. "Mum!"

He grabbed me by the chin and forced me to look into his eyes. "The pool has her, Viv. The blood trees have taken her in. She's one of them now. They both are."

I stopped fighting, trembling as the water dripped off me. "You knew?"

He dropped his eyes. Nodded. "These communities," he said. "There's always a contract. I'm so sorry, Viv…" He sank to his knees and buried his face in my stomach. "How was I to know? I'd already promised; made my trade before I met you."

I ran my hands through his hair and held him to me. I didn't blame him. I'd known it too, had done it myself. All those years, just surviving. I'd been so tired that I'd let down my guard in favour of an easier life here at the commune. "We should leave," I said, but I didn't move.

Phillip got to his feet and grasped me by the arms. "Or we could stay? Rebuild. There are more people on the way. It's why I went to town."

"The myth at the water tap? That was you?"

He nodded again.

It all made sense now: the trees, the dizzying spell of their blood fruit, Marelle and the generations of her family who had settled nearby to nourish the pool…and Phillip, Mum, even me—we'd all been complicit.

Above me, the leaves of the blood trees whispered in my ear. The people weren't gone entirely; their lives had simply been extended. They'd evolved into something different. *Something new.*

And my mother had been happy, hadn't she? She was *still* happy.

Phillip's auburn eyes burned into mine. "Viv?"

"What was it like in town?"

"Worse," he said. "The desalination plants have broken down."

I lifted my chin to the blood fruit trees, feeling strangely lighter. "Okay, then. We'll stay."

REMEMBERING FRANK

by Kealan Patrick Burke

Although I had seen him around social media long before that, my first real correspondence with Frank Errington was over ten years ago when he signed up for my newsletter. Something I grew to appreciate about Frank was that if I announced a new book, he ordered it on blind faith. If I did a subscription drive or giveaway, his was always one of the first names to appear on the signup form. If I floated an idea for feedback, his voice was always among them. Whenever a new book came out, he was often one of the first to review it. And while his reviews of my work were invariably positive, the emails he sent to me, in which he went on at greater length and on a more personal level about what he loved about the books, often kept me motivated when my drive was at its lowest. That was something else that struck me about him: despite being more passionate about books and the business of reviewing than almost anyone else in the indie community, I don't think he was ever truly aware how much his passion meant to us, the writers. And when he wasn't validating our efforts with kind words of praise, he was offering constructive criticism to help make the next book better. He would always do such in a manner suggesting he didn't think it appropriate, that he might be crossing a line, when nothing could have been further from the truth. When someone is that well-read and has that passion about books, you ignore their critique at your peril. I learned to trust his instincts to the point that I often called upon him for assistance when a book was not yet ready for public consumption. His input proved invaluable, and it galls me that I'll never get the chance to properly express to him how much that meant to me.

But Frank could be a crank too. I rarely heard him talk about social issues, politics, religion, etc., but one could glean a modicum of his feelings on certain subjects by either his blunt refusal to engage, or his comically cryptic responses to my social media posts in which I exercised no such restraint. Sometimes I got the sense I was exasperating him by being silly, or by trying too hard to be relevant on Facebook (the bane of many a writer these days). I got the sense he'd have been quite content for me to delete all social media apps and just get back to the business of writing rather than wasting my time arguing with strangers. I think he was probably right. Rather than use his own online presence for popularity or jousting with trolls, Frank was there to connect with the writers and readers he liked. He was there for books, always and forever, and I admire that a great deal about him.

When I heard he was sick, I do as I often do, and wished him well while assuming he would be fine. Any real concern was offset by his trademark joviality and good humor, even while acknowledging that he had found himself in a rather precarious situation. I monitored his updates with increasing worry, and then for a while it seemed, no news was good news.

Until it wasn't.

I was sorrier about Frank's passing than I can adequately express here. When you find someone who shows so much unbridled passion for your work, they transcend the mantle of mere reader. In the end, I thought of him as a friend, and the subsequent outpouring of grief and affection for him in the wake of his death shows I was far from alone in feeling that way. He was a welcome and valued member of our community, and one I still think of every time I open the Excel document where I keep a small but precious list of reviewers I trust to be fair and objective about my books. Although Frank's gone, I can't bring myself to remove his name from that list. To me, he's out there somewhere, still reading, still reviewing, and maybe shaking his head in frustration whenever I write a line he doesn't like or push a story in the wrong direction or tell an online troll where to stick his opinion.

Mostly, I think of him among endless tomes of his beloved books, smiling, in a library with no closing time.

LIMINAL

by Alan Baxter

As I raced from the cab this morning I had no idea it would be my last taste of fresh air. I may have paused to savour it otherwise. Gail always told me I rushed through life like I was trying to reach the finish line instead of putting the end off for as long as possible. *You'll race yourself into an early grave, and you'll still lose.* I'd laughed at that, assumed it was the nagging anyone would expect from their wife. Now? Now I miss her so much it hurts.

As I bolted through security, carry-on only as usual, my watch showed I had seven minutes. I ducked and weaved through departures, people scowling and muttering in my wake, but made it to the gate with four minutes to spare. The brunette guarding the air bridge smiled, her uniform so neatly pressed she looked like a shop mannequin.

I'd made it. I may have been rude to Gail, told her to get off my back, stop telling me to live life and not take work so seriously. I paid the bills, didn't I? And she'd winced at that, snapped, *Screw you!*, because she relied on my wage. But I was the one who told her to pursue her creative dreams. Maybe I resented that a little, after all. *Screw you, too, love*, was my response, and I ran for the taxi, not even a kiss. My lips are cold with its absence now.

But here I was. Even if I was more curt with the taxi driver than necessary, insisting he drive faster, skip the yellow lights, because I had a damned important flight to catch. His face had darkened, *I'm not breaking the law because you're late, buddy.* And we sat in icy silence as I willed the traffic to part, the lights to change, hating him.

I look back now and remember that with shame. Have I always been such a dick? Probably.

People have feelings, Gail used to remind me, so often it became almost rote. Implying along with it that maybe I didn't.

Then the brunette, maintaining her smile, said, "This boarding pass is invalid, Sir."

"What?" I stared, confused, unable to process the words for a moment. "What do you mean invalid?"

"This is not an acceptable boarding pass."

I grabbed my phone back, checked the details, the date. It was all correct. I tapped up the email itinerary and confirmation, turned the screen to show her.

She leaned forward, read a moment, then stood straight. Still that damned plastic smile locked in place. "It's not valid." I drew breath to argue, but she went on. "Perhaps go to the help desk at the end of this hall, near security, and ask them."

I looked at my watch. "The flight closes in three minutes."

She looked through me, as though I were no longer there and asked the next person in line to step up.

Stunned, I sprinted to the end desk with a sign above that read INFORMATION.

"I'm in a real hurry. I must catch this flight, I have an incredibly important meeting in Melbourne, but the woman up there said my pass is invalid."

The man at the counter, young and chiselled, sandy hair close-cropped, nodded and smiled. He took my phone and perused it. "She's right. This is not valid."

"It says right there it's for flight QS459. That flight is on the departures board, look! It says 'Gate closing.' I have to get that flight."

"I'm sorry, Sir. Maybe take this up with your travel agent."

"My travel…what?" Frustration burned inside me. "I booked online with WebFlight. I always do, dozens of times a year. I spend half my life in airports, and I've never had a problem. The flight is about to close!"

The man nodded, rictus smile. "It's always best to arrive at the airport with plenty of time in hand."

Anger overrode any politeness and I yelled, "I want to see your manager, right now!"

He said pleasantly, "Yes, Madam?"

An elderly lady, impeccably dressed, stepped forward, stood right beside me, so close I could smell her shampoo. "Hello, dear. The loudspeaker said my flight to Hobart has been delayed, but I missed the rest."

The man leaned forward and pointed. "Can you see the big screen up there? It'll be updated with all the gate and time details, so just keep an eye on that. Hopefully the delay won't be too long."

"Will you please get your manager, right now!" My voice was loud, braying, but neither of them so much as blinked. Gail's words echoed in my brain, *I'm surprised more people don't just ignore you when you get so abrasive.* Abrasive! It stung then, but here it bore an altogether different hurt.

I looked around, watched people milling about, lining up, going about the usual business of an airport. Not one of them spared me a glance.

I briefly caught the eye of a young man in shorts and t-shirt strolling by. "Can you believe this?" I said, desperate for someone to acknowledge the ridiculousness of my situation.

He half-smiled, raised a slight shrug, then frowned. He looked left and right of me, no longer meeting my gaze, then shook his head and walked on. His frown melted away within a couple of steps.

I turned a slow circle. The departures screen no longer showed flight QS459. I'd missed it. I'd miss the meeting, which meant we'd lose the account. Which meant I would probably lose my job. *Last chance*, O'Reilly had told me. Too many deals I hadn't been able to close. I worked so damned hard, but perhaps I'm just no good at it after all. I deflated utterly. I saw Gail's smile in my mind's eye, a little bit *I told you so* and a little bit *You should try to slow down, be nicer.*

I walked slowly to a bar in one corner, *Murphy's* in yellow neon above a falsely dim interior. It was almost deserted, just four or five hardened drinkers having pre-lunch, pre-flight beers. I sat heavily onto a bar stool and when the bartender looked over, I said, "Double Jack Daniels on ice, please."

He nodded. "You got it."

I stared at my hands resting on the bar, fingers interlaced. I'd have a drink, take a moment, then go and fix this. Screw the expense, I'd simply buy a new ticket, right there at the check-in desk, for the next available flight to Melbourne. Surely it would only put me a couple of hours behind at most. I'd ring Cindy Bellaver and give her a sob story she couldn't resist, tell her I was so sorry and I would be there soon and the meeting would go ahead as planned. I hadn't lost the account yet.

Where was my drink? I looked up, saw the barman standing not one metre away, staring into space.

"Hey, mate. Did you forget my JD?"

He ignored me. I stood up, moved to stand right in front of him, staring into his pale green eyes. "Mate! My drink?"

He looked suddenly to his left and smiled. "Yes, madam?"

A woman with skin like polished mahogany, wearing a tailored business suit and high heels, approached the bar. "Pinot grigio, please, whatever's your best."

"You got it." He turned and poured the drink right away, sat it on a coaster in front of her and made casual small talk, ignoring me completely. Fear settled in my gut. Gail, what should I do now?

"Can you not hear me?" I demanded. "See me?"

My heart began to race, my breath came shallow and sharp. Neither the barman nor the woman so much as glanced at me. I reached out, poked her in the upper arm with some force, one index finger jabbing in, but I hardly felt her. Without breaking stride in her conversation with the barman she absently brushed over the spot with one well-manicured hand.

In a daze, I walked back out into the main concourse, hundreds of people wandering in all directions, and yelled at the top of my voice, "WHAT'S HAPPENING?"

A few heads turned, but none caught my eye and all looked away again, indifferent. I felt cold and lost, all I wanted was Gail's arms around me. I hadn't had a hug when I left either, too busy, too late, too rude. Her parting shot, *Screw you!* and a door slamming. That lack was like a hole in me.

Then I spotted the shadows.

Formless, undulating blobs of darkness. I thought perhaps anger, frustration, was causing issues with my vision. Maybe a headache coming on, and who could be surprised by that? When I turned to look, nothing was there. I looked away and saw them again, bulging from the high metal beams of the atrium ceiling, from angles where walls met. If I looked directly at them, nothing. But from the corners of my eyes, the edges of my peripheral vision, they were undeniable, bleeding and swelling in. And from whatever angle I looked, they all seemed to be reaching for me.

I chose to ignore them, and ignore the fearful nerves rippling through me. I needed to get things sorted out and went back through security, over to the Qantas main desk. I stood for a moment as the woman there seemed to be reading her monitor. After a few seconds, I cleared my throat. Loudly. Nothing.

"Excuse me!" My voice was another shout, my cheeks reddened at the brashness, but she didn't so much as blink.

I drew breath to shout again, thinking next I would reach over to shake her by the shoulder, when she looked up with a smile and said, "Can I help you?"

"Oh, thank goodness! Listen, I really need—"

"I was wondering if there was a chance to get an earlier fight?"

I turned so fast I staggered. Right behind me, almost pressed against me, stood a tall man, late 50s or so, in jeans and jumper, tan leather boat shoes. His bald head glistened under the fluorescents. I sidestepped, appalled at his invasion of my space, but knew he had no idea I was there. Neither did the woman behind the desk.

I moved back a little, on the edge of tears. As I turned again, I saw another swelling bubble of darkness rising behind the woman's chair. When I snapped my eyes back it was gone, but I knew I hadn't imagined it. I walked out into the busiest part of the departures hall, where passengers headed into the security area and through to the gates. I stood erect and stationary, right in the path of the moving crowd. Not one person caught my eye, but not one bumped into me either. They seemed to drift a little left, a little right, oblivious, like water around a rock. I began trying to collide with someone, anyone, but they always slipped by. I reached out to push or poke, but my hand made no contact with anything. It was like trying to grab a sunbeam. Horrified, I ran for the exit doors.

I skidded to a stop when they didn't open.

Trembling in near-panic I waited, and soon enough someone approached from the other side. The doors slid open and I bolted through. A wall of cold, icy enough to snatch my breath away, tore through me and my vision blurred momentarily. As I regained my equilibrium, I found myself facing the departures hall, just inside the doors. I tried again and again at three different exits, all with the same result.

I was overcome with a crushing weight of guilt, remembering Gail and our words as I rushed from the house. Why had I been so rude? I could just as easily have hurried out with a kind word instead of a harsh one, paused for that last hug. And I didn't even pat Wesley. I missed my beagle in that moment with a physical ache that made me gasp.

I collapsed onto the floor near the exit I couldn't use, and I wept. I had no recourse, no idea what to do. No one saw me, heard me, could even touch me. My world reduced to one busy, noisy, artificial building. As I lifted my face from my palms, I caught glimpses of those bulging shadows again, bigger now, far bigger. They hung pendulous above me, swelled from every corner like fungus in vibrant bloom, only they were so black. More than that, they were an absence of light, of colour. An absence of everything. Wherever I looked appeared normal and mundane, but at every peripheral point the cold darkness loomed.

And here I am. Before long those shadows will surround me. And then what?

So I'm writing it all down, because what else is left? I can't feel the floor beneath me any longer, sound is becoming muffled. It seems all I can touch is what I brought in with me, my small carry-on messenger bag and its contents. So I tap furiously at my iPad and I'm aware of those smooth and globular arcs of darkness approaching from every side. I don't imagine anyone will find this, but when there's no time left I'll throw it away from myself and maybe someone will stumble across it.

I want to scream Gail's name in the hope someone hears me. I want to fill this hole inside me with her love, find a way to stop up the howling void where my heart should be. Even the brush of a stranger's hand would be a balm, but there's nothing. Just the encroaching darkness.

As I type these words, staring hard at the brightness of my screen, it's almost at my toes, inches away. Cold emanates from it, such bone-deep, all-consuming cold.

It's only millimetres from me now.

If anyone finds this iPad, please tell Gail I lov

SUBLIMINAL

by Shane Douglas Keene

For Frank Errington.

Across the silent threshold of
transition, I am breath,
a sound you don't hear,
an idea that isn't yours,
a poignant, unexpected
memory of near things
far from you now

but maybe not as far as
you think, when you hear
that whisper, see that shadow,
feel that chill and think,
"ghost," it may be me,
no ghost at all

subliminal I, stardust and
memories, and so, so many
tales to tell;

let me whisper them to
you.

NOBODY'S DAUGHTER

by John McIlveen

oster Square, despite its name, is triangular in shape. The plot of grass acts as a median in our small city of Riverside, Massachusetts, separating a variety of buildings—the post office, the town hall, and a five-story, nondescript business center. A tribute to a forgotten historical figure, the square is adorned only by two Revolutionary-period cannons, two benches, four large, neglected flower urns, and a statue. It is well tended and attended by humans and pigeons alike. All in all, Foster Square is nothing special…except for the statue. The statue makes it special.

It is a life-size rendering of a young woman seated on the ground, arms held out before her, palms up as if in meditation, her legs folded beneath her to her right. Her dress, modestly draped over her knees, speaks of spring. Her fine features, full lips, hair flowing mid-back in a slight wave, offer softness to the exquisitely carved black granite. Her beauty is not that of goddesses or princesses, but of suppleness and youth: the all-American girl.

A small commemorative plaque on the base reads *"Nobody's Daughter."*

She arrived four years ago, on a Saturday, with no celebration but for a brief article in the weekly paper. The town accepted the anonymous gift, for she was tasteful and added beauty to the otherwise ordinary square.

I often have lunch on Foster Square, save for inclement days. I am a loner. I overhear conversations about the origin of the statue, or as to who the young lady is. They amuse me. Most are off the mark, others painfully close, none of them fully accurate.

For the true story, we must backtrack fourteen years to a young man named Ammar Sardell. At sixteen, Ammar was bright, adventurous, and mildly rambunctious. He walked the line, though the opportunity to veer to either side reared often for him and his friends, Chris Tremblay and Jimmy Ruiz. All three lived in the same mid-town tenements converted from abandoned mill buildings two decades earlier.

Always open to adventure, they often searched old structures or tried to impress one another at parkour, an activity that the more daring took to an extreme, often falling—sometimes from great heights—with painful or fatal results. Fortunately, Ammar and his friends were not so foolish.

One bitterly cold evening in November of 2003, Ammar, Chris, and Jimmy, tired of watching Comedy Central, moved to the basement of the tenement to waste time and smoke a couple of joints. The boiler room door was secluded in a darkened alleyway at the rear of the building. Though locked, Jimmy could quickly manipulate the door using a switchblade. Jimmy was not only his name but also his talent; a sad portent into a future of repeat stays at Massachusetts Correctional Institute – Concord for forced entry.

The three boys darted inside, intent on the storage room where management stockpiled furniture, decorations, and office surplus; a comfortable place to do little. They bustled through the boiler room, weaving around pipes and rumbling machinery, but Ammar caught sight of something that made him pause and backpedal.

Seated on a piece of cardboard beside a large water heater was a young woman, legs splayed and back to the wall. Her hands palms-up on her legs, her eyes closed as if afloat in a state of enlightenment. She wore an oversized, thick winter coat and a tattered woolen hat pulled low over her ears. Ammar stepped closer. He recognized her from somewhere or sometime.

"Hi?" he said.

Nothing.

"What the hell, Sardell? Come on!" Came a distant voice.

Hesitant, Ammar watched her.

"Just go," she said, emotionless, no room for a response.

Ammar went.

Ammar returned shortly after midnight; images of the girl had hijacked his thoughts and claimed his sleep. He breached the door in reasonable time—but with less dexterity than Jimmy—and entered the heat and clamor of the boiler room. Safety lights nestled high amidst pipes and conduit dispersed conical shafts reminding him of UFO retractor beams.

He returned to the water heater to find her still there, eyes closed, a depleted backpack as a pillow. Her stillness ignited a spark of fear within him until she hitched, shaking her body, and freeing his breath. Her thin, dirt-streaked face was pretty, freckled across the cheeks and nose, and again begged recollection.

A discarded Taco Bell wrapper lay near her leg. He had the impression it was retrieved, not purchased, and a profound sadness swept over him. Ammar left and soon returned with two bottles of water, four slices of American cheese, an orange, and two apples. He left the offering beside her and returned home.

She preoccupied his thoughts throughout the night and during the following day, making school and communication difficult. At work he stocked shelves and faced cans, garnering accolades from his boss for not socializing. He begged off hanging with Chris and Jimmy.

"I feel like shit, man," he lied, and hurried home.

She was not there that day, nor for the next six days, but late the following Saturday evening as Ammar walked home from work, he noticed her moving purposefully down the dim alleyway. She paused at the boiler room door and then entered the building.

Ammar followed. He triggered the door latch, and with light steps, made his way to the water heater.

"Shit!" she said when Ammar appeared. She hastily pushed something between the wall and the water heater.

"Hi," Ammar said, maintaining a buffer between them so not to intimidate her, but also for escape if perchance she turned feral.

She stared warily, her eyes seeming to cycle in and out of focus…and then a flicker.

"Hey Amma-what-cha-face," she said, offering a lackadaisical wave.

"You know me?"

"Fuck, yeah. Saint A's. You were a skinny little shit. Taller now but still skinny. From Arabia or something."

Saint Augustine's school. It seemed so long ago, another lifetime, though it had only been three years. A better place and time before the planes hit the towers and his father took off to parts unknown, foreclosing on their American dream.

His mother had lost her job when the semiconductor industry crashed. She was never able to match her previous esteemed position and was forced to mop floors and swab toilets in office complexes, burying her self-respect deep inside to fester like a tumor. They moved to *The Mills* and he transferred to public schooling.

"Afghanistan," Ammar corrected.

"Whatever."

She was drunk or high and Ammar experienced a blend of sympathy and revulsion. She freed a half-smoked cigarette and a lighter from her coat pocket and lit up. He studied her brown eyes, her freckles, and a memory of a younger, fresher, and much rounder cheeks arose. Her beautiful face, once plump with adolescence, now reduced to this drawn visage, was utterly heartbreaking.

"Wait, you're Selene Carras!" Ammar barked, unable to govern his surprise.

"Shocking, huh?" Selene looked away. "Smack…it seduces you and makes you ugly."

"You're not ugly, just…thinner."

Selene shrugged. "You bring me food the other night?"

Ammar nodded.

"You expect a blowjob or something?"

Ammar had often fantasized about it, but not in this situation. "No, I just figured you were hungry."

"Really?" She pinned him with curious eyes and he wondered if she was insulted or grateful.

"I'm not like that," Ammar said.

"You gay?"

"No."

She studied him at length. "Thanks," she said sincerely. "Now get the fuck out of here so I can ride."

"Do you have to?"

"Try and stop me," Selene said.

Ammar returned the next day. Although Selene was gone she tormented his thoughts. At Saint A's, she had been a year ahead of him, but very much in his field of vision. She had seemed an infectiously happy child of wealthy parents, the personification of youth and spirit with her mile-wide smile and effervescent personality. Boys liked her and girls envied her.

Near the water heater, under the edge of the cardboard, he found a discarded orange syringe. He crushed it under his sneaker.

What had happened to her? Where were her parents?

Selene took the rotisserie chicken and bottled iced tea Ammar offered her. It was nearly a week later. He had sensed she'd be there, and if not, the meal would have tasted fine to him.

"Why are you doing this? I'm not looking for sympathy."

Ammar shrugged and pointed to the cardboard on which she sat. "Can I?"

"Suit yourself, hero."

Ammar sat.

Selene pulled a section of skin from the chicken, put it in her mouth and chewed. She wiped her nose, looked around the room as if confused, and then started crying.

Ammar felt useless. He wanted to hold her and comfort her but was afraid she'd think he wanted more. "What can I do for you?" he asked.

"Stay a while. I don't want to be alone."

Ammar obliged, a silent sentry while Selene drifted off, still there when she jerked awake, panicking, short of breath.

"Can you lend me twenty bucks?"

236

Twenty was all Ammar had left before payday and he knew what it would be spent on. He looked at the barely touched chicken, making sure she noticed.

"What for?"

"Woman stuff."

"CVS is down the street. Walk with me and I'll buy it, or I'll go get it for you."

Selene stared at him with sleepy eyes and then lay down, spouting out a melodramatic *Fuck you*.

"Can I ask a personal question?" asked Ammar.

"Do I have a choice?" Selene muttered into her cardboard bed.

"Yes."

She was silent long enough Ammar thought she'd fallen to sleep. "What?" she finally asked.

"Have you tried getting help?"

"For what? My life is perfect." She huffed with derision, then conceded, "No one wants to help me."

"I do," said Ammar.

"There's always a price."

He wiggled his fingers. "No strings."

Selene huffed again. "Right."

"What about your parents?

Selene snorted. "What about them?"

"Where are they? If I remember, they were wealthy."

"They're alive and well, living out their plastic fantasy in Castle Carras." Selene sat up and slumped against the wall, her arm draped over a metal junction box at the base of the water heater.

"You don't get along with them?"

Selene's expression emphasized how foolish his question was.

"What went wrong? You seemed so happy at Saint A's."

"Nothing *went* wrong that wasn't always wrong," she sneered. "Tricked you all, didn't I?"

"What happened?"

"Long story, talking about it won't help. Go away now, I'm tired and need my beauty sleep." She lay down again. "Gonna change the world tomorrow."

"When will you be back?" Ammar asked.

"I don't know."

"Come back tomorrow night."

"Why?"

"I want you to."

She opened one eye. "Why?"

"Promise you will."

"Go away."

Ammar waited until Selene was snoring lightly, her arms and legs twitching from inner energy or demons. He retrieved a throw pillow from the storage room, gently lifted Selene's head, and slid it beneath.

She watched him as he left the room.

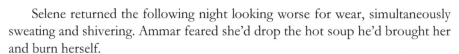

Selene returned the following night looking worse for wear, simultaneously sweating and shivering. Ammar feared she'd drop the hot soup he'd brought her and burn herself.

"Why do you care?" Selene asked.

"I lived in Afghanistan until I was eleven. When war and death surround you, you do anything to stay alive. I don't understand why you do this…*to yourself?*" He gestured to her arm. "Life is valuable. You are valuable. You don't deserve to live this way…or die this way."

"Maybe I do." She sipped, clutched her stomach, and setting the soup down, grimaced.

"You okay?"

"Hardly," she said, teeth clenched. The pain subsided and she smiled—the first in the two weeks since he'd found her. It was sweet, heartwarming, and Ammar was relieved her addiction hadn't progressed to where her teeth had started falling out. A glimmer of hope.

"Have you tried going home?"

She raised a shaking hand and pulled her hat off to reveal greasy, stringy hair.

"Tried once, can't now. His majesty changed the locks."

"Because of you?"

"I stole money…almost a thousand."

"What for?"

Selene gave him a look that asked *really?* "Before that, he said I'd left the family in shambles, ruined the good Carras name, and then he slammed the door in my face."

"Why?"

"Because I did. Got picked up for prostitution. Got to make a living, you know." She shrugged it away but Ammar knew she was watching his reaction. It was a gut punch, not because he hadn't expected it, but because the mental imagery was so painful. "I was seventeen. They caught me with a high-profile lawyer. He was an acquaintance of my father's, but he didn't know me…at least at the time. They never mentioned his name in the paper. I was released to the street."

That she talked about it so easily showed the depths to which her self-respect had fallen. She wiped her nose and clenched her stomach again.

"Still care?" she challenged.

"Yes." He knew there was more to it. "How'd you end up on the street the first time?"

"I ran."

"Why?"

"My father slapped me across the face…hard. I thought he snapped my neck."

"What'd your mother do?"

"Like always, cowered and sniveled like a dog."

"She didn't protect you? What about your brother…Mark?"

Selene released a loud and sharp laugh; a gunshot. "Ha! He's why my father slapped me." She tucked her chin to her chest and mimicked in a deep voice, *"How dare you accuse your brother of such…rubbish?"*

Another gut punch.

"What did he do?" Ammar asked, knowing the hideous truth.

"Raped me," Serene said, blasé—as if she had said *he crossed the street.*

Mark Carras, everybody's buddy. Solid bodied with chiseled handsome features…beautiful on the surface, repugnant beneath.

"Your fucking brother?" Disbelief and outrage contorted Ammar's face.

"Precisely, but he preferred blowjobs."

Ammar stared at her, aghast. "He did it more than once?"

"A hundred, two hundred, a thousand times…as long as I can remember. It's not something you keep track of. He's seven years older than me. He had plenty of time."

No fucking wonder she shoots up, Ammar thought. He wanted to hurt Mark Carras and the hateful people who had parented them. How did they not know what was happening under their roof, or was denying it easier than dealing with it? It seemed *too* bizarre and Ammar felt a fragment of doubt, but the broken soul slumped against the wall made it believable.

"I'm sorry they did this to you." He hoped she recognized his sincerity.

She pulled a battered pack of Winstons from her pocket, jiggled a torn cigarette from it, threw it to the floor, freed another, and lit up. She blew smoke toward the ceiling. "Shit happens."

"It's not right."

"Which matters, how?" She dug at a hangnail.

"You be here tomorrow?" he asked.

"I don't know, hero," she said, drowsy.

"Maintenance doesn't usually come in weekends," Ammar said.

Her eyes cycled between agitation and exhaustion until they closed.

The horrors Selene had suffered tormented Ammar through the night and he fought the urge to check on her. Despite her being eighteen, he had embraced a sense of responsibility for her and feared she would go in search of another fix. He tossed and turned enough to awaken his mother in her bedroom across the apartment; not easy since she would collapse into bed each night under the weight of total fatigue. He felt guilty. She was scheduled to work seven to three on Sunday and was gone when he arose at eight.

Ammar dressed, brushed his teeth and hair. He scanned the refrigerator, grabbed a leftover burrito, took two bites and tossed it, noting never to eat burritos again after brushing.

Multiple scenarios played out as he headed for the basement: Selene gone, Selene blitzed on smack, Selene with a man, Selene lifeless. He pushed the thoughts away.

What he did find was Selene lying on the floor, her body shaking, and her face drenched in enough sweat to dampen the cardboard beneath her. A puddle of vomit near her head also clung to her hat and matted her hair. Ammar was no authority on addiction, but he knew what he was seeing. It had been two to four days since she had last shot up.

Ammar knelt and gently rested a hand on her.

"Ffffuuuccckkk! My fucking head. Don't touch me," Selene croaked.

"You're having DTs," Ammar said.

"No fucking shit," she said between rapid breaths. "I need some candy, just a taste. Get me some, please. Just this once."

"I don't have money," Ammar said. Not entirely true, but he had no intention of feeding her craving, not that he'd know where to find any.

"You said you care. You don't fucking care or you'd get me some."

"Sorry, can't do it."

"Then just kill me, pleeese!"

"Can't do that either."

"You're an asshole. I hate you."

Ammar rose and headed for a paper towel dispenser near a utility sink.

"Don't fucking leave me!" Selene demanded.

Ammar smiled despite himself, returned and gently wiped vomit from her face. She pulled away but then let him press the cool paper towel to her forehead. He remained with her for two hours, fearing maintenance workers would show up and formulating an explanation in case they did.

Selene drifted in and out of a troubled sleep. Ammar wanted to do something for her, but being sixteen and financially limited didn't present a lot of opportunities. He couldn't take her to a movie or a meal looking the way she did, not that she'd eat anything.

"Hey," she croaked.

"Hi," said Ammar.

"This sucks."

"I can't even guess. You impress me."

She rolled her eyes. "I puked?"

"A little."

"Oh, God, I'm fucking disgusting. How can you stand looking at me?"

"I've seen you looking better," he admitted. "Hey, I work four to eight today, my mother works until four. Come up to the apartment and hang for a while."

"I don't think your momma would like catching you with a whore." Selene laughed, dry and raspy, as if her laughter had sat idle too long and had rusted. She rocked in place, lightly kneading her arm.

"Don't call yourself that," Ammar said, but she was right. His mother was devout. If she found a woman in their apartment who'd been arrested for prostitution, she'd have him doing Salat at the mosque in minutes. "Nothing personal, but I figured you'd like to shower, maybe sit after and watch TV."

"Do I smell bad?"

She reeked of sweat, vomit, and addiction, but he had acclimated to it. "You don't smell good, but I've smelled worse."

"What the fuck. Help me up…slowly." She extended her hand.

Ammar led her to the fourth-floor apartment, getting curious glances but passing no one he recognized.

Selene entered the bathroom and closed the door behind her. "Can I take a bath instead?"

"Of course."

"You have a washer and dryer?" she called from the bathroom.

"Yeah."

Ammar retrieved his robe from his bedroom, returned to the bathroom and timidly knocked. Selene opened the door and stood before him, naked and unabashed. Ammar reflexively averted his gaze from her as she dropped her soiled clothes into a pile at his feet.

"There's more in my backpack," she said. "Can I?"

"Yeah." He held the robe out to her, which she grabbed.

He stole a glance as she closed the door. She was painfully thin, childlike. Anger seared in him, toward her father, her mother, her brother, at the bastard lawyer and anyone else who had ever hurt her. He loaded her clothes into the washing machine set behind billfold doors near his bedroom. Her small collection of possessions was as heartbreaking as everything else about her.

He sprawled on the couch and watched *Lizzie McGuire* and *The Proud Family*, swapped the wash to the dryer and watched half an episode of *Kim Possible* before Selene emerged from the bathroom. She dropped onto the couch beside him, looking smaller than ever in Ammar's oversized robe, a towel wrapped around her head like a turban. He smiled.

"Welcome back. I was ready to send a search team."

"I had to scrub the tub. Had a ring like Saturn."

Again, her bluntness knocked him off center. "Feeling better?" he asked.

"I feel like shit, but I feel like clean shit, so that's better. The bath helped a lot," she said, holding his gaze for the first time since he'd brought her the soup.

"Your clothes should be done soon."

"Sending me packing already?"

"No! Just saying. My mother doesn't come home until four."

She smiled and removed the towel from her head, her arm visibly trembling. She shook her head, fanning her hair out, increasing her appearance from twelve to fifteen years old. Two small lesions near her lips and a mild darkness beneath her eyes confirmed her addiction, yet were evident of a relatively new dependency…as addictions go.

"In the bathroom cabinet, there's—" Ammar struggled.

"What?" Selene pressed.

"You know…woman things. You said—"

"I lied," she admitted, shrugged. "I haven't had a period in months. Benefits of smack. You have a brush?"

He retrieved one of his mother's brushes, thoughts of lice crossing his mind. He'd boil it once Selene left. She ran the brush through her hair with a quivering hand as they shared small talk, the *Power Rangers* flickering on screen.

"In another life, I would do this five hundred times every morning," she said.

Ammar looked at her familiar spray of freckles. She was still pretty, but the wholesome beauty had dampened. She set the brush on the couch and turned to him.

"We can fuck if you want," she said.

A flicker of panic and a stream of thoughts sped through Ammar. *What do I do? What if mom comes home early? How do I explain a woman wearing nothing but my robe?* She spilled a drink? She puked? At least that was somewhat true.

He had often deliberated when and how his first sexual encounter would transpire, and while the prospect was certainly appealing, Selene's condition, childlike appearance, and his mother's many warnings about STDs were huge deterrents.

Seeing his hesitance, Selene said, "Yeah, I don't blame you."

"No! I want to. You're very pretty, but if it happens, I want to be sure it's what we want and that you don't feel obligated."

She searched his eyes. "Are you for fucking real?" she asked.

"I think so."

"Will you hold me for a while at least?" she asked, almost plaintive.

Selene curled against Ammar and he held her, reverberations of her dependency humming through her and into him.

"You know," Selene said, breaking a long silence. "Right now, at this moment, I feel like I could kick this thing and someday maybe have a normal life."

"I'd like that for you. I think you can," Ammar said. "How'd you get started?"

"Mother's Vicodin. Heavy-duty stuff, ten milligrams of hydrocodone per tablet. Life was warm and fuzzy on *vikes*, not so much once the bottles were empty." She rubbed her forehead and then took Ammar's hand. "Vicodin's hard to find on the streets. Heroin and meth are easy. You don't need a prescription. Someone told me it gave the same high."

"Does it?"

"Yes and no. It's the best-worst feeling ever. I love it, I hate it. I don't recommend it."

When the sweats and shakes again took ahold of Selene, she lay down, restless, agitated, often crying out. "I want to rip off my skin," she groaned, fingers clawed.

Slightly after noon, she leveled out. Ammar made peanut butter and jelly sandwiches, and Selene ate a quarter of hers with mouse-like nibbles before her stomach knotted. It was the most Ammar had seen her eat since he'd found her and it encouraged him.

At two-thirty, Selene carefully dressed and stuffed her few extra items in her backpack. "I need to go—before I can't," she explained.

Ammar followed her to the parking lot where she kissed him sweetly.

"See you soon, hero?" she said.

"Hey, I need a favor!" Ammar said.

"What?"

"If you get the urge to use, don't, okay? I promised to hang with Chris and Jimmy after work, but I'll be home later. Promise you'll come back here. I'll help you through it."

"I know you will." She kissed him again and walked away.

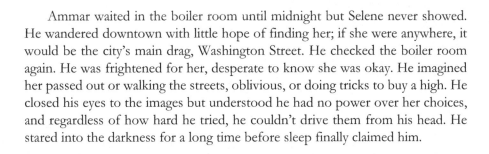

Ammar waited in the boiler room until midnight but Selene never showed. He wandered downtown with little hope of finding her; if she were anywhere, it would be the city's main drag, Washington Street. He checked the boiler room again. He was frightened for her, desperate to know she was okay. He imagined her passed out or walking the streets, oblivious, or doing tricks to buy a high. He closed his eyes to the images but understood he had no power over her choices, and regardless of how hard he tried, he couldn't drive them from his head. He stared into the darkness for a long time before sleep finally claimed him.

Ammar's mother had already left for work when his alarm woke him. His first thought was of Selene. He had an hour to dress and get to school. He hurried through his morning routine, grabbed his book bag, and sped out the door.

Exiting the apartment complex, he turned for the alleyway between the buildings and froze, panic congealing his legs.

Outside the boiler room door, a police cruiser and ambulance idled, red and blue lights flashing and strobing defiantly. A crowd of onlookers had gathered, crowding yellow barricade tape that read *"POLICE LINE"* and *"DO NOT CROSS."*

Coaxing his legs, he walked and then ran toward the scene. As he neared, he saw a stretcher near the ambulance, covered by a sheet…completely covered.

"No…no, no…no no!" He tried to duck beneath the tape. A police officer stepped in front of him and corralled him backward.

"Please stay behind the line, son," he said, but Ammar surged forward again and the officer grasped his arm.

"No, no!" he said, trying to string his words together. He bounced on the balls of his feet, staring at the small shape outlined beneath the sheet, child-small.

Who else could it be?

The officer spoke to him but Ammar was beyond hearing. Near the doorway, a maintenance man stood looking troubled and pale.

"Roger!" Ammar yelled.

Roger glanced his way and sullenly turned back to the officer, without acknowledging Ammar.

"Wait! Is she dead?" Ammar asked, but he knew. His words got the officer's attention.

"How do you know it's a she?"

"I know her. She's homeless!"

"Wait here. Don't move."

The cop walked to the other officer, spoke, and then both policemen returned. They gently led Ammar away from the crowd and the stretcher, though his eyes couldn't leave it.

"Is it her?" Ammar asked.

"I don't know son, can you tell us who you think it might be?"

"Her name is Selene Carras. She's homeless but it's not her fault."

The officers shared a glance. "Please wait near the cruiser. We may need to ask you a couple questions."

The questions were quick and perfunctory. *How long have you known her? When was the last time you saw her? What? How? Who?* They answered none of Ammar's questions, acting deaf to them. The paramedics loaded the stretcher into the ambulance and drove away, not confirming who lay beneath the sheet. He knew.

Ammar suffered through school and work in a daze, thinking only of the girl he had met a month earlier…now gone forever.

His mother was asleep when he arrived home, but sleep evaded him, not from wondering when he'd see Selene again, but knowing he never would.

He dozed sporadically until his mother's activity dragged him from his stupor. He joined her at the table where she, already in her janitorial garb and kerchief, drank coffee and read the paper.

"You're up early. Can't sleep?"

"No," He leaned to kiss her cheek.

"You okay?" she asked, ever intuitive.

"Yeah."

"Coffee on the stove."

"You know I don't drink the stuff, Mom."

"Forgot you're an alien. You hear about the homeless girl they found dead in the basement?" she asked, seeming slightly animated.

"Yeah, it's freaking sad," Ammar said, hoping she'd mention it no more.

"Poor thing, just looking for a place to stay warm and she gets electrocuted."

"What? What do you mean electrocuted?"

"Says it here." She pushed the paper forward, looking at him oddly. "Daughter of some local bigwig. We clean his offices on Thursdays."

Ammar grabbed the paper. The article buried on page four read:

Woman Electrocuted In
Tenement Basement

The body of a homeless teen was discovered in the basement of a Riverside apartment complex early Monday morning by the complex maintenance head, Roger Demeister. The deceased, identified as Selene Marie Carras, estranged daughter of local financier Alexei Carras, appeared to have inadvertently come in contact with exposed electrical conductors after forcing her way into the building's boiler room. Police Captain Greg Foley said there will be an investigation, but believes no foul play is involved.

Reportedly, Selena Carras had run away from home in 2001 after a family dispute resulting from an arrest. Alexei Carras believed his daughter had fled to the West Coast.

Selena Carras is survived by her parents, Alexei and Dorinda Carras, of Riverside, a brother, Mark Carras, also of Riverside, and a number of aunts, uncles, and cousins residing in Greece. Holland Funeral Home will be handling Services.

Ammar read the article three times, saddened and confused. It was the last line *Holland Funeral Home will be handling Services* that troubled him. Would they be pretentious and insincere enough to put on airs after the way they had abused, neglected, and denied Selene? Would they shower their deceased daughter with traitorous love and provide a beautiful funeral only to impress observers?

Ammar intended to be present at Selene's funeral.

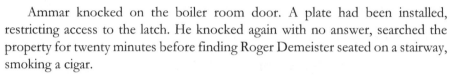

Ammar knocked on the boiler room door. A plate had been installed, restricting access to the latch. He knocked again with no answer, searched the property for twenty minutes before finding Roger Demeister seated on a stairway, smoking a cigar.

"Hi, Roger."

The maintenance man looked at him and nodded. He still appeared pale.

"Ammar, right?"

"Good memory," Ammar said. The only time he recalled talking to the man was the day he and his mother had moved in.

"I remember the names of the people I like...and the people I don't like. You I like. You don't cause trouble."

It was difficult telling Roger's age. He was short with ropey arms, his hair graying at the temple and mostly gone, wrapped around the back of his head like a laurel wreath. He released a stream of cigar smoke from beneath a walrus mustache.

"Thanks," said Ammar. "Roger, can you tell me what happened to Selene Carras yesterday morning?"

"Electrocuted. Fucking shame, poor kid dying like that. Excuse my French."

"I know, but what happened?"

"You know her? You were pretty upset."

So he did notice me, Ammar thought. "She was a friend."

"She was troubled," Roger said.

"She was still a good person."

Roger shrugged. "Fair enough. Stupid shit luck, as far as I can tell. She knocked the junction box cover off the water heater when she tried to sit or something—bumped into the element. She was still holding onto a copper water line when I found her; 277 volts makes every part of you contract. No letting go of that pipe until I tripped the breaker. Pretty much cooked her from the inside out, poor kid."

"Oh God!" Ammar said, choking out a sob. He turned and fled without another word.

Ammar entered the Greek Orthodox Church unnoticed, sat in the last row, and counted seventeen heads in attendance including himself. Selene's casket, a

246

beautiful exhibition of craftsmanship, was a light-colored hardwood, maybe hickory, and polished to splendor. A spray of pink and white roses covered most of the lid. Its opulence was obscene to Ammar and he hoped Selene couldn't see such an insult. Mark Carras was seated in the front row, as broad-shouldered and handsome as Ammar remembered. Alexei and Dorinda Carras sat to Mark's right. The man was solid, a fireplug with granite hair and an emotionless face that appeared to be carved of the same. Dorinda Carras, also emotionless, looked dead inside, a petite husk of a human devoid of life. To Mark's left sat a woman with lustrous hair and an enviable figure, even in black dress. *His wife?* Ammar wondered.

At the conclusion of the service came the next insult, when Mark lined up as a pallbearer.

Ammar followed the procession along a side road on the outskirts of Riverside to a cemetery he never knew existed. He stood back during the ceremony, standing last in the short line of people offering condolences to Selene's remaining family. Ammar stepped before Alexei Carras who met his eyes and offered his hand. Ammar didn't shake.

"Hello," Alexei greeted in his businessman's voice. "Did you know Selene?"

"Better than you did, it seems," Ammar said.

The man's brow furrowed and his hand fell to his side, all professional composure. "Excuse me?"

"She was your daughter," Ammar said.

"Yes."

"No, she was your *daughter!*" Ammar repeated, louder, tears forming at the unfairness of it all.

Dorinda and Mark Carras looked at Ammar. Alexei stood straighter, pulling his shoulders back, but Ammar wasn't intimidated.

"How does this concern you?" asked Alexei, civility gone.

"Why didn't it concern you?" asked Ammar, his voice rising. He pointed at Dorinda Carras. "You knew! You both knew what your son was doing to her, but you hid it and let it continue! All to protect your image!"

"You best leave!" said Mark Carras.

"Why? So no one finds out? She was your sister!" Ammar sputtered. "Your *SISTER!*"

The beautiful woman in black looked at Mark and then at Ammar. Ammar saw Mark Carras' punch coming and ducked from most of it, though he'd probably have a sizable bruise on his cheek.

Dorinda Carras burst into tears. She moved from her husband, striking at his hands as he tried to hold her at his side. Ammar wondered if maybe she didn't know.

"Who the hell are you?" Alexei Carras roared.

"Who the hell are *you?*" Ammar responded. "*Nobody.* You are *nobody!*"

Ammar turned and left the cemetery.

There is a statue downtown on Foster Square, a tribute to a young woman who deserved better. It faces southwest, toward the offices of Carras Financial. I saved a long time to buy it; it wasn't cheap. It's made of polished black granite, meticulously sculptured. Its resemblance to a young Selene Carras is striking. The artist used a photo in my freshman yearbook from when Selene was a sophomore.

I often wait on the park bench until *Nobody* leaves work. He could leave by the back door, but he never does. Sometimes he pauses to look at the statue, other times he walks by, averting his gaze. I've never seen him walk past without looking at *some* point. Some days he looks at me…some days not.

I heard that Nobody's wife left him. Now *he's* an empty, lifeless shell.

Selene's autopsy showed signs of previous use but no opioids were found in her system.

She was clean. How's that for a kick in the ass?

There is a statue on Foster Square

A tribute to Nobody's Daughter…

Who deserved so much better.

REMEMBERING FRANK

by John Palisano

Words have so much power. As writers. As reviewers. As champions of practitioners of both, our literary circle lost a true ally in Frank. His reviews meant so much to so many because you could feel the passion in every word. His was not a love affair of convenience, but of pure joy.

My own friendship with Frank began as with so many others—online. He reached out early, as my first novel was published and released. I was struck at how detailed and thoughtful his reviews were. Not only were his reviews graceful and intelligent, but they remained genuine and encouraging.

For anyone who's endured a harsh review, in person or print, having a person like Frank get behind your work felt like you'd made it. In an era where handicapping and finding things wrong with a book seem to be the go-to stance, Frank lifted and shouted to anyone who'd hear when he'd read something he connected with. I still feel lucky and blessed…and a little bit shy…about a few of the nice things he said about me. Like the time he said he had read my collection twice. Hearing that shocked me, the thought someone would take the extra time to do so. But that was Frank's passion for the horror genre.

What about Frank as a person? I looked back on some of the messages he'd sent me, and his public persona as a reviewer was no act. The same passion he had for books crossed over into Frank as a person. His wisdom about storytelling kept a very fine gray line with his wisdom about people. I'll cherish his notes to me most of all. He was and is a treasure. He's terribly missed.

His body may be gone, but his words…the positive and encouraging words he took time to write and post on so many books…so genuinely strong…are as powerful today as they were while he was with us, and they will stay that way for countless years to follow.

Rest in peace, dear friend. You're missed.

EVERYDAY KINTSUGI:
THE GLORY OF HER BROKEN PARTS

by Mercedes M. Yardley

Her grandfather told April her first lie.

"There is an ancient Japanese art called Kintsugi," he said. "It is when you take something broken and repair it with gold. This turns it into a beautiful thing of even more value. Pottery has been fixed this way for many generations. People are fixed this way, too. Take the flaw and turn it into something better. Can you imagine that, April? Taking the worst part of yourself and working it into something admirable?"

This made April's dark eyes shine. She wanted to be loved in all of her imperfections. She wanted to stand in the glory of her broken parts. Her mother, ever so strict and exacting, railed against her because she wasn't smart enough, wasn't disciplined enough, didn't have skin that glowed with the luminance of pearls and a voice that commanded the oceans. At first April shrank in fear, but then she remembered the promise of Kintsugi.

"I will let the damage become something better," she said aloud, and she drew the horsehair of her bow far too loudly against the violin, and drew her eyeliner on with too heavy a hand. She took off her clothes in front of boys and girls and teachers. She traded her school uniform for something that looked nice on the back of a motorcycle or inside a police car.

Crash crash crash. Break break break. She told lies and stories and pressed false charges and faked miscarried babies. She stole wallets, hearts, social security numbers, and government secrets. She knew that the more she broke, the more she would shine. She destroyed documents. She sabotaged marriages. She sold her soul and intel and the diamond necklace that had been her only birthright.

Her mother's tears were made of gold.

There was a bomb, a terrible thing, that had burned the clothing from her grandfather's back and seared it to his skin. Now there was a new bomb, the ultimate Kintsugi, that would shatter everything apart so it could be mended with so much gold that the mind dazzled.

"I can save all of us, repair mankind completely," April said, her eyes fiery and her hand smashed on the bomb's button. But this is modern-day America, not fifteenth-century Japan, and when you pulverize something as badly as April had done, there are no more parts to gently piece together. You end up with handfuls of rubble. You end up with dust. There's nothing left to repair, and even if there was, this is the age of disposability. You take that chipped piece of pottery and you toss it in the other teeming piles of refuse, and never think of it again.

HUSH, LITTLE BABY

by Rob Smales

I'd just left Jones Memorial with Dicky Carlton—my partner at the time—so we were in the area when dispatch sent out the call. Just lucky, I guess. Anyway, dispatch reported a woman with an infant who wouldn't stop crying, who didn't have a car to get the kid to the doctor. Said she'd sounded kind of young, panicking, the whole nine yards. I gave fifty-fifty odds it was a nothing call. Doctors get them, EMTs do too: first-time mothers who can't get the kid to stop crying and it turns out to be bad gas, or constipation, something like that. They get scared, make the call, and wind up feeling silly about it afterward. Honestly, I like those calls. The relief on their faces when the kid rips a big burp and quiets right down…

We hit the lights and hustled to the address, a run-down apartment building we'd become familiar with. I grabbed the kit when we got there, and Dicky hit the button for number 304—the name beside the bell was *Deal.* The door buzzed, and we were inside and trooping up the stairs—we'd been there before; we knew it was a *really* slow elevator. Not halfway up, I realized the heat in the building was broken—or maybe the super had just turned it off to save money. The January cold had turned the whole place into a big icebox. By the time Dicky pushed open the door on three, I'd already revised my fifty-fifty estimate to something a little more serious. It had to be around forty degrees on those stairs, and cold like that could be bad for the little ones.

The door to 304 opened as we got there, and dispatch had it right: Mrs. Deal couldn't have been more than twenty-two, twenty-three tops. She stepped back to let us into the apartment, and I saw right away she was holding the kid, just a swaddled bundle on one arm with the finger ring of a pacifier sticking out of the little gap at one end.

"Hi," she said as I put the kit down. We were standing in the living-room side of an open kitchen/living room, and she'd put a space heater along one wall that kept the room tolerable. Barely. "Uh, hi. This is kind of embarrassing, but I think I called you guys out here for nothing."

I'd half come to that conclusion already. The pacifier was in place, the kid had obviously stopped crying, and Mom looked a little embarrassed. "Don't worry about it," I said. "It happens. He let out a whale of a burp? Or was it the other end?"

"*She* didn't do either, as far as I know." She rocked the bundle slightly. "She just stopped."

I waited for Dicky to say something, but he was being strangely quiet for Dicky.

"I didn't panic *right* away," she said with a little laugh. "The books all say to wait awhile, to let them cry and they'll usually sort the small stuff out."

"Hey," Dicky whispered. I glanced at him; he was staring at me with a half-frown, obviously sniffing the air.

"But after she hadn't eaten for a week, I started to get nervous."

I took Dicky's hint and sampled the air. In summer, we'd have had the odors of the building: maybe a hundred laundry hampers and the family down the hall frying up some of their world-famous garlic-and-onion goat. With the cold we only had this apartment to deal with, and even then, the scent was deadened, but I caught it. Almost fruity. Rotten. *Bad.*

Then her words hit me.

"Your daughter hasn't eaten in a *week?*"

"Three, actually." The young lady bent to nuzzle into the gap above the pacifier. "You were being a stubborn little stinker, weren't you?"

Oh, God.

"What do you want to do?" Dicky stage-whispered, and his eyes were huge. Dick Carlton could handle any injury the world threw his way, but the crazies freaked him out. I never learned why. I'd seen some pretty fucked-up things in Iraq and knew stress could do funny things to people. There was this one guy over there. A land mine had blown off both of his legs, and he just sat there holding one of them like a teddy bear, telling it about the ball going through Buckner's legs in the '86 World Series while he bled out. Damndest thing. So I understood people sometimes say crazy stuff, but it doesn't mean they're crazy. Dicky, though…didn't get that. He wouldn't even glance at Mrs. Deal, just stared at me, looking ready to bolt. He'd be no help here.

I put my back to the woman, who'd started singing "Hush Little Baby" to whatever was in that blanket. "You go out where she won't hear and get on the radio," I whispered. "Get some cops, but tell them not to come all lights and sirens. She's not violent or anything, so they're just a precaution, okay?"

"Got it," Dicky said, and if not for the singing behind me, I might have laughed at the relief on his face. He moved fast, but paused at the door and looked back, guiltily. "You sure? I mean…" He jerked his chin toward the singing woman. "You gonna be okay with…"

"I'll be fine," I said, and he was gone before I'd finished the third syllable. I turned, and it was just me and Mrs. Deal.

And the baby.

She was still bent slightly, gazing into the swaddling with a little smile on her face. If it had been a painting, the scene could have hung in a museum under the title *Mother with Child*. It wasn't a still life, though: she was sort of dancing as she sang, pausing the song and dipping the bundle like a ballroom partner at the end of every line.

"And if that diamond ring turns brass." Dip. "Mama's gonna buy you a looking glass." Dip. "And if that looking glass gets broke." Dip.

I'd seen mothers do that before—hell, my mother probably did it with me—and for the kid it's like an amusement park ride. Every dip brings little shrieks and laughter. But not this child. The little mother swung her baby with energy, and dipped it with vigor, but that little bundle stayed just as silent and motionless as it'd been since I arrived. I took a breath—and instantly regretted it, tasting the funky fruitiness of the air on the back of my tongue, and knowing what gave it that flavor.

"And if that billy goat gets cross." Dip.

"Ma'am?" I said.

"Mama's gonna buy you a rocking horse." Dip.

"Miss?"

"And if that rocking horse turns over." Dip.

"Miss, may I see the baby?"

She straightened, standing there frozen with her back to me for the space of a breath. Two. Then her voice came quietly, all the bounce gone out of it, like she was trying to lull the child to sleep. "Mama's gonna buy you a dog named Rover." No dip this time. No dance. Mrs. Deal just kept her back to me, the small swaddled thing in her arms out of my view as she crooned quietly. "And if that dog named Rover won't bark—"

"Miss," I interrupted, a little louder. "May I see your baby?"

For a moment, she said nothing. "Why?" She'd said it in that quiet, lulling voice, but there was no inflection, no hint of lift at the end of the word, like it was a question. If she'd put some power behind it, it might have sounded defensive, or even argumentative, but the word came out flat and unemotional. The change from her happy singing, coupled with her absolute stillness, was unnerving. I had a second there when I wished I'd gone out in the hall with Dicky; just hot-footed the fuck out of there and let the cops deal with Deal. But we're here to help people, right? That's the job.

I said, "You called an ambulance for your baby, right? If I'm not going to take her for a ride or anything, then I need to verify that she's all right. Okay?"

"She's stopped crying. She's fine."

She was so still, and that voice hadn't changed. It was really creeping me out. I kept talking, hoping to swing her around toward normal, the way she'd been when she'd opened the door. My voice went bouncy and cheerful, like I was unconsciously trying to show her the way back from wherever she'd gone in her head. I cranked up the bullshit machine.

"Oh, I know. *You* know she's fine, *I* know she's fine, but the folks downtown…look, all they care about is numbers and paperwork. You wouldn't *believe* the paperwork I have to wade through in this job. But you made an official call, so I have to fill out a call response sheet, and it asks on that sheet if I've verified that no one at the scene required medical attention."

She hadn't spoken or looked at me, but she'd turned her head slightly, cocking an ear my way. Anything was an improvement over that damned statue-like stillness.

"Now, if I fill out that sheet saying I *verified* no one needed medical attention and it gets out that I *didn't*—you know, see with my own two eyes sort of thing—it could mean my job. And I really need this job."

She'd turned her head farther, was maybe looking at me from the corner of her eye.

I spread my hands. "So, if you could let me take a look at her—for that stupid form, you understand—I'd really appreciate it."

There. It was total bullshit, but most people don't know anything about the job, just what they see on TV. But I'd turned it into her doing me a favor. We were on the same side, just her and me against the man, so—

"Mama's...gonna buy you...a horse...and...cart..."

She was still using that soft, singing-the-baby-to-sleep voice, and the dip she made was in slow motion and deeper than the others, but it was progress. I was so jittery, though, I jumped when the pacifier fell to the floor with a little *thunk*.

"Got it." I darted forward, scooping up the little piece of pink rubber and plastic. I went past her to the kitchen side of the area and rinsed it off in the sink. When I turned back to her, she'd spun to face where I'd been, blocking my view and keeping herself between me and her silent little charge.

She shuffled in a slow sort of dance again, with that low, slow song. "And if...that horse and cart...fall down...you'll still be the sweetest little baby...in...town..."

I edged toward her, holding out that pacifier like an invitation, some proof I was authorized to be there; like I belonged. But I didn't belong, and we both knew it. At some point her whole world had shrunk to just that frigid little apartment and the tiny bundle in her arms, and it didn't matter if I was holding a med kit or a binky. I was an intruder, and I'd never be anything else.

"So hush, little baby...don't you cry...your daddy loves..."

Her voice trailed off and her shuffling halted again. I waited a few seconds, thinking it was just a long pause, and she'd finish the song. I planned to ask to see the kid again, but instead of another word, Mrs. Deal made a sound. It was a small sound, a little moan in the back of her throat, but it was a sound I'd heard once before. Hearing it again shriveled my stomach.

I'd met a war widow when I got back from the Middle East, a woman who'd come to meet my plane, convinced her letter had been a clerical error. The army makes them all the time, she'd said, transposing a pair of digits in a serial number, or confusing two men with the same last name. So there was no way, just *no way* they'd gotten it right and it was *her* Tommy Murphy coming home in a box. *Her* Tommy Murphy was in a hospital somewhere, or maybe he was just fine and with his unit, but his letters weren't getting through to her for some reason. She knew I'd been in Tommy's unit, and she knew I knew where her Tommy Murphy was. She'd even brought me a picture to verify we were talking about the same Tommy. We were…and so was the army. The sound she'd made right then, when my words knocked down all the little walls she'd built up inside herself and all the grief they'd been holding back suddenly rushed through her in an overwhelming flood, *that* was what came out of Mrs. Deal right then.

Your daddy loves…

I said, very quietly, "Where's your husband, Mrs. Deal?"

She straightened. "He'll be back in a few days." Her voice had lost any sing-song quality, gone spooky flat again. "Most of him. There was an IED, and…anyway, he's coming home. From Afghanistan. They sent a letter."

"I'm sorry, ma'am."

She stepped away and started pacing, bouncing the bundle as if comforting a finicky baby, though not a sound came from that blanket. "It's not even like we're at war," she said, and suddenly she was cheerful again, like she'd been when we'd arrived, though I could see the strain around her dark eyes, hear the ragged edge to her voice. "It was just a *police action*, sort of a silly little thing in the grand scheme. But there was Dennis, getting blown up by a homemade bomb, seven thousand miles from home." She shook her head, and her smile said it was almost funny, but her eyes…didn't. She made an amused little *tss*. "So like him." Those wounded eyes shot to the table, a closed envelope sitting in its exact center. "They sent a letter," she said again, and her tone was anything but flat. She sounded like someone trying to cheer up a pet, or a very young child, where a happy tone is much more important than the message itself.

"When?" I asked.

"Excuse me?"

"When did the letter come, Mrs. Deal?"

"Three weeks ago," she said, and then she went on, her words picking up speed like a little kid running down a hill, going faster and faster because they're already falling and their feet are trying to catch up. "But there are delays—always delays with the army. It's always 'hurry up and wait'—and he won't be home for another week. But that's *fine*, it's all *fine*. Just another week for it to be just me and—"

"So," I interrupted, because unless it's a really short hill, those running kids usually fall, hard, and this little mother looked like she had a hell of a lot of hill in front of her. "The…uh…the letter arrived right about the time your baby stopped feeding?"

She whirled toward me, bundle held tight to her chest. Her mouth dropped open in almost comic surprise, but her eyes burned fever bright. "You know," she said, "that *never* occurred to me before. Of course! How could I have missed something *that* obvious? Especially with all her crying. For three weeks it's been nothing but crying and crying, and there wasn't anything I could do to stop it."

Someone had been crying in this apartment for three weeks, I knew, but I very much doubted it had been whatever was left in that blanket.

"So, the letter," I said. "It made her sad."

"*Very* sad," she said.

"And she cried."

"Cried and cried."

"And she wouldn't eat?"

"Not a drop. But she was still crying, and the books say to let them cry, so that's what I did."

My throat had gone dry, and while I was trying to maintain that bouncy, cheerful *you and me against the man* tone of voice, what came out was far too raspy to qualify. "Well, then, I'll…uh…I'll make sure to include all that in the report. Extenuating circumstances, first-time mother, all that. That's terrific. But still—for that form—may I take a look at your baby? Please?"

She never even blinked at my tone. "Of course!" she said. Game show hosts only wished they could sound as cheerful. "Of course! I'm sorry I called you out here for nothing, but really, I wouldn't want you to get into trouble over this." She stepped toward me, holding out the blanket-wrapped little shape. While her whole face was stretched in a wide, almost desperate grin, the eyes in that face were the eyes of every soldier I'd lied to on my tour through the Middle East; men to whom I was trying to offer comfort, telling them they would make it home. They always knew the truth though.

Her face was offering the lie, but her eyes *knew*.

I looked straight into those eyes as I accepted the little bundle—so light I remember thinking, *Straw! All this time it was just a straw doll!*—and said "Thank you," though I don't think there was actually any sound. I stared into those eyes as I stepped back a pace. Her hands hung in the air between us, thin fingers twitching and grasping, as if without the baby to hold they didn't know what to do. "Thank you," I whispered again. And I looked down.

The eyes staring up at me were huge and dark and round, and far too large for the wizened little face around them. Cheeks that should have been chubby were sunken. Tiny lips that should have been shaping either laughter or cries were stretched back so tightly her white little gums showed. The skin was so thin and fine the sockets in the skull around those eyes were clearly visible. I couldn't tell if this was from malnourishment or if some of it had happened when the little body started to desiccate, the cold in the apartment slowing decomposition enough that the little figure had time to dry out like a steak left uncovered in the fridge.

What I could tell, however, was that this little girl was very, very dead.

"See?" said Mrs. Deal, like a game show host revealing a big prize. "She's just fine." In my peripheral vision her hands reached toward me, trembling fingers already seeking the comfort of that pink blanket. "She's fine." The happy host was still there in her voice, but had started sounding a little less happy, a little uncertain. "Now give her back."

Still staring down into those huge little eyes, I retreated a step. I tried to say something, tried to say *anything*, but the words wouldn't come.

"Give her back," she said, alarm swelling in her voice.

I shook my head and retreated another step, my rump bumping lightly against the sink-edge.

"Hey!" Panic boosted her voice, higher and louder. "She's *fine*! Give her back. *Now*!"

Behind her the apartment door opened and two uniformed cops walked in fast, slowing when she spun to face them, spreading their hands a bit and trying to look nonthreatening. "Mrs. Deal," said the older one. "We're gonna need you to remain calm, okay?"

"What are you talking about?" The game show voice was gone now. She was all panic, all the time. "I called an ambulance, not the police! My baby's fine!"

The cop who was doing the talking looked at me then, raising his eyebrows in a silent, desperate question.

I shook my head.

His eyes closed for a moment, and he took a long, slow breath. "Mrs. Deal, we're going to take care of your baby." Behind him, his partner motioned me toward the door.

I followed his suggestion as Mrs. Deal shouted "My baby's *fine*," moving quietly around the outside of the room rather than walking right past her, staying out of reach. I think she might have started for me when I came into view, but I couldn't look at her. All I know is the cop slid between us, blocking her path as soon as I was past her.

"*Where is he going with my baby?*" she shrieked, but the cop just repeated, as flat and implacable as smooth water, "We need you to remain calm, Mrs. Deal."

Dicky was waiting in the hall. "I heard almost the whole thing," he said. "I figured you had it under control, so I didn't come in. I briefed the cops, though, so—"

A wail split the air, a terrible sound, full of more pain and anguish than can be expressed with mere words. I'd last heard it in that airport when I'd shattered a young wife's hope.

"Jesus *Christ*!" said Dicky Carlton, but I kept walking, kept carrying that little bundle away from the woman making that terrible sound.

I made it halfway to the stairs before I threw up.

Karen Deal was the baby I carried out of that apartment. I didn't find out her name until I got her to the coroner—they'd done a records search before I even got there. Dr. Black was on that night, and he immediately gave her the once-over, verifying my death pronouncement. He was the one filling out the death certificate, and this is what makes this Karen's story, the part that made me run out of there faster than Dicky Carlton had fled that apartment. The part that still keeps me up at night even though that was close to a dozen years ago now.

"That's odd," said Doc Black.

"What?"

"Her eyes," he said, and my stomach gave a twinge. "The corneas should have hazed just hours after death, when her system stopped pumping moisture through them, but these look perfectly normal."

"I noticed that," I said, stepping a little closer. "Is she not dead? Some kind of coma, maybe?"

He sighed. "No, she's gone. The cold will make it harder to pinpoint exactly when, and starvation was under way, but this little girl died of dehydration. With a hungry, crying infant, the process would have been accelerated by the crying itself. Maybe the mother didn't feed her for twenty-one days, but it really only would've taken four or five. A week, tops. But the way she died should have accelerated the hazing, not—what the hell?"

"What?"

He fumbled with something. "I've never seen…"

I stepped up beside him. "What?" I said. "What is it?" He dropped the sterile gauze pad he was holding and scooped up another. He blotted and pointed. I looked.

As I watched, moisture collected in the corner of one eye, and then the other. It collected, then overflowed, trickling down her cheeks. Dr. Black patted them dry and it happened again. Then again. I have no idea how long it went on because I turned and ran. I ran, but I can never get away from the memory of little Karen Deal, almost three weeks dead, tears silently falling from her perfect brown eyes.

THE GARDEN OF DELIGHT

by Alessandro Manzetti

Puerto Juárez, Cancun – Mexico
November 2, 2066

They say it was the asteroid Uxor-77, crashed in the Indian Ocean five hundred miles from Perth, that changed this world so much. Even here, in Mexico. The seas and oceans have become black, thick as oil, dotted with rows of skulls like sailing race buoys, and people seem to have gone insane; forbidden dreams frying in the broth of their overheated brains, and everyone sleeping with an axe under their pillow. They are hungry, more than yesterday, more than ever. Living today is like floating through yesterday's remains, strewn and beaten like delicious pheasants, and hung by the ankles from tribal structures to drain their fluids above apocalyptic purple-and-blue tufts of grass. Memories seem red, like liquid poppies, as if they were painted by Manet's brush, staining the heretic canvas of the Apocalypse, the burned fields and human menageries.

Meat, milk—all animal proteins—have become poison. They slowly burn your stomach; in a few days your tongue is boiled and swells like that of India's sacred cows, then your eyes explode and it's over. What matters now is survival.

Uxor-77 is the wide vagina of the Apocalypse; it has rock armor and pulsates at a depth of thousands of feet, its outer folds dilating rhythmically, like the sharp lips of an oyster, spreading in the womb of Mother Earth, with macabre tremors and radioactive orgasms. That "green death" would like to take possession of your body and mind; it's always waiting for each of us every morning to crawl down our throats at first breath, like an invisible snail, to fuck us.

The green death moves inside the flesh, in the land, water, and air. Even inside thoughts, which run too fast now, colliding with each other, shattering the armor of archetypes and taboos. I've seen people on the street cutting out their own tongues with a knife, tearing them away, obsessed by their boiling glands. They make their bodies bleed, until they've drained them completely. Finally, they wait for the fat mutant rats to strip their flesh from humanity, and then become carcasses, surrealist sculptures lit by the intermittent electric neon of neuron clusters released, leaking from crushed brains, which, like translucent glue, drip down the drains, finding a new route.

These fat rats are a new kind of predator, the pinnacle of evolution, the breed chosen by this crazy world to replace us. They have thick skin, and their skulls have changed, have become oblong, and now contain bigger brains and many more ideas than before. Their eyes, lit by the dreadful, psychedelic frequency of the Apocalypse, make each night seem like an inverted sky with green stars that blink, opening and closing their eyelids, while the sky above, the real one, is now covered by a thick blanket created by Uxor-77. Night, here in Mexico, as it is elsewhere, is suffocated by a white, gelatinous cover, up there, in front of the moon that has almost disappeared, against a black background; darkness pours into the streets, at the edges of the harbor, on the houses with walls covered by fleshy mushrooms, a new and unknown species, that reflect, with their phosphorescent blood, the artificial lights of the city, still operating, intermittent hopes, mostly burned out.

Everything has changed. People, betrayed by the new traps of their own planet and the indifference of their gods and leaders, rely on ancient traditions and ancestral rites, on sorcerers who wear latex masks and predict the future by reading wounds on the bodies and mouths of the desperate, forced to adapt to the needs of cannibalism, to the new philosophies focused on swallowing human livers, entrails, and preserves made of muscles. Proteins are the new gold of this century; bullion of flesh, stored in many little living Fort Knoxes, walking on two legs, staggering on roadsides with the severed heads of their fellow men and women inside shopping bags. Children who are still breastfed are not poisonous like most other infected humans and animals; they can be eaten without risk, without consequences. Their flesh is healthy and tender, easy to digest. People go hunting night and day, forcing mothers—those who still resist the bite of the green death—to stay awake for days, to remain seated behind the front door with sawed-off shotguns in their laps, to protect their nests. They wait for the predator, the hungry—a neighbor, a relative, or a stranger. Even their husbands. It doesn't matter which monster turns the light off tonight, which one eats the flesh of their sons.

The epidemic began six months ago. The army of hungry people, now out of control, those whom we call *youth eaters*, are getting bigger and stronger. They like to experience the magical orgasm of having survived the Apocalypse by eating newborn flesh, even if it's only enough for one more week of life. Nothing better than that kind of flesh, which still smells of milk, of the biological matrix of the mother, who has just forged those tasty nerves, those little muscles and bones to be chewed, until the tip of the tongue seeps into the fresh marrow, tasting the fragrant pulp that screams of youth.

Rico, my five-month-old only child, was taken by the youth eaters three weeks ago, while Celeste, my wife, was asleep in her chair with the rifle in her lap. She hadn't slept for three days until that moment. Those three bastards, after having taken care of my son, even swallowing his clothes, too thrilled by the fever of the cannibal, bit one of my wife's ankles too; they tasted her because Celeste still appeared to be immune to the green death. She looked too beautiful to resemble a daughter of the Apocalypse. But in her blood, as well as in mine, the venom of Uxor-77 already flowed. We are both in stage one of the epidemic impact, as they call it. We will become youth eaters in about a month, or maybe our eyes will explode before that; it would be better to die that way to avoid becoming, sooner or later, part of those cannibal bands that, gathered around the old neighborhood fires, stuff their mouths with skewers of infants.

That sad night I was on patrol at the harbor; it was my turn and that of Florentino, in his usual belt stuffed with hand grenades, and old Ignacio, very familiar with the flamethrower, with all his teeth covered in gold; at night his smile is one of the few things that still shines in this ghost town. I couldn't do anything for my Rico. I cried so hard I tore the muscles in my neck and made the hordes of dogs yelp as they encroached upon the landfill to the south, where human fingers stick out of thousands of black bags piled in gloomy, soft pyramids of the twentieth century, as if those tormented carcasses, stuffed inside, wanted to run away.

Today is *el Día de los Muertos*, and Celeste wants to see her little Rico before the green death makes her go totally crazy. The earthly body of my son is inside the stomach of those three motherfuckers, of course, but we can see his soul sucking milk from the branches of the Chichihuacuauhco trees, the place that hosts all the children who die so early, not yet weaned off their mothers' breasts. So says Celeste—she really believes this story. We need to reach the Isla Mujeres, a few sea leagues from here, where Ixchel, the goddess of fertility, takes care of the dead children's garden, near the southern tip of the island, the first part of the Mexican territory to be illuminated by sunlight in the morning. The Maya knew how to choose their sacred sites, as well as how to enjoy human flesh, thanks to special recipes, during their festive banquets. An ancient pre-Colombian cult is back in vogue in this crazy world, together with other witchcraft, old and new, absurd rituals that make the fat mutant rats seem more advanced and human than us. I don't think all this was caused only by the crash of asteroid Uxor-77.

The Apocalypse seemed to have started before; there were clear signs. The ultimate goal of human evolution may be self-destruction, something that has been hidden in the genetic code of our species from the beginning, protected by a primordial password, back to a time when we still walked on all fours and lived in the trees, away from large fangs. A kind of backdoor, a virtual red button on the command console, a golden key to turn in its seat, a procedure capable of launching into the planet's ass hundreds of nuclear missiles when the countdown reaches zero. But this doesn't matter now.

We go from house to house, gathering the others and moving together toward the harbor to leave for Isla Mujeres. We defend ourselves with weapons and sticks from the attacks of the fat rats constantly on the hunt, immune to the poison that flows in our blood. We are nothing more than food on the move, waiting to eat or be eaten. Every street is an open-air butcher shop, where the screams are queens, like opera divas, while the squares are filling up with disgusting dens built with fleshless bones, white as marble, human remains, pieces of flesh too hard or too old to be eaten, assembled by the glue of cartilage. In those revolting places, the damn rats mate and breed, with the Apocalypse sonar pulsating inside their bellies, encouraging them to become millions.

Celeste is with me, together with a crowd of young women, their useless breasts swollen with milk protruding from red, sleeveless dresses with full skirts, typical of el Día de los Muertos, accompanied by a few husbands who have survived and chew their tongues in order to resist the green death that is about to erupt inside their bodies. All these people want to see the souls of their devoured children eat and play in the Chichihuacuauhco garden on the island, protected by Ixchel. The signs of the goddess are painted on the women's cheeks: two small semicircles, blue painted on their faces with fingertips. Those signs represent the magical, infinite vagina of Ixchel who continues to take care of the dead children to repopulate the planet; they will be ready when our species is totally extinct. Something cyclical, eternal. So says the myth, and today people will believe anything just to escape from reality, from what surrounds us, from the gruesome Apocalypse unleashed by Uxor-77, the dark bride from outer space that came here to mate with death in a sulfur mist.

The old fishing boat of Iker the Iberian is waiting for us; he's a son of a bitch who could only be fucked by the green death. Instead of his right ear, ripped off by the teeth of a barracuda, there is a thin sheet of dilithium that goes down to his neck, containing a radio transmitter and a telescopic antenna. He calls it his "magical seashell" and says it guides him during his sea journeys. But I know that he imagines hearing, thanks to this strange device, the voice of Flora coming from hell, his wife who died ten years ago. Her voice, a whisper, is the breath of the sea he likes to listen to; it is the North Star that tells wonderful stories to sailors, shaking her breasts to confuse their minds and senses.

Iker's boat is the last one to sail toward Isla Mujeres. The others have already left. We can see them in the distance, with their painted hulls for el Día de los Muertos: vaginas and blue skulls, sometimes submerged by the waves, while the red clothes of the women seem like many small sails driven by the wind. Iker shouts at us to hurry, to get on board, crossing the narrow walkway, while his strange crew, the Ortiz twins with their messed-up hair, work with their flamethrower to keep away two hordes of rats approaching, too close, threatening our group. Before boarding the *Flora Belly*, Celeste and I take a last look at the houses of the city in the southern area of the harbor.

We see, in the narrow alleys, people running and climbing on balconies, with their gnawed legs dangling down, while from the steep slopes rivulets of human blood drip, mixing with the green manure of the cursed rats, phosphorescent like their eyes.

"Come on! Hurry up!" Iker shouts. "Manu, cast off now!" They slowly moved away from the harbor. Celeste observes the black sea, thick like oil, ground with effort by the boat's engines. We see some shadows beneath the oily surface of the water, long and sinuous bodies, similar to big snakes with two heads; swimming upstream, they seem to observe us with their primitive senses, maybe able to detect our smell, our voices swaying on the deck of the boat. They are new mutant creatures, other daughters of Uxor-77. They made a killing of our mackerels, tunas, marlins, and mahi-mahi. The sea has no more colors, just like everything else. It is nothing more than a dark aquarium of death. The people of my city call this new species of predator "snakes of the devil;" someone caught them and saw the real appearance of these monsters out of water. Their bodies are a horrendous dichotomy of steel and jelly, a Giger's merging of teeth, muscles, and sex organs mechanically combined. Heretical beasts.

Iker boasts of having eaten several specimens of them, ripped apart their flesh and cooked it in a pan with hot sauce. "Their heads are good, but they must be cooked for a long time," he likes to say whenever someone brings up the topic. But these are his same old stories, which no one believes now. His madness seems to be the only way for him—his gasoline—to move forward and escape the Apocalypse. I should learn from Iker.

"What are you thinking about?" I ask Celeste, almost resigned to her silence. She hasn't said a single word for days. I imagine she continues to think of Rico's soul sucking milk from the branches of Chichihuacuauhco trees; it has become her obsession, and today, at el Día de los Muertos, she'll see her son again. Celeste really believes in the story of Isla Mujeres, in the dead children's garden, and that's fine with me. I'm with her, ready to believe anything, any sorcery or miracle, if it's useful; if it can help her in some way.

"Will he be playing with the others? Has his hair grown?"

She spoke to me, finally; her blue eyes seem to look at me, but she's not really seeing me. In her mind lives Rico's ghost who, with his small fingers, moves the gears of her thoughts back and forth, making them creak, her voice broken by emotion. Celeste is nothing more than a doll now, with a tape recorder instead of a heart, that continues to rewind the memories of yesterday, the advanced mechanics moving her skeleton with grace, echoing her vocal cords, making it look like she's still alive.

"I'm sure he's fine, on the island, along with the other babies."

The beach is covered with empty turtle shells, it's hard to get to the north side of the island to reach the sanctuary. We walk among groups of pilgrims of death, while the stone idols of Ixchel, Ixchebeliax, Ixhunie, and Ixhunieta, with their bared breasts ramming the wind, watch us from above with strange, intrigued and hungry glances, practically licking their lips of death. "Living flesh!" Maybe that's what the goddesses are thinking, who now seem to descend upon us with their long shadows, pointy from their indestructible, eternal nipples. Ixchel is the most fascinating, no doubt, with her jaguar ears, her snakes and jade jewelry that gather around her firm body, a dragonfly carved on her abdomen, which seems to have just flown out of her sacred vagina, and an overturned jar in her hands, which, I guess, pours her amniotic fluid onto the beach, like an invisible waterfall.

Celeste has moved away from me; she's leading the group now, near the edge of the beach, anxious to reach the Chichihuacuauhco garden. She seems to have wings on her ankles. I start to follow the path, leaving Ixchel's view who, like a stone mermaid, slows my pace and my mind, shaking her invisible rattles, ancestral castanets, inviting me to fly into the purple cathedral of her womb and be suffocated by pleasure like other dragonflies imprisoned there. A good way to die, always better than living the reality, outside, here, especially after the crash of Uxor-77. Then I start to run, because from those turtle shells scattered everywhere, thousands of coral snakes are emerging, awakened by the heat of the afternoon and by the human smell. Iker had warned us about that damn beach, which he called "Little Normandy." The reptiles attack the last of the group, raising their heads, loading their venom glands with the deadliest of poisons.

During these pilgrimages of death, there are always the disillusioned, the slower ones; many of them allow snakes to spit venom in their blood, without resistance. Ernesto, the butcher, chose that quick death. He's tired of following the ghost of Regina, his wife, who tore out all of her hair and now walks on all fours, just like the fat rats of the apocalyptic harbor. The youth eaters have driven many people insane. Ernesto, sitting on the sand, is overcome by the snake coils and clenches his hands and teeth, while the cables of his neck muscles are tightening until they snap one after another; he seems to be praying. For a moment I can see, in the core of his eyes, the jellyfish of relief caressing his brain with their transparent, hypnotic tentacles. He's tasting the morphine of the end. Then I reach the group, on the ascent to the sanctuary, without looking back.

The women, with their red dresses, sit in small groups around the Chichihuacuauhco trees. Observing them from a distance, they look like a bunch of tomatoes in a dry field. Then they begin to hum, lulling in their arms something invisible. Is this the garden of the dead children? Is Rico here? I don't see anything but charred oak bombed by the radioactive rain, drooping psychedelic agaves, a carpet of ferns disintegrated into powder, from which emerge the ruins of ancient walls, a stump of an altar with a strange hunting scene carved on its pedestal, topped by an iguana that moves only its eyes; it seems to be made of stone too. Where is the goddess and the milk of the dead?

I approach Celeste and her red circle of women who tremble as if they are sharing the intimacy of a nest. She holds tight against her chest her illusion, the small ghost of Rico. I think back to when Uxor-77 had not yet crashed on the planet and remember her thin fingers on my lips, shutting off my most painful thoughts. The old shop of my father, a retailer of batteries for holographic systems, was close to bankruptcy; I was ruining everything. "It'll be fine, you'll see," she said to me. I can still see, thanks to the torches of memories, her mango skin, her queenly Byzantine thighs, her swollen belly, and the breasts that were beginning to fill with milk. "You, me…and him, nobody else." She always repeated these words. Then the asteroid came, with its fiery trail that scarred the sky for days.

The Apocalypse was revealed, together with its fat rats and the most horrible animal mutations; it was time for the youth eaters, for sleeping with an axe under the pillow…and then again that awful night, Rico's carcass and his soft fleshless ribs, his cradle splashed with blood by a cannibal Pollock. I still hear, from that moment, the Morse code of madness that engraves lines and dots in the matrix of my brain: A.P.O.C.A.L.Y.P.S.E.

It had to end this way, here, in the Chichihuacuauhco garden during el Día de los Muertos, to celebrate ghosts, both those who live inside your head and those sitting on the roots of these death oaks, between photographs, toys, and dolls whose heads rotate 360 degrees, necklaces, mechanical laughter, laser guns of spaceships that turn on and off, drones in the shape of parrots, sad chants, red dresses, women's heads with no more hair, and the dead who suck the black milk of the Underworld. But there are things I can't see here, and others that I see too well. I would like to become stone, like the remains of this macabre place, this overturned Eden, just like that iguana who doesn't waste too much energy living, continuing to look at me with pity.

Celeste, with her hand to her forehead, protecting herself from the sun, looks up and smiles. "What did I tell you, his hair grew!"

I see nothing, like the other men who are with me, but this piece of adrift planet that sucks the poison from its apocalyptic land, where Uxor-77 laid its phosphorescent eggs, and this group of women with their breasts still swollen with milk who are cradling ghosts. A psychedelic, absurd celebration of el Día de los Muertos, while the idol of the goddess Ixchel, the primordial uterus, the chipped totem of motherhood, seems to turn its face toward us; its breasts of stone, which are immune to Earth's gravity, appear larger than before. The milk in the stone and that of the branches of the Chichihuacuauhco trees flows at the edges of the consciousness of men, splitting into a thousand elusive streams, without ever filling our jar of senses; we don't have eyes powerful enough to see it. Besides, we're in Isla Mujeres.

"You see him, don't you?" Celeste reads my face, realizing I'm blind to this parallel reality, although I'm nodding to her. What is she caressing? The transparent skull of Rico, or something else? And what are the other women seeing now? For whom, or what, are they singing their nursery rhymes? Bonifacio, one of the husbands of these pilgrims of death, lies down on the ground; he seems to be trying to see something through the sparse grass and the little dunes of agave dust. Perhaps he imagines the dead children of Chichihuacuauhco have become small as ants, or he's just going insane. Maybe I'm mad like him, and I'm watching from a sick place in my mind, going back in time, where Celeste, on the kitchen chair, stretches as she always does, hoping to see, from the window overlooking the harbor, a boat docking, full of children with their flesh sewn, as it should be in nature, driven by a captain with a scar on his throat from ear to ear, who wears a conquistador's helmet and, balancing on the bow, waves a white flag. As if to say:

"The Apocalypse, the war, is over, folks! Come and take your children back."

Still, I'm sure to be right here, on the Isla Mujeres, in that place called Chichihuacuauhco, holding my face in my hands, hoping my brain will drip down through my nose to get it over with quickly, both to live and to think. But the goddess has different plans for me. Celeste's back suddenly seems shocked by high voltages; she's having convulsions. She gently puts Rico's body on the ground, Rico's imaginary body, then gets on all fours to release the kilotons of death, triggered by the now unstoppable epidemic in her body. I've seen this macabre scene a thousand times in the city. I try to get closer to her, but she strikes me with her whirling arms, which move with non-human speed. Her eyes, which now resemble two supernovae, explode; her blue eyeballs, attached to the whitish tails of nerves, like the tentacles of jellyfish, are projected a few feet, living artillery rockets. The blood gushes from her face; Celeste is now a human fountain that sprays its sap, its red fluid, until she's dry. After all, it's better to die this way than become a youth eater and bite babies, constantly on the hunt like those fat rats.

I want to see Rico for the last time, like all these women, indifferent to my wife drowned in her own pool of blood, who continue to sing for their children and hold their hands. Until sunset, after that the children will become invisible; so says the legend.

What are they really seeing?

I gather Celeste's eyes from the ground and squeeze them in my hands. Maybe it will work this way. And it's true, after just a few seconds of darkness, I see the real Chichihuacuauhco garden, the milk dripping from the branches, the mammillae, sunflowers that stain the ground with their expressionist yellow, and Ixchel, in the flesh, who fertilizes this magic little piece of the planet with her amniotic fluid, which continuously drips out between her legs.

And then I see the children, everywhere, hundreds of them, with their intermittent shadows, their black and white bodies that pulsate thanks to an alien radio frequency. Their flesh, torn away during their terrestrial lives, finished between the teeth and in the stomach of youth eaters, has returned to their bones, as if nothing had happened. But they seem to have almonds instead of eyes, maybe to make them forget what they have seen, and their mouths are smeared with blood, like those of predators.

Rico, who must have caught my scent, comes close to my shoes, pushing himself forward on hands and knees. Celeste was right, his hair grew. I lean toward him, I take him in my arms, I cradle my son and sing an old song. Then he opens his mouth—he has the teeth of a wolf—and clings to my chest.

Bite, my little one.

REMEMBERING FRANK

by Paul F. Olson

I didn't know Frank well. We didn't talk daily, swap long e-mails, text each other, or run into each other at conventions. In fact, we never actually met in person. But he was one of my favorite people all the same.

The thing that struck me immediately about Frank was that he was brimming with all of the qualities that are in such desperately short supply today. Kindness. Dignity. Optimism. Humor. Heart. A note from Frank was an occasion for celebration. He always left you with a smile. That's a special gift. Yes, he loved horror. Yes, he was a passionate, insightful reviewer. But more importantly, he was a passionate, insightful human being. He was always encouraging, never disparaging, and even in the face of devastating health challenges, he chose to connect rather than retreat, build rather than destroy, and do what he could to leave the world a better, dare I say happier place.

The story I wrote to honor Frank is called "You Can't Eat Just One," and interestingly, the title was a gift from Frank himself. A few years back, he used that phrase in a review of my short story collection, saying the tales were like potato chips, you couldn't eat just one. It was one of the nicest things any reviewer ever said about my work, and I couldn't think of a better jumping-off point for my story. As I began, I envisioned a fairly dark and ominous tale, but something unusual happened along the way and the end result was…well, considerably brighter. I'm fairly sure that was Frank at work again. It had to be. When I think of Frank, I invariably think of kindness, light, and love. When you come right down to it, those are the only things that really matter in this world, and I have no doubt that he was beside me as I wrote, making sure I didn't lose sight of that. So thanks, Frank, for looking over my shoulder and helping make the story—*your* story—what it needed to be.

I miss you.

THE TENTH CIRCLE

by Jason Parent and Kevin Rego

Time isn't linear—at least not when you're dead. I've spent a thousand lifetimes waiting for a chance to live one. Soon, I will have it.

———————◆———————

"Is that a Ouija board?" Kel asked. She pulled a rectangular box from the shelf in my mother's basement.

"I don't know." I stood and dusted my hands off on my jeans. "I've never seen it before. Can't say I'm surprised, though. Mom got into all sorts of shit before the end—herbal remedies, homeopathic nonsense…anything to cure the rot inside her. She tried Jesus, Buddha, Allah, and all the others too, without any luck, so it wouldn't surprise me if she looked for guidance from"—I made hand quotes and conjured my best spooky voice—"the spirit realm. Sad, really."

I stared at the cement floor, watching a spider tiptoe across Kel's sneaker, remembering Mom before the cancer struck her, before her mind crumbled under desperation and the maddening sensation that she was being eaten alive from the inside out. A hell of a way to go. Long and full of pain. Not only for her, but for me, who had to watch every step of the way, sidelined.

"When my time comes, I hope it's quick."

Kel kissed my cheek and stroked my arm. "When your time comes, science will have found a cure for death, so you've got nothing to worry about."

She had done her best to lighten the mood, but thinking of Mom in her final days always made me fume. Mom had spent a fortune on those quack doctors and, after that, the televangelists, who filled her head with promises and pipe dreams of paradise in the afterlife when all that awaited her was a race with a box to see which would decay first. "I'd like to kill every last one of them."

"What?" Kel asked.

"Nothing."

Kel swiped her hand over the box, making a streak through the dust, then blew off the rest. Her eyes lit up with a smile that made her whole face shine, the one that reminded me of Christmas, pancakes, and all life's true blessings. The one I'd fallen in love with. But I knew what was coming.

"Can we try it?"

"Try what?" Mickey asked as he plodded down the stairs, each heavy step causing the old wood to groan. He pushed his thick-rimmed glasses up the bridge of his nose and squinted at the box in Kel's hands. "Are you two playing games while me and Lauren do all the work?"

In her high, nasally voice that skyrocketed my blood pressure like oxygen injected into an artery, Lauren called from the top of the basement stairs, "What's going on down there? Are you two farting around while Mick and I do all the work?"

"I found a Ouija board!" Kel shouted. "Let's try it!"

"I don't know how I feel about talking to spirits in my recently deceased mother's house," I said in barely more than a whisper. My mom had been dead for several months, but I'd been slow to put the house on the market. And before that, she'd been in the hospital so much that it could hardly have been said that anyone had lived in the house, aside from a few dust bunnies and her nasty cat, which, at that moment, was probably pissing on my apartment wall or shredding the arm of my favorite chair.

"Won't it be weird playing it in his dead mom's house?" Lauren called. Tact had never been her strong point, but the question at least showed some common sense.

Kel looked at me, her cheeks reddening while her laugh lines smoothed away. But when I shrugged, unable to ever say no to her, they returned with a vengeance. "Yay!" she shouted, pumping a fist in the air as if she were thirty going on eleven. She ran up the stairs, muttering something about cleaning off the kitchen table.

Mickey gave me a sideways glance and shrugged. "I think we all could use a break." His eyes took in all the still-unfinished work. "Damn, your mother had a lot of shit."

"Maybe we can summon her up, and you can let her know how you feel about it." I sighed. "Come on." Letting out another long breath, I headed after Kel.

When I reached the top of the stairs, Lauren and Kel were already seated at the table. I went around them to the fridge and pulled out the twelve-pack I had bought for the occasion. Moving old-lady furniture and incinerating old-lady underwear worked up quite a thirst.

I tossed a beer to Mickey, who, with a gut built on hops and barley, would never turn one down. I placed a bottle in front of Kel and another in front of Lauren.

Lauren crinkled her nose as if in disgust. The expression, along with her other sharp features and beady eyes, made her look like a fruit bat. "Um, may I have a glass?"

I turned around before rolling my eyes and opened one of the cupboards, its shelves cluttered with dishes stacked without any semblance of order. "We still need to pack the dishes," I said under my breath as I reached for a caramel-colored, diamond-patterned glass that had probably been four for a dollar at Savers. I handed it to Lauren.

She turned her nose up at it. "Never mind. Out of the bottle is fine."

Holding back my annoyance, I sat down and drew my key ring from my pocket. With the bottle opener attached to my keys, I popped the lid from my beer. I then slid my keys over to Kel, who sat at my left. The game box—if summoning spirits could be called a game—sat in the center of the table, unopened, and no one moved to change that.

After everyone had taken a few gulps from their beers, Kel gave me a nudge. "Well?"

"Well what?" I took another swig. "This is your show."

Undeterred, Kel pulled the box toward her and opened it. She rubbed her hands together, face beaming, and drew out a board and a triangle with a circular hole in its middle. The board itself had numbers on it ranging from zero to nine, all the letters of the alphabet, and the words *yes*, *no*, *hello*, and *goodbye*.

When I saw another word printed on the box itself, I nearly spit out my beer. "Who are we supposed to talk to with this? Optimus Prime?"

Mickey chuckled. Kel looked at me curiously, and Lauren just frowned.

"Hasbro! I get it." As Mickey laughed, his moobs jiggled. He looked at Lauren, and with an air of pride, likely thrilled with the opportunity to know something know-it-all Lauren did not, he said, "Hasbro is the same company that makes—"

"I know what they make," Lauren snapped.

I cleared my throat. "I think the point Mickey is trying to make is that Hasbro sells kiddie toys. And as much as My Little Pony seems to have been created by demons straight out of Hell, the company hardly seems the obvious choice for mass-producing a device for communing with the netherworld."

Kel frowned. "Ouija boards have been around for over a hundred years. There have been many recorded instances of people using them to contact spirits."

"Okay…" I emptied my bottle, placed it on the table, and folded my hands in front of me. As much as I wanted to appease Kel, I remained guarded. Something about the whole thing was making me uneasy, though nothing I could put my finger on and nothing to do with my mom. Summoning her would, at worst, subject me to another lecture on how I should be doing more with my life and popping the question to Kel. She would probably be right on both counts.

Shaking off the thought, I said, "So…who should we contact? Prince? David Bowie? Morgan Freeman?"

Lauren tsked. "Morgan Freeman isn't dead."

"He's not? Dude's been in like a thousand movies, plus voiceovers, so I figured he must be a thousand years old."

Kel patted my hand. "Hon…not Morgan Freeman. Let's just see where the board takes us."

"Okay."

"Just…try to take it seriously."

"Do we need to shut the shades or something?" Mickey asked. "It's like broad daylight in here."

Ignoring him, Kel placed the pad of her forefinger on the triangular pointer. Mickey followed suit, a big, dumb smile across his face. Lauren sighed and graced us with her participation. Reluctantly, with a tremor in my hand I hoped the others wouldn't notice, I touched the planchette. Nothing happened.

"Now what?" Lauren asked.

"Oh spirits of the…what did you call it, babe?" Kel asked. "Oh yeah, I remember." She took in a breath then, in a booming voice, said, "Oh spirits of the netherworld, we seek your knowledge and guidance. If any spirit can hear us, please give us a sign."

Again, nothing happened. I could feel my shoulders slowly drop. Mickey's gaze darted to each of the cracks in the ceiling, looking for only God knew what. Lauren rested her cheek on her hand, looking about as interested as a cat beckoned by a stranger. Only Kel remained focused, her gaze fixed to the planchette.

More relaxed and hoping to put an end to the game, I said, "This is stu—"

The pointer twitched. The movement was slight, but it drew everyone's attention. I swallowed then held my breath.

For a moment, nothing else happened. My heart jumped when the planchette began to slide. Slowly, millimeter by millimeter, it slid over a word. *Hello.*

Kel sat up straight, eyes beaming. "Hello, great spirit! Are you a kind and benevolent force?"

"That seems like a catch-22," Lauren said. "Would an evil spirit be inclined to admit—"

The pointer slid over another word. *Yes.*

I looked each of the others in their eyes, trying to determine who had moved the arrow. All I knew was that it hadn't been me.

"Everybody keep your fingers on the arrow," Kel instructed. Pausing, she grimaced then whispered, "What should I ask it?"

"Ask its name," Mickey whispered back.

"Morgan Freeman, aka Optimus Prime," I said, and Mickey covered his mouth to stifle a chuckle.

Lauren sneered. "Morgan Freeman wasn't the voice of Optimus—"

"Hush!" Kel said firmly. The charade was apparently important to her, so I wiped the shit-eating grin off my face, cleared my throat, and leaned forward, donning the most interested face I could muster.

"What is your name?" she asked the dome light on the ceiling fan.

Again, a moment of silence passed before the planchette moved. In a painstaking crawl, it spelled out my name.

"Not cool, guys," I said. "Who's moving it?"

Lauren smiled. "It could just be a coincidence."

"Oh, don't tell me you're buying into this bullshit too. You're too smart for that."

Kel shot me a glare, and I realized that in a backhanded way, I had just implied she was stupid. I looked away and shut my mouth.

"Are you saying you want to speak to my boyfriend or that you are my boyfriend?" Kel asked.

When the planchette didn't move, Mickey opened his mouth to speak but tripped over the words. At last, he said, "You have to ask it, like, yes or no questions. You know, like in *Jeopardy*."

Lauren rolled her eyes. "That's not how *Jeopardy* works."

"I know. I just mean that you should ask it questions it can answer easily."

Kel held up a finger, silencing the room. "Okay. Do you have a message for my boyfriend?"

My eyes began to blur. A dull hum rang in my ears. I was only somewhat aware the planchette was moving again, that my finger was still on it, but my vision worsened and my hearing dulled. What I did see of the room before me was like a scene from a black-and-white television, the signal poor and the picture distorted between lines of dead space. The sound of Kel's voice vanished, replaced by the crackle of static.

I blinked, and my heart exploded in my chest. I lost my breath and trembled all over, for in that half a second my eyes were closed, I saw a face flash under my eyelids. The memory of it quickly faded, but it had been somehow familiar despite its sinister shark grin, rows and rows of triangular teeth, and eyes as black as pits.

I, of course, dismissed it as a sort of mini-nightmare, but the fog surrounding me had yet to lift. I tried to raise my hand to rub my eyes, but it didn't move. The forefinger of my other hand remained pressed against the pointer, moving along with it, though I couldn't feel a thing.

My body remained seated at the table. I wanted to scream out for help but was unable to move or make a sound. The others seemed none the wiser. My heart thudded faster and faster as panic made me sweat.

Then I heard a voice. Though somehow familiar, it didn't belong to any of my friends. *I've been waiting a long time for this—my moment, my one chance in many circles.*

I ignored the voice, deep and malevolent as it was. Dismissing it as unreal, I focused on moving a finger. The sort of psycho-paralysis, combined with the voice I had heard, meant one of three things. I was either physically ill, mentally ill, or... As if those two options weren't bad enough, the third was beyond my ability to grasp.

I have you. What was yours is now mine again. What's mine can now be yours forever. A cackle devoid of mirth sent shudders down my spine. I looked at the others, who were smiling and laughing. I wanted to hit them, to hurt them, to strangle them for not lifting a finger to help me as I filled with a hatred for them beyond anything I had ever felt before.

No, not my hate. Not mine.

Some force worked itself inside me, filled me with the skin-crawling sensation that my flesh was merely the costumed housing of another, one who embodied everything that was vile and loathsome.

My hand wrapped around the planchette as if on its own volition. I ripped it from the others' fingers. Like a puppet on strings, I leapt from my seat, onto the table, then onto Mickey, knocking him off his chair and tackling him to the ground. Pinning him with my weight, I drove the arrow though his lenses, popping them loose from their frame while the planchette jabbed again and again into his eyes. A laugh, not mine, rose from my throat.

My hand reached for a bottle I hadn't realized was near me. Mickey's beer must have fallen in the attack. I grabbed it by the neck and bludgeoned Mickey's head with it until it broke. With the jagged edge still attached to the bottleneck, I punctured his neck and basked in the arterial spray.

As I stood, bottle still in hand, I turned toward Lauren. She was standing, backing away from the sight I must have made. I could feel my teeth pressed tightly together. Was I smiling?

I swiped at her eyes, and she screamed. Her hair swung over her face as she turned with the blow, but given the lack of blood, I figured I couldn't have done more than cut her superficially.

That wasn't good enough for the force behind my motions, a force I couldn't consider or comprehend, even as I tried to stop it. I pressed myself against Lauren's back, pinned her against the kitchen counter, and slid her hand toward the sink.

I could see what I was doing and knew what I was about to do, and it made me dizzy. But my eyes remained open, cruel cameras forcing me to watch and record the horrors my body was compelled to commit.

My arm slid over Lauren's. My hand clamped over her wrist. I forced her hand into the sink and then down the garbage disposal. I flipped a switch.

I heard her screaming above the hum, growing louder and louder. With a snap, the world came in crystal clear. I felt my weight holding her down. My jaw hurt from clenching. My body was mine again.

I turned off the switch and pulled Lauren's arm free. I vomited when I saw the mess of it I had made, tears beading out of the corners of my eyes. Lauren's face was pale white. Her chest beat in succinct, rapid motions. Her breaths were short as her eyes glazed over and rolled back. Her skin was cool and clammy to my touch.

I leaned her against the cabinet, the need to call for help blaring through the mania fogging my brain. I scanned the counter, searching for my cell phone, then

I looked at the table and, finally, at Kel. She stood watching me, hand over her mouth, tears pouring down her cheeks.

I reached out for her but froze when she recoiled. I was coated in blood and was starting to realize how everything must have looked to her.

"What have you done?" she asked, her voice soft and muffled by her hand.

"It-it-it wasn't me," I blurted, but of course it had been. Even if I wasn't in control, my body had been the vessel. I could think of no way to explain it, but I had to try. "I was…I was…possessed!"

Had that been what happened? It sounded right, and though I'd never believed in spirits, it seemed the only thing that made sense. Why did we have to open that stupid box? Why couldn't we have just left well enough alone? Then a thought caused me to lunge at her. "Run! I'm not sure if I'm in control or if it's just temporary."

Kel kicked me in the shin, but instead of running for the door, she circled the table. She pulled her cell phone from her pocket.

"Kel," I said, leaning over the table and reaching for her. She was going to call the police. She was going to call them and send me away for something I hadn't done, or at least hadn't intend to do. That wasn't fair. It was her fault this had happened. Not mine. She was the one who wanted to play with that fucking board in the first place. She was the one who believed in spirits.

"Hon…you know me. I didn't do this. I *wouldn't* do this." But the fear in her eyes, the tremor in her fingers—she was afraid of me. Not whatever had been controlling me.

Me.

My heart felt as though it wouldn't go on. "You believe me, don't you, honey?" I asked through tears. "Don't you?"

She shook her head and pressed 9-1-1.

I reached for her with both hands, Lauren's blood—or maybe it was Mickey's—dripping from my fingertips. "Hon, please. Put the phone down. Let's talk about this."

"My boyfriend just killed two people, and he's coming after me!" Kel shouted into the phone.

Without thinking, I charged at her and slapped the phone out of her hands. "I didn't do it," I said over and over again, pulling her close as she beat against my chest. The more she fought, the harder I squeezed, drawing her closer, never wanting to let her go. She mumbled into my chest, wet with her tears and the blood of our friends. But I refused to let her go until she calmed down.

After what seemed like an eternity, Kel finally quieted. She leaned into me, her weight suddenly heavy. I thought she had fainted, so I carried her to the couch. There, I rested her head against a throw pillow and let her sleep.

I had never before seen her sleep with her eyes open. She was so still, so quiet.

The police were coming, and they would read the scene as Kel had. And Kel... I sobbed into my hands. I had done that myself. Whatever had possessed me could claim Mickey and Lauren, but Kel was my own damnation.

I plodded into the basement and grabbed an extension cord off a tool bench. Then I plodded back upstairs and upstairs again, to the second-floor landing overlooking the foyer. A railing separated the landing from a drop-off of about fifteen feet. I tied one end of the cord around the railing and the other around my neck, then I jumped over the rail.

My neck didn't snap in the fall, but the cord held. I clawed at the makeshift noose as it dug into my skin. Pain burned down my throat. My eyes bulged in their sockets. I couldn't breathe.

And as my air supply ran out, my legs kicking and thrashing, my fingernails carving trenches into my skin, I heard the voice again, growing louder with each breathless second. I was sure it was laughing.

I laughed as his soul, my human soul, passed me on its way to Hell, while I made my escape. Ages I had waited, for while human time is linear and has a definitive end, the eternity of the dead is circular. Around and around I went after my first death, sent to Hell for sins committed in a mortal lifetime beyond that day in my mother's basement, the day Kel and I played with a Ouija board with no effect. After my true death, I toiled in torment in a lake of fire with billions but smartly, gaining power, rank, wisdom, knowledge, influence, and above all, the means and will to escape. I went from tortured soul to torturer to demon of a higher class, always bound by one rule: to be damned for eternity.

But all loops have loopholes for those clever enough to find them. I waited for eternity's spiral to circle back to the beginning and progress back to that time my stupid human form called out to the spirit realm. I took control then. My euphoria from killing those two humans was so intoxicating, I could barely keep from killing Kel. But my mortal form needed to do that, to commit the ultimate sin that would ensure his damnation, then take his own life so I could assume his form beyond possession and into true inhabitation.

So as my mortal soul left its vessel, my demon soul reentered it, imbuing that recently dead shell with new, supernatural life. Hand over hand, I climbed up the rope around my neck then over the banister. I severed the binds that tethered me with more ease and gaiety than those I'd severed during my escape from Hell, binds my mortal soul will now endure anew.

A true chicken-and-egg scenario, I know. A paradox, and so be it. I'm here to stay, for the one thing our gods loath to interfere with in the human world is that blessing and curse of free will. Free will that is now mine to exercise.

Yes, I am free—free to kill, rape, feed, fuck, and conquer as I please, blessed by an unholy angel with immortality in mortal form until all life comes to an end. Only then will Hell have me again. For the millennia between, my fun is just beginning.

OLD FRIENDS

by P.D. Cacek

The old man is dying.

The old man is dying in a white room that smells faintly of alcohol swabs and disinfectant and, if I take a deep enough breath, of urine and decay. A single lamp burns on the bedside table, illuminating a face I barely recognize.

It's been so long since I've seen him.

The old man is dying as I stand at the foot of his bed and watch. He has outlived all his kith and kin and is dying alone...except for me.

We'd met one night when the old man was still a boy—a very precocious and imaginative boy who had somehow convinced his parents to take him to a movie that he'd said all his friends had already seen.

It'd been a lie, of course, but whether his parents believed him or not it didn't matter. It wasn't a school night and they'd also wanted to see the film so hand in hand, they took him to see a man stitched together from the bodies of the dead and brought to life. His mother had wanted to leave immediately after the first disinterred corpse, but his father was made of sterner stuff and began a whispered mantra "it's just a movie" that lasted until the flames consumed the man-made creature.

When the lights came on, the boy was still staring that the blank movie screen and might have stayed that way if his parents hadn't pulled him from the theater.

All the way home his mother kept wondering out loud what sorts of parents the boy's friends had if they'd allowed them to see such a horrible movie. The boy didn't say anything because he didn't hear his mother, the images he'd seen filled his head, blocking out everything else.

It was late when they got home and his parents were tired, so the boy was sent off to brush his teeth and say his prayers and to sleep tight and not let the bedbugs bite. His mother wished him pleasant dreams as she turned out the light and closed his bedroom door.

But it was too late for that. I was there.

He didn't say his prayers the way he usually did, kneeling beside his bed with his eyes closed in the hope that the Almighty would take it as a sign of piety. He didn't curl onto his side and sleep. He lay flat on his back, awake and wide-eyed, and watched the room he'd known all his life change into something darker...frightening...dangerous.

That first night I just stood in a shadowed corner of that room and watched as he gathered in all the images he'd seen until there was no room left inside his head and all he could do was flail at the covers and scream. I was very small then, too, and eager, oh so eager, but I waited, biding my time until it was my time, and watched his parents rush in to comfort him.

It was just a bad dream, his father said. It was that movie, his mother chided; I knew we should have left. Oh, he's okay, his father again, aren't you, sport?

Back and forth, back and forth until the boy who'd become the dying old man nodded and lied again. He was fine, he said, but kept glancing to the shadows that concealed me. I think he knew I was there because he asked his parents to leave the door open and the hall light on...just this once, please?

His father looked appalled at the idea of a son of his needing to have a light on, but his mother took it as yet another sign that she'd been right about the movie and his friends' parents. I could hear them still arguing once they got back to their own room—after leaving the hall light on and his door open.

I did nothing that first night but watch; I didn't need to do more than that.

After that night a tap on the wall, a hooked fingernail drawn across the bedsprings beneath him, the gentlest of pressure on the loose floorboard would send him into screaming fits. He called me the monster, after the creature in the movie, and I was always under the bed or in the closet or had somehow gotten outside to claw at his bedroom windows. His mother thought they should take him to the doctor. His father thought he should just "grow up and be a man." Neither solution would have helped.

Nor did the small night light his mother bought him despite his father's booming protestations.

Through childhood to manhood, he was never able to sleep in the dark again.

Perhaps it was because I stayed too long. While others of my kind stay but a few years, we had almost two decades together. I was there to keep him awake during those blurry sessions of late-night studying and kept him company the night before he left his family's home for one he'd occupy with his new bride.

I followed him to the hospital when his first child was born and hovered when they brought it home, but by then there were real fears that diminished mine.

I can't remember when I left, but I'm here now.

The old man opens his eyes and looks at me but without recognition. The disease that is taking him took his memories first. He doesn't remember me. When he turns his head I follow his gaze to the shadow the lamp has thrown against the opposite wall. The shadow is small and withered, shrunken like him.

It's my shadow.

The old man is dying and so am I.
We had our time together but it's over.
When the old man closes his eyes I take his hand.
Shh, I tell him, you're not alone...I'm here.
And he smiles.

TOMMY THE DESTRUCTO-BOT
VS.
THE BULLIES FROM FUTURE STREET

by Todd Keisling

1 - WELCOME TO FUTURE STREET

War came to Future Street one crisp autumn day, dressed in tinfoil and copper tubing, with pneumatic pistons driven by the steam of one child's bloodlust. Immaculate lawns were stained scarlet, and trees were splattered with the goopy entrails of Ricky Johnson and his gang of idiots.

Newspapers and network reporters spent years discussing, speculating, and eulogizing the death of a neighborhood wrought by the hands of a mechanical menace once known as Tommy Slone. The families of Future Street slowly dissolved into the folds of time, each one packing up their things and bidding farewell to their old suburban homes, determined to put the horrors of that day behind them once and for all. Their legacy was a cul-de-sac of empty houses, with For Sale signs lost in the overgrowth of weeds, and unkempt lawns that would never hide the scar of what happened that autumn morning.

Only one house remained occupied, owned by a recluse everyone chose to avoid, and she had nothing to say. She barred the door from solicitors and interviewers, threatening them with a cool gaze that could crack stones and wither flowers. Instead, the odd sculptures in her backyard spoke for her in ways no one could understand, a bizarre gallery erected in memoriam to the battle fought that day.

War came to Future Street dressed as a twelve-year-old. His name was Tommy Slone, a boy who dreamed of becoming a robot.

2 - TOMMY SLONE: KING OF FREAKS

"Hey freak."

Tommy Slone clenched his teeth as he stepped off the bus, wiped his sweaty palms on his jeans.

"Maybe he didn't hear you?"

"I know he heard me. Hey nerd, are you deaf too?"

Tommy didn't turn around. He knew their voices well enough to pick them out of a crowd. Ricky Johnson's sneering face sprang to mind, followed by the dimwitted Nicholas "Muffin" Arnstead. Tommy wondered if Joey and Vincent Prewitt were with them, but a short burst of laughter followed a moment later, and Tommy had his answer.

A stone whizzed past Tommy's head, ricocheting off Mrs. Future's fence with a dull plunk. Tommy peered over his shoulder. All four bullies waited at the corner, sitting on their bikes with backpacks slung over their shoulders. Muffin clutched a slingshot in his hand.

"Nice shot," Ricky said, nudging Muffin's shooting arm. "Ten points if you can hit him."

"Twenty," Muffin said.

"No way," Joey chimed in.

"Make it fifty," Vincent said. "He's a king of freaks. Kings are good for it."

Muffin readied his next shot, and Tommy jerked his head down just in time. The stone shot over the top of his head, ricocheted off the top of the fence, and struck a window.

Oh no. Old Lady Future's gonna be pissed. Tommy sucked air through clenched teeth, gripped his backpack, and shuffled forward along the sidewalk.

"Hey," Ricky shouted, "where do you think you're going?"

Muffin dropped a handful of pebbles and wiped his hands on his dusty jeans. "A hundred points if you smash his face, Rick."

Ricky cracked his knuckles and swept back his greasy black hair. "Hundred points for the King of Freaks. I can do that." He trudged across the street. "Hey, Slone. I'm talkin' to you, retard!"

Tommy's cheeks burned. He hated that word, hated what it meant, and hated those four boys more than anything else for using it. But beneath all that hate, fueling the fire that burned in his face and forced tears to the corners of his eyes, was a sense of shame, embarrassment.

Sometimes he couldn't make words like everyone else did. They got stuck on his tongue, the sounds on repeat like a broken record. He had to wear a shoe lift on his left foot to correct the length of his leg, earning him the ridicule of his peers for shuffling instead of walking.

His mother's words echoed in his head. *You're special and different, and other people can't deal with that, so they try to hurt what they don't understand.* Her explanation had been enough—for a while, anyway, until he was old enough to understand his deficiencies and why the kids at school laughed at him all the time.

Every day at school was a minefield of jeers, jokes, and mockery for Tommy Slone. Some days he wondered if they were right. Maybe he really was a king of freaks.

"I'm talking to you, shithead."

He glanced over his shoulder and saw the bully lumbering toward him with the urgency of a Mack truck. Ricky Johnson was every middle-schooler's nightmare: big for his age, built solid, with the temper of a bucking bull at a rodeo. He carried a switchblade. Some say he killed his old man; others said he'd been arrested three times before sixth grade.

Fuck you, Tommy wanted to say, but the words stumbled on his lips. "F-F-Fuh-Fuh—"

"Shut up, retard."

Ricky smacked the failing words from Tommy's mouth and the glasses from his face.

"A hundred points for Ricky!"

Vincent's voice, maybe. Or was it Joey? Tommy couldn't tell. Everything swam before him. He shuffled forward, determined to make his way home, but Ricky pushed him back against the fence.

"Not so fast, retard. You're worth a hundred points." Ricky looked at his friends. "Anyone else wanna beat my high score?"

"I do," Muffin said, his size ten sneakers scraping across the pavement.

Ricky took hold of Tommy's arm, held him in place. "Hey guys, look at this. The retard is crying!"

Tommy couldn't help himself. The tears were there, spilling down his cheeks, betraying his last ounce of dignity. Ricky laughed, and soon the others joined him, their raucous voices like a barbershop quartet from Hell. Tommy sank to his knees, sobbing.

"Hey, what about—"

A door slammed open behind them, the sudden crash silencing the words in Ricky's throat.

"Which one of you boys cracked my window?"

An old woman's voice. Ricky let go of Tommy's hands, and Tommy took the opportunity to seek the sidewalk for his glasses. He found them, pushed them on his face, and whimpered when he saw a crack in the lens.

"I'm talking to you," the old woman said, but Ricky and his gang weren't listening. They beat feet toward the corner, and a moment later they were gone.

"I suppose you know who cracked my window?"

Old Lady Future stood over him, her black sundress dripping from her shoulders like bat wings. She wore a red flower above her ear, contrasting the shiny silver hair pulled back in a bun. She looked down at him through a pair of thin-rimmed spectacles.

"N-Nuh-Nuh-No, ma'am." Tommy strained so hard to force out the words that he saw colors dance before him.

"Nonsense. Don't lie for them after what they did to you." Tommy opened his mouth, but Old Lady Future silenced him with her index finger. "You live just down the street, don't you? You're Tommy Slone?"

He nodded, wiping his nose. She offered a grim smile and extended her hand. "I'm Mercedes Future. Now that we're not strangers, let me walk you home."

3 – THE FATE OF SNITCHES

Tommy followed the old woman around the corner, holding her hand like a toddler, and he didn't care who saw them. Holding her hand was the least of his worries, especially after what he'd endured in the last five minutes. Old Lady Future walked in silence, her dark dress scraping along the sidewalk behind them like dead leaves in the wind, and Tommy thought about what she'd said.

Don't lie for them. Why had he felt compelled to? He'd seen so many others cower in the shadow of those four boys, only to be so reticent when asked by their teachers where those bruises came from. No one liked a snitch, a rat, a tattletale—but no one liked Tommy all that much, either, so what difference would snitching make? And still his first instinct had been to lie and cover for them. *That's not right,* he thought. Bullies like Ricky and Muffin and the Prewitt brothers thrived on the understanding and fear of others. They needed to be shown they couldn't treat other kids like they were dirt.

Mrs. Future tugged at his hand, pulling him back to reality.

"This is home, yes?"

"Y-Yes."

She smiled, nodding as she let go of his hand. Tommy looped his fingers around the straps of his backpack and mumbled "Thank you" under his breath. He was halfway across the lawn when Old Lady Future called to him. He paused, turning back to her, his heart rising in his throat. *She's going to want to talk to Mom,* he thought. *Please no, I don't want to—*

Don't lie for them.

Tommy gulped. "Y-Yes, muh-ma'am?"

"What those boys did was wrong, Tommy. You know that, right?"

He nodded. Mrs. Future's smile faded. There was a warmth in her gaze, but something else that Tommy couldn't place, something grim and calculating and maybe even sinister.

"If you ever want to do something about them, come see me. I can fix you, Tommy. And then you can fix them. We could water my garden with their tears. Would you like that?"

Tommy stared, unsure of what she meant. He opened his mouth, prepared to stammer his way through a question, fearful his curiosity would get him into even more trouble—

"Tommy? Sweetie, are you okay?" He turned, the color draining from his face. His mother stood in the open doorway, confused by the presence of the neighborhood recluse. "Is everything okay out here?"

"Everything is just fine, Mrs. Slone." Mercedes Future swept a silver strand from her forehead and offered Tommy's mother the brightest of smiles. "I was just asking your son about the wonderful flowers in your bed." She pointed to the blooming daisies along the sidewalk. "They're beautiful."

"Oh, well, thank you, Mrs. Future." Mrs. Slone held out her hand. "Come along, Tommy. I'm sure you have homework."

Before Tommy joined his mother, he looked back at his unlikely savior. Old Lady Future stood with her hands clasped as if in prayer, smiling. She lifted a finger to her lips and winked before shuffling her way along the sidewalk.

Tommy understood all too well.

4 – THE AMAZING DESTRUCTO-BOT

Upstairs, Tommy waited for the inevitable visit from his father. Mr. Slone had arrived home not long before and judging by the way things had fallen silent downstairs, Tommy suspected his mom was having a chat with his old man. About the odd appearance of Old Lady Future in their front yard. Maybe about the crack in Tommy's glasses. Or perhaps about the reddened, hand-sized marks on their son's tear-stained cheeks.

Tommy sighed, hoping his mind was just playing kickball with his fears. To keep his imagination busy, he retreated to his bed, and reached to the nightstand for his stack of comics. Comic subscriptions were one of the few luxury expenses his parents allowed, and though his tastes were varied, his absolute favorite series was *The Amazing Destructo-Bot*.

He pulled last month's *Destructo-Bot* from the stack and ran his fingers along the bright yellow lettering. The cover showed the daring Destructo-Bot, part man and part machine, punching a random thug through a wall. Destructo-Bot didn't have guns or knives, laser beams or explosives to fight crime; he used his fists and colossal strength to make the bad guys pay for their infractions.

And boy, did they pay. Tommy flipped ahead to the comic's climax, where Destructo-Bot smashed his way through the walls of a casino vault to punish would-be thieves known as the Yardley gang.

He skipped back to the beginning of the action, replaying the scene in his mind, imagining himself in place of the hero, lifting Ricky Johnson with one hand and knocking the bully's head off with an iron-gloved fist. He saw himself tearing off Muffin Arnstead's arms like an insect and using the bleeding limbs to beat Joey and Vincent Prewitt to death.

In Tommy's mind, he was a different sort of Destructo-Bot, with a body covered in bloodstained armor, and a face mask like a smiley face—because he was a nice guy, and not a king of freaks anymore.

In Tommy's mind, he was a protector, a fighter who'd sacrificed his humanity to save the world from bullies like Ricky Johnson. Because the world deserved better than the bullies on Future Street.

Mr. Slone opened the door and stuck his head into the room.

"Hey, champ."

Tommy looked up, smiled.

Mr. Slone walked in and stood at the edge of his son's bed. He held a brown envelope in his hand. "You got something in the mail today."

"C-cuh-comics?"

Mr. Slone grinned as he handed over the envelope to his son. Tommy promptly tore open the flap. Inside was this month's issue of *The Amazing Destructo-Bot,* the cover depicting its titular hero strapped to a table while a scientist operated a bizarre machine. The byline read "DESTRUCTO GETS AN UPGRADE!"

"Looks like an exciting one," Mr. Slone said. He took a seat on the edge of the bed. "But listen, champ…your, uh, your mom wanted me to talk to you. Can you put that down for a minute so we can chat? You know, man to man?" Mr. Slone ruffled Tommy's hair. "Your mom said you had some red marks on your face. Like someone had slapped you." Mr. Slone tilted his head to study his son's cheeks. Tommy wanted so badly to look away, but he knew that would only arouse his old man's suspicion. "Did someone hurt you, Tom?"

"Nuh-Nuh-N—"

Don't lie for them. Old Lady Future's commanding voice chimed in his head. He looked away from his father, seeking comfort in the comics at his side. What would Destructo-Bot do? *He'd tell the truth,* Tommy thought. *And he'd do more than that. He'd stop the bullies from hurting anyone else.* Visions of decapitating Ricky Johnson flashed before him. If only life could be like his comic books. He wouldn't have to shuffle his feet or stumble because of his stupid shoe lift. He wouldn't stammer his words, and no one would mock him for his speech impediment. In the world of Destructo-Bot, Tommy could be a normal kid with a normal life.

"Champ?"

"S-Suh-Sorry."

"It's okay, bud. You were going to say something?"

Don't lie for them.

"Yuh-Yes."

Mr. Slone nodded, the smile fading from his face. "Yes, someone hurt you?"

Tommy glanced back at his comics. In the world of Destructo-Bot, Tommy could be brave. He could stand up to the bullies just like his hero.

Over the next hour, Tommy told his father what had happened earlier that day at the bus stop. His heart was racing by the time he'd finished, his eyes sheathed in tears, his cheeks burning with embarrassment and rage. Mr. Slone pulled him close, kissed Tommy's forehead, and whispered that everything would be okay.

And while Mr. Slone retreated downstairs to tell Mrs. Slone and discuss what to do next, Tommy cried into his pillow. Not out of terror, for tomorrow there would surely be hell to pay, but out of anger that he could do nothing about whatever Ricky Johnson had in store for him.

Here in the real world, Tommy realized, the bullies of Future Street always won.

5 – THE COWARDLY RICKY JOHNSON

The next morning, Ricky and his gang cornered Tommy as soon as he stepped off the bus, with Muffin throwing his arm around the kid like they'd been friends for years. Ricky gripped Tommy's collar and pulled the boy close.

"Need to talk to you, freak. Inside. Now."

Tommy didn't struggle. He knew the score, knew there was no point in trying to fight them. He was outmanned, not that he could've taken even one of them on himself, and he followed them inside toward the restroom. Once there, Vincent and Joey stood guard at the door. Muffin pushed Tommy to the tile floor and laughed as the boy cried out from the impact. Ricky produced his famous switchblade—the sharp blade protruded with a swift *shick* sound—and pointed the tip at Tommy's face.

"Did you rat me out?"

"Nuh-Nuh—"

"Spit it out, you fucking retard. Did you rat me out?"

Retard. Lightning flashed in Tommy's mind, sparking the rage that conjured such violent daydreams the day before, and he summoned all his courage to speak. He glared at Ricky, pushing himself back against the restroom stall, and exhaled.

"Y-Yes, I did. Wh-What are y-you going to d-do about it, y-you fuh-fucking cuh-cuh-coward?"

The sound of his words surprised no one more than Tommy himself. He felt vindicated and powerful as he watched their stunned expressions. Ricky blinked, slack-jawed, the switchblade wavering in his hand. Muffin shot a look over his shoulder at the Prewitt brothers, who gaped with amazement at the outburst.

The moment was short-lived, as the rusty wheels in Ricky's head slowly cranked back into position. "The fuck did you say to me, retard?"

Muffin smirked. "Called you a fuckin' coward, Ricky."

The Prewitt brothers punctuated the room with their hyena laughter, struggling to silence themselves and failing miserably. Ricky's cheeks erupted in red splotches, his eyes suddenly feral, and Tommy dry-swallowed. *Probably shouldn't have said that,* he thought, but deep down, he heard Old Lady Future say, *Nonsense.*

Ricky reached out and nicked the tip of Tommy's nose with the blade. A dollop of blood oozed from the wound and plopped on Tommy's shirt.

"You think I'm a fuckin' coward now, retard?"

Tommy tried to speak, but Ricky didn't wait. He cut a gash across Tommy's cheek. A thin curtain of blood trailed down Tommy's face.

"Ricky—" Muffin began, shooting a worried glance at the Prewitt brothers, who were too stunned by what was happening to react.

"How 'bout now?"

Another flick of the knife. Blood seeped down Tommy's brow and into his eyes.

"I could cut your whole fuckin' retard face off."

Go ahead, Tommy wanted to say, but this time he held his tongue. He'd pushed his luck as far as he was willing to, and he was already paying a price. Instead, he closed his eyes and dove into himself, waiting for Ricky to do whatever he was going to do. Warm blood ran down the contours of Tommy's face and dripped off his chin.

"Ricky, stop it, man."

Muffin Arnstead again, only this time Joey and Vincent Prewitt joined him in protest. "Yeah, Rick, enough's enough. He's bleedin' pretty bad, man."

A cold silence fell over the five of them, broken only by the piercing ring of the morning's first bell. Ricky looked at his gang, then back at Tommy. He put away the switchblade, grabbed Tommy's backpack, and dumped its contents over the bleeding boy. The latest issue of *The Amazing Destructo-Bot* fell to the floor along with two textbooks.

"I ain't no goddamn coward," Ricky mumbled. He reached down and picked up the comic. "You remember that, freak."

Tommy looked away, his eyes clouded with tears as he listened to the slow ripping of the comic's pages.

"We ain't done, you and me. Next time I see you, you're dead." Ricky tossed the shredded remains of the comic at Tommy's feet. "Let's get out of here."

Tommy waited until they were gone before collecting his things. When he was done, he tried to stop the bleeding on his face. Staring at his reflection in the mirror, at the gashes carved into his skin, Tommy decided Ricky was right: they weren't done.

6 – MAD SCIENCE

Tommy remembered what Old Lady Future told him the day before in front of his house. *I can fix you, Tommy. And then you can fix them.*

He had the anger and drive to resist the oppression of the bullies from the other side of Future Street, but he lacked the body, the strength. Maybe his street's namesake could help him. Looking at the wounds on his face—which would surely need stitches—Tommy decided he was angry enough to find out. They'd hurt him for the last time, and he'd make them pay.

How, exactly, was another matter altogether, but he was determined to find out.

Tommy snuck out of the restroom and crept along the empty hallway toward the school's back door. His head was filled with a humming nest of angry hornets, and the thought of staying at school only compounded his anxiety.

The morning's first classroom bell rang and students flooded the halls, but if anyone saw the young man with bloodstained paper towels pressed to his face, they made no sign of acknowledgment. Tommy Slone was as invisible that morning as he'd always been. No one paid attention to the social lepers at his school, not even the teachers, and he was on his way back to his neighborhood long before anyone noticed his absence.

The morning was overcast, the sky threatening rain, but Old Lady Future was outside in her front lawn trimming the hedges that demarcated her yard. She wore the same black dress, with the same red flower perched in her hair, and she didn't seem at all surprised when Tommy rounded the corner.

Old Lady Future lowered her chin, surveying the damage. Tommy met her eyes, summoning all his courage not to look away. He'd heard so many stories about the neighborhood recluse: that she was a magician, a sorceress, that she danced naked in the moonlight with devils. Perhaps the most intriguing to him, however, was not that she was a witch, but a scientist of sorts. A different kind of sorceress, one that made magic through the laws of nature and physics.

"You're hurt."

"I-Is it tuh-true?"

Mercedes Future waited, watching the stammering young man work the words from his lips.

"Y-yuh-you can fuh-fix m-me?"

"I can." She reached out and took his chin in her hand. "But there's a price." She traced a finger along the gash on his forehead, and he winced. "It will hurt, too. More than what they did to you. And what is done cannot be undone. Do you understand, Tommy?"

He thought he did and said as much. Old Lady Future smiled. "So be it. Follow me."

The inside of the Future estate was dim, lit only by a few sparse lamps, its walls and hallways lined with shelves of books. Every room they passed revealed more books, vaults of knowledge overtaken with dust and forever frozen in time. This rare glimpse into the private life of Old Lady Future sparked a hint of envy within him. Here was an entire house full of books, cut off from the judgmental outside world, and wouldn't it be so great to live here among the pages?

"D-duh-did you ruh-write all these?"

"Some of them," she said, leading him through a sparse kitchen toward a door in the corner. "My laboratory is just this way." Old Lady Future opened the door, revealing a brightly lit staircase leading down to the basement.

"Luh-Laboratory?"

"Yes, dear boy. Where I will fix you."

Unlike the parts of her home he'd seen, the basement was luminous, spotless, free of dust and clutter, and every item there had a purpose and place. Electronic gadgetry lined the walls, from computer monitors and televisions to amplifiers and equalizers. Thick bundles of cable were coiled around the support beams in the center of the room, stretching to the machines scattered around the perimeter. A soft hum filled the room, punctuated with errant beeps and boops, and a thin spidery arm of electricity arced between two antennae perched atop an unused console television. A gurney sat off to the side, adjacent to a narrow table covered in wires and electrodes.

Mercedes sensed the boy's confusion and placed a comforting hand on his shoulder. "I'm a doctor. Of the scientific variety. Used to be. The neighbors think I'm mad, and I'm fine with that." She walked toward a rack on the far wall and retrieved a white lab coat. "Most of these machines, I made myself. Well, with my late husband. He was the engineer, and I was the…visionary."

Questions raced through Tommy's head, complimenting the uneasiness arising in his gut. What happened to her husband? What did she mean by "used to be?" They were questions he wanted so badly to ask, if only his voice would cooperate, but his nerves got the better of him. There was too much to take in all at once in this laboratory, his mind suddenly fatigued by the possibilities of what she might have in store for him here. Had he made a mistake?

The cuts on his face ached. He made a fist, transforming the pain into anger. Ricky Johnson had to be taught a lesson, along with the rest of his gang, and Tommy was prepared to pay whatever price was necessary. It's what Destructo-Bot would do.

"I had a dream of marrying man and machine, of complementing cogs with tissue and supplementing flesh with wires. They laughed at me, said it couldn't be done, but my late Arnold believed in me." She sighed, wiping a tear from her eye. "He's in the garden now."

Something she'd said yesterday occurred to Tommy. *We could water my garden with their tears.* Had Arnold Future done the same?

Mrs. Future shrugged on the lab coat and wheeled the gurney toward the center of the room. Tommy watched with unsettling curiosity as she connected a series of wires to the gurney, muttering to herself while a computer whirred to life on the side of the room, its monitor flickering with a series of blank vitals—pulse rate, blood pressure, brain waves, and something that looked like viscosity levels. He strained to get a better look, but Old Lady Future beckoned him toward the gurney.

"Jump up, Tommy. We're almost ready to begin. Are you afraid of needles?"

His instinct was to nod—he was absolutely terrified of them—but on second thought, he shook his head. Mercedes smiled softly.

"There's no shame in it, dear boy. I'll need to use one to administer a sedative, which you'll want. I need you asleep for the worst of it."

She wheeled over a small cart of tools. Tommy's eyes fell upon the small circular saw nestled between a hammer and pair of pliers.

"Now," Mercedes Future said, "how would you like for me to fix you?"

Tommy hesitated, realizing this could be his last opportunity to change his mind, but he remembered what she'd told him before: *Don't lie for them.* If he backed out now, wouldn't he just be lying for them by lying to himself? Lying because what he really wanted, deep down, was to make them pay for what they'd done to him, to the other kids in school, and to make sure they'd never hurt anyone ever again. Just like his hero would do.

With a heavy sigh, Tommy Slone set down his backpack and pulled the ripped pages of his latest comic from the pouch. He placed the halves together on the gurney and showed the old woman what he wanted. After a few seconds of studying the image, Old Lady Future looked at him and nodded. "I can do that."

Tommy smiled and climbed onto the gurney.

7 – REMOVING THE BAD PARTS

A storm rolled in over the cul-de-sac while Old Lady Future worked on amputating Tommy's malformed limb.

In that time, Tommy's parents were notified of his absence, and the police were called. Ricky Johnson and his cronies were questioned separately when security footage revealed them forcing Tommy into the restroom. They offered four wildly different accounts of what transpired in the restroom, ranging from "innocent teasing" to "trading comic books," and were all suspended by the end of the day.

As the storm roiled overhead, the search for Tommy continued apace. No one thought to call on Old Lady Future, and why would they? Mercedes Future was a creepy old woman who was rumored to have killed her husband and buried him in her garden.

While the rain fell, so did Tommy's blood down the basement drain. A metal piston replaced his leg, complete with a steel foot that also served as a venting apparatus. His vocal cords were enhanced with copper tubes, aluminum alloy, circuitry, and amplifiers. Gears, wires, and other mechanical detritus lay strewn about the floor.

When she was finished, Old Lady Future stepped back to survey her work. She'd removed Tommy's bad parts, which now lay in a gory pile near the drain, and replaced them with machinery of her own making.

But something wasn't right. She tilted her head, looking over the parts that remained, and then back to the torn comic book.

Mercedes smiled. There were still improvements to be made.

8 – AND THEIR TEARS WILL WATER HER GARDEN

The following morning, while the local police had their best detectives scouring the town for possible leads, Ricky Johnson and his henchmen conducted a search of their own. After their separate interrogations the day before, Ricky had called them each that night, instructing Muffin, Joey, and Vincent to meet him the next day.

"I'm gonna find that freak before the cops," Ricky growled. "Gonna finish what I started. Show him I'm not a fuckin' coward."

They waited at their usual corner, just across the street from the privacy fence that lined Old Lady Future's property. The air was crisp, a fine autumn morning that went unappreciated by the quartet, and while Ricky was in the midst of a soliloquy so violent that even Muffin Arnstead begged him to calm down, there came a shrill puff of steam beyond the edge of the fence.

No one noticed at first. It was just an air horn piercing the day like a train announcing its arrival, even though the closest railway was thirty miles away. Ricky went on, working himself up into a rabid frenzy.

"I'm going to cut out his eyes, you know. Pop one out with my knife, then the other, and then I'm gonna make him eat 'em—"

The fence exploded, startling them from Ricky's sermon. Ricky collapsed in a heap, covering his head instinctively as the shockwave blew over them.

"Was that a fuckin' bomb?" Muffin shouted, but no one heard him. Their ears rang with a fury that, had they lived longer, would have transformed into tinnitus. As the dust settled, an abomination stepped through the hole in Old Lady Future's privacy fence.

Joey was the first to see what became of Tommy Slone. He screamed, pointing toward the terrible figure standing across the street. Vincent, Muffin, and Ricky followed the direction of Joey's finger, and joined him in staring agape at the mechanized monstrosity birthed by the awful vision of Mercedes Future.

The remains of Tommy Slone stood before them. His bad leg was replaced with a steel enclosure, fitted with a piston that rose and fell erratically whenever he moved. Steam shot from his metal foot, now measured evenly with his good leg, and together they supported a hulking torso of meat and bits of a rusted barrel. Tinfoil and wires wrapped his arms, connecting to the electrodes on Tommy's neck. Twin pipes jutted from his back, venting clouds of white steam. Lights dotted Tommy's shoulders, blinking red with the boy's rage. A flat square panel of steel was embedded where his jaw used to be, with a protruding speaker in his throat that uttered a dissonant growl when he saw the quartet trembling across the street. Old Lady Future had done nothing to the boy's eyes—they glowed with a hateful energy all their own.

"YOU FUCKING COWARDS."

The mechanical voice boomed overhead, shattering the windows of neighboring houses. Ricky and his cronies staggered to their feet, exchanging glances in panic, waiting for someone to do something. Instead, they cowered as the mechanized King of Freaks stomped across the street, took hold of Ricky Johnson's throat, and tore the bully's head clean off. Ricky's blood pattered upon the metal protrusions of Tommy's chest like a warm summer rain.

Tommy the Destructo-Bot held Ricky's sagging, dumbfounded head in his metal hands and crushed the skull like a pumpkin. Bits of skull and gray matter splattered Tommy's face, and a bellowing laugh erupted from the speaker in the boy's throat.

Joey Prewitt fainted, a fact which did not save him in the end, as Tommy crushed the bully's skull underfoot while disemboweling Vincent Prewitt with a single punch. Muffin tried to scream, but the air was forced out of his lungs when Tommy heaved him into the air. With one swift wrenching motion, he twisted Muffin in half, the snapping of his spine like the pop of kindling in flames.

"IT IS DONE," Tommy boomed, tossing Muffin's broken body aside. "YOU WILL NEVER HURT ANYONE AGAIN."

A puff of steam shot from the pipes in Tommy's back. The lights lining his stitched and swollen shoulders dimmed, fading from bright red to pink to a dull yellow. He turned back toward Old Lady Future's house, and found the mad scientist waiting for him at the opening in the fence. She applauded his work as he slowly trudged across the street.

"Well done, Tommy. A brilliant display."

"THANK YOU, MA'AM."

"Do you remember what I told you?"

"WHAT IS DONE CANNOT BE UNDONE."

Mercedes Future nodded. "And there is a price, my boy. You've done well. Now, you must go to my garden and sleep. Until you're needed again."

"UNTIL I AM NEEDED AGAIN."

"Yes, Tommy. Please, come with me."

He followed her through the hole in the fence and around the corner of her home where the backyard opened into a lush flower garden. A gazebo stood in one corner, lined with a colorful display of fauna, and in the center, overgrown with weeds and moss, was a series of metal sculptures. When Tommy drew closer, he realized they weren't sculptures at all, but other metal figures much like himself: former people, covered in alloy and wires, their bodies stitched together like patchwork quilts. A menagerie of experiments, testaments to the bizarre and beautiful insanity of their creator.

"Would you take your place, my boy?"

"YES, MA'AM."

Tommy looked back toward the fence and the street beyond, feeling a hint of sorrow for his parents, but the sensation passed. They would be okay without him. And here, in the safety of her backyard, he would always stand guard over his childhood home.

Until I am needed again, he thought, his cheeks flushed with a sense of pride. A hero of flesh and wires.

A sentinel. A Destructo-Bot.

Future Street's unsung hero. The amazing Tommy Slone, King of Freaks.

REQUITAL

by Richard Thomas

O*pen your eyes, Graysen.*
  The shack is filling with a heat that rises up from the desert, a weight on my chest slowly spreading to my limbs, as a flicker of this journey unfurls in black and white photos, one horrible image after another. My breath is shallow, hard to summon up from the depths, and then I'm sitting upright on the cot, the thin blankets green and itchy, coughing up blood into my open hands. Sand sifts in through the open frame, the actual wooden door painted red, splintered into sections, and scattered over the front yard. Emaciated, and nude, I squint, looking out the opening into the pale sunlight, unwilling to turn toward the corners of the empty hut, the shadows filled with memories.

And the girl.

Always the girl.

She smiles in the darkness, blonde hair pulled back into pigtails, red ribbons holding the braids tight. Today it's a light blue dress, ringed with daisies at the waist and collar, her black patent leather shoes buckled, shimmering somehow, the dainty little socks as white as bone. Her hands are behind her back, a grin holding her face intact, and I know what she's hiding. I don't want to see it again, but soon enough she'll show me. Yesterday it was a mad dash into the desert where I collapsed in the blazing sun, dust filling my mouth, my skin turned to parchment.

Today?

The car.

I close my eyes, and I'm flying down the highway, the wind in my hair, the windows open, the beat-up Nova purring across the desolate landscape, the girl and house no longer in the rearview mirror. Jeans and a white t-shirt, scuffed boots, my hands grip the wheel as I push the accelerator down, lunging forward. The blacktop spirals forward like a slick of oil, and I chase it—anything to be out of that room, away from her. I click the radio on. Static, up and down the dial, as flashes of faded billboards and dying cactus fill my periphery vision.

I look in the side mirror, and there's nothing back there, a smile as blood fills the cracks between my teeth, my gut clenching suddenly in knots. Under my fingernails, there is so much dirt and grime; I can never seem to get it out. Eyes to the horizon, I cough again, a mist of red spraying the windshield, wiping my mouth as I sneer.

Dammit.

I never smoked a cigarette in my life.

Eyes to the side mirror, the rearview mirror, and the world framed in the windshield shimmers like I'm under water.

It feels good to be moving.

For a moment, I can almost forget why I'm here.

This particular black and white photo comes in several different versions— the grandmother in Alsip growing old and feeble, finally made obsolete; the neighbor hurt on the job, unable to work, abandoned by insurance and company alike; the sister and her addiction, garnering no sympathy, an inability to empathize. But closing my eyes won't help.

I want to be hungry, I want to pull over and order a cheeseburger and fries, a large coke, a diner filled with shiny, happy people. I want to say hello to Mabel or Alice and have her smile and put her hand on a cocked hip, call me Hon or Shug, a bell dinging in the window, the counter filled with cowboys, and truck drivers, and that one haggard salesman with his tie loosened, dingy white shirt unbuttoned.

I want it so bad that it aches.

Instead, I get one more photo—and it's Jim from accounting, and his wife. Jennifer? Julie? There are doctors and beeping lights, the cold tile holding wheels that squeak, as machines are pushed around, a flurry of footsteps filling the cold, sterile air. There was a child, I was told, but whether it was a boy or a girl, I can't tell you. I should know those details. If I was anything resembling a human being.

I take a breath, the road unfurling, and yet, the desert stays on my right, the horizon forever looming, the mountains to the left quiet in their dismissal.

On that particular day, something was due. It's not important what it was— report, numbers, article, paper, results, opinion, facts. I grip the steering wheel harder, knuckles white, pushing the car down the never-ending highway, that diner always just out of reach.

A sharp pain in my ribs causes me to let go of the wheel, gently massaging the spot, knowing it won't do me any good. A cough rattles into my fist, and I rub the red on my shirt.

Here we go.

What did I say? I can't remember.

I yelled at my secretary, it's coming back now, the desk, the glass windows in the office spilling the city for miles in every direction. My back was to her, as I screamed, face red with rage, fists clenched at my sides. Tan, standing tall, the suit custom-made, the tie special-order, the ring on my left finger platinum, the watch shimmering gold.

Never sick a day in my life.

She pleaded with me.

Stockholders, I said. I can't count on him.

Her lips pursed.

You don't understand, I argued.

Rubbing my temples, I never looked at her once.

Make it happen.

Not long after that, she was a ghost too. Marlie. Or Mary. Dammit. What was her name? The road turns to the right, as the Chevy hugs the dotted yellow line, and I cough again, slow with my hand, spattering the dashboard, and it's the mirrors again, the road behind me empty, the back seat slowly filling with shadows.

No, not yet.

This one, it hurts less, it's almost bearable.

And then it shifts, the pain, my hands curling into claws, as my mouth opens in a silent gasp.

This is how it goes, I know.

I can't hold the wheel, so I ease off the gas, the car drifting to the right, trying to bat at the controls, to keep this ton of steel from veering off the shoulder and into the desert, but this will fail too, I know, and then we hit something.

Rock, hole, curb, turtle—who the fuck knows.

Doesn't matter.

I'd like to say there was disorientation and then darkness, but not here, not now. That would be a gift.

Out of reflex I stamp my right foot toward the brake, but it's too late. And then we roll. I push my foot against the floor to try and brace myself as glass shatters, shards imbedded in my face and neck, my eyes closed tight. The car dents and shudders, my right leg snapping at the ankle, something pushing into my chest, the steering wheel fracturing my ribs, and then it stops.

I'm briefly granted a respite, the darkness finally slipping in, and for a moment, I forget it all. But not for long. It's the pain that brings me back.

The sun fades while I bleed, as I labor for breath, in and out, a stabbing pain when I try to inhale, my hands throbbing, a dull panic all the way to the bone, a whimper escaping my split lips.

When I open my eyes, in the last remnants of daylight, as I count the pulsing horrors that riddle my body, a dozen voices scream out in suffering.

I hear footsteps in the dirt, and gravel, and glance to the open window.

It won't be the cancer that gets me. Maybe not even the accident. And certainly not old age. I see four legs saunter up to the car—gray fur, and paws with sharp black nails. I hear a panting that I had thought was in my head, my own struggle for breath, but no, it's something else. The heavy breathing turns to a low growl, and then the four legs turn to eight and then sixteen.

So, this is how it happens, I laugh.

Points for originality.

And amidst the musky smell of mangy fur and sour urine, I see her black patent leather shoes. The shiny buckle. And the dainty white socks. And then I smell the gasoline.

When I turn to the window they're gone.

Out of the frying pan, and into the fire.

There is a spark, and I start screaming.

Open your eyes, Graysen.

The shack is filling with a heat that rises up from the desert, and I run my fingers over my body searching for the new marks—gently touching my ribs, covering my eyes and feeling my face for cuts, mottled flesh, rotating my ankle in slow, little circles.

There is the cot upon which I lie, the same itchy, green blankets and the door open to the elements, sand slipping in, a single red scorpion ambling over the threshold. As always, I am naked, and alone. My lips are cracked, mouth dry, so I sit up and contemplate water. There is a well outside, I think. There used to be, anyway.

I know, I say to the critter as it skitters toward me. It's not your fault, it's merely in your nature. It heads between my bare feet and under the cot, to a tiny hole in the back of the room, where it disappears.

Water.

I turn to the corner first, take a deep breath, and nod at the girl.

Today she is in a pair of denim overalls, her feet bare, with a pink t-shirt under the straps, ruffles at the edge of the sleeves, and a silver necklace that looks like a daisy. Always the daisies.

Her hair is loose today, down past her shoulders, and she smiles a little, eyes on me the entire time, taking a single step toward me. Her hands are still behind her back, but I don't need to see. I've been shown already, so many times.

But I'd like to mark our progress.

She'd like to see me suffer.

Before I can find my way to the well outside, my throat clutching, forcing down a swallow, a tarantula the size of my fist meanders through the door, and I back up a bit, uneasy with the way its legs move, undulating over the faded wood floor, skimming the dust, the hair on its legs making my skin crawl. It looks so meaty—the idea of my bare foot squashing it sends a shimmer across my flesh, as my stomach rolls, my top lip pulled back in a snarl.

It follows the path of the scorpion, but this time I pull my feet up, letting it move past me, under the cot, and into the hole in the wall, which seems to have expanded.

Eyes to the girl, but she's gone now.

I'm not surprised. So much work to do.

I stand up, licking my lips again, my swollen tongue gently prodding the cuts and sores that line my mouth, trying to find any moisture at all. The photos spiral into the air, one after another, back to my childhood, fanned out like a hand of cards, as the memories come rushing back. I want to open my eyes, to push the images away, but open or closed, it doesn't matter, as these visions force their way into my mind. The magnifying glass and the ants; the pet hamster set on a record player as it spins around and around; the egg found in a henhouse and squashed, its pale flesh wrapped around that singular bulbous blue eye; the cat buried up to its neck, so trusting in its innocence as the riding mower started up; the family dog wolfing down the steak while I waited for the poison to take effect.

And then I hear a woman scream.

The flash of red stands in the doorway—the desert fox still, as if stuffed—black beady eyes on me, ears turning this way and that. It barks once, and looks around, as if wondering where it is. It opens its jaw wide again, and then screams into the room.

It is unholy.

And then it's gone.

When the rattlesnake slithers into the room I know there won't be any water for me today, and I can hardly swallow. It's getting difficult to breathe, the snake's tail shaking like a baby's rattle, winding its way across the sandy floor, and then darting under the cot and through the hole.

Too easy, I know.

I close my eyes for a second, and when I do there is a cavalcade of clicking insects, scurrying through the door in a wave of tiny bodies. Centipedes in red and brown, beetles with their iridescent shells, a flurry of wasps and bees filling the air with a dull buzz. I cover my eyes and cower in the corner, but they only dance about the room and then disappear.

And then they get larger, the creatures of the desert, progressing up the food chain. A pack of dogs, sniffing and yipping, fills the room in a clutch of mania—coyotes and jackals and wolves circling each other, snapping and tearing out mouthfuls of fur, their eyes wide in a seething mass of hunger and anxiety, as I push back against the wall. They weave in and out, like some biting, dying ocean of gnashing teeth, and yet they hardly seem to notice me at all.

What I'd give for a single glass of water.

What I'd give to not be torn limb from limb.

In their sudden absence the soft red glow of the sun descending fills the empty doorframe, and a shadow lurches past, a head of horns leaping, and landing, and then leaping again. It passes by, never entering. As I hear the dull thud of its movement push on down the road, it screeches as if caught in a trap, and then suddenly it goes quiet.

When the darkness fills the opening again, it is much larger, blocking out the light bit by bit until there is no sunlight left to give. And yet, it still is not in sight. A smell wafts into the room, something thick and meaty, and I gag in the growing night. Whether on two legs or four, hooved or clawed, the thick odor of rotting flesh and fetid liquid spills across the room, filling my mouth with a bitter, itching sensation. It is the smell of burning carapace, the sickly-sweet copper of blood crescendoing across a flat surface, the burning rot of diseased flesh slipping from the bone.

I hold my hand to my mouth and close my eyes, trying to remember the shine of her buckle, the gentle fabric of the pristine sock, as my flesh is painted crimson, skinned alive— flayed for the desert to feed on in primal hunger.

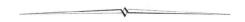

Open your eyes, Graysen.

The shack is filling with a heat that rises up from the desert, and I do not open my eyes this time. I sob in my solitude, understanding so many things now.

And yet, there is more.

I have not been enlightened just yet.

There are depths to be plumbed, dark sparks that were pushed so far down that I thought they'd never see the light of day again.

The girl is here, but I refuse to look at her, whatever romper or summer dress she might be wearing today. Her innocence is a skin she wraps around her like a snake, ready to shift and molt at a moment's notice.

I can see her anyway, and this time she holds her hands out, something in them, reminding me why we're here.

I don't want to see it.

I won't open my eyes.

You will, she says.

When the perfume drifts to me, it is as if I have awoken in a field of flowers— a basic pleasure that was taken from me such a long time ago. It takes me back to my youth.

The citrus is a sharp note in the dry, acrid desert—the orange and plum making my mouth water. The jasmine and rose are a lightness that washes over me, so I inhale deeply, the tension finally unclenching. The patchouli and sandalwood conjure up slick flesh and burning incense, the images spiraling back.

No, please.

My first love.

I try to sit up, to open my eyes, and yet, there is only the darkness. And then I feel her touch.

It is such a simple mercy.

Her hands run over my scarred, withering flesh and she whispers in my ear, unintelligible words, a cacophony of gentle incoherence. Her eager mouth and gentle tongue press up against my neck, and my heart beats a rabbit-kick in a ribcage crisscrossed with scars.

What, speak up, say it again?

She pushes me back down, her lips brushing my mouth, my eyelids, my cheeks, and then she bites, drawing blood. Pushing me down harder, my head strikes the wood of the cot frame, her mouth at my neck where the whispers turn to threats.

My eyes are open now, and yet, I cannot see.

Her fingernails run down my arms, beads of crimson rising to the top of my leathery flesh, and I am so weak now, so vulnerable. No, I say.

If only it was that simple, she replies.

The photos appear now, in black and white—flashes of skin across so many years, in the back seats of cars, in dingy apartments where beer cans litter the floor, and then later, on glorious sheets made of Egyptian cotton, the thread count in the thousands, instrumental music in the background, candles burning in the muted darkness.

Not yet, she said.

The others, the same. An echo into the void.

Not tonight

Wait.

Please.

And the notes change now, to something musky, my stench rising to the surface—the salty tang of panic, my sour mouth gasping fear and confusion layered over shock.

Her hands are so strong, in the dark, and I am vulnerable to her base defilement, flipping me over, her strength growing, as the air grows foul. There is something else with us now, whatever love becomes when it is betrayed, the jasmine wilting, the fruit rotting in a liquid covered by buzzing flies, and she takes from me now, what I took from her then.

I plead for her to stop, asking for forgiveness. But it does me no good.

Open your eyes, Graysen.

The shack is filling with a heat that rises up from the desert and the girl holds out her hands, the scroll unfurling, to the floor and out across the empty room, the scripture filled with so very many transgressions.

YANK

by Somer Canon

Tanya stepped out onto her front porch with her coffee and smiled at the glorious glow of the morning light. It had been dreary, even violent, the last few days with constant rain and storms. The sunlight was a welcome sight and a balm to the sour mood she'd been in.

Humidity thickened the morning breeze and instead of feeling refreshed by a dying sigh from the cool night, she was brushed with a warm moistness that wasn't very refreshing. She smiled as she likened the sensation to that of being licked by a giant tongue. Her moment of peace was interrupted, though, when she noticed several of her neighbors out in their yards, knelt in their HOA-approved brown mulched flower beds, weeding furiously.

Catherine Mayfield, the head of the Homeowners Association, was a cat-eyed control freak who would leave notices in mailboxes over the slightest infraction of the rules. Heaven forbid a dandelion should appear or a mailbox be anything but the one approved brand. Catherine lived for infractions and fines and Tanya had, so far in her two years living in the otherwise wonderful neighborhood, only received three warnings from the HOA Burgermeister. One notice was for unapproved zinnias in her front flowerbeds that she'd planted during her first spring in her new home. She'd spent the day at the home improvement store and bought thirty dollars' worth of the pretty flowers. She was panicked and sad when she got the notice in her mailbox informing her that the zinnias were a non-compliant yard décor, and that if she did not remove them in twenty-four hours, she would be fined seventy-five dollars. All that fuss for a few little flowers.

Sighing, Tanya stepped off of her small porch to assess the damage the storms had done to her yard and to see how much weeding she would have to do before her shift at the hospital. She set her coffee cup down and walked through her thankfully small yard, picking up sticks that had blown off of neighboring trees. She walked to the side of her house, to the small shed where she kept the tools necessary to maintain her yard to HOA standards, and pulled a long, brown paper yard waste bag out and put the sticks inside. It wasn't enough to warrant calling the city to come for the bag, so she rolled the top closed and placed the bag back in the shed. She then got her flowery gardening gloves and her gardening trowel and trudged to the mulched flower bed, expecting to see weeds such as nettles and lambsquarters destroying her previously compliant garden.

What she saw instead caused her to utter a curse to herself. Feathery weeds, almost a foot high, had completely invaded the flower bed so much so that she could barely see the regulation brown mulch between their delicate fronds. It was going to take forever to pull them all. Tanya prayed they had small, shallow roots. Normally, she would have thrown the weeds into her grass and gone over them with her lawnmower to keep everything in line with what was expected, but there were far too many and their wilting bodies would be visible to any HOA spies driving around looking for anything out of place.

She trotted back to the shed to get her yard waste bag. She heard a sharp cry from one of her neighbors and looked in the direction of the sound to see if help was needed. Someone must have grabbed a nettle stem without their gloves on. When she saw nothing out of the ordinary, she continued to her task, not having a second to waste before she was due at work.

Tanya knelt down, the moist soil squelching under her weight, and grabbed one of the weeds by the stem and pulled. It resisted. Frowning, she tightened her pinching grip and pulled harder, hoping the stem didn't break. That would leave the roots intact for her to dig out with her trowel, costing her more time. She pulled and pulled and finally there was a strange popping sound. The weed came free, sending Tanya falling back onto her butt.

"Damn!" She huffed, looking down at the quickly withering weed in her gloved hand. By the time she dropped it into the yard waste bag, it had turned brown and shriveled into a tiny ball.

Strange weeds.

As she knelt down, this time armed with her trowel, she heard another sharp cry from a neighbor, but judging from the echoing nature of the sound, it was from the next street over. Everybody in the neighborhood was just as frantic to get their gardens into compliance before work to avoid Catherine's finicky wrath. Tanya didn't have the time to stop and wonder what was making the neighbors yell.

She jammed her trowel into the ground and pulled at a handful of the fine-leafed weeds. They wouldn't give at first, so she dug deeper and at a more precise angle with the trowel, hoping to cut through the root system to free the flora vermin from her flower bed. She wiggled the trowel deeper into the soil until she felt the iron tip finally break through something. With that, the handful of weeds came free, but before she had time to celebrate, there was a terrible, breathy shriek that came not from another neighbor, but from her flower bed. Startled, Tanya stared down at the ground trying to talk herself out of a certainty that she had indeed heard the ground scream. She looked at the shriveling handful of weeds in her hand and then back at the hole in the ground from where she had pulled them. There was something, a dark viscous liquid, pulsing up from the hole, like an oozing wound.

Stunned, she reached a hesitant hand out to the strange liquid and dipped a gloved finger into it, soaking the fabric. Upon inspection, the liquid was a deeply dark green, and it smelled of dead and rotting flowers. It reminded her of when the blooms from the gift shop at the hospital would begin to wilt and die, mixing with the already pungent stenches of the hospital. She could handle the antiseptics and bodily fluids, but the thick, perfumed smell of rotting flowers stuck in her gullet every time.

And what of that strange shriek she heard rise from the ground when the weeds were finally jerked free? She leaned closer to the strange hole and as the stench of floral decay filled her nose, she heard another shriek, this time from across the street. They were short screams, more like the yelp of a startled dog. She decided she had misheard one of her neighbors kneeling down on a pebble or tripping over something.

The hole in the ground continued to gently spew the green goo. Tanya eyed it suspiciously and decided that logic was the best way to describe that little piece of weirdness. It had rained a lot. This goo was surely just from the storms causing the ground to end up being waterlogged.

She shook her head and took a cleansing breath. She was so flustered to get her yard back in order before she got reprimanded, that she was hearing things and making herself afraid of ordinary groundwater.

Tanya adopted a stiff upper lip and plunged her trowel again into the earth. From behind her, another scream. She shook her head, wondering why she and all of her neighbors bowed before the tyranny of the HOA, why they were so frantic to avoid the attentions of Catherine that they were hurting themselves to do something that could have reasonably waited a day or two, or at least a few hours until after the workday had ended.

Shaking her head and playfully planning to move to a neighborhood that outright banned HOAs, she grabbed another handful of the weeds and worked to yank them free of the soil. When the trowel tore through their roots and the weeds came free, there came again that screeching yip. But this time she was certain it was coming from the ground. As the ooze again began bleeding out of the hole once occupied by the delicate weeds, Tanya stared for a moment. Something was amiss.

Another scream from a neighbor, but this one sounded different. This one was not a short, percussive yelp, but a strangled scream. Enough to leave any throat raw.

Tanya jumped up and looked around, hoping to locate the screamer so she could help. Before she could do so, she noticed Albert Knauer, her retired neighbor across the street, standing and backing away from his flower bed. Tanya wondered what had Albert looking so stunned or disoriented. She noticed the dirt in his flowerbed was kicking up, shifting and moving about as if something had been buried beneath the mulch and was struggling to find the surface.

"Hey, Albert! Hey!" Tanya called out.

The man must not have heard her. His eyes were fixed on the writhing subterranean thing. She looked around, hoping the other neighbors were also witnessing the strangeness. She saw they too were backing away from their flower beds, all lost in what they were seeing in their own yards and not what was going on around them. She felt the ground beneath her own feet start to shift.

Heart in her throat, Tanya turned to see the earth in her own flower bed start to push upwards. The little feathery weeds were wriggling and bouncing as the ground beneath them moved and stirred. Tanya could see that whatever was under there, the weeds were part of it. Mulch flew everywhere, and Tanya put a hand up to protect her eyes from the flying shards. She, like her neighbors, took slow, cautious steps away from the roiling dirt, curious but also afraid.

Fear took precedence when something enormous rose out of the ground. It was nearly as long as her flower bed, which the HOA stipulated could be no longer than twenty-five feet, and hers came in at an acceptable eighteen feet. It was shaped almost like an enormous log, with no discernable front or back, no head and no tail. Although it was obviously alive and mobile, the thing also didn't appear to be breathing. It would have looked downright unassuming in a forest, just another rotting, fallen tree trunk resting on the ground. The feathery weeds were growing from the top, looking like sun-worshippers, reaching for the light in religious revelry. Photosynthesizing for the enormous thing just under the dirt, perhaps.

Tanya gaped in awe for only a moment before she turned to flee the massive thing, but before she could get in more than a single step, a woody tentacle reached out from the thing and wrapped around her waist, holding her in place. She screamed, trying to wrench herself free. She twisted, pulled, and clawed at the strange tendril, but she may as well have been trying to cut down a tree with her fingernails.

Another, smaller, woody tentacle reached out and wrapped around the upper part of her right arm. She felt a hard jerk, looked down, screamed again.

It had ripped her arm right out of the socket.

She watched in horror as it placed the arm in the brown paper yard waste bag.

Yet another woody tentacle reached out and wrapped around her left leg. She screamed and fought with her one remaining arm, doing her best to get away. The thing gave a powerful jerk that sent her head whiplashing forward and nearly knocked her unconscious. When her senses cleared slightly, she saw the thing using several smaller woody arms to fold her leg that it had just ripped from her body, and stuff it into the yard waste bag.

The main tentacle around her waist tossed her aside. She fell onto the soft, moist grass, watching the thing wiggle and burrow itself back under the mulch. The pain was all that existed in her world for a moment. Fear was forgotten, the attack of the disappearing beast seemed to have happened an eon ago. Her entire being lived in a bubble of agony that invaded every cell, every sense.

Tanya was a nurse and should have been prepared to act, but the sharp anguish and the loss of a leg and arm kept her on the ground. She briefly rose above her misery and looked around at her neighbors and saw that they had their own strange, organic hulks. Albert's body was lying motionless on his lawn next to his head. Donna Reilly was writhing on her grass, missing all four of her limbs. Franco Amara was still in the clutches of his hulk, and from the sounds of it, several other neighbors were having a similar experience.

Tanya looked at her own damage. Tattered wounds, the skin in ribbons, massive blood loss and tissue damage. Her yard waste bag was soaked in blood and her foot, still wearing her sensible, and comfortable sneaker, was sticking out of the top. All for what? A lawn that met the exacting standards of the goddamn HOA?

Hearing the screams and moans of her neighbors, fellow victims of whatever had risen from the earth, Tanya laid back and stared up at the sky. The warmth was leaving her, literally pulsing from her and darkening her lawn. She smiled. Catherine would be writing notices to a bunch of corpses for non-compliant yard décor.

The sky was blue and clear, save for a few wisps, like memories of the dark, bloated storm clouds of the past few days. A warm breeze blew over her, and she could smell the wet earth. It was such a beautiful day.

LONE GUNMAN

by Jonathan Maberry

— 1 —

The soldier lay dead.
Mostly.
But not entirely.
And how like the world that was.
Mostly dead. But not entirely.

— 2 —

He was buried.

Not under six feet of dirt. There might have been some comfort in that. Some closure. Maybe even a measure of justice.

He wasn't buried like that. Not in a graveyard, either. Certainly not in Arlington, where his dad would have wanted to see him laid to rest. And not in that small cemetery back home in California, where his grandparents lay under the marble and the green cool grass.

The soldier was in some shithole of a who-cares town on the ass-end of Fayette County in Pennsylvania. Not under the ground. Not in a coffin.

He was buried under the dead.

Dozens of them.

Hundreds. A mountain of bodies. Heaped over and around him. Crushing him down, smothering him, killing him.

Not with teeth, though. Not tearing at him with broken fingernails. That was something, at least. Not much. Not a fucking lot. And maybe there was some kind of cosmic joke in all of this. He was certain of that much. A killer of men like him killed by having corpses piled on top of him. A quiet, passive death that had a kind of bullshit poetry attached to it.

However, Sam Imura was not a particularly poetic man. He understood it, appreciated it, but did not want to be written into it. No thanks.

He lay there, thinking about it. Dying. Not caring that this was it, that this was the actual end.

Knowing that thought to be a lie. Rationalization at best. His stoicism trying to give his fears a last handjob. *No, it's okay, it's a good death.*

Except that was total bullshit. There were no good deaths. Not one. He had been a soldier all his life, first in the regular army, then in Special Forces, and then in covert ops with a group called the Department of Military Sciences, and then freelance as top dog of a team of heavily armed problem solvers who ran under the nickname the Boy Scouts. Always a soldier. Pulling triggers since he was a kid. Taking lives so many times and in so many places that Sam had stopped counting. Idiots keep a count. Ego-inflated assholes keep count. A lot of his fellow snipers kept count. He didn't. He was never that crazy.

Now he wished he had. He wondered if the number of people he had killed with firearms, edged-weapons, explosives, and his bare hands equaled the number of corpses under which he was buried.

There would be a strange kind of justice in that, too. And poetry. As if all of the people he'd killed were bound to him, and that they were all fellow passengers on a black ship sailing to Valhalla. He knew that was a faulty metaphor, but fuck it. He was dying under a mountain of dead ghouls who had been trying to eat him a couple of hours ago. So…yeah, fuck poetry and fuck metaphors and fuck everything.

Sam wondered if he was going crazy.

He could build a case for it.

"No…"

He heard himself say that. A word. A statement. But even though it had come from him, Sam didn't exactly know what he meant by it. No, he wasn't crazy? No, he wasn't part of some celestial object lesson? No, he wasn't dying?

"No."

He said it again, taking ownership of the word. Owning what it meant.

No.

I'm not dead.

No, I'm not dying.

He thought about those concepts, and rejected them.

"No," he growled. And now he understood what he was trying to tell himself and this broken, fucked up world.

No. I'm not *going* to die.

Not here. Not now. Not like this. No motherfucking way. Fuck that, fuck these goddamn flesh-eating pricks, fuck the universe, fuck poetry two times, fuck God, fuck everything.

Fuck dying.

"No," he said once more, and now he heard *himself* in that word. The soldier, the survivor, the killer.

The dead hadn't killed him, and they had goddamn well tried. The world hadn't killed him, not after all these years. And the day hadn't killed him. He was sure it was nighttime by now, and he wasn't going to let that kill him, either.

And so he tried to move.

Easier said than done. The bodies of the dead had been torn by automatic gunfire as the survivors of the Boy Scouts had fought to help a lady cop, Dez Fox, and some other adults rescue several busloads of kids. They'd all stopped at the Sapphire Foods distribution warehouse to stock up before heading south to a rescue station. The dead had come hunting for their own food and they'd come in waves. Thousands of them. Fox and the Boy Scouts had fought their way out.

Kind of.

Sam had gone down under a wave of them and Gipsy, one of the shooters on his team, had tried to save him, hosing the ghouls with magazine after magazine. The dead fell and Sam had gone down beneath them. No one had come to find him, to dig him out.

He heard the bus engines roar. He heard Gipsy scream, though he didn't know if it was because the hungry bastards got her, or because she failed to save him. Impossible to say. Impossible to know unless he crawled out and looked for her body. Clear enough, though, to reason that she'd seen him fall and thought that he was dead. He should have been, but that wasn't an absolute certainty. He was dressed in Kevlar, with reinforced arm and leg pads, spider-silk gloves, a ballistic combat helmet with unbreakable plastic visor. There was almost no spot for teeth to get him. And, besides, Gipsy's gunfire and Sam's own had layered him with *actual* dead. Or whatever the new adjective was going to be for that. Dead was no longer dead. There was walking and biting dead and there was dead dead.

Sam realized that he was letting his mind drift into trivia. A defense mechanism. A fear mechanism.

"No," he said again. That word was his lifeline and it was his lash, his whip. *No.*

He tried to move. Found that his right hand could move almost ten inches. His feet were good, too, but there were bodies across his knees and chest and head. No telling how high the mound was, but they were stacked like *Jenga* pieces. The weight was oppressive but it hadn't actually crushed the life out of him. Not yet. He'd have to be careful moving so as not to crash the whole stinking mass on them down and really smash the life out of him.

It was a puzzle of physics and engineering, of patience and strategy. Sam had always prided himself on being a thinker rather than a feeler. Snipers were like that. Cold, exacting, precise. Patient.

Except…

When he began to move, he felt the mass of bodies move, too. At first he thought it was simple cause and effect, a reaction of limp weight to gravity and shifting support. He paused, and listened. There was no real light, no way to see. He knew that he had been unconscious for a while and so this had to be twilight, or later. Night. In the blackness of the mound he had nothing but his senses or touch and hearing to guide every movement of hand or arm or hip. He could tell when some movement he made caused a body, or a part of a body, to shift.

But then there was a movement up to his right. He had not moved his right arm or shoulder. He hadn't done anything in that quadrant of his position. All of his movements so far had been directed toward creating a space for his legs and hips to move because they were the strongest parts of him and could do more useful work longer than his arms or shoulders. The weight directly over his chest and what rested on his helmet had not moved at all.

Until they did.

There was a shift. No, a twitch. A small movement that was inside the mound. As if something moved. Not because of him.

Because *it* moved.

Oh, Jesus, he thought and for a moment he froze solid, not moving a finger, hardly daring to breathe, as he listened and felt for another twitch.

He waited five minutes. Ten? Time was meaningless.

There.

Again.

Another movement. Up above him. Not close, but not far away, either. How big was the mound? What was the distance? Six feet from his right shoulder? Six and a half feet from his head? Something definitely moved.

A sloppy, heavy movement. Artless, clumsy. But definite. He could hear the rasp of clothing against clothing, the slither-sound of skin brushing against skin. Close. So close. Six feet was nothing. Even with all of the dead limbs and bodies in the way.

Jesus, Jesus, Jesus.

Sam did not believe in Jesus. Or God. Or anything. That didn't matter now. No atheists in foxholes. No atheists buried under mounds of living dead ghouls. There had to be someone up there, in Heaven or Hell or whatever the fuck was there. Some drunk, malicious, amused, vindictive cocksucker who was deliberately screwing with him.

The twitch came again. Stronger, more definite, and...

Closer.

Shit. It was coming for him, drawn to him. By breath? By smell? Because of the movements he'd already made? Five feet now? Slithering like a snake through the pile of the dead. Worming its way toward him with maggot slowness and maggot persistence. One of them. Dead, but not dead enough.

Shit. Shit. Shit. Jesus. Shit.

Sam felt his heartbeat like a hammer, like a drum. Too fast, too loud. Could the thing hear it? It was like machinegun fire. Sweat stung his blind eyes and he could smell the stink of his own fear and it was worse than the reek of rotting flesh, shit, piss, and blood that surrounded him.

Get out. Get Out.

He twisted his hip, trying to use his pelvis as a strut to bear the load of the oppressive bodies. The mass moved and pressed down, sinking into the space created as he turned sideways. Sam pulled his bottom thigh up, using the top one as a shield to allow movement. Physics and engineering, slow and steady wins the race. The sounds he was making were louder than the twitching, rasping noises. No time to stop and listen. He braced his lower knee against something firm. A back. And pushing. The body moved two inches. He pushed again and it moved six more, and suddenly the weight on his hip was tilting toward the space behind the body he'd moved. *Jenga,* he thought. *I'm playing Jenga with a bunch of fucking corpses. The world is fucking insane.*

The weight on his helmet and shoulders shifted, too, and Sam pushed backward, fighting for every inch of new space, letting the weight that was on top of his slide forward and into where he'd been.

There was a kind of ripple through the mass of bodies and Sam did pause, afraid he was creating an avalanche. But that wasn't it.

Something was crawling on him. On his shoulder. He could feel the legs of some huge insect walking through the crevices of jumped body parts and then onto his shoulder, moving with the slow patience of a tarantula. Nothing else could be that big. But, this was Pennsylvania. Did they have tarantulas out here? He wasn't sure. There were wolf spiders out here, some orb-weavers and black widows, but they were small in comparison to the thing that was crawling toward his face. Out in California there were plenty of those big hairy monsters. Not here. Not here.

One slow, questing leg of the spider touched the side of his jaw, in the gap between the plastic visor and the chinstrap. It was soft, probing him, rubbing his skin. Sam gagged and tried to turn away, but there was no room. Then a second fat leg touched him. A third. Walking across his chin toward his panting mouth.

And that's when Sam smelled the thing.

Tarantulas did not have much of a smell. Not unless they were rotting in the desert sun.

This creature stank. It smelled like road kill. It smelled like…

Sam screamed.

He knew, he understood what it was that crawled across his face. Not the fat legs of some great spider but the clawing, grasping fingers of a human hand. That was the slithering sound, the twitching. One of *them* was buried with him. Not dead. Not alive. Rotting and filled with a dreadful vitality, reaching past the bodies, reaching through the darkness toward the smell of meat. Of food.

Clawing at him. He could feel the sharp edges of fingernails now as the fingers pawed at his lips and nose.

Sam screamed and screamed. He kicked out as hard as he could, shoving, pressing, jamming with knees and feet. Hurting, feeling the improbably heavy corpses press him down, as if they, even in their final death, conspired to hold him prisoner until the thing whose hand had found him could bring teeth and tongue and appetite to what it had discovered.

Sam wrestled with inhuman strength, feeling muscles bulge and bruise and strain. Feeling explosions of pain in his joints and lower back as he tried to move all of that weight of death. The fingers found the corner of his mouth, curled, hooked, tried to take hold of him and rip.

He dared not bite. The dead were filled with infection, with the damnable diseases that had caused all of this. Maybe he was already infected, he didn't know, but if he bit one of those grublike fingers it was as sure as a bullet in the brain. Only much slower.

"Fuck you!" he roared and spat the fingers out, turning his head, spitting into the darkness to get rid of any trace of blood or loose flesh. He wanted to vomit but there was no time, no room, no luxury even for that.

And so he went a little crazy.

A lot crazy.

All the way.

— 3 —

When the mountain of dead collapsed, it fell away from him, dozens of corpses collapsing down and then rolling the way he'd come, propelled by his last kicks, by gravity, by luck. Maybe helped along by the same drunk god who wanted more of the Sam Imura show. He found himself tumbling, too, bumping and thumping down the side of the mound, the jolts amplified by the lumpy body armor he wore. Kevlar stopped penetration of bullets but it did not stop the foot-pounds of impact.

He tried to get a hand out before he hit the pavement, managed it, but at the wrong part of his fall. He hit shoulder-first and slapped the asphalt a microsecond later. Pain detonated all through him. Everything seemed to hurt. The goddamn armor itself seemed to hurt.

Sam lay there, gasping, fighting to breathe, staring through the fireworks display in his eyes, trying to see the sky. His feet were above him, one heel hooked over the throat of a teenage girl; the other in a gaping hole that used to be the stomach of a naked fat man. He looked at the dead. Fifty, sixty people at least in the mound. Another hundred scattered around, their bodies torn to pieces by the battle that had happened here. Some clearly crushed by the wheels of those buses. Dead. All of them dead, though not all of them still. A few of the crushed ones tried to pull themselves along even though hips and legs and spines were flattened or torn completely away. A six-year-old kid sat with her back to a chain link fence. No legs, one hand, no lower jaw. Near her was an Asian woman who looked like she might have been pretty. Nice figure, but her face had been stitched from lower jaw to hairline with eight overlapping bullet holes.

Like that.

Every single one of the bodies around him was a person. Each person had a story, a life, details, specifics. Things that made them people instead of nameless corpses. As he lay there Sam felt the weight of who they had been crushing him down as surely as the mound had done minutes ago. He didn't know any of them, but he was kin to all of them.

He closed his eyes for a moment and tried not to see anything. But they were there, hiding behind his lids as surely as if they were burned onto his retinas.

Then he heard a moan.

A sound from around the curve of the mound. Not a word, not a call for help. A moan. A sound of hunger, a sound of a need so bottomless that no amount of food could ever hope to satisfy it. An impossible and irrational need, too, because why would the dead need to feed? What good would it do them?

He knew what his employers had said about parasites driving the bodies of the victims, about an old Cold War weapon that slipped its leash, about genetically modified larvae in the bloodstream and clustered around the cerebral cortex and motor cortex and blah blah blah. Fuck that. Fuck science. This wasn't science, anyway. Not as he saw it right then, having just crawled out of his own grave. This was so much darker and more twisted than that. Sam didn't know what to call it. Even when he believed in God there was nothing in the Bible or Sunday school that covered this shit. Not even Lazarus or Jesus coming back from the dead. J.C. didn't start chowing down on the Apostles when he rose. So, what was this?

The moan was louder. Coming closer.

Get up, asshole, scolded his inner voice.

"What can't I just lay here and say fuck it?"

Because you're in shock, dickhead and you're going to die.

Sam thought about that. Shock? Yeah. Maybe. Concussion? Almost certainly. Military helmets stopped shrapnel but the stats on traumatic brain injury were staggering. Sam knew a lot of front-line shooters who'd been benched with TBI. Messed up the head, scrambled thoughts, and...

A figure lumbered into sight. Not crawling. Walking. One of them. Wearing mechanic's coveralls. Bites on his face and nothing in his eyes but hunger and hate. Walking. Not shuffling or limping. Not even staggering, like some of them did. Walking, sniffing the air, black and bloody drool running over its lips and chin.

Sam's hand immediately slapped his holster, but there was no sidearm. He fumbled for his knife, but that was gone, too.

Shit. Shit. Shit.

He swung his feet off of the mound of dead and immediately felt something like an incendiary device explode in the muscles of his lower back. The pain was instantly intense and he screamed.

The dead mechanic's head snapped toward him, the dead eyes focusing. It snarled, showing blooding, broken teeth. And then it came at him. Fast. Faster than he'd seen with any of them. Or maybe it was that he was slowed down, broken. Usually in the heat of combat the world slowed down and Sam seemed to walk through it, taking his time to do everything right, to see everything, to own the moment. Not now.

With a growl of unbearable hunger, the ghoul flung itself on Sam.

He got a hand up in time to save his skin, chopping at the thing's throat, feeling tissue and cartilage crunch as he struck, feeling it do no good at all except to change the moan into a gurgle. The mechanic's weight crashed down on him, stretching the damaged muscles in Sam's back, ripping a new cry from him, once more smothering him with weight and mass.

Sam kept his hand in place in the ruined throat and looped his other hand over, punching the thing on the side of the head, once, twice, again and again. Breaking bones, shattering the nose, doing no appreciable good. The pain in his lower back was incredible, sickening him even more than the smell of the thing that clawed at him. The creature snapped its teeth together with a hard porcelain *clack,* but Sam kept those teeth away from him. Not far enough away, though.

He braced one foot flat on the floor and used that leg to force his hips and shoulders to turn. It was like grinding broken glass into whatever was wrong with his spine, but he moved, and Sam timed another punch to knock the ghoul over him, letting his hips be the axle of a sloppy wheel. The mechanic went over and down and then Sam was on top of him. He climbed up and dropped a knee onto the creature's chest, pinning it against the place where the asphalt met the slope of corpses. Then Sam grabbed the snapping jaw in one hand and a fistful of hair at the back of the thing's head with the other.

In the movies snapping a neck is nothing. Everyone seemed to be able to do it.

That's the movies.

In the real world, there is muscle and tendon and bone and none of them want to turn that far or that fast. The body isn't designed to die. Not that easily. And Sam was exhausted, hurt, sick, weak.

There was no snap.

What there was…was a slow turn of the head. Inch by inch, fighting against the ghoul's efforts to turn back and bite him. Sam pulled and pushed, having to lean forward to get from gravity what his damaged body did not want to provide. The torsion was awful. The monster clawed at him, tearing at his clothes, digging at the Kevlar limb pads.

Even dead, it tried to live.

Then the degree of rotation passed a point. Not a sudden snap, no abrupt release of pressure. More of a slow, sickening, wet grinding noise as vertebra turned past their stress point, and the point where the brain stem joined the spinal cord became pinched inside those gears. Pinched, compressed, and then ruptured.

The clawing hands flopped away. The body beneath him stopped thrashing. The jaws snapped one last time and then sagged open.

After that Sam had to finish it, to make sure it was a permanent rupture and not a temporary compression. The sounds told him that. And the final release of all internal resistance.

Sam fell back and rolled off and lay side by side with the mechanic, their bodies touching at shoulder, hip, thigh, foot, Sam's fingers still entwined in the hair as if they lay spent after some obscene coupling. One breathed, the other did not. Overhead the moon peered above the treetops like a peeping Tom.

— 4 —

The moon was completely above the treetops by the time Sam got up.

His back was a mess. Pulled, strained, torn or worse, it was impossible to tell. He had a high pain threshold, but this was at his upper limit. And, besides, it was easier to man up and walk it off when there were other soldiers around. He'd seen his old boss, Captain Ledger, brave it out and even crack jokes with a bullet in him.

Alone, though, it's easier to be weaker, smaller, to be more intimate with the pain, and be owned by it.

It took him half an hour to stand. The world tried to do some fancy cartwheels and the vertigo made Sam throw up over and over again until there was nothing left in his belly.

It took another hour to find a gun, a SIG Sauer, and fifteen more minutes to find one magazine for it. Nine rounds. Then he saw a shape lying partly under three of the dead. Male, big, dressed in the same unmarked black combat gear as Sam wore. He tottered over and knelt very slowly and carefully beside the body. He rolled one of the dead over and off so he could see who it was. He knew it had to be one of his Boy Scouts, but it still hurt him to see the face. DeNeille Shoopman, who ran under the combat callsign of Shortstop. Good kid. Hell of a soldier.

Dead, with his throat torn away.

But goddamn it, Shortstop's eyes were open, and they clicked over to look at him. The man he knew—his friend and fellow soldier—did not look at him through those eyes. Nothing did. Not even the soul of a monster. That was one of the horrors of this thing. The eyes are supposed to be the windows of the soul, but when he looked into Shortstop's brown eyes it was like looking through the windows of an empty house.

Shortstop's arms were pinned, and there was a lot of meat and muscle missing from his chest and shoulders. He probably couldn't raise his arms even if he was free. Some of the dead were like that. A lot of them were. They were victims of the thing that had killed them, and although they all reanimated, only a fraction of them were whole enough to rise and hunt.

Sam placed one hand over Shortstop's heart. It wasn't beating, of course, but Sam remembered how brave a heart it had been. Noble, too, if that wasn't a corny thing to think about a guy he'd gotten drunk with and traded dirty jokes with. Shortstop had walked with him through the Valley of the Shadow of Death so many times. It wasn't right to let him lie here, ruined and helpless and hungry until he rotted into nothing.

"No," said Sam.

He had nine bullets and needed every single one of them if he was going to survive. But he needed one now really bad.

The shot blasted a hole in the night.

Sam sat beside Shortstop for a long time, his hand still there over the quiet heart. He wept for his friend and he wept for the whole goddamn world.

— 5 —

Sam spent the night inside the food distribution warehouse.

There were eleven of the ghouls in there. Sam found the section where they stored the lawn care tools. He found two heavy-bladed machetes and went to work.

When he was done he was in so much pain that he couldn't stand it, so he found where they stacked the painkillers. Extra-strength something-or-other. Six of those, and six cans of some shitty local beer. The door was locked and he had the place to himself.

He slept all through the night.

— 6 —

When he woke up he took more painkillers but this time washed it down with some trendy electrolyte water. Then he ate two cans of beef stew he cooked over a camping stove.

More painkillers, more food, more sleep.

The day passed and he didn't die.

The pain diminished by slow degrees.

In the morning he found a set of keys to the office, and found a radio in there, a TV, a phone, and a lockbox with a Glock 26 and four empty magazines, plus three boxes of 9mm hollow points. He nearly wept.

The phone was dead.

Sam turned on the news and listened as he loaded bullets into the magazines for the Glock and the single mag he had for the SIG Sauer.

He heard a familiar voice. The guy who had been here with the lady cop. Skinny blond-haired guy who was a reporter for a ninth-rate cable news service.

"This is Billy Trout reporting live from the apocalypse…"

Trout had a lot of news and none of it was good. His convoy of school buses was in Virginia now and creeping along roads clogged by refugees. There were as many fights among the fleeing survivors as there were between the living and the dead.

Typical, he thought. *We've always been our worst enemies.*

At noon Sam felt well enough to travel, though he considered holing up in this place. There was enough food and water here to keep him alive for five years, maybe ten. But that was a sucker's choice. He'd eat his gun before a week was out. Anyone would. Solitude and a lack of reliable intel would push him into a black hole from which he could never crawl out. No, the smart move was to find people.

Step one was finding a vehicle.

This place had trucks.

Lots of trucks.

So he spent four hours using a forklift to load pallets of supplies into a semi. He collected anything that could be used as a weapon and took them, too. If he found people, they would need to be armed. He thought about that, then went and loaded sleeping bags, toilet paper, diapers, and whatever else he thought a group of survivors might need. Sam was a very practical man, and each time he made a smart and thoughtful decision, he could feel himself stepping back from the edge of despair. He was planning for a mission, and that gave him a measure of stability. He had people to find and protect, and that gave him a purpose.

He gassed up at the fuel pump on the far side of the parking lot. A few new ghouls were beginning to wander in through the open fence, but Sam kept clear of them. When he left, he made sure not to crash into any of them. Even a semi could take damage and he had to make this last.

Practical.

Once he reached the crossroads, though, he paused, idling, trying to decide where to go. Following the buses was likely pointless. If they were already heading south, and if Billy Trout was able to broadcast, then they were alive. The last of the Boy Scouts were probably with them.

So he turned right, heading toward the National Armory in Harrisville, north of Pittsburgh. If it was still intact, that would be a great place to build a rescue camp. If it was overrun, then he'd take it back and secure it.

It was a plan.

He drove.

There was nothing on the radio but bad information and hysteria, but there were CDs in the glove compartment. A lot of country and western stuff. He fucking hated country and western, but it was better than listening to his own thoughts. He slipped in a Brad Paisley CD and listened to the man sing about coal miners in Harlan County. Depressing as shit, but it was okay to listen to.

It was late when he reached Evans City, a small town on the ass-end of nowhere. All through the day and into the evening he saw the leavings of the world. Burned towns, burned cars, burned farmhouses, burned bodies. The wheels of the semi crunched over spots where thousands of shell casings littered the road. He saw a lot of the dead. At first they were stragglers, wandering in no particular direction until they heard the truck. Then they walked toward him as he drove, and even though Sam didn't want to hit any of them, there were times where he had no choice. Then he found that by slowing down he could push them out of the way without impact damage to the truck. Some of them fell and he had to set his teeth as the wheels rolled over them, crushing and crunching things that had been people twenty-four hours ago.

He found that by driving along country roads he could avoid a lot of that, so he turned the truck out into the farmlands. He refueled twice, and each time he wasted bullets defending his truck. Sam was an excellent shot, but hoping to get a head shot each time was absurd, and his back was still too sore to do it all with machetes or an axe. The first fuel stop cost him nineteen rounds. The second took thirteen. More than half a box of shells. No good. Those boxes would not last very long at that rate.

As he drove past an old cemetery on the edge of Evans City he spotted smoke rising from up ahead. He passed a car that was smashed into a tree, and then a pickup truck that had been burned to a shell beside an exploded gas pump. That wasn't the source of the smoke, though, because the truck fire had burned itself out.

No, there was a farmhouse nearby and out in front of it was a mound of burning corpses.

Sam pulled the truck to a stop and sat for a while, studying the landscape. The moon was bright enough and he had his headlights on. Nothing moved except a tall, gently-twisting column of gray smoke that rose from the pyre.

"Shit," said Sam. He got out of the truck but left the motor running. He stood for a moment to make sure his back wouldn't flare up and that his knees were steady. The SIG was tucked into his shoulder holster and he had the Glock in a two-hand grip as he approached the mound.

It was every bit as high as the one under which he'd been buried. Dozens upon dozens of corpses, burned now to stick figures, their limbs contracted by heat into fetal curls. The withered bones shifted like logs in a dying hearth, sending sparks up to the night where they vanished against the stars.

Sam turned away and walked over to the house.

He could read a combat scene as well as any experienced soldier, and what he was seeing was a place where a real battle had taken place. There were blood splashes on the ground and on the porch where the dead had been dropped. The blood was blacker even than it should have been in this light, and he could see threadlike worms writhing it in. Sam unclipped a Maglite he'd looted from the warehouse and held it backward in his left hand while resting the pistol across the wrist, the barrel in sync with the beam as he entered the house.

Someone had tried to hold this place, that was clear enough. They'd nailed boards over the windows and moved furniture to act as braces. Many of those boards lay cracked and splintered on the floor amid more shell casings and more blood spatter. He went all the way through to the kitchen and saw more of the same. An attempt to fortify that had failed.

The upstairs was splashed with gore but empty, and the smears on the stairs showed where bodies had been dragged down.

He stepped to the cellar door, which opened off of the living room. He listened for any kind of sound, however small, but there was nothing. Sam went down, saw sawhorses and a door that had been made into a bed. Saw blood. A bloody trowel. Pieces of meat and bone.

Nothing else.

No one else.

He trudged heavily up the stairs and went out onto the porch and stood in the moonlight while he thought this through. Whoever had been in the house had made a stand, but it was evident they'd lost their battle.

So who built the mound? Who dragged the bodies out? Whose shell-casings littered the yard?

He peered at the spent brass. Not military rounds. .30-30s, .22, some 9mm, some shotgun shells. Hunters?

Maybe.

Probably, with a few local police mixed in.

Why come here? Was there a rescue mission here that arrived too late? Or was it a sweep? The armed citizens of this rural town fighting back?

Sam didn't know.

There were dog footprints in the dirt, too. And a lot of boot and shoe prints. A big party. Well-armed, working together. Getting the job done.

Fighting back.

For the first time since coming to Pennsylvania with the Boy Scouts, Sam felt his heart lift. The buses of kids and the lady cop had gotten out. And now someone had organized a resistance. Probably a redneck army, but fuck it. That would do.

He walked around the house to try and read the footprints. The group who had come here had walked off east, across the fields. Going where? Another farm? A town? Anywhere the fight took them or need called them.

"Hooah," he said, using the old Army Ranger word for everything from 'fuck you' to 'fuck yeah.' For now it meant 'fuck yeah.'

East, he thought, was as good a direction as any. Maybe those hunters were protecting their own. Sam glanced at his truck. Maybe they could use some food and a little professional guidance.

Maybe.

He smiled into the darkness. Probably not a very nice smile. A hunter's smile. A soldier's smile. A killer's smile. Maybe all of those. But it was something only the living could do.

He was still smiling when he climbed back into the cab of his truck, turned around in front of the old house, found the road again, and headed east.

REMEMBERING FRANK

By Hunter Shea

Frank always gave my monster stories love and though we never met face to face, I knew he had that inner child magic glowing within him. I'd like to think that the next time we meet, it will be under the stars, or perhaps one with the stars, hoping for a glimpse of something that will bring us right back to those fairy dust years where anything and everything was possible.

A TATTOO FOR JOEY

by Tom Deady

Grampa," the little boy squealed, running up the driveway and throwing himself into my arms.

I caught the boy with a grunt and hoisted him up. "How's my big boy doing? Ready for some big fun this weekend?"

Joey nodded, beaming, as his mother—my daughter, Monica—walked up to meet us. "Dad, I can't thank you enough for taking Joey on such short notice," she said, kissing my scruffy cheek. She placed his duffel bag on the ground at the bottom of the front steps, smoothing her Journey concert t-shirt. "Hey, you painted the porch."

I turned to look at my handiwork. The two-story Cape Cod style house was in good shape, but it was a never-ending battle. "Are you kidding," I said, a bit out of breath, "we are going to have a 'boys only' weekend. No girls allowed, right Joey?"

"Girls have cooties," the six-year-old crowed.

The three of us shared a laugh, then Monica got serious. "Dad, are you sure you're up for this? You haven't had Joey overnight since…" She let the words dangle there unspoken.

I waved dismissively. "That was almost a year ago. I'm fine. I'm more worried about you. Is everything okay? You were a bit…evasive on the phone."

My daughter's face clouded, but she tried to brighten it up with a smile. It didn't work. She brushed a stray lock of her long brown hair behind her ear. "Al is away on business, stuck in Atlanta. He was supposed to be home today, but they didn't close the deal in time. He has to stay until Monday to sign the papers." Her brows knitted until they almost touched. "I'm flying down to meet him."

I watched my daughter carefully, with the scrutiny of a dad. Again, she tucked a lock of hair absently behind her ear. *That's her tell, her nervous signal.* There was more, and I wasn't going to like it. Al Winthrop was a dirtbag, always had been as far as I was concerned. "Spill it, Monica. Whatever it is won't change my opinion of Al. We've already been over that."

Monica sighed, glancing at Joey to make sure he wasn't listening. He'd brought a toy helicopter out of the car with him and was flying it around the driveway, making the accompanying *wop-wop-wop* sounds to go with the maneuvers. "Al doesn't know I'm coming," she said quietly, "and I doubt he'll be happy to see me."

I nodded, also checking on my grandson before speaking. Kids had a way of picking things up even if you didn't think they were paying attention. "You don't think he's alone, do you?"

Monica dropped her eyes and shook her head. She wasn't quick enough, I had caught the glisten of tears building before she looked away. "How about you stay with Joey and I fly down there to have a chat with him," I said angrily, only half-kidding.

Monica shook her head, eying me. *Is that doubt on her face?* I reached out and gently tilted her head up to meet my gaze, tamping down my rage as the first tear slipped out of her eye. "I think it's over, Dad," she said shakily, falling into my arms.

I patted her back, tightening my embrace. "Joey and I will be just fine," I said too loudly. "We've got a busy schedule of blanket forts, cartoons, and pizza. You go have fun and we'll see you when you get back."

Monica wiped her eyes and kissed me, then crouched in front of Joey. "You be good for Grampa, okay, kid?"

Joey nodded, a fearful look crossing his face. "Why are you sad, Mommy?"

"Because I'm going to miss you," she said, scooping him into her arms and squeezing until he cried uncle.

They finished their goodbyes, and I sent Joey inside. Monica looked at me for a long time. "Dad, are you sure you're all right?"

A seed of anger took root. *One little visit to the psych ward and I'm marked for life.* I buried the thought and forced a smile. "We're both going to be fine."

Finally, she nodded and got into her Camry with a wave and a toot of the horn.

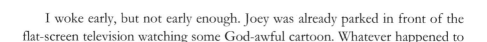

I woke early, but not early enough. Joey was already parked in front of the flat-screen television watching some God-awful cartoon. Whatever happened to *The Flintstones* or *Scooby-Doo?*

"What do you want for breakfast, champ?" He finally answered me the third time—when I was standing in front of the television. I got to work on pancakes, wondering what sorcery it would take to get him away from the boob tube. I placed my hands on my hips and stretched, trying to shed the morning aches I'd become accustomed to.

We ate our pancakes while Joey explained the entire history of the silly show he'd been watching. I tuned him out, nodding where appropriate, and cringing at the veritable pool of maple syrup his soggy pancakes were floating in. After much negotiating, he brushed his teeth and got dressed. He wandered back into the living room looking for the remote, which I had already hidden.

"Grampa, I can't turn on the TV," he said mournfully, as if losing the remote were akin to his puppy dying.

"That's correct, oh, wise one," I said grandly. "Now is the time of day when all great adventures begin. So, we shall begin ours." *A nap would be a grand adventure.* This got to him and I smiled when his eyes widened.

"What's our adventure, Grampa? Are we going to hunt for buried treasure? Slay dragons?" His face glowed with the endless possibilities.

"I can't promise dragons," I said with a grin, "but I do know a place where we can see many creatures of all shapes and sizes." His smile erased my desire for a nap. I had an adventure to create.

We arrived at the zoo early enough to beat any crowds—if people even crowded into zoos these days. I parked the car and we walked up to the main gates. It looked more like a theme park than the zoos I'd visited as a kid. I was hoping something extraordinary would be going on and luck was with me. I tapped Joey on the shoulder and pointed to the sign:

"GIANT REPTILES FROM AROUND THE WORLD!"

It didn't matter if he could read it or not, the pictures that accompanied the words told the story. There were alligators, crocodiles, sea turtles, Galápagos tortoises, and… I really was in luck: a Komodo dragon.

I paid for the tickets, grabbed a map of the zoo, and Joey and I set forth on our quest. For the next three hours, I was as much a six-year-old as Joey. We marveled over the incredible array of creatures the zoo had on exhibit. We exited exhausted—my morning aches and pains now amplified—but deliriously happy. It was a day he'd never forget.

"Grampa, I'm hungry," Joey moaned from the back seat.

I glanced in the rearview mirror. He was wide awake and grimacing as if he hadn't eaten in days. A moment ago, he'd been heavy-lidded and well on his way to a nap. I stole a look at the car's digital clock. *Shit.* It was almost two in the afternoon and he hadn't eaten since breakfast. Well, except for the sno-cone and some popcorn.

"Hang on, big guy. We'll stop for a snack, okay?"

He nodded. "Cracker Jacks," he said, and I still had hope he'd fall asleep.

Five minutes later, Sal's Quick Stop came into view. We were only a few minutes from home, but Joey was wide awake and muttering about being hungry. I pulled into the lot and helped Joey out of his car seat. "Cracker Jacks and something to drink, then home we go, right?"

Joey nodded, tightening his grip on my hand as we crossed the parking lot and entered the little store. The air conditioning was cranking, and I shivered at the sudden temperature change. We went to the candy aisle and perused the selection. After a minute or two I realized I had a problem: there weren't any Cracker Jacks.

"Hey, did you ever try these?" I held up a bag of cheese curls. He shook his head and repeated his demand for Cracker Jacks. I watched him carefully. The way his forehead was creased and his rapid blinks meant one thing: there was a meltdown on the way. *Is that how I looked?* I shook the thought away, desperately searching the shelves for the box with the stupid sailor on it and the cheap made-in-China prize inside.

"Grampa, I need Cracker Jacks," he whined, too loud for the little store.

I closed my eyes, the little tic in my temple going like mad. I took a deep breath and opened my eyes. *Was that there a minute ago?* I reached out and snatched the box from the shelf. The picture was the same caramel-coated popcorn and the same red stripes. But instead of the sailor there was a baseball player taking a mighty swing with an oversized bat. The box read, "Ballpark Snacks—Special Prize Inside!"

"Joey," I nearly screamed with relief, "here we go."

His face exploded in a smile, then he reached for the box, the smile fading quickly. "These aren't the right ones," he mumbled, the meltdown signals reappearing.

"No, these are better than regular old Cracker Jacks," I told him with no uncertainty. "Look here," I pointed to the box. "There's a special prize inside, not just the same old prizes you usually get."

He took the box dubiously, then nodded firmly. I took his hand, glancing back at the shelf. *Dodged a bullet. It's the last one.* The temperature seemed to drop even further, and I rushed him up to the checkout, anxious to get back outside in the sun.

Joey didn't take my hand as we exited; he was too busy trying to tear the box open. "Whoa, whoa, sonny." I snatched the box from him and took his hand. "We'll be home in five minutes and you can eat your snack like a civilized young man." He grumbled but didn't give me a hard time. I stood for a moment before crossing the lot back to the car. The afternoon sun felt like heaven on my face after the chill of the store. I took a deep breath and was hit with a sudden, profound sadness. The beautiful day, the aroma of freshly cut grass, my grandson's tiny hand in my own...it all felt somehow hopeless. Somehow not enough. *Just like last year.* I shook the thought away and stepped off the curb. The blaring horn nearly stopped my heart as I stumbled backward dragging Joey with me.

The car screeched to a halt. *Where did he come from?* A young man jumped out looking from me to Joey with wild eyes that held both fear and anger. Once he saw we were both unhurt, his anger gained control.

"What the hell, man? Watch where you're going!" He looked again at Joey, who had started to cry when he spotted a small scrape on his knee. "Who the fuck lets *you* watch their kid?" He got back into his seventies-era Plymouth

Satellite and pulled away, AC/DC cranked on the stereo and his middle finger waving out the window.

"Joey, it's okay. Let me see that knee." I made a big deal of examining it, partly to calm him down but mostly because I wasn't sure if my legs would hold me if I attempted to stand. I should have given that asshole a piece of my mind. He was driving way too fast in a parking lot full of pedestrians.

"I'm glad you're not hurt."

I turned to see an elderly woman looking down at us. Her stern countenance held none of the compassion of her words. "You could have both been killed stepping into traffic like that. An old fool and a young fool," she huffed.

I got to my feet, shaky legs and all. "Why don't you mind your own fucking business, you dried up twat."

She recoiled, a look of such puritanical outrage on her face, that I nearly burst out laughing. "I never," she muttered.

"And you never will," I replied. "Now kindly fuck off."

She sputtered something I didn't understand and stormed off.

"Let's go, Joey. The adventure continues," I said through a burst of giggles.

Joey eyed me curiously, but I didn't care. He'd probably heard those words before, and if he hadn't, well, today was as good a day as any to hear them.

"Grampa," Joey said between crunches of his knock-off Cracker Jacks, "why were you so mean to that lady?"

We were back home and he was all set up on the couch with his snack and a sippy-cup of milk on a fold-out TV tray.

I sighed. Having regained my composure, I was embarrassed. "That was a mistake, son. I was mostly mad at myself for almost getting us hurt, then I was mad at the driver for yelling at me. I was wrong to take out my anger on that poor woman. Do you understand?" *Even though she was a dusty old cunt.* He shrugged, already bored with the conversation. So much for teaching him a life lesson.

"Can I open my special prize now?"

"Sure, kid, let's see what you got," I replied with enthusiasm so insincere I was surprised he didn't pick up on it.

Joey tore into the wrapper and tossed it aside to examine his prize. It was one of those fake tattoos that you wet your arm to apply. They never worked right, half the stupid thing staying stuck to the paper when you peeled it away. *Great, he'll pitch a real fit when it doesn't come out perfect.* While Joey stared at it like it was the Holy Grail, I picked up the wrapper to throw it away. I glanced at the picture of the kid in the baseball uniform, then did a double take, bringing the picture closer to my aging eyes. I picked up the empty box and compared the picture of the boy to the one on the wrapper. I squinted, going back and forth between the two, holding them so close they were almost touching my nose.

The boy was the same on both, yet *not* the same. It was why they were different that was driving me crazy, like those games in the newspaper where you have to find ten differences between two pictures that looked the same. Finally, I saw it. *Or it saw me.* It was the eyes—isn't it always? The boy on the box looked determined but happy as he swung the bat. The boy on the prize wrapper looked gleeful, but in a demented way. *Like I looked last year?* Like he might be hitting someone's skull instead of a baseball. I threw both on the table and clasped my hands together so Joey wouldn't see them shaking.

"Tattoo, eh?" *Does my voice sound weird?* "What's the picture, a dragon? Cool hot rod?" But I already knew it was neither of those.

Joey held it up, his own eyes shining with a mad glee, and there was the kid in the baseball uniform. "Can I put it on, Grampa?"

I stared at that tattoo for a long time without answering. Chainsaws were shredding up my guts, every instinct telling me to grab that vile thing and rip it into tiny pieces then burn it. But that would be crazy. What would Monica say?

"Grampa?" Joey's voice held a question, but he wasn't asking if he could put on the tattoo. He was asking if Grampa was losing it.

"Sure, of course. Let me see those instructions." I held out my hand, unable to hide the tremors. Joey's face scrunched up when he saw the trembling old-man hands reaching toward him, but he gave over the instructions. I read them slowly, more to kill time than anything else. A dull ache had started at one temple and was creeping across my forehead. *Maybe it's a stroke*, alarmed at the hopeful note that accompanied the thought. Feeling like I was walking the last mile, I trudged over to the kitchen sink with Joey in tow. I helped him wet the waxy paper and hold it on his thin forearm.

The five minutes I waited for the tattoo to be ready passed endlessly. It was long enough to enjoy a slideshow of vivid images of what might be.

The tattoo contains acid and burns through his flesh while he writhes in pain.

The tattoo is some super-adhesive and when I pull the paper off, Joey's skin comes with it, exposing raw muscle and snaking veins.

The tattoo is somehow poisonous and I'm powerless as pus-filled sores bubble across his entire body.

"Grampa?" That question again.

"Yes, it's time." I was not surprised to feel a tear zigzagging down my cheek. I peeled the paper off slowly, expecting something, expecting anything. When it came off with a wet slurpy sound, I saw it was just a silly tattoo of a kid in a baseball outfit swinging a bat. Now the fear was real. Not fear for Joey but for my own sanity. It was not just like last year, I realized, it was worse. I should have called Monica.

"Thanks, Grampa, it's so cool!"

Joey looked at the tattoo with the wonder only a six-year-old has. Then he looked at me with the honest adoration saved only for grandparents, and my silly fears melted away. Calling Monica and last year's incident slipped into that place where bad dreams go upon waking, and I basked in the role of best Grampa ever.

"Make sure you don't touch it until it's dry, or it might scrape off, okay?"

Joey nodded solemnly. "Today was fun, Grampa. Thanks." He hugged my legs, careful to not touch the part of his arm with the tattoo to my clothes.

I put a hand on his back and tousled his hair with the other. "It was a fine adventure, wasn't it?"

We spent the rest of the afternoon constructing an elaborate blanket fort in the living room. Monica called before bedtime, and Joey talked a mile-a-minute about the zoo and everything we saw, finishing breathlessly about the special prize. Finally, he handed me the phone.

"Sounds like you had quite a day," Monica said, and I could almost hear her smile coming through the phone.

"It wasn't just a day, it was an *adventure*," I replied with a wink at Joey. He didn't notice; he was staring intently at his tattoo. "What about your day?" I asked quietly.

"Al doesn't know I'm here yet," she said, suddenly sounding old and tired. "I've been playing Nancy Drew and following him around, but he's been with clients all day, *male* clients, and they all just had dinner at the hotel restaurant." She paused, and I thought I heard her sniffing back tears. "What if I'm wrong, Dad?"

"It's not a crime to be wrong, honey." *I'm shredding Al's face off with a cheese grater in my mind.* "It's not like your suspicions are unwarranted." *He's screaming as I pour Tabasco sauce on the tattered remains of his face.*

"I know, but what kind of wife does it make me?" Now she couldn't hide the tears.

"One who is concerned about her marriage, that's all." *His skin hangs in bloody strips as I stand there laughing.*

"What's so funny, Dad? Is it Joey?"

I was laughing out loud. Something hard and cold settles in my chest. "Yeah, we made a cool blanket fort, and he wants to sleep in it. Is that okay?"

"Dad?" Her tone was even, but I heard the accusation in it. "Are *you* okay? Do you need me to come home?"

"Don't be silly, Monica." I laughed. "We're having the time of our lives here. You do what you need to do, and we'll be here when you get back. I'm thinking about taking him to Canobie Lake tomorrow, where we'll probably eat too much crap and come home with bellyaches."

"Make sure he wears sunscreen, okay?"

She sounded convinced. Thankfully, most of the zoo was shady, so we didn't need no stinkin' sunscreen. I almost giggled but managed to hide it with a cough.

We said our goodnights, and I set to the task of getting Joey ready for bed. Monica never answered about him sleeping in the fort, so that was as good as a yes for me. I stayed with him, reading books to him until he conked out, then it was off to bed for me. I was exhausted.

I woke the next day feeling refreshed and mentally planning my day as I lay in bed. I'd have to pick up a few things at the grocery store, maybe run over to the True Value for—*Joey.* I looked at the clock on the night table. The dial glared accusingly at me, telling me it was after nine. I rolled out of bed, listening for the sound of the television, and rushed downstairs.

How could I have forgotten I was minding him?

"Joey, you up?" The blanket fort was intact and the television was off.

"Grampa?"

It was Joey, but where was he? His voice sounded so far away. Had he gone outside alone? Monica would kill me...

"Joey, where are you?"

"In the fort," he replied.

Impossible. I hurried over and yanked the blanket-door open. *He's not there!*

"Joey?"

"Grampa, I feel funny." Barely a whisper.

I pulled the fort apart, tossing the blankets aside. I felt like the big, bad wolf going after one of the little pigs. "There you are," I breathed, my legs wobbly with relief. *Why hadn't I seen him before. He was right inside the fort.* "Not feeling good?"

He sat up slowly, which was a red flag because Joey didn't do *anything* slowly. "I feel...tired." His eyes squinted, and he looked up at the ceiling. "Not exactly tired, I can't..." His words trailed off, so I didn't hear what he'd said.

I knelt beside him and placed a hand on his forehead. "You don't have a fever. Does anything hurt?"

He shook his head. His bottom lip stuck out and his eyes glistened. "I'm scared, Grampa. I feel like I'm going away." His tears came, fast and furious as a summer thunderstorm.

I reached out and pulled him to me, and for just a second, he felt...diaphanous. Like he was there, but not *all* there. *I feel like I'm going away.* The words passed quickly through my thoughts, but not before my heart went into overdrive.

Call Monica, Hugh, your gears are slipping again.

I carried Joey to the kitchen and got him seated at the table. "Let me get you some cereal, okay? You'll perk right up." I fixed him a bowl of Rice Krispies and set it in front of him.

He was staring at his tattoo, an oddly suspicious look on his young face. "Grampa, look, my tattoo is changing." He held his arm up to me.

It's probably peeling off already.

I leaned in, not seeing what he meant, then I recoiled. Yesterday, the baseball kid had been nothing more than a black-and-white silhouette. Now, some of the pinstripes on his uniform were a bluish-black, and the bat looked brown. "Wow, that *is* a special prize." I wished my heart would slow down.

Joey nodded, munching on his cereal.

I couldn't pull my gaze from the tattoo. *How did it work?* "Must be some kind of new ink," I mumbled, more to myself than Joey. The shrill ring of the phone yanked me from my reverie.

I answered the call and my first thought was that someone was pranking me. All I heard was a weird moaning. Before I could hang up, the sound changed to a wet sob. "Monica? Is that you?" More noises came that I recognized as the devastating sound of heartbreak.

"Dad," she finally choked out.

"It's okay, hon. We'll figure this out. Come home."

Fucking Al. Dead man walking.

"I'm at the airport," she said between sobs. She was getting control of herself. "I caught him red-handed. It's over."

"I'm so sorry," I cooed, hoping she couldn't hear the murder in my voice. "We can talk when you get here. What time is your flight?"

"They're boarding now. I just had to let you know."

"I'm here for you, and you've got a great little boy who can't wait to see you."

I could chain up that motherfucker, Al, in my basement and work on him for days.

"I have to go, Dad. I'll see you soon."

I made sure Joey was okay then went into the living room. A cold, deadly rage snaked through me. I clenched my fists so tight my knuckles ached. I tried to take deep breaths, but what felt like a steel band tightened around my chest. I folded up the blankets we'd used to make the fort.

Keep busy. That's the ticket.

"Grampa, when is Mommy coming home?" Joey called from the kitchen.

Now I'm not good enough? I flexed my hands, then shook them out. "She's on her way. That was her calling from the airport. She'll be here before you know it." *Please don't ask another whiny question.*

"Why didn't she want to talk to me," he wailed.

"Because your—" *I caught myself before I said it*—*because your dad was batter-dipping the old corn dog down in Hotlanta and your mom is a little upset. Jesus, get a grip, old man.* I pressed my hands to my forehead, trying to clear my jumbled thoughts. "She had to run to catch her plane, but she said she loves you and can't wait to see you." The words were monotone, robotic. But he was six, he'd never know.

I went back into the kitchen and put on a smile that hurt my face with its insincerity. "Joey?"

"What?" he answered.

Where is he hiding.

A chair scraped, and I gawked as Joey came into view. "No…" He hadn't been there a second ago, and now— "Joey, are you okay?" I squeezed my eyes shut, then opened them slowly. It didn't help. Joey was…faded.

The bowl slipped from his hands, shattering on the tile floor.

I looked down at his bare feet. "Don't move, Joey. You'll cut your feet." I had slippers on but was still careful to avoid as many of the ceramic shards as I could. I hauled him up into my arms and my bowels almost let go. There was nothing to him.

"Grampa, what's happening?" His voice sounded distant.

Impossible. His mouth is right next to my ear.

I set him back down on the floor, a safe distance from the broken bowl. "It's the tattoo," he cried.

I looked at his arm. The baseball kid's uniform was in full color, blue pinstripes with an orange logo. His hair was blonde. The bat he held had words on it now, but they were too small for me to make out. The only thing not fully formed was the kid's face. What would happen once those details filled out? "We have to wash it off. It's…it's making you sick."

"I don't feel sick, I feel…"

I didn't hear the rest; it was too faint. I got him to the sink and turned the water on. I sat him on the counter and pulled his arm under the faucet. Grabbing a washcloth, I began to wipe the tattoo off. When I looked, it was still there, just as bright.

Are the kid's eyes blue now?

I pushed the lever all the way to hot and doused his arm in dishwashing soap. I rubbed. Hard. Joey began to squirm and cry about the water being too hot. *His voice is stronger.* I scrubbed harder, ignoring his cries. When I pulled the cloth away, the tattoo was still visible, but it was back to just black ink and faded quite a bit. Joey's arm was a scalding red.

I put my hands on his cheeks. "Joey, do you feel better? Do you feel more…*here*?"

He nodded, still sobbing.

"Thank god," I whispered. "Let's get you dressed and you can watch television for a bit before your mom gets home, okay?"

He sniffled some more but nodded.

By the time I got him dressed, the tattoo was darkening, growing clearer. Black against a background of blistering red. I watched Joey carefully for any signs that he was slipping away, fading, whatever it was that was happening.

We went downstairs, and I gave him the remote for the television. We'd had enough adventures, and I just wanted Monica to get home so—*so he won't be my problem anymore.* The volume of the TV went higher, and I glanced at the screen. He was watching some nonsense cartoon. I couldn't figure out what was going on other than it was a bunch of loud jibber-jabber. I clasped my hands over my ears, the constant babble sending waves of pain into my skull.

"Joey, turn that damn thing down," I bellowed, unable to hear my own voice over the gibberish of the cartoon. "Joey?" He wasn't on the couch…but he was. I had to squint to see him.

He's fading…going away again.

I stumbled across the room, snatching the remote from the arm of the couch and powering off the television. The sudden quiet left my head buzzing. Joey was staring at his tattoo, which had begun to fill in with colors again. Tears rolled down his translucent face.

"Grampa?"

His voice was a thousand miles away, barely audible over that damn buzzing. "Come on, Joey, quick!" I took his hand, unsure if I had it or not until I was dragging him behind me into the kitchen.

"Grampa, you're hurting me!"

So faint. *I'm going to lose him. There'll be nothing left but that tattoo.* The thought of that kid and the bat made my bladder let go. Hot piss soaked my pants and ran down my leg. I held Joey's arm up. The baseball kid was in full color, the features of his face clear for the first time. His gleefully malevolent expression taunted me. Then he grinned wider.

I have to save him before he disappears.

I yanked open a drawer, spilling utensils across the floor with a dizzying clang. I reached down and plucked the carving knife from the mess and went to work on Joey's arm.

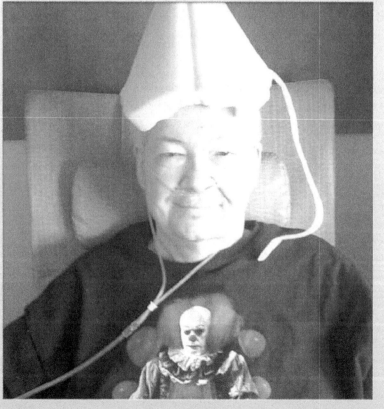

WHATEVER HAPPENED TO SOLSTICE YOUNG?

by Nicholas Kaufmann

There are times, on dark nights when I'm alone, when the wind blows through the eaves of my house and sounds like a voice whispering my name. A familiar voice. I suppose it should frighten me, and I suppose if I were anyone else it would, but it doesn't. Instead it gives me a strange kind of comfort.

It's not unusual for me to hear it while staying up late into the night in my living room recliner, grading my students' papers and sipping my evening tonic, a Balvenie DoubleWood on the rocks. If the dean of the university ever found out I drank while grading he would have a conniption, but how does the old saying go? What you don't know can't hurt you? Except I know that's not true. The wind likes to remind me of that.

When it whispers my name, it draws me back to long ago, to that terrible autumn of my youth, so defined by heartache and terror. It began with a simple childhood crush. It began with Solstice Young.

Luminous, with an effervescent smile that could chase the clouds from the sky and the ever-present fragrance of honeysuckle, hibiscus, and lemon—I loved Solstice Young with the wholesome, unconditional love only a child could have for an adult. In the fall of 1983, when the school year was new and the leaves had just started to turn the color of fire and saffron, I was twelve years old and Solstice Young was twenty-two. That ten-year gap might as well have been a chasm of eons, and had she not been the music teacher at my sleepy little town's school I likely never would have laid eyes on her. But I did, I saw her every day for third period, right before lunch, and it felt like a blessing. For a kid who excelled at the art of faking stomachaches to get out of school, that autumn was the only time I can remember actually being excited to go every day.

My love for her bloomed the first day I walked into her classroom, which was one of the smallest in the school. Even in 1983, music classes weren't given much respect. The administration and the school board always seemed on the verge of cutting its funding altogether. They hadn't yet, but in their twisted need to show their contempt they moved the music class to the smallest classroom they could find, a cramped, closet-like room where only half the ceiling lights worked. But somehow Solstice Young made the room feel so much bigger and brighter than it was. She festooned it with all kinds of musical instruments and tacked cardboard album covers to the walls: Fleetwood Mac's *Rumours*, *Led Zeppelin IV*, David Bowie's *The Rise and Fall of Ziggy Stardust*, Blondie's *Parallel Lines*, Roxy Music's *Avalon*, Duran Duran's *Rio*. We knew what music was back then.

At the time, I had never listened to any of those albums, although I knew Keith, my older brother, owned at least one of them. I remembered him coming home with *Rumours* one day, that unforgettable yellow sleeve art burning itself into my mind—a man and a woman holding hands in mid-dance, he with his leg up on a small ottoman, she circling him with her arms outstretched in almost mystical abandon. The man looked like everything I wanted to be when I grew up, dashing and debonair in his boots and vest like a bearded storybook pirate, and the woman—well, there was something about her that was very like the teacher standing at the front of the classroom.

She'd written her name on the chalkboard in a delicate, feminine script—Miss Young, with the *i* in Miss dotted by a smiley face she'd drawn. She wore a white cotton peasant blouse and a long, flowing skirt with a paisley pattern. Her dark blonde hair was long and streaked with highlights, with a single, braided strand that hung near her ear. A spray of summery freckles dotted the bridge of her nose and spilled onto her cheeks. Her big, blue eyes were bright with the enthusiasm of someone about to teach children for the very first time, the polar opposite of the jaded, tired, permanently annoyed eyes of those who have been teaching for years. I should know. I see those tired eyes in my own mirror quite often.

When Solstice Young smiled, dimples creased her face and it was like the sun was shining right on you. How I loved to make her smile. When I look back with the mind of a teacher, I can see how she humored us, laughing at all the students' corny jokes even if they weren't funny, and smiling as she listened to countless ridiculous questions and rambling, nonsensical stories. Even mine. But I prefer to remember it differently, to remember her smile as genuine, her heart so big it could encompass the whole class. That's how I want to remember Solstice Young now that she's gone. *If* she's gone.

I was too young at the time to understand what an unusual name Solstice was. I assume now that her parents were Beats or hippies, and given how she dressed and the way she spoke of musicians with the same reverence a preacher would when speaking of Jesus, that was probably the case. I didn't know anything about her except that she wasn't from our little town, where everybody knew everybody. This implied, astonishingly, that she'd *chosen* to come there after graduating from whatever university she attended. It meant she'd *chosen* to teach at my school, and to my feverish, lovesick mind that meant destiny had brought us together. All I cared about, all I lived for, was her attention. Even a table scrap was a meal to me. I raised my hand in class regardless of whether I knew the answer. I volunteered to transcribe notes from sheet music onto the chalkboard for her. I studied extra hard what words like *adagio* and *larghissimo* meant so she would see what a good student I was.

One night in early October, when I was in the family room reading a chapter on Italian Baroque composers, my father came in with a can of beer and shooed me to the far side of the couch. He plopped down where I'd been sitting, picked up the remote, and turned on the local news. There was no point in complaining about the interruption. Nothing came between my father, his post-dinner beer, and the evening news. The house could burn down and he wouldn't get up until the can was empty and the broadcast was over.

I tried to ignore the television, but the word *murder* caught my attention. I looked up from my textbook as the anchor reported that the dead body of a middle-aged woman, one Maisie Talbot of Fox Hill Road, had been found behind the bus station early that morning. Her throat had been torn open by a wild animal. The authorities were urging caution.

"Wild animal my ass," my father muttered, sipping his beer. "I bet it's one of those pit bulls they're always talking about on the news. One killed a kid a few months ago. You ask me, they should all be put down. That's what you do with vicious animals like that."

The next day in class, Solstice Young played Simon & Garfunkel's "The Sound of Silence" for us on the record player. As the haunting opening notes floated through the classroom, she said, "There's something so dark and seductive about the music, don't you think? And that first lyric, 'Hello, darkness, my old friend,' there's a resignation there, a giving up of one's self. But not out of fear. Out of love." She closed her eyes and sang along with the record without an ounce of shyness or timidity, swaying to the music like a charmed snake. "Take my arms that I might reach you," she sang out and hugged herself tight. Her blouse slipped off of one creamy, bare shoulder, but she didn't even care. She was a million miles away, and whatever she was imagining in that moment was hers and hers alone.

Afterward, the other kids laughed in the hallway about it. Even Craig Maberry and Bob Moore, my two best friends, thought it was weird, but not me. I thought it was magical. I felt like I had caught a glimpse of the real Solstice Young, the one no one else saw.

But as much as I wanted to impress her, I couldn't play music. I made such a mess of trying to perform "Hot Cross Buns" on the recorder along with the rest of the class that she had to come to my rescue.

"You've got your finger on the wrong hole," she said, gently moving my hand. "Here, put your finger on this hole instead. That's better, isn't it?"

Then, without warning, her cheeks flushed and she started laughing as if she'd said something funny. It was a different laugh from her normal one. This one was dark and full of secrets, and though I didn't understand what was so funny, the sound of it reached deep inside me and grabbed hold.

I stared at her hand on mine as I played the notes. The warm, perfect feel of it overwhelmed me. Her sleeve pulled back on her arm, and I noticed an angry-looking white scar along the length of her wrist, crisp and straight as if from a razor. The sight of it frightened me, but I forgot it a moment later when she squeezed my hand approvingly. I very nearly fainted. Surely it was a sign, a way of letting me know that she favored me above all the others, that somehow she knew of my love for her and returned it. It didn't matter that she moved on to Billy Mears next and did the same for him, I was still swooning from her attention, still inhaling the mystical fragrance that drifted in her wake like incense.

I didn't know if that combination of honeysuckle, hibiscus, and lemon was a perfume or soap or just her natural scent, but it was like catnip to me. When I smelled it in the hallways of the school I would slow my gait, hoping to catch even a glimpse of her.

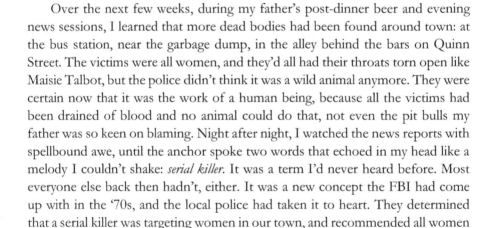

Over the next few weeks, during my father's post-dinner beer and evening news sessions, I learned that more dead bodies had been found around town: at the bus station, near the garbage dump, in the alley behind the bars on Quinn Street. The victims were all women, and they'd all had their throats torn open like Maisie Talbot, but the police didn't think it was a wild animal anymore. They were certain now that it was the work of a human being, because all the victims had been drained of blood and no animal could do that, not even the pit bulls my father was so keen on blaming. Night after night, I watched the news reports with spellbound awe, until the anchor spoke two words that echoed in my head like a melody I couldn't shake: *serial killer*. It was a term I'd never heard before. Most everyone else back then hadn't, either. It was a new concept the FBI had come up with in the '70s, and the local police had taken it to heart. They determined that a serial killer was targeting women in our town, and recommended all women stay inside after dark until the killer was brought to justice.

During those same weeks, I hid my childish adoration of Solstice Young from everybody, including Craig and Bob, but somehow my brother Keith knew. He was two years older than me and attended the same school. He was also the cruelest person I knew. When we passed each other in the hallways at school, he would greet me with a punch in the arm, or stuff me into my locker, all to the delight of his cackling friends. But his favorite brand of torture was to throw my love for Solstice Young in my face every chance he got.

"I saw Miss Young's tits," he told me once, taking obvious pleasure in the shock on my face. We were in his bedroom. He had Pink Floyd's *Wish You Were Here* spinning on the turntable and there was still a pungent, herbal odor in the air from the joint I'd seen him toss out the window when I barged in on some business or other. I had surprised and embarrassed him by catching him in the act, and now he wanted to get back at me with these hurtful words.

"Shut up!" I yelled. My anger was quick and possessive. "You did not!"

"I did," he said, a merciless grin on his face. "It was just last week, in the hallway at school. She was rushing somewhere with an armful of books. She dropped one of them, and when she bent down to pick it up I could see right down her blouse. She wasn't wearing *anything* underneath. I saw *everything*. It was all right there on full display. *Everyone* in the hallway saw."

"Shut up!" I yelled again. I shoved him, and forgetting whatever business had brought me to his room, I ran into my bedroom and slammed the door. I threw myself onto the bed and cried into my pillow. I didn't know why I was crying, except that it felt as though my brother's story had sullied Solstice Young somehow, abused her in some way she didn't deserve, as if she were no different from the lewd naked women in the magazines Keith kept hidden under his bed. But she *was* different. She was special, and the way Keith had talked about her made everything feel thorny and wrong and ruined.

October was nearing its end. The foliage was gone, leaving behind bare trees like skeletal, grasping hands. The grass faded to a lifeless brown. The air turned cold and bitter, and on some days it would sting your face if you didn't wrap up in a scarf. The hothouse bloom of summer was long dead, and everything was about to change.

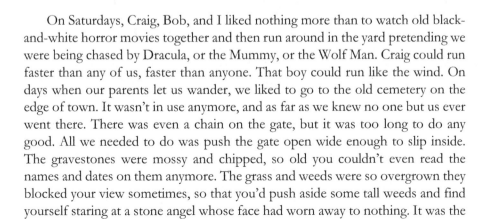

On Saturdays, Craig, Bob, and I liked nothing more than to watch old black-and-white horror movies together and then run around in the yard pretending we were being chased by Dracula, or the Mummy, or the Wolf Man. Craig could run faster than any of us, faster than anyone. That boy could run like the wind. On days when our parents let us wander, we liked to go to the old cemetery on the edge of town. It wasn't in use anymore, and as far as we knew no one but us ever went there. There was even a chain on the gate, but it was too long to do any good. All we needed to do was push the gate open wide enough to slip inside. The gravestones were mossy and chipped, so old you couldn't even read the names and dates on them anymore. The grass and weeds were so overgrown they blocked your view sometimes, so that you'd push aside some tall weeds and find yourself staring at a stone angel whose face had worn away to nothing. It was the perfect setting for us to horse around in, laughing and shrieking and hiding from Frankenstein's lurching, stiff-armed monster.

But our favorite part of the old cemetery was the moldering, abandoned chapel that stood amid the graves. Its wooden walls had rotted through and were covered with clinging, brown weeds. Its roof had collapsed in places, and the spire had partially crumbled to leave only a twisted, mold-black arm that reached yearningly toward the sky. The three of us would watch the chapel from behind a row of graves, knowing the front door had fallen off its hinges ages ago and daring each other to go in. We were too scared to do it, of course, but it was enough just to imagine what the inside of the chapel looked like—dark, dusty pews draped with sheets of cobwebs; the altar probably smashed to pieces by beer-fueled older boys or else made home to families of mice, or better yet, thousands of crawling, chittering insects; empty holes where the stained glass windows had been, looming like the black eye sockets of a skull.

The sun sets early in October, and by the time we started back from the old cemetery it was already dusk. When we reached Main Street, we stopped to point and laugh at the young couple we saw kissing against the brick wall of an antiques shop. My laughter died away when I saw that the woman whose back was pressed to the wall and whose lips were pressed so passionately to someone else's was Solstice Young. My chest tightened and my stomach dropped to my feet. The man she was kissing was a little older than her, with dark hair and a stubbly jaw. He was dressed in jeans and a leather jacket over a Black Sabbath concert t-shirt. As he slid his hand up from her waist to twine his fingers in her hair, I saw he wore a big gold ring in the shape of an upside-down pentagram, that most metal of symbols. He looked exactly like the kind of guy parents didn't want their daughters dating, and so of course Solstice Young, who marched to the beat of her own drum, was kissing him right in front of everybody. Right in front of me.

The man ended the kiss and began to pull away. She bit his bottom lip and pulled it with her teeth. When she let go, she looked at him with a devilish smile that seared itself into my mind. It bored down deep in me and awoke something I'd only ever felt before when sneaking peeks at Keith's hidden magazines. But even that delicious, furtive pressure had been only a shadow of the urgency I felt now in every beat of my heart. I watched, rapt and envious, as she took the man's hand and led him down the sidewalk.

"Who was that with Miss Young?" I asked, watching them vanish into the darkening twilight.

"That must be her boyfriend," Craig said. "I heard her talk about him before."

"When?" I demanded, prickly and defensive.

"Remember when I had to stay late at school for detention?" Craig said. I did. He'd hidden a piece of chalk inside Mr. Palmer's eraser so that it drew a line across the chalkboard when he tried to erase a geometry lesson. Mr. Palmer had been so angry he hurled the chalk across the room, shattering it against the far wall. Snotty little Jessica McCrum ratted Craig out and he got a detention. I felt bad for him having to be there with all the druggies, dopers, space cadets, and juvenile delinquents, but we all agreed the practical joke with the chalk had been so funny it was worth it. "When they let us out of the detention room, Miss Young was talking to Miss Nugent in the hallway. She said she met a guy who was new in town like her. I guess they've been going out for a while now."

Miss Young had a boyfriend! I railed furiously against the idea, tried to tell myself she didn't really like him, but I'd seen the way she looked at him. You couldn't fake that kind of longing. Believe me, I knew.

I went into a funk. I didn't want to get out of bed the next day, but it was Sunday and my parents dragged me to church. I didn't want to get out of bed on Monday, either. The idea of seeing Solstice Young was too much to handle, but my parents made me get up and go to school. I considered skipping music class, but once I smelled that familiar fragrance outside her classroom it lured me in, filling my head with promises that she wasn't dating that guy after all, that it was all a misunderstanding, that she was still...

Still what? Mine? But she wasn't. She never had been. I knew that, I wasn't crazy. I was just a pimply-faced kid and she was in her twenties. What did I think was going to happen? That we'd get married and live happily ever after like in some stupid story? I paused in front of the door as cold, hard reality weighed down on me, snapping my heart in half under its burden. Then I took a deep breath and forced myself to enter the classroom.

The first thing I noticed was that she looked different. Tired, paler, with bags under her eyes like she hadn't slept all weekend. I tried to feel indifferent about it, but instead I felt bristly and resentful. Even at twelve years old, I could think of things that a boyfriend and girlfriend did together that would cause them not to get enough sleep. She was spacey and uncoordinated throughout the class, forgetting what she was talking about, writing the wrong word on the chalkboard, telling us to read a chapter we'd already read. I supposed her mind was elsewhere. I supposed this was what love did to people.

It went on like this for several days. We moved up from playing "Hot Cross Buns" on the recorder to playing "When the Saints Come Marching In," but I was still hopeless. It didn't help that I was distracted by jealousy. Solstice Young had to correct my fingers again, and like a trained dog my heart leapt to attention in her presence, but this time when she touched my hand her skin felt cold and clammy. As she moved my finger from the wrong hole to the right one—there was no laughter from her this time—her sleeve pulled back to reveal the scary white scar on her wrist again...and something else. There was another scar on her wrist, pink enough to still be new, only this one was in the shape of a crescent. It reminded me of the mark I'd left on Keith's arm when I was little and he was too rough with me and I bit him.

349

She leaned over to get a better look at my hands, and the neck of her blouse fell open. Remembering Keith's story and how bad it had made me feel, I looked away quickly, but not before I saw it. A second crescent-shaped scar on the swell of her breast. I thought feverishly of Solstice Young with her boyfriend's bottom lip between her teeth…

Biting…

and the same urgent feeling I'd felt on Main Street came rushing back a hundredfold, an unbelievable pressure screaming for release. I thought I would go mad from it.

Every day she looked a little worse, her rosy skin turning white as paper, the brightness dulling in her eyes. Her hair turned limp and stringy. Sometimes she seemed barely strong enough to lift the textbook. But instead of feeling sorry or concerned for her, I grew angrier. This, I decided, was her punishment for betraying me. I wince now when I think about it, my white-hot rage that she had chosen, reasonably and correctly, a man her own age over a mooning child, but a broken heart clouds the mind and at twelve years old I didn't know any better. The changes came over Solstice Young so gradually that nobody else at school noticed, only me. She was my world, and I saw everything. If she needed help, if she needed someone to see what was happening and do something about it, then I failed her. That's something I have to live with.

But I don't think she did. I don't think she wanted that at all.

Eventually, Solstice Young stopped coming to school. We had a substitute music teacher, Mrs. Hanson, a stern harpy who always seemed angry to be there and whose pinched face and resentful sneer cured me of any further schoolboy crushes on teachers. No one knew what had happened to Solstice Young, not even the other teachers. With a killer on the loose everyone feared the worst, though no one said it out loud. I went into a funk even deeper and darker than before. Nothing mattered. The world could stop turning and fall into the sun for all I cared. Solstice Young was dead, I was sure of it. Craig and Bob tried to get me to come play with them, but I refused. All I wanted was the safety of my bed and the comfort of my tearstained pillow. Finally, my parents told me it was either go play with my friends or be forced to see a psychiatrist, so I went with Craig and Bob, begrudgingly, to the old cemetery on the edge of town.

This time, when we dared each other to go inside the chapel, I didn't chicken out. I ran right in, not caring what I would find, not even caring if I died in a roof collapse or at the hands of the serial killer. Neither fate awaited me. The interior of the chapel looked like I had imagined it, full of dust and cobwebs and water damage from the holes in the roof. I was surprised, however, to find a thin metal cross still standing on the altar, badly rusted but upright. The sight of it brought my simmering anger to a boil. There was nothing good in this world. The cross was a lie. *Everything* was a lie. I picked up a rock from the floor, and with an angry shout I threw it at the cross. The rock knocked it off the altar, and the cross broke apart on the floor with a loud crash.

The sound brought my friends running. I don't remember what happened after that. My fury was too overwhelming. I found out later from Craig and Bob that I had fought them and yelled curses at them. They had to run and get my brother Keith, who came and dragged me out of there. I don't recall anything between throwing the rock and being at home again, listening to my parents whisper frantically about whether I was developing a nervous condition.

But as the days passed, they never found Solstice Young's body the way they did the other victims. This was a balm of sorts for my anguish. It meant there was a chance she hadn't died at the hands of a serial killer, that her final moments hadn't been filled with fear, a thought that had tormented me to the point of utter devastation. It left hope alive that she had simply skipped town with her boyfriend to establish a new life, safe and happy, somewhere else. That thought stung me with a fresh pang of possessiveness, but at least it meant she was alive. I could be happy for her, if nothing else.

The murders grew more frequent. The police found more bodies every day, and not just women anymore. Men and children had been added to the roster. "Children!" my mother had wailed, nearly collapsing in horror at the news. "What kind of a monster would kill children?" No one had an answer for that. Perhaps if they had, things would have turned out differently. As it was, it was only a matter of time in a town that small before the killer struck someone close to me. When you're a child, you think bad things only happen to people on the news. You think it can't touch you, but it can, and there's no way to prepare for it. It flattened me, pounded me into the earth like a hammer, when they found Craig Maberry's bloodless body in the woods near the school.

Poor Craig. Always the class clown, he'd been given a detention again, this time for making faces in Spanish class. It was hardly fair, he was only trying to make Abby Berger laugh because she was so scared about the killer, but rules were rules. It was early November and the sun had already set when detention let out. The police reckoned the killer got him on the walk home from school.

I was inconsolable. If the earth had opened up under my feet to swallow me, I wouldn't have fought it. I was a zombie at Craig's funeral. I couldn't look at anyone, not even Bob, who was just as shell-shocked as I was. It was a closed-casket service. They couldn't reconstruct Craig's neck well enough to display the body.

The town put a curfew in place. No one was allowed outside after dark unless it was an emergency. But once Bob and I had recovered from the shock of Craig's death, we didn't let that stop us from coming up with a plan to honor our fallen friend. In secret, whispered phone calls we decided we would go to the old cemetery and write in chalk on the inside of the cemetery wall, where only the brave and the intrepid would see it, *Never forget: Craig Maberry was here first.* There was no way our parents would let us do this, of course. They hadn't been letting us do *anything* lately. So it would have to be done at night, after they'd gone to bed. It meant breaking curfew, but that didn't matter to us nearly as much as honoring Craig. With the fearless bravado of the young, which others might call foolishness, we agreed to sneak out of our houses at midnight and meet at the cemetery gates.

When the time came, I clambered down the trellis on the side of our house with a pocketful of chalk and ran full-speed through the empty streets toward the cemetery. It was freezing out, the coldest night of the fall so far, and my panting breath turned to clouds of vapor before me. A strange, chilled fog wound through the streets and clung to the lampposts, diffusing their light into an eerie haze. When I passed the brick-walled antiques shop on Main Street, I thought suddenly of Solstice Young, and my heart ached at her absence. At the cemetery gates, I waited for ten minutes, shivering in the cold, but Bob didn't show. I figured he'd either chickened out or had been caught by his parents. But I was determined to complete our mission, with or without him.

Inside the cemetery, the fog enveloped the gravestones and turned them into dark, huddled shapes like a crowd of ghoulish onlookers. I was about to pull the chalk from my pocket when the sound of the chain clanking against the gate stopped me. I turned, thinking Bob had joined me after all, but the figure I saw through the veil of fog was too tall, the size of an adult. It was covered head to foot with gray funeral shrouds that made it almost indistinguishable from the haze around it. I ducked down behind a tombstone in terror, then peeked over the top. I held my breath so the vapor wouldn't give me away. No clouds of breath came from the shrouded figure, but they issued from a second shape that emerged from the mist beside it.

Bob.

Now I knew why he hadn't shown up. The shrouded figure had caught him. I wanted to signal Bob, let him know I was here, but I was too scared. I didn't want the figure to see me. But something was wrong with Bob. He wasn't trying to get away. His face was slack and expressionless. His eyes stared blankly into the fog. The shrouded figure reached over to put a hand on Bob's back, and something glimmered on one of its pale fingers. A ring—one I'd seen before. A gold ring with an upside-down pentagram.

Bob was passive and compliant as the shrouded figure guided him into the old chapel. I released my breath and the vapor burst out of my mouth in a heavy cloud. For a moment I was too terrified to move, but I had to. It was Bob. I had to try to help him somehow.

I followed them, but it was like a dream. My feet wouldn't move as quickly as I wanted, and the cold, impenetrable fog was a wall holding me back. When I finally reached the chapel, I stayed just outside the doorway and peeked in. A thick odor of decay hung in the air. The shrouded figure was leading Bob toward the far end of the chapel where, to my horror, I saw a second figure waiting. This one was covered in gray funeral shrouds, too, but was smaller and slighter than the first. The taller one passed Bob wordlessly over to the smaller one. Bob's expression never changed, not even when the second figure stroked his face, pushed his head to the side, and bent its cowled head to his neck. I heard the sound of teeth ripping into tender flesh. Too terrified to move, I looked away, unable to watch, but I could still hear it. The slurping, sucking sound. I put a knuckle between my teeth and bit down. It was the only way to stop myself from screaming.

When the sound stopped, I dared to look again. Bob's lifeless body lay on the floor, his throat torn and glistening, his eyes open and sightless. I know there was no way I could have helped him, that I would have died, too, but the crushing guilt I felt upon seeing him like that has never left me. I watched as the second figure approached the first, and their shrouded faces met in a horrible kiss. The taller one took the smaller's arm, lifted its upturned wrist to its mouth, and I heard the awful sounds again.

This time, I didn't look away. A charge ran through me. Not of terror, but of something else, something carnal, as one shrouded figure bit the wrist of the other…

Biting…

and drank from it, as if to share in the taking of Bob's blood.

The smaller figure suddenly turned its shrouded head toward the doorway where I stood. It was too dark to see inside the shroud, but the chill that came over me told me *it* had seen *me*. I turned and ran.

My mother had wanted to know what kind of a monster would kill children. I knew the answer now. Even through the confusion and the fear, I knew. Of course I did. How many old movies had I watched on a Saturday afternoon in which undead creatures rose from their graves to feast upon the blood of the living and turn a chosen few into creatures like themselves? But I'd never thought they were real, just actors who wore long capes and spoke with Eastern European accents—not *this*, not real creatures who could come to my town and kill people I knew. I ran, and when I remembered the cross that had stood tall and proud on the chapel's altar before I broke it, the cross that could have stopped or hindered these creatures if the stories were true, I was overcome with a despairing shame. My own careless rage had created a sanctuary for them. I'd given them a safe place to hide. Me.

I ran all the way home, climbed up the trellis, locked the window behind me, and the bedroom door too, for good measure. I spent the rest of the night with the covers drawn up to my neck, sobbing for Bob and staring at the window. I waited for the shrouded figures to appear, convinced they had followed me home, but they never came. After an eternity, the sun rose again.

In the morning I told my parents I was going to stay home from school, and because they thought I was still in mourning, they didn't argue. After my father left for work, and after my mother left to run errands with my assurance that I would be fine at home alone for an hour, I sneaked out of the house again. I returned to the old cemetery, but this time I went through the woods. It took longer, but I couldn't risk being seen on Main Street carrying a can of gasoline from our garage. My father's words echoed through my head like a drumbeat: *They should all be put down. That's what you do with vicious animals like that.*

I knew enough about these creatures to understand what had to be done, and since I was the one who had inadvertently given them a place to hide, it was up to me to do it. I marched into the old chapel, confident I would be safe in the light of day while the creatures slept in their hidden spots, and poured gasoline on everything, pausing only to note that Bob's body was gone. Standing in the doorway, I pulled from my pocket a book of matches I'd taken from the kitchen. I lit one, used it to light all the other matches still in the book, and threw the blazing matchbook into the chapel. It had been a dry autumn, and with the help of the gasoline the old wood went up fast. I didn't stick around to watch it burn. I couldn't risk getting caught. I ran and made it back home before my mother returned.

When my father turned on the news that night, I heard the chapel had burned to the ground. The police blamed teenage hooligans inspired to vandalism by heavy metal music, that all-purpose bugaboo of the 1980s, but no one was ever arrested for it. No one ever came to question me. I wasn't even on their suspect list. I never told anyone what I'd done, or why. When my parents told me Bob had been killed, that his body had been found discarded in a corner of the cemetery, I had to pretend I didn't already know and cry all over again. I did a pretty good job of it.

The murders stopped after that. The townsfolk theorized that the killer had moved away, or had died and was lying in the morgue without anyone being any the wiser. I grew up, graduated high school, and left town to attend a university where, inspired by my memories of Solstice Young, I studied to be a teacher. When I graduated, I focused on getting a job teaching at the college level. I wanted older students. I didn't want any twelve-year-olds mooning over me the way I had over her. It would have been unbearable.

Along the way I met women my own age, but no relationship lasted long. None of them measured up to my memories of Solstice Young. She was never far from my mind, even as the gulf of time between my childhood and adulthood stretched wider. Whenever the mood hit me, which was frequently, I would search for her name in newspapers, phone books, and, later, on the Internet, confident that any Solstice Young I found would be her. After all, how many Solstice Youngs could there be in the world? But I never found anything. I never found out what became of her. On dark nights when I'm alone—and I'm always alone now, because no love runs as deep as first love—and the wind whispers through the eaves like a beckoning voice, I tell myself I still don't know. But I do. I do.

They say smell is the strongest sense that's tied to memory, and I have generally found this to be true. The scent of fresh-cut grass reminds me of Saturday afternoons spent running from imaginary monsters in the backyard with Craig Maberry and Bob Moore. (Had we known there were real monsters to run from, how foolish we would have felt.) The odor of dry, dusty earth brings back memories of our secret playground, where we would run shrieking with laughter through the tombstones. When I followed Bob and the shrouded figure into the chapel all those years ago, I smelled the stench of decay in the air, but I smelled something else, too, beneath it. The fragrance of honeysuckle, hibiscus, and lemon.

It makes me think about how there were two of those creatures in the chapel, not one. It makes me wonder who Craig, the boy who could outrun anyone, might have seen coming for him out of the woods the night he died. Someone he would have recognized. Someone he wouldn't have run from. A familiar face within the shroud.

They say what you don't know can't hurt you, but it can, and there are still so many important things I don't know. Was Solstice Young's boyfriend, he of the upside-down pentagram ring, the start of it all? I suppose if I were cursed to undeath for all eternity, I would want her by my side forever, too. She had that effect on people. Or was it possible they were turned by a third creature I never found?

I wonder sometimes if she was an innocent victim, or if it was a choice she made. Because despite her sunny exterior, there was a darkness to Solstice Young that I had been blind to as a child. She was a woman of contradictions, just like her name. After all, a solstice could be the longest day, or the longest night.

And then there's the biggest question of all: Were they in the chapel when I burnt it down? I didn't dare go back to look for bones. The murders stopped, it's true, but that didn't mean they were dead. Creatures like them aren't tied to a single location, a single town. They might have moved on.

The reason I wonder is that on some nights it's not just the familiar voice on the wind whispering my name that catches my attention. There's a familiar scent, too, a fragrance that slips tantalizingly between the window and its frame. It brings back memories of a young woman I thought had burned as brightly as the sun, but who had felt such despair that she had once dragged a razor down her wrist, who had stood before the class with her eyes closed and spoken unashamedly of how seductive the darkness was, and who might have given herself over to it in the end; a young woman I had loved so completely that I could forgive her anything. And whenever I smell it—*hello, darkness, my old friend*—I open the window and invite it in.

BOYS DON'T CRY

by Chad Lutzke

Allen, Maurice, and I were in Maurice's car eating burgers bought with the money he'd been tossing in the console the past two months—spare change from when he'd run and grab smokes for his mom. I could smell the olives from Maurice's burger while he talked. I hate olives.

Allen was in the back seat complaining about how his burger tasted like pepper and maybe he should have gotten cheese on it and that next time he will.

"He just dropped there on the front steps...and that was it." Maurice was talking about his dad's heart attack.

"Damn, dude. I'm sorry, man," I said. "No wonder your mom drinks."

"She's not an alcoholic, dude. She has like one glass of wine before bed."

"Yeah, I get it."

"Check this out." We turned around, and Allen had a french fry sticking out of his fly.

"Seems about right," I said.

"Awww, man!"

We polished off the burgers and flipped a coin for the soundtrack on the ride downtown, using the only quarter Maurice kept in his console that could never be spent—his lucky quarter. It was easy to spot from the others because it'd been painted with dark-pink nail polish. Morgan's friend did that. Maurice sure was into that girl. I think he read too much into it, like when a girl writes on your arm in school. He never really did have a chance with her, but he tried. Just like with his board. No way was his giant ass ever going to land anything. But he tried.

I lost the coin toss, always did when he used that quarter. So, Maurice ejected the Minor Threat tape and swapped it for NWA. I hid that pain-in-the-ass quarter in my pocket, lit a smoke, and rolled the window down, pretending I was somewhere else, while Eazy-E declared his love for malt liquor.

Maurice pulled into an empty church parking lot. We'd never been there before. We scoped it out, looking for handrails, banks, curbs, steps and gaps. There weren't any, but we did find a two-foot wall, so Allen and I took turns ollying over it while Maurice did his thing—tried to pop two-inch ollies. We never made fun of him, though. You gotta start somewhere. Every one of us.

"Jex! Check that out," Allen pointed at the church. It was covered in enormous windows--frankensteined glass made with a dozen different colors. "It's an upside-down cross."

I looked at it. Maurice looked at it. At the bottom of the window was a large, red sword.

"It's a sword," I said.

"They should fix it. I mean...it's a church. Ya know? How did they not notice that when they were putting it up?"

"It's just a sword, man." I went for the wall again and fell on my ass, road rash on my palms. I wiped the pebbles from my skin and sat on my board, watching cars pull into the parking lot of the funeral home next door. I'd been inside twice. Once for my grandfather's funeral, another for my grandmother. I hated that place. It smelled like flowers and new carpeting.

Allen sat on his board next to me, and we shared a smoke under the sun while Maurice kept at it. Trying and failing.

We watched the mourners spill out of their cars, eyes to the ground, thoughts on the dead.

"You wanna go inside?" I asked Allen.

"The funeral home?"

"Yeah, pay our respects."

"We don't know anyone. We weren't invited or whatever."

"You don't have to know someone to mourn, or offer a smile to the people in there."

Allen seemed to think about it a moment, flicked the spent smoke across the parking lot. "Yeah, okay."

"Just don't act like a dick. No joking around."

"I won't, man."

Maurice skated over, and we told him what we were doing.

"I hate those places," he said.

"So do I," I told him. "But it's not about us."

Maurice shrugged. "I guess."

We tossed our boards in the trunk and walked toward the funeral home. The closer we got, the more I wondered if the whole idea was disrespectful. A well-intended smile for the living and a moment of silence for the dead from us might come off as insensitive. We had no business being there.

But still we walked.

The door was held open by a block of wood, and the smell of flowers hung like a cloud near the entrance. It was thick and triggering, and just like that I was a little kid again, following my parents inside to see my grandparents tucked neatly in their coffins.

A man wearing a carnation on the breast of his black suit nodded at us—either an employee or distant relative of the deceased. Either way, he didn't know we didn't belong.

As we entered, the smell of flowers stuck to my tongue like old perfume, and I could hear a church organ somewhere in the distance. People were gathered in the halls, loitering near different doors leading to rooms where sad families whispered and hugged, offering gentle back pats to those who entered.

Nobody looked at us. They were too busy reminiscing over those who now lay in coffins.

Allen snickered at a woman's hat, and I elbowed him in the ribs. Everything was a joke to him, even then.

The first door we came to was open. Rows of chairs filled the room with mourners peppered throughout. At the far end of the room, in front of the audience of chairs, was a casket. It was open, and I could see the profile of a clay face with white hair. An old man.

"We goin' in?" Allen whispered.

I didn't answer, just put one foot in front of the next. It felt like I wasn't in control, like my feet just moved forward regardless of what I might have to say about it.

I expected people to stop us as we walked through the aisle formed by chairs, but nobody did. And nobody stared. We were the least of their worries.

As I drew closer to the casket, my hands dove into my pockets. I do that when I'm uncomfortable. It gives me solace, I guess—occupying my hidden hands with keys, loose change, or the ribbed, steel wheel of a lighter. This time I had a lighter in one pocket and Maurice's lucky quarter in another.

I rubbed the shit out of that quarter. But not for luck. It settled me.

I kept waiting for my feet to give in and turn, walk out of there and get back on my board, but they kept on, until all three of us stood there at the casket looking in.

We'd climbed Mount Everest and now looked down at the accomplishment. Was this really about paying respects? Heartfelt condolences? Or did we just want to see a dead body and have a story to tell? Once that thought entered, I felt like a dick for staring at a man I knew nothing about.

"He looks fake," Allen whispered.

It was true. The dead always look like something's lying underneath them, with its claws dug in behind their jaw, stretching their face toward the satin pillow.

I kept waiting for the old man's eyes to open, like he knew we were looking down at him and that our being there was such a tasteless thing it'd wake him. It bothered me that no one knew we didn't belong, and I almost wanted the guy to raise up, and like Donald Sutherland at the end of *Invasion of the Body Snatchers*, point us out.

"Dude, let's bail," Maurice said.

I didn't move. I looked at the man's clay-flesh and wanted to touch it, to feel the chill of Death. But why? For a story to tell? *Hey, Jess! Guess what! I touched a dead body.*

I took a hand out of my pocket and buried it in the coffin, felt the silky texture of the white satin.

"Dude." Maurice whispered.

I pulled my hand out, hung my head, and walked away, through the aisle made from chairs, out the door, and down the hall. Allen and Maurice followed.

Until we got in the car, none of us said anything. Was that shame? Or were we still paying our respects, a moment of silence?

Maurice started the car.

"Flip for music?" I asked.

Maurice grinned. "Good luck." He opened the console and rummaged for his lucky, dark-pink quarter. "Dude! Did you take my quarter?"

I pulled my pockets inside out, revealing all I had was a lighter and some lint. After entertaining him with a brief search through the car—and our pockets again—I grabbed a different coin and we flipped.

I won.

I put my tape in, rolled the window down, lit a smoke, and smiled against the highway wind.

Godspeed, old man.

IMPRINT

by John Palisano

A train powers though the rain.
A commuter stays glued to his book.
Words on the page…
An imprint from a dark brain.
He's rereading every story, every word again.
He has to write to this author,
to tell him how this is affecting him,
that the work struck a nerve.

A car rides on fumes toward the Mojave.
A driver keeps straight over the rise,
wheels on the asphalt.
They imprint on the dark rainy road.
He's counting every mile, every foot again.
He tells his story to his phone,
describes how it is burning inside him,
that the work needs to be born.

Stories come like lightning.
Filled with people we instantly know.
As real as flesh and blood that we can touch,
much better, sometimes, sometimes …

Like electrical wires firing,
downed in a storm,
scattershot and ready to strike,
ideas spark and travel.
Lighting the darkness,
if even for a blink.
But in that second,

one can see everything.
Every contrasting detail.

And the story they show imprints…
Transfers.
To be told once more.

WE BARE ALL

by Wesley Southard

Morty wept as he stared out the window.

At ninety-three, it was how he spent most of his time, alone and afraid inside his ramshackle cabin. These days his brain was like a kaleidoscope. A reflective mix of anger and sadness, shame and despair.

The one sentiment he didn't feel was hope.

Through a teary prism, Morty sucked down what was left of his homemade sour mash and continued to examine the desolate road beyond his yard. Outside, the midday sun strained to break through the dense tree tops, keeping his small plot of wooded land in relative darkness. There were days Morty never saw the sun at all. The gloom was normal—it matched his woeful outlook. Nowhere to go, and nothing to do. He was so close to the end, and there was only so much time before he was finally gone...before they were all gone.

Who would take care of the town then?

His ears suddenly perked up. Morty quickly wiped the thin layer of grime away from his window. He gasped.

"Sweet Jesus..."

A car! An honest-to-goodness car! Driving toward town!

Heart fluttering with excitement, he shifted his interest to the rough patch of hardened dirt at the corner of his lot.

It was time to start tilling.

While Karl, Dana, and Deangelo laughed among themselves inside the car, Aaron studied the gaudy billboard as it raced toward them. It was the same one he'd seen a dozen times since they'd passed through Atlanta, only this one boasted a different girl. Different girl, same three block letter words stretching across its hot-pink background:

WE BARE ALL

They must have been produced sometime in the nineties—possibly the eighties—because Aaron was positive hair that big didn't exist these days. Curls and waves so high, so full of Aqua Net, it had to be a health code violation. On this particular poster, the blonde's pencil-thin eyebrows were curled in a coy, knowing stare. Her frosted, glittery lipstick, now sunbaked, could have once blinded unsuspecting drivers.

He leaned forward as it whipped past and became yet another fast-food advertisement on the back side. Brazen anticipation off Exit 11.

"No fucking way!" Dana yelled.

Kurt retorted, "Yes fucking way!"

Aaron blinked away the sunlight and the world came rushing back.

Dana turned all the way around in the front passenger seat to face Kurt. "There's no way in hell you slept with *four* different women in the same night, you goddamn liar!"

Kurt slapped the open seat between himself and Aaron. "Why would I *lie* about that? Daddy don't lie!"

"Whoa!" Deangelo stopped him. With one hand on the wheel, he pointed with a rigid finger, keeping his eyes on the road. "Damn it, Kurt, how many times are you going to keep doing that?"

"Doing what?"

"I've told you time and again, you nasty bastard. Stop calling yourself *Daddy*. It's fucking gross. Last I checked, that was rule number two for this trip."

Dana nodded. "That's true."

Kurt barked out a laugh. "Man, piss on you both. Daddy does what Daddy wants. Just because it's *your* bachelor party vacation doesn't mean *you* get to make up all the rules. You're not in charge."

"That's where you're wrong," Deangelo declared. "I *am* in charge. And, for your information, this is *not* a bachelor party."

Dana raised an eyebrow. "Well, I mean, you are getting married in two weeks."

"Correct."

Kurt added, "And all of us are your best friends."

"For the most part, yes."

"And we're driving all the way down to Florida because—"

"Because it's summer and it's the perfect time to visit the beach and get sunburned with said friends."

"Do black folks get sunburned?" Dana asked, grinning.

Deangelo smirked. "Nah, we just get better looking."

Eleven hours into a fourteen-hour drive and Aaron was fully ready to toss himself out the window. Witty banter could only get you so far, but when the hours roll into double digits and those stories and jokes had been on repeat since junior high, there was only so much a man could take. He never wanted to come on this trip or party or whatever the hell Deangelo was calling it. He wanted to spend the only week he had off this year drinking himself into a stupor. Ever since Kenzie left, it was all he could do to cope with the loneliness. At least he wouldn't be lonely for the next week, thanks to Deangelo. But by no means did that imply he would stay sober.

Another billboard flew past.

"My dude, face it," Kurt said. "It's a fucking week-long beach bachelor party."

Deangelo growled. "I said it's not a goddamn bachelor party!"

Dana cocked her head. "Chesya wouldn't let you have a bachelor party, would she?"

Deangelo sighed and rubbed his eyes. "No. You have no idea the hell I went through to convince her to let us do this. Months of begging, and even after she agreed she made damn sure to remind me every single day that this *is not* a bachelor party. No partying, no dance clubs, no strip joints. Those are the rules, and I plan to stick by them."

"No strip clubs?" Kurt whined. "We're driving to Daytona Beach, the strip club capital of the South!"

"And we won't be seeing a single one."

Kurt crossed his arms and muttered, "Maybe not *you*."

Dana said, "Man, you're really pussy-whipped, aren't you?"

Deangelo side-eyed her. "At least I have a pussy to whip me. What's your excuse?"

"Me? I'm perfectly happy being single right now, thank you very much. I don't need another sad, nagging woman to control my every move."

"Yeah? How's Carrie doing these days?"

Dana sighed. "I don't know. Haven't seen her since the split. I see no reason to be friendly after the shit she pulled."

"Uh-huh. Can't say I blame you."

Kurt laughed in the back seat. "Take some advice from the best-looking one in this car: stay single. I've never needed a woman to hold me down."

Eyeing him from the rearview mirror, Deangelo said, "I don't think that's your choice."

"Hardy-fucking-har."

While the other two laughed, Arron remained silent, inwardly rolling his eyes. Kurt's hand clasped onto his shoulder, making him jump.

"You see, Aaron and I, we don't need that shit holding us back. We're grown-ass men, carving out our own destiny, flying our own ships, piloting our own boats. Ain't that right, A-man?"

Without looking, Aaron nodded.

"Damn straight. Don't worry about Kenzie, man. She was a grade-A bitch."

Pinching his face, Aaron angrily turned to Kurt.

Kurt asked, "What? Everyone knows I'm right."

"He's not wrong." Deangelo nodded.

Dana added, "Hate to admit it, Aaron, but for once Kurt isn't lying…unlike what he said about four girls in one night."

Kurt yelled, "I wasn't fucking lying! It was sophomore year in college!"

"Bitch, I've been with *far* more women than you, and I can say with the upmost confidence you have never slept with more than four women in your whole life!"

This time Aaron actually rolled his eyes. He turned back to the window, letting the blazing midday sun warm his tired face. Outside, the kudzu-covered oaks and maples zipped by in an emerald blur. At least three to four more hours of this shit. God help him, he needed a drink—and fast.

Another billboard approached, this one in faded neon purple. Same girl, but with a few more words posted beneath her.

COLDEST BEER IN GEORGIA

"Can we stop?" Aaron immediately asked.

Deangelo glanced back in the mirror. "You okay?"

"He speaks!" Dana quipped.

Aaron wiped the sweat from his brow. "I want to stop."

"Why?" Deangelo asked. "Need a piss break? I guess I could use one myself. Anyone else?"

"No, I'm thirsty."

"Thirsty? We've still got plenty of water and soda in the cooler."

Aaron groaned. "I want a beer, D."

"Hell yeah," Kurt agreed. "A cold beer sounds great!"

"Man, my black ass ain't stopping in the middle of Nowhere, Georgia for no beer." Deangelo vehemently shook his head. "I'm liable to get fucking shot down here."

Aaron grabbed the headrest and pulled himself forward. "Look, D, I've kept quiet this whole time. Not a peep. I'm hot, I'm tired, and I'm cranky. All I want is a damn beer. That's it. Just one. Is that too much for your best man to ask for?"

Deangelo drew out a long breath through his teeth, unhappy with being cornered. "Man, the shit you get me in to. If I get lynched by some men in white hooded robes, I'm going to come back and haunt your white ass."

"That's fine. I'll just make you watch Chesya and I when we get frisky."

"You mother—" Deangelo huffed, then whispered, "Are you sure this is a good idea?"

"What do you mean?"

Deangelo rolled his eyes. "You know damn well what I mean. We don't need you getting drunk. Sober trip, remember? Rule number three."

The vein in the corner of Aaron's eye twitched. "It's just one drink, D. One and that's it. I swear."

Deangelo shot him a questionable look. "Just one?"

"Yes. Just one. In fact, everyone gets one. My treat."

"Fuck. Fine. Where am I going?"

Aaron pointed. "Exit eleven. Two miles ahead."

Dana eyed him, a small grin spreading across her lips.

Deangelo shook his head. "Well, wherever we're going, they better have a gas station. You can fill it up. Also your treat."

For the first time in a long while, Aaron grinned. "Works for me."

Tooty slid the red checker across the board and exclaimed, "King me, old man!"

Albert didn't answer. Sitting across the small folding table from her, he continued to stare down at his feet. His glazed eyes focused on something Tooty couldn't quite see. Beside his rocking chair, old Phil snored and kicked in his sleep.

Tooty waved her hand. "Albert? Are you okay, dear?" When her husband didn't respond, she snapped her fingers, wincing at the arthritic pain in her knuckles.

As if coming out of a dream, Albert lifted his head and blinked. "Huh?"

"Daydreamin' again? I said king me, old man."

Albert nodded, embarrassed. "Yeah, yeah, sorry." He placed a checker piece on top of hers and proceeded to rub the salt-and-pepper stubble across his chin.

Tooty watched her husband a few moments as his mind roamed elsewhere. "Want to talk about it?"

Frowning, Albert shook his head.

She reached out and took her husband's hand, rubbing his thin, liver-spotted skin with her thumb. "It'll be okay, hon."

Albert finally brought his eyes up to meet hers. He shrugged. "Will it?"

Letting him go, she sighed and carefully sat back in her creaky, wicker chair. "I think so. Just got to keep the faith. Without that, what do we have?" She nodded. "They'll come. They'll come."

Giving her an unsure smile, Albert nodded back.

She pointed at the board. "In the meantime, it's your move. Get to steppin'."

Old Phil abruptly woke and lifted his head. Both Tooty and Albert heard it, too.

A moment later, a car came driving past their house.

Grinning, Tooty couldn't grab the gardening tools quick enough.

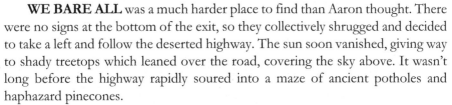

WE BARE ALL was a much harder place to find than Aaron thought. There were no signs at the bottom of the exit, so they collectively shrugged and decided to take a left and follow the deserted highway. The sun soon vanished, giving way to shady treetops which leaned over the road, covering the sky above. It wasn't long before the highway rapidly soured into a maze of ancient potholes and haphazard pinecones.

Deangelo grumbled. "This better be the best damn beer of your life, Aaron."

It was another seven miles of bitching and complaining before they saw any signs of life. A small clapboard shack sat a few yards beyond the tree line, blanketed in thick gray shadows. They were undoubtedly lost, but Deangelo refused to slow the car, instead hitting the gas with a little more zest. As they passed by, an old man in overalls and no shirt stumbled out of the house. Obviously drunk, he halted next to a dirt patch on the front lawn and watched them drive by. He lifted an arm and waved.

Kurt whistled. "I'll bet that old coot knows what squirrel tastes like."

Dana watched as they sped on. "Yeah…he's probably been with more women than you, too."

"Oh, piss off. Cousins don't count." He paused. "Right? Like, they don't count, right?"

"You're a sick puppy, Kurt."

Deangelo called out, "Hey, Aaron, does this bar actually exist, or are we heading for someplace where you plan to make us squeal like pigs?"

His patience running thin, Aaron's eyes continued to roam the dense forest, searching for anything that resembled a town. Maybe Deangelo was right. Maybe **WE BARE ALL** didn't exist anymore, bulldozed away or left to rot somewhere after years of begging travelers to come observe God's gift to lonely truckers. Unfortunately, a lukewarm soda would have to tide him over until they passed over into the Sunshine State.

A few minutes later, a small wooden sign appeared on the right side of the road.

"Welcome to Prancer, Georgia," Kurt snickered. "Population forty-six."

Dana rubbed her arms. "Seems like a very specific number."

"Are we really about to drive around this place for a damn beer?" Deangelo moaned.

Aaron squeezed the driver's shoulders. "Shut up and drive."

With an exaggerated sigh, Deangelo turned onto to the roughly paved road into town.

A few minutes later, the sky overhead opened up as they exited the forest and entered the small community of Prancer. Brilliant sunlight gleamed across the road, bleeding over the dozens of small homes which lined the street. Much like the shack a few miles back, these residences had suffered similar dilapidation. Dwellings leaned in all directions, windows covered in hazy, ruffled plastic, lawns yellowed and overgrown with dandelions and crabgrass. Their owners, appearing no worse for the wear, relaxed in rocking chairs on their front porches. Smoke drifted from pipes. Frail, delicate hands knitted. Tired dogs kicked in their sleep.

"Salt of the earth," Dana muttered.

"Won't be long before they return to it," muttered Kurt.

"Don't be rude. These people have probably never been outside of this town. This is all they know."

Kurt shook his head. "Man, that's fucking depressing." He rolled down his window and yelled, "Yo! Want to come to the beach with us? Sand and bikinis, baby!"

An old couple playing checkers on a card table turned to watch them go. Their eyes grew wide with surprise.

"Jesus," Dana yelled, rolling his window up with the front controls. "Leave those poor people alone!"

"I'm just having some fun. Hell, that's probably the most excitement they've had in years."

Aaron turned back around as they passed. Their game forgotten, the old couple were now both standing and heading down their front steps. Each one held a gardening tool as they headed for a small dirt patch on the front lawn of their home.

Deangelo grumbled. "We could have already been in Florida by now, getting some fresh squeezed OJ at the Welcome Center."

Aaron punched the back of the driver's seat. "Quit your bitching. Look—there's a gas station right up there."

Deangelo squinted. "Looks like the gas station from that movie...the one with that guy who wears people's faces." He steered into the parking lot and pulled up to the only pump on the lot.

Unbuckling himself, Aaron popped open his door. "Tell you what, if they have any extra faces in there, we'll get you a newer model. How's that sound?"

"I would be highly shocked if they've ever even seen a black man around here, much less carried their detached faces."

The other two got out and began to stretch. Deangelo remained in the car.

"You coming?" Aaron asked.

"Hell no! Just pump the gas and let's get the fuck out of here, please."

"Fine."

Upon realizing the gas pump had no credit card reader, Aaron filled the tank and casually strolled toward the small station house. Dana and Kurt followed.

Inside, the florescent bulbs audibly buzzed above the rows of dusty shelves. Unlabeled cans of food and various Georgia-themed knickknacks lined the homemade display racks. Yellowed soda bottles sat inside ancient refrigerators, long out of date, as were the candy bars displayed by the register. The smell of old fried chicken permeated the air. Dana and Kurt eyeballed the items, giggling as they sauntered through the aisles.

Aaron stepped up to the front counter. "He...hello?"

The dirty white sheet covering the back room fluttered open. A wild frock of white hair poked out, followed a moment later by a confused face. With a tangled gray beard and a wrinkled blue t-shirt which read "Been there, licked that," a sleepy looking old man stepped out toward the counter. His eyes were suddenly full of shock, and his open mouth looked just as surprised. Only a handful of jagged teeth remained inside the man's blackened gums.

"Well I'll be damned…" he croaked.

"Hello, sir," Aaron said. "I'm very sorry to bother you, but my friends and I just filled up our vehicle and need to pay for the gas."

The old man rubbed his eyes. "Wait…you boys…came to visit?"

"Well, yes. Only for a bit. We saw the billboards all the way down I-75."

A wide smile ruptured across his face. "You boys goin' to the titty club?"

Aaron cracked his own smile. "Um…I believe it's a gentleman's club, but yes."

Dana and Kurt walked up behind Aaron.

"What's this about titties?" Kurt asked.

"I knew it," Dana said, beaming. "We're going to that strip club, aren't we? I saw the advertisements, too."

Kurt put his palms up. "Wait—the bar we're going to is a *strip club*? A-man, brother, I knew I loved you for a reason!"

The old man giggled with glee. "Ah, shucks, you boys are goin' to love it! Biggest titties in all of Georgia! Girls so pretty it'll make you pop a woody right there through your Bugle Boys!"

Kurt giggled right along with the old man. "Holy shit, I love this guy!"

Dana asked, "What if we're not able to sport wood, sir?"

The old man tossed Dana a sharp, mean glare before turning around toward the back room. "Helga! Helga, woman, get out here! We've got guests!"

"What?" a frail voice answered.

"Woman, we've got some fine young men who've come to see the titties!"

A few moments later the sheet parted, and a tiny old woman shuffled out. Much like her husband, her face was alight with glee. "Well, I'll be! Look at this! Two strappin' young men came to visit Prancer!"

Dana shifted from foot to foot, visibly uncomfortable.

The old man said, "I was just tellin' them about We Bare All."

"Did you tell them about the titties, Harold?" She turned to Aaron, wagging a gnarled, arthritic finger. "Young man, let me tell you, the girls down the street, they've got the biggest and best titties in the whole state. You won't believe it! Those girls are young and pretty and willing to give ya a darn good time, yes sir."

"Welp, I'm sold!" Kurt gleefully exclaimed.

Grinning, mostly from disbelief, Aaron let his eyes jump from face to face. Never in his life had he heard the elderly speak with such open crudeness. Part of him wanted to laugh along with Kurt, but the whole exchange made him terribly uneasy. He wondered if it was some sort of prank the locals played on outsiders, to entertain themselves on the rare occasions someone younger than sixty-five stumbled into town. But the two before him seemed genuinely thrilled they were there.

Aaron said, "Well, it's not so much the, um, the nudity we're looking for, ma'am. We're mostly just looking for a cold drink. That's all."

"You're in luck then!" the old woman declared. "Coldest beer in the state—cheapest, too!"

The old man craned his neck, looking past them to the car outside. "That colored fella, he with ya?"

Aaron raised an eyebrow, expecting the man's jovial attitude to evaporate. "Uh, yes, that's our friend."

Rubbing his bearded chin, the old man nodded solemnly. "Welp, I imagine they'll be happy to see him, too. Helga, does that old colored couple still reside on Turkey Hill Road?"

"The Barrys? Haven't seen them in a spell, but I believe so."

Aaron asked, "Excuse me?"

The old man waved it off. "'Tis nothing. Tell ya what, you boys go to the titty bar and have yourselves a grand ol' time. Tell 'em Harry sent ya." He winked. "That'll get ya the special treatment."

"Okay, sure." Aaron was growing more uncomfortable by the second. "Here's thirty bucks for the gas."

Harold shook his head. "On the house, young fella." Before Aaron could protest, he added, "Seriously, go now."

"Well…okay then. If you insist. By the way, where is this place? We haven't seen a sign since leaving the interstate."

The old man pointed out the window. "Up the street there, about three blocks or so on the left. Ya can't miss it."

"Great. Thanks again. You two have a good day."

The three headed for the front door, back out into the heat.

"Thank *you*!" the old man called. As the front door closed, the couple embraced each other with a big hug.

They were coming. She could feel them. Could taste their energy and their youthful vigor. She inhaled, their potency coming at her like waves.

Without turning her head, she slowly moved her eyes until she found the others sitting next to her in the darkness.

Quivering, they, too, could feel it. Eternity was ending.

Not much longer now.

"That old guy was such an asshole," Dana sulked.

Watching the rows of ramshackle homes crawl by, Aaron wasn't even listening. He was focused on the road, so absorbed in his own thoughts he could barely hear anything outside of his racing heartbeat. The embrace of alcohol was so close he could practically taste it. One beer was all he wanted…maybe two…maybe more.

Shit, he thought miserably. *You've got a problem, man.*

He was never much of a drinker before Kenzie came along. His ex was quite the partier, a social butterfly, and it took her a long time to convince him to break out of his cocoon. He loved his *own* friends—hers, not so much. It always took a few drinks for him to finally feel comfortable around them at bars and clubs. Soon, a few became several. Then several became a dozen. By the time he realized he had a problem, half of every paycheck was being pissed away at bars. He supposed this vacation was just as much for him as it was for celebrating Deangelo's last two weeks as a free man.

Just one. That's it. In and out. Poof. Ghost.

"What do you mean?" Kurt asked. "I thought he was pretty damn funny."

Dana pinched her face in disgust. "He completely wrote me off and kept giving me the stink eye."

"Well, they probably don't get a lot of women down here looking to go to strip clubs."

"But I like women!" she huffed.

"He doesn't know that!"

Deangelo stomped on the brakes. All four pitched forward in their seats. "The fuck did you say?"

Kurt shrugged. "What?"

"Did you say *strip club*?" he spat. "You motherfuckers are about to get me divorced before I even get married!"

"What's the big deal?" Dana asked.

"How many times do I have to tell you chuckleheads? No strip clubs! My woman made it *very* clear. You know she don't play like that."

Along the street, dozens of old people stepped out of their houses, eyeballing their stalled vehicle. While many watched with gleeful smiles, others hurried around the sides of their homes, garden tools in hand. An old woman in a pink floral nightgown hobbled down the sidewalk in the opposite direction. She waved happily.

Aaron leaned forward. "Look, D, I'm buying the drinks, okay? Nothing will show up on your bank statement. She'll never know."

The driver shook his head, unconvinced. "She's going to know, man."

"No, she won't. I promise."

Deangelo sighed. "Aaron, if I didn't love you so much, I would beat your ass right here on the street and give these people something to watch."

Aaron sat back with a grin. "Shut up and drive."

Another block, another round of happy, elderly faces, and the club finally appeared behind a copse of cypress trees. The building was so much smaller than Aaron had imagined, about the size of a large garage. The outer layer of aluminum siding had been sunbaked into a muddy, bourbon brown, peppered with patches of copper-colored rust. Dozens of metal signs advertising beer and liquor were posted across the front, some of which Aaron was quite sure no longer existed. The massive neon sign attached to the roof which bared the club's name was turned off.

Deangelo pulled into the small, empty lot and chose a spot near the front door. He leaned forward and stared at the three giant words hovering above them. "Yeah? If I'm going to destroy my relationship, they better fucking bare it all."

"Hell yeah! Daddy likes!" Kurt excitedly leapt out of the car.

Dana rolled her eyes and followed.

Aaron placed a hand on his best friend's shoulder. "It'll be fine. Calm down. It's just a drink. If you don't want to look at the women, then look at me instead."

Deangelo barked out a dry laugh. "Man, if some girl is going to put her chest in my face, I'm sure as hell not going to stare at your ugly ass."

Aaron laughed. "That's the spirit."

"Hey…just one drink. I mean it, that's it. Seriously, I'm worried about you."

Shaking his head, Aaron stopped himself from snapping. He took a deep breath and closed his eyes. "One drink."

"All right, let's get this over with."

They both stepped out of the car. The sweltering southern heat accosted them, instantly making them sweat. A light breeze ruffled the cypress vines, sending an empty potato chip bag spinning across the lot. Other than their footsteps, the town was eerily quiet.

Dana approached the front door. "Is this place even open?"

Kurt giggled. "We're about to find out!" He pulled open the door and the other three followed him inside.

Unlike the sunlit parking lot, the building's interior wasn't as easily visible. The overhead bulbs were all turned off, and the only light came from the waxy, frosted windows near the front door. The front waiting area was small and cramped, filled with dirty leather couches and padded lounge seats. Metal chairs were stacked on top of tables. The stench of old sweat and liquor buried itself in Aaron's nose, and something about it made him feel at home. The door slammed shut behind them.

On the other side of the dance stage, three faces all turned toward them at once.

Deangelo yelped, throwing his arms across the others. Aaron's skin prickled with nervous energy. Dana and Kurt stepped back toward the door.

Three women sat silently beside the stage. They stood, revealing their scantily clad bodies, minimally adorned in lacy bras and panties. An old man with a long white ponytail stood up straight behind the bar against the back wall, while another old man peeked out from inside the DJ booth on the far right wall. All five seemed just as shocked to see them.

Aaron called out. "Sorry to intrude, but are you guys…open?"

The woman closest to them pushed her chair back and slowly strolled over. Aaron eyed her curiously. He wasn't generally into strip clubs. He found them gross and uncomfortable and could always feel the eyes of the dancers' boyfriends watching from the back corner. Not to mention the drinks were incredibly overpriced. But something told him this time would be different. Other than the four of them, the club was dead as a doornail. No one to judge his stares—and, boy, was there a lot to look at.

The young woman walking his way could have been a supermodel had she lived anywhere but the backwoods of South Georgia. Her hair was impeccably done, long chestnut waves steadily flowing into loose curls across her pale, freckled shoulders. Much like the billboards miles back, her lipstick was bright and glossy, with light flecks of glitter accenting their plumpness. Aaron did his best not to glance down, but he had to admit, the pervy old couple at the gas station weren't lying. The other two women had sashayed up behind her, a blonde and a redhead, both equally as gorgeous and out of place.

With a grin, the brunette took Aaron's hand in hers. "Sugar, for you...we're always open."

The lights suddenly snapped on above them. Dozens of smaller bulbs exploded across the wooden walls, showering the room with bright, fluorescent neons. A small whine of static from the speakers, and a moment later Metallica's cover of "Turn the Page" came echoing out. Spotlights blazed, illuminating the small, glassy stage and the two vertical brass poles attached to it. Above, a disco ball whirled to life, dotting the scene with glittery life. The living wrinkle inside the deejay booth gave them all a hearty thumbs up.

Aaron allowed himself to be led past the dusty couches toward the back bar. A quirky smile on his lips, he caught a whiff of the brunette's perfume. He couldn't quite put his finger on the scent, but it was absolutely intoxicating. He turned back and saw the other two women take Deangelo and Kurt's hands, all of them following him back. Kurt was unable to contain his glee. Deangelo, on the other hand, appeared miserable, his eyes flittering across the walls. Behind them, Dana walked by herself, frowning.

When they reached the back, the ponytailed bartender playfully smacked the polished wooden bar top. "Boys, boys, boys! What'll we be havin' today?"

Kurt leaned in over Aaron's shoulder. "Y'all got Yuengling?"

The old man pointed and winked. "Coldest in Georgia!"

Aaron was impressed. "That sounds fantastic. Four bottles, please."

The barkeep's smile faded when he leaned past and saw Dana. He broke open the cooler behind him and took out their ice-cold bottles, handing them each one but giving Aaron two. Aaron handed Dana hers, along with a shrug.

She rolled her eyes and turned her focus back on the other women.

"How much?" Aaron asked

"Oh...fifty cents apiece sound good?"

Shocked, Aaron said, "Are you serious?"

The old man winked again. "For you boys? It's my treat."

"Holy shit!" Kurt laughed. "Daddy says we hit the jackpot in this town! Dirt cheap beer and gorgeous women? Heaven on earth, baby!"

The women giggled and led them back to the plush chairs surrounding the dance stage.

Deangelo leaned into Aaron's ear. "One beer, man. We're gone in twenty."

The brunette glanced back to him with a wry smile.

Aaron nodded. "One and twenty. Got it."

Two hours and roughly ten beers later, the four weary travelers were absolutely trashed. Nobody had spoken in over an hour. Instead, they stared intently at the three women gyrating masterfully on the glittery stage. Dozens of empty bottles were scattered about the floor and circular side tables, their owners slumped in the chairs beside them. Kurt appeared to be having the time of his life, whistling and laughing, tossing bill after bill onto the stage. Deangelo, though quiet, had greatly loosened up, a small grin plastered on his goateed face. Only Dana appeared to be having a bad time. Once she recognized the strippers had zero interest in her, she continued to drink and play on her phone. Aaron would somehow have to make it up to her later, but for now…

The music ebbed and flowed, as did Aaron's vision as he tried to focus on the brunette. Her primal scent invaded his senses, rolling like Atlantic waves, splashing, enveloping his every thought. Their eyes were locked onto one another's, unbroken for some time. Another cold beer was thrust into his fist and a moment later it was draining into his mouth. Fuck Kenzie, fuck Florida, fuck the beach, and fuck this stupid "not a bachelor party" vacation—this was all that mattered.

Tito & Tarantula's "After Dark" twined seductively through the speakers, forcing the brunette to slow her silky movements. Aaron was enraptured. By the time the guitar solo echoed through the room, his beer was empty and his mind was just as gone. He shifted in his seat, trying his best to hide the erection straining inside his shorts.

Fully nude, the brunette lifted her eyebrows and nodded behind him. His vision blurred, Aaron turned his head and located a small side room by the bar. Lights flickered beyond the curtain door. He turned back and playfully pointed to himself. The brunette giggled and then climbed down from the stage. Aaron drunkenly stood and took her soft hand as she guided him away. Just before he lifted the curtain and stepped inside, he glanced back to his friends.

Kurt was already disappearing into another side room, while Deangelo was helping the remaining dancer down off the stage.

While he was being led away, the old bartender causally stepped around the bar and strolled toward Dana. The wrinkled old deejay followed as the curtain fell in Aaron's eyes.

The private room was tiny and cramped, not much bigger than a walk-in closet, and the only light was a small strobe which rapidly flickered above their heads. Before he could speak, Aaron was shoved down onto a wide, circular couch. The alcohol sloshing around in his stomach nearly expelled the moment his ass hit the cushions. He belched and quickly covered his mouth. The single speaker hanging from the ceiling began to play Twista's "Slow Jamz," and the brunette found the easy beat and swayed, swinging her sizeable hips to and fro, her breasts following. Aaron reached for his wallet, but she gently smacked his hand away. Resigned to the idea that everything in this miserable town was free, he let his head fall into the backrest and allowed the music to take him away...

The brunette straddled him and sat on his legs, pressing her ample chest into his face. Her scent overpowered him, smothering him like a warm, wet blanket. Sweat poured down his face and stung his bloodshot eyes. His arms shook. He was unsure what do with his hands. Every breath shuddered uncomfortably out of his throat. She flipped around and pressed her ass against his painfully constrained crotch. Aaron nearly lost his mind. She leaned back and tossed her soft locks into his face. Her perfume enveloped him. He inhaled deeply as it sent a rush of adrenaline through his body, flaring every nerve. The strobe blinked faster. Aaron closed his eyes, shaking uncontrollably. It was all too much, yet not enough.

Over the music, she whispered, "Do you want me to—"

"Yes!" he cried.

Without thinking twice, Aaron spun on his side and fell backwards onto the couch. With her back to him, she sat on his beer-bloated stomach. A moment later she extracted his cock through his zipper. Her hand was warm and quick, and though he couldn't see her work, it was obvious this wasn't her first time. That didn't bother him—in fact, it only drove him wilder. His legs shook beneath her.

What would Kenzie think? This...is...fucking...insane!

The pressure grew and grew. As he neared the edge, he sat up on shaking elbows and leaned to look around her.

His eyes went wide.

While his cock was in the blur of her right hand, in her left she held a small clutch of glowing blue eggs.

Before Aaron could question what he was seeing, he came. Thick ropes of ejaculate arced into the air. Acting swiftly, the brunette moved her other hand over to catch it. The fresh sperm dropped across the eggs, making their soft blue lights immediately grow brighter.

Aaron opened his mouth to protest, but he instead collapsed backwards, his brain shutting down like an engine.

As darkness overcame him, he heard the brunette shout, "I've got it!"

Two more voices hollered the same words.

———————————⟡———————————

Aaron awoke to the sound of banging. The strobe light was off, the room now pitch black. He stood on shaking legs and went to put his cock back into his pants but found it was already stuffed back inside. Dazed, he stumbled out of the room.

The main area of the club was much like they had found originally it. The lights, the sounds, the life—all gone. The only movement was from Deangelo. He stood on the far side of the room, angrily bashing a folded metal chair against a closed closet door.

"D…what's going on? What happened?"

Deangelo spun around and yelled, "*You stupid motherfucker! I could kill you!*"

From inside the closet he heard, "Is that Aaron?"

Aaron stumbled toward him. "What…why is Dana in the closet?"

"I don't know!" Deangelo screamed. Sweat poured down his face and neck. "Just help me get the door open!" He dropped the chair and then wedged his fingers into the small gap he had created in the doorframe.

Aaron joined him and after a few moments of pulling, the lock snapped and gave away. The door swung open.

Dripping in sweat, Dana staggered out and furiously shoved Deangelo. "Why did you leave me, you pricks? I was in there for fucking hours!"

Aaron rubbed his throbbing temples. "Wait…what? Hours?"

"Yes! When you assholes went off for your private dances, those old fuckers blindsided me and hit me over the head with something. I didn't even get a chance to defend myself. The next thing I know I'm waking up in this fucking hotbox. What the hell were you guys doing in there for so long?"

Aaron shifted awkwardly where he stood.

Deangelo growled and punched the closet door shut. "Did they…"

She shook her head. "Thankfully, no."

"Shit," Aaron blurted, tapping his pockets. "Where's my phone?"

Deangelo shook his head. "Fucking gone, same as ours."

"Hello?"

They all three jumped as Kurt drunkenly stumbled out from his private room. "Where… Fuck, my head. Where is everyone?"

"We are leaving! Now!" Crying, Dana ran to Kurt and grabbed his wrist, then dragged him toward the front door.

Aaron and Deangelo quickly followed.

When they stepped outside, Aaron was surprised to discover it was well past dark. Crickets and cicadas chanted, filling the world with their angry, strident songs. Without hesitating, they all jumped back into the car. Deangelo revved the engine, and a moment later they were peeling out of the empty lot.

"Goddamn it, Aaron," Deangelo yelled, "you stupid, selfish fuck! What did I say—what did I fucking say? I said one beer and twenty minutes! We were already supposed to be at the condo by now!"

Aaron rubbed his tired eyes. "I'm sorry. Please…stop screaming. My head hurts so bad."

"Absolutely not! Sorry ain't going to cut this time, asshole!" Deangelo began to cry. "Oh my God…what have I done? What have I done?"

"Just…just let me think." Aaron turned to ask Kurt what he had done, but the man had already passed out in his seat, his head resting against the window, snoring.

"D, please get me out of his fucking hillbilly town," Dana moaned. "Please!"

"I'm working on it."

The main strip of town passed by in a flash, as did its elderly residents. Aaron pressed his head against the window to look.

Bathed only in lantern light, the owners of each home stood on their front lawns, cheerfully waving at their car. Below their ecstatic faces, each local held the hand of a small, nude toddler. Some were boys, others were little girls, but they were all caked head to toe in fresh, wet earth. The children appeared dazed and lethargic, their eyes unseeing, as if they had just woken from a long sleep.

Dana muttered, "What in the fuck…"

A gleeful chorus of 'Thank you' and 'You saved us' called out into the night.

Deangelo immediately floored the gas.

His arms buried deep in the cold earth, Morty pulled with every ounce of strength his frail body could muster. When her small head finally ruptured the loose dirt, he let go of her wrists and reached beneath her arms. One final pull and Morty carefully extracted his little girl from the ground. In the hole below, the remains of a large, blue egg sat in pieces.

"Jesus, Mary, and Joseph…you're so beautiful. So precious." Tears spilled down his bearded cheeks as he placed her on her feet. He spat into his handkerchief and gingerly wiped the smudges of soil from her pale, expressionless face. "I've waited so long for you."

Behind him, the car he saw earlier screeched around the corner and raced as fast as it could down the narrow highway, away from Prancer.

Morty waved as they passed. "Thank you so much! God bless you!" He turned back to his little girl and hugged her hard. His chest hitched, this time with sobs of joy. "God bless you all."

———————————

Somewhere beyond the cabin, three feminine shapes raced through the forest on foot. Their eternity had ended. They were finally free.

Before long, they disappeared into the night.

IT STARTED WITH A SINGLE NOTE

by Evans Light

The piano, a Kohler & Campbell upright fashioned from brown cherry, is a birthday gift from Mother and Father for their children, Timothy and Emma Lee. The instrument is far from fancy, although Mother thinks the fluted legs make it look more expensive than it actually was.

Mother and Father purchased the piano with hopes of uncovering innate musical talent within their seven-year-old twins, but two years of lessons, tortuous practice sessions, and hours upon hours of bitter complaints from both children thoroughly proves otherwise. So they give up, and the piano is left to collect dust and framed family photos atop its lid as it sits neglected in the far corner of the living room.

Father is at work and the kids are at school. Mother is cleaning house, feeling listless and bored. She lifts the piano's fallboard to dust off the keys, more out of habit than any real need. As she slides the dust cloth along the keyboard, she accidentally depresses one of the keys just enough to lift a hammer and strike a string.

The unexpected note brightens the stillness of the empty room, both startling and thrilling her. It's as if that particular note is electric, sending a jolt right into her heart. The sensation is pleasurable, addictive, and she immediately wants to feel it again.

Mother slides the bench out from the piano and takes a seat, her outstretched finger trembling with excitement as she gently presses a random key. The tone that sounds from within the cabinet isn't the same as before. The room doesn't brighten, no electricity is felt.

Mother continues to peck, one key at a time, searching frantically for that special note. After a half-dozen tries she finds it, hidden among the ebonies. A look of near-orgasmic pleasure spreads across her face. The room brightens once again as though a door in the sky has been cracked open to allow a small glimpse of Heaven.

Cleaning house is now the last thing on her mind. Her dust cloth drops to the floor as Mother plays that single note over and over again. But the intensity of the sensation it brings diminishes somewhat with each repetition and lasts only as long as the note.

She wants more.

She needs more.

Mother's fingers dance frantically up and down the keyboard, playing that first note while desperately seeking a second, anything to prolong the sensation of bliss. She finds a second note, and eventually a third, each lengthening the melody and enhancing its effect.

The children come home from school to find themselves left without greeting as Mother sits at the piano in the living room, mesmerized, intently working out her special song. Father comes home from work to a dark and dinnerless house, his wife brushing off all inquiries about her day as she plays the same handful of notes over and over while tirelessly searching for the next and the next.

Father makes dinner, helps the children with their homework, and tucks them in bed. He retires to his own bed, worried and alone, closing the bedroom door to muffle the sound of his wife replaying the same bit of tune endlessly in the living room, wondering if she's lost her mind.

He awakes the next morning to find her fast asleep, still seated at the piano with her arms crossed, head resting upon them atop the keyboard. He carries her to bed and wakes the children for school, fixing them breakfast and walking them out to the bus. Before he leaves for work, he stands in the bedroom door watching Mother as she sleeps, wondering if she was still playing the piano in her dreams.

Months pass and seasons change, but Mother's obsession with the song does not. She relentlessly seeks the rest of the tune, as though treasure was buried beneath those black and white keys.

As she feels her way through the melody, it becomes more complex. No longer does a single finger suffice, both hands must be employed as octaves and chords emerge. Not only is the correct sequence of notes required to produce the magic, but the correct rhythm and tempo is essential to prevent the euphoria and light from fading away.

Her husband's protestations and her children's pleas are but intrusions on her singular quest. They bring in family and friends to try to pry her away, even a doctor drops by to make sure she's sane. She's fine, she insists, only pursuing her passions.

Eventually, Father and the children give up and go on about their lives. Mother's there but she's not, not as they need her to be, but they all gradually acclimate to the change.

Mother spends years at the keyboard laboring to finish that single song, leaving her post only to attend to the most essential necessities, utterly committed to obtain whatever wonders lay just out of reach on the other side. Her visions of Heaven become increasingly clear the further into the song she plays. Each strike of her finger upon the keyboard is purposeful, determined to tear down the wall between this world and the next with the powerful melody she's stumbled upon. She's a musical archaeologist, as she digs out each new series of notes from where they lie buried beneath limitless combinations.

Before they leave home for their first year of college, Timothy and Emma Lee help Father move the piano to the most remote room in the house, so he can watch television in the evenings undisturbed by the noise. Mother worries more about damaging the piano than she does about her kids leaving home, fretting and pacing as they roll it down the hall. Excited to get back to her music after the unwelcome intrusion, she forgets to tell her children goodbye while Father helps them pack up the car. He stands alone, waving at the end of the driveway, as they pull away.

Father sometimes forgets he has a wife, as two or three days often pass in between his encounters with Mother as she staggers around the house, lost in her musical addiction. He pities her, pities himself, but knows her obsession has become unstoppable.

Years pass and the twins, adults now, come to visit with Father. Mother, hair now silver, remains hunched in the back room over her keyboard, as always. She fails to notice her children's arrival as they say their hellos before heading back into the living room. There they sit and visit with Father, barely aware of the tinkling music that emanates from Mother's piano room, that endless background noise of their lives.

As they talk about times gone and those yet to come, the room grows noticeably brighter, even though the sky beyond the windows remains cloudy and gray.

For the first time in decades, there is a change in Mother's never-ending song. Father and the twins stop talking, intrigued by the development. As they listen, the music grows louder, more assured. A shriek of joy from the piano room echoes down the hallway.

The music begins to swell, the song's complex tempo is different, now somehow alive. Father and Timothy and Emma Lee squirm as the song crawls into their ears, like a physical being struggling to find a way inside. As it succeeds, they begin to sense all the song contains, all that Mother has felt and known these many years. The melody is the heartbeat of the earth, all the waves of the world breaking in time. It is the beginning and the end, and everything in between.

Father and the twins fall silent, listening intently, unable to do anything else as the music washes over them, absorbing them as they absorb it.

The light in the room grows ever brighter, not from outside the windows but streaming through the hallway door. The atmosphere within the room shifts, the air redolent of fresh cherries and timber, growing warmer by the moment.

The song continues to surge, sliding and shifting, an invisible serpent winding its way through every room in the house. It morphs into something they've never heard before, never experienced before, not even Father throughout decades of hearing Mother play.

Timothy and Emma Lee rise from their chairs, following Father as he leaves the room, heading down the glowing hallway toward a melody that a mere two hands could never play.

The sound takes on physical form, becoming both flowing colors and twirling shapes as the three approach the piano room. A kaleidoscope of light swirls through the half-open doorway, furtive and alive.

The music is glorious, transcendently baroque and staccato. The intensity of the light and brilliance of the colors emanating from it forces Timothy and Emma Lee to shield their eyes. Father, now sick with worry, bursts through the door. A luminescence emanates from the piano so dazzling that Mother's form is lost within its glow.

As the three enter the room, every note on the keyboard plays at once. Eighty-eight notes take flight, infinity upon infinity, as though a flock of birds has been rustled up into an endless blue sky.

The piano room grows silent and dark as Mother's pink cotton nightgown flutters down to rest upon an abruptly vacant piano bench. On the floor beneath sits mother's matching slippers, both empty.

Father walks to the piano and sets the lid down to cover the keys, casting a sorrowful gaze at the remnants of his family gathered around him. It's as though he's closing a coffin.

"I'm so sorry," Emma Lee says, reaching to take her father's hand.

Father pulls it away before she can manage, brusquely wiping tears from his eyes.

"Sorry?" he exclaims, voice full of unexpected indignation. "She found what she was looking for. Be sorry for the rest of us, for we can only hope to be so fortunate."

REMEMBERING FRANK

by Chad Lutzke

I wish I could remember the exact circumstances regarding the first time I met Frank. It wasn't in person, unfortunately. But he had reviewed a book of mine, then another. By that time, whenever he heard another was being released, he made sure he got a copy for review, shooting me a message to let me know he was ready and willing.

By the time he passed, Frank had reviewed six of my books. He loved every one of them, even the one I thought he wouldn't: *The Same Deep Water as You*. That book was an experimental departure for me. It wasn't horror, but it was dark—a coming-of-age tragic romance with beer, skateboarding, punk rock, and falling in and out of love.

I figured the book would alienate those within Frank's demographic. He was in his late 60s. But Frank Errington, God bless him, loved that book, giving it all the stars and stating it was filled with bits of wisdom.

Frank really got it.

Now, I'd already really liked him. But it was at that point I realized just how hip, how open-minded the man was, particularly for his age. The same can't be said for many of us. Young or old. We can be a close-minded bunch. But Frank? He just wanted to hear a good story. Light or dark. Clean or bloody. Still today, on the front page of his blog are the last few reviews he did. One of those for my work, where he said, "We just seem to be on the same wavelength…" That's every writer's dream, to connect with the reader. And it's one of the reasons why I miss Frank's presence within the community and why being asked to take part in a tribute was an easy YES from me.

I'm guessing most stories in this tribute are horror because that was Frank's wheelhouse. That was his tribe. So, mine may be the outlier. The one that's neither bloody nor scary. And I'm okay with that, because this one isn't for the reader but 100 percent for Frank. And I think he would have liked it.

So, to celebrate Frank's eclectic and hip taste, I wrote a story using characters from that beer-drinking, skateboarding, tragic romance just for him.

Here's to you Frank. May you somehow, somewhere be able to read it.

NECROPHONE

by David Price

Red light on. Okay, it's blinking, recording. Deep breath, look into the camera…let's do this.

Hi, I'm Steven Cross. Some weird stuff has happened to me lately. It's really shaken me up, kind of made me question the truth of…well of everything, I guess. What is reality, you know? Forces are in play here that I used to believe were just imaginary. I'm still not sure. I still wonder if I'm losing it or having some sort of psychotic break. And it's made me wonder how much I can trust my memory, so I thought maybe I should make a record that explains what's happened to me so far, just in case. In case of what, I don't know. I'm just feeling more paranoid lately. All right, let me start this story where it begins; with the death of my grandfather.

I hate funerals. It's the finality, you know. This is it, your loved one is going into the ground for good, or at least until the gates of Hell open up and the dead rise again. Still, if there's one thing worse than funerals, it's wakes. I really hate wakes. What's with the open casket, would you tell me? I don't get it. What is the deal with everybody standing around in a room with a dead body surrounded by flowers? It's morbid. Look, I know the person is dead, that's why I came to the wake in the first place. So let's just close the casket and put a couple of pictures near it, you know? It boggles my mind that we pay people to put makeup on corpses so they look good enough for public viewing. Doesn't anyone else see anything wrong with this?

You see, my ninety-nine-year-old grandfather died. That's what I'm talking about here. He was ready to go. His wife, my grandmother, died twenty-four years ago. That's a long time to live without your spouse. They were married fifty-one years, too. Imagine that, you're married for fifty-one years, your wife dies, and you live twenty-four more years. I can hardly grasp that. Somehow my grandfather lived almost a hundred years, spent half his life with his wife and just about half of it without her. And there wasn't a day after she died that he didn't miss her. He told me that, probably more than once, on one of my all-too infrequent visits. We never visit our grandparents enough, do we? It's like we think, despite all evidence to the contrary, that they'll live forever. They've always been there, you know? Maybe his house had something to do with it. I don't know how long my grandparents lived there, but it was a long, long time.

It wasn't that big, I still don't know how my mother, her sister and brothers all grew up there at the same time. Over the course of my life, going there for holiday visits and whatnot, the house never changed. Not at all, well, at least not in any significant way. Nothing was ever remodeled. I suppose there were repairs from time to time, but nothing major. When you walked in the side door (they didn't use the front door as a regular entrance), you entered a kitchen that could have existed in 1955 with green Formica countertops, painted white cabinets and a yellow linoleum floor. There was a small square wooden table with a couple of old metal and green vinyl chairs, but I never ate at it, as far as I can remember. Dinner was served in the dining room, which was dominated by a long walnut table, probably an antique by today's standards, leaving just enough space left over to walk around the table. It sat eight comfortably, ten not-so comfortably. The dark wood chairs had a kind of lattice back, and the flower pattern that had been originally printed on the red satin padded seats had long since faded away. Only two of those rickety chairs had armrests, and those two special seats were placed at the ends of the table. There was a built-in china cabinet in the corner of the dining room, nothing fancy, just kitty-cornered into the wall and painted white.

Despite the dining room table seating ten, I still had to sit at the kids table, a folding card table set up in the living room, until I was well into my twenties. Man, I hated the kids table. I couldn't wait to finally get a place at the big table. Of course, I didn't realize there's only one way to get a seat at the big table—someone has to die. The most memorable thing in the room though, was this piece of furniture that was like a cabinet, long as the table and on legs. I'm pretty sure my mother calls it a buffet. It seemed like my grandparents kept everything in there, from paperwork to pictures and bottles of booze. Seemed like anything of importance was kept in that buffet.

After my family flew in from various parts of the country for the funeral, we spent a night reminiscing at my grandfather's house. We sat around that dining room table, drinking forty-year-old scotch that Gramps must have been saving for some special occasion. Maybe he was saving it for us, for that night. That's sentimental, cool, and creepy, all at the same time. We went through my grandfather's stuff; mostly family pictures and paperwork. It's amazing how many memories are collected in a lifetime, and it all seemed to fit in that buffet. As I sorted through some of my grandfather's papers, I noticed something about expenses for the cottage he built up in New Hampshire. I glanced at it, but the handwritten message on the back was far more interesting. It was the first draft of a last will and testament, dated the year his wife died. It said that, since he wouldn't be around much longer, he needed to make sure his affairs were in order. I guess when his wife died, he felt closer to his own mortality. After thinking his time was near, he lived another twenty-four years.

I passed that will around until all my cousins had a chance to look it over. Something directed me to that paper. Everyone had that feeling, as if it was something we were meant to see. Maybe it was supposed to say something like, *"Don't be sad, I've been ready to die for a long time."* It was as if Gramps was speaking to us from the other side.

All right, so at the wake, everyone and their brother showed up. Luckily, death for a ninety-nine-year-old isn't too sad. We should all live that long, right? If you haven't accomplished what you wanted to in a hundred years, you weren't even trying. My grandfather was not a lazy man, so I'm sure he checked off all the stuff on his bucket list. The sadness comes when you realize that the strong, opinionated, crusty old man that you all loved for so long is now gone, and you are never going to see him again. It's the aching pain of loss.

My brother wanted to deliver the eulogy. He has a good heart that way, but everything happened so fast that he didn't have time to write anything down. At breakfast, I got a notebook, started writing and continued to work on it at the funeral home. I was a pallbearer and I was supposed to help carry the casket out to the limo, but I was too busy writing the eulogy for my brother. It all worked out, because my brother delivered one heck of a speech. People laughed and cried at all the right parts. Just family attended the church, which is why funerals are different. A much smaller crowd shows up to bury the body. My grandfather was a World War II vet, so there was a flag-folding ceremony, and a soldier played "Taps," which was gut-wrenching. There's closure at a funeral.

How final is death, though? Religions have sworn to have that answer for thousands of years. Mediums claim to communicate with the dead. Is there a Heaven, Nirvana, or afterlife? Are we reborn? What about all those near-death, light-at-the-end-of-the-tunnel experiences? I never really knew what to think about that life-after-death stuff. It all sounds like bunk to me, but on the other hand, so many people believe in it that maybe there's something to it. I've always wondered if human beings actually had souls. If so, does the soul travel to some mystical plane, populated with beings of light? Can souls get stuck on earth and become ghosts? These questions become more important after you've lost someone close to you.

I bet you're wondering if I went to a psychic or something. It wasn't like that. My wife got me this new smartphone for Christmas. A few days after we buried my grandfather, I was sitting in his house in the rocking chair he had received as a retirement gift, taking a break from packing up the detritus of a long life, and I started fiddling with my new phone. As I scrolled through the App Store, one particular app called "Necrophone" caught my eye. It didn't strike me right away what it was, but I clicked on it to see what it did. According to the description, the Necrophone app was a device to speak with the dead.

I read over the bizarre description. It claimed to be the number-one App in the Spirit World. Use this app to get one last chance to say goodbye to loved ones, it said. There were restrictions, of course. The app would only work within one lunar cycle of the deathday of the person you were intending to contact. That was the word it used, "deathday," kind of like the opposite of birthday. Apparently, there is a waiting period for spirits before they transition into their next incarnation. Your belief system contributed to how the spirit was "sorted" after death. It read like a lot of mumbo jumbo to me. I scrolled down to the bottom. The company was Higher Powers, and the app was updated on the date of my grandfather's death. It was version 999.0 and had a five-star rating with over one billion reviews. All this for only $1.99. It was worth a look.

I downloaded the app, not really expecting much. When I opened it up, it asked for the full name, birthday, and deathday of the soul I wished to contact. It reminded me that the app would only work within one lunar cycle of the deathday. I decided to test that claim and entered a date from three months ago. Sure enough, I got an error message stating, "The date you entered is not within one lunar cycle of today's date. The soul you wish to contact has moved on." I corrected the date and received this message, "Availability has been confirmed. To contact the spirit press SEND."

I stared at that last line for a while. I got out of the rocking chair and paced around his small living room. I'm not sure for how long; could have been seconds, or it could have been hours. What started as a joke didn't feel so freaking funny anymore. This felt real. I finally sat down in the old orange recliner chair— Gramps's chair. The matching couch sat across the room from me. Was orange upholstery cool back in the day? The Red Sox were playing on the TV. Gramps had always loved baseball, so it seemed fitting to have it on while I sorted through his stuff. I muted the volume, but since my grandfather had been hard of hearing, the closed captioning continued to scroll across the screen. My finger shook over the send button on the phone. What if it worked? I realized that thought terrified me. What do you say to the dead and what do they say to you? How do the dead feel about being dead? It was stupid; the whole thing had to be some kind of prank. The screen would go black for a few seconds and then a screaming zombie would jump out. That's probably what would happen, so why be afraid?

I pushed send, and a voice answered, "Hello? Is this…God?"

"What? I mean, no, this is Steve. Gramps, is that you?" I replied.

"Steven? Number one?" That's what my grandfather called me every time I visited, because I was his first grandchild. *Here comes number one.* A wave of vertigo hit me, so I sat down before I fell over. "How did you…how did you get this number?" he said. "I am pretty sure I'm dead, Steven."

My breath hitched, just like I was a little kid again. I swallowed hard and tried to pull myself together. "Yeah," I cleared my throat, "yeah Gramps, you died…in your bed. We buried you, um, three days ago." God, this was so hard. I coughed to cover up a sob.

"Three days, you say? Has it been that long? It could have been three hours or three weeks because I have no sense of time."

"Oh…" I struggled to think of what to say to him. "Uh, is it better, where you are? Have you met Gram, and your brothers?"

"I am all alone here, Steven. I have not seen anyone since I arrived."

"Oh, well, are you in a tunnel, or something. I think you're supposed to go into the light." Why did I just say that? If he went into the light, my chance to talk to him would be lost.

"No, I am not in a tunnel and there is no light, Steven."

"You're not? Uh, where are you then? What's it look like?" Maybe I was supposed to use the Necrophone app for some higher purpose. Maybe I was supposed to help my grandfather find his way.

"I am in a room, I suppose you would say. There is no light, although I can see just fine. There is a chair in the center of the room and a small table beside it with a telephone on it. There is a door on one side of the room. On the other side of the room, there is an elevator. That describes my surroundings."

I looked up. The closed captioning continued to scroll over the baseball game. Someone on the opposing team, the Tigers, had just hit into a double play to get the Red Sox starting pitcher out of a bases loaded situation and end the inning. Fenway went wild. "Wow." This was surreal. Was I really getting a description of an afterlife waiting room from my deceased grandfather? "Have you tried the door?"

"I have, Steven. It is locked."

"What about the phone? Maybe you could call out to let them know that you're there and the door's locked?"

"The telephone has no dial tone. It appeared not to function at all until you called me."

"What about the elevator?"

"I am afraid to push the button, Steven."

"Why? Just make sure you push the up button, right?"

"There is no up or down button. There is only a call button."

"Oh. Well, maybe you can choose the direction once you get inside? I bet it has one of those old-fashioned levers inside, or maybe an elevator man."

"Somehow, Steven, I don't believe you get to choose the direction of the elevator. That's already been decided. If there is an elevator operator, then he must be Charon. Do you know who that is?"

"Yeah, I do." Gramps had shared his love of mythology with me at an early age, especially Greek mythology. "He's the ferryman on the River Styx who brings souls to the land of the dead."

"Yes, he does."

"Ah, well, what are you worried about anyway, Gramps? You've been a decent, hardworking man all your life. You were a great father and grandfather. I'm sure the elevator will take you up."

"I'm not so sure about that, Steven."

"Why would you say that? I'm sure it's all about the big picture, not every little detail."

"This is not about little details, Steven. It's about the war. I did things that I've never mentioned to anyone. When we came back, we all told ourselves that it was war, and these things were best forgotten. We carried on and made lives for ourselves. Some days I even managed not to think about the things I did over there. But now that I'm here, the war is all I can think about."

"I don't know what to say, Gramps. You said that you were lucky and never saw any action."

His voice wavered. At first, I thought I was losing the connection, but then I realized it was a mixture of sadness and guilt. "I lied. I lied to protect my family from what I did. I lied to myself to forget the horror."

I stood up, my nerves making me jittery. This was unreal. I reached up to run my fingers through my hair, and found I was still wearing a baseball cap. I took it off and tossed it onto the orange couch. Gramps hated it when you wore a hat indoors. There were family pictures all over the house, but the living room was especially covered in them, on the walls, on the shelves, and over the mantel of a fireplace that had never been used as long as I'd been alive. I picked up a picture that was fairly famous in our family. Myself, my brother, and our three male cousins were behind the house at an old tree. My youngest cousin, who couldn't have been more than four at the time, was on his brother's shoulders. My brother sat on a low limb, and I hung upside down from that same limb. Our other young cousin stood in front, hands behind his back and smiling gleefully. Gramps took that picture. A tear escaped my left eye and rolled down my cheek. "What about forgiveness? You believe in that, don't you?"

"I did when I was alive. At least I told myself I did. I always had some doubt. As I wait here, it feels as though a man is judged by the worst of his deeds, not the best."

This call had taken a turn for the worse. My dead grandfather was afraid of going to Hell. What was I supposed to say to console him? I didn't know what he did in the war, and I didn't want to know. If he believed it was enough to put the fate of his immortal soul in jeopardy, who was I to argue otherwise? It occurred to me the app said it would only work for one lunar cycle after the deathday. "Gramps, I got this…" He wouldn't know what the hell an app was. He never had a cell phone, or a computer, for that matter. "I got this thing on my cell phone. It's an app, which is like a computer program. It's how I contacted you. According to Necrophone, I can only contact you for one lunar cycle after you died."

"Interesting. Do you have a point, Steven?"

"Well, I was thinking that at the end of twenty-eight days, maybe the door unlocks."

"Or maybe the elevator doors open," Gramps said.

"Yeah, I suppose that could happen, too." I didn't know how to offer any more hope than an unlocked door could provide. My phone had been getting warmer, heating up during the entire conversation, but now it was almost too hot to hold. Communicating with the spirit realm must have taxed the battery. "Gramps, I think my phone is overheating. It might shut off on its own. If that happens, I want you to know I didn't hang up."

"Listen, number one, will you be able to call me again?"

"I think so, as long as the app doesn't stop working and my phone doesn't burn up. This is so unreal, you know?"

"I understand. Promise me something, then. Call me every day until those twenty-eight days have passed. It will help me count off the time I have left here."

"I promise, Gramps. I'll call you every day." I had no idea if Necrophone would work again, but I hoped it would.

"Excellent. We can talk about all the great times we had together."

"I would really like that, Gramps."

"Goodbye, number one. I love you."

"I love you too, Gramps." Trickles of salty tears ran down my cheeks. I wiped them away self-consciously. "I'll call you tomorrow, okay?" My voice cracked, just a little.

"I look forward to it." The line went dead. I wanted to call him right back, to make sure it was real, but the heat was so intense I couldn't hold the phone any longer. I put it down and the screen flickered out. Crap, I hoped my phone wasn't fried. Replacement smartphones weren't cheap, and somehow I knew that Necrophone wouldn't be in the App Store again. That was a once-in-a-lifetime shot.

In a couple of hours the phone cooled down. When I tried to turn it on again, however, nothing happened. I hooked it up to the charger and the empty battery screen appeared. Well, at least that was something. Maybe it wasn't completely cooked. I watched some TV, trying to keep my mind away from what happened. I checked the phone every so often and according to the battery meter, it was charging. After a couple of hours, it showed a full charge. I pushed the power button and turned it on. I called my brother, just to see if it worked. I didn't tell him about the conversation with our dead grandfather. I scrolled to the last page and the Necrophone app was still there. Okay then. Tomorrow, I would see if it worked again.

I didn't mention the incident to my wife when she got home from work. I decided not to tell anyone. It felt like a secret, one I shouldn't share. I was the secret-bearer and any wrong move could take it away from me. Somehow, I knew if I showed someone else the app, one of those screaming faces would jump out. Necrophone was for me and me alone. To show it to another person, or even talk about it, would break the spell.

To my surprise, I didn't dream that night, or maybe I just didn't remember any dreams when I woke up. I thought about my grandfather all day while I was at work. I tried to remember the times we spent together when I was younger. It wasn't that easy; the memories seemed to blend together.

When I got home, I opened the app, stared at the send button again and I froze. I'd felt this way before. Twenty years ago, a bunch of us drove to a quarry to dive off an eighty-foot cliff. Staring over that cliff to the still water far below terrified us. No one wanted to be the first to jump. Well, I always wanted to go skydiving, so I kicked off my shoes and jumped. I counted on the way down. One Mississippi, two Mississippi, all the way to seven before I hit the water. Now, you'd think the second jump would be easier, right? It wasn't. The second time felt like tempting fate or spitting in Death's face. I wanted to prove I had more nerve than that to the girls, though. I jumped four more times before we decided to stop for the day.

I looked at the send button just as I had stared off that cliff, daring to tempt fate, twenty years ago. I mustered up the courage to jump off again. He answered on the first ring.

"Steven?"

"Yeah, hi Gramps. How'd you know it was me?"

"You're the only one who has called me. Why did you call back so soon?"

"It's the next day, Gramps. It's been about twenty-four hours since we talked."

"Has it really? It seems like I just talked to you a few minutes ago."

"No Gramps, it was yesterday."

"Hmm, I have been lost in my memories all that time. You've heard the phrase, 'My life flashed before my eyes.' It seems all I can do here is reflect on the past. It's so vivid, Steven. It's like you are watching the movie of your life."

We talked about the New Hampshire cottage that day. My grandfather built it himself, with help from his brothers and brother-in-law. There were so many memories associated with that place. I talked about all the times I helped him work on it. My grandfather always woke up with the sun and drank coffee while reading the newspaper. After he was done with the paper, he cooked bacon and eggs. We'd stumble out of our rooms when the smell of sizzling bacon woke us, usually around 7:00 a.m. Gramps would greet us with a hearty "Good afternoon!" Yup, that was my Gramps, "Good afternoon" at seven in the morning. After finishing whatever chores he had for us, we had the rest of the day to ourselves. If we didn't mess around, we could get those projects done by ten or eleven in the morning. Then we could spend the rest of the day at the lake. The best memories I had with my grandfather were of those summers. Sure, there were holidays and vacations mixed in there too, but the cottage dominated my thoughts of time spent with him.

He knew every last detail of those summers. Gramps talked about a time I barely remembered when I was sixteen and climbed up on the roof to kill a hornet's nest. I went up there, armed with hornet spray, and doused the nest until the can was empty. A couple of angry hornets chased me off the roof. The next day I went back up and knocked the lifeless nest down. He didn't laugh at the time, but Gramps told me that every time he thought about the face I made as I ran from the angry hornets, he chuckled to himself. I never knew that.

It got easier to call him every day. I looked forward to it. Eventually, we ran out of shared memories, but he had plenty more that didn't involve me. Gramps told me all about his fifty-year marriage to his wife and all the compromises a man has to make to keep the peace. He told me about the difficulty of raising four kids with very different personalities and trying to make sure they all turn out all right. He worked a couple of jobs to support those kids and give them everything they needed. He talked about his dreams, too. He did a good job fulfilling those dreams. His biggest regret was that he buried two of his own children. Living to the age of ninety-nine can have that effect, though. If you make it to such a ripe old age, you've outlived many of the people you knew, maybe even some you raised. That was the hardest thing. Even now, all those talks with Gramps while using the Necrophone app, it's all a blur. I consider those talks a blessing. I mean, who gets a chance to do that?

Three days before one lunar cycle had passed, Gramps told me that he worked up the courage to go over to the elevator.

"Did you push the button?" I said.

"No, I just stood there and listened. It moves. I heard it going up and down. Occasionally, I heard whimpers or crying. One time I heard laughing. At times, in the distance, I could hear the faint sounds of joyful singing. Other times I heard wails and moans. I'm scared, Steven."

"Well you shouldn't be, Gramps. I know so much more about you now than I did before. You were a good man. You were a great son, brother, husband, father, and grandfather. Not every man can hope to have lived the life that you did. It was an honest life. If there is a God, what more can He ask from one of His children?"

"I still have not told you what I did in the war."

"I know, I know, but how bad can it be? No matter what it was, I'm sure God forgives you. Look at all the good you did. Look at the family you raised. It has to be enough." Then he told me about his actions during the war, or his war crimes, I guess you could call them.

The next day I tried to learn as much as I could about the Catholic Church's definition of "mortal sin." According to the church, committing a mortal sin was serious and considered a grave offense. Mortal sins were the ones that sent you to Hell. The more I read about them, the more depressed I got. I suspected

Gramps already knew all this stuff, which was why he was worried. Man, the Catholic Church had a lot of rules, and things were not as clear as I hoped. There was all this stuff about being excommunicated at the moment of committing the mortal sin, remission, penance, and many other confusing ideologies. One thing was clear, if you died in a state of mortal sin, you went to Hell directly upon death. Since Gramps was in that waiting room, his own personal purgatory, I assumed his soul's fate was not set in stone.

I talked to Gramps later that day, but there was a weight between us now. I knew what he did in the war and why he worried that he might be punished for it. We only had a couple of more chances to talk before his time would be up. I told him I was doing all I could on my end. I read something about plenary indulgences, which was how the Catholic Church once allowed the wealthy to buy their way into Heaven. What was even stranger was that it was unclear if this practice still existed. Pope Pius V banned indulgences five hundred years ago, but there were rumors that the church had reinstated this controversial practice, perhaps due to the poor world economy. One article said that these indulgences could be purchased for loved ones who had already died and that this would ease the transition from Purgatory to Heaven. Oddly, indulgences reminded me of the fare paid to Charon for passage across the River Styx and into the realm of the dead.

If you had asked me about all this stuff a few weeks ago, I would have scoffed at it and called it a bunch of crap. Things were different now. I told Gramps I had an appointment with a priest in the morning to discuss this whole indulgence thing and see if it was for real.

I met Father Benoit in his office in the rectory. "You're not a regular here, Steven Cross. This must be important. What can I do for you?"

"Ah, well, good question." I had rehearsed this in my head but now it sounded too stupid to say. "My grandfather died recently."

"Oh, I'm so sorry for your loss, Steven. How old was he?"

"Ninety-nine."

"Well, he certainly lived a full life. Was he a strong-willed man?"

"The strongest."

"Then you must be in need of some spiritual guidance. When such a steady patriarchal presence departs, it is not uncommon for the surviving family members to feel…shall we say 'lost,' for a while. I will do my best to help you through this difficult time."

"Ah, that's not exactly it, Father."

"No? Well, give me the whole story then, and I will see what I can do." So I did. Well, sort of. I didn't mention Necrophone, of course, but I brought up the whole thing about the war and my grandfather's fear of dying in mortal sin. He asked me how I knew what my grandfather had done in the war, so I told him it was a deathbed confession.

"Yes, mortal sins indeed," Father Benoit agreed. "Did your grandfather ever confess these sins to a priest and do penance?"

"He did, but he felt like the penance wasn't enough, and that he was never truly absolved. He was terrified on his deathbed, Father."

"Hmm, well, what do you think I can do now? He's been dead for a month. If your grandfather was concerned, he should have spoken to his own priest. I wouldn't worry, though, Steven. If the rest of his family loved him as much as you obviously do, I'm sure his good works absolved him in the eyes of God."

"Yeah, well, he wasn't as sure about that, or he wouldn't have been so scared. Father, I've done some research. What about plenary indulgences?"

"Indulgences? The church banned those hundreds of years ago, Steven."

"I know that's the official stance, Father, but according to some sources on the internet, the practice still exists."

"You can't believe everything you read on the internet, Steven."

"I know. Look, let's cut to the chase, okay? My grandfather told me about a CD he had that nobody knows about. His last wishes were that I cash it in and buy one of these indulgences, just to make sure he didn't go to…you know, the wrong place."

"And how much would this CD be worth?"

"Fifty thousand."

"Fifty? And you would be willing to sign this over to the church?"

"As long as the church keeps quiet about it, yes. The rest of the family might not understand, but I promised my grandfather I would do it."

"I see. You will need an appointment with the bishop. I should be able to get one for you in a few weeks."

I panicked and blurted out, "No! It has to be tomorrow morning. His time is almost up."

Father Benoit raised an eyebrow. "What do you mean, 'His time is almost up?'"

"Um, uh…he specified that this had to be taken care of within twenty-eight days of his death."

"Then why did you wait until the last possible moment?"

"I…I couldn't find the CD." I wasn't very good at this lying on the fly thing, but I was doing my best. "And since he asked me this on his deathbed, I wasn't sure it really existed. It…it wasn't where he said it would be, but I found it yesterday, so I called you. Can you please get me an appointment tomorrow morning? It has to be in the morning."

"This is most unusual," Father Benoit said. "But considering how serious the matter is, I may be able to get you an appointment with the bishop. Give me your phone number and I'll get in touch with you after I've made some calls."

My grandfather was very nervous now. I told him about my consultation with Father Benoit, who would arrange a meeting the bishop. Fifty grand was nothing to sneeze at, not even if you were the Catholic Church. I had a lot to do in very little time, but I was all in. Gramps put his trust in me and I promised to succeed. I hated hearing him like that, in fear for his immortal soul. It broke my heart.

I waited and waited for Father Benoit to call, but he didn't. My wife could tell I was agitated, so I told her I was having trouble with a customer that was driving me nuts, which was believable enough. At 9:45 p.m., my phone finally rang.

"I'm sorry it's so late, Steven."

"No, no, it's okay. Do I have an appointment with the bishop?"

"He has agreed to meet with you at 11:30 in the morning. Don't be late. The bishop is a very busy man and he's squeezing you in between appointments. I gave him all of your details and he said he'd take care of it."

"Really, he's going to grant an indulgence?"

"That's correct, provided you fulfill your end of the bargain."

"Oh, I will, don't worry. Thank you so much, Father Benoit. You've taken a huge load off my mind. You're a lifesaver."

"Glad I could be of service, Steven. Take care."

"You too, Father. Thanks again."

It occurred to me that the whole indulgence thing could be one giant swindle. I focused so much on getting one that I hadn't considered it before. Did the church really have the power to grant salvation with a piece of paper and a nod? Was I going to waste fifty thousand dollars?

The bishop told me that an indulgence was a very unusual request in this day and age, but not completely unheard of. He had a very official-looking document from the Vatican, signed, sealed, and delivered. It granted Gramps full redemption and remission into the church. The bishop also said it guaranteed his admission into Heaven, but there was a catch. He told me he wouldn't give it to me until the mortal sins were confessed to him. Normally the sinner did this, but in the case of indulgences, a family member could act as confessor. So far, I'd avoided thinking about it, never mind speaking about it. The bishop gave me no choice, so I told him.

Gramps' unit was in Belgium during the bloodiest American campaign of World War II, the Battle of the Bulge. The second day of the conflict, German forces captured the U.S. 7th Armored division near the town of Malmedy. SS Colonel Joachim Peiper gave the order to have more than three hundred American POWs shot and killed, a decision which would later have him executed for war crimes. The American army was outraged. Two weeks after Malmedy, Gramps' unit captured sixty Germans troops in the Belgian town, Chenogne. The prisoners were locked inside of the town hall, but the American soldiers wanted revenge.

Gramps was on guard duty when some angry soldiers stormed over. They were pissed about the Malmedy massacre and they intended to exact their own pound of flesh. The building was torched with a flamethrower, all sixty prisoners still inside. Gramps shot a few of the prisoners as they tried to jump from windows. The whole unit watched the building burn, listening to the piercing screams of sixty men. It was impossible to cover up, so the Allies reported that the German POWs were shot due to an order to take no prisoners.

That was Gramps's war crime. He shot and killed German POWs trying to escape from a burning building. The bishop accepted the story I told as confession of the mortal sin and granted me the indulgence. I left his office.

In all the excitement, I left my phone at home. I had to rush back to call Gramps and give him the great news. He had died at 2:07 in the afternoon so his twenty-eight-day cycle would be over in a couple of hours. An eighteen-wheeler rolled over on the interstate, which left me stuck in a massive traffic jam. I would never make it in time. With my car's GPS I calculated an alternate route home. The problem was, the new route wasn't a highway and went through a bunch of cities. All the red lights I hit drove me nuts. I rocked back and forth in the driver's seat, saying, "Come on, come on," as the minutes ticked away. It was going to be close. I almost ran over a woman pushing a baby carriage across the street.

I got home and called Gramps with only minutes to spare. "I got it, Gramps! I got it! Did anything come through on your end?"

"What do you mean, Steven?"

"Oh, I don't know. I thought you might get a gold coin or something, to give to the ferryman, you know?"

"No, nothing appeared, Steven, but I'm sure that's just myth. You didn't fail, that's what is important. I don't want to burn like those German prisoners did." Over the phone, I heard a mechanical whirr. "The elevator is coming for me, Steven."

I had doubts again. I wanted to tell him not to get on that elevator. I wanted to scream that I thought we just got scammed, but I couldn't do it.

"The doors are opening. I love you, number one."

"Don't hang up! Leave the phone off the hook as you go in. I want to hear it."

I heard him greet the elevator operator, who I imagined was Charon. I heard the doors closing and yelled, "I love you too, Gramps!"

"Goodbye, Steven," I heard distantly. I strained to hear as much as I could. I tried desperately to detect another sound, and then I heard it. Far, far away, there were voices. They were so hard to make out, so distant, so faint. There was a click and one of those recorded operator voices said, "Thank you for using Necrophone. We hope you had a positive experience and would consider using us again in the future." I didn't think so.

In the light of day, I like to think those were the voices of joyful singing, and it cheers me up to imagine Gramps reunited with all the family that went before him. He deserves salvation.

But when I lay down at night, in the dark, I think those voices were the wails and moans of the damned, and I shiver, my eyes moist with tears. I've never been one to pray, not even when I was a kid. I pray every night now, afraid of the judgment that will one day be passed on my life.

So that's it. I don't know what's real anymore. I used to be more grounded, putting my faith in science, in stuff I thought I knew to be true. Paranoia has started to creep into my daily life. Did I talk to my dead grandfather on my smartphone? Did I really spend fifty thousand dollars on a piece of paper that is supposed to get him into Heaven? Does all that religious stuff I once thought of as simple superstition actually have some merit? Mortal sin, Purgatory, plenary indulgences, that stuff can't be real. Can it?

SCAREMONGER

by Greg Chapman

Justin opened the bedroom cabinet door where he was hiding and couldn't believe his eyes. He was looking down at a cityscape, the same one he had seen a day earlier with his friends, when he'd felt happy.

Cold sweat ran down his face as he gripped his phone with trembling hands and scrolled through his contacts in a desperate search for help.

He was coming and there was nothing Justin could do but say goodbye.

Justin hadn't spoken with his sister Juliette in so long, and he wanted to hear her voice one last time. He made to press the call button when he heard a knock at the front door. Justin froze.

"Mr. Clarke, it's Dr. Harvey. Can you open the door please?"

The psychologist's voice boomed through the apartment.

Justin cleared his sister's contact from the screen and brought up the keypad. He pressed 9-1-1.

"Mr. Clarke? You know I'm only here to help you."

Justin pressed up against the back of the cabinet. He had to believe there was no way Dr. Harvey could get inside. The house was locked up tight and Harvey was just a man.

Dr. Harvey pounded on the door, the sound reverberating down the hall and into the cupboard, into Justin's soul.

"Open the door, Justin. There's no need to be afraid. I can help you."

Justin's thumb hovered over the dial button, but he couldn't bring himself to press it. Fear had taken hold of him like a strangler's hands around his throat. Dr. Harvey hadn't helped him conquer his fear at all; he'd chained him to it.

"Just come out of that cupboard, unlock this door and we can talk. That's all I want—to talk."

How did Dr. Harvey know he was hiding? Justin's heart pounded as he hovered twenty storeys above the city.

It was Dr. Harvey; he didn't know how, but his therapist was showing him his greatest fear.

Justin tried to straighten his trembling legs. The cupboard shifted above the rooftops and Justin gripped the sides, his fingernails breaking in desperation. The breeze flooded the cupboard turning his sweat to ice and clamping around his heart.

"You should have let me help you, Justin."

Justin screamed at the sound of a voice behind him. Dr. Harvey appeared at his shoulder, from the darkness of the cupboard. The doctor smiled and a small spider crawled out from between his teeth.

"I could have helped you."

Justin tried to scream again, but fear had claimed his voice, robbed his body of blood. Dr. Harvey reached out with a fleshless hand and pushed Justin in the chest. As he fell out of the cupboard into the stark light of day, down hundreds of feet onto the streets below, he prayed not for his own soul, but for his sister's.

That it would always protect her from fear.

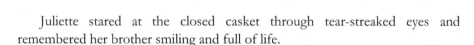

Juliette stared at the closed casket through tear-streaked eyes and remembered her brother smiling and full of life.

The church was filled with people all slumped in mourning. The priest stood beside the coffin, his robes gleaming white in the morning sunlight, as if in defiance of their sadness. Juliette watched him wave the thurible incense around her brother's coffin and tried to imagine what he looked like inside.

What did someone who threw themselves from the corner window of the twentieth floor of a hotel look like?

Juliette stared at the coffin and wondered what had driven Justin, a man so full of potential, to take his own life. The eulogy she'd written and was supposed to read, was now being delivered by her uncle, an endless drone. The priest's final offerings of consolation were a foreign language.

Nothing made sense anymore.

When the ceremony was done and the coffin taken from the church to the hearse, the people came to Juliette to offer their condolences. What she wanted from them was that understanding, the reason why her brother had left her the only child, the last remaining member of the Clarke family.

With each long embrace, from each friend and acquaintance, Juliette felt as if she were dying too, the mourners taking a piece of her soul. It wasn't until her boyfriend Dale held her hand that she was pulled back to the land of the living.

"How you holding up, Jules?" he said, and kissed a tear from her cheek.

"I don't know."

He squeezed her hand. "Ready to go to the cemetery?"

Juliette watched the black hearse with its mahogany coffin wind down the church road, the slow procession of cars like scarab beetles trailing behind. She shivered.

"I...can't."

"It's okay. I'm here," Dale said.

She squeezed his hand back and pulled him close. "Why? Why did he do it?" she asked him, asked the world.

"God knows." He led her down the church steps. "Come on. I'm with you every step of the way."

She let him guide her away from the church. Ahead, down the highway, was the cemetery, and the inevitability she feared. A young couple, friends of Justin whose names she couldn't remember, nodded at her solemnly. The two men came forward.

"My name is Ryan, and this is Alex. Justin was our friend. We just wanted to tell you how sorry we are. Justin was such a great guy."

"One of the best," Alex added.

Juliette accepted their embraces. "It's so hard to believe he's gone."

Ryan frowned. "He seemed so happy when I ran into him a few weeks ago. He told me he'd met someone who'd changed his life."

"A girl?" Dale asked.

Alex shook his head. "No, he mentioned he'd met some counsellor who'd helped him get over his agoraphobia."

Juliette shivered again. "Agoraphobia? Are you...are you making some sort of sick joke?"

"Babe..." Dale said and squeezed her hand again as the two men gaped in embarrassment.

"What? No, we'd never..." Alex held up his hands to placate her.

"Then what are you talking about?' Juliette said, her voice rising in the churchyard. "He never had that...not since he was little. He got over it."

Ryan very carefully touched her shoulder. "He always suffered with it, right through college. He never told you?"

Juliette tasted the saltiness of her tears. "We...haven't been in touch for years. Not since Mum and Dad died when we were just teenagers."

"So...you said Justin found a way to get over his fear of heights?" Dale asked the pair.

"Yes," Alex said. "The last time we saw him was at Sydney Tower. He'd never looked so happy, and he couldn't stop telling us about this guy who'd helped him."

Juliette wiped the tears from her eyes. "What guy?"

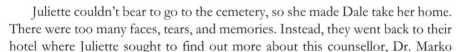

Juliette couldn't bear to go to the cemetery, so she made Dale take her home. There were too many faces, tears, and memories. Instead, they went back to their hotel where Juliette sought to find out more about this counsellor, Dr. Marko Harvey. She would go to Justin's grave when she understood.

She Googled the name and found a glossy website—*Dr. Marko Harvey, Psychotherapist*. Harvey's image was large on the screen, his neatly parted hair and teeth were too perfect. Juliette watched one of his videos and immediately took a dislike to him. He looked and acted so fake, like a televangelist. There were so many slogans, all spouting about how he could help people conquer their fear.

"Fear is just a construct in our minds," Harvey said in one video. "It's a wall that's blocking your path in life. I can help you turn your mind into a hammer, so you can knock that wall down." He ended the sentence with a trademark smile.

"That guy looks creepy, like Ted Bundy," Dale said, startling Juliette. "Oh, sorry Jules, I didn't mean to scare you."

Juliette pushed her laptop closed. "It's okay."

Dale gently massaged her shoulders and she stood to move away, unable to handle physical contact.

"Are you okay, babe? If you want to talk about it—"

Juliette looked down on the city, the cars and pedestrians the size of ants. She imagined Justin watching them closing in as he fell.

"I'm going to go see that Dr. Harvey tomorrow, try to get him to tell me why Justin killed himself."

"Are you sure you want to do that Jules? Maybe you just need some time…to mourn. Trying to find answers will only make things harder."

Juliette whirled on him. "He jumped out a fucking window Dale! He was always happy. He had a good job, his own apartment. Yet, for some reason, he killed himself."

Dale frowned. "Maybe…maybe he wasn't happy. You said it yourself, you hadn't seen him in years."

Jules pushed past him. "Well if anyone knows why he did it, it'll be Dr. Harvey. I don't care what you say, I'm going to see him."

Dr. Harvey's offices were only three blocks away from the hotel. She left at 8:30, after breakfast, the tension between Dale and her unresolved. He'd never understand her need for the truth because his mourning was completely peripheral. He was only mourning for her. The only way she could grieve was to know the truth.

She entered Dr. Harvey's offices unannounced. A man and a woman sat near the reception desk, their faces forlorn. A pang of guilt pricked inside Juliette as she considered her own selfishness. She was about to turn and leave the offices when the receptionist spoke up.

"Can I help you?" she said.

Juliette faced her. "I want to speak to Dr. Harvey."

"Do you have an appointment?"

"No, I'm not a patient."

The receptionist flashed Juliette a smile, trying to remain professional. "Do you have a referral?"

Juliette stepped closer to the counter. "I'm not looking to become a patient..." She stopped for a moment to compose herself. "My brother is...was... Justin Clarke was his name."

"I'm sorry, miss, but we can't discuss our clients' details for confidentiality reasons."

"Justin killed himself a week ago."

The receptionist blanched, and her eyes darted to the couple waiting. Juliette glanced at them over her shoulder and saw the horror in their eyes.

"Miss, I'm sorry, but we can't discuss our clients without their permission."

Juliette clenched her fists. "He's dead, you fucking bitch, so how can I get his permission?"

The receptionist's jaw dropped as Juliette backed away, enraged. She heard the couple exchange whispers, but she was already heading out the door. It had just started to rain when she walked onto the street, but the heavy drops on her face did little to temper the anger inside. She'd speak to Dr. Harvey one way or another, and she wasn't afraid of the consequences.

At 6:00 p.m., Dr. Marko Harvey exited his offices onto Mary Street. Juliette, who'd been waiting in a nearby coffee shop, followed him to a car park four blocks away. From behind, Dr. Harvey looked more like a businessman than a therapist, with his clean-cut suit and briefcase. Juliette wondered if he was therapist at all, and the thought led to even darker notions of Justin succumbing to Dr. Harvey's wiles. Maybe she was overreacting, like Dale said. What if Justin had simply been unhappy? The man walking just twenty feet in front of her held the key. She kept her distance, right until the moment Dr. Harvey removed his keys and unlocked his car, a black Mercedes-Benz. Juliette approached him as he opened the door.

"Dr. Harvey, I need to speak with you."

The therapist turned, a scowl on his clean-shaven face. "Who are you?"

"My name is Juliette and I want to talk to you about my brother, Justin Clarke."

Harvey looked her up and down, but Juliette saw no emotion, no tell. "You're Justin's sister?"

"That's right. He was a patient of yours."

Dr. Harvey smirked. "He told you I was treating him?"

Juliette frowned. Did he not know about Justin's death? "I haven't spoken to him for years. I came back home to bury him."

The therapist's eyes widened. "Excuse me?"

"He died a week ago."

Dr. Harvey put his bag down. "Truly? Oh, I'm so sorry to hear that."

Juliette tried to read his expression, desperate to know if his shock was sincere.

"What were you treating him for?"

The man straightened. "I'm a therapist. I help people with anxieties. Unfortunately, I can't talk about specific clients."

"I'm his next of kin—in fact, I'm his only surviving relative."

"I'm very sorry, but I can't discuss your brother's case. I'm even more sorry to hear of his passing."

Juliette folded her arms. "Perhaps I'll go and see a lawyer."

His eyes narrowed and Juliette saw coldness there. "If you think that's necessary," he said. "Again, I apologise, but I have another meeting at the hospital."

He got in his car and closed the door. Juliette stepped out of the way as he reversed, but he never looked her in the eye or watched her in his mirrors. The thing Juliette found most disconcerting however was that Dr. Harvey never asked her how Justin died.

That night Dale slept on the couch while Juliette tossed and turned in their bed, alone with her thoughts.

Her mind filled with visions of Justin falling and striking the concrete, reduced to a pulp of broken bones, of Justin crying out to her from inside a darkened space, and finally his endearing smile becoming a wound oozing brackish blood.

Listless, she sat up in bed, skin slick with sweat, heart slamming against her chest. The darkness was like a cage. She moved to the edge of the bed and wondered if it was just a physical reaction, but her thoughts were so palpable.

Juliette tiptoed from the bedroom to the kitchen to get a glass of water. Seeing Dale asleep on the couch, she opened a cupboard for a glass, careful not to disturb him. The glass slipped through her clammy fingers and smashed on the tiles. Cursing herself, she stepped away from the shards of glass and looked to Dale. To her surprise, he was still asleep. The crash had been so loud, but he hadn't even rolled over. Skirting away from the jagged mess on the floor, she walked into the lounge room towards the linen cupboard where the dustpan was kept. As she slinked by her boyfriend, she noticed how still he was. She stopped, staring at him, scanning for the tell-tale rise and fall of his chest.

"Dale?" she whispered.

Dale's chest was still, and Juliette heard no breathing.

"Dale?" she said more urgently, a quiver of panic setting in.

She reached out and gripped his arm and found it icy cold.

"Dale!" She shook him and her nails left tiny red crescents in his skin.

His arm slumped off his chest and dangled to the floor.

Juliette recoiled, waiting to scream. She questioned whether her lover was dead, and pressed her hand to his chest, to feel the beat of his heart. Feeling nothing, she reached out a trembling hand to his throat.

When Dale's eyes opened and his face transformed, Juliette's scream finally came.

But her boyfriend's face was now Dr. Marko Harvey's, and it was smiling with morbid glee.

"Your brother was right—you are terrified of death," Dr. Harvey said.

It was then the nightmare shattered, leaving Juliette to wake in bed, terrified of just how deep her grief was taking her.

The fact Dale answered Juliette's screams wasn't so much of a relief for her that he was alive, but rather a confirmation of the vividness of her dream.

She could barely look at her lover that morning. He should have been dead on the couch—had been dead. She realised she had to get away, to clear her head. The dream and her obsession with Dr. Harvey proved she wasn't coping. She told Dale as much and asked him for some space. He agreed to return home early on his own and leave her in peace, in the hope she would come home feeling closer to being healed. They said their goodbyes on good terms, but still Juliette couldn't shake that vision of him lifeless on the couch.

After he'd gone, she caught the train into the city and tried to self-indulge. The shopping centre was the distraction she needed. She bought several new outfits and sampled some fragrances. It was lunchtime before she realised she'd not had a single thought about her brother. For the first time in days, she felt hopeful. Famished, she walked to the food court and was trying to decide what to eat when she saw someone she'd never expected to see.

Dr. Marko Harvey was seated at a table enjoying a meal with an elderly couple. All three were smiling, sharing in each other's company. With her eyes locked on the therapist who'd plagued her dreams the night before, it took Juliette several moments to notice the man and woman sitting with him.

The couple's smiles drew her attention, the way the laugh lines framed their eyes. Juliette covered a gasp with her hands as her long-dead parents turned to smile at her. Dr. Harvey was smiling too, that knowing smirk, but when Juliette looked to the other diners in the food court, they seemed oblivious to the impossibility that was taking place.

"Would you care to join us, Juliette?" her dead father said.

"Oh, that would be lovely," her mother said.

Juliette flinched and stared. Only Dr. Harvey and her parents stared back. Everyone else enjoyed their meals and conversation.

"I… I'm dreaming again," Juliette muttered.

"Are you?" Dr. Harvey said, and he stood to walk over to her.

"Don't…don't you come near me." Juliette looked to the other diners for recognition of the strangeness that was taking place, but they were blind to it.

"That's not very polite dear," her dead mother said.

Dr. Harvey wrapped an arm around Juliette's shoulder and smiled back at her mother and father. During the macabre conversation, Frank and Beatrice's skin had begun to blanch and crack with decomposition. A horrible sight only for her.

"Frank and Beatrice have been telling me all about your thanatophobia," he said.

The word didn't make sense to Juliette. Nothing did.

"It started when her pet dog was run over by a truck when she was six years old," Frank said as he pushed a forkful of salad into his rotting mouth.

"Oh, yes, that poor little puppy," Beatrice said, frowning. "What was the little thing's name?"

"Suzie, I think," Frank said, chewing. "Is that right, Juliette?"

Juliette swallowed down a wave of nausea. The whole world was moving, but simultaneously standing still. "What is going on?"

Dr. Harvey stepped in front of her and squeezed her shoulders. "It's only lunch with your mum and dad. I don't see why you're so upset?" The therapist's eyes were so pale, as was his skin. His teeth were perfectly white, but beyond them his mouth was a cave of equal darkness. He turned to Frank and Beatrice. "It must be the whole Justin thing."

Juliette's parents put their cutlery down and gaped at her.

"Just like her brother," Beatrice said, nodding her decrepit head.

"She's always had a fear of death," Frank said. "And Justin was afraid of heights. Bea and I were afraid of losing them." He ate some more salad. "That dog was the start of it for Jules. Then her best friend died, then my mother and Bea's parents, then us and now...Justin."

Dr. Harvey rubbed Juliette's shoulders. "It all makes sense. I thought when Justin told me about your fear, he was just trying to ignore his own problems, but it seems to me your fear is even greater than his."

Juliette's throat tightened as she stared at her parents. They were rotting in their seats while everyone around them kept on eating. In the blink of an eye the other diners became corpses too, but they had no idea of it or anything else. She tried to wrench free of Harvey's grip, of her parents' eyes, but she was powerless.

"What...are you?" she said to the therapist.

He smiled and a centipede emerged where his tongue should have been. "The man who's going to save you from your fear of death, just like I saved Justin from his acrophobia."

Frank shook his fork in his bony hand. "Oh, that boy and his fear of heights—why were our kids so afraid, Bea?"

"I have no idea Frank, but I bet Dr. Harvey does—don't you, Dr. Harvey?"

The centipede slid across Harvey's cheek and burrowed into his ear. 'Oh, the answer's simple isn't it, Juliette? Everyone's afraid of something.'

Juliette shrieked and came to in the food court. Dozens of people stared her way, confused looks on their faces. Juliette fled the court, ran from their gazes back into the street to return to the hotel. The face of Dr. Marko Harvey stalked her. Even when she closed her eyes, he was there. Unless she did something soon, she believed he would take her soul.

It wasn't until Juliette was back in her hotel room that she felt safe. Even though the room was locked, she still checked that all the windows were sealed tight. She sat in the middle of the lounge room and tried to call Dale on her mobile phone.

She needed to hear his voice, just to feel something normal, something that was real and not a dream. She was still shaking from the last dream, but what frightened her the most was the extent of her imagination. Her dreams had been few and far between, and certainly never of a horrific nature. Before she would have put it down to grief, but the reappearance of Dr. Harvey and his sinister nature left her wondering—and afraid. She tsked when Dale's phone went to voicemail.

"Dale, it's Jules. I need you to call me back as soon as you land."

She ended the call and then immediately followed her voicemail with a text: PLS CALL ME. SCARED.

Minutes turned into over an hour, and she realised she hadn't moved. She didn't want to do anything but wait for Dale's call. The lounge room darkened as the afternoon sun drifted down and it only amplified her despair. Every time she thought she would drift off to sleep, she forced herself to play a game on her phone or surf the web. In the back of her mind, however, she was desperate to connect with Dale, to know he was okay.

A knock at the door jolted Juliette to attention. She sat up and felt her flesh tighten with goosepimples.

"Who's that?" she said and instantly bit her lip for making a sound.

"Juliette, it's me."

Juliette stood and moved closer to the male voice coming from the other side of the door.

"Dale?" she said.

"Juliette, please, open the door."

She held her phone up and pressed triple zero on the keypad. "I'm going to call the police."

The sound of sobbing echoed in from under the door. "Juliette, please, you have to let me in—he's coming for me."

Heart pounding, Juliette strained to hear the voice, a voice she thought she knew.

"Justin?" she said.

"You have to let me in! Please! He's coming!"

"Dr. Harvey?"

A thud shook the door. "Why won't you let me in? I'm your brother!"

Juliette covered her ears as the pounding kept coming. "No! You're not here! You're dead!"

"Why did you stop speaking to me? Why didn't you help me?"

The pounding became so forceful that the hinges started to separate from the wall.

"Stop! Stop it! I'm sorry!" Juliette said.

"I'm falling, Juliette!"

The window inside the hotel room shattered and the wind threw shards towards Juliette. A body flew in, crashed into the television, and rolled onto the floor. Juliette screamed as she recognised her brother's face beneath layers of shattered glass and blood. His eyes, wide and white, gazed up at her.

"Juliette…" Justin wheezed.

"No! You're not him! You're not my brother! You're dead!"

Justin crawled onto his belly and pulled himself towards her. Rivulets of blood streamed from his eyes and mouth.

"Help…me…"

"Get away! Don't you touch me!" Juliette backed away and collided with the kitchen bench. Justin, somehow alive, got to his feet and staggered towards his sister. His body was broken and every movement of his limbs released the sound of bones grinding together. Juliette saw the knife block on the kitchen bench and grabbed a large kitchen knife. She waved it in her brother's face. He stared at it and then smiled—an all too familiar smile. The smile became a chuckle.

"You're going to kill your own brother?" Justin said.

Juliette looked from the blade to her brother and then back again. It shook in her hand.

"Juliette—who is so scared of death? The same Juliette who screamed for hours when her dog died? Who left town when her mummy and daddy were mangled by a B-double truck? Don't make me laugh!"

But Justin did laugh, long and heartily. He bent backwards laughing, but when he finally stopped and stood upright, he wore the face of Dr. Marko Harvey. Juliette gripped the knife with both hands.

"No! You get away from me!"

Dr. Harvey took a step closer. "Are you sure I'm here. Are you sure you're not dreaming again?"

"You…you gave me the dreams."

He held up a finger and then plucked a chunk of glass protruding from under the fingernail. "You're half right. All I'm doing is showing you your fear. Just like I did with Justin."

"You killed Justin!" Juliette swiped the knife at him, and he stopped moving.

"He killed himself."

"*What are you? What do you want?*"

"Everyone has to face their fears eventually. I am that fear."

Juliette's head bloomed with fear and confusion. She tried to focus her mind, tried to ignore Harvey's words. The knife trembled between her and her brother's killer. Harvey opened his arms.

"Come and embrace your fear," he told her.

Juliette focused on the hard edge of the knife. She straightened her arms and released a primal scream. The blade disappeared into Dr. Harvey's chest and he let out a gasp of shock, his cocky smile wiped away in an instant. She pulled the blade free and a torrent of foul liquid spilled out onto the floor. The fluid, which swam with dead beetles, centipedes, and barbed wire, swarmed around her feet. She recoiled. The thing that was Dr. Harvey fell into the pool and immediately began to deteriorate. Its face became a dark cave and its eyes like endless tunnels. From its mouth came one final insult.

"You'll always be afraid."

It was over. She was free. The knife slipped from her hands and splashed into the murky pool that spread about her feet.

Juliette began to sob. The grief came in a flood of tears. She put her head in her hands and shook with relief. She imagined Justin smiling down on her, grateful the thing that had been haunting them was gone.

Something brushed Juliette's leg. Looking down, she saw she was almost ankle-deep in the remnants of Dr. Harvey. The fear returned like an artic breeze, crawling in time with the rising black pool. She let out a cry of terror and tried to pull her legs free, but the wire coiled, and the insects crawled higher and higher, faster and faster. She toppled into the pool and like quicksand, it dragged her down.

"No!"

The wire burned around her wrists as a million insect legs squirmed towards her screaming mouth.

"You'll always be afraid," a voice uttered from the pool.

The quagmire enveloped her face, pouring into her mouth and nose, filling her inside and out. Taking control of her...body, mind, and soul.

Like it took control of Dr. Harvey.

And Justin.

And all the other phobia sufferers around the world.

Beneath the blackness, Juliette understood the only thing left to fear...was fear itself.

THE HAPPIEST PLACE ON EARTH

by Curtis M. Lawson

N athan couldn't count the hash marks. There were too many of them—
countless rows of five. Regardless, he scratched another onto the wall
with his pencil. It was force of habit now to mark the days, and there
was a bit of comfort that came from the routine. At one time he would
have gotten into trouble for drawing on the walls, but there were no adults here
anymore. There were no people here at all, except for him.

The radio played in the corner. Every morning it was the same song—a cover
of "Wild Horses." It was his favorite part of the day.

Nathan got dressed, moving his head along with the music. The song ended
as he slipped on his sneakers and the news followed. It was bad news, as it had
been for a while. The world was coming apart at the seams. People were getting
violent over things he didn't understand—politics, race, and religion.

The voice on the radio explained that the violence wasn't really about any of
those things though. It was about people losing their jobs and food shortages. It
was about the threat of war. It was about gangs, governments, and corporations
exploiting tragedy. Nathan didn't understand any of that either, but he liked
hearing that voice, even when it sounded afraid.

The news report always ended with the voice backpedaling, talking about
how everything wasn't really as bad as it seemed. Things would get back to normal
soon. Cooler heads would prevail. There was nothing to be afraid of.

Nathan was young, but he knew a lie when he heard it.

The radio went silent, save for the soft hum of static. Nathan left it on, as he
always did.

He wasn't sure how long he'd been squatting in the happiest place on Earth,
but he remembered that he used to love going outside and exploring the grounds.
This place was a dream—an empty amusement park all to himself. He'd ride the
rollercoasters and go-karts from dawn to dusk and binge on cotton candy and
funnel cakes. At some point though, the rides stopped working and the food went
rotten. A shroud of darkness hung over the park now, even in the day, and it was
not an empty darkness.

Phantoms lurked in shadowed corners and sea monsters growled from the
cavernous recesses of dark water rides. Dead presidents with vinyl skin and steel
bones screeched hate from their podiums in a language of static and feedback.

And then there was the obsidian fog surrounding the park—that dark and terrible mist that consumed all it touched.

The monsters rarely attacked in the day, but the days were getting darker and shorter, and the terrible creatures in the park were growing bolder. He couldn't stay hidden away in the castle forever, as much as he might like to. He needed to salvage supplies. He needed to move his body—to stretch and run and leap.

Nathan pulled the curtain aside, exposing a set of three arched windows. From this vantage point, he could see from the leafless trees and desiccated bushes outside the castle, all the way down the main thoroughfare. There was a time when the front gates were visible, but the ring of heavy, black fog that encircled the park had grown tighter by the day.

The fog didn't concern Nathan this morning though. Not as much as the things that haunted the park. He watched from the window, looking for shifting shadows or lifeless objects that moved with unnatural power. Everything looked dangerous from up in the castle. It was impossible to tell if a shadow moved because of shifting light or because it possessed a life of its own.

He grabbed his spear—a kitchen knife fastened to a broomstick with a zip-tie—from the side of his bed and hung it across his back with a harness made from window shade cord, then slung his backpack over one shoulder. Nathan left the castle suite and descended the stairs, running one hand across the smooth mahogany railing and the other hand across the rough faux-stone wall. He concentrated on their textures, appreciating the contrary sensations. He'd always taken such simple sensations for granted, but now Nathan made a point to focus on little details he would have previously overlooked.

The front gate opened to an overcast day. Ragged standards fluttered in the wind, their colors faded. Shadows of flags danced across the ground. Nathan avoided the shadows, fearful they might transform into black serpents or amorphous phantoms.

In front of the castle was a bronze statue of a well-dressed man holding hands with a cartoon mouse. The man's arm was pointing out toward the horizon, a smile on his face, as if he were gazing out over all the wonder and magic that future held. Nathan stood beside the statue and tried to see the same thing— some promise on the horizon. There was only shadow and fog.

Nathan didn't bother with the main thoroughfare. It had been picked clean some time ago. Instead, he walked to a small pond near the castle. There were fish here in the shallow water and they were easy to spear. Some of them were ugly prehistoric-looking creatures with jagged underbites. Others bore rich, crimson stripes, warning of their toxicity. Others still were adorable and cartoonish with big, sad eyes.

Nathan took off his shoes, rolled up his jeans, and stepped into the water. With his spear poised above the surface, he watched for any fish he might catch. One of the ugly ones swam toward him. It was a silver-scaled beast with teeth like needles and a body like a javelin. A barracuda—that was the name that came to mind. He'd written a report on them for school once, and this sure looked like the same thing.

The monstrous fish rushed toward him, leaving rippling trails in its wake. Nathan tensed, fearing that if his spear missed, the beast might bite off one of his toes. He stabbed at it and felt his spear tip cling against the concrete bottom of the artificial pond. His eyes closed instinctively, and he waited for the inevitable pain from its snapping jaws.

He felt no pain. Nathan opened his eyes and saw the barracuda flailing and struggling in the water. His spear had pierced its back fin and held it pinned. An audible sigh of relief escaped his lips.

Careful not to let the fish free, Nathan backed away to shore. He kept the tip of his spear pinned against the concrete and dragged the barracuda along while keeping a safe distance. His prey's rage turned into panic. It tried to turn and swim the other way. The fish flailed and tugged until its fin ripped free from the spear tip. With a ruined fin, the barracuda couldn't make it far, however. Nathan stabbed the crippled fish again, this time in the center of its body.

The fish lost its fight, and Nathan brought it to shore. He was careful to drop it far away from the pond so it might not flop its way back into the water. It seized on the ground, bleeding out and unable to breathe.

Nathan smiled. It was a big fish, and it would be enough food for him and Baba. Truthfully Baba never had an appetite, but Nathan felt guilty showing up without enough food for both of them.

The multi-tool in Nathan's backpack had all the accessories he needed to clean the fish—a sharp blade, a fish-scaler, and a pair of pliers. He stabbed the barracuda once more, putting the creature out of its misery, then went about the work of cleaning and gutting it. It wasn't something he enjoyed, but his father had taught him how at a young age and he was able to disassemble his prey with a cool detachment.

Focused on his blade and the fish, Nathan didn't immediately hear the ticking behind him. Even when he did, his subconscious shrugged it off as ambient noise. Only when the ticking gave away to a brassy alarm bell did Nathan realize what was happening.

He turned, nearly dropping the fish, and saw a massive crocodile crawling out from the pond. The monstrous reptile regarded him with cold, black eyes. A guttural growl played like a sustained bass note beneath the ringing sound that came from inside the beast. It shook its head back and forth until the alarm stopped. Both Nathan and the crocodile stood silent for a moment, the only sound the echo of ticks and tocks from deep within the reptile's belly.

The crocodile charged. Its speed was scary, even on land. Nathan tossed the flayed fish at the beast. It paused to devour his offering. Nathan grabbed his backpack and spear and ran off before it could decide it wanted him as dessert.

Nathan didn't dare to try another fishing spot. Instead, he raided a hotdog stand—one of the few that wasn't overrun with feral cats. The freezer had thawed out long ago and the meat inside was rotten, but he managed to salvage a package of stale rolls and a few packets of relish.

Baba didn't seem very thankful for the meal. He stood still and silent, never even glancing at the food. This was the monkey's way though—ever quiet and stoic.

"Sure, the fish would have been better, but I don't see you getting off your butt and finding us lunch," Nathan said to the monkey.

One side of a bun broke off as Nathan squeezed relish into the slit. Once it was slathered with the green spread, he pushed the broken piece back on. The relish held it together like paste.

"This is why you're so sluggish. You never eat."

The filthy, man-sized monkey sat in the chair across from Nathan and stared blankly into the distance. It showed no reaction to his words.

"It's not so bad," Nathan said after taking a bite.

The first bite hadn't tasted like much of anything, so Nathan concentrated on the next one. He tried to remember the smell of pickles and the hard chewiness of old bread. The taste and texture of both intensified with each chew.

"Okay, maybe it is pretty bad," he said with a laugh.

Nathan took his time with lunch. In between bites, he told Baba about his run-in with the crocodile, exaggerating the encounter to make himself sound more heroic. In this version, the reptilian monster had sneakily stolen the flayed barracuda and then run off. Nathan told Baba that he pursued the beast with his spear, ready to carve it into crocodile steaks, and that it narrowly escaped into the water. Baba was unimpressed, his expression never changing.

"Okay, maybe it didn't happen exactly like that," he admitted, then changed the subject.

Nathan reported the mist had overtaken just a little more of the park, the same way it did every day, and that things were getting even worse outside. That's what the man on the radio said, at least.

"This place might not be what it used to, but hey, it was still be the happiest place on Earth I suppose that's something, right?"

Nathan forced a smile, but it was short-lived. Despair pulled at the corners of his mouth like gravity. He reached across the table and placed a hand on Baba's matted paw.

"And, hey, we have each other."

He wished Baba would say something to reinforce his optimism—a single utterance or even a reassuring wink. He couldn't, of course. Baba wasn't a real monkey or even a person in a monkey costume. He was just an empty mascot. Even so, Nathan left him with a hot dog bun and a few relish packets, in case he changed his mind and got hungry.

Nathan returned to the castle, weary of the shadows and the monsters within the park. What little light penetrated the gray skies dimmed into blackness, and night enshrouded the park. Nathan closed the curtains and waited for the radio static to give way to the sound of an acoustic guitar.

There were different songs at night, not just that Stones cover his dad used to sing to him. It was all acoustic stuff though, accompanied by a melancholy voice. The singer always sounded on the verge of crying, like the music was the only thing keeping him together but also threatening to break him apart.

Nathan went to bed with the radio playing. The music was his talisman against the things in the dark.

The mist had rolled in further overnight. Nathan looked out the window and there was less to see today than there had been yesterday. He wondered how long it would be until the black fog swallowed the castle and him along with it.

Music swelled beneath the radio static as Nathan marked another hash mark on the wall. He closed his eyes and concentrated on the sound of "Wild Horses." He never sang along, even though he felt the urge. The man on the radio only played or spoke in the morning and night. Singing over that would ruin it.

A news report followed the song. Stuff was still bad outside, but help was coming. The government had a plan.

"We just need to make it a while longer," the voice on the radio proclaimed. "By the time you're back, everything will be normal again."

Nathan didn't want to leave the castle. The hotdog buns and relish could sustain his hunger, but he still needed batteries. He feared the radio might go dead at any moment, and he couldn't bear the thought of being without it, even for a day.

He crept out from the castle and made his away across the eastern bridge to the futuristic section of the park. The water below the bridge had once been clear and blue, but now it was gray and brackish. Nathan was careful not to let his mind wander, always listening for the *tick-tock* sounds of crocodiles in the water or trolls growling beneath the bridge. His eyes scanned for malevolent shadows that might peel themselves off the ground and take on a third dimension.

The section of the park across the bridge was a 1960s B-movie utopia, or it had been at one time. Now it was like an abandoned human colony on an alien world. Double arches supported a huge sci-fi sculpture of armored cable, cathode tubes, and mad science arrays. An unnerving hum came from the sculpture. Electricity arced between the metal arches at random intervals and stray lightning bolts shot down from the array. The pathway beneath was painted in black carbon and riddled with cracks.

417

Nathan veered off the paved road and gave the sparking archway a wide berth. Still, he flinched with each snap of electricity. Somewhere close by a radio broadcast played in a shop or café. He could hear the man on the radio giving soft assurances that everything was okay.

The entire section of the park was blanketed in the shadow of Mount Cosmos, an enormous structure that extended into the sky like a snow-white peak. Its design reminded Nathan of a bio-dome city-state on some far off world. Dark fog engulfed more than half of the building, the black mist in stark contrast with the sprawling, ivory architecture.

There was a rollercoaster in there. Nathan had gone on it once when he was younger—when he and his family had come here before the bad times. The ride had scared the hell out of him. It was huge and fast, and spooky synthesizer music played in the darkness beyond the rails of the track. Even now, he could hear the faint echo of that music and the clicking of a rising coaster.

Nathan stepped through the shattered glass door of a nearby shop. A feral cat sat upon the counter, eating astronaut ice cream from a chewed and torn package. It let out a warbled mew, warning Nathan to keep his distance. He took the animal's warning and kept to the aisles, searching for anything of use.

There were plenty of clothes—plenty in his size even. He stuffed a few t-shirts and a pair of flip-flops into his backpack, along with a pair of swim trunks.

The cat mewed at him angrily, raising its hackles. Nathan imagined it yelling at him for shoplifting.

"Oh yeah?" he asked. "Did you pay for that astronaut ice cream?"

The cat hissed, then went back to its snack. Nathan turned away from the animal and rooted through shelves full of toys, looking for anything that might have the batteries he needed. He ripped open package after package, only to find battery compartments crusted with white corrosion. Every battery was swollen and leaking.

He cursed and moved to another aisle. Flashlights, ray guns, and laser swords hung from pegs. Nathan unscrewed their handles and popped open their battery compartments. Each time he was met with disappointment.

The feral cat hissed and cried at the counter. Nathan ignored it at first. The cats only got violent when you challenged them for food. Otherwise, they were just loud. He yelled for it to shut up, then turned around to see what it was mewling about.

His mouth hung open and a toy ray gun fell from his hand. The mist had rolled into the store. It pushed through the broken front door, then poured across the floor and climbed the walls. Racks of clothes and shelves of toys vanished into its nebulous dimensions.

The feral cat arched its back and hissed at the ebony fog. Dark and wispy tendrils reached out like probes and the cat swatted at them with its claws. The mist wrapped around the animal's leg and snatched it off the counter. A loud, discordant mew was cut short as the cat vanished into the wall of fog.

Nathan grabbed as many of the laser swords as he could manage and ran for the emergency exit of the shop. He slammed his body into the push bar and kept running out into the street.

Up ahead Nathan could see the double archway before the bridge. It sparked and barked in an erratic display of electrical chaos. He didn't know how close the hungry mist was and he didn't dare turn around to find out. Could he make it around the archway before those black tendrils dragged him into oblivion?

Nathan decided not to chance it. He ran straight through the double arches and beneath the sci-fi sculpture array. The hair on his arms stood on end and electricity hummed in his ears. Lightning bolts rained down all around him, and the ground shook with the force of their impact. Crisscrossing blue sparks arced across the outer arch like a gate.

All but one of the laser swords slipped from his grasp as Nathan dove beneath the wavering lines of electricity that barred the outer archway. He rolled to his feet and stumbled onto the bridge. His body trembled with adrenaline and tingled with electricity.

He thought back to the time he'd been dared to lick a nine-volt battery—the shock, the metallic taste. He dwelled on the recollection as he raced across the bridge.

Halfway across, Nathan dared a backward glance. The tidal wave of fog had come to a stop, but it had devoured nearly half of Futureland. Even Mount Cosmos, that titanic ride that scraped at the heavens, had been lost to the terrible mist.

Nathan ran back to the castle. He didn't bother to listen for the ticking of approaching crocodiles or the jerky movements of living shadows. He didn't keep an eye out for food or supplies.

When he made it back to the castle, Nathan raced upstairs to his suite and slammed the door behind him. He dropped the toy laser sword on the floor and stared out the window that overlooked the park. The mist had rolled in as fiercely on all sides. Half of the park was gone, lost to the oblivion that lay behind that black veil.

Nathan collapsed into bed. He cried in silence and waited for the radio to play its goodnight songs.

White corrosion leaked from the bloated, ruined batteries in the laser sword, just like all the others. Nathan cursed as he tossed them into a trash barrel near his bed. Static played in the background and he wondered how many days of power the radio had left.

The opening notes to "Wild Horses" came over the speakers. Sobs broke up the vocals and the music would pause as the singer took deep, audible breaths.

News from the outside world followed the music. The man on the radio sounded desperate and afraid—worse than Nathan had ever heard him. He muttered a string of bad news.

People were killing each other over canned food and gasoline. The hospitals had shut down and the doctors had all gone home. The pharmacies had been raided and there was no medicine to be found. Neither the police nor the military were responding—it was every man for himself.

Bad news was usually followed up by backpedaling. The man on the radio would gather his composure and assure that everything would go back to normal soon. This time though, he didn't do that. A crying apology ended the transmission instead.

Nathan added a hash mark to the wall and looked out the window. The mist had rolled further in overnight. Not as fast as it had while he was scavenging the day before, but more quickly than usual. Most nights it encroached upon the park by inches, but this time it was by yards.

A terrible thought occurred to him. What if the fog had claimed Baba?

Nathan got dressed and hurried out of the castle, taking only his spear for protection. He rushed down the steps, nearly tripping on his flip-flops, then ran past the dead bushes and toward the western half of the park. He raced across the bridge, shouting Baba's name.

A ticking sound brought Nathan to a halt as he stepped off the bridge. A low growl accompanied the mechanical ticks and tocks. Nathan readied his spear and turned around slowly.

The monstrous crocodile who had nearly killed him two days prior hissed and snapped in the water, the back half of its enormous body lost in the fog. Smokey, black tendrils lashed around its neck and its front legs. Terror shone in its primal eyes as it clawed at the cement riverbed.

From where Nathan stood, he could see it was a losing battle. With every thrashing movement and snap of its terrible jaws, the crocodile was pulled deeper into the nothingness behind the black fog. It growled and bellowed and Nathan wondered what it was trying to say. Was it raging with anger, making violent threats to the end? Was it asking for his help? Did it want him to save its life, or was it begging for the mercy of death before it succumbed to whatever terrible fate awaited it in the mist?

Nathan didn't move to help the crocodile. He stood stricken with fear and watched as its scaled flesh and gnashing teeth fell behind the white veil. Its bassy growls went silent and the constant mechanical ticking from its stomach ceased.

The mist lurched forward, its dark volume staining the water and the air like black ink spilled onto a drawing. Nathan turned and ran.

His throat and lungs burned by the time he made it to Baba. The monkey was still there, sitting at the same bistro table as always. Nathan hunched over, grabbing his knees, and took a moment to catch his breath.

The fog was rolling in quickly from the west and the rust-colored mountains that rose so high just two days ago were gone. Baba seemed oblivious to the approaching doom. He just sat there wearing the same expression as always.

"We need to get out of here, buddy."

Baba didn't move.

"We'll go back to the castle," Nathan said, pointing toward the white and blue spires in the center of the park—the place farthest away from the mist. "We'll be safe there."

Nathan placed his hands under Baba's arms and pulled him out of the chair. He dragged the monkey away from the approaching fog, Baba's limp legs dragging against the ground.

"You gotta help me out, Baba! You're heavier than you look."

The monkey did nothing. He didn't stand and walk on his own. In fact, he stopped moving altogether.

Nathan tugged at Baba, but it was like he was nailed to the spot. He pulled again, then saw that Baba's own shadow held him in place. It had come to life on the ground, acquiring depth and some facsimile of mass. Its paws gripped Baba by the ankles and pulled against Nathan.

"Let him go!" Nathan screamed.

The shadow did not concede. It pulled harder, dragging both child and monkey toward the rolling wall of fog. Nathan dug his heels into the ground, but his flip-flops had little traction.

"Let go of my friend!"

The shadow monsters never made a sound, but this black mockery of Baba threw its head back like a laughing mime. It pulled even harder and Nathan's feet skidded across the pavement. The distance between them and the fog eroded.

Tendrils darted out from the mist like the probing black tongues of some terrible alien. Baba's shadow reached its tail out to one of the tendrils. It became one with the fog and then dragged Baba's legs through the dark veil.

"I can't do this alone, Baba."

Nathan pulled at the monkey, trying to wrestle him away. The mist would not relinquish its grasp though. It held Baba tight and slowly rolled forward, overtaking the monkey inch by inch. Baba smiled a static grin at Nathan, even as the fog devoured it.

"I can't do this alone."

The black mist rolled over Baba's face. Nathan dropped the monkey's hand and backed away. The monkey's outstretched arm vanished into the great nothingness.

Nathan's bottom lip trembled. His face was wet with tears. At first, he couldn't remember what that felt like—the warm and wet feeling of ugly crying. He concentrated on it. It was important to feel, even the bad stuff. He willed the sensations—the weight and warmth of fat teardrops and the saltwater taste as the tears ran into his mouth.

Nathan ran from the mist, through the receding streets and byways, and back across the western bridge. He stopped outside the castle, in front of the statue of the well-dressed man and the cartoon mouse. He looked up into the man's eyes, desperate for some assurance or comfort, but there was only madness within the man's gaze. The statue stared out at the encroaching fog with a look of insane wonder and happiness—a look of sublime hope, as if he saw God on the horizon. The mouse grinned from ear to ear. There was something sinister and suspicious in that smile as if it knew just what horrible thing came their way—as if it had been waiting for it.

Nathan left the well-dressed man and the cartoon mouse to their fate. He raced through the castle gates, up the steps, and into his suite. Praying it might make some sort of difference, Nathan locked the door and pulled the curtains shut. He fell into bed and waited for the radio to play its nightly transmission. It did, but this time it skipped the music and didn't bother with the news.

"Things are bad, little man. Really bad. If it was just me..." The man on the radio broke into a sob and it took him the better part of a minute to regain his composure. "If it was just me, I'd stay here right next to you. I'd die by your side if that's what it took."

Nathan had never heard his father sound so sad. It broke his heart.

"I have your sister to worry about too, though. I can't help you, anymore. I've tried... God, I've tried... But I can still help her. I can try to get her someplace safe."

Nathan reached out and stroked the radio. The red indicator light faded in and out.

"We need to leave in the morning, So I need you to find your way back to us. I need you to wake up for me, Nate. Okay, buddy?"

Sobs and sniffles crackled over the radio static.

"I don't know the way home, Dad," Nathan whispered. "And I can't do this alone."

"I love you, Nathan. I'll always love you."

Nathan woke up to complete silence. No radio static filled the room. No cats mewed outside, and no monsters growled in the distance. The indicator light on the radio cast no glow. He tweaked the antennae and turned the volume up and down, but it was dead.

The black fog had penetrated the castle overnight. It rolled under the door and through the windows, lazily eating away at the floor. The mist climbed the walls, erasing the hash marks Nathan used to keep track of the days.

Nathan hugged the radio and closed his eyes. He tried to remember the smell of his father's aftershave and the texture of his stubble when he'd kiss him goodnight. These things were important to him, even now.

He clutched the radio, pretending to hold on to his father and sang the words to "Wild Horses" until his voice was lost in the mist.

THE RECALL

by Joshua Viola

*B*e fruitful and multiply.

Four words of good advice that held for thousands of years before the multiplying got out of hand. More births meant more deaths. Not to mention the spikes: war, pestilence, plague. You do the math. It's a simple progressive curve and you don't even need software to plot it.

Just take a look at the line outside the Pearly Gates. Within a couple thousand years of the Kid getting hammered to that cross, the queue of the faithful stretched farther than you could see. A lot more souls than the heavens had ever been designed to support, which added a ream of structural and load-bearing stress issues to the already difficult processing mess.

I'd tried to tell the folks Upstairs we weren't ready for what they had planned, but I always got the same response: *Mike, we appreciate the input, but we really just need you and your team to do your jobs and process those coming in and those going down. Simple as that.*

No, not so simple, actually.

First, there's admissions. Admissions are the domain of the Gatekeeper, and so is the waiting area. If you know Pete, you know he wasted no time making it clear that he and his crew were overwhelmed.

Easy enough to see why, what with the admission interviews, background checks, sign-offs at every level, and all the filing and cross-filing that had to be adhered to, no exceptions.

That was the job—check all the boxes, take care of every item on every list, make the applicants *whole* again, and only then let them through the Pearly Gates so they can walk the Streets of Gold.

Or send them down.

Try keeping up with all that when you're dealing with a few hundred thousand new deaths every day.

Can't be done.

But don't try telling Him that.

Still, we managed, more or less, testing out different methods of crowd control and entry access management. Some of them worked, some of them didn't, but at least we were doing the job.

Then word came down from A-level: They were kicking the End Times into high gear, and *fast*. You-Know-Who wrote the damned (sic) memo and had the gall to close it, absolutely without irony, with the words:

The Rapture is coming. Is your department ready?

Well, we weren't, not by a long shot, but a few of us had been giving the matter some pretty serious thought, not to mention sending some pretty serious memos and white papers Upstairs.

Even when the rules were first etched into the tablets, nobody Upstairs really expected rigorous adherence. It just wasn't in their nature. Certainly, they weren't going to stick too closely to all ten of the things. Most of them got their ticket punched for the train going down before their bodies were cold.

And that was part of the plan—a ten-step program for weeding through the arrivals and streamlining the admissions process.

But He would only let us go so far—all the forgiveness and state-of-grace clauses just made more work for Pete and his crew at the Pearly Gates.

We tried to get some help from Upstairs, some utterances that would either make things stricter or more clearly relaxed, but neither J^{PRIME} nor J^{SON} was willing to bend too much. The Kid has His my-way-or-the-highway moments.

Don't even get me started on the Ghost.

Between the three of them, it's a wonder we've still got jobs.

The problem wasn't that His followers had been fruitfully multiplying for a few thousand years; it was that they'd been learning things all that time. Things that got the birth rate/death rate equation so far out of whack: improved hygiene, medicines, surgery, better food, warning labels on cigarette packs, seatbelts. Every life-extending technique made the bottleneck worse.

But it was transfusions and transplants that really gummed up the works, not that we knew it until the big-R began.

Our hearts sank the instant Gabe blew the first Recall note. The End Times were here and we were about to have a crowd at the Pearly Gates like nothing any of us had ever seen before. No way we were ready, and even before the second note it looked like Pete was going to take his halo upstairs and tell J^{PRIME} to shove it.

Probably would have done it, too, except things got so bad so fast that neither he nor any of the rest of us could do anything but watch.

It was the body parts that got to us first.

Say you're a good person, hold pretty firmly to the Big Ten—enough to be more likely than not to gain entrance, anyway. You live a good, clean life, and don't think too much about always doing the right thing.

Like checking the organ donor box on your driver's license.

Then, say there's a bad person—smoker, drinker, maybe a drug user, never said no to fatty foods or a second helping of ice cream. And this person powers their way through a pretty shitty and irredeemable life: spouse-abuser, maybe, kicker of dogs and small children, worshipper of graven images, banker, politician, whatever.

Even bad people get good medical care. If they can afford it. So when your heart is ready to give up the ghost after a few decades of double cheeseburgers for breakfast, you get a new one.

Won't make any difference to your terminal ticket. You're headed down, no question, but what about that new heart? Say it came from that good person. Doesn't he or she deserve to have their heart with them, beating with excitement as they stroll those golden streets?

It became clear very quickly that the top three thought those hearts needed to be called Home because Gabe hadn't hit note four before a buttload of bad people with good people's hearts inside their sinful chests heard something like a trumpet and then damned (as it were) if their shiny new hearts didn't tear themselves right out of their stitched-up chests and head for the skies.

Those skies were raining hearts on the waiting area before Gabe got his horn really heated up.

And not just hearts.

Pete and his crew, trying hard to keep order in the rapidly evolving (don't tell Him I used that word) chaos, found themselves getting pelted with legs and arms, eyeballs and livers and kidneys. Good thing—if you could find a good thing in all that mess—that whole head transplants hadn't been perfected before the Recall was sounded. Transfused blood was a real bear. About all I can tell you is that enough sinners got enough good blood to slick the waiting area with red.

Cleanup on cloud nine!

Maintenance will be scrubbing for a millennium, maybe two, but, frankly, some of it just isn't going to come out. They've got no beef—scrubbing's a picnic compared to trying to tag every organ and drop of blood and match them with their original owners.

I swear, every one of us on duty was ready to trade all our benefits for a job down below. No tagging or matching or paperwork there—no questions at all. Just a quick sneer and then a snap-assignment to one of the Circles and *Next!*

Sounds like Heaven to me, and at this point I don't care Who hears me say that.

Some of it was funny, though, if you've got the same sense of humor that most of us here develop over time. Like this one guy and a prostitute.

She was doing it on top with a little more energy than usual. The guy had a ring of suture scars around the base of his manhood, and while they threw her a little at first—not that she risked her pay by letting him see any of her unease—she found, to her surprise, that the ridge added a little something extra to her chores.

But only a little. She was writhing in the throes of her performance's peak when the worthy penis was called Home from the most unworthy man's body.

For the first time in her career, the prostitute's screams were genuine.

Complicating all of it—like we needed any more complications—was the ocean of the Saved who rose whole. Most of those were from a millennium before medical progress became a factor, but that still meant a few million moderns, all of them ready after holy preparation for the big rapturous moment of their Ascension. Some of them—more than you might have expected—hadn't accepted transfusions or transplants or vaccines or any of the benefits of modern medicine.

Even those who bent the medical rules and ignored the proscriptions against prescriptions, were arriving in large numbers. They hadn't smoked, hadn't drunk, hadn't cheated on their spouses, hadn't done much of anything—sure hadn't had any *real* fun.

And every one of them expected to be let right in. They'd earned entry, hadn't they?

Well, yes and no.

Trying to explain to even one of them that there was paperwork and bureaucracy to deal with before they got to see what lay beyond the Pearly Gates, that they'd just have to wait their turn, and do so while standing ankle-deep in bits and pieces of their fellow Saved was an exercise in futility.

When you're dealing with millions of them, it's not even that. It's a bad joke, is what it is, and they may think the joke is on them, but they'd be wrong.

The joke's on those of us who have to deal with it. We're standing *knee*-deep in blessed entrails, and how much fun do you think that is?

The more Gabe blew, the worse things got.

The strictest of the believers started organizing before the Recall Song was half-finished. Among their good deeds back on Earth, they never missed a chance to vote against the very sorts of bureaucratic regulation and over-reach that was keeping them from their Promised Land, and they weren't going to take it. They demanded to see J^{PRIME} and see him *right this instant*.

Fat chance.

He and the Kid, not to mention the Ghost, weren't about to deal with any of this one-to-one or even one-to-millions. Not their style. They're great delegators, always have been, and they sure weren't about to change.

This was *their* mess, but it was *ours* to clean up.

By the time Gabe blew his last note the skies had cleared a bit, but that only meant everything coming our way was already here for us to trip over. Or slip on—Pete went down hard when he took a mighty stride right into a big pile of Recalled kidneys and tumbled ass over halo through a stream of sanctified blood. Nothing funny about it—which didn't keep a couple of us from tucking our faces into our robes so he wouldn't hear our chuckles.

But that was about the only laugh we got that day, and the thought of the work that lay ahead told every one of us we weren't likely to laugh much, if at all, ever again.

Insult to injury came quick.

Gabriel had barely started cleaning the spit out of his mouthpiece when the Revelation Seven started tuning up *their* horns. We all knew what that meant. No more fun times down on Earth: Here comes the Wrath!

Bad as the Wrath was going to be—and it would be *bad*—I didn't think it would be as bad as the headaches and annoyances and absolute madness of what we were trying deal with up here. Not even close.

Which is why I'm calling it quits.

Whatever disadvantage the Wrath has for those left behind, it has certain career advantages for someone as skilled at processing souls as I am.

The Wrath's going to last a while on Earth, but nowhere near as long as dealing with the waiting room chaos to come. And once the Wrath is finished, there'll be an even bigger number of admissions waiting in the anterooms of the Circles.

By the time the last of the Revelation Seven's notes have sounded, I plan to be well-established in the crew processing *those* souls. Nice, cushy job, no tough decisions or judgments, God knows (He does, you know,) no kidneys and hearts and blood and penises to keep track of.

Line them up and let them in—the kind of work I was made for.

Whether He likes it or not.

A FEE FOR FABLES

by John Boden

— 1 —

*I*ts movements were graceful yet jerky in a way, perhaps like a spasming man underwater might look. Every movement had a soundtrack of whisper; the papery skin making contact with another patch of papery skin. In the dim of dusk, it appeared to be made of hornet nest. Crepe of dusty gray and threaded with black.

The only buzzing was the sound of her heart as she lay in bed and peered through the space between the bottom of the blind and the window ledge. Her nightgown sticking to her sweat-sheened skin. The whisper-skinned thing walked around out at the edge of the yard. Its bulbous head nodded slightly and its too-long neck seemed to struggle to keep it upright.

It turned and though she couldn't tell if it had eyes, seemed to gaze right at her window, directly into her room. Her breath hitched and she held a gasp behind small teeth. It held up an arm that ended in an appendage with only two long digits, one of which it jammed upwards in a swift and unexpected motion, impaling the lower part of its face. Then, with another flurry of movement, dragged the inserted finger sideways, tearing a ragged wound in its face. The wound opened, bits of the mâché-like flesh dangling or dancing away on the light breeze. The corners rose as it smiled. Black things shined and wriggled within. Beetle backs and static squirming. It seemed to stare right at Marcy's window, tilting that large head forward to exaggerate the fact it might be looking into her paling face.

She lay as still as possible. Not breathing or blinking. She heard a voice flutter through the screen of the window. It was a small thing of moth wings and blowing sand that said, "I know you see..."

— 2 —

Marcy woke with the sun and pulled the blanket over her face, not the whole way, just to the bridge of her nose. A modern Kilroy. The aroma was both comforting and slightly repulsive: sour perspiration, something slightly salty and acidic stitched to another smaller fungal reek. She breathed deep and embraced the fragrances with sighing lungs. A wheeze and cracking bones symphony when she moved to sit upright. Movement at the window drew her attention. Marcy felt her pulse quicken and she went cold. She slowly peered out into the yard, and with relief, found it was only the crow out there again. It stood on the sill and tapped the glass three times and disappeared. Her heart replies in kind from within its cage of weakened ribs and sagging skin. Another sigh and the blankets were tossed aside, a womb torn apart to leave her vulnerable and raw.

There is no crueler thing to do but get up and face another day.

— 3 —

In the husk of the kitchen, Marcy sits and takes another sip of the brown in the chipped mug. She cannot taste it. Her tongue tingles and dances as the memory of words and speech skulk upon it. She's been alone so very long. She hears a soft voice by her ear, *"I know you see me."*

She feels the tear run down her cheek as she struggles to decide whether it was recollection of the dream or vision she had last night, or a plea with the world to just acknowledge she exists. She decides it's both, and words begins to trickle from her mouth:

"Consequence is this old ratty string around my finger, hardened by the dried sweat and saliva of days, or weeks.

I chew on it anyway, this jerkied life.

I felt the stale fetuses of repercussions grind and mash between molar and gum.

I swallowed and felt them grow in my belly.

When not stillborn, they might've been beautiful monsters.

That was my hope.

I ought to also have known better,

I have shoeboxes under my bed.

Filled with the brittle bones of hope,

as delicate as a dead bird.

I fill my hands with them sometimes at night,

rub them along the flesh of my jaw.

Smooth and sharp at the same time.

Like words that smell like teeth."

Marcy raises the mug to her lips and bites its edge with slightly crooked teeth. She feels the ceramic against enamel and it makes her spine shiver a bit. Her jaw clamps a little harder and hears the vessel crack and feels the bits stick to her teeth and lips. Marcy places it on the table and looks at the chipped spot along the top edge, then to its twin on the other side of the mug. She wipes her mouth with her hand and stands. Marking Xs on a calendar would be easier.

— 4 —

"The moon smiles in the window when I'm not looking. The moment I turn to catch it, the smile swerves into sneer and the night goes out. I'm not bothered. The best darkness is the absolute kind."

Marcy watches the red numbers of the clock as they change, each minute dying with a silent dignity. She rolls closer to the window and grips the bottom of the blind between her crooked fingers, raising it slightly, slowly. The shed stands at the far corner, bathed in silver moonlight. The dried corn stands tilted and stooped in the garden that died of neglect. She feels a tingle in her shoulder, when she notes movement from the corner of her view. The thing moves into her line of sight with sure but slow steps. She squints and notes the differences a day makes. The braided sash of dark hair that hangs from its shoulders and neck like Jacob Marley's sins. It comes as close as the edge of the garden before stopping. Marcy stares at her visitor for long minutes that sting like hours. It makes no movements, no gestures. Just quietly staring and daring. Marcy rolls away from the window to take a bottle of pills from her nightstand. She swallows two and gulps the last of the tap water in the glass that has been there for a week. She closes her eyes and tries to remember the fable that her sentinel reminded her of before the herd of slumber tramples her down.

— 5 —

Her bones ache a little more than usual. She worries that maybe she had walked in her sleep and fallen. The bruises on her calves and the back of her arm are dark plum and just as tender. She winces as she strokes them.

"Better be more careful, old girl."

She empties the last of the shredded wheat into the bowl and eats it without milk. Expiration dates always break her heart. She crunches and stares at the black phone mounted on the wall, covered in dust, while behind her tired eyes she sees rivers and boats. It is only as she approaches her mouth with the last piece of cereal that she notices her fingernails are the color of bruise. She sighs and finishes her breakfast. It's the most important meal of the day.

— 6 —

Marcy sits on the porch, her sentinel appearing just before eleven. She sips at her glass of water and watches as it paces the edges of her property. Bits of its papery skin dancing on the breeze, whispered muttering dancing from its mouth. Marcy finishes her water and rocks quietly for a moment. The being stands still at the foot of the porch steps and looks up at the old woman. The mouth bent upward into a smile of sorts. She sees it has eyes now, but realizes they are a pair of wasps sitting idle on either side of its head. It doesn't move and the breeze dies and all she can hear is the oceanic whispering beneath its skin. She feels the buzz within again and it begins to rise like tide. She closes her eyes and sees churning waters, sees a thin pale hand, and hears the clinking of chains...of change. She stands and goes inside.

— 7 —

It is early evening when Marcy returns to the porch. The creature has not moved at all, it still stands at the base of the steps. Marcy sighs and smiles, squinting up to the sky as she does so.

"All these days, I knew it but didn't. I kept thinking of stories. Of rhymes and tales. Poetic portents that I paid no attention to. I nearly didn't put it together. When you get old, you get ignorant. Or maybe we start that way and just idle, willfully so. You fill your head with stories your whole life and never once realize that there's a fee to be paid. A life poorly written is a life unlived. A life spent alone is a diary entry of the lonely doomed."

Marcy steps down closer to the thing and it tilts its head toward her. Is it nodding? That wound of a smile moving slightly. It holds out its right arm and the hand at the end of it. Marcy holds out a gnarled hand of her own and opens it, two coins falling to land in the upturned palm of her visitor.

Everything stills and Marcy releases the breath she's been holding for so very long. She opens her eyes and finds her creature gone.

— 8 —

"The neighbor was on her walk and noticed the flies. She called it in. said she hadn't seen the old bird in a few days." The young man in the white uniform blathers.

"Her name was Marcy Oates and I'd put it as at least a week, maybe more like two." The red-faced man's eyes are rimmed with wet.

"Did you know her?" the other man asks, a tint of shame across his features.

"No, I'm just the sensitive type." Red Face snaps, a little snottier than needed. The two slowly roll the old woman from the bed where she's been lying for some time. Her flesh is blue and purple and splitting in spots. The sheets stained dark in their mourning ruin. Flies buzz to get at their squirming brood.

"Marcy Oates." Red Face mumbles again as he scribbles on the pad in his hand.

"Natural causes, looks like." The other man chimes in.

Red Face nods and flips his tablet closed and gets back to trying to wrangle the body into the vinyl bag and onto the stretcher. They manage to get her out the front door and down the porch steps before Red Face stops. His eyes are stuck on the two coins laying in the dead grass at the foot of the steps.

ANNIVERSARY

by John R. Little

It was sixty years ago to the day when they first met.

Jimmy Lamars didn't need any help remembering, because it was not only the anniversary of the day they met—a year later they married on the same day. August 1.

To add to that, August 1 was also his birthday.

He'd wandered down to the beach that day when he turned twenty-three, expecting nothing but an afternoon of reflection and peace. Jimmy had just changed jobs, and the new one wasn't really working out for him. They expected him to work long hours and to be available on weekends. He wasn't too into that, because he was finding he had almost no time to himself. Who wanted to be locked into a career that left him no free time to enjoy his life?

He was twenty-three for Christ's sake. His life was just beginning, and he knew it.

"Not me," he said as he took his sandals off and walked slowly out to the water. The beach sand was squishy between his toes, and he loved the feel of the blistering sun beating down on him.

It was a hot day, maybe the hottest of that summer.

Hibbon's Cove was off the beaten path. He had driven fifty miles from Bangor to reach the secluded area just south of Bay Harbor. He'd found the place by accident two summers earlier while wandering along the Maine coastline.

Jimmy never told a soul about Hibbon's Cove. He'd been there a half dozen times since then, to walk in the refreshing water, watch the tides come in and out, and to just be alone with his thoughts. It was the perfect place to go when he needed to make a big decision.

He was already a heavy man, more than 220 pounds, and when he was walking his beach alone, he never had to worry about anybody laughing at him.

It was his own private paradise. Until that day.

Gail Sommers had also tripped across Hibbon's Cove by herself. Well, in her case, it was her and two girlfriends who had found the quiet little beach together. She was twenty-one and her two besties were both leaving Bangor to move to

New York City. They'd only given her two weeks' notice until they were going to the Big Apple to "find themselves." Whatever that meant.

They hadn't asked her to join them, which hurt, but she also knew she wouldn't have gone. Maine was where she'd been born and where she would probably live her entire life.

"I'm going to miss you guys so much," she had said as they walked the lonely beach. Trish and Amber smiled and nodded. It was during that walk Gail realized that although they were her besties, she wasn't theirs.

Secretly, she couldn't help thinking it was the same as always.

According to her daddy, Gail was big-boned. That sounded like something she was born with, so it wasn't her fault she was bigger than the Barbie dolls walking with her. They were twigs compared to her, and when they didn't invite her to go to New York with her, she knew it was because they didn't see her in the same league as them.

Walking on the deserted beach and understanding that fact made Gail horribly sad.

Ten days later, Trish and Amber left with a small trailer dragging along behind Trish's car (the one her own daddy had given her for her eighteenth birthday), and they hit the road.

They never answered Gail's phone calls or letters. This was before emails and texting, but she later knew they would have ignored those too.

Hibbon's Cove should have been a sad place for her, but it wasn't. It was a place of transition for her, moving from being a dumb girl who had no clue to a woman who was starting to understand how the world worked.

From that day, Gail thought of the Cove as a place she could just be herself, without worrying what anyone else thought about her.

On August 1, *that* first day of August sixty years ago, Jimmy and Gail both walked on the sand at Hibbon's Cove, each expecting to find nobody else to share the beach with, and so each was shocked to see another person there.

Jimmy saw Gail first, and his initial reaction was to want to cover his belly, but he had left his t-shirt in the car. He had nothing to hide behind, and his belly fat spilled out over his bathing suit like always.

He wanted to just turn around and leave, but he could tell that Gail saw him. If he left now, he'd look like—what?—like a freak? A coward? He didn't even know, and he didn't have much time to think about it.

The girl was walking toward him.

He looked at her and tried to smile. He felt trapped, mentally as well as physically, since his feet were being sucked into the wet sand as waves spilled over his toes. It felt like quicksand, and for a moment he was afraid he'd be sucked right down, but of course no such thing happened.

After hesitating, he started to walk toward her. She was smiling at him.

When they got closer to each other, she said, "I thought I was the only person who knew about this place." She laughed.

He felt a wave of relief wash over him. Something about that laugh just set his mind at ease.

"And I thought that, too."

They stared at each other, as if they were the only two humans left in a dead world.

Jimmy didn't know what to say. He just wanted to see that smile again.

Gail had smiled because she was afraid. It was an odd habit she knew she had, but there was nothing she could do about it. She smiled in lots of other circumstances, too, but this time it was due to fear.

Who was this strange man who was encroaching on *her* beach?

"I'm Gail," she finally said.

"I'm Jimmy."

He didn't know if he should offer to shake hands. That might be weird.

Gail was calming down. She liked the sound of his voice. It wasn't scary. In fact, he seemed as nervous as she was.

It took them ten minutes before they both shook their jitters and were able to be comfortable.

Neither one knew this was the start of a lifetime together.

Now, Jimmy was turning eighty-three on this August 1.

Gail was eighty-one, going to turn eighty-two on December 14.

They'd woken that morning, full of the normal pains and problems they woke up with every day. Growing old was not for the meek, especially when serious health problems came along for the ride.

Jimmy was taking a chemo-break. It'd been two years since the cancer first showed up in his bowel. At times he considered himself lucky to have lasted until then without any serious problems, but once that bit of cancer showed up, everything changed.

Hastily arranged surgery removed part of his bowel, along with his prostate and his bladder. Those organs were collateral damage; they couldn't get the bowel cancer out without taking those, too.

Since then he wore a couple of bags stuck to his body all the time, taking care of his piss and shit.

Maybe that would have been okay if that was all there was to it, but oh no, the cancer had other ideas. After some initially promising checkups, the cancer showed up again. This time in his liver and a spot on one of his lungs.

Jimmy was subjected to radiotherapy and lots of chemo sessions. Lots.

Sometimes the chemo nauseated him, and he wouldn't eat for days on end, even when pushed to it by Gail.

The last rounds, though, were different chemicals, and these ones made him want to eat nonstop.

Weird.

He'd ballooned back up to 275 pounds, and he supposed he would die one day soon, way too big for a standard casket.

Have to make those arrangements before it's too late, he'd often think to himself. But he hadn't ever followed through on that. He didn't want to leave the funeral details to Gail, but it felt like if he went to chat to the local undertaker, he'd be giving up.

Gail's health problems weren't life-threatening, but they were equally debilitating.

She'd had her right knee replaced ten years earlier, and now she'd had to have the left one replaced. She could barely walk, even with crutches, but at least she knew that was temporary. After a few months, she'd be waddling along the same as she always had.

Gail never commented about Jimmy being so overweight. After all, from the day they'd met, she'd never been slim. Now, although she knew she tipped the scale at 204, she wouldn't ever mention that to him.

Jimmy loved Gail with all his heart.

Gail loved Jimmy just as much.

Sixty years together didn't seem nearly enough, but both knew they'd be lucky to celebrate sixty-one.

That morning, Jimmy creaked to life when the dawn sunshine reached down from their bedroom window. He'd been dreaming about that long-lost day when they first met.

It hurt to move at all, and it took a lot of energy just to roll over to face Gail. He was breathing hard and took a moment to catch his breath.

Gail smiled. She knew the effort it took him. It was almost as bad for her.

"We should go to Hibbon's Cove," he said.

She frowned and said, "What are you talking about? It's been years."

Jimmy nodded. "I think it's been twenty years since we were there."

He wondered how that was possible. It was their special place, but somehow, they seemed to have forgotten all about it.

"Twenty years? Really?"

"Yes, maybe twenty-one or twenty-two." He wasn't sure.

"It'd be awfully hard on us," Gail said.

Jimmy shrugged. "Easier today than next year." He paused and added, "I think we deserve to see it one last time."

Gail nodded, knowing she would do anything for the man she loved.

"Should we pack a lunch?"

"Yes. Tuna sandwiches and Coke."

She smiled. That was the same lunch they'd taken almost every time they'd gone to visit the Cove when they were young.

She remembered them running out to meet the tide, catching the waves that crashed over their bodies, laughing as the powerful water pulled them every which way, and grabbing each other's hands to help them stay stable.

Jimmy leaned over and gave his wife a long kiss. He didn't care how much it hurt.

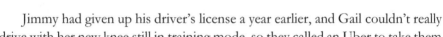

Jimmy had given up his driver's license a year earlier, and Gail couldn't really drive with her new knee still in training mode, so they called an Uber to take them to Hibbon's Cove.

It took them more than a few minutes just to get themselves out of the car. The Uber driver had to help pull each of them out in turn, and he asked, "Are you sure you folks will be okay? You don't look too…"

Stable? Healthy? Alive?

Jimmy didn't know how he had planned to finish that sentence, but he supposed any of those words would fit.

"It's okay," he said. "We come here all the time."

"Okay, well, you can request me when you want to go back home, if you want."

Jimmy nodded and didn't look back as he and Gail shuffled down the skinny little path that led through some trees and eventually down to the Cove.

"Think anyone else has found our little paradise yet?" he asked Gail.

She smiled and looked at him. He still loved that smile.

There was nobody else on the beach, which is what they expected. They set the bag of sandwiches and cans of Coke down and looked out to the water.

It was as beautiful a day as either could remember. The sky was pure blue, a deep blue that somehow seemed to reflect the deep color of the water below. The beach was empty of people, empty of garbage, empty of all signs of humanity.

Jimmy liked that.

It was low tide, so the ocean seemed a very long way from them.

He hesitated, unsure he could walk that far. He didn't have to look at Gail to know she was thinking the same thing. She had brought a single crutch to use on her left side, but it was as hard for her to walk as it was for him.

It wasn't just his cancer or her knee. Their bodies were old, and they just couldn't support their heavy weights like they used to.

Fuck it, he thought. He looked at Gail and smiled.

"We'll never come back. This is our only chance. We can't miss this last chance."

Gail didn't answer for a moment, and he was afraid she would say no.

Finally, she nodded and said, "It's our life."

The first steps were easy enough. The sand was mostly dry, and they didn't really sink in. Jimmy's feet seemed to have some kind of memory, as if they were young and happy to be in the sand.

Twenty years? Really?

Gail used her crutch but was struggling to move. He wanted to take her hand and help, but with him being a bit unstable himself, he was afraid he'd make both of them fall.

They moved slowly, occasionally glancing at each other and smiling support.

The sun bounced off Gail's hair, and it almost brought tears to Jimmy's eyes. She was beautiful.

He had dropped his shirt, so he was wearing only shorts. He no longer owned an actual bathing suit. Gail was wearing an old dress she didn't care about. It was bright yellow, perfectly matching the sun.

The sun itself was beaming down and was hotter than Jimmy could ever remember. Was it always this hot? He was sweating, rivulets of water flushing down the rolls of his upper body.

He didn't see any sweat falling from Gail. *Figures*, he thought.

Gail didn't notice any of that. All she could think of was trying desperately to put one foot in front of the other without falling. She didn't want to look like a fool in front of Jimmy. She'd done that quite enough times in her life, thank you very much.

She never would have tried this without his encouragement. She wanted to look back, to see how far they'd walked out, but she was afraid that if she did, she'd lose her nerve.

She had to be strong for Jimmy.

Jimmy was breathing hard. He was already worn out, and they'd only covered about half the distance to the water.

"Wish it wasn't low tide," he said softly.

"We would have come no matter what," Gail said.

He grunted.

She added, "Back in the day, we'd have run out to the water in seconds. At least this way we get to enjoy the walk."

Jimmy burst out laughing in spite of himself. "Yes," he said, "it's a beautiful walk."

And it was.

His one and only love was walking with him on an amazing afternoon. How could he complain about that?

"It would have been nice to have a cool breeze," he said.

"Sure would."

Jimmy wondered how long they'd been walking, but he wasn't wearing his watch. It wasn't waterproof and he was firm in his belief that he'd be out sitting in the water very soon.

Another ten minutes passed, and they reached the water.

It started with little pools that had held the last of the retreating water. Jimmy wondered if that meant the tide was still going out or if it was coming in now. He hated that his memory was failing. Even ten years ago he would have known how the damned tides worked. Now it was just a big puzzle.

"Oh, it's cold!" said Gail.

"It always feels that way," Jimmy answered. "But, you're right. I'd forgotten that, too."

"It's nice on my toes."

He nodded. "Let's keep going."

They walked more, and Jimmy tried to convince himself it was getting easier. His feet were all wet now, water up to his ankles. The cool water was soothing the pain in his feet, but it wasn't helping the pain in the rest of his body.

He felt weak, and he gritted his teeth to try to gain control of himself. He would *not* fall down in front of Gail.

"Should we stop here?" she asked.

"Just a little farther," he whispered. He wanted to stop there, too, but it would be like they were little two-year-olds splashing in the water on their first trip to the beach.

He was a man, not a baby.

He walked another step and Gail followed.

"Just up to our knees," he promised.

She didn't answer, and he wasn't sure if she was okay with that decision or not, but he really needed them to go a little farther. Just a bit. Far enough that he would leave the toddler area behind him.

"Remember we'd come out here with our Frisbee and stand fifty feet apart, throwing it to each other? Other times we'd toss a football," said Jimmy.

"We'll not be doing that today, my dear."

"Oh, I know. It's just the good memories flooding me."

"Me too."

"Sometimes we'd go a bit deeper and you'd stand on my shoulders, looking like the Statue of Liberty. I'd crouch down and then push you up as high as I could, and you'd do a freedom dive into the water."

She smiled, and this time she reached out and took his hand.

"I remember," she said.

They stood still and looked out together. The water wasn't up to his knees, but they'd gone as far as he could manage. He was exhausted.

He turned to her and smiled. A tear fell down his cheek.

"Jimmy? What's wrong?"

He was choked up with emotion and couldn't answer her. He just shook his head. Then he sniffed and tried to get control of himself. He made a downward motion with his hands and both of them took some very cautious movements to lower themselves to sit on the sand.

Jimmy was almost out of breath. He tried to take a deep long breath, but it was hard. *That* was the effect of the chemo, he was sure.

He looked back to shore. From the perspective of sitting there, the shore looked forever away.

"Are you okay?" Gail's voice sounded concerned.

"I'm fine. I just needed to catch my breath. How are you doing?"

"Well, I don't know how I'm going to get back up, but right now I feel fine!" She laughed. She'd used her crutch to get herself down to the sandy ground. Now she set it on the other side from her. She kept a hand on it so it wouldn't float away.

Jimmy watched the waves lap at them. When they slapped his belly, it sounded like a tiny cheering section.

Clap, clap, clap.

He tried to shimmy himself a little bit closer to Gail, but he couldn't manage it. The sand was sucking his body down, and his eighty-three-year-old muscles didn't have the strength to argue.

Gail said, "I think we were sitting right around here when you asked me to marry you."

Jimmy opened his mouth in surprise. He'd forgotten about proposing to her here, but that was right! That was exactly right!

"You're as beautiful now as you were then."

She smiled and then looked out to the water. "I think the tide is coming in."

Jimmy glanced over and saw waves that looked a little bit bigger than he'd expected. They continued to slap at his belly. "I think you're right. Might make it easier to walk back."

"I'll take all the help I can get!"

*If I can't move my whole body over…*he thought. He lay down and supported himself on his right elbow. Then he could reach her with his outstretched left arm. He just wanted to touch her.

"Sixty years," he said.

She was lost in thought and didn't reply.

They sat for thirty minutes, each swimming in their own memories of the many wonderful times they'd spent in this same water. They'd make comments occasionally, but all they really needed was to touch hands.

Gail was also lying down now, trying to regain some of the strength she'd lost by walking out this far. Her knee throbbed and screamed to her brain to not be so fucking stupid, but she ignored that, preferring only to think of wonderful memories with her husband.

"Do you think we should go back?" asked Gail.

Jimmy really didn't want to, but he knew she was right. They'd done what they came for, and the memories of this day would have to satisfy them in the future.

That's not such a bad thing, he thought.

He was still lying down, and he pulled his legs toward himself.

They hurt and didn't want to move. The tide was indeed coming in, and he was surprised that his legs were totally covered. How did that happen?

He took a different strategy and leaned over to his right, bringing his left arm around as if he was going to do a push-up.

As if.

That didn't work, either. He didn't have the strength to push himself up.

Not even close.

"Sweetie, I think I'm going to need you to help me up."

Jimmy was embarrassed at having to ask for help.

Getting old really sucks.

He kept trying to move his body around to get some traction, but nothing seemed to work. He was stuck lying in the water and had no way to help himself.

"Good thing I've got you here," he said.

He glanced over at Gail, but she was struggling, too. That's when he noticed her crutch had somehow gotten loose and was floating independently toward the shore.

He'd have to help her walk, once they got up.

That's okay. I'm still her knight in shining armor. I can do that.

Now, Gail was struggling with her own breathing. She'd pushed and pushed but she was too frail to get her own body lifted off the sandy bottom.

Stupid fat woman.

She never called herself fat out loud, but she'd used that term her whole life in her deepest, most private thoughts. Now, she was glad the word hadn't slipped out. She felt totally useless. What kind of a woman can't even stand up?

She was out of breath and hadn't moved an inch.

In frustration, she looked over at Jimmy. He was squirming around, having as much trouble as she was.

She needed his help, but he needed hers.

"This is ridiculous," she said.

The water lapped on her belly, and she wanted to yell at the damned ocean. It was like the tide was laughing at her.

How the hell could we both be stuck out here?

More importantly, how can we get back to shore?

Gail tried to turn herself over, to try to crawl, but she couldn't make the transition. She had no muscle power to push her body over. It was like trying to use a pitchfork to turn over Mount Everest.

"Jimmy, what are we going to do?"

Jimmy had no answer for her. He kept squirming as much as she was, but he wasn't having any more luck than her.

Finally, he stopped. He was overcome with the effort and saw black spots in front of his eyes. He knew he was about to faint, but he couldn't allow that. The water was only a foot or so deep, but it was enough for him to drown.

He pressed his eyes closed, as if that would somehow stop him from blacking out, and maybe it worked. He kept conscious. Barely. In a corner of his mind, he heard Gail calling to him, but he couldn't make out any of her words.

Jimmy wanted to just turn back the clock and not have this crazy idea of going out into the water.

What was he thinking?

Water splashed onto his face, and he flashed his eyes open.

"The water," he mumbled.

"What?"

He took as deep a breath as he could. "Water is rising. Fast."

Gail noticed for the first time. The water level had been rising so slowly, it hadn't registered, but she could see it was higher now. *Much* higher.

"Oh, God…"

"Don't panic," said Jimmy.

"But, what can we do?"

"I…I don't know."

Gail tried to look back toward shore, to see how far away her crutch was, but she couldn't see it. Water was lapping in her face, too.

"Jimmy, I'm afraid."

He didn't hear her. A larger wave had splashed onto his face, and he'd started choking from the water he'd swallowed.

With the tide coming in, his body wasn't as pinned to the sandy bottom, but it didn't seem to matter. He still couldn't find the energy to move his body around or to sit up. He was paralyzed, with no energy reserves. The cancer treatments had sucked all the life from him, and now it was leaving him for dead

The next wave came quickly, and then the next.

Gail couldn't really see much, because she was battling her own fight. It seemed like the waves had just started a battle that only they could win.

Her knee was killing her, but she knew it was old age that had sapped all her strength.

After another dozen waves splashed over her harder and harder, she knew she wouldn't last long.

All she wanted was to hold Jimmy's hand one more time.

She reached out, but she wasn't sure if she was touching him or if it was just her imagination.

The waves kept rolling over the two lifelong lovers, and eventually they both stopped fighting.

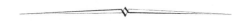

It was three days later when Allan and Theresa Gilson walked through the pathway to find their way down to Hibbon's Cove. It was their own private beach. As far as they knew, nobody else ever came here.

This was their third wedding anniversary. They'd made a habit of coming to the beach each August 4, and they hoped it would be that way their entire lives.

After all, this was where they had met, five years earlier.

They laughed and ran down to the beach. As they got close, they flipped off their sandals and kissed, a long loving kiss that would start their little anniversary off on the right foot.

As they broke the kiss, Theresa pointed out a bag that was sitting on the sand. They went to look and found there was some sandwiches and a couple of cans of Coke.

"That's odd," Allan said.

"I guess somebody else knows about this place after all."

"I guess."

They looked around. It was Theresa who saw them.

"Over there."

They ran two hundred feet down the beach and out toward the water. As they got close, they could see the two bodies. A man and a woman, partly eaten by birds and crabs. Their bodies were partially under the sand, and great patches of skin were peeled off. Their faces were horrible. Grotesque. Barely recognizable as human.

Theresa and Allan couldn't help tears falling from their eyes when they saw that the corpses were holding hands.

REMEMBERING FRANK

by Terry M. West

Tribes form. Even in the solitary pursuit of writing. It's easy for a socially awkward or painfully shy writer to disappear in plain sight or be taken for an arrogant snob. It's easy to be an outsider. Without effort.

You try to surround yourself with like-minded souls to sympathize or encourage. And those relationships may strengthen or falter given the opportunities you or an ally receive. Or don't receive. At the end of it all, it's just you and the keyboard. That's how it always ends, when you think about it. People go up the ladder and some never look back or only long enough to wave *ta-ta*. Others give up the quill altogether because they don't feel like they're getting anywhere.

After a long creative sabbatical that was broken around 2011, I got back on the Horror Writer Express (coach seating, of course). I made a conscious decision to worry about the work and not the bullshit and politics of it. I can come across as a pretty sociable fellow, but that's taken years of practice and performance. I'm Spidey cracking wise in the middle of taking on the Sinister Six. But even with all that bravado and *fuck anyone but the readers*, it's hard sometimes to see the kids on the playground that you can't join. And you know it's really not *them*.

See, that's what I loved about Frank. I didn't have him in my life as long as most of the contributors here paying their respects. We'd been connected on social media which can mean everything or nothing. We were united pretty closely on politics. I knew he was a well-regarded reviewer. He knew I was an author.

When my collection, *Gruesome*, was released, it had an introduction by Hunter Shea. And Frank loved Hunter (shit, who doesn't?). So he requested a review copy of it and wrote it up for his blog. It was a good review and it made me feel so much more in the *club*, I guess you could say. His kind words helped me tremendously. It helped with sales and it definitely helped my self-esteem. We communicated here and there after that. I tried to share his articles/reviews whenever I saw them. He'd do the same for me.

I think if more people were as genuine and giving as Frank was, we'd all run in much happier circles in this crazy club of ours. What impressed me the most about Frank was how hard he worked on his reviews, despite the health issues and treatments that plagued him. He was devoted to the genre and its writers. As devoted as one would be to family. And God knows, we loved him.

I didn't have him in my life nearly long enough. And if I'd known him twenty years, I'd probably feel the same. I'm jealous of those who were able to spend time with him. I would have loved to shake his hand and tell him, eye to eye, what he meant to me. To all of us. And I'm confident that would speak for all of us. But I think he knew.

God bless you, Frank. You were cherished, my friend. I'll miss that disarming smile of yours and the mischievous twinkle in your eye.

VARIANCE

by Kenneth W. Cain

They followed Jackson everywhere. Even in the middle of the night, they would be out there desperately looking for him. He knew that even before he started thinking about escape.

Do they even sleep?

Jackson didn't, not lately. He lay awake most nights, and even when he did get some sleep, he woke far earlier than Tessa. Not that it mattered. No one would bother him in that house. They kept things peaceful there, and right now, peace was the last thing he needed. What Jackson needed was chaos, not that having them following him around everywhere wasn't a kind of chaos. It just wasn't the sort he needed at the moment.

Even now he imagined they were communicating through their tiny earpieces, trying to locate him, sending orders to spread out to cover more ground, search the city in a grid-like fashion. They were intolerable men and women, always by his side. He'd had trouble shaking them as of late too, and that was all he really wanted. To get away from them and figure out what was going on in his head, clear his thoughts.

They're worse than my mother.

Careful not to wake Tessa, he slipped on his robe and snuck into the bathroom. He hefted the lid off the back of the toilet and secured a bottle of vodka he'd hidden there weeks ago, then he replaced the lid. A long swig ensured that he could maintain the numbness he'd started feeling earlier this afternoon a little longer. It was cheap vodka—bottom-shelf stuff—but it didn't taste bad, even if the bottle was sweating toilet water. Besides, toilet vodka was better than chugging large bottles of mouthwash any day. And he should know, given that two bottles of mouthwash served as his first drinks of the day, mostly because he was brushing his teeth at the time. A weak concoction, it was enough to start the numbing process. He also found it easier to explain his minty-fresh breath to Tessa than he did the alcohol. She'd been on his case a lot ever since his last relapse, and frankly he didn't want to hear it. Not today. If only the mouthwash had sated his addiction.

Even that wasn't a huge problem. He kept bottles hidden throughout the house, because that's what alcoholics do—even when they aren't drinking every day, they hide little secrets. It was his failsafe, an "I'll drink you later, when I have a bad day" sanctuary. Even that alone, the act of hiding bottles—some in the toilet, one behind the washer, a few outside buried in the garden—was an addiction. There were seven bottles on the property he knew about, perhaps more he'd forgotten, but those would do him no good, anyway. When he wasn't "self-medicating," he was collecting and hiding, taking half-empty bottles out of the kitchen and running off with them while no one was looking. That in itself was a herculean task given how watchful they were of his activities. Not one of those men or women who followed him around would let him take a sip, not even if his life depended upon on. Tessa had instructed them well.

He hadn't consumed a single drop since his migraines went away. When they returned with a vengeance last week, he'd tried not to drink. A few times, he took the toilet vodka out, stared at the bottle, felt it in his hands, but he hadn't tasted it. Once, he even took the lid off, smelled the spirits, and actually got a boner from that sweet aroma. But still, he hadn't partaken of it. For some reason, the mouthwash threw him off the wagon, and he'd been drinking all day ever since. Thankfully, he'd gotten pretty good at hiding his drunkenness, so he was able to fool everyone around him, at least for a while.

It was Dr. Hamlin who first referred to his drinking as self-medicating. Hamlin had prescribed Jackson these tiny blue pills to ease his pain, but they never seemed to work. Or maybe they did but then their effectiveness stopped after some time. Whatever the case, it always came to a point where he felt getting soused was his only escape. He realized only now that he'd already consumed all of the little secrets he knew about, save for this bottle of vodka. And he needed the alcohol now more than ever, because it was working on his migraine. He felt numb…for now.

I'm going to need a refill soon.

He snuck out through the kitchen. With the staff not yet at work, he went unseen. From there, he made his way through the house to the back lawn and encountered some security personnel, though they didn't appear to notice him. He tiptoed along the side of the house and hid among some bushes, where he overheard two men talking about the most recent Nationals game. He saw others too, men and women stationed here and there, all of them wide awake and ready should he require their help.

They're everywhere. He stayed where he was for now. *I need a distraction.*

Better yet, he needed a clear path off this property. Without that, he wouldn't get far without them. And if they caught him, they'd take away the alcohol; that much was certain. They would never let him drink, let alone get drunk.

Jackson tiptoed across the lawn. Perhaps they were distracted or didn't anticipate anything at this early hour. Whatever the case, he made it almost the entire way to the front gate without being seen. There he waited, unsure of what to—

The gate opened. A car rolled through, stopping to chat to a security individual. He didn't care who it was or why they were here. All Jackson cared about was the opportunity, which he used to squat-run through the gate unseen, staying down to make sure he kept out of sight. Only once he was well down the sidewalk did he relax and start walking upright again. He must have looked rather foolish, but he didn't think anyone saw him, so he celebrated his escape with a swig of vodka.

Crap. It's almost gone.

He wandered along, unaware of his appearance. He suspected he didn't look so sanitary in his robe. If anyone saw him like this, that would only serve to cement in the public's mind just how far he'd sunk. Sure, this was rock bottom, but it was necessary. Truthfully, he hadn't felt like himself in months. But everything started to make sense this afternoon, when he snuck into the kitchen for a nip of cooking sherry.

He drank the rest of the vodka and tossed the bottle into a nearby trashcan.

Something bigger than migraines was wrong with him, that was what he felt. It was almost as if the alcohol had unlocked something inside of him, perhaps a power or maybe some internal insight, something cosmic even. He couldn't be sure, not yet, which was why he needed more alcohol fast. Before he could worry about that, he needed to work on making himself invisible, near as he could. Because once the security found out he was missing, they'd be out looking for him in droves.

Plenty of vagrants camped out under the bridges. He walked among them mostly unnoticed until he found what he was looking for.

"Hey, buddy," Jackson said.

The drowsy man looked up at him. "Whaddaya want?"

"Can I buy that jacket and hat off you?" Jackson dug into his pockets for his wallet and fingered out two Franklins.

"What? Sheesh. No—" The guy saw the bills, recognized the profile on them, and changed his mind fast. "You betcha." He couldn't shrug off the coat fast enough.

"How about that, too?"

The guy looked down at the ground, at the half-empty bottle of whiskey. "Hmm… I don't kn—"

"I'll throw another hundo your way."

The guy bunched up the jacket and slapped the hat on top, then plopped them down in Jackson's hands. Reluctantly, the man retrieved the bottle and shoved it into Jackson's fist. Jackson extended the bills and the man snatched up the cash.

"Say, do I know you?" The man scrutinized him up and down. Did people like this even watch TV? "You look familiar."

"Nah. I'm a nobody like everyone else here. We good?"

Without another word, the man staggered away, no doubt rushing off to wait for the liquor store to open. Jackson watched him until he was well out of sight.

After sliding the jacket over his shoulders, Jackson instantly became aware of the filth and stench rising from the cloth. The coat smelled like Death himself had worn the garment and soiled it. And the hat wasn't much better. Who knew what critters might be rejoicing the second he put it on his head? For now, he didn't have any other options because he couldn't risk anyone recognizing him.

He staggered out of the alley, bounced off the corner of the building, and struggled for a brief second to stay on the sidewalk. There weren't many people out this early in the morning, a few people walking their dogs or jogging, maybe heading home from an unruly night of partying or catching an early breakfast. A woman hurried by, her expression grave, obviously frightened by his appearance. He must have looked homeless because she took a wide berth to avoid him, which was fine by him. The breeze of her passing left sweet-smelling scents in the sweltering night air among hints of sewer gas and rat waste. She made it twenty yards before she looked back with disgust.

Well screw you too, lady.

A TV program flashed in a nearby window, what looked like an electronics store. He stumbled across the street until he was in front of the window and steadied himself on the glass. Leaning there, he took a long slug off the whisky. Despite everything, it didn't taste that bad. He'd expected much worse, a sort of urine taste given the condition of the man he'd gotten it from. It wasn't the good stuff, what he preferred to drink, but something the stores kept in the discount aisles because it could peel paint off the walls. And truth was, Jackson didn't mind the heartburn that followed. It kept him awake, conscious of his surroundings, able to make quick decisions.

He observed the animated news anchor. That didn't intrigue him so much as his own dim reflection in the glass, the man staring back at him.

What am I doing here?

His defined eyebrows and powder-blue eyes had served him well over the years. They'd helped him secure jobs, gain confidence from men in high places, even with the ladies. And though he couldn't see it with this hat on, he'd had thicker hair back then though, and hadn't needed a godforsaken comb-over. God, he hated getting older. He doubted he could score even an intern these days, despite his position. Struggling to see his younger self in the reflection, he squinted but failed to see any semblance of himself. Yet he'd glimpsed something for sure.

A quick sip of whisky made him waver. He righted himself and leaned back against the glass, studying his faint blurred reflection more closely.

What was that?

He didn't have a clue until he pushed back, wobbling on both legs. His eyes widened in anticipation of a fall. Only his reflection hadn't reciprocated.

What sort of witchcraft is this?

No, that wasn't it. This wasn't magic. This was…

You're drunk, idiot.

He took a big swig and forced an awkward smile to his face as he observed the reflection's effort. Now he saw it quite well. With his free hand, he felt his face and realized his reflection didn't match his expression. Not exactly. This was what he'd been feeling all day, as though he weren't truly himself, not entirely. Like he was harboring—

An imposter?

Why hadn't he noticed it before?

He swirled the bottle in his hand, considering this question, and it hit him. Whatever *this* was, the alcohol somehow weakened its ability to hide from him. Sensing this truth, Jackson took a long drink and rested his forehead against the glass, staring into the dark pitted eyes of his reflection.

"How did you get in there?"

No answer, but he hadn't expected one. He wasn't even sure it could communicate with him.

"Hey, buddy," a man said from behind him. "You okay?"

Of course he wasn't. He decided to ignore the guy, seeing the man's unwavering concern behind his reflection in the window.

Just go away.

He didn't though, so Jackson grunted. That must have been enough because the guy moved on.

Returning his attention to his reflection, Jackson thought back over the years, searching for clues. He remembered tearing his ACL in his senior year of college football.

One of the doctors could have transplanted something inside of me then?

Or maybe it happened earlier than that. Perhaps as far back as his childhood. Maybe even birth. After all, he'd had these migraines for as long as he could remember.

"How patient were you in selecting a host?"

Again, no answer. Somehow this all felt so…

Familiar.

Like he'd done this before, perhaps many times even throughout his life. Though he could recall no such encounter.

What does that mean?

Was this *thing* somehow wiping his memories? Selecting what he would and would not remember? The magnitude of this notion froze him. His legs weakened. All of his fingers—

"Whoa." The bottle had nearly slipped right out of his hand. Almost as if something were controlling him, trying to make him drop it. He tightened his grip and took another drink.

"I'm right. This isn't the first time, is it?"

Had this thing chosen him, groomed him, convinced him that these were his choices? If so, it must not have expected him to develop a fondness for alcohol. But how did it get there?

His parents had what most people referred to as *old* money. He never questioned where it came from, or why he'd attended the finest schools, as he always assumed they'd inherited the money. So he had no reason to question their intentions. Until now.

Could they be in on this?

Could everything down to his very beliefs, his worries, all his wants and desires, have been fabricated by some...*parasite?*

Christ.

Maybe whatever was growing inside of him released some sort of anesthetizing agent, a chemical that kept him sedated while it further secured its hold over him. Whatever the case, it had failed this time.

He waved the bottle at his reflection. "Tonight, I have this to stop you." Lifting the bottle to his lips, dissatisfaction filled him when he realized he'd near emptied it. Angered, he kept his voice low. "I know you're in there. Now answer me."

His reflection remained silent. That man only gazed back at him with troubled eyes.

"Excuse me," a woman said.

When he turned, he was met by a soft face and a bright smile. There were more people out now. Daybreak was approaching.

What time is it?

He nearly lost his balance when he glanced off at the horizon, staring at the tip of the Washington Monument, seeing how the sun painted its edges a bright orange.

"I thought it was you," she said. "Do you mind?"

She showed him her cellphone. Without fully understanding, he nodded, sliding the bottle inside the jacket so she wouldn't see it. She huddled up beside him, and he wrapped one arm around her shoulders, almost using her to support himself. Surely she could smell the coat, the alcohol, all of it. But she didn't seem to notice any of it.

She raised her phone, he put on his best fake smile, and she took the selfie. "Thank you," she said, bowing once as she went on her way.

He watched her for a few seconds, somewhat troubled by her intrusion. If she recognized him, others would too. And if word got out where he was, he would need to run. He hoped she didn't post that photo to social media. Not because of the way he looked, but because they scoured social media for that sort of thing. If they saw that picture, they'd find him. Now he regretted taking the photo, and if he hadn't been drunk, he might not have. But he needed to stay inebriated, so he was at the mercy of his drunkenness to a degree. Still, he had to stay ahead of this. Hurrying away, he took a left, then a right. He had no idea where to go or how to get there, only that he needed to keep moving and should stick to the back alleys—

A strange thought occurred to him. Had Tessa never noticed any of this? She was the person closest to him. It unnerved him to think she hadn't seen anything out of the ordinary.

All these years and not a single complaint.

Well, that wasn't entirely true. She'd found a bottle or two, and she'd caught him drinking the mouthwash on more than one occasion. She had plenty to say on each occasion.

What if she's in on this, too?

His frustration erupted. "Why won't you answer me? I know you're in there."

Still, there was no response.

"All right then, I'll just drink you out."

He spotted a liquor store at the end of the alleyway and walked with purpose. As he returned to the sidewalk, he passed store windows. He glanced into each store as he passed and barely caught it—his reflection shaking its head. He came to an abrupt stop, steadying himself before the window of a law office.

"I knew it."

He waited but nothing came. If nothing else though, seeing his reflection shaking its head had been a brief validation of his worst fears. Something was inside of him. Either that or he'd gone completely mad.

In the background, the morning's earliest birds chirped. Cars began their morning commute, their engines rumbling down the road, their wheels crunching displaced gravel. Someone laid on their horn, jarring him out of his thoughts. If not for that, he might not have felt the extra weight in his jacket pocket.

"Ah ha!"

He removed a flask. The vagrant had forgotten about it. After uncapping it, he gave a sniff. It smelled potent, but he took copious sips and breathed deeply afterward. Brandy wasn't as tasty, but it would do the trick to keep this imposter at bay.

Tipping the flask as if toasting his reflection, Jackson said, "Why are you here?"

No answer, as expected. But he did recall several instances where he'd gone against his gut feeling.

Like Sandra Holloway.

He'd chickened out with proposing to Sandra. At least that was how he remembered it. Although he did love Tessa, he hadn't at the time. Everything that followed happened too fast: engaged after only three months, married after six. Yet he could recollect little else about those days.

She'd been so agreeable, too.

What she'd identified as true love seemed nothing of the sort now. But maybe she wasn't in on this so much as she might be hosting her own parasite.

Oh, Tessa…

Other instances bothered him: the career path he'd chosen, the place they called home, his children. But when he saw himself on a TV, a recent discrepancy bothered him. He'd long supported conservation, sharing his concerns with Tessa. Together they'd weighed the pros and cons of a program that might someday save this planet. Yet, when the time came for action, he'd opposed all of it. Were there special interest groups involved? Yes, of course, as always. This had been something else though, something that felt like…like being drunk. Like losing control.

Afterward, he and Tessa celebrated the variance. They had laughed that night, and made love. This decision, it would affect millions, and they'd felt so happy…

What have I done?

He realized then he hadn't been the only one. The vote hadn't even been close. His reflection scrutinized him. He did so right back.

"You're trying to exterminate us, aren't you?"

No answer.

"And I've done nothing to stop you."

Right then, his reflection grinned, something that physically made him shiver.

He struck a finger at his reflection and took two quick tugs off the flask. "Well, I won't do it anymore." He stood tall. "Do you hear me?"

At first, only silence. Then an alarming voice penetrated his thoughts. *No.*

Silence returned, followed by the awful pain behind his right eye. He pinched the bridge of his nose until the ache subsided.

"You can hurt me all you want, but this ends here."

He drank the rest of the brandy and returned the empty flask to his pocket. His eyes fell on the liquor store down the street. He would refresh himself as soon as the store opened.

Laughter invaded his thoughts, and the pain returned tenfold. *You will try and fail,* the voice said.

Jackson shook a fist at the window. His reflection shook one back. But his anger subsided when he noticed the lights whirring behind his reflection.

They're close.

He spun on uneasy legs and ran, but made it only five yards before he tripped and fell. Somehow, he knew it wasn't an accident. A few people stopped and watched him scramble back to his knees. He didn't care, rising and stumbling back down an alleyway. Half a dozen vehicles peeled to a stop behind him. A quick glance back revealed that several bystanders had pointed out his escape route.

Jackson was well ahead of them by the time they entered the alley. As he ran, he checked several doors, finding all of them locked. With no other path, his only option was to continue down this alley. He neared the end, seeing the street, and considered where to go next. A black four-wheel drive vehicle screeched to a halt at the end of the alley. Two agents leaped out and came at him. Now he had no choice but to fight.

He dodged them best he could, his equilibrium off, trying to force his way around them. One of the agents seized his left arm and pulled. Another took his right. Together, they brought his escape to a quick end.

As they led him to one of the vehicles, he watched the other agents deal with the growing crowd, especially those who had taken pictures or videos with their cell phones. None of it would ever be seen.

"This way, Mr. President," a woman said.

They led him to one of the vehicles, gentle but insistent. He ducked inside and the door closed. Seconds later, the motorcade raced off toward home.

The agent in the passenger seat turned to him, rested his arm on the divider, and lifted his shades. "That was a close one, sir."

Disappointed, Jackson answered. "Yes—"

The man's face twisted with anger. "You be quiet!"

Jackson shuddered, realizing only then that these men weren't here for him, but for his parasite. Dejected, he leaned his head against the cool glass. Even in the early morning light, he could see a wicked grin spread across his reflection's face in the window.

I AM THE DOORWAY

by Stephen King

Richard and I sat on my porch, looking out over the dunes to the Gulf. The smoke from his cigar drifted mellowly in the air, keeping the mosquitoes at a safe distance. The water was a cool aqua, the sky a deeper, truer blue. It was a pleasant combination.

"You are the doorway," Richard repeated thoughtfully. "You are sure you killed the boy—you didn't just dream it?"

"I didn't dream it. And I didn't kill him, either—I told you that. They did. I am the doorway."

Richard sighed. "You buried him?"

"Yes."

"You remember where?"

"Yes." I reached into my breast pocket and got a cigarette. My hands were awkward with their covering of bandages. They itched abominably. "If you want to see it, you'll have to get the dune buggy. You can't roll this"—I indicated my wheelchair—" through the sand." Richard's dune buggy was a 1959 VW with pillow-sized tires. He collected driftwood in it. Ever since he retired from the real estate business in Maryland he had been living on Key Caroline and building driftwood sculptures which he sold to the winter tourists at shameless prices.

He puffed his cigar and looked out at the Gulf. "Not yet. Will you tell me once more?"

I sighed and tried to light my cigarette. He took the matches away from me and did it himself. I puffed twice, dragging deep. The itch in my fingers was maddening.

"All right" I said. "Last night at seven I was out here, looking at the Gulf and smoking, just like now, and—"

"Go further back," he invited.

"Further?"

"Tell me about the flight."

I shook my head. "Richard, we've been through it and through it. There's nothing—"

The seamed and fissured face was as enigmatic as one of his own driftwood sculptures. "You may remember," he said. "Now you may remember."

"Do you think so?"

"Possibly. And when you're through, we can look for the grave."

"The grave," I said. It had a hollow, horrible ring, darker than anything, darker even than all that terrible ocean Cory and I had sailed through five years ago. Dark, dark, dark.

Beneath the bandages, my new eyes stared blindly into the darkness the bandages forced on them. They itched.

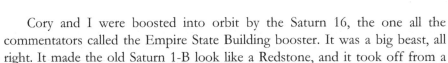

Cory and I were boosted into orbit by the Saturn 16, the one all the commentators called the Empire State Building booster. It was a big beast, all right. It made the old Saturn 1-B look like a Redstone, and it took off from a bunker two hundred feet deep—it had to, to keep from taking half of Cape Kennedy with it.

We swung around the earth, verifying all our systems, and then did our inject. Headed out for Venus. We left a Senate fighting over an appropriations bill for further deep-space exploration, and a bunch of NASA people praying that we would find something, anything.

"It don't matter what," Don Lovinger, Project Zeus's private whiz kid, was very fond of saying when he'd had a few. "You got all the gadgets, plus five souped-up TV cameras and a nifty little telescope with a zillion lenses and filters. Find some gold or platinum. Better yet, find some nice, dumb little blue men for us to study and exploit and feel superior to. Anything. Even the ghost of Howdy Doody would be a start."

Cory and I were anxious enough to oblige, if we could. Nothing had worked for the deep-space program. From Borman, Anders, and Lovell, who orbited the moon in '68 and found an empty, forbidding world that looked like dirty beach sand, to Markhan and Jacks, who touched down on Mars eleven years later to find an arid wasteland of frozen sand and a few struggling lichens, the deep-space program had been an expensive bust. And there had been casualties—Pedersen and Lederer, eternally circling the sun when all at once nothing worked on the second-to-last Apollo flight. John Davis, whose little orbiting observatory was holed by a meteoroid in a one-in-a-thousand fluke. No, the space program was hardly swinging along. The way things looked, the Venus orbit might be our last chance to say we told you so.

It was sixteen days out—we ate a lot of concentrates, played a lot of gin, and swapped a cold back and forth—and from the tech side it was a milk run. We lost an air-moisture converter on the third day out, went to backup, and that was all, except for nits and nats, until re-entry. We watched Venus grow from a star to a quarter to a milky crystal ball, swapped jokes with Huntsville Control, listened to tapes of Wagner and the Beatles, tended to automated experiments which had to do with everything from measurements of the solar wind to deep-space navigation. We did two midcourse corrections, both of them infinitesimal, and nine days into the flight Cory went outside and banged on the retractable DESA until it decided to operate. There was nothing else out of the ordinary until…

"DESA," Richard said. "What's that?"

"An experiment that didn't pan out. NASA-ese for Deep Space Antenna—we were broadcasting pi in high-frequency pulses for anyone who cared to listen." I rubbed my fingers against my pants, but it was no good; if anything, it made it worse. "Same idea as that radio telescope in West Virginia—you know, the one that listens to the stars. Only instead of listening, we were transmitting, primarily to the deeper space planets—Jupiter, Saturn, Uranus. If there's any intelligent life out there, it was taking a nap."

"Only Cory went out?"

"Yes. And if he brought in any interstellar plague, the telemetry didn't show it."

"Still—"

"It doesn't matter," I said crossly. "Only the here and now matters. They killed the boy last night, Richard. It wasn't a nice thing to watch—or feel. His head…it exploded. As if someone had scooped out his brains and put a hand grenade in his skull."

"Finish the story," he said.

I laughed hollowly. "What's to tell?"

We went into an eccentric orbit around the planet. It was radical and deteriorating, three twenty by seventy-six miles. That was on the first swing. The second swing our apogee was even higher, the perigee lower. We had a max of four orbits. We made all four. We got a good look at the planet. Also over six hundred stills and God knows how many feet of film.

The cloud cover is equal parts methane, ammonia, dust, and flying shit. The whole planet looks like the Grand Canyon in a wind tunnel. Cory estimated windspeed at about 600 mph near the surface. Our probe beeped all the way down and then went out with a squawk. We saw no vegetation and no sign of life. Spectroscope indicated only traces of the valuable minerals. And that was Venus. Nothing but nothing—except it scared me. It was like circling a haunted house in the middle of deep space. I know how unscientific that sounds, but I was scared gutless until we got out of there. I think if our rockets hadn't gone off, I would have cut my throat on the way down. It's not like the moon. The moon is desolate but somehow antiseptic. That world we saw was utterly unlike anything that anyone has ever seen. Maybe it's a good thing that cloud cover is there. It was like a skull that's been picked clean—that's the closest I can get.

On the way back we heard the Senate had voted to halve space-exploration funds. Cory said something like "looks like we're back in the weather-satellite business, Artie." But I was almost glad. Maybe we don't belong out there.

Twelve days later Cory was dead and I was crippled for life. We bought all our trouble on the way down. The chute was fouled. How's that for life's little ironies? We'd been in space for over a month, gone further than any humans had ever gone, and it all ended the way it did because some guy was in a hurry for his coffee break and let a few lines get fouled.

We came down hard. A guy that was in one of the copters said it looked like a gigantic baby falling out of the sky, with the placenta trailing after it. I lost consciousness when we hit.

I came to when they were taking me across the deck of the *Portland.* They hadn't even had a chance to roll up the red carpet we were supposed to've walked on. I was bleeding. Bleeding and being hustled up to the infirmary over a red carpet that didn't look anywhere near as red as I did...

"...I was in Bethesda for two years. They gave me the Medal of Honor and a lot of money and this wheelchair. I came down here the next year. I like to watch the rockets take off."

"I know," Richard said. He paused. "Show me your hands."

"No." It came out very quickly and sharply. "I can't let them see. I've told you that."

"It's been five years," Richard said. "Why now, Arthur? Can you tell me that?"

"I don't know. I don't know! Maybe whatever it is has a long gestation period. Or who's to say I even got it out there? Whatever it was might have entered me in Fort Lauderdale. Or right here on this porch, for all I know."

Richard sighed and looked out over the water, now reddish with the late-evening sun. "I'm trying. Arthur, I don't want to think that you are losing your mind."

"If I have to, I'll show you my hands," I said. It cost me an effort to say it. "But only if I have to."

Richard stood up and found his cane. He looked old and frail. "I'll get the dune buggy. We'll look for the boy."

"Thank you, Richard."

He walked out toward the rutted dirt track that led to his cabin—I could just see the roof of it over the Big Dune, the one that runs almost the whole length of Key Caroline. Over the water toward the Cape, the sky had gone an ugly plum color, and the sound of thunder came faintly to my ears.

I didn't know the boy's name but I saw him every now and again, walking along the beach at sunset, with his sieve under his arm. He was tanned almost black by the sun, and all he was ever clad in was a frayed pair of denim cutoffs.

On the far side of Key Caroline there is a public beach, and an enterprising young man can make perhaps as much as five dollars on a good day, patiently sieving the sand for buried quarters or dimes. Every now and then I would wave to him and he would wave back, both of us noncommittal, strangers yet brothers, year-round dwellers set against a sea of money spending, Cadillac-driving, loud-mouthed tourists. I imagine he lived in the small village clustered around the post office about a half mile further down.

When he passed by that evening I had already been on the porch for an hour, immobile, watching. I had taken off the bandages earlier. The itching had been intolerable, and it was always better when they could look through their eyes.

It was a feeling like no other in the world—as if I were a portal just slightly ajar through which they were peeking at a world which they hated and feared. But the worst part was that I could see, too, in a way. Imagine your mind transported into a body of a housefly, a housefly looking into your own face with a thousand eyes. Then perhaps you can begin to see why I kept my hands bandaged even when there was no one around to see them.

It began in Miami. I had business there with a man named Cresswell, an investigator from the Navy Department. He checks up on me once a year—for a while I was as close as anyone ever gets to the classified stuff our space program has. I don't know just what it is he looks for; a shifty gleam in the eye, maybe, or maybe a scarlet letter on my forehead. God knows why. My pension is large enough to be almost embarrassing.

Cresswell and I were sitting on the terrace of his hotel room, sipping drinks and discussing the future of the U.S. space program. It was about three-fifteen. My fingers began to itch. It wasn't a bit gradual. It was switched on like electric current. I mentioned it to Cresswell.

"So you picked up some poison ivy on that scrofulous little island," he said, grinning.

"The only foliage on Key Caroline is a little palmetto scrub," I said. "Maybe it's the seven-year itch." I looked down at my hands. Perfectly ordinary hands. But itchy.

Later in the afternoon I signed the same old paper ("I do solemnly swear that I have neither received nor disclosed and divulged information which would...") and drove myself back to the Key. I've got an old Ford, equipped with hand-operated brake and accelerator. I love it—it makes me feel self-sufficient.

It's a long drive back, down Route 1, and by the time I got off the big road and onto the Key Caroline exit ramp, I was nearly out of my mind. My hands itched maddeningly. If you have ever suffered through the healing of a deep cut or a surgical incision, you may have some idea of the kind of itch I mean. Live things seemed to be crawling and boring in my flesh.

The sun was almost down and I looked at my hands carefully in the glow of the dash lights. The tips of them were red now, red in tiny, perfect circlets, just above the pad where the fingerprint is, where you get calluses if you play guitar. There were also red circles of infection on the space between the first and second joint of each thumb and finger, and on the skin between the second joint and the knuckle. I pressed my right fingers to my lips and withdrew them quickly, with a sudden loathing. A feeling of dumb horror had risen in my throat, woolen and choking. The flesh where the red spots had appeared was hot, feverish, and the flesh was soft and gelid, like the flesh of an apple gone rotten.

I drove the rest of the way trying to persuade myself that I had indeed caught poison ivy somehow. But in the back of my mind there was another ugly thought. I had an aunt, back in my childhood, who lived the last ten years of her life closed off from the world in an upstairs room. My mother took her meals up, and her name was a forbidden topic. I found out later that she had Hansen's disease—leprosy.

When I got home I called Dr. Flanders on the mainland. I got his answering service instead. Dr. Flanders was on a fishing cruise, but if it was urgent, Dr. Ballanger—

"When will Dr. Flanders be back?"

"Tomorrow afternoon at the latest. Would that—"

"Sure."

I hung up slowly, then dialed Richard. I let it ring a dozen times before hanging up. After that I sat indecisive for a while. The itching had deepened. It seemed to emanate from the flesh itself.

I rolled my wheelchair over to the bookcase and pulled down the battered medical encyclopedia that I'd had for years. The book was maddeningly vague. It could have been anything, or nothing.

I leaned back and closed my eyes. I could hear the old ship's clock ticking on the shelf across the room. There was the high, thin drone of a jet on its way to Miami. There was the soft whisper of my own breath.

I was still looking at the book.

The realization crept on me, then sank home with a frightening rush. My eyes were closed, but I was still looking at the book. What I was seeing was smeary and monstrous, the distorted, fourth-dimensional counterpart of a book, yet unmistakable for all that.

And I was not the only one watching.

I snapped my eyes open, feeling the constriction of my heart. The sensation subsided a little, but not entirely. I was looking at the book, seeing the print and diagrams with my own eyes, perfectly normal everyday experience, and I was also seeing it from a different, lower angle and seeing it with other eyes. Seeing not a book but an alien thing, something of monstrous shape and ominous intent.

I raised my hands slowly to my face, catching an eerie vision of my living room turned into a horror house.

I screamed.

There were eyes peering up at me through splits in the flesh of my fingers. And even as I watched the flesh was dilating, retreating, as they pushed their mindless way up to the surface.

But that was not what made me scream. I had looked into my own face and seen a monster.

The dune buggy nosed over the hill and Richard brought it to a halt next to the porch. The motor gunned and roared choppily. I rolled my wheelchair down the inclined plane to the right of the regular steps and Richard helped me in.

"All right, Arthur," he said. "It's your party. Where to?"

I pointed down toward the water, where the Big Dune finally begins to peter out. Richard nodded. The rear wheels spun sand and we were off. I usually found time to rib Richard about his driving, but I didn't bother tonight. There was too much else to think about—and to feel: they didn't want the dark, and I could feel them straining to see through the bandages, willing me to take them off.

The dune buggy bounced and roared through the sand toward the water, seeming almost to take flight from the tops of the small dunes. To the left the sun was going down in bloody glory. Straight ahead and across the water, the thunderclouds were beating their way toward us. Lightning forked at the water.

"Off to your right," I said. "By that lean-to."

Richard brought the dune buggy to a sand-spraying halt beside the rotted remains of the lean-to, reached into the back, and brought out a spade. I winced when I saw it. "Where?" Richard asked expressionlessly.

"Right there." I pointed to the place.

He got out and walked slowly through the sand to the spot, hesitated for a second, then plunged the shovel into the sand. It seemed that he dug for a very long time. The sand he was throwing back over his shoulder looked damp and moist. The thunderheads were darker, higher, and the water looked angry and implacable under their shadow and the reflected glow of the sunset.

I knew long before he stopped digging that he was not going to find the boy. They had moved him. I hadn't bandaged my hands last night, so they could see—and act. If they had been able to use me to kill the boy, they could use me to move him, even while I slept.

"There's no boy, Arthur." He threw the dirty shovel into the dune buggy and sat tiredly on the seat. The coming storm cast marching, crescent-shaped shadows along the sand. The rising breeze rattled sand against the buggy's rusted body. My fingers itched.

"They used me to move him," I said dully. "They're getting the upper hand, Richard. They're forcing their doorway open, a little at a time. A hundred times a day I find myself standing in front of some perfectly familiar object—a spatula, a picture, even a can of beans—with no idea how I got there, holding my hands out, showing it to them, seeing it as they do, as an obscenity, something twisted and grotesque—"

"Arthur," he said. "Arthur, don't. Don't." In the failing light his face was wan with compassion. "*Standing* in front of something, you said. *Moving* the boy's body, you said. *But you can't walk, Arthur.* You're dead from the waist down."

I touched the dashboard of the dune buggy. "This is dead, too. But when you enter it, you can make it go. You could make it kill. It couldn't stop you even if it wanted to." I could hear my voice rising hysterically. "I am the doorway, can't you understand that? They killed the boy, Richard! They moved the body!"

"I think you'd better see a medical man," he said quietly. "Let's go back. Let's—"

"Check! Check on the boy, then! Find out—"

"You said you didn't even know his name."

"He must have been from the village. It's a small village. Ask—"

"I talked to Maud Harrington on the phone when I got the dune buggy. If anyone in the state has a longer nose, I've not come across her. I asked if she'd heard of anyone's boy not coming home last night. She said she hadn't."

"But he's a local! He has to be!"

He reached for the ignition switch, but I stopped him. He turned to look at me and I began to unwrap my hands.

From the Gulf, thunder muttered and growled.

I didn't go to the doctor and I didn't call Richard back. I spent three weeks with my hands bandaged every time I went out. Three weeks just blindly hoping it would go away. It wasn't a rational act; I can admit that. If I had been a whole man who didn't need a wheelchair for legs or who had spent a normal life in a normal occupation, I might have gone to Doc Flanders or to Richard. I still might have, if it hadn't been for the memory of my aunt, shunned, virtually a prisoner, being eaten alive by her own failing flesh. So I kept a desperate silence and prayed that I would wake up some morning and find it had been an evil dream.

And little by little, I felt them. Them. An anonymous intelligence. I never really wondered what they looked like or where they had come from. It was moot. I was their doorway, and their window on the world. I got enough feedback from them to feel their revulsion and horror, to know that our world was very different from theirs. Enough feedback to feel their blind hate. But still they watched. Their flesh was embedded in my own. I began to realize that they were using me, actually manipulating me.

When the boy passed, raising one hand in his usual noncommittal salute, I had just about decided to get in touch with Cresswell at his Navy Department number. Richard had been right about one thing—I was certain that whatever had gotten hold of me had done it in deep space or in that weird orbit around Venus. The Navy would study me, but they would not freakify me. I wouldn't have to wake up anymore into the creaking darkness and stifle a scream as I felt them watching, watching, watching.

My hands went out toward the boy and I realized that I had not bandaged them. I could see the eyes in the dying light, watching silently. They were large, dilated, golden-irised. I had poked one of them against the tip of a pencil once, and had felt excruciating agony slam up my arm. The eye seemed to glare at me with a chained hatred that was worse than physical pain. I did not poke again.

And now they were watching the boy. I felt my mind side-slip. A moment later my control was gone. The door was open. I lurched across the sand toward him, legs scissoring nervelessly, so much driven deadwood. My own eyes seemed to close and I saw only with those alien eyes—saw a monstrous alabaster sea-scape overtopped with a sky like a great purple way, saw a leaning, eroded shack that might have been the carcass of some unknown, flesh-devouring creature, saw an abominated creature that moved and respired and carried a device of wood and wire under its arm, a device constructed of geometrically impossible right angles.

I wonder what he thought, that wretched, unnamed boy with his sieve under his arm and his pockets bulging with an odd conglomerate of sandy tourist coins, what he thought when he saw me lurching at him like a blind conductor stretching out his hands over a lunatic orchestra, what he thought as the last of the light fell across my hands, red and split and shining with their burden of eyes, what he thought when the hands made that sudden, flailing gesture in the air, just before his head burst.

I know what I thought.

I thought I had peeked over the rim of the universe and into the fires of hell itself.

The wind pulled at the bandages and made them into tiny, whipping streamers as I unwrapped them. The clouds had blottered the red remnants of the sunset, and the dunes were dark and shadow-cast. The clouds raced and boiled above us.

"You must promise me one thing, Richard," I said over the rising wind. "You must run if it seems I might try…to hurt you. Do you understand that?"

"Yes." His open-throated shirt whipped and rippled with the wind. His face was set, his own eyes little more than sockets in early dark.

The last of the bandages fell away.

I looked at Richard and they looked at Richard. I saw a face I had known for five years and come to love. They saw a distorted, living monolith.

"You see them," I said hoarsely. "Now you see them."

He took an involuntary step backward. His face became stained with a sudden unbelieving terror. Lightning slashed out of the sky. Thunder walked in the clouds and the water had gone black as the river Styx.

"Arthur—"

How hideous he was! How could I have lived near him, spoken with him? He was not a creature, but mute pestilence. He was—

"Run! Run, Richard!"

And he did run. He ran in huge, bounding leaps. He became a scaffold against the looming sky. My hands flew up, flew over my head in a screaming, orlesque gesture, the fingers reaching to the only familiar thing in this nightmare world—reaching to the clouds.

And the clouds answered.

There was a huge, blue-white streak of lightning that seemed like the end of the world. It struck Richard, it enveloped him. The last thing I remember is the electric stench of ozone and burnt flesh.

When I awoke I was sitting calmly on my porch, looking out toward the Big Dune. The storm had passed and the air was pleasantly cool. There was a tiny sliver of moon. The sand was virginal—no sign of Richard or of the dune buggy.

I looked down at my hands. The eyes were open but glazed. They had exhausted themselves. They dozed.

I knew well enough what had to be done. Before the door could be wedged open any further, it had to be locked. Forever. Already I could notice the first signs of structural change in the hands themselves. The fingers were beginning to shorten…and to change.

There was a small hearth in the living room, and in season I had been in the habit of lighting a fire against the damp Florida cold. I lit one now, moving with haste. I had no idea when they might wake up to what I was doing.

When it was burning well I went out back to the kerosene drum and soaked both hands. They came awake immediately, screaming with agony. I almost didn't make it back to the living room, and to the fire.

But I did make it.

That was all seven years ago.

I'm still here, still watching the rockets take off. There have been more of them lately. This is a space-minded administration. There has even been talk of another series of manned Venus probes.

I found out the boy's name, not that it matters. He was from the village, just as I thought. But his mother had expected him to stay with a friend on the mainland that night, and the alarm was not raised until the following Monday. Richard—well, everyone thought Richard was an odd duck, anyway. They suspect he may have gone back to Maryland or taken up with some woman.

As for me, I'm tolerated, although I have quite a reputation for eccentricity myself. After all, how many ex-astronauts regularly write their elected Washington officials with the idea that space-exploration money could be better spent elsewhere?

I get along just fine with these hooks. There was terrible pain for the first year or so, but the human body can adjust to almost anything. I shave with them and even tie my own shoe-laces. And as you can see, my typing is nice and even. I don't expect to have any trouble putting the shotgun into my mouth or pulling the trigger. It started again three weeks ago, you see.

There is a perfect circle of twelve golden eyes on my chest.

SURVIVAL 101

by Jeremy Hepler

The pounding on the front door startled Nora. She stopped brushing her teeth and stared into the small mirror above the bathroom sink. It was 10:30 p.m. She was in her cow-print pajama bottoms and a white t-shirt, tired after a long day's work at Allied Foods, ready to lie down and fall asleep listening to Jimmy Kimmel ramble on about Trump. She'd never had a random visitor in the twenty-two years she'd lived on Silver Fish Road. Her riverside house was thirty miles from the nearest town, a good ten-minute drive from the closest neighbor.

Following a second series of pounds, a man yelled, "Is anyone home? We need help."

Nora set her toothbrush on the sink ledge and hurried to the living room. As she approached the front door, someone slapped the living room window three times and she froze.

"Please help us!" It was a woman this time.

The desperation in the woman's voice caused Nora's chest to tighten, her pulse to quicken. What the hell was going on?

The man pounded on the front door again.

Nora's eyes nervously bounced back and forth from the door to the window. She'd watched enough ID Channel to be leery of blindly opening the door. The man and woman could be criminals. Meth heads. Or worse. And what if there were more than two? Nora chewed on her lip. But what if they *were* in danger? What if they were hurt? She put her hand to the small of her throat. She wished she wasn't alone. She wished Beth was with her. Beth would've made her feel confident, protected. But Beth had moved out two weeks earlier after receiving an email from *needtosee123@gmail.com* containing several pictures of Nora in bed with another woman. Beth had packed her belongings and moved out while Nora was at work, never giving Nora the chance to deny or explain the pictures. She left a short note and printed copies of the pictures on the kitchen counter.

I know what you've been up to. Don't try to lie your way out of it and say they're old pictures or it's not you in them. The handmade quilt on the bed is one of a kind. We bought it at the flea market last year, so I know it's our bed. And look at your hair. It's chopped short with red streaks. You just did that last month. You know I've been burned before and won't stand for it. Don't bother calling.

Nora had called and texted Beth multiple times anyway, but Beth hadn't responded.

The woman slapped on the window again, and the man pounded on the front door so hard the cheap deadbolt partially splintered away from the frame. Panic kickstarted Nora's legs and she rushed to the kitchen and grabbed a carving knife out of the cutting block on the counter. She would've preferred the 9mm Beth had bought her for her forty-fifth birthday in December, but the gun was in her truck, under the driver's seat.

Clenching the knife, she slowly made her way back to the front door and hollered, "What's wrong?"

"Please, let us in," the man answered.

"Do you need me to call the sheriff?"

"We don't have that much time," the woman yelled. She was on the front porch with the man now and sounded hysterical. "It's not that far behind us."

It? Nora thought. Coyotes, black bears, and cougars frequented the riverside area, but none of those typically attacked humans. They usually ran. "What are you talking about?"

"For the love of God, lady, just open the damn door!" the man screamed.

"Please don't let us die out here," the woman added.

Nora flicked on the porch light and looked out the peephole. The man had a shaved head and thick goatee flecked with gray. His face was slick with sweat. His Colorado Rockies t-shirt soaked around the neck and armpits. The woman flanking him had frizzy shoulder-length brown hair and large eyes. She was breathing fast and shallow and repeatedly checking the dirt road behind them. Her pink tank top sloughed off her small shoulders. Both of them appeared to be around thirty years old. Healthy and clean-cut. Legitimately scared.

"All right," Nora said. "I'm unlocking the door."

"Hurry," the woman pleaded.

Nora cocked the knife head-high as she unlocked and opened the door. The man glanced at the knife, gave Nora a thankful nod, and then ushered the woman toward the doorway. In her eagerness to get inside, the woman tripped over the footboard and fell to her knees. When the man didn't respond, Nora helped the woman up.

"Thank you," the woman said.

Nora was about to ask the woman if she was okay, but the woman's eyes suddenly widened, and she pointed over Nora's shoulder. "Look! It's right there!"

The man cut his eyes toward the thicket on the far side of the dirt road. Nora looked the same direction and searched the darkness but saw nothing suspicious. When the man turned his attention back to Nora, he had a determined look in his eyes. He grabbed her by the shoulders. "I've got to do what's best for my family." He jerked her outside onto the porch, headbutted her in the nose, and thrust her toward the porch steps.

A bright white flash exploded in Nora's brain. Like a flash bang had gone off in there. She dropped the knife, and although temporarily blinded from having her nose broken, she instinctively threw her hands out in front of her as she smacked onto the cement porch and tumbled down the four steps. Needles of pain stung her right hip and shoulder when she landed on the drought-hardened ground. She laid motionless for a moment, blood trickling from her nose, her mind struggling to catch up with the situation, to piece together a coherent thought.

She wiped the wet from her eyes as her vision came back into focus and rolled onto her stomach. When she pushed herself up into a crawling position, a wave of dizziness washed over her. She closed her eyes and hung her head, waited for the sensation to pass, and then blotted her nose with her t-shirt and looked at the front door. It was closed.

As she pulled herself upright using the handrail, the kitchen light popped on. The woman's face appeared in the window. She pointed at the thicket again. "Run! Run!"

Nora looked back over her shoulder and saw an animal crossing the road, heading toward her, crouched low like a stalking lion. When it stepped into the glow of the porch light, Nora could tell it was a cougar. A juvenile. Seventy to eighty pounds. Tan hide. Long curved tail tucked between its legs. A heart-shaped face with alert ears. Its golden eyes were locked on her.

She ascended the stairs and jiggled the locked doorknob. She banged three good times, slammed her shoulder into the wood twice. "Open the fucking door!" She glanced over her shoulder. The cougar moved closer, taking slow measured steps, preparing to pounce.

Realizing her carving knife was on the ground at the foot of the steps a few feet from the cougar, Nora scanned the porch for something else to defend herself with. Two stacks of terra cotta pots she planted herbs in every spring stood in the corner. A broom leaned against the house beside them. She slid her eyes to the cougar. It had stopped with its front paws on the bottom porch step. She'd crossed paths with a fair share of cougars over the years, but they'd never looked at her the way this one was. It seemed to be smirking. And the delightful, hungry look in its eyes told Nora it not only intended to slash her to pieces, but that it would also thoroughly enjoy the task.

Nora hurried to the corner of the porch, picked up a terra cotta pot, and hurled it at the cougar. "Get out of here!" She'd played league softball for twenty-plus years—third base—and was known for her arm strength and accuracy. Beth, who played first base, had jokingly dubbed her Miss Guns.

The cougar moved back, and the pot hit the bottom step. Shards smacked its face and side, but its eyes never left Nora. As she grabbed a second pot, it bypassed the steps in a single bound and rushed her. She twisted and ducked when it lunged for her head. It slammed into the house behind her and fell onto its back, knocking her to her knees. She crawled forward a few feet and stood as the cougar rolled onto its belly. Then she reared back, let out a guttural howl, and threw the terra cotta pot at the cougar's face as hard as she could.

The cougar angled its head down, and the pot shattered on the top of its skull. It whined and staggered back on wobbly legs, blood streaming down its face from a gash above its right eye. Nora leapt off the porch and ran toward the driveway carport. Toward her truck. Her gun. If she could reach the gun, she had a chance. Beth had taught her how to shoot it fairly well.

She glanced back when she reached the tailgate and saw the cougar jump off the porch. She hopped in the cab and locked the doors. Seconds later, the cougar slammed into the driver's door. Nora screamed as it stood on its hind legs and propped its front paws on the window. Their faces were inches apart, separated by a thin sheet of glass. A line of blood split the cougar's face in half. It glared at Nora like a vengeful executioner, like it wanted her to know she would die a horrible death.

She frantically searched under the seat for her gun holster, but when she found it and pulled it out, it felt light. Too light. Just a holster. No gun. Her hands began to tremble.

"No. No. No. No. No."

She tossed the holster onto the passenger seat and shoved her hand deeper under the seat. She waved it around, reached, wanted, hoped, but felt nothing.

"Goddamnit!"

She rose up and looked out the driver's window. The cougar was gone. She looked in the driver's side mirror. Nothing. She scurried to the passenger window and looked outside. Nothing. In the mirror. Nothing. Out the cracked back window. Nothing. She felt claustrophobic, trapped, as though floating on a flimsy raft in the center of an ocean teeming with bloodthirsty sharks.

She picked up the empty holster and threw it at the windshield, hard. "Fucking bitch!" Her eyes welled up. Beth had taken the gun to spite her. She just knew it. Nora had never been a gun girl, or an any weapon girl like Beth, for that matter. When she hadn't expressed enthusiasm about the gun and asked if it was a joke-gift, Beth had become angry, calling Nora spoiled and ungrateful, like she had countless times in their four years together.

Nora buried her face in her hands and cried. She regretted not being grateful about the gun. She regretted calling Beth a bitch. Beth had been so good to her, constantly surprising her with flowers and gifts. Always showering her with praise and attention. Being supportive when Nora's mother called each week to remind her that lesbians go to Hell. Maybe if Nora had been more grateful and appreciative, Beth would've given her a chance to defend herself when it came to the pictures. Then she wouldn't have been alone when desperate strangers had banged on the front door. Or trapped in a truck without a gun while a demented cougar lurked outside, plotting her death.

She pulled her face out of her hands and yelped when the cougar leapt into the truck bed. She craned her neck and watched the cougar lower into an attack stance, aimed at the back window. She was fumbling to unlock the door when the cougar crashed paws-first through the glass like a diver entering the water. It landed on the passenger seat and slid onto the floorboard.

Nora grabbed a large chunk of glass off the seat and pressed her back against the driver's door as the cougar righted itself and turned toward her. It glanced at the shard in her right hand before meeting eyes with her. It knew her intentions as well as she did it. She raised the shard, squeezing it tight enough to draw blood from her palm. "Come on!" The words came from such a primitive place in her brain that she didn't recognize them as her own.

A deep growl bubbled in the cougar's throat and it lunged at her, landed on her. She wrapped her left hand around its throat, pushing to hold its open mouth at bay. Razor-sharp claws slashed into her arms. Cougar spittle sprayed her face. Screaming in pain and fear, she somehow managed to scrape the shard down the cougar's leg. It jerked its head sideways and clamped down on her right wrist hard enough for teeth to hit bone. But she didn't drop the shard. She let go of the cougar's throat and jammed her left thumb into its eye. It immediately released its grip on her right wrist, and she stabbed the shard into its side, wedging the tip tightly between rib bones. It wailed in agony and fell onto the floorboard, nipping and pawing at the bloody shard.

Nora quickly unlocked the driver's door, hopped out of the cab, slammed the door shut, and ran to the front porch. The kitchen light was still on, but the woman was no longer watching from the window.

Nora picked up the carving knife and glanced back to see if the cougar was coming. It wasn't. Not yet. She needed to get back inside her house. Her cell phone and truck keys were in her bedroom. And she had a better chance of fighting off the man and woman inside the house than she did a cougar out here in the open. Besides, maybe she would only have to fight off the man. He'd been the one to break her nose and throw her out of the house. The woman had wanted to help her, felt sorry for her, pointed out where the cougar was and urged her to run.

She sprinted to the back of the house and stopped in front of a knee-high pile of bricks. She and Beth had hidden a spare key to the back door under the bricks after accidentally locking themselves out of the house one day when they'd gone for a riverside walk. She'd never used the key, or even looked for it, but it had to be there.

She dropped the knife between her legs and started quickly setting bricks aside. As she worked, her eyes constantly bounced left to right, checking for the cougar. Her nose throbbed and bled into her gaping mouth. The slashes on her arms and shoulders burned. Her bitten wrist screamed for relief. Time seemed to slow to a crawl. When she finally reached the bottom of the pile, she saw the magnetic key box poking out from under a broken brick. The key clanked around inside when she jerked the box free, and a slight smile found her face.

The back door had no deadbolt or chain. Unless the man and woman had pushed a couch or chair up against the door or were holding it closed, Nora should have easy entry. She unlocked the door, twisted the knob, and lightly pushed. The door swung open. She held the knife out in front of her with both hands like a sword and stepped inside.

"Where the hell are you?" she called out.

Silence answered her. No lights were on. The front door, which was closed when she'd retrieved the knife, was wide open now. Maybe they left, she thought. Maybe they saw the cougar was injured enough that they could escape. Maybe they didn't want to stay and face the consequences of what they'd done to her. Or…maybe they wanted to make her *think* they had left. Maybe they were hiding somewhere in the house, waiting to ambush her.

Flicking on each light she passed, Nora cautiously made her way to her bedroom. Her heart hitched when she entered the room and saw that her truck keys and cell phone weren't on the nightstand where she'd left them. She cursed, ran back into the living room, and was ten feet from the front door when a cougar leapt onto the porch and sauntered into the open doorway. A different cougar. Uninjured. Bigger. An adult with the same tan color hide as the juvenile. Around one hundred and forty pounds. Anger burned in its eyes.

Shaking her head in disbelief, Nora slowly backed away. The cougar matched her step for step, keeping the distance between them the same. Nora stopped when her back hit the wall separating the kitchen from the living room. The cougar stopped, too.

"What do you want?" Nora yelled. Tears streamed from her eyes, mixing with the blood smeared across her face. She grabbed a framed photo of her mom off the wall and hurled it at the cougar. "Leave me alone!"

The cougar dodged the photo, and as its teeth and nostrils flared in disapproval. The woman appeared in the doorway behind it. She had blood on her loose tank top and jeans, a gun in her hand down by her side. The cougar jerked its head the woman's way when she walked into the house.

A small flame of hope flickered in Nora's heart. "Shoot it," she said. "Shoot it now."

But as the woman moved farther into the living room, the flicker faded. Nora saw the woman's gun was a 9mm with a custom pink handle. The gun Beth had bought. The gun that should've been under the truck's driver's seat.

"How did you…" Nora trailed off when the woman stopped, spread her legs shoulder-width, and took aim.

The woman held eye contact with Nora for a second before shooting twice, hitting Nora in the right kneecap and left thigh. Nora dropped the knife and crumpled to the ground, grabbing at her legs, the pain so intense she couldn't scream. Or breathe. Or anything.

As she lay bleeding, the juvenile cougar walked through the front doorway. It moved with an awkward gait. Its head was slumped, face and ribcage matted with blood, eyes far less ferocious and eager than earlier.

Nora glanced at the adult cougar, which was walking toward the woman. It stopped in front of her and in a blur of motion, a CGI shifting of shape, morphed into a naked man with a shaved head and thick goatee. *The* man. Nora's mouth fell open. Her eye's bulged.

The man eyed Nora, then looked at the juvenile cougar. "Finish her off, Sam."

"He can't," the woman protested. "He's injured. I just pulled a fucking piece of glass out of his side, remember?"

"He's hurt, not injured," the man argued. "He'll be fine. Do as I said, Sam."

Sam slowly made his way toward Nora while the woman scolded the man. "I thought you had everything planned out to the *T*. You said she'd be an easy target."

"She was. I made sure her girlfriend wouldn't be here. I made sure she didn't have a gun. I made sure no one would be within earshot to hear her scream." The man shook his head. "The boy just needs practice."

Sam crouched beside Nora, lowered his face to within an inch of her neck, opened his mouth wide enough to swallow the moon. He'd been licking his wounds. His breath smelled of blood. Nora didn't have the will or strength to fight him. She felt paralyzed not only by the pain dominating what seemed like every nerve ending in her body, but also by the horrifying truth. The man had been planning her demise for months. Watching her. Stalking her. He'd been the one who had emailed Beth the doctored pictures. He'd stolen her gun. He wanted his son to rip her to pieces.

And, dear God, he'd just turned from a cougar into a man.

As Sam bit into her neck, she closed her eyes and tried to focus on the man's and woman's argument rather than the tearing sound of her own flesh.

"He wasn't ready for this," the woman said. "He's only ten years old. He just learned how to control the changing a few months ago, for God's sake. We should've kidnapped her and tied her up like the others."

"We can't spoon feed him forever," the man said. "He has to learn to track and hunt if he's ever going to survive on his—"

Nora lost consciousness.

HOMESICK

by Richard Chizmar

Timmy Bradley hates his new house.

He hates the slippery, shiny floors and the long, winding hallways and the big fancy rugs. He hates the stupid, ugly paintings on the walls and all the weird looking statues that sit on the furniture. He hates just about everything.

Including the strange way that his father and mother have been acting ever since they moved here. To this house.

He sits alone in his bedroom—lights off, door closed—looking out the window at the darkened city. Crying.

Timmy misses his old house and the way things used to be when they lived there. He misses his friends and Sarah, and he even misses his school. But he *especially* misses the way that his father—even though he'd been busy back then, too; after all, his father had been the governor of Massachusetts for goodness' sake—used to take time out to play with him each and every day. That's what they had called it back in those days—"time out." No matter what was going on, his father always found a few minutes to go out for a walk with Timmy or play a card game or watch some television. Sometimes he would even take Timmy along on a short trip when it didn't interfere with school and his mother said it was okay.

None of this happens anymore.

His father is always surrounded by people now. And on those few occasions when he *is* alone or just with the family, his father is always so quiet and serious. And distant. Nothing at all like the goofball who once danced around Timmy's bedroom with a pair of Jockey shorts on his head or the father who once bounced on his bed so hard that the frame broke and they laid there giggling for what had to be fifteen minutes.

This house has changed him, Timmy thinks.

He moves away from the window. He sits on the edge of his bed and stares at the back of the bedroom door. He is no longer crying.

Timmy knows that his mother is trying to make things better for him. She, too, is much busier now, but *still* she plays with him a lot more often than before and seems intent on kissing him on the cheek at least a hundred times each day. Or at least it feels like a hundred times.

And, of course, once or twice a week she gives him her little speech: "You have to understand, Timmy. Daddy's job was important before, but now he's the president. For the next few years he's going to be very, very busy with real important things. But you'll get used to it here; it's such a beautiful house. It really is…"

That is part one of the speech; some days he gets part two; other days, he gets both: "…And soon you'll meet new friends and find fun and exciting things to do. You just have to be more patient and remember, we *all* have to make sacrifices. Especially your father. Don't you think he'd rather spend time with us than go to all those stuffy meetings and dinners? Of course he would. He misses us, too. Just remember, sweetheart, he's the president now, and that's a very big deal…"

Timmy almost always comes away from these talks feeling sad and lonely and a little guilty. Jeez. What *can* you say to all that talk when you're only twelve years old?

Some days—usually on those days when his father smiles at him the way he used to or spends a few extra minutes with him after dinner—Timmy thinks that his mother might be right. That things might turn out okay after all. He thinks this because sometimes if he concentrates long and hard enough, he can remember not being so happy in their old house for those first few weeks after they'd moved in.

Back then, like now, there were so many adjustments to make. All the fancy stuff he wasn't allowed to touch. All the secret service men and the stupid security rules he had to memorize. The stiff, new clothes he had to wear and all the dumb pictures he had to dress up for. And, worst of all, he remembers, all those boring parties he had to go to.

When Timmy thinks back to all those things and how, over time, he'd learned to live with them, he sometimes thinks he is just being a baby. A big, fat crybaby, just like he'd heard his father whisper one night last week when he thought Timmy wasn't listening: "I've *got* to get going now, dear. I'll talk to him later. Besides, he's just being a baby again."

Timmy sits back on his bed and listens to his father call him a baby. (*He's just being a baby again. Being a baby.*) Just thinking about that night hurts his feelings all over again, makes his face red and hot and sweaty. And it also makes him angry.

Who is he to call me a baby? Timmy thinks. *He's* the one who messed everything up. *He's* the one who made us come here in the first place.

Timmy looks up at the picture frame on his dresser at the pretty smiling blonde girl in the photo. His stare locks on the wrinkled pink envelope sitting next to it.

Dear Timmy,

I got your letter and the package. Thanks so much; it's sooo beautiful. This letter is so short because I have to eat dinner in a couple of minutes. My mom says I have to stop mooning over you, can you believe that she actually said that...that I was mooning over you? Anyway, she said that I was wrong to promise you that we'd still go steady and she made me go to the dance with Henry Livingston this past weekend. I ended up having a lot of fun. Henry sure can fast dance. Not as much fun as I would have had with you, but what can we do?—you being there and me being stuck back here. Henry asked me to go to the movies with him on Friday and I told him yes. He's a bunch of fun, not like you, but what can we do? So, I guess we're not going steady or anything anymore. My mother's making me show her this letter before I mail it, so she'll know I "broke it off." Sorry. Those are her words, not mine. I miss you, Timmy, and I'll write again soon if my mom lets me. She said she has to think about it. Please write back as soon as you can and don't be mad, okay?

Love, Sarah

P.S. Henry said to say hi and don't be mad at him.

Timmy feels the tears coming and looks away from the picture. But it's too late. He's already crying. Again. Jeez, maybe he *is* a baby. Maybe his father is right about him after all.

But that doesn't matter now. Timmy no longer cares *what* his father thinks. Besides, he knows this is different than last time. Last time they moved he didn't get sick, he didn't cry, he didn't have nightmares. This time is different, he thinks.

He looks at the bedroom door and wonders what is happening downstairs. He figures it is just a matter of time now. If all goes according to his plan, he'll be back in Massachusetts in time for soccer season. Back holding hands and walking home from school with Sarah. Back playing video games and tag-team and rollerball with all his friends (except for that backstabber Henry Livingston).

Timmy looks at the clock on the wall. It is after seven o'clock—Sarah and Henry are probably inside the movie theater by now—and he wonders again why it is still so quiet outside his bedroom.

Just be patient, he thinks. Just like his mother always says, *You have to be more patient, Timmy.* To pass the time, he tries to imagine everything as it has happened. Inside his head, he watches himself as he...

...pours the poison directly into their coffee, careful not to get any on the edge of the cups or on the tray. Then he swirls it around real good with his finger until all the white powder disappears. Finally, he pretends to stretch out on the sofa and read a comic book, but he really waits and watches them take their first sips, then tiptoes upstairs to his room.

He looks at the clock again. He can't imagine what's taking so long.

He walks to the window and sits down with his back to the door. He wonders what movie Sarah is watching. He thinks of her there in the dark, eating popcorn and sipping soda, Henry's fingers touching her hand. Closing his eyes, he whispers a quick prayer. He asks only that everything goes according to his plan. That soon it will all be over and they will send him home again. Back to Sarah. Back to his friends. Back to his old house.

A few minutes past eight, when he hears the loud, angry voices and the heavy footsteps outside his door, he knows that his prayer has been answered. He is going home.

CLARK! STOP!

by Josh Malerman

A gas station. Shut down for the night. Lights off.
A grocery store. Stickers on the window.
Street lamps. Three.
A hardware store. *BILLY'S.*

Two parked cars. Rusted out. Both.

A bar. *WILLY'S.* No people out front. No racket from within. Pink neon OPEN sign is on, though. Paints most the downtown pink.

High full moon.

Telephone wires above the street.

A post office/police station.

Speed limit sign.

25 m/p/h.

But Clark is going 40.

Who cares? Town is empty. One-block town. Who cares? Fifteen over. There's not even enough time to slow down. So Clark doesn't. Doesn't even want to.

But it isn't the bar's neon that colors the one block after all.

It's the red light up ahead.

Clark sees it so Clark slams on the brakes.

Sees a cop car, parked, as he slows. Sees someone sitting in it, too.

Clark's Volvo comes to a stop just about level with where the sidewalk ends. His heart is beating hard, despite having nothing in the Volvo that could get him in trouble. How much trouble could a public speaker, self-help, family man get into anyway?

None.

That's how much.

So calm down.

And yet, he did speed by a cop in a one-block town and now he's sitting at the town's one light and the cop is probably writing down Clark's license plate number before pulling out just as silently as he sits there and even if you have absolutely nothing to hide, it's a rattling thing, speeding by a cop. Especially in their town.

It's always their town.

It is. But this one feels especially owned.

Clark is trying not to look into the rearview mirror, trying not to look at the cop car. But that's what he's doing. Looking in the rearview mirror at the cop car. He sees the shape of the man, the brim of his hat, sees him shift in his seat, too, in case there was any question whether or not the body is real.

Some towns set up mannequin cops. Not this one.

Clark listens to the soft purr of the Volvo's engine. He's always liked the way it sounds. Hell, he loves this car. Even loves the way the turn signal clicks.

But no turn signal right now.

Red light.

Sit still.

Silhouette of the cop in his car. In Clark's rearview. Behind him and to the left. Otherwise the street is empty.

The town is empty. Otherwise.

Clark turns the radio down. Just a notch. Just so that he's not distracted. Doesn't suddenly, accidentally, drive through this light.

Clark thinks of Helen.

No real reason to, she just pops into his head. Helen. His ex-wife. His dead wife. Died in a car accident.

Clark ran a red light that day. Ford truck smashed into the passenger side. Helen's side. Sometimes she drove, too. But that day the passenger side was Helen's side. That day.

Long light.

It *is* a long light. Or maybe it's not. Maybe it's been twenty seconds and Clark just feels like the cop has had enough time to draw a pretty detailed sketch of the newcomer. The man at the red light. Clark.

Clark catches himself staring at the rearview. So he stops.

Stops.

Stop.

Red light.

Still.

Ahead is open, empty road. Only thing keeping Clark from experiencing it is this light. This one circle of red in all this tiny town and all this huge world. One circle of red, like when the sensei stops a pupil from advancing by placing only his pinkie under his nose.

Helen.

Crushed her. The Ford. Clark isn't afraid to talk about it. Talks about it all the time. Mostly at his seminars. It works well there. Packs a punch. The crowd gets real interested when the man who has all the answers reveals his own terrible tragedy, his own reason to pack it in. People like to know that he's got problems, too. That he's not just up there on stage espousing the golden slabs of life and living. People like to know that he's suffered, too. The Helen story does that. Boy does it.

Clark is adjusting his tie. Loosening it. He's always liked driving the Volvo in a suit jacket and tie. Likes the looks of his thin white hands gripping the wheel by the blue dashboard lights. Likes to see the shirt-cuffs coming out of the jacket just so. Makes him feel like a success in business. That's important to Clark. Believing in himself.

Light is still red.

Clark shakes his head. Wonders if the cop saw that, wonders if the cop is thinking this stranger in town is getting impatient. Why would he be impatient? What's the problem with stopping at a light for a spell? Not enough people enjoy stopping for a spell. That might be a thought a small-town cop might have.

Clark rolls down his window. Smooth gliding sound. The Volvo. Clark loves it. Fresh air enters. Air from all that open space ahead. Hell, even the short distance the head-beams reveal looks like infinite open space to Clark. If he squints, he thinks he can see another speed limit sign about a hundred feet past the light. Probably says something like 50. The way out of town. Off this street.

Come on.

Long light.

Or is it?

Clark looks to the rearview mirror. Sees the cop shift in his seat again. Just shifting in his seat is all. No doubt watching the prissy Volvo idling and the prissy driver at the wheel. Clark wonders if there's a white line under his car, a sign, too, in his blind spot, that reads:

STOP HERE FOR LIGHT

It's possible he missed that. Possible he's pulled up too far. That might be something to get pulled over for. He places his hand on the shifter. Thinks he might go in reverse a few feet. Thinks again. Sits still. The cop is going to wait until the light turns green, wait for Clark to pull away, then he's going to slowly creep out after him. Isn't that what they do? It's like they don't like it when you're already pulled over, like that ruins half the fun.

A shriek from somewhere outside. Not the radio. Clark turns the radio down another notch. Sure sounded like a scream. Sure sounded like a girl. He looks in the rearview mirror, past the cop, back to that bar. He's expecting to see a woman tripping out the meager wooden door. She would know the cop. And depending on what she knew about him, she'd either twirl a carefree hand in his direction and stumble off toward home or she'd straighten up, quick, frightened that he knew she'd been drinking.

But there is no girl.

And yet…

A scream.

Helen.

Yes, of course Helen screamed. She screamed before the Ford hit them. She screamed,

Clark! STOP!

But Clark didn't stop. Not that time. He did this time. He's still stopped. Is starting to feel like he's still *stopping*. Like the time between noticing the red light and coming to a complete stop is infinite, that whole idea about an infinite number of points between A and B. A) Clark spotted the stoplight. B) Cark stopped. But maybe it hadn't happened yet. Maybe he's still rolling along those infinite points, an endless and linear series of red circular saucers floating in a black emptiness, continuing on into forever.

Come on.

Clark clears his throat. Wonders if the cop heard it. Wonders if the cop is wondering why the stranger in town is getting antsy at a standard red light. Maybe there's something in the trunk? Maybe there's someone curled up (tied up) on the front seat?

He cleared his throat after all.

Stop, it.

Stop.

In the distance, beyond the strength of the headlamps, but still there in the headlamps' fringe, a figure rises in what must be an empty field. An empty lot. An empty.

Clark gasps not because the figure is particularly frightening but because any movement at all is somewhat shocking.

It's a figure for sure. A figure cut by the moonlight, a figure cast against the dark but cloudless sky and open fields framing it like an oil painting forever.

Clark can't take his eyes off it. What else is there to look at? The light is still red. The cop is still sitting in his car. The miles aren't changing on the odometer. The street is still empty.

You heard a woman scream.

Is it a woman standing there in the field?

Yes. It is.

Is she facing him? Facing the stoplight?

Yes. She is.

Clark loosens his tie a little bit more.

He turns the radio up a notch. Then back down a notch.

"Fucking light," he says, and he quickly looks to the rearview mirror. The cop definitely shifted in his seat. The cop definitely heard him say *fucking light*. Now we've got an angry antsy stranger in town. The kind of Volvo driving, cuff-caring, stiff who thinks he's bigger than this town and can't stand being stopped for a minute or more here, *here*, in this town.

Clark doesn't even know the name of it. This town.

Helen.

He saw the Ford before she did. He saw the light, too. But while Helen was prattling about picture frames for the foyer, Clark was crunching numbers, considering odds, wondering what the chances were that he would survive a car crash, the same crash that would kill Helen, if he were to run a red light.

Intentionally.

He remembers the exact thinking he thought:

It's a numbers game. Whether the odds are in your favor or not, there are *odds.*

Yes, that was it. Those words came clear as a third eye to him as he and Helen approached that intersection, just before the Ford came barreling into the passenger side and crushed Helen's body into his, crushed her so immediately that he'd never be able to extricate the sight of her seemingly two-dimensional figure with the words *Clark! STOP!*

The figure, the woman in the field ahead, is moving. Dancing? Maybe. Maybe drunk.

The light is still red.

Clark is thinking of Helen.

The woman is moving like she's dragging something, or like she's been injured in a bad way and Clark can't help but imagine the woman is Helen. Surely it's just some field-jockey, trashed, stoned out of her mind, a sight the cop has seen a hundred times. Perhaps she's imagining herself galloping gracefully toward the intersection, just coming out of some wavy dope funk, dragging something. Yes, dragging her Time and Dignity toward the bar where she's gonna pour some tequila on them both and set them aflame.

"Helen?"

Now Clark's done it because now Clark's flat out said her name and his window is still open, and the cop probably heard it and maybe he heard just enough of a tremor in Clark's voice to detect that, uh oh, this guy intentionally ran a red light many moons ago with a mind to murder his wife.

The figure's head perks up at the name Helen.

Clark loosens his tie even more.

He's tapping his fingertips on the steering wheel.

I know sorrow, Clark likes to tell the crowds who come to hear him speak about self-confidence. He likes to start the "Helen Segment" that way. *I know sorrow…too. Just like you. I know of a loss resonating at a frequency so low…so deep…that at times I thought I would no longer be able to hear it, though it would be there ever still. I lost my wife.* Gasps from the crowd. Always. *An autumn afternoon's drive and on the way back, we approached a small town, the last we'd encounter before turning onto the gravel road to home.* "Home" not "House." Warmer that way. *There's a stoplight there, at the Percy Lodge, where families flock to buy flavored coffee, maps of the state parks, and framed photographs of the gorgeous woods. I even saw a family, that day, as we rolled toward the light, saw a mother holding her young son's hand on the sidewalk, saw a father pointing at something on a shelf through the window.* A pause here. Always. A deep breath. *A light we'd obeyed one thousand times but this once, this one oversight.* Another pause. Longer. Or about the same. *I lost my Helen that day. I was the one driving. Blame me, I say, blame me.*

That usually did it. That set the table. Until it seemed the tears would never stop. Stop.

The light is still red.

Clark looks to his fingertips on the wheel. They're a faint red from the indomitable light suspended not ten feet ahead. Clark feels like he's part of a painting, one small piece of a still life. Or perhaps the centerpiece. The focal point. Like the cop can't look anywhere else.

Still life.

Clark still has his life. Helen does not. Clark gambled. Played the odds. Let the Ford smash right into them.

Ran the light.

The silhouette stumbles into the road now, though Clark can't see her features yet. She looks thin. Too thin. And still walks like she's dragging something.

Bum leg, Clark thinks. *Shit-canned. Probably fell off a barstool.*

Clark gives the Volvo a little gas. The engine revs. He looks to the mirror and sees the cop shift once again. That damn hat, makes the man look like a state trooper. Something scarier about a state trooper. *Gibbons Police* doesn't intimidate like *Michigan State Trooper.*

Though he can't see her features, the figure ahead has stopped in the middle of the road. Clark imagines she's going to cross it. But she doesn't. She just stands there. Everything in this town takes a long time, he thinks. For fuck's sake, he thinks.

"Hey, lady!" Clark calls out the window. "Get out of the road!"

Because the light's going to change. Because it has to. And when it does, Clark wants to go.

Clark looks up to the light.

Come on come on come on.

The light must be broken. And it's okay for motorists to stop and look both ways before passing under a broken red light. In fact, it's starting to feel like Clark is *more* suspicious for sitting this long rather than running it. The cop must be wondering what Clark has to hide, obeying the rules so rigidly like this.

Can't you see the light's broken? The cop is going to say. *What's the matter with YOU?*

Suspicious.

No, nobody was suspicious of him after the accident. Not even Helen's difficult parents shot him an accusatory glance. Accidents happen. Losing your wife in one of them happens, too.

Clark removes his tie.

He turns the radio up a notch. Commercial. Turns it back down.

Helen was too much. In every way, Helen was too much. What was that saying she used to say? The one about being...

Being me is like being anybody else. Only more so.

That got a rise out of every dinner guest they entertained. Not because it was funny. Clark knew that. People laughed because what else was there to do?

CLARK! STOP!

He should stop. Stop thinking about Helen. Stop thinking about cops and the past and the present and the woman standing in the middle of the road. He should focus instead on the purr of the Volvo's gorgeous Swedish engine. Wait for the light to change…and split.

Splat.

That was the inane cartoonish word that crossed his mind when he decided to run that light, when he decided to chance it with the Ford. *Splat.* As if the collision would create an explosion of colors with round edges, a funny horn sound, a drum hit. But nothing went splat. Instead, it was a crunch. And suddenly Helen, mashed, half her natural width, was pressed against him, eyes closed, as if she'd rolled over on him in bed, dreaming beneath a cider press.

Nobody suspected him. Nobody at all.

And didn't that mean something? Didn't that mean he was justified? In some cosmic, karmic way?

Clark shakes his head again and realizes the woman is now standing just beyond the reach of the indefatigable red light. This means she's gotten closer.

And the light hasn't changed.

He looks to the mirror. The cop still sits in his car.

The woman steps under the light. There's something wrong with her. Like she's been hurt in a bad way.

Clark…

Clark suddenly feels ill because this word, his name, *has* been spoken.

The woman said it. Said his name.

He puts the Volvo in reverse.

The cop shifts in his seat.

The woman steps closer, she's coming toward the car and Clark sees she's been hurt bad, smashed, like she was standing in the wrong place as two swinging logs met.

Clark puts the car in park and places his hand on the door handle, ready to get out.

Clark…stop…

It's the woman again. Saying what Helen said way back when and Clark removes his hand from the door handle and shifts the car back into drive.

The light is still red.

We'd passed through that light one thousand times, he'd told the audiences, the people looking for a reason to remain optimistic in a world where men risk their own lives to kill the women seated beside them in cars.

It's Helen, gamely crossing the intersection.

It's Helen. Clark has no doubt.

And she doesn't look good. She looks just like she did in that memory of his, when everything became bright noise and bent metal and he saw, for a moment, Helen's features, as she was squashed to half her width.

It's her and she's dragging (*the truth?*) toward him, under the light, unable to raise her hands but somehow pointing at him all the same, pointing, as if to say, he did it, officer, he did it he did it he did.

Clark considers running her over. Running the light and running her over and trying to outrun the small-town cop, too. Maybe if Clark does it fast enough the cop will have to stop and check on the woman, check on Helen, and by the time he determines she's twice dead Clark will be well out of town, far beyond the infinite red light that holds him.

He gives the Volvo a little gas. A little more than he means to. The engine revs loud. In the mirror he sees the cop move, but not much. Still not getting out of his cruiser, still not pulling out, pulling up next to him, asking him why the hell he's obeying the rules so tightly because the only people who do *that* are people with something really terrible to hide.

Helen's close now, awful under the red light, a still life of that ghastly image Clark has held so tight to his body that nobody has ever seen it but him.

Clark unfastens his seatbelt. He must get out of here. Must get out of the car. He can't just sit here as this woman (Helen) inches toward him, with the red light like the eye of God above him and the cop the hand of God waiting to move, to pounce, to cup Clark up and drop him into a prison cell for the rest of his life.

I know sorrow, too. Like you.

Sometimes the attendees had questions, and sometimes those questions stuck with him.

Clark reaches into the glove box, mistaking the situation for one in which he has been pulled over. He's looking for his registration and proof of insurance before he realizes nobody has pulled him over, the cop hasn't moved. He's thinking of one particular question that has really stuck with him over the years, asked by a bearded man wearing a red button-down shirt.

Do you feel guilty that you survived?

Clark looks up suddenly because the woman is now at the passenger side of the Volvo. She's opening the door. Clark can hear broken bones working beneath her creased, rice paper skin.

"Hey! Don't come in here!"

But she's opening the door. She's coming in. She's sitting beside him on the passenger seat.

Of course I felt guilt. But guilt is selected. Guilt is preferred. And I... I did not choose it.

But the bearded man in the red (*stoplight*) button-down asked another question, one that haunted Clark in many hotel rooms in many cities he got to by car.

When *did you choose not to choose it?*

And as though added by a third voice, Clark heard, *before or after?*

Before or after the accident?

"Before!" Clark yells, pressing against the woman, the thing, as she leans into him, her battered features as thin as the spines of his self-help books.

"HELP!"

The light is still red.

The light is still red, the light is still red, like forever and dead, the light is still red.

"HELP!"

When *did you choose not to choose guilt?*

Before?

or

After?

Clark is out of the car. Doesn't remember opening the door. Stumbles across some gravel. Red pebbles. Red stones. Everything is red.

Clark is racing up the street, to the police cruiser, then banging on the driver's side window.

The officer is asleep in there.

Clark is banging hard. Clark is waking him up.

The officer opens his eyes. He looks surprised. As if woken from a particularly steady dream. No changes in there, no change of pace. He's quickly rolling down the window and facing this stranger in town, this one-block town.

"Hold on now," he says. "Just hold—"

"I killed my wife," Clark says, putting both hands through the cop's open window, palms up, asking to be arrested, shirt-cuffs perfectly extended beyond the ends of his sports-jacket sleeves. A voice is telling him not to do this. *Clark! Stop!* But his mouth is moving, he's already confessing. "I killed my wife. I killed my wife! The light's not changing… I killed my wife…"

TIRED OF WALKIN'?

by Michelle Garza and Melissa Lason

The hour was getting late so she sped up, not terribly concerned with getting pulled over. She figured her looks could get her out of most speeding tickets and when that didn't work, she'd just phone her daddy's lawyer. The highway was growing dark, signaling to Barbie her father's plane would be landing soon. He was away on business which granted her the freedom to roam, and roam she did, but she would make damn sure to get home before he did. She couldn't afford to get cut off from the shared bank account like her shithead brother.

She cranked the stereo and felt the wind blow in through the open window. The scent of cigarettes filled her nose, making her bite her lip, and the claws of addiction came climbing up her back. She'd kicked smoking only five months before and the smell of the damn things was still too enticing. Her headlights revealed a stranger on the roadside in a long black coat, walking along with thumb extended. She snickered as she slowed the sports car down to a crawl beside the hitchhiker.

She killed the radio and called out the passenger side window, "Tired of walkin'?"

He turned and in the gathering darkness she could make out the hint of a grin beyond the burning cherry of a cigarette. Two dirty fingers held it up to his lips, and smoke hung around most of his face, obscuring it, but she could see his smile. He had crooked, black teeth and dry lips. It made Barbie's stomach turn to think of how filthy he must have been.

"Sure am," he said, reaching for the door handle.

"Then run a while!" She cackled and hit the gas. The car raced forward; his hand fell away, but the cigarette stayed between his lips.

She watched him in the rearview mirror while she laughed uncontrollably. He didn't react the way most drifters did, just stood stone-still and watched her go. It was a little disappointing he didn't run after her, or flip her off, or helplessly toss rocks from the shoulder of the road at the fading taillights of a car she knew he could never catch.

"Party pooper," she said.

With the stereo cranked back up, she focused on making her way homeward as quickly as she could. The cornfields on each side of the road blew by in a blur of tall shadows against the dark sky; an occasional streetlight left yellow orbs on her peripheral vision. With her windows down she could smell the damp earth and feel the cold wind of approaching winter filling up the space of the tiny car. She reveled in the night and daydreamed of parties, drinks, and trashy men. An empty void in her chest ached to turn her car around and go back to Ronny's party. Thinking of him being drunk and his eyes roving sent a punch of jealousy through her gut.

Barbie eased off the gas pedal and let the car slow almost to a stop as she flipped down her vanity mirror, her eyes glancing back and forth from her reflection to the road before her and back again. In the small light attached to the mirror, she studied herself for a second before closing it. She wasn't as pretty as some of the other girls, but she was definitely more adventurous, and her daddy's money was very alluring. It eased the sinking feeling in her stomach and beat back the depression she felt settling in on her after recalling her competition for Ronny's affection. He'd have to be crazy to cheat on Barbie.

She pressed the gas pedal down until her car was just above the speed limit and continued her trek homeward, back to the rich part of town and the fancy neighborhood where she lived. A place Ronny would never be welcomed with his long hair and tattoos, and of course his low-class blood.

Beyond the reach of her headlights stood a long, dark shadow on the roadside. Barbie grinned, hoping this second hitchhiker in the gravel and dirt would give her a good laugh. She slowed down a bit, piloted the car close to him and was about to shout out the window when she smelled his cigarette and noticed the drifter's long coat dancing in the wind, the black-toothed smile visible on his face. She shook her head and blinked slowly. It was impossible for the guy she had left in the dust miles back to now be ahead of her. Barbie felt a pain in her chest, her lungs burned, and she choked on her own words before they came from her mouth. Panic filled her with static fear as the car came to a halt, her body unresponsive to an alien fear gripping her. The door was pulled open. He came crawling into the car like a spider, long and spindly, his coat draped around him like a black veil, stinking of dirt and smoke, shielding most of his face from her; for that and the lack of light she was grateful. Barbie didn't want to look at him. She didn't want to see him, because she knew no human could have traveled as quickly as he had.

"I took yer advice," the drifter beside her said, a cigarette still dangling from his dry lips.

The noxious fumes of the smoke crawled up her nose, replacing the stench of him for only a moment before the reek of decay knotted her stomach. He took a long drag from the cigarette and slowly pulled his coat aside as he exhaled a cloud of dirty smoke into the interior of her car. A startled yelp escaped her when the hitchhiker turned his face to her, revealing what he really was, a thing her preacher granddaddy warned her about whenever she visited him in the nursing home. An entity of pure darkness housed in a gnarled body etched with scars. In his milky eyes she felt the pull of eternity, a promise of death and suffering, a place where time was stopped and replaced by endless torment.

"I ran for a while, and then the wind just picked me up and blew me along like a fallen leaf, like smoke on a breeze. Looks like this car ain't as fast as you thought. Though I haven't met a human alive who could get away from me, no matter what they were drivin'."

The thing lifted his hand.

Barbie felt her head spin as a filthy, elongated finger ran along her cheekbone. Smoke billowed from his mouth as he caressed her face; an endless cloud of filthy air filled the car. Her vision went dark as his words invaded her ears and ate into her mind like a ravenous worm. She struggled not to black out as a piercing pain, like an ice pick being driven straight into her brain through her ear canal, swallowed her in fear. The voice of the beast sitting beside her became distorted, hard to cling to or recall, but what she *could* understand sank into her terror-stricken brain.

"I'm a drifter you might say. I walk the darkness between worlds, looking to hitch a ride with pretty little things like you."

"Wake up!" Barbie's eyes fluttered and the blinding light of the sun jarred her awake.

Her father, Jim, sat beside of her, his arms folded across his chest.

"What? How?" she asked.

"You came stumbling in last night," the old man said, "long after I got home…stinking of cigarettes."

Barbie was confused, shocked she made it home without remembering what happened after the incident with the hitchhiker.

"You swore you'd never do that again. I can't believe you'd lie to me like that."

"Daddy, I'm so sorry…" Barbie tried desperately to think of a way out of admitting she was hanging out with a crowd her father would never approve of.

"You swore you wouldn't smoke anymore!"

She breathed a sigh of relief. He still didn't know where she'd been, or who she'd been with.

"You've gone months without those damn things, and suddenly you start smoking again?"

"I'm so sorry. I promise I won't do it again," she whispered harshly as she reached for his hand.

He took it and asked, "What were you up to?"

"I was at the country club with the girls. I guess I had too much fun and slipped up by smoking a few of Martha's cigarettes."

"You can still have a good time without those cancer sticks," he said.

"You're right. I'm sorry. Don't be mad at me."

Jim gave in, a smile raising the edges of his lips. "Okay, honey. I can't stay mad at my Barbie doll."

He left her bedside, and she stayed tucked beneath the sheets. She worried he was only waiting for her to feel better before ripping her a new asshole for disobeying him. Her night out could cost Barbie his trust, and she couldn't afford to be shunned by him and end up getting cut out of his will. Her stomach ached and her mouth tasted like a barroom ashtray. She was thankful he seemed to be buying her story about being with the other goodie-goodies of the neighborhood; she just prayed she wouldn't have to ask Martha to corroborate her story to her father. It continued to worry her for a while but what ate at her more was not being able to recall what took place after the drifter crawled into her car. Where did any memories of what transpired after his spindly fingers slid down her cheek go?

She looked to the window. The sun shone brightly through a crack in the curtains, but its rays didn't soothe the sickening feeling welling up inside of her. She sat up and a shock of pain twisted her stomach. She dry-heaved and ran for the bathroom.

Barbie hugged the toilet as a burning mouthful of vomit escaped her. It stank terribly and only nauseated her worse. Her stomach cramped, and she readied herself to throw up again, but something thick seemed to be caught in her chest, agonizingly lodged somewhere between her throat and gut. She whined and opened her mouth, wishing to God whatever it was would just come out. Not being able to breathe frightened her, and the pain grew to an unbearable degree as a thick chunk finally came up her throat. She closed her watering eyes as she coughed it out into the toilet with a splash of wretched water hitting her face.

She breathed deeply, relieved she had emptied her stomach of whatever was making her feel so horrible, cursing the cheap vodka she let Ronny pour down her throat. Barbie stared down into the toilet to see a handful of cigarette butts floating in her vomit. She flushed the toilet and fell back against the bathroom wall, trying to stifle a ragged cry. An irritating itch at the back of her throat made her worry she might have to puke again but her mind was preoccupied. She recalled the voice of the thing in the black coat, the drifter of worlds, and like a broken record it repeated the thing's words in her mind. Tears gathered in her bloodshot eyes; she gripped the sides of her aching head.

...looking to hitch rides with pretty little things like you.

Barbie held her stomach. Cold sweat ran down her face. In her bedroom she could hear her cell phone's chime indicating a text message waited to be read, but she couldn't move, couldn't think. Her mind kept replaying the memory of the drifter crawling into her car. She felt an exhaustion eating away at her, down to her bones. A cold pain in her joints.

With some struggle, she stood and returned to her bed. She found her phone on the bedside table, swiped the screen, and saw a handful of messages she had missed, along with a recent one from Martha.

"Fuck," she whispered, and tossed the phone onto her bed.

She didn't have it in her to speak to Martha, to keep up the appearance of being a goodie-goodie after experiencing something so unexplainable, something so terrifying. She lay her head down, choking again on the feeling of something caught in her throat.

Barbie wondered if she would ever stop feeling sick and violated, if she could ever look at herself in the mirror again without recalling that thin finger, reeking of death and cigarettes, sliding down her cheek. The memory of its eyes, two evil white orbs buried in hollow cheeks, made her paranoid. She felt as if those eyes could still see her.

She shivered and pulled her comforter up over her head, her damp hair stinking of sweat and smoke, and rode the waves of torment, both physical and mental. Then she heard someone whispering, and started weeping. She fought to contain her sobs, but when the voice continued, she realized it only stopped when she hiccupped or cried. The voice was coming from her own lips.

Stewart parked on the street, but made sure not to sit directly in front of the house. He ran his fingers through his hair and lit a half-smoked cigarette from the overflowing ashtray. He watched his father's car leave the driveway of the mansion he once called home.

"Fuckin' asshole."

The taillights of the car faded in his rearview mirror. Content the old man was gone, he made his move. He quickly got out of his car, grabbed a backpack from the backseat, and hurried toward the gaudy front doors. His hands shook as he slid the key in the lock and turned it, laughing at his father's arrogance, as if mere banishment would keep Stewart away. The old fuck should have changed the locks after tossing his son in the streets to fend for himself. At least that's what Stewart thought when he planned to rob the place.

The house was dimly lit—only the light at the top of the staircase was on. It beckoned him upward to his father's study where he could get his hands on the valuable collectibles and access the old man's safe. He would be in and out quickly, and ready to party.

He paused at the foot of the stairs, staring up hazily at the glow. It was like spying a glimpse of Heaven peeping through dark clouds. It was the promised land, to him, anyway. After running out of money and drugs, being so close to getting what he needed made him swear angels were singing from the floor above him. He wiped nervous sweat from his upper lip and ascended the steps.

Jim drove furiously. He couldn't even recall stopping at any red lights or stop signs in his haste to get to the house where he knew his daughter had actually been hanging out thanks to a GPS unit in her cell phone, the phone he paid for. The house—if it could be called one, being a drug den in a white-trash neighborhood—looked abandoned. He marched up to the screen door at the front of the house and pounded on it. He wasn't a small man, and though he had come from a well-off family, he wasn't afraid to throw fists when he needed to. He wasn't surprised when no one came to answer the door.

"Open this goddamn door!"

He kicked the screen door and his loafered foot went through it. Cursing, he wrenched his foot free and grabbed the broken door and attempted to yank it free of its hinges. He stopped to peer through the holes he had battered through the old screen and realized the wooden door beyond was left open.

"Open up, you scumbags!" he yelled into the dark house.

He rammed his hand back into the hole left by his foot and felt around for the lock. He unlocked it and yanked the screen door open, then rushed into the house and through a living room with stained shag carpet and trash littering the floor. He was disgusted by the stench of the place, stale beer, old food, and cigarette smoke. How could Barbie even want to step foot in such a place?

"Come out here!" Jim yelled as he made his way through the small house, kicking open a door that led into a filthy kitchen.

He headed down a hallway that required him to turn sideways in order to squeeze through, navigating his way around mounds of junk and filth. He looked into a bathroom but found it empty save for a cockroach calmly sitting on the sink. The tiny critter was more like a roommate than a pest. At the end of the hallway was the lone door he hadn't kicked open. When he got there, he squinted at it, plotting to break it down, determined to get his hands on the bastard who had lured his daughter into such a hell. Jim figured the cheap old piece of shit couldn't withstand a couple of forcible kicks, so he pushed his way past another mound of junk and let his wrath rain down upon the door.

It flew inward, hit the bedroom wall, and bounced back to shut in his face. His momentary glimpse of the room inside startled him. There was a corpse of a man tied to a bed. He knew the guy must be dead because of all the blood. It was spattered everywhere. Jim couldn't tell what the guy actually looked like, only that he had long hair.

"What the *fuck*?"

He reached out and slowly pushed the door open again. He didn't step inside, but just stood there in shock of what he was seeing.

The bed was soaked in crimson, red pools coagulating in the filthy carpet, flies buzzing as they flew in through the open window. Seeing that pale, bloodless body tied to the bed with two empty eye sockets sickened Jim. Had his daughter been here? Was Barbie a part of this atrocity?

He carefully stepped inside and navigated the room, avoiding the bloody carpet, to get close enough to see the extent of the corpse's injuries and whether there were any clues as to his daughter having been involved.

The dead man's chest and abdomen were riddled with stab wounds. A cigarette butt had been jammed deep into one of the eye sockets, a detail he'd missed at first glance. There was a hole in the victim's chest that was larger than Jim's fist, a jagged pit where a heart once beat.

Jim shuffled back a step, realizing there were cigarette butts everywhere, littering across the entire floor, soaking up copper-scented blood. His mind replayed his reaction when Barbie had come home, how badly she had smelled of smoke. It sent a shock through him.

He stepped back out through the doorway and ran to the bathroom. The cockroach that had been chilling out there scurried away, crossing the filthy countertop and then down the wall, where it hid behind an overflowing trash can. The grimy toilet seat had been broken off and the bowl looked as though it hadn't been cleaned in years. In the few inches of water at the bottom of the bowl sat the heart, apparently the same one that had been removed from the corpse's chest in the other room. Its blood mingled with piss and shit stains, causing Jim to puke into the sink. Even when he finished, he couldn't get that smell out of his nostril, off his tongue. It smelled and tasted of cigarettes…and death.

He ran the faucet to rinse the chunks of his vomit down the drain, then made his way back to his car and sped away, intent on asking his daughter what she had really been up to last night. To verify whether or not he needed to call his lawyer. There was no way in hell he was going to let Barbie see jail time over some scumbag living in the slums. He hoped the murder took place after she left, but he had a terrible feeling it hadn't.

"That scumbag must have hurt her. If he put his hands on her…"

Jim screamed, his mind a jumble of possibilities, and memories of his innocent little girl, the sight of the dead guy tied to a bed, and the unbelievable quantities of blood soaked into filthy decades-old carpet.

He kept his foot on the gas pedal, and the trashy neighborhood blurred by his window until it was gone. He hit the highway, his mind fixated on his daughter and the dead man. His hands trembled with fear and rage. How could both of his children turn out to be such fuckups? His heart pounded in his chest and his vision began to darken. His blood pressure was skyrocketing; his ungrateful offspring would be his downfall. What would his friends and neighbors say when the police hauled Barbie through the front door of his mansion in handcuffs, then convicted her of cutting some scumbag up and stuffing cigarettes butts into his empty eye sockets? How could he keep the situation under control? It would ruin him; even if she never spent a night in jail, he could kiss his business partners goodbye.

A thunderous crashing sound startled him, like a sudden earthquake had split the highway beneath him. It caused his heart to seize up in his chest for a second before returning to pound against his ribcage as his car skidded out of control. He felt his pants go warm, wet as his bladder let go. His instincts kicked in and he gripped the wheel, righting the car's path before it went hurdling off the side of the highway and into a field. He stepped on the brakes and the car fishtailed, stopping only when it hit a telephone pole on the roadside.

He gasped as he climbed out of the car and stared at the blown tire for what felt like eternity before his hands finally ceased shaking. He started walking up the side of the road, retrieving his cell phone to call for help when he realized he was fucked; its screen was crushed in the accident. His forehead ached. He lifted his hand and felt a lump forming there, but he was more concerned for his daughter, the nightmare of a situation he found himself in.

"When I get home, you better have a good explanation," he said to the vision of his daughter in his mind.

She had looked like death warmed over when he left her. Now he worried why she looked that way.

Stewart lifted his backpack, heavy with his old man's loot that he had gathered from the study. He grinned proudly, and in his mind ran his own delusional version of how the scene would play out once his father returned. The old man would walk through the door and his jaw would comically drop when he realized he'd been robbed. His desk left in shambles; the gold hourglass given to him by his own father, gone; the box of imported cigars, empty; and half a bottle of brandy drained onto the soft cushion of his favorite chair. His eyes would quickly glance over to the safe that he kept hidden behind an expensive mahogany shelf of leather-bound books, and he would fall to his knees and scream at the sight of it standing open, emptied of all the cash he kept stashed inside.

Stewart patted his pockets, the thick stacks of money promising him many days of partying, the likes of which he hadn't taken part in since the old fuck tossed him into the cold streets.

"This is what you get for turning your back on your own son," he said, and the addiction in his veins both congratulated him and urged him to hit the streets, to score.

Stewart slung the backpack up onto his shoulder and then dug into his front pocket until he pulled out a nearly flattened pack of cigarettes. He withdrew the last one and lit it. His father hated when he smoked in the mansion, even though the hypocrite was always up here puffing on his cigars. It would be the icing on the cake. The smell would waft downstairs and lead the old man up to face his defeat. He took a long, satisfied drag and released the puff of smoke slowly, watching it defile his father's sanctuary.

"Got another one of those?"

The voice startled Stewart, his bravery dwindling to cowardice in an instant. He turned quickly and saw the silhouette of his sister standing in the doorway to the study.

"Goddamnit! Fuck, Barbie, you trying to give me a heart attack?"

"I just need a smoke." Her voice sounded hoarse, like she just woke up from a three-day hangover.

"This is my last one."

"Then give me a drag."

"Get outta my way, and don't say a fuckin' word to Dad until I leave. I want him to find out by seeing my handiwork."

Barbie didn't move. She just stayed there, waiting for Stewart to hand her the cigarette.

"I said, get the fuck outta my way."

"And I said to give me a drag off of your cigarette! I smoked all mine."

"Yeah, sure. You quit months ago. You're just wasting time so Dad can call the cops, right?"

Barbie stepped closer to Stewart and, in the dim light of the study, he could see she was pale and sweaty, her lips dry. She held her hand out, and he shrunk away from her long thin fingers.

"Is he home?" Stewart asked. "You're just stalling for him, aren't you, you fuckin' rat?"

Stewart tried to shove his sister out of the way, but she wouldn't budge. She felt heavier than her usual petite self, too, like she had swallowed a sack of bricks.

"Get outta the way!"

Barbie snatched the cigarette hanging from his lips and shoved him back.

Stewart tumbled over the arm of their father's favorite chair and hit his head on the heavy wooden desk that he had just cleared of its valuables. The backpack tangled around him, and he struggled to get back on his feet, cursing his little sister as he did.

"You really don't want to fuck with me, Stewart."

"What's your skinny ass gonna do?" he asked, though he internally wondered if she wasn't knocked up by how heavy she felt when he had pushed her. She looked like she'd spent all day hunkered over a toilet.

"It isn't just me anymore," she said, gripping her gut.

"I knew it; you're a whore. Probably got pregnant by some golf caddie, right?"

His sister didn't answer. She just smoked the cigarette feverishly until the filter lit. She tossed it at Stewart and waved a cloud of smoke away from her face. Stewart leaped back when a spark from the dying cigarette lit the brandy he had dumped on the chair. Flames ate into the cushion, and smoke filled the room as he attempted to make his escape. The streets were calling to him, promising him a fix and a loose woman.

Barbie stepped into his path.

"I need to hitch a ride with someone, but you, you look like a fuckin' lab rat with your eyes all glassy," Barbie said, her voice distorted and gravelly.

Stewart's mouth popped open. He was ready to tell his sister off, but her lips spread into a grin that went so wide it split her cheeks.

"I got yer number," she said. "You like to shoot shit into yer veins. What kind of ride would that be for me? There's no power in that, nothin' that would excite me...save for maybe skinnin' a few of your junkie friends before I hit the highway."

Barbie's eyes turned white, milky as a dead man's.

Stewart stepped back. "What the fuck?"

"You'd be too much like your bitch sister. I sure showed her a good time. Took her for a ride and showed her what a real party was, but her body is far too weak. I need someone strong."

Stewart shook his head, praying this was some drug-induced hallucination caused by his need for a fix. His sister reached up, starting to peel her own face off, and Stewart felt himself losing consciousness. His vision blurred as he fell to the floor and began to put together the pieces, that this person wasn't his sister at all, but something had taken control over her, possessed her.

"You don't look strong," she said. "You look like a piece of shit."

Stewart couldn't move, or scream. Something in Barbie's white eyes held him captive.

She moved in closer and stood over him, picked up a picture of their father in a gold frame. It was from an article about him in the local newspaper that proclaimed him a dominant business figure, a man of real power.

"Now there's a body I'd like to be in. He looks like he's goin' places, places I want to be...but first, I need a ride."

Jim walked along quickly, his anger and disgust driving him onward. He didn't care about his wrecked car. He was too fixated on getting back to Barbie. Evening was coming, and he worried he wouldn't make it home until long after dark. By then the house could be swarmed with police.

On the horizon, he saw two headlights, like yellow eyes staring at him, promising him a faster way to reach his daughter. He hadn't been so desperate in all his life. He stuck out his thumb and swallowed the lump of embarrassment rising in his throat.

The car slowed and it wasn't until he reached the passenger side window that he realized it was familiar to him. He leaned in the opened window and couldn't believe his luck, running into his no-good son out here, staring at him with a wide grin on his face. Cigarette smoke hung in a stinking cloud around Stewart's face. Jim could only imagine what he would want in return for a ride; he felt his checkbook wailing in agony. It would be costly, for sure, both in terms of cash and pride. He would have to endure it.

"Hey, dad, tired of walkin'?" the thing in the car said.

REMEMBERING FRANK

by Matt Bechtel

My contribution to this anthology, "Cozzy's Question," is Bob Booth's last story.

He began plotting it when he entered Hospice, about two weeks before he passed. After a few days of "spitballing" it with him—discussing characters and plot points as we so often did—his story consumed me. Compounded by the fact that he was fading quickly, I asked Bob if I could take a crack at writing it. He was in so much pain that he could barely speak, but he smiled, nodded, and told me, "Have at it."

The story that poured out wound up taking a very different direction, and halfway through I realized I was writing it entirely for myself. However, upon completion and getting feedback from a few trusted readers, I realized the story was worth sharing, even though it had been borne from my own grief. White Noise Press originally published it as a stand-alone chapbook in 2014, and it was later included in my collection, *Monochromes and Other Stories* from Haverhill House Publishing in 2017.

Which was when Frank read it. And in his review of *Monochromes* for *Cemetery Dance,* he wrote of "Cozzy's Question," "By far, my favorite tale is this Twilight Zone-esque story which actually made me tear up for a moment."

Revisiting that review made me tear up for a moment. Because you see, Frank and Bob missed each other; Frank's first Necon was a few years after Bob passed. But Bob once famously said of the convention he founded, "You either get Necon or you don't," and make no mistake, Frank Michaels Errington GOT it and GOT us. One year, while he was enduring his own hero's trial, Frank scheduled a dialysis treatment at a nearby clinic so he could take a three-hour break and return to Necon immediately thereafter. Hell, there's a reason why Necon's annual "Year's Best Books Kaffeeklatsch" has been renamed in his honor—such was his love for our community and tribe, and such is our love for him. And that kind of love endures forever.

The original dedication of "Cozzy's Question" read, "Dedicated to our family (all of you)." Honestly, that's why I find the story's inclusion in this anthology so appropriate—because even though he never shared a Saugy and a drink with Bob on this side of the veil, Frank is, and will always be, one of us.

WHAT ARE LITTLE GIRLS MADE OF?

by Christa Carmen

Sugar and spice and everything nice. That's what little girls are made of.

At least, that's what the nursery rhyme says. Constance and Michael Tiverton had always believed that particular verse. When they had their first child, however, a daughter they named Nadia, they became convinced that little girls were made of worry and fright of things that go bump in the night.

Though Constance and Michael both had anxious dispositions, Nadia gave new meaning to the term worrywart. As a toddler, Nadia bit her nails and twirled her hair, sucked her thumb and chewed her lip. By her fifth birthday, she'd shed those more benign habits in favor of what would be her primary method of self-soothing.

The doctors called it excoriation, a type of impulse-control disorder characterized by the repetitive and compulsive picking of the skin, picking that could result in tissue damage, if the sufferer was unable to control his or her symptoms. Nadia's parents called it what it looked like—picking—and had lost count of the number of times they'd been forced to say, "Nadia Tiverton, if you don't stop picking at your fingers, you'll pull every inch of your skin clean off!"

When Nadia started kindergarten, everything from the weather to the mood of the family's capricious cat could send her into a spiral of worry and despair. Once, when a hurricane warning kept her class indoors at recess, Nadia became so convinced of impending disaster, of the classroom's big bay windows imploding in a shower of glass, of the storm reaching in its giant, terrible hand of wind and rain and lifting her out, up, and away, that she'd peeled massive strips of skin off each of her fingers before Ms. Wendy could inform them that the hurricane had been downgraded to a regular old tropical storm.

On the day Nadia was to make her First Holy Communion, such was her nervousness at the prospect of walking down the aisle before God and the rest of the congregation that she spent the moments before mass working a dangerously substantial flap of skin loose. The depression in her thumb was so deep, it issued forth a stream of bright red blood that soaked the front of her heretofore pristine white dress. Her mother, father, and the entirety of French Creek Church, were horrified by the sight of seven-year-old Nadia walking down the aisle, pale and trembling, covered in blood, and looking for all the world like the murder victim of a violent ghost who called the narthex home.

By the time Nadia entered high school, there wasn't a student, male or female, who had not experienced firsthand the fallout of Nadia's gory habit. Unlike Nadia's parents—and *most* of her teachers—her classmates were neither kind nor diplomatic in their suggestions that she refrain from picking at her skin.

"Here comes Nadia," the girls would sneer from in front of the locker room mirrors, as they smeared gloss across their lips and rolled up their shorts in preparation for gym class. "Hurry up and open the tampon machine…she'll need ten! One for each finger."

On the field, while Nadia picked at her cuticles, and waited to be chosen last for softball, lacrosse, or soccer, the boys would sing under their breath:

Little Miss Nadia, French Creek's biggest freak,
She'll pick her fingers and spring a leak.
Don't follow after her to use a bat or ball,
'Cuz you can bet it'll be a bloody free-for-all!

Or:
Miss Nadia Tiverton in a blood-speckled dress,
Could get none of the boys to touch her chest.
If ever a boy dared to look her way,
She'd open up a wound and the blood would spray!

At night, alone in the dark, the fingers of one hand tearing at the fingers of the other, blood splattering the once-white sheets, Nadia would promise herself there'd be no more picking. She'd curb the horrible habit once and for all, starting tomorrow.

But each morning, as the first beams of sunlight streamed through her bedroom window, thoughts of war and death, of losing her parents in an accident or getting kidnapped, of plummeting college acceptance rates and fake news and politics and nuclear weapons, Nadia's fingers would react to her fears, first by scratching, then by prodding, then pinching and peeling and pulling and picking and tearing, until the prospect of a day without bleeding slipped through her fingers like sand, as impossible to believe in as glass slippers or fairy godmothers.

By the start of her junior year, Nadia Tiverton had been to the emergency room six times for self-inflicted injuries so serious, they required stitches. On her sixteenth birthday, at which no one but her cousin and the daughter of her mother's friend from next door showed up, Nadia wished her parents' admonishment ("You'll pull all your skin clean off!") would just come true. Maybe, if she stripped herself of every square inch of skin, all her impulsive worrying and catastrophizing would cease.

The thought dissipated along with the smoke from the sixteen birthday candles (plus one for good luck), but Nadia found it returned more and more as time wore on. It revisited her as her fears ballooned, as those troubles resulting from her excoriation disorder grew.

Most of Nadia's nailbeds were so damaged from the constant trauma that the fingernails had fallen out, and once gone, refused to grow back. The few nails that remained were discolored and malformed, yellow with rot and ridged from years of abuse. The fingers themselves were a nightmare of scars, and had the shriveled, shrunken look of flesh left too long in stale and stagnant water.

Nadia hid her hands from the prying eyes of others whenever she could, donning gloves in the wintertime, and stretching shirtsleeves over fingertips to the point where the fabric shredded. But these were temporary barriers only, erected to delay the inevitable. A shaky dam at the mercy of a pummeling river. The eye of an ever-present storm.

In the spring of her junior year, Nadia's classmates began to exude excitement over the impending prom like voracious shrews emitting a heavy, heady musk. Nadia had no delusions that an invitation to the dance was in her future. She'd never attended a sleepover, never gasped over a shared bowl of popcorn at the latest slasher flick, but she knew who Carrie White was, and the blood-covered prom dress was not a look any girl aspired to.

The night of the dance, after insisting to her parents that she was fine, that she didn't want to go out for ice cream, didn't want to play cards or watch television or submit to any of the other well-meaning distractions they proposed, she sat at her vanity and inspected herself in the mirror. She tried to picture herself in a fancy dress, and held back her hair, imagining the way a stylist could have manipulated the golden tendrils to fall just so.

The lumpy gauze around her fingers ruined the effect. With a whimper, she let her hair fall back to her shoulders. Still staring at herself in the mirror, she started unwrapping the bandages, piece by piece.

What are *little girls made of?* she thought, adding another piece of gauze to the pile beside her.

Perhaps the girls at the prom are made of sugar and spice and everything nice, but surely I am not.

Fingers liberated, she gripped a flap of skin.

Surely I could see what I am *made of, if I could just get a look beneath my skin.*

Nails squeezing the wayward ectodermal tissue, Nadia pulled. The skin peeled away from the muscle in a wide, neat strip, crested the fingertip, and continued peeling, as if Nadia was yanking at the finger of a glove she no longer wished to wear.

What are little girls made of? she thought again, rather wildly. *Of worry and fright of things that go bump in the night.*

Adjusting her angle, she pulled again, and the skin around the second finger gave way.

Of muscle and bone, she sang to herself, *and the terror of being alone.*

The skin that had covered the rest of her hand came away easily enough. With a jerk, the entirety of the skin encasing her arm followed suit.

"Of tendon and blood," she said, now out loud, "and of washing away in a flood."

The skin around her shoulder pulled free with a wet ripping sound, and took the top portion of the skin across her chest and stomach with it. The skin of her second arm went after that, which allowed her to use both hands now, to pull. She stepped out of the skin that had sheathed her legs as if bidding farewell to an old pair of pants.

"Of disappointments and fears, and of too many tears…"

Nadia gripped the flap of skin at the base of her neck. She set her jaw, closed her eyes, and pulled. The upward motion, the removal of the mask, was like that of a younger Nadia on a past Halloween, but oh-so-much-more gratifying. At the point of her closed eyes, the skin caught, resisted, threatened to hold fast.

She grunted, and pulled harder, stifling a scream.

The last of the skin suit tore free.

Nadia Tiverton stood, a crimson statue of raw and gleaming muscle, at the center of the room. She smiled at her reflection, at the fact that there was—at last!—no more pesky skin at which to pick.

Every inch of it had been pulled clean off.

She walked out of the bedroom, downstairs, and through the foyer toward the door.

"Nadia, is that you?" her father called from the living room.

"Sweetheart," her mother said. "Where are you going?"

"I'm going to the prom after all," said the girl who had no skin. "To be sugar and spice and everything nice, and a girl who is trapped no more."

And with that, she opened the door, and stepped out into the night.

FRUITS OF LABOR

by Robert Ford

Every once in a while, he would remember his *Christian name,* as his mother used to call it, but those times weren't often. For over twenty years, he had simply been called "Stone" by the other people, like him, living on the streets. There was no reason to use anything else.

He crawled from the small hutch of cardboard he had slept in the night before and blinked at the overhead sky. It was overcast and gray, and Stone wondered if the sun would burn it off as the day wore on.

The cardboard shelter wasn't where he normally stayed—only a makeshift spot behind an alley dumpster to spend the night and get some sleep as he scoured the lines of the city. The house-dwellers going to and from, they didn't see the order of the lines—they only saw direction—and it saddened Stone.

Realizing the order in that chaos so long ago is what had set him free. All of those people consuming and taking… *Take, take, take,* that's all they did. He used to think that way, that pushing papers here and there and attending meetings deemed important and valuable actually meant something.

But they didn't. They contributed nothing.

Locusts. All of them were locusts. Consuming and eating and moving onto something else when the fields of their attention were empty.

To live is to give.

Stone had seen that phrase on a church sign years ago and it had lodged in his mind like a piece of gravel in the tread of a work boot. The thought made him glance down at his bare feet. To describe them as dirty would be a weak and unworthy attempt. No, Stone's feet were caked and covered to a burnt brown color with texture like the bark of an ancient pine tree. He pulled the hem of his tan canvas pants lower toward his ankles, and the scent of what was beneath wafted toward him. The flesh of his calves itched, and he moved, carefully getting to his knees, and stood to stretch.

His thick tumbleweed beard itched too. Stone ignored it at first, and then ran a hand over his face and down over the coarse hair and thick clusters nested within. It had started a month ago, after he had spent a few days sleeping in Haddon Park in the middle of the city. It had been beautiful there, surrounded by the tall, peeling sycamore trees that framed the long curving pond. He had stared at the reflection of the moon flickering in the water and the black shadows of the ducks as they swam.

The wood ticks had come for him in the night as he slept, slowly making their way to a new home in the wild thicket of his beard hair.

Stone had let them be—after all, they were only doing what they were meant to do—and now they grouped among the graying strands of his beard and fed, shiny and swollen like overripe green grapes. He ran a hand down over them again, the sensation against his palm like touching a collection of polished marbles. There was a soft popping sound, faint and muffled, as one of the ticks burst and thin pus squirted over the salt and pepper hair of his beard like morning dew.

In the distance, a church bell rang.

Stone considered walking toward the sound to watch the people gather, but he decided against it. He'd seen enough house-dweller sheep in his life and besides, he had his own flock to attend to.

He'd been counted among the sheep long ago—another lifetime. A nice job and a nice house, and cars and a wife and a daughter.

All nice. Everything was nice.

But it wasn't truth. It was an illusion painted to perfection. Treasured baubles that only existed in his mind.

It's time.

As life went on, one by one, all of those nice things had been taken away. He'd turned over the reasons—still did during some nights as the darkness dragged on—why all of it had been stolen.

The wheel of fate. Karma. Bad luck. God's will.

At times, there were not enough tears to drown the thoughts. He could still hear the phone call, like some emergency broadcast on loop, the day truth was revealed.

A car accident, sir. Your wife and daughter were—

A car horn blared from the street, and Stone shook his head. He twisted, stretched his arms over his head, and lifted his backpack from the cobbled-together cardboard shelter. Stone slung the strap over his shoulder and headed toward the tunnels—his real home and the home of his flock.

It took close to an hour to reach the tunnel from here, but Stone didn't mind. After all this time, the sidewalks and alleyways were familiar friends. He took his own path, through torn chain-link fences and abandoned yards, overgrown with weeds and concrete blocks scattered like broken teeth.

He reached the entrance to the subway tunnel and set his backpack to the pavement.

It's time.

Easing down to the pavement, Stone withdrew a harmonica from the front pocket of his stained denim jacket, and began to play—a slow, mournful harmony that grew in tempo and pitch. He drew breath from his tired lungs, exhaled into the hobo harp, making it sing. The ticks in his beard wriggled and grew antsy from the noise.

As Stone stared into the shadows of the tunnel, he began to see them appear and walk into the light. One by one they came closer and sat, cross-legged and silent, gathering at the song he played.

Three at first, then four more, another five—the people he had grown to love and care for during his years on the streets all gathered around him and sat in a circle. Their expressions varied from mild amusement and smiling eyes, to the too-familiar vacant stare of someone wondering how they came to arrive at living homeless.

Stone played a few moments longer and then tucked his harmonica back into the torn pocket of his jacket. His smile was safely hidden behind his beard, but it was there as he scanned the faces of the people surrounding him. He gave a nod.

To live is to give.

Stone had given in life. Love and affection and attention and money. And the selfish mechanic of existence had decided to take more. What he had given wasn't enough. A cosmic parasite intent on siphoning away everything.

Stone studied their expectant, hopeful faces. How it had come to be, Stone couldn't remember, but gradually, over time, they had all started to view him as provider, protector, guider.

Shepherd.

He stepped closer to Rags, the young brunette woman who had come to live among them several years ago. Stone remembered her arrival well—bruised and beaten like a dog bound for a shelter—as his flock had welcomed her in with open arms. They had cared for her as Stone had taught them—nursed her body and healed her mind—and here she was before him, fire in her eyes once again.

Looking skyward, Stone uttered a silent request. He raised his arms out to his sides and began to weep at the silence from his unheard prayers. Tears fell along his cheeks, creating trails through the grime lighter than the surrounding skin.

Stone nodded slightly, and sadly, at the expected silence, and his attention turned toward the darkness of the tunnel and what lay beyond. Stone repeated his plea for help and soft whispers began at the back of his mind. Murmurs layered on top of one another, making the words indecipherable—a choir discussing a legion of forbidden secrets.

Inside the hairy froth of his beard, the gluttonous crowd of ticks began to release their parasitic grip. One by one, they began to writhe and move and march. They crawled north until they dragged themselves over the skin of his weathered lips, their spindly legs as soft as the tickle of a baby's eyelashes.

An assembly line of engorged ticks continued along Stone's face and neck, making their way down his arms, until they began to reach his calloused, filthy hands. The people gathered around Stone's feet began to sway.

He turned to Rags and offered her a plump tick, filled so tightly the flesh was smooth as a green tomato, and the young woman took it into her mouth and chewed. Her eyes closed as she savored the delicacy.

One by one, Stone fed the group of homeless birds the parasites of his love. One by one, they took his offerings, biting into the too-full ticks. Stone watched the filled sacks burst inside their mouths like well-made confections packed with strawberry jam.

Gradually, the creeping sensations along his hands slowed and then stopped, and Stone felt the people licking at his fingertips, their mouths hungry still, yearning like newborn calves for their mother's teat.

What does one give when they have nothing left? What does one offer other than themself?

Stone smiled at his flock and bent to the cuffs of his pants. His attention was on the tattered end of his left leg first, and he took time and care to peel it up from his ankle, cautiously moving the fabric away from the odd, bulging form around his leg. The musk rolling from Stone's legs was earthy and dank. He grabbed the pants cuff and pulled, tearing the worn cloth along the stitched seam.

Pale green curls of vine sprung free and Stone released a deep sigh at the release of pressure. He pulled harder and the cloth tore higher, up to his thigh. Stone turned to his other leg, repeated the process, and stood, his pants in tatters of cloth.

Stalks embedded into the flesh of his calf muscles bulged beneath Stone's mud-colored shins. Pale green, sun-hungry vines twisted into thin branches and groups of broad leaves. Stone saw the flock's expression change. Their hungry faces filled with awe.

A skinny post of a man everyone called Nails reached out timidly toward Stone and plucked a tomato from the vine. The group's focus turned to watch Nails place the tomato between his lips and tenderly bite into the fruit. It popped, and a small mixture of juice and seed slopped over the man's lower lip.

Nails closed his eyes and inhaled through his nose, almost sensually, as he chewed. Nails opened his eyes again and the rest of them began to reach for Stone's legs. Each time a ripe tomato was pulled from the plants, Stone trembled as shivers rolled through his body.

One by one, they took of him, eating tomato after tomato, until his vines were empty, barren of fruit and blossom.

Stone was empty. A void. A dry field.

The moist sound of them chewing the fruit grown of his flesh and blood continued until they were silent again. Stone looked down at their faces, still full of hope and light and…hunger. *Still* hunger.

Stone smiled and nodded at his abandoned children, the lost souls looking to him for guidance. For salvation. He pushed the sleeve on his left arm up toward his elbow, exposing his wrist and forearm.

Protector. Shepherd. Provider.

Stone did the only thing he could do. There had never been a choice.

He brought his wrist toward the matted tangle of his beard and put his mouth against the gritty, salty skin before biting down. Blood spilled onto his lips, and Stone clenched his teeth harder and wrenched his head to the side. A flap of skin tore away like the first bite of a fresh apple. He turned and offered his bleeding wrist to his flock and they clambered over one another to drink.

He stood, giving his life, until he couldn't. The muscles in his thighs felt watery and as weak as a newborn kitten's. Stone fell to his knees on the warm pavement. His head swam, and distantly, he felt someone bite into the soft flesh of his right wrist. He spread his arms wide.

They clawed at him, clutching fistfuls of his grungy clothes. The vines along Stone's legs, now stripped of fruit, broke and snapped under the attention of their clenching hands. The green plant smell mixed with the hot penny scent of his blood. He let himself fall backward into the fold and watched the sky overhead darken as the shape of their silhouettes descended upon him.

Stone closed his eyes and smiled and let his sheep feed until darkness arrived.

YOU CAN'T EAT JUST ONE

by Paul F. Olson

Nikki Setterlind was beginning to suspect that she was not normal. To be honest, there were more than a few signs, but the most obvious one was this: too many things annoyed her these days. On her good days, it felt like half of everything she saw, heard, or thought about ticked her off. On the bad days, the percentage was much higher. Her friends at school flitted around like they always had, with their same old vapid smiles. They were like blissful little butterflies, unaware and uninvolved, going from flower to flower with scarcely a thought in their heads: beautiful wings, tiny brains.

Nikki, on the other hand, seemed to have evolved into another kind of creature altogether, something awkward and gangly—an ostrich, perhaps, stalking around a barren desert, cocking her head angrily left and right, glaring at everything that annoyed her, which was most things, most of the time. She was bugged by her parents. She was bugged by her older brother, Dan. She was bugged by her boyfriend, Drew LaCroix, who really wasn't her boyfriend anymore. She was bugged by her teachers, by her soccer coach, by the movie selection on Netflix, the games on her phone, the posters on her wall, not to mention the wall itself, her entire bedroom, and, for that matter, the whole damn house. Last night, she had almost thrown her laptop across the room, fiercely irritated at the way everybody in the world called it "The Ghost of Christmas Future" when Charles Dickens had quite clearly named it "The Ghost of Christmas Yet to Come."

Yeah, she thought. That was not normal.

This had been going on for several months now, and others had begun to notice. Her friends, Alyssa Chase and Tana Gorensen, had both remarked in recent days how "hormonal" she had become. Mr. Ebert, her algebra teacher, told her she needed to "lighten up" in class. And yesterday morning, in the midst of a frankly ridiculous argument over scrambled eggs, her mother had thrown up her hands in exasperation, and said, "What's wrong with you, anyway? You're becoming such a curmudgeon."

While she had agreed with the sentiment, Nikki was shocked by the image. To her, a curmudgeon was impossibly old and decidedly male, like that ancient crank, Tommie Koski, who ran the antique shop in Kelly's Corners with a permanent sneer in his voice and a perpetual scowl on his face. Could you even have a fourteen-year-old curmudgeon? A *female* curmudgeon?

It wasn't until the following afternoon that the answer to that question hit her with a nasty jolt. She was riding her bike home after school under a dark and lowering October sky. Earlier in the day, a wind-driven mix of rain and sleet had swept through the area, and the streets of Patterson Falls were slick. She was slowing down to make a cautious turn onto Cedar Street when she suddenly remembered that stupid fight with her mother and the truth hit home.

There were indeed female curmudgeons. Oh, yes. There were *lots* of them, but that's not what people called them. They had a different name for them, something uglier. And as for age, that had absolutely nothing to do with it. Young, old, or in between, a female curmudgeon was a bitch.

So that was what she was. Or maybe it was what she was turning into. Either way, it was not good. It meant she was destined to be a bitch, and that was a pretty crappy destiny. She needed to do something about that. She needed to fix it.

Are these the shadows of the things that will be, or are they shadows of the things that may be only?

That made her laugh, but without much humor.

"Ghost of Christmas Future, my ass," she muttered.

She began to peddle faster, in a hurry now to get home and return to the one thing that still made her happy these days: her books. At the moment, that meant one book in particular—a Kate Morton novel she had picked up Monday at the little lending library Mrs. Norman operated in the vacant lot across from her house on Coakley Street. She had read a few Mortons before and enjoyed them, but this one was something special. She had fallen in love with it immediately, and by the time she reached page one-hundred, *The Clockmaker's Daughter* had become her new favorite novel. The whole thing felt like an embarrassment of riches, with its abundance of characters, shifting perspectives, crisscrossing timelines, and a haunted, melancholy atmosphere. It was like nothing she had ever read before, and she was enchanted.

But her dream of reading was interrupted a block from home when she saw her father's pickup heading her way. He spotted her, too, stopped in the middle of the road, and waved her over.

"Throw your bike in the back and hop in. I want to show you something."

Nikki felt a surge of annoyance and disappointment. "I really don't have time, Dad."

"Nonsense. You're fourteen years old. You've got nothing but time."

"I really—"

"Fifteen minutes tops. Humor the old man."

Nikki sighed and hefted her bike into the pickup bed, where it joined some pieces of old scrap lumber, a spare tire with no air in it, and a motley collection of toolboxes that had been sliding around back there since Nikki was in the first grade.

Her father headed back toward downtown, which made Nikki's heart sink, sure that he was going to take her to the Dairy Hut for an ice cream cone. For years it had been a Setterlind tradition to get in one last ice cream run before the Hut closed for the season on Halloween. Nikki had always looked forward to those excursions. Today, however, it just felt like another inconvenience.

But her father drove right by the Hut and pulled up instead into a parking space half a block down, in front of a building that looked like it should have been torn down fifty years ago. With peeling paint, a sagging second story, and a display window covered with plywood, the place definitely looked ready for the wrecking ball. Nikki vaguely remembered it being a shoe store a long time ago. Her mother had taken her there to get a new pair of sneakers before her first day of kindergarten, and the saleswoman had given her a red balloon.

"What are we doing here?"

"I thought you might want to see Patterson Falls' new bookstore."

"New...*what?*"

"I just signed the last of the contracts with the new owner, a guy from downstate. I'm going to be renovating the place over the winter, in time to get it opened up next May."

"A bookstore? Here?"

Her father grinned. "Slight exaggeration. It's not an honest-to-goodness bookstore. It's a coffee shop, really. And a smoothie bar. And a gift shop. But in the back, he wants to have an entire section of bookshelves—new releases and bestsellers, some classics, and a stock of Michigan books, of course. So not a *real* bookstore, but the closest thing we've ever had around here."

He pulled out his phone and opened a photo album containing a half-dozen blueprints. Nikki couldn't make heads or tails of them at first, especially on the small screen, but her father patiently took her through them one by one, expanding the images and pointing out where things would be. After that, he opened the glove compartment and took out a manila envelope containing a tarnished key.

"Want to see the inside?"

"I guess," Nikki said with a shrug.

For the next fifteen minutes her father walked her around the place, showing her where the coffee bar would be, the booths, the tables, the display space for Conley Lake sweatshirts and hats, but none of it really registered with Nikki. The building was filthy, and it smelled of dust and mildew and animal urine. It bore no resemblance at all to the former shoe store, though all she really remembered of that place were some mirrors and a bench by the front door—and the balloon, of course. She tried to act interested but had trouble working up much enthusiasm, even when her father took her to the back and showed her where the book department would be.

"You don't seem very excited by all this," he said at last. "I thought you'd be happy to have a place in town that sells books."

"I am," she said, unsure why she was lying to him.

Later, when they got home, she raced for her room and grabbed *The Clockmaker's Daughter* off the nightstand, eager to immerse herself again in the world of Birchwood Manor. But she read only a few pages before putting the book down with a sigh, finally realizing why the thought of the new business didn't excite her the way it should.

By all rights, someone who read as much as she did should have been over the moon at the prospect of a bookstore in Patterson Falls—even a fake, wannabe, poseur bookstore meant to appeal way more to the summer people than to the year-round residents. And she would have been excited, except for some strange reason she found herself feeling sorry. Not for herself. For Marie Norman.

That made absolutely zero sense, of course. There was no connection between the new business, which was nothing but a moldy old building now and wouldn't even be open for another seven or eight months, and Mrs. Norman's little lending library, which had been around nearly as long as Nikki could remember. To think that the new one would be competition for the old was just silly. And competition for what? Mrs. Norman didn't sell her books. She didn't make a dime from her endeavor. To say that the new place would be competing with her was like saying McDonald's competed with the guy down the street who grilled up some burgers and invited you over to eat.

Nikki returned to the book but still had trouble concentrating. Eventually, she stopped trying and went down to help get dinner on the table instead.

Nikki had never been inside Mrs. Norman's house, but she had a pretty clear picture of what it would be like. It would be stuffed full of old-lady knickknacks and sad framed photos of her dead husband. The refrigerator door would be covered with little cat magnets holding up the greeting cards sent by grown children who never visited. And all of it would be smothered beneath a heavy blanket of flowery smells: sachet, bath powder, potpourri.

She had steeled herself to face all of that, but now it appeared she wouldn't get the chance. She had been knocking on Mrs. Norman's door for several minutes without an answer. The dead silence that greeted her filled her with a vague sense of unease.

Until two months ago, none of this would have been necessary. Back then, Mrs. Norman had been outside every time Nikki came to visit the little library across the street. It had been that way for years, from the time Mrs. Norman had installed her very first display unit—that red wooden box with a peaked, shingled roof that looked like a birdhouse on steroids mounted atop a stout wooden post—and in the years since, as she added a second display next to the first (green), then a third (blue), and a fourth (yellow). Whenever Nikki arrived, Mrs. Norman would be there ahead of her, puttering away: organizing the books inside the displays, adding new titles, repairing the shelves, polishing the glass doors, touching up the paint, brushing dead leaves or pine needles off the roofs, trimming the grass around the posts. But that had all changed and Nikki had not seen the woman since…it seemed hard to believe, but at least since the middle of August.

At first, she had assumed it was just bad timing, that she happened to be visiting when Mrs. Norman was cleaning her house or doing laundry or downtown shopping for groceries at the SuperValu. As time went by, sure, she began to have some doubts, but even then she had refused to think too hard about it. It was just a run of bad luck, that's all.

Now, knocking and knocking and getting no answer, she wasn't so sure.

Nikki stood on tiptoe and peered through the little octagonal pane of glass in the middle of the door. There wasn't much to see, just an empty entryway. On the left was a staircase, on the right a coatrack with a single brown sweater hanging on it. Beyond that, there was a doorway leading somewhere and a long hallway leading somewhere else. There were no lights on, no movement, no signs of life.

Nikki shivered. She knocked one more time, but her heart was no longer in it. She turned around on the stoop and looked at Mrs. Norman's front yard. Her breath caught in her throat as she noticed what she had failed to see before— what perhaps she had not *wanted* to see. The lawn, normally mowed every week in the summer and fall, trimmed and raked and kept as neat as a pin, had grown long and shaggy. Dead October leaves were scattered across the grass and piled in messy windrows along the edges of the weed-choked garden.

She hurried down the sidewalk and across Coakley Street to the library Mrs. Norman had lovingly built and tended to for so long.

The four display units looked exactly as they always had, clean, orderly, and fully stocked, as if Mrs. Norman had just left a minute ago after finishing her daily maintenance.

The units were nearly identical copies of the Little Free Libraries that had sprung up in towns and cities around the world in recent years. They operated the same, too, with a simple *Take a book, leave a book* philosophy. But Mrs. Norman had never officially affiliated herself with the international movement. Above the door of each unit, where the Little Free Library sign would normally have been posted, there was instead a hand-painted sign reading FOOD FOR THE SOUL. And below that, slightly smaller: BETCHA CAN'T EAT JUST ONE. Back when Nikki had first discovered this marvelous place, she had not understood the joke. She had asked her father about it, and he had explained about the Lay's potato chips ads from the old days. But even before that, she'd had a pretty good idea what Mrs. Norman was getting at. Books were like junk food, seductive, irresistible, powerfully addicting.

Taking a deep breath, Nikki opened the glass front door of the yellow unit. There, on the bottom shelf, was another door, this one smaller and made of balsa wood, with a cheap, tiny lock to keep out snoopers. Mrs. Norman had installed this door almost two years ago, painting it with a row of little daisies and three words: NICOLE'S PRIVATE STASH.

"I have to do something for my best customer," she had said. "You know that most of the people who stop here are summer folks—cottagers and tourists on their way out to the lake. I can count the number of locals on my fingers, and most of them come only once or twice a year. But you, my dear, you're here twice a week like clockwork. That kind of loyalty deserves to be rewarded, so I set up this special area just for you, and I promise to always keep it stocked with books I think you'll like."

Nikki dug into her pocket and pulled out the little silver key Mrs. Norman had given her that day. Her hands had begun to tremble, and it took her three tries to fit the key into the lock.

The last time she had been here, just four days ago, she had picked up the Kate Morton book and left an Agatha Christie and two Dean Koontz novels in its place. If what she now feared was true, she would open NICOLE'S PRIVATE STASH and find those same three books sitting there, right where she'd left them.

She gritted her teeth and opened the door.

With a surge of relief, she saw that her books were gone, replaced by four fat hardcovers. She took them out one by one, running her hands across the glossy covers. There was another Kate Morton, a novel by Ruth Ware, a volume called *The Complete Short Stories of F. Scott Fitzgerald,* and a monstrous doorstop of a book by someone called James A. Michener.

Nikki wobbled on her feet, nearly overcome with relief. A moment ago, she had been absolutely certain that Mrs. Norman was dead. These books, these *gifts,* proved that she was not. It had just been a matter of bad timing, after all.

She loaded the hardcovers into her backpack and replaced them in the display with the paperbacks she had brought to trade. She was in the process of relocking the little wooden door when she heard footsteps behind her.

"I don't think you're s'posed to be messin' around here."

She turned and saw an old man standing a few feet away, eyeing her warily. He was wearing a faded Detroit Tigers cap and a denim jacket with the collar turned up against the chill.

"The kids were up here this past weekend," the old man said. "I talked to the son. He said they're gonna be puttin' the place on the market soon, so I'd leave my hands off all their stuff if I was you."

Nikki stared at him in confusion, unable to process what he'd just said; he might as well have been speaking Finnish.

"Kids?" she said.

"Yeah. Her kids. Marie's kids. They've been up a few times lately, takin' care of business. There's always lots to do when…" He trailed off with a half-hearted shrug.

"When what?"

"When…well, y'know. When someone dies."

Nikki felt her heart beating faster. "When someone dies," she repeated softly. "Is…is Mrs. Norman dead?"

"Well, yeah."

There was a strange, distant roaring inside Nikki's head now, and a wave of nausea swept over her.

Mrs. Norman couldn't be dead. That was impossible. She had just left four new books for Nikki to read. Those books were in her backpack right now. She could feel the weight of them pulling at her arm. Mrs. Norman wasn't dead. She had just been here. Sometime in the last four days, she had been here.

An empty house…an uncut lawn…

The old man was giving Nikki an odd look, and she heard the sound of her own voice speaking to him from far away. "How long ago did she die?"

"Ohhh, that's kinda hard to remember," the old man said, scratching the side of his nose thoughtfully. "It was back in the summertime, for sure. Weather was hot. End of August, maybe? Just before Labor Day?"

Nikki broke away and sprinted for her bike, the heavy backpack banging against her leg as she ran. As she climbed onto the seat, she looked back and saw the old man staring at her in surprise or anger or maybe just total confusion.

She saw something else, too. It lasted for only a second, the length of a single breath, but in that brief time she saw someone standing next to the fourth library unit, the yellow unit, the final unit in the row. She detected a flash of color, a hint of white hair, part of a hand. Not a person. The suggestion of a person.

Then, as quickly as that, it was gone.

It took just a few minutes to find the obituary in the online edition of the *Conley Lake Chronicle*, from the first week of September: *Marie Adele Norman, 83, of 639 Coakley Street, Patterson Falls, died peacefully August 27, at Marquette General Hospital.* And with that, everything began to make sense. Those final days of August were the time each year that her family split up and scattered to the four winds. It was when her mother and father took their annual long weekend to watch the Cubs play in Chicago, when her brother went to basketball camp downstate, and when Nikki herself visited her aunt in Green Bay. That explained it, how Mrs. Norman could have died and she had missed the news.

Of course, there were no details on the cause of death. In the *Chronicle,* no one ever died of anything specific. You went one of two ways, peacefully or unexpectedly, or else died of religious euphemism: *went to be with his Lord, returned to her heavenly home, was called to sing in the angel choir.*

Nikki read the obit carefully, chewing her lower lip to keep from bursting into tears as she learned all about Mrs. Norman's life: her late husband of forty-two years, two children, five grandchildren, and one great-grandchild. Her birth in Minnesota so long ago. Her thirty-year career as a secretary at Barlow's Insurance and her retirement job behind the cash register at Kendrick's True Value. She had belonged to the Patterson Falls Women's Club and the Conley Lake Beautification Committee, and according to the obit, "enjoyed sharing her favorite books with one and all through the small lending library she built close to her home."

That *did* bring the tears, and Nikki angrily closed her laptop, pushing it away so she could no longer see the screen.

"Goodbye, Mrs. Norman," she murmured. "I really didn't know you at all, but you were just about my best friend."

She unzipped her backpack, took out the four books she had found in NICOLE'S PRIVATE STASH an hour ago, and stacked them on the desk. They made an impressive mountain of words, a fortress of paper and ink.

Something brushed the back of her neck. Nikki cried out and whirled around in her chair. She thought for a second that she saw a shadow flicker across the carpet near the door, but decided it was a just an illusion.

Tears in the eyes could do that. And she suddenly had plenty of tears.

"It's a cliché because it's true, Nicole. There is nothing, nothing more wonderful than a book."

It was half an hour past midnight, the temperature was four degrees above freezing, and Nikki was pedaling through a town so quiet it appeared to be utterly empty, as if all the inhabitants had been spirited away by magic. The only things moving besides her bike were the autumn leaves in the street, which skittered and swirled as she rode past.

In the silence, Mrs. Norman's voice came to her with startling clarity. Nikki could remember the conversation perfectly, though it had happened long ago, on an exceedingly warm summer day. They had been sitting next to the little library—there had been only one unit back then—Nikki sprawled in the grass, Mrs. Norman perched in a plastic lawn chair, both of them sipping from glasses of ice-cold limeade.

"Books are the only perfect creation of humankind," Mrs. Norman had said. "They are the most glorious thing you can possess or give to someone else. They're the best gift—the perfect gift, really."

"Is that why you have this?" ten-year-old Nikki had asked, gesturing to the display unit towering above her.

Mrs. Norman smiled. "I've always given books away, you know. Even during those years I worked for John Barlow at the State Farm office. Back then, I kept a little wicker basket full of books next to my desk. Anyone who came in to pay their premium or file a claim walked out with their paperwork, one of John's little free desk calendars, and a book or two from me. Giving books away is part of who I am, Nicole. It's what I've always done, and I always will."

"But why? I mean, you know, I like to read and all. Books are fun. But what make them so special?"

Mrs. Norman looked surprised. "My dear, a book is like a tiny little miracle that you can hold in your hands. Every book, no matter what it is, who wrote it, or what it's about, contains wonders without end. There's a whole world, a complete universe, all of it, right there between the covers—earth and sea and sky, lives and hearts and souls. Do you understand?"

Nikki hadn't—not then, not for a long time—but she had nodded cautiously nevertheless.

"You listen to me, Nicole. There are only two things in all of existence that contain the entire universe inside them. One of them is a book."

Nikki looked up at her, wide-eyed. "What's the other?"

Mrs. Norman smiled gently, leaned over, and tapped Nikki's chest, just above her heart.

"You, my dear. You."

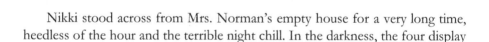

Nikki stood across from Mrs. Norman's empty house for a very long time, heedless of the hour and the terrible night chill. In the darkness, the four display boxes on their pillars looked like shadowy creatures huddled together for warmth.

Finally, after a length of time that might have been five minutes or an eternity, she approached the yellow unit. In her right hand she gripped the key to NICOLE'S PRIVATE STASH. Her left cradled a stack of three books against her chest. She suspected it was no longer necessary to bring books to trade, but she had done so anyway, without even thinking about it.

It's what I've always done, and I always will.

Rather than open the door right away, Nikki surprised herself by reaching up and grasping one of the little cedar shingles on the roof of the display. She wiggled it back and forth, trying to pull it off. At first it wouldn't budge, but after a while it gave a little, and with some more work it actually began to jiggle loosely in her hand. She gave it one last sharp tug, and the tiny shingle came free, leaving a ragged line along the right edge of the roof, like a mouth with a missing tooth.

Nikki walked a short distance away, turned her back, and began to count slowly to one hundred. Her breath puffed out in front of her as she whispered each number into the still night air.

When she was done, she walked back to the library and found that the roof had been restored. Of course it had. She had expected nothing less. The shingle she had removed was still gripped loosely in her hand, but there was another one, a new one in its place. She reached out slowly and touched it, finding the wood smooth and surprisingly warm beneath her hand.

Nikki uttered a short laugh, the sound jarring in the night air. Then she opened the glass door and put the key into the lock on her private compartment.

There were two new books inside. It was too dark to read the titles or make out the authors' names, but that didn't matter. They were her books now. They had been chosen for her, and whatever they were, they would be perfect.

She replaced the books with the ones she had brought and locked up the panel again.

As she turned away, she once again sensed a presence nearby. It was impossible to see, but she felt it clearly. It was as if someone was standing right next to her in the darkness, shoulder to shoulder, hip to hip. There was a gentle movement in the air around her. Rise and fall. Breathing. Heartbeat.

A tingling warmth spread through her, and she realized that for the first time in over two months she did not feel annoyed, irritated, irked, bugged, bothered, or angry about anything.

"I understand now," she said to the night, and with that the sensation passed, leaving her alone again.

On the way back to her bike she noticed something sticking out of the top of one of her new books. She pulled it out, expecting it to be a bookmark of some kind, but it turned out to be a single piece of white paper, tri-folded like a letter.

She opened it up and peered at it closely, the paper almost touching her nose, but could make out only a few vague markings. Intrigued, she knelt at the edge of the sidewalk, took out her phone, and turned on the flashlight app.

She blinked at the page in confusion. It appeared to be some sort of secret message, a communiqué written in code. On the right side of the page was a long list of numbers and measurements. On the left, there was a series of small sketches—simple lines and arrows at the top, growing increasingly more detailed and complex as they marched down the page, until you reached the final drawing at the bottom. As soon as she saw it, her confusion vanished and she broke into a grin.

Nikki turned one last time to look at Mrs. Norman's displays, then down at the paper in her hand, which showed her everything she needed to know to build her very own.

Overcome with gratitude, she placed her new books and the plans into her backpack and slipped it over her shoulders. Then she raised her eyes skyward and took a long, deep breath. The world around her was cold, dark, silent, but thrumming with possibilities. After a moment, Nikki climbed on her bike and pedaled toward them.

COZZY'S QUESTION

by Matt Bechtel

It had been a rough few years for Cozzy, but she had never woken up like this before.

"YOUR TIME HAS COME! YOU MUST GIVE ME YOUR ANSWER!"

The booming words jolted her from her sleep. Her ears had become so keen that even a whisper or a single footstep toward her hiding place would have startled her awake, so someone yelling at her like an overzealous quiz show host was more than enough to get her heart racing. Still, she had learned it was best not to give away her position until she was certain there was imminent danger; as such, she patiently waited, listening to the rain splatter against the top of the long-abandoned construction tube that she now called her bed.

Nothing. Not another word. Just the gentle, insistent rain teeming down upon her makeshift roof.

I must be hearing things, Cozzy thought, allowing herself a cathartic ears-to-tail stretch as she nestled back in and closed her eyes once more.

"YOUR TIME HAS COME! YOU MUST GIVE ME YOUR ANSWER!"

There it was again! Unmistakable! Who could possibly be asking her this question?

That was when it dawned on her—no one. Who would ever ask anything of an alley cat (although Cozzy hated that term, and besides, she spent most of her time in the park)? As much as it seemed directed at her, she must have been overhearing someone else's conversation; in fact, her discarded aluminum-siding-tube-bed often amplified nearby sounds. Still, just to be certain, just to calm her nerves, Cozzy decided to poke her head out and see with her own diamond-shaped pupils what it was her ears were hearing.

Her exposed head was met by a falling sheet of rain and the warm smile of an old man sitting on the park bench across the path.

"Hello, Cozzy," he greeted. "How can I help you?"

Cozzy shook the water out of her now-soaked ears, certain the old man had called her "kitty" and she'd misheard. *Yeah, sure thing old-timer,* she thought to herself as she started to slink back into her tube. *Got a saucer of warm milk with you?*

"I'm sorry, Cozzy, but I don't have any food with me. If I could give you any, I would."

Cozzy stopped cold in her silent tracks and slowly emerged from the safety of her tube. The park was deserted, perhaps from the deluge or perhaps because few people ever came to this remote corner, which sat as an unfinished construction site. As the rain pelted her matted fur against her slender frame, Cozzy locked eyes with the old man and asked, *Who are you, and how can you hear my thoughts?*

"How can you hear mine? Do you see my lips moving?" he replied.

She hadn't noticed until he called it to her attention, but the assaulting raindrops were becoming too much. Out of instinct, Cozzy darted under the bench upon which the old man sat. As he peered at her through the wooden slats, Cozzy gingerly pushed her face toward his leg and inhaled. She smelled nothing. *Who are you?*

"Just an old friend of an old friend of an old friend. I'm here to help you; you have an important question to answer."

Cozzy sniffed at his pants leg again and the same nothingness greeted her. That was when she noticed that, somehow, unlike every inch of her flea-infested coat, his clothes weren't the least bit wet. Cozzy had heard plenty of tall tales before, from her family and even from other neighborhood cats, but she'd always been skeptical. Still, she was skeptical enough to know that she didn't know everything.

Are you a ghost? she finally asked.

He chuckled. "I think I like that term about as much as you like 'alley cat!' But yes, that's one thing you could call me."

What's another?

"Spirit. Advisor. Friend, I hope. I meant what I said, Coz. I'm here to help you."

Help me? You can't give me food and you can't stop the rain; what on earth are you going to help me with?

"Exactly that," he answered. "Everything. Everything on earth. You've been asked a very important question, Cozzy—*THE* question, the most important question ever asked. And the voice won't stop until you give it an answer."

Oh really? And what question is that?

"Do you want the world to end?"

Cozzy blinked hard and shook the water from her sopping ears again. *What did you just say?* she asked.

But the old man had vanished.

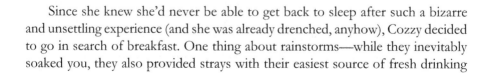

Since she knew she'd never be able to get back to sleep after such a bizarre and unsettling experience (and she was already drenched, anyhow), Cozzy decided to go in search of breakfast. One thing about rainstorms—while they inevitably soaked you, they also provided strays with their easiest source of fresh drinking water. Cozzy positioned her body atop a gutter grate—a trick she'd learned long ago, as the grate didn't allow for any puddles or pooling beneath her—and dropped her mouth into the small stream flowing alongside the curb, lapping herself a better drink than she'd had in days.

As she drank, Cozzy couldn't help but laugh to herself. Drinking water used to be so easy—walk up to your bowl, drink your thirst away, and if it dried up too soon, meow incessantly until someone refilled it for you. If that was too boring, just wait for the granddaughter to do the dinner dishes…

"Jillian!" Grammy yelled. "Why do you insist on letting her do that? She has her own bowl, you know!"

"She likes it!"

Cozzy craned her neck around the neck of the faucet and lapped at the trickling water Jillian had set for her. While she knew it was the same water that waited for her in her bowl at all times, something just always seemed special about getting to drink straight from the tap. It was funny how it upset Grammy so much; seriously, what did she care?

"I know you just do that to extend your time doing the dishes so you don't have to dive into your homework yet!"

"Nuh-uh!" Jillian exclaimed, "It's not homework time yet! We still have to have dessert first!"

Cozzy arched her back and Jillian responded by scratching the base of her tail, just as she wanted. Cozzy continued to drink, contented in the knowledge that she had trained her family so well.

Papa stood up from his seat at the dinner table with an overfull grunt and an offer for his granddaughter. "Finish the dishes and I'll start scooping the ice cream. Deal?"

Mid-drink, Jillian scooped Cozzy into her arms, nestled her face into the scruffy back of the cat's neck, and then gently lowered her to the linoleum floor. Cozzy pretended to wail in protest; even though she'd been full for a solid thirty seconds, she couldn't let her family know that she wasn't deeply disappointed!

"I know, Cozzy," Jillian whispered into her ear, "but I'll let you drink straight from the faucet again tomorrow night, I promise!"

A car drove by, careening through a standing puddle far too fast, splashing a cascade of water across the entire sidewalk and anyone unlucky enough to be near the side of the road. Cozzy was the only one there; of course, it didn't really matter since she was already soaked to the bone.

The extra dousing was punctuated by the voice again. *"YOUR TIME HAS COME! YOU MUST GIVE ME YOUR ANSWER!"*

You know what? At least have the decency to let me get some breakfast first!

Cozzy slinked her way through an empty gas station to a nearby shopping center that housed four different restaurants, all of whom kept their dumpsters tucked neatly away in the rear employee-and-deliveries-only parking lot behind the buildings. This was always her first stop for food each day. Sometimes Cozzy had to do things to eat that she wasn't proud of, but four restaurants times three shifts equaled a lot of bags and one well-placed claw swipe could turn an overstuffed dumpster into a buffet. This morning was no exception, and the food was still relatively fresh by garbage standards.

"Do you even remember what kibbles taste like, Cozzy?"

Her head snapped up from the chicken carcass she was munching. It was the old man again.

If you're asking me that, you already know the answer.

"Just how long has it been?"

I'm not sure. I've never been great at keeping time. Maybe two years? I know I've been out here through two winters on my own.

"I'm sorry about what happened to your family."

People die. That's what they do. I've come to accept it.

"That's true," the old man agreed, "everyone dies. Not just people—cats, dogs, fish, trees—all life, eventually, dies. But you, Cozzy, you get to decide if that day is today."

I still don't get what you're talking about.

"I know you've heard the question. That's why I'm here. That's how this has always worked—you get the question, I show up to explain the situation, and when you're ready, you make your decision."

Her chicken bones picked clean, Cozzy turned her attention to what appeared to be the discarded end of a serving of meatloaf. This bag had turned out to be quite a score and Cozzy knew it was best to eat as much as she could before one of the owners discovered her and chased her away.

Actually, I've just heard the demand for an answer, she corrected. *But you're telling me the question is 'do I want the world to end?'*

"Yes."

Cozzy sat silently, not eating, not moving, and barely breathing.

"Yes," the old man repeated.

So I decide I want the world to end, and...

"And that's it," he finished for her. "The end of everything, all of it, in the blink of an eye. The Apocalypse, Armageddon, Ragnarök, or whatever you want to call it—the end of all life on earth. Because you say so."

But...why?

"Because that's the way it's always been," the old man said, "since the first cats joined the first humans down here. That's always been your place and your role. Some cultures almost got it right, like the Egyptians; they worshipped you as gods because they recognized a link between felines and the afterlife. The truth is this world's fate has always lain with you."

Yeah, but why me? Why not a lion, or a tiger, or a house cat that, you know, actually has a house? Why do I have to take a break from sifting through garbage to decide the fate of the world?

The old man shrugged. "Because your great-great-great-great...aw to heck with it, I have no clue how many generations back it goes! Because you're descended from the first who was asked, Cozzy. It's in your blood."

Yeah, well, I'm still not sure you're asking the right cat... Cozzy began to answer, looking up from her piece of meatloaf for the first time in minutes, but he was gone again.

Suddenly, a sound like a gunshot exploded just behind her head. Cozzy shot straight up into the air before seeing one of the restaurant owners with rocks in his hand. His first throw had barely missed her and had crashed into the side of the metal dumpster. Cozzy tore off as soon as her paws touched the wet pavement and before he could aim again.

It hadn't always been like this for Cozzy. For a long time, life was good...very, very good. As good as it could be, actually.

Grammy and Papa had adopted Cozzy from the local shelter the day she was weaned, which also happened to be Jillian's fourth birthday. All Jillian wanted more than anything else that year was a kitten, but her and her mom's apartment wouldn't allow pets (how absurd!). However, there were no such silly rules at Grammy and Papa's house, and since Jillian's mom worked third shift at the hospital and she spent most evenings at her grandparents', Cozzy very quickly became *their* cat (all three of them). It was the precocious Jillian who'd named Cozzy, and though her name didn't make much sense for a female cat, she'd come to love and appreciate its quirkiness.

As Cozzy had told the old man, she was never good at keeping track of time, but she guessed she'd lived in the comfort and love of her family for at least a decade. Jillian had certainly grown up a lot, and not just physically (but darn if she hadn't gotten *so* much taller!). Again, silly, stupid, arbitrary rules had kept Cozzy from attending her dance recitals and school plays, and even her middle school graduation, but she always felt as if she was there and a part of Jillian's accomplishments because she'd watched her practice and rehearse so often in the living room (not to mention she'd always, *always* sneak into the celebration photos afterwards!).

It was around that time Papa started getting sick. Cozzy was the first to realize it, though she didn't know just how sick he would get. She sensed enough to spend as much time as she could curled at Papa's feet at the end of the couch, then at the end of his and Grammy's bed, and then finally at the end of the special mechanical adjustable bed the nurses brought in. She honestly didn't realize just how sick he was until he stayed home with her and watched Jillian's eighth-grade graduation from his laptop.

No one needed to tell Cozzy when Papa passed away; she had dozed off on the couch and was awakened by the sound of Grammy crying at the kitchen table. No one else was there yet, although Cozzy knew that Jillian and her mom would come crashing through the door at any moment and wrap their arms around her. Still, until they got there, Cozzy nuzzled her face against Grammy's shin and rubbed herself back and forth against her legs. Almost instinctively, Grammy dropped a hand away from her eyes and stroked her fingers back and forth across Cozzy's arched spine. Cozzy knew it wasn't as good as one of her granddaughter's hugs, but she knew Grammy understood and appreciated it; after all, they were family.

Again, Cozzy was never good at telling time (she never understood why Grammy and Papa insisted that "the middle of the night" was no time to go outside), but she did understand that Papa had been sick for a long time before he passed because she could feel a sense of relief from the rest of her family. "He's finally at peace," she overheard them say. "He's in a better place now." They were all horribly sad, but there was an odd comfort and calm that blanketed her family.

Things were very different with Grammy.

One night, just like every other night, Grammy had put down fresh kibbles and water for her, put a load of wash into the dryer, turned on the late news, and tucked herself into bed. Only she didn't wake up in the morning; in fact, she never woke up. Cozzy had meowed and meowed at her and even batted the edge of her blanket the way she knew Grammy *hated*, but she couldn't rouse her. That was how the nice lady next door, who visited every morning for coffee and used to carpool to choir practice with Grammy, found them.

It just didn't make sense. Papa had been sick, but Grammy had been fine. From her hiding spot under the dresser Cozzy heard one of the paramedics say "her heart gave out" when speaking with the neighbor, but again, it didn't make sense. After all, Grammy's heart had been fine! She still loved Cozzy, Jillian, and everyone the same as always! There was no sense of calm this time, no sense of relief. Just rage. Rage…and sensible fear. The house was empty. Cozzy couldn't stay there on her own, and Jillian's and her mom's apartment wouldn't allow her. She knew the next words out of the paramedic's mouth after he saw her food and water bowls would be, "Call the shelter."

But he had left the screen door propped open. She darted through it in a flash, leaped down her front steps without even touching a single one, and scrambled away as quickly as her four legs could carry her.

"YOUR TIME HAS COME! YOU MUST GIVE ME YOUR ANSWER!"
I know! Cozzy thought, as loudly as she could.
"YOUR TIME HAS COME! YOU MUST GIVE ME YOUR ANSWER!"
I said I know! I heard you the first dozen times! Geez!
Cozzy took the long way to the park in case the rock-throwing restaurateur had decided to follow her (one could never be too careful). The voice boomed

repeatedly inside her head the whole way, and apparently, it was becoming impatient. Rather than head directly back to the unfinished construction site, she meandered along the outskirts of the playground. On nice days when she was up for it, Cozzy sometimes stole beneath the tall hedges that framed the area and watched the kids play.

It's abandoned today because of the rain, she explained to the old man.

He chuckled. "You knew I was here this time!"

I could sense you. You don't survive out here as long as I have if you allow anyone or anything to sneak up on you. Plus, I figured you were due to come back since the voice won't shut up.

"I know it's not my place to ask, but are you any closer to making your decision?"

As close as I was the first time I heard the question.

"I'm sorry you're stuck with this responsibility," the old man said. "It's a heck of a spot. It's not a fair position to put you in."

Cozzy glared at the old man through the dripping rain from the bush fronds. *Fair?* she asked, incredulously. *You don't have to talk to me about fair. It wasn't fair to watch Papa suffer like he did. It wasn't fair to have the night steal Grammy from us like some cowardly thief. They were good people. They were my people, and I was their cat, and we were a family, and now...*

Cozzy's indignation simply wore out. She turned her eyes to the merry-go-round.

There are usually kids here to watch, she explained again. *Families. But not today. It's raining today, and I can sense it'll be snowing again soon. And I don't know how much more of this I can take. And you, or whoever or whatever, are asking me if I want all of this to keep going?*

The old man let her words hang in the air, like the suspended drops of rain that paused on the shrub before finding their way to Cozzy's tired, threadbare coat. Finally, she looked up at him through wet eyes with what she realized was her last breath of indignation.

Life isn't fair, she told him. *Why should death be?*

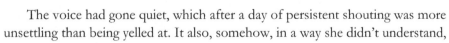

The voice had gone quiet, which after a day of persistent shouting was more unsettling than being yelled at. It also, somehow, in a way she didn't understand, let Cozzy know it was time.

She had made her way back to her refuge of the aluminum siding tube and tucked herself away from the rain's assault, but somehow, in a way she didn't understand, she understood that wasn't right. The voice had gone silent as soon as she'd taken shelter. She knew that actions and words had meanings beyond themselves. She couldn't do this hiding within abandoned construction equipment.

Cozzy took a deep breath, pushed herself from her hiding spot into the driving rain, and with all the strength and little majesty she had left, she jumped atop the empty tube and closed her eyes. As soon as she did, the voice returned.

"YOUR TIME HAS COME! YOU MUST GIVE ME YOUR ANSWER!"

I know, Cozzy thought, much differently this time.

"YOUR TIME HAS COME! YOU MUST GIVE ME YOUR ANSWER!" it demanded.

No.

"YOUR TIME HAS COME! YOU MUST GIVE ME YOUR ANSWER!" the voice repeated.

Cozzy opened her eyes and looked straight up into the blinding storm. *You're not listening to me.* She steeled herself. *My answer is no. No, I do not want the world to end.*

"WHY?" the voice bellowed.

No one said I had to give an explanation, Cozzy defiantly spat back against the rain.

"WHY?" the voice bellowed again.

Who cares? Cozzy screamed to herself and to whoever or whatever was listening. *The why doesn't matter!*

"WHY?" the voice insisted.

THIS IS WHY! Cozzy's mind screamed. She closed her eyes and let the memory overflow her more than the downpour…

A few days before Papa had passed, they were all in his bedroom with him—Grammy, Jillian, Jillian's mom, and Cozzy, curled at Papa's feet as always. Her whole family had tears in their eyes, although they weren't really crying. If there was such a thing as being so happy and so sad at the same time, that's what they were. Papa had a huge smile on his face, and he reached out and took his granddaughter's hand. He'd been somewhat loopy for a while and half asleep even when his eyes were open, but on this night, with them, he was all there.

"This world is yours, Jillian," he told her. "It's all yours. It was made for you. You are so brave, and so strong, and you make me so proud! There is nothing you can't do, so don't you ever let anyone tell you any differently. Go out there and grab it. Reach for the stars, because they're yours for the taking."

This world isn't mine to end, Cozzy thought, her eyes clenched. *It belongs to Jillian, and all the granddaughters and grandsons. And I would never turn a good man like Papa into a liar.*

Cozzy didn't open her eyes until she noticed that the wetness on the back of her neck felt different. It wasn't the teeming rain anymore; it was a soothing, slightly rough, but entirely caring feeling she hadn't experienced in years. She couldn't place the physical sensation, but she felt something else as well…something more important, something more powerful, and something else she hadn't felt in a long, long time.

She felt safe. And loved.

Cozzy opened her eyes, and to her shock and panic, they were completely out of focus, so much that she couldn't see. Frantically, she blinked repeatedly, trying to regain all her senses at once.

Before she could see clearly, something deep inside of Cozzy suddenly recognized the sensation against the back of her neck—it was another cat's tongue. Her mother was bathing her. As soon as she realized that, her eyesight cleared.

She looked directly up and into a face she hadn't seen in years. The features had aged and she was an adult, but it wouldn't matter if twenty years or two thousand years had passed—Cozzy would always, *always* instantly recognize that face.

It was Jillian.

Jillian's eyes welled and her hands flew to her mouth. A handsome man who radiated kindness stood beside her and wrapped his arm around her shoulder.

"What is it, sweetheart?" he asked.

"The kitten," she whispered. "The first of the litter…it looks just like Cozzy!"

"Cozzy?" a young, excited voice asked. "Who's Cozzy?"

Jillian took the hand of the young woman who'd piped up. "Cozzy was Grammy's and Papa's and my cat when I was your age!"

"Grammy doesn't have a cat!" another young voice declared.

"No," the kind man explained, "not Grammy Sara. Grammy Sara's parents."

"Oh, the one's we're named after?" the boy asked again.

Jillian beamed at him. "That's right, Bobby. The Grammy and Papa you and your sister are named after. We looked everywhere for Cozzy after Grammy passed away, but we could never find her."

The young girl wrapped her arms around her mom's waist, and her father tousled her hair. "Well Wonder-Twins," he declared, "I think we know which kitten of Angel's litter is going to join our family! Agreed?"

Mary looked up at her mom. "Can we name her Cozzy, too?"

Jillian beamed, and struggle as she might to stay awake, a yawn overwhelmed Cozzy. As she drifted off to sleep nestled against her mother's body, she heard Jillian say, "Sure! Although we don't even know if that kitten is a boy or a girl yet! But geez, wouldn't it be funny to stick *another* little girl kitty with that name?"

It seemed much later when Cozzy awoke; she'd been through so much she doubted she'd ever be able to explain, and yet still, she had no clue how much time had elapsed. There were a number of other kittens squeezed into the plush, towel-lined box with her and her mother, all of them asleep. When she looked up this time, the only face she saw was that of the old man.

"I'm proud of you, Cozzy," he told her. "You did good. Not that any of us ever doubted."

Where am I? she asked.

"Your next life!" he said. "What, you can accept all those ghost stories you heard over the years, but it's too hard to believe that cats actually *do* get nine lives?"

You mean…?

"Look Cozzy, I'd be lying if I said I understood all of this, and I've been around a *lot* longer than you! Like I told you, this is how it works. At the end of each of your lives, you decide whether or not the world ends. You say no, the world goes on and you come back again. Then, after nine times, you pass the torch to the next cat in line. I'd tell you more about what awaits you after that, but that's a surprise I refuse to ruin…nor do I have the words to properly describe!"

How did you know I'd say no? Cozzy asked. *I mean, after everything, how did you know?*

The old man smiled at her, genuinely and proudly. "You cats! You're stubborn, pigheaded, independent, opinionated, and it's not in your blood to quit, no matter what…just like humans. That's why you get asked the question."

Will I…will I remember all of this? Cozzy asked.

"Nah," the old man replied. "You couldn't fully enjoy this life if you did. And if any cat ever deserved to enjoy her next life, it's you."

Cozzy started to nod off again, but she shook her new small head violently to stay awake for another moment. *Wait, don't go yet!* her mind screamed. *I have one more question!*

"What is it, Cozzy?"

How did I…before I forget, how did I end up here? With Jillian again?

The old man smiled as another colossal yawn pushed the kitten towards sleep. "It is highly unusual," he admitted. "Normally, there's a much longer gap between lives than this, but this opportunity presented itself and whoever or whatever is in charge decided that reuniting you and Jillian was too good to pass up. That you deserved it…both of you."

Cozzy yawned again as sleep began to overtake her. The old man reached out a hand that wasn't really there and gently pressed it against the top of her tired head as she drifted off.

"Not everything is unfair," he told her.

AFTERWORD

by Kenneth W. Cain

When our little writing group (the Mid-Atlantic Dark Fiction Society, aka MADS, and the Pennsylvania chapter of the Horror Writers Association) decided on this project, I was a little nervous at first. This was to be my first foray into editing a charity anthology, and not only that, but one that meant a lot to me personally. Rightfully so, I wasn't sure quite what to expect. I knew Frank had a great reputation in the horror community, but we were about to ask several authors to allow us to use their work for nearly nothing in return. I was pleasantly surprised (but actually, not) by just how many people wanted to be part of this anthology, no matter how small the role. Many more wanted to contribute but were unable to, showing just how grateful the genre was to have Frank in their lives.

See, the thing is, Frank moved so many people with his words, his presence, how he carried himself in general, that people literally jumped at this opportunity. It was humbling to say the least. And who was more gracious than a guy like Frank? There, that's the important part; to understand that whatever names end up on the cover, many more people took part in making this project what it is. It's the whole of the contribution that matters. So I would be remiss not to mention Jacque Day and Somer Canon, both who worked so hard to make sure this book was top notch, proofreading and offering advice on stories. Personally, I'd like to thank them both for their contribution. And of course, there's Todd Keisling, who came up with the idea when MADS was still tossing around the idea of putting out an anthology from our group. Todd's guidance and advice during this project, as well as his incredible design work, was impeccable. There are many more to thank, including several members of MADS for their sacrifice. Also, a big thanks to Tom Deady for his help with the project. And, I owe a big thanks to Pete Kahle from Bloodshot Books, who didn't even blink when we approached him with this idea.

That said, none of us did this for recognition. We did this for Frank. Because he deserved it. Because he made us all feel special, even when his criticism of our work didn't align with what we'd hoped. Frank loved this genre, and he loved the people in it even more. And he didn't play favorites, because Frank Michaels Errington was one of us.

Rest in peace, dear friend. May we see you again someday.

ABOUT THE AUTHORS

ALAN BAXTER is a multi-award-winning author of horror, supernatural thrillers, and dark fantasy. He is also a martial arts expert, a whisky-soaked swear monkey, and dog lover. He creates dark, weird stories among dairy paddocks on the beautiful south coast of New South Wales, Australia. Find him online at www.warriorscribe.com, on Twitter @AlanBaxter, and on Facebook.

MATT BECHTEL is the chairperson of the Camp Necon writers convention. His first collection, *Monochromes: and Other Stories*, was published in 2017, and he has sold stories to PS Publishing and the New England Horror Writers, among others. He lives with his wife, author Sheri Sebastian-Gabriel, and their family. Find him at www.matt-bechtel.com.

JOHN BODEN lives a stone's throw from Three Mile Island with his wonderful wife and sons. A baker by day, he spends his off time writing or watching old television shows. He is the author of *Jedi Summer with The Magnetic Kid*, *Detritus in Love* with Mercedes M. Yardley, *Spungunion,* and *Walk The Darkness Down*. His not-really-for-children children's book, *Dominoes*, has been called a pretty cool thing.

GEOFF BROWN is an award-winning Australian writer and Australian Shadows Award finalist-editor. He is the co-founder of Cohesion Press, and runs ghost tours through a haunted 1800s lunatic asylum. He occasionally works as a story consultant for Blur Studio and Tim Miller, director of *Deadpool* and *Terminator: Dark Fate.*

KEALAN PATRICK BURKE is the Bram Stoker Award-Winning author of *Kin* and *Sour Candy*. Visit him on the web at www.kealanpatrickburke.com or on Twitter @kealanburke.

The winner of both a Bram Stoker and World Fantasy Award, **P.D. CACEK** has penned more than a hundred short stories, seven plays, and six published novels.

Her most recent novel, *Second Lives* from Flame Tree Press, will soon welcome a sequel, *Second Chances*, due out in November 2020.

KENNETH W. CAIN is an author, an award-nominated editor, and a graphic designer. His most recent releases have been through Crystal Lake Publishing, and his novel, *From Death Reborn*, is forthcoming from Silver Shamrock Publishing. www.kennethwcain.com

SOMER CANON is a minivan-revving suburban mom who avoids her neighbors for fear of being found out as a weirdo. When not peering out of her windows, she is consuming books, movies, and video games that sate her need for blood, gore, and things that disturb her mother.

CHRISTA CARMEN'S debut collection, *Something Borrowed, Something Blood-Soaked*, is available from Unnerving, and won the 2018 Indie Horror Book Award for Best Debut Collection. She lives in Rhode Island with her husband, their daughter, and a bluetick beagle named Maya. Find her online at www.christacarmen.com.

CATHERINE CAVENDISH first started writing when someone thrust a pencil into her hand as a child. She writes mainly supernatural, Gothic, ghostly and haunted house horror. Her books include *Garden of Bewitchment, The Haunting of Henderson Close,* and the *Nemesis of the Gods* anthology, among others. Find her at www.catherinecavendish.com and on social media.

Two-time international Bram Stoker Award® nominee **GREG CHAPMAN** is the author of several novels, novellas, and short stories. His books include *Hollow House* and the collections, *Vaudeville and Other Nightmares* and *This Sublime Darkness: and Other Dark Stories*. Based in Queensland, Australia, he is also a horror artist and current president of the Australasian Horror Writers Association.

RICHARD CHIZMAR is the author of *Gwendy's Button Box* with Stephen King, and the multi-award-nominee *A Long December*. His fiction has appeared in dozens of publications, including *Ellery Queen's Mystery Magazine* and multiple editions of *The Year's 25 Finest Crime and Mystery Stories*. Chizmar's work has been translated into many languages, and he has appeared at numerous conferences as a writing instructor, guest speaker, panelist, and guest of honor. Learn more about him at RichardChizmar.com.

TOM DEADY was born and raised in Malden, Massachusetts, not far from the historic (and spooky) town of Salem. He has endured a career as an IT professional, but it was his dream to become a writer. His first novel, *Haven*, won the 2016 Bram Stoker Award for Superior Achievement in a First Novel. He has since published *Eternal Darkness, Weekend Getaway, Backwater*, and *Coleridge*, as well as several short stories. He resides in Massachusetts where he is working on his next novel.

T. FOX DUNHAM lives in Philadelphia with his wife, Allison. He's a lymphoma survivor, cancer patient, modern bard, and historian. Fox is an active member of the Horror Writers Association, and has published hundreds of short stories and articles. He is host and creator of What Are You Afraid Of? Horror & Paranormal Show, a popular horror program on PARA-X RADIO.

ROBERT FORD is author of the novel *The Compound*, the novellas, *Ring of Fire, The Last Firefly of Summer, Samson and Denial*, and *Bordertown*, and the collection, *The God Beneath my Garden*.

DOUNGJAI GAM is the author of *glass slipper dreams, shattered*, and *watch the whole goddamned thing burn*. Her short fiction and poetry have appeared in *Lamplight*, *Wicked Haunted*, and *Nox Pareidolia*, among other places. Born in Thailand, she currently resides in New England with author Ed Kurtz.

CHRISTOPHER GOLDEN is the *New York Times* best-selling author of *Ararat*, *Red Hands*, and *Snowblind*, among many others. With Mike Mignola, he created the comic book series *Baltimore* and *Joe Golem: Occult Detective*. With nearly a dozen Bram Stoker Award nominations, he has won twice. He is also a Shirley Jackson Award nominee. Learn more about him at www.christophergolden.com.

One of the most popular and influential writers of color in modern horror fiction, **J. F. GONZALEZ** is the author of *Primitive*, *Up Jumped the Devil*, *The Corporation*, *Back From The Dead*, *They*, *Bully*, *Screaming To Get Out and Other Wailings of the Damned*, *Shapeshifter*, the best-selling *Clickers* series (co-written with Mark Williams and Brian Keene), and *Survivor*, considered the seminal work of extreme horror. His short fiction and academic writing about the history of horror literature appeared in over two hundred magazines and anthologies during his lifetime. His forthcoming posthumous works include collaborations with Gabino Iglesias, Wrath James White, and Brian Keene.

MARK ALLAN GUNNELLS loves to tell stories. He has since he was a kid, penning one-page, Twilight Zone knockoffs, though he likes to think he has gotten a little better since then. He loves reader feedback, and above all he loves telling stories. He lives in Greer, South Carolina, with his husband, Craig A. Metcalf.

JEREMY HEPLER is the Bram Stoker Award-nominated author of *Cricket Hunters*, *The Boulevard Monster*, and numerous short stories and nonfiction articles. He lives in central Texas with his wife and son, and is currently working on his next novel. Follow him on Twitter, Facebook, Instagram, or Goodreads.

PETE KAHLE is the author of the epic alien sci-fi/horror novel, *The Specimen*. In 2015, he founded Bloodshot Books, a small press dedicated to cross-genre fiction that mixes the best of horror, science fiction, mystery, and thrillers. Pete is also an insane fan of the New York Jets, despite living deep in the heart of enemy territory near Gillette Stadium. Years of disappointment in his team could very well have led to his morbid outlook on life.

NICHOLAS KAUFMANN is the best-selling co-author of *100 Fathoms Below*, with Steven L. Kent. His fiction has been nominated for a Bram Stoker Award, a Shirley Jackson Award, a Thriller Award, and a Dragon Award. He lives in Brooklyn, New York.

SHANE DOUGLAS KEENE is a poet, writer, and musician living in Portland, Oregon. He is one third of the Ink Heist podcast and co-founder of inkheist.com. He wrote the companion poetry for Josh Malerman's serial novel project, *Carpenter's Farm* in 2020, and has many more forthcoming works. He lives with his wife and two small dogs who are convinced they are royalty.

TODD KEISLING is a writer and designer of the horrific and strange. He is the author of several books, including *Devil's Creek*, *Scanlines,* and *The Final Reconciliation*, among other shorter works. He lives somewhere in the wilds of Pennsylvania with his family where he is at work on his next novel. Share his dread on Twitter: @todd_keisling, Instagram: @toddkeisling, and at www.toddkeisling.com.

STEPHEN KING is the author of more than sixty books, all of them worldwide bestsellers. He is the recipient of the 2018 PEN America Literary Service Award, the 2014 National Medal of Arts, and the 2003 National Book Foundation Medal for Distinguished Contribution to American Letters. He lives in Bangor, Maine, with his wife, novelist Tabitha King.

CURTIS M. LAWSON is an author of unapologetically weird fiction. His work ranges from technicolor pulp adventures to bleak cosmic horror and includes *Black Heart Boys Choir*, *The Devoured*, and *Those Who Go Forth Into The Empty Place of Gods*. Curtis hosts the Wyrd Transmissions Podcast. He lives in Salem, Massachusetts, with his wife and son.

EVANS LIGHT is author of *Screamscapes: Tales of Terror*, the upcoming *I Am Halloween*, and more. He is editor of *Doorbells at Dusk* and the ongoing *In Darkness, Delight* horror anthology series, and is co-creator of *Bad Apples: Halloween Horrors* and *Dead Roses: Five Dark Tales of Twisted Love*.

JOHN R. LITTLE has been writing dark fantasy and horror stories for decades. He considers himself very fortunate to have been nominated for the Bram Stoker Award four times and to have once won for his best-known book, *Miranda*.

CHAD LUTZKE has published dozens of stories, and his books have earned praise from Jack Ketchum, Joe R. Lansdale, Richard Chizmar, and Stephen Graham Jones, as well as his own mother. You can find him lurking the internet at www.chadlutzke.com.

JONATHAN MABERRY is a *New York Times* best-selling multi-genre author, five-time Bram Stoker Award-winner, and comic book writer for Marvel, DC, Dark Horse, and IDW. His vampire series, *V-WARS*, was a Netflix original. He sits on the board of the Horror Writers Association, and serves as president of the International Association of Media Tie-in Writers and editor of *Weird Tales Magazine*.

JOSH MALERMAN is the *New York Times* best-selling author of *Bird Box* and *Malorie*. He is also one of two singer-songwriters for the rock band The High Strung, whose song, "The Luck You Got," serves as the theme song for the Showtime series, *Shameless*. He lives in Michigan with his favorite person in the world, Allison Laakko.

ALESSANDRO MANZETTI of Rome, Italy, is a two-time Bram Stoker Award-winning author. His work has been published extensively in English and Italian in the forms of novels, stories, poetry, essays, and graphic novels. His most recent English-language novels are *Shanti: The Sadist Heaven*, published in 2019, and the 2018 novel, *Naraka: The Ultimate Human Breeding*. Manzetti's stories and poems have appeared in Italian, USA, UK and Polish magazines. www.battiago.com

JOHN M. MCILVEEN is the best-selling author of the paranormal suspense novel, *Hannahwhere*, winner of the 2015 Drunken Druid Award (Ireland) and nominee for the 2015 Bram Stoker Award. He is also penned the story collections, *Inflictions* and *Jerks*. He lives in Haverhill, Massachusetts, with his wife, Roberta Colasanti.

JOHN MCNEE is a Scottish horror author of the books *Prince of Nightmares*, *Grudge Punk*, and *Petroleum Precinct*, and the new collection, *John McNee's Doom Cabaret*. In reviewing his debut novel, *Prince of Nightmares*, for Cemetery Dance, Frank Michaels Errington described McNee as "a skilled craftsman" and "someone to keep an eye on."

TIM MEYER dwells in a dark cave near the Jersey Shore. He is an author, husband, father, podcast host, blogger, coffee connoisseur, beer enthusiast, and explorer of worlds. He writes horror, mysteries, science fiction, and thrillers, although he prefers to blur genres and let the story fall where it may.

LEE MURRAY is a multi-award-winning author-editor from Aotearoa-New Zealand. Her work includes military thrillers, the Taine McKenna Adventures, the supernatural crime-noir series *The Path of Ra* (with Dan Rabarts), and the debut collection, *Grotesque: Monster Stories*.

PAUL F. OLSON is the author of the novels *Alexander's Song* and *The Night Prophets* and the collection, *Whispered Echoes*. He co-edited the anthologies *Post Mortem: New Tales of Ghostly Horror, Dead End: City Limits,* and *Better Weird,* published the magazine *Horrorstruck,* and was co-creator and original editor of the *Hellnotes* newsletter.

KELLI OWEN is the author of more than a dozen books, including *Teeth, Waiting Out Winter,* and the *Wilted Lily* series. An editor and reviewer for over a decade, she writes fiction that spans the genres from horror to thriller and back. Visit her at kelliowen.com.

JOHN PALISANO writes in many disciplines. Details at johnpalisano.com

JASON PARENT is an author of horror, thrillers, mysteries, and science fiction, though his many novels and short stories tend to blur the boundaries between these genres. His work has won him praise from both critics and fans of diverse genres alike. His latest novel is *The Apocalypse Strain*. Visit his website at authorjasonparent.com, and follow him on Facebook, Twitter, and anywhere books are sold.

DAVID PRICE lives in Massachusetts with his two children. He is the author of *Lightbringers* and *Dead in the U.S.A.*, and has edited several horror anthologies, including the *Wicked* series for the New England Horror Writers.

ANTHONY J. RAPINO resides in northeastern Pennsylvania, where he teaches English, writes speculative fiction, and sculpts three-dimensional horror. His novel, *Soundtrack to the End of the World*, and story collection, *Greetings from Moon Hill*, are available now. Proof of psychosis can be found on his website: www.anthonyjrapino.com.

KEVIN REGO was born in Fall River, Massachusetts, to immigrant parents from the Azores. He has worked in film, both in front of and behind the camera, and has performed on stages all over the world. In his diverse career in the entertainment industry, he has acted, directed, scripted, stage managed, and performed more death-defying stunts (his first love) than Batman.

HUNTER SHEA is the product of a misspent childhood watching scary movies, reading forbidden books, and wishing Bigfoot would walk past his house. He doesn't just write about the paranormal—he actively seeks out the things that scare the hell out of people to experience them for himself. His novels can even be found on display at the International Cryptozoology Museum. To follow his shenanigans and sign up for his Dark Hunter Newsletter, go to www.huntershea.com.

MICHELLE GARZA AND MELISSA LASON have been dubbed the **SISTERS OF SLAUGHTER** for their work in the horror and dark fantasy genres. Their work has been published by Thunderstorm Books, Sinister Grin Press, Bloodshot Books, and Death's Head Press. Their debut novel, *Mayan Blue*, received a Bram Stoker Award nomination.

ROB SMALES is the author of the collection, *Echoes of Darkness*, and editor of the dark humor anthology, *A Sharp Stick in the Eye (and other funny stories)*. His most recent publication is the coming-of-age horror novella, *Friends in High Places*. He hails from Salem, Massachusetts, where he lives, writes, and occasionally sleeps.

WESLEY SOUTHARD is the Splatterpunk Award-winning author of *One for the Road, Resisting Madness, Slaves to Gravity* with Somer Canon, and many more. He currently lives in South Central Pennsylvania with his wife and their cavalcade of animals. Visit him at www.wesleysouthard.com.

JEFF STRAND is the author of the novels *Pressure, Dweller, My Pretties,* and a bunch more. Frank Michaels Errington was always kind to them, though the dude did make some snarky comments to Jeff in person. You can visit his Gleefully Macabre website at www.JeffStrand.com.

BRETT J. TALLEY is the author of several acclaimed horror novels, short stories, and collections. Twice nominated for a Bram Stoker Award, Talley's works include *That Which Should Not Be, He Who Walks in Shadow, The Fiddle is the Devil's Instrument,* and the *Limbus, Inc.* trilogy. Find him at brettjtalley.com

SARA TANTLINGER is the author of the Bram Stoker Award-winning *The Devil's Dreamland: Poetry Inspired by H.H. Holmes,* and the Stoker-nominated *To Be Devoured.* She serves as a mentor for the HWA Mentorship Program, and co-organizes the HWA Pittsburgh Chapter. Find her on Twitter @SaraTantlinger and saratantlinger.com.

RICHARD THOMAS is the award-winning author of three novels, three short story collections, and 150+ stories in print, as well as the editor of four anthologies. He has been nominated for the Bram Stoker, Shirley Jackson, and Thriller awards. Visit www.whatdoesnotkillme.com for more information.

PAUL TREMBLAY has won the Bram Stoker, British Fantasy, and Massachusetts Book awards. He is the author of *Survivor Song, Growing Things, The Cabin at the End of the World, Disappearance at Devil's Rock, A Head Full of Ghosts,* and the crime novels *The Little Sleep* and *No Sleep Till Wonderland.* His essays and short fiction have appeared in the *Los Angeles Times, Entertainment Weekly* online, and numerous year's-best anthologies. He has a master's degree in mathematics and lives outside Boston with his family.

TONY TREMBLAY is the author of two short story collections and one novel, *The Moore House,* nominated for a Bram Stoker Award. He is the host of The Taco Society Presents television show, an interview program with an emphasis on horror, and is a co-founder of NoCon, a genre convention held yearly in Manchester, New Hampshire. Tremblay lives in Goffstown, New Hampshire, with his wife.

JOSHUA VIOLA is a four-time Colorado Book Award finalist and co-author of the *Denver Moon* series with Warren Hammond. His comic book collection, *Denver Moon: Metamorphosis*, was included on the 2018 Bram Stoker Award Preliminary Ballot for Superior Achievement in a Graphic Novel. He is owner and chief editor of Hex Publishers.

Bram Stoker Award-winning author **TIM WAGGONER** has published over fifty novels and seven collections of short stories. He writes original horror and dark fantasy, as well as media tie-ins, and recently released a book on writing horror fiction called *Writing in the Dark*.

TERRY M. WEST is an American horror author. He is best known for *What Price Gory, Car Nex, Transfer,* and his *Night Things* series. He was a two-time finalist for the International Horror Guild Awards and he was featured on the TV Guide Sci-Fi hot list for his YA graphic novel series, *Confessions of a Teenage Vampire*. www.terrymwest.com

DOUGLAS WYNNE is the author of the novels *The Devil of Echo Lake, Steel Breeze,* and the SPECTRA Files trilogy, *Red Equinox, Black January,* and *Cthulhu Blues*. He lives in Massachusetts with his wife and son and a houseful of animals. You can find him online at www.douglaswynne.com.

STEPHANIE M. WYTOVICH is an American poet, novelist, and essayist. Her work has been showcased in *Weird Tales, Gutted: Beautiful Horror Stories, Fantastic Tales of Terror,* and many others. Wytovich is the poetry editor for Raw Dog Screaming Press, and Dark Regions Press published her debut novel, *The Eighth*. Find her on Twitter @SWytovich.

MERCEDES M. YARDLEY writes whimsical horror and wears poisonous flowers in her hair. She is the author of *Beautiful Sorrows, Pretty Little Dead Girls,* and the Bram Stoker Award-winning *Little Dead Red*. You can reach her at mercedesmyardley.com.

ALSO FROM
BLOODSHOT BOOKS

HOW MUCH DO YOU HATE?

Eddie Brinkburn's doing time for a botched garage job that left Sheraton's brother very badly burned.

HOW MUCH DO YOU HATE?

When Sheraton's gang burn his wife and kids to death, Eddie soon learns the meaning of hate.

HOW MUCH DO YOU HATE?

And that's how the prison psycho transfers his awesome power to Eddie. A power that Eddie reckons he can control. A power that will enable Eddie to put the frighteners on Sheraton...

Available in paperback or Kindle on Amazon.com

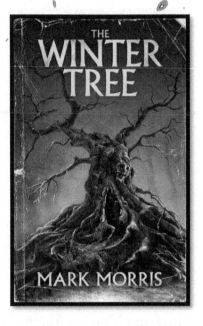

**FINALLY IN PRINT AFTER MORE THAN THREE DECADES, THE NOVEL
MARK MORRIS WROTE <u>BEFORE</u> *TOADY***

EVIL NEEDS ONLY A SEED

Limefield has had more than its fair share of tragedy. Barely six years ago, a disturbed young boy named Russell Swaney died beneath the wheels of a passenger train mere moments after committing a heinous act of unthinkable sadism. Now, a forest fire caused by the thoughtless actions of two teens has laid waste to hundreds of acres of the surrounding woodlands and unleashed a demonic entity

EVIL TAKES ROOT

Now, a series of murders plague the area and numerous local residents have been reported missing, including the entire population of the nearby prison. But none of this compares to the appearance of the Winter Tree, a twisted wooden spire which seems to leech the warmth from the surrounding land.

EVIL FLOURISHES

Horrified by what they have caused, the two young men team up with a former teacher and the local police constabulary to find the killer, but it may already be too late. Once planted, evil is voracious. Like a weed, it strangles all life, and the roots of the Winter Tree are already around their necks.

Available in paperback or Kindle on Amazon.com

There's a monster coming to the small town of Pikeburn. In half an hour, it will begin feeding on the citizens, but no one will call the authorities for help. They are the ones who sent it to Pikeburn. They are the ones who are broadcasting the massacre live to the world. Every year, Red Diamond unleashes a new creation in a different town as a display of savage terror that is part warning and part celebration. Only no one is celebrating in Pikeburn now. No one feels honored or patriotic. They feel like prey.

Local Sheriff Yan Corban refuses to succumb to the fear, paranoia, and violence that suddenly grips his town. Stepping forward to battle this year's lab-grown monster, Sheriff Corban must organize a defense against the impossible. His allies include an old art teacher, a shell-shocked mechanic, a hateful millionaire, a fearless sharpshooter, a local meth kingpin, and a monster groupie. Old grudges, distrust, and terror will be the monster's allies in a game of wits and savagery, ambushes and treachery. As the conflict escalates and the bodies pile up, it becomes clear this creature is unlike anything Red Diamond has unleashed before.

No mercy will be asked for or given in this battle of man vs monster. It's time to run, hide, or fight. It's time for Red Diamond.

Available in paperback or Kindle on Amazon.com

January 12, 1888

When a day dawns warm and mild in the middle of a long cold winter, it's greeted as a blessing, a reprieve. A chance for those who've been cooped up indoors to get out, do chores, run errands, send the children to school… little knowing that they're only seeing the calm before the storm.

The blizzard hits out of nowhere, screaming across the Great Plains like a runaway train. It brings slicing winds, blinding snow, plummeting temperatures. Livestock will be found frozen in the fields, their heads encased in blocks of ice formed from their own steaming breath. Frostbite and hypothermia wait for anyone caught without shelter.

For the hardy settlers of Far Enough, in the Montana Territory, it's about to get worse. Something else has arrived with the blizzard. Something sleek and savage and hungry. Wild animal or vengeful spirit from native legend, it blends into the snow and bites with sharper teeth than the wind.

It is called the *wanageeska*.

It is the White Death

Available in paperback or Kindle on Amazon.com

ON THE HORIZON FROM
BLOODSHOT BOOKS
2020-21*

Fort – Rob E. Boley
Birthright – Christine Morgan
Revival Road – Chris DiLeo
Marmalade – Roland Blackburn
BioTerror – Tim Curran
Cracker Jack – Asher Ellis
Normal – Benjamin Langley
The Obese – Jarred Martin
Our Carrion Hearts – Brian Fatah Steele
Cluster – Renee Miller
Pound of Flesh – D. Alexander Ward
Crimson Springs – John Quick
Popsicle – Christa Wojciechowski
Schafer – Timothy G. Huguenin
The Amazing Alligator Girl – Kristin Dearborn
Fairlight – Adrian Chamberlin
Ungeheuer – Scott A. Johnson
Teach Them How to Bleed – L.L. Soares
Blood Mother: A Novel of Terror – Pete Kahle
Not Your Average Monster – World Tour
A Life Transparent (Monochrome Trilogy #1) – Todd Keisling
The Liminal Man (Monochrome Trilogy #2) – Todd Keisling
Nonentity (Monochrome Trilogy #3) – Todd Keisling
The Abomination (The Riders Saga #2) – Pete Kahle
The Horsemen (The Riders Saga #3) – Pete Kahle

* other titles to be added when confirmed

BLOODSHOT
BOOKS

READ UNTIL YOU BLEED!

Made in the USA
Las Vegas, NV
15 May 2021